ENDSINGER

ALSO BY JAY KRISTOFF

Stormdancer
Kinslayer
The Last Stormdancer

c.1

ENDSINGER

JAY KRISTOFF

THOMAS DUNNE BOOKS ST. MARTIN'S PRESS NEW YORK

THOMAS DUNNE BOOKS.
An imprint of St. Martin's Press.

ENDSINGER. Copyright © 2014 by Jay Kristoff. All rights reserved. Printed in the United States of America. For information, address St. Martin's Press, 175 Fifth Avenue, New York, N.Y. 10010.

www.thomasdunnebooks.com
www.stmartins.com

Designed by Steven Seighman

Map artwork © David Atkinson: handmademaps.com

Kanji designs: Araki Miho: ebisudesign.com
Clan logo design: James Orr

The Library of Congress Cataloging-in-Publication Data is available upon request.

ISBN 978-1-250-00142-9 (hardcover)
ISBN 978-1-250-02295-0 (e-book)

St. Martin's Press books may be purchased for educational, business, or promotional use. For information on bulk purchases, please contact the Macmillan Corporate and Premium Sales Department at 1-800-221-7945, extension 5442, or write to specialmarkets@macmillan.com.

Simultaneously published in Great Britain by Tor, an imprint of Pan Macmillan, a division of Macmillan Publishing Limited

First U.S. Edition: November 2014

10 9 8 7 6 5 4 3 2 1

For Jack, Max and Poppy.

Raise your fists.

MONS OF THE SHIMA IMPERIUM

TIGER CLAN (TORA)

FOX CLAN (KITSUNE)

DRAGON CLAN (RYU)

PHOENIX CLAN (FUSHICHO)

THE LOTUS GUILD

THE SHIMA ISLES

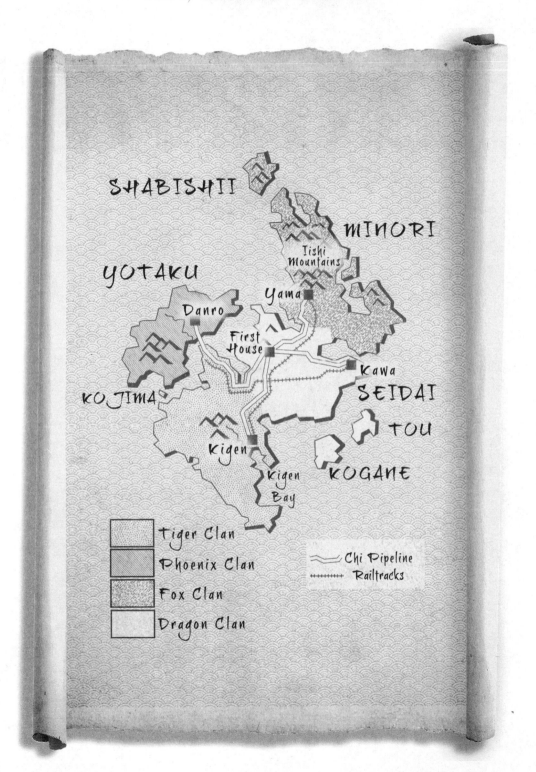

KIGEN

DOWNSIDE

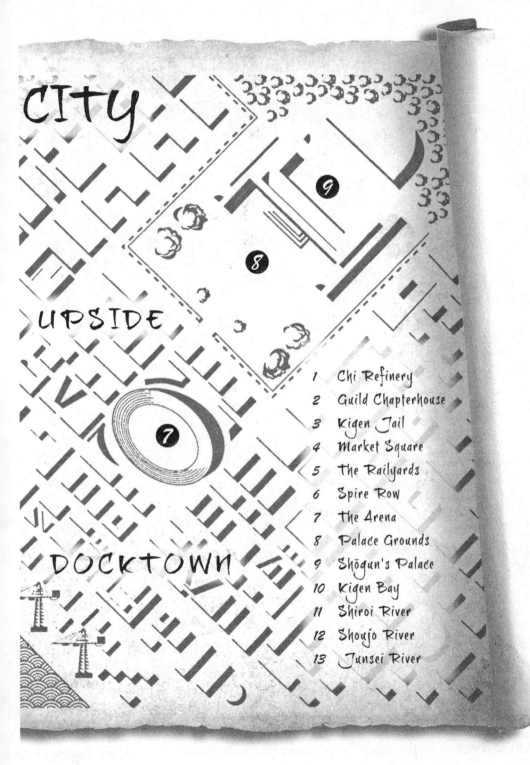

CITY

UPSIDE

DOCKTOWN

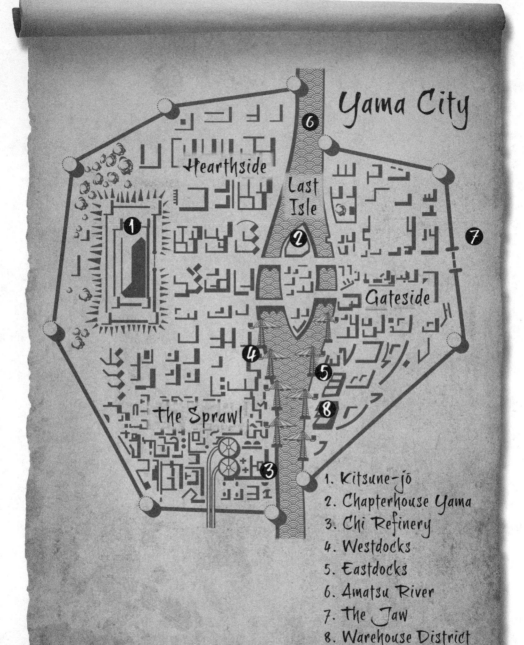

Yama City

Hearthside

Last Isle

Gateside

The Sprawl

1. Kitsune-jō
2. Chapterhouse Yama
3. Chi Refinery
4. Westdocks
5. Eastdocks
6. Amatsu River
7. The Jaw
8. Warehouse District

There's a time when the operation of the machine becomes so odious—makes you so sick at heart—that you can't take part. You can't even passively take part. And you've got to put your bodies upon the gears and upon the wheels, upon the levers, upon all the apparatus, and you've got to make it stop. And you've got to indicate to the people who run it, to the people who own it, that unless you're free, the machine will be prevented from working at all.

—MARIO SAVIO

LOTUS WAR CHARACTER REFRESHER

WHO THE HELLS ARE ALL THESE PEOPLE?

Yukiko—A young girl with the ability to speak telepathically to animals (a gift called "the Kenning"). Yukiko forged a powerful bond with the thunder tiger, Buruu, and has become a figurehead of the Kagé rebellion. Her telepathic ability has been growing, granting her astonishing abilities and causing agonizing headaches, but its cause—her pregnancy to the Tiger Daimyo, Hiro—promises to be more painful still.

Last known whereabouts: Yukiko traveled north, seeking the truth of her growing power. Discovering the female thunder tiger Kaiah and a gaijin lightning farm, she returned to Shima in time to help thwart Hiro's marriage to Lady Aisha and save the rebellion from ruin.

Buruu—A thunder tiger (aka arashitora). Yukiko's best friend and loyal companion. Buruu is the last of his race in Shima. His feathers were clipped by Shōgun Yoritomo, and until he molts again, he cannot fly without the aid of mechanical wings built for him by the Guild Artificer, Kin. He is referred to by other arashitora as "Kinslayer," though he hasn't revealed why.

Last known whereabouts: with Yukiko.

Kin—An Artificer (engineer) of the Lotus Guild who built mechanical wings for Buruu. Kin tried to join the Kagé rebellion but found no acceptance among them. During the attack on Hiro's wedding, Kin and the False-Lifer Ayane betrayed the rebellion and handed over its leader, Daichi, to the Lotus Guild.

Last known whereabouts: after his betrayal, Kin was accepted back into the Guild.

Akihito—A former hunter of the Imperial Court, and Yukiko's friend since childhood. Trapped in Kigen city after Yukiko left, he found two siblings—Hana and Yoshi—both of whom possess the Kenning. During the attack on Hiro's wedding, he rescued the pair from yakuza thugs, and brought them into the Kagé rebellion.

Last known whereabouts: aboard the sky-ship *Kurea*, with the other Kagé members.

Hana—A Burakumin (clanless) street waif, Hana served as a maid in Kigen palace. Inspired by Yukiko, she joined the Kagé and helped liberate Michi from her prison. She possesses the Kenning, and her mother was a gaijin captive of a Kitsune soldier. Her left eye was torn out by a yakuza gangster, but her right eye glows like rose-quartz. She has no idea why.

Last known whereabouts: aboard the sky-ship *Kurea*, with the other Kagé members.

Yoshi—Hana's brother, Yoshi is a streetwise thief who crossed the yakuza, resulting in his lover's murder and his sister's maiming. He is half-gaijin, like his sister, and also possesses the Kenning, though he primarily uses it to speak to rats.

Last known whereabouts: aboard the sky-ship *Kurea*.

Jurou—Yoshi's lover, tortured and killed by yakuza gangsters.

Last known whereabouts: an alley in Kigen city.

Daken—Yoshi and Hana's cat. He died trying to save Hana from the yakuza.

Last known whereabouts: yakuza warehouse.

Kaiah—A female arashitora, discovered by Yukiko near the gaijin lightning farm. Kaiah and Buruu share a troubled past—she refers to him as "Kinslayer" and treats him with contempt. She agreed to help Yukiko and the rebellion out of a desire to defend Yukiko's unborn children.

Last known whereabouts: with Yukiko.

Ayane—A member of the Lotus Guild, part of the False-Lifer sect. Inspired by Kin's rebellion, Ayane traveled to the Iishi Mountains, seeking to join the Kagé, but she was met by cruelty and distrust, eventually suffering a brutal assault at

Isao's hands. This attack prompted Kin to betray the rebellion and sell Daichi to his former masters.

Last known whereabouts: after Kin's betrayal, Ayane was accepted back into the Guild.

Yoritomo-no-miya—Shōgun of Shima. Daimyo of the Tiger clan. A lunatic who came too young to power, and was ultimately consumed by it.

Last known whereabouts: Yoritomo was slain by Yukiko.

Aisha—Yoritomo's sister. Last daughter of the Kazumitsu Dynasty. Secret ally of the Kagé rebellion. Aisha's neck was broken by Yoritomo when he discovered her rebel sympathies.

Last known whereabouts: in order to spare herself the indignity of being married to Hiro, Aisha begged Michi to end her life. She died in Kigen palace.

Michi—Maidservant of the Lady Aisha. Secret member of the Kagé rebellion. Swordmaster. Michi passed up a life of love and happiness with the Tiger Lord Ichizo (Hiro's cousin), murdering him in her attempt to rescue Aisha. When begged by her Lady to end her suffering, the girl tearfully complied.

Last known whereabouts: aboard the sky-ship *Kurea*, with the other Kagé members.

Hiro—AKA "The Boy with the Sea-Green Eyes." Daimyo of the Tiger Clan. Hiro has been propped up as Tiger clanlord by the Lotus Guild—they also replaced his arm with an iron prosthetic after Buruu tore it off. It was the Guild's intention to marry Hiro to Aisha and cement his claim to the Shōgun's throne, but the plan was thwarted. Hiro is Yukiko's former lover, and desires nothing more than to see her dead.

Last known whereabouts: Kigen city, in the ruins of his palace.

Daichi—Leader of the Kagé rebellion. A former member of the Kazumitsu Elite who rebelled against the Shōgunate after Yoritomo mutilated his daughter, Kaori. Daichi has blacklung—a degenerative lung disease caused by lotus pollution, characterized by coughing fits and black saliva. He was betrayed by Kin during the attack on Hiro's wedding, and captured by the Guild.

Last known whereabouts: a Lotus Guild prison cell.

Kaori—Lieutenant of the Kagé rebellion. Daichi's daughter. She bears an awful knife scar on her face, courtesy of Yoritomo-no-miya. She helped spearhead the attack on Hiro's wedding that ended in her father's capture.

Last known whereabouts: aboard the sky-ship *Kurea*.

Kensai—Second Bloom of the Lotus Guild, and Voice of the Guild in Kigen city. One of the most powerful and influential Guildsmen alive, Kin's adoptive uncle, and chief designer of the iron behemoth known as the Earthcrusher—a mechanical giant intended to end the gaijin war and destroy the Kagé rebellion.

Last known whereabouts: Lotus Guild Chapterhouse in Kigen city.

Piotr—A gaijin doctor who helped Yukiko escape captivity at the lightning farm. Piotr was friends with a captured rebel Guildsman, and vowed to get a message to the Guildsman's lover after he died. Piotr traveled back to Shima with Yukiko, Buruu and Kaiah.

Last known whereabouts: the Kagé stronghold in the Iishi mountains.

Isao—A young member of the Kagé. He spied on Yukiko while bathing, discovering she bore the tattoo of the Shōgun on her arm. He was knifed in the back by Kin during the attack on Hiro's wedding, as punishment for the cruelty he'd shown to Ayane.

Last known whereabouts: dead in a Kigen basement.

Blackbird—The dashing captain of the sky-ship *Kurea*, and a rebel sympathizer.

Last known whereabouts: on his ship, flying the Kagé from the ruins of Kigen.

PART ONE

BIRTH

Through darkness he walked,
Holy Lord Izanagi. Maker and Father.
His beloved lost; great Lady Izanami, Mother of All Things,
Deep in Yomi's black, sorrows strung about his neck, he searched
    for his love.
And yet what he found, after miles and trials untold,
He then left behind.

—from the Book of Ten Thousand Days

PROLOGUE

The thing inside their mother wanted out.

Swollen and heavy as stone, Lady Sun fell westward into the waiting oceans. A chill followed her descent, coiled in the mountain shadows, creeping toward the dusty little farm and its withered fields. The wind brought the brittle bite of approaching winter, the vapor from the deadlands stirring like a lover at its touch, rippling with the sound of their mother's screams.

Tetsuo and Hikita crouched together in the dirt, all grubby faces and threadbare rags. The children had fled the house when the noise became too much. Their mother's agonized cries had reduced little Tetsuo to tears, and Hikita took his younger brother's hand and led him out into the dark and quiet. Hikita knew he must be strong. He was the man now. Thin shoulders only ten summers old, carrying the weight of his family and the weight of the world.

Their neighbor had arrived with the midwife, and now the women clustered about the bed as Mother wailed, stepping outside only to dash buckets of red water onto cracked earth, or wring bloody rags between their fingers. Hikita would watch them then, his eyes hidden behind soot-smeared glass, black and empty as the dusk above their heads.

He knew what another mouth meant for his family. Knew their pitiful stead wouldn't have enough good earth left next season to feed three, let alone four. But the baby was coming, whether he willed it or not. There was nowhere else for it to go, after all.

Tetsuo stabbed at the ashen earth with a stick. The blood lotus crop around them swayed and rolled, voices whispering in the husk-dry leaves.

"Do you think it will be another boy?"

"Only the Maker knows," Hikita replied.

"I would like a sister."

"I would like the cur who put that baby in her to be at her side. I would like Father to still be alive." Hikita scowled, climbing to his feet. "Like has nothing to do with life."

He stared at the Tōnan mountains to the west; jagged fists raised against the setting sun. Between Hikita's feet and those stone roots, miles of deadlands stretched into the dark—cracks in the earth running twenty feet deep, wreathed in choking fog. Through the fumes, he could see a broken wagon here, a collapsed barn there. Farmsteads run to ruin, swallowed by the blackness spreading from the Stain. He knew somewhere in those mountains loomed First House, the heart of Guild power in Shima. The ones who fed the lotus with the blood of round-eyes, or so the radio sometimes said. The ones who were bleeding this land dry for the sake of fuel and flowers.

Sometimes, when the sky-ships flew overhead, the windows would rattle and little Tetsuo would wake from his sleep, thinking demons were rising from the hells. But Hikita knew the oni had better things to do than trouble the sleep of foolish boys. The Endsinger's children dwelled below the earth, deep in the Yomi underworld. It was men who stained the clouds in their roaring machines. Men who turned the sky to red, the land to ashes, the rain to black. Not demons. Not gods. Just men.

A trembling wail split the dusk, Mother shrieking, throat raw. Hikita scowled again, lifted his kerchief and spat. Brother or sister, it didn't matter. He'd hate that child. Hate it as he hated its father, with his smooth talk and smoother smile. A dog who took advantage of a widow's loneliness, left her in dishonor, a bastard in her belly. He'd kill him if he saw him again. Show him that though they lived on the Stain's edge, in the poorest lands in all the seven islands of Shima, they were still Ryu clan. The blood of Dragons still flowed in their veins.

The windows began rattling and Hikita looked up, expecting to see a Guild sky-ship lumbering out of the dusk. But the sky was an empty, fading red, scabbed with storm clouds. The rattling intensified, the earth trembling so violently he fell to his knees. Tetsuo crawled across the bucking soil, a great belly-sore rumble beneath them. The brothers held each other as the island shook, Tetsuo crying out in fear.

"Another earthquake?"

The fifth in as many weeks. The rumbling stilled, choking slowly, until the skitter of rotten earth into the deadlands' fissures was the only noise. A thin cry began: a newborn's first bewildered plea as it was dragged from bloody warmth into this world of men. Kicking and screaming.

"It's here!" Tetsuo cried, the tremors forgotten. He slipped from Hikita's embrace and dashed into the house, dirty heels beating the verandah like drums.

Hikita stood slowly, listening to the hungry wails from their newest mouth.

He could hear his mother crying, the joy in her voice as she called for him to come meet his new sister. And the boy shook his head and licked the ashes from his lips, looking across the tall stalks of blood lotus to the desolation around the mountain's feet.

He blinked. Squinted in the gloom.

Tiny lights. Blood-red. A pair, shining between the lotus fronds. The crunch of little feet in dead leaves and deader earth. Hikita peered into the dark, the wails of his new sibling filling his ears. The deadlands' fumes were an oil-thick shadow, rippling like black water. The lotus stalks bent gently—something moving through the crop—and the tiny lights flickered out, once, twice, winking like the long-lost stars in the skies overhead.

No, not winking, he realized.

Blinking.

A figure shuffled from the stalks, covered in black earth and ashes. It stood two feet high, but its arms hung long and low, back bent as it shuffled forward and snuffled at the air. Its eyes were scarlet, casting a bloody light over heavy brows, hairless skull, swollen lips. It saw the boy, lips splitting into an idiot grin like a toddler who'd just found a new playmate. But its teeth were yellowed fangs, tusks protruding from its lower jaw, and Hikita realized beneath the mask of dirt and ash, its skin was midnight blue.

"*Uh-uuhhhhhhhh,*" it said, holding out its arms.

Hikita's eyes were fixed on the talons set in those grasping fingers, sharp as katana.

"*Gn-uhhhhh . . .*"

"Oni," he breathed. "Lord Izanagi save me."

The demon flinched at the Maker God's name, eyes growing bright and wide. It loped forward, knuckles dragging in the earth, a shriek of rage spilling from crooked fangs.

Hikita screamed. Screamed with his sister, here on her birthing day in the shadow of those broken peaks, amidst the rot creeping like a cancer across the island's skin. Screamed as if it were his final breath. As if it were all he was, and all he ever would be.

As if the world itself was ending.

1

SCHISM

Lightning burned the skies to white, glinting on black glass all around her.

Buruu and Kaiah loomed over her, their thoughts a raging storm in her mind.

And in her head, in her belly, only pain.

YUKIKO . . .

What is she talking about?

- TELL HER. -

Tell me what? Who is "they"?

YUKIKO, YOU ARE WITH CHILD—

"Yukiko."

The girl opened her eyes, the sweet scent of burning cedar in her lungs. It took a moment to remember where she was. Who she was. What had brought them to this.

She knelt beside a firepit in a simple house at the heart of a village in the trees. A bone-deep cold had slunk down from the mountains, hungry as ghosts, stealing through the Kagé stronghold and bringing the freezing promise of winter to come. Yukiko could smell it in the air, waiting at the edge of the stage. Storm clouds and white frost and black, black rain.

Six others sat around the flames. The bleeding remnants of a beheaded rebellion.

Soldiers without a captain?

Or sheep without a shepherd?

Kaori stared at Yukiko across the fire, steel-gray eyes bloodshot and circled with shadows. A long fringe was draped over the scar running forehead to chin, skin pale and drawn. She sat on Daichi's cushion at the head of the circle—as his daughter, everyone assumed Kaori would take charge now the leader of the rebellion was gone.

No, not gone, Yukiko thought.

Taken.

Other Kagé sat beside Kaori: Maro, the only other remaining member of the original council, long hair bound in warrior's braids, a leather patch over his missing eye. Beside him sat the Blackbird, the sky-ship captain who'd flown them from Kigen's smoldering ruin. The man's scowl was almost hidden beneath an enormous straw hat, his beard as thick as hedgerows. Then there was Michi of course, small and razor sharp, a chainkatana and wakizashi marked with the sigils of a noble Tiger household across her back. Little Tomo, the black and white pup she'd rescued from Aisha's chambers, sat in her lap, gnawing a knotted rope.

Lightning arced across an angry horizon.

The forest's pulse pounded inside Yukiko's head, the Kenning as loud and bright as she could ever remember. She tried to dim it, filtering it against a wall of herself. She could feel every living thing around her: swooping owls and fleeing mice and every life between, and burning above them all, the minds of every man and woman and child in the treetop village. Her hand strayed to her belly, to the two sparks of impossibly knotted heat she could sense inside her.

Inside me.

There was no room in her head for a thought that shape. No world where it could make any kind of sense.

Akihito took her hand, his massive paw swallowing hers whole. She squeezed his fingers in return. After months spent believing he'd died in Kigen jail, seeing him again had felt like coming home. They'd sat together on the Blackbird's ship during the retreat from Kigen, the big man speaking of his missing months, his injured leg, finding the street-urchins Hana and Yoshi. Yukiko spoke of the gaijin lightning farm, the sea dragons, the Razor Isles. And at the very end, she'd hung her head and spoken about what was growing inside her, swelling the Kenning beyond anything she'd ever known.

She'd told him who the father was. He hadn't even blinked. Just wrapped her in one of those fearsome Akihito hugs, kissed her brow, and told her everything would be all right.

He sat beside her now, hair tied back in cornrows. His right shoulder was wrapped in bandages, the Shōgun's tattoo burned from his flesh. Yukiko remembered Daichi doing the same to her, here in this very room. The thought of the old man chained in some chapterhouse filled her heart with flame, her mind with burning images of the boy who'd betrayed them all. Selling out the Kagé leader. Returning to the Guild he'd once fled from. A boy who'd said he loved her.

She sighed, brushing her hand across her eyes.

Gods, Kin, how could you?

She could feel Kaiah circling high overhead, the female thunder tiger delighting in the rumbling storm. Buruu was curled up on the landing outside, watching her with wide eyes. Anxiety written in the sway of his tail, the tilt of his head. He feared for her.

ARE YOU WELL, SISTER?

Feared for the twins inside her.

My Gods.

She tried to swallow with a mouth dry as dust.

Twins . . .

"Yukiko," Kaori repeated. "Are you well?"

She blinked. Shook her head. "I'm sorry. I'm just tired."

"We're all tired. Sleep when you're dead."

"I'm fine." She sat up straighter, tossed the hair from her eyes. "Go on."

"So," Kaori said. "We must plan our next steps. With Hiro's wedding foiled, the alliance between the Tiger and Dragon clan has crumbled. Daimyo Isamu of the Fox clan refused to even attend Hiro's wedding, so we can assume the Kitsune have no love for the Tigers either. This presents opportunity. An opportunity to purge the Guild from Shima once and for all."

"We have bigger problems," Yukiko said. "This Earthcrusher you spoke of will march soon, with Hiro leading the assault. Even if he doesn't have Aisha to tie him to the Kazumitsu line, fear of this machine might still make the other clanlords swear allegiance. Hiro already has the Phoenix armies at his command, and their Daimyo imprisoned. If the other clans unite with him and march north to the Iishi, we have nothing to throw against them."

"And the Guild know exactly where we are," Michi said softly. "The betrayer will have told them."

The puppy climbed off the girl's lap, began snuffling at the corner.

Yukiko nodded, swallowing bitter rage. "We have to assume Kin told them everything. This forest won't hide us anymore. I think we should seek permission from the Fox Daimyo to move to Yama city. They have a fortress there, at least. A fleet. An army."

"You asked us to place our faith in strangers before," Kaori said. "Look where it led us."

". . . Are you saying Daichi's capture is *my* fault?"

"I'm saying my father is in Guild hands because we trusted the strangers you brought to our door. From now on, the Kagé stand alone."

"We can't win this alone, Kaori."

"No? Not even with the mighty Stormdancer at our side?"

"Kaori, I know you're angry at—"

"My father is a captive because we put faith in your beloved Kin. And your once-lover Hiro is leading an army up here to annihilate us. Forgive me if I don't place much stock in your judgment, Stormdancer."

"Kaori, I loved Daichi too—"

"Don't do that," Kaori snapped. "Don't speak about him like he's already gone."

Michi's puppy began dancing in circles and barking at the roof, his tail a blur. "Tomo!" Michi hissed. "Hush!"

Yukiko and Kaori stared at each other for an age, the crackling fire the only sound between them. Kaori's stare was almost hateful, finally broken as she turned to Akihito.

"What of the children you brought with you, Akihito-san? The gutter-waifs from Kigen? Two more fighters with the Kenning could be formidable allies, considering we now have two thunder tigers. If one could be taught to ride the female . . ."

The big man cleared his throat, cast an uncomfortable glance at Yukiko. "I'm not sure we can ask much of them. Yoshi has a bad concussion, probably a fractured skull. Hana is shaken up pretty badly. She's not sleeping." He grimaced. "Her eye is hurting something fierce."

"Her eye is cause for concern," Kaori nodded.

"It'll heal," Akihito shrugged. "She just needs time."

"No, Akihito-san. Not the one plucked from her socket. The one that glows."

"Oh." A nod. "Right."

"What does your gaijin say about the girl, Stormdancer?" Maro asked. "The way he reacted when he first saw her . . ."

Yukiko was still staring at Kaori, shock at her words settling in her bones.

"Yukiko," repeated Maro. "What does your gaijin say?"

She looked out to the silhouette on the landing. Piotr stood gazing into the forest, his wolf skin wrapped against the growing cold. His pipe illuminated the deep scars on his face, his blind eye, dark cropped hair and a pointed beard. Cinnamon-and-honey-scented smoke spilled from pale lips, lightning glinting on the iron brace at his knee.

Buruu was swacking his tail against Piotr's legs, falling stone-still whenever the gaijin turned to glare. As soon as Piotr turned away, Buruu would swack him again. Piotr had helped them escape the lightning farm, and they both owed him a debt—the thunder tiger was just showing affection in the most annoying way he knew how.

"It's hard to understand him," Yukiko said. "Piotr's Shiman is broken at best. He talks about Hana like she's . . . touched or something. I saw a gaijin woman at that farm who had an eye like Hana's. Same color, same glow. They treated her like a holy woman."

"You should speak to her," Michi said. "Hana is strong as iron. And we'll need to wield every weapon we have against Hiro and his Earthcrusher. Whether we fight here or in Kitsune lands, two stormdancers are better than one."

Yukiko nodded wearily.

Little Tomo barked again, flaring the headache in Yukiko's head.

LITTLE WOLF, IF YOU KEEP BARKING YOU WILL BE A LITTLE MEAL.

Burru growled, long and low. Tomo tucked his tail and wisely fell silent.

"There's also this," Yukiko said. She produced a battered leather wallet, held it up to the assembled Kagé. "It's a letter. From the Artificer who fixed Piotr's leg. He was a captive of the gaijin, taught Piotr how to speak Shiman. If you can call it speaking . . ."

"A letter from a Guildsman?" Kaori narrowed her eyes. "To whom?"

"His lover."

"Guildsmen do not have—"

"It's all true, Kaori. What Ayane told us. There *is* a rebellion within the Guild. Piotr's Artificer was a member. This is a letter to his lover, a woman named Misaki, asking her to fight on and bring the Guild down." She removed the worn paper from the wallet, held it up to the firelight. "*And I will pray for you, for all the rebels that remain, that you may finish what we have started: Death to the Serpents. An end to the Guild. Freedom for Shima—*"

"Death to the Serpents?" Michi frowned.

Yukiko shrugged.

Kaori's voice was a low hiss. "My father is being tortured in some Guild hellpit right now because of that spider-legged bitch, Ayane. You expect us to believe anything she said?"

"Lies work best hidden between truths. If there's a group within the Guild looking to take it down from the inside, if this Misaki exists—"

"You'd have us take up arms beside chi-mongers?" Michi was incredulous.

"You just said we're going to need every weapon we can get, Michi."

Akihito frowned, rubbing his scarred thigh with dinner-plate hands. "If the Guild have a rebel faction, some of those we killed in the attack on Kigen could have been . . ."

"I know." Yukiko stared at the fire, thinking of the Guild ships she'd destroyed over the Iishi ranges. "They're just like us. They see the wrong of it. And we've been murdering them."

THERE IS NO MURDER IN WAR.

Buruu's thoughts rolled over her like storm clouds.

Tell that to the ones they loved.

YOU CANNOT BLAME YOURSELF, SISTER. YOU DID NOT KNOW.

But I know now. We can't go on like this, Buruu. Whether they can add to our strength or not, we can't keep killing them. It's just wrong.

"May I see it?" Kaori held out her hand. Yukiko passed over the letter, watched the older woman scan it with steel-gray eyes, her expression cold as snow.

Tomo barked again, one high-pitched yap that made Yukiko flinch. A curse rose on her lips, and she turned on the dog, pouring into his skull, ready to shout for silence.

. . . silver razors . . .

She blinked, pupils dilating.

. . . red eye watching bad badbad . . .

SISTER, BEWARE!

Buruu was on his feet, knocking Piotr aside and leaping onto the roof of Daichi's cabin. Two tons of muscle and beak and talon smashed the eaves to splinters, Maro crying out in alarm, Tomo yelping, the assemblage scattering as the ceiling partially collapsed.

"Maker's breath, what the hells is the matter with him?" Kaori cried.

Buruu landed amidst shattered timbers, shaking his head like a wolf savaging prey. As the Kagé stood dumbfounded, he opened his beak and spat onto the decking a crumpled ruin of silver clockwork and delicate spider legs, set with a windup key and a glowing red eye.

"Izanagi's balls," Michi hissed.

The council gathered around the ruined machine, no more than a handful in size. One of the delicate legs twitched, blue sparks popping as the light in its eye slowly died. Buruu growled, a bass rumble felt deep in Yukiko's chest. The night fell deathly still.

"What the hells is that?" Kaori hissed.

Michi crouched low to the boards, eyes on the ruined machine. Her terrified puppy leapt into her arms, tail between his legs, eyes fixed on Buruu. The thunder tiger snorted once, tail moving side to side with easy, feline grace.

GOOD EYES, LITTLE WOLF. PERHAPS I WON'T EAT YOU AFTER ALL.

"It's a Guild surveillance drone," Michi said. "Kigen palace was full of them."

Akihito nudged the thing with his boot. "What do they do?"

"What they see, the Guild knows."

The big man's eyes widened. He lifted his warclub and pounded it a little flatter. Michi clutched a terrified Tomo to her breast. "Gods, it's dead, Akihito!"

The big man shrugged apology, smashed it once more for good measure.

"Where in the hells did it come from?" Yukiko asked.

"Stowed away on the *Kurea*, maybe?" Akihito looked at the Blackbird.

"Amaterasu's tits, man." The captain raised one eyebrow. "Why on earth would the Guild have drones aboard my ship? If they knew I was a Kagé sympathizer, they'd have locked me in a torture cell faster than a Docktown strumpet lifts her kimono when the navy hits town."

Michi scruffed her puppy's ears to calm him. "One of the False-Lifers I killed in Aisha's bedchambers had a thing like this hidden in the orb on her back." She looked directly at Kaori. "Maybe this one belonged to the False-Lifer you kept prisoner here?"

Yukiko's heart sank. "Ayane . . ."

". . . She was spying on us," Kaori breathed. "Even locked in her cell, that bitch could see everything!" She hurled the ruined machine into the firepit, voice rising with fury. "Who knows how long it's been watching? And you want us to lay with these snakes, Yukiko?"

"Kaori, just—"

"Just what? The Lotus Guild has murdered our allies and friends! Butchered thousands of gaijin. If there *is* a rebellion within it, they're a pack of cowards, sitting on their hands while this country rushes toward the brink." Kaori turned to Maro. "Get to the transmission station. We broadcast this news tonight. Name this Misaki openly. We'll see what the clanlords think when they find out the Guild itself has an insurrection brewing inside it."

"You can't do that," Yukiko said.

"You do not tell me what I can and cannot do, Stormdancer."

"What do you think the Guild will do if you name her openly? They'll kill her, Kaori!"

"One less chi-monger. Perhaps her death will spur her comrades into action."

"Are you serious? Since when were we about murdering innocents?"

"Innocents?" Kaori spat. "Is that a joke?"

"The Guild rebels can be our allies! We're on the same godsdamned side!"

"Is that so? And what were our 'allies' doing while the Guild turned the skies to blood and the rivers to tar?"

"Read the letter! They've been working for years, waiting for—"

"Waiting!" Kaori roared. "Waiting while *thousands* died. Birds dropping from the skies, forests razed, gaijin turned into fertilizer. Waiting for *what*? An invitation? A perfect moment that would never come?"

"It's *wrong*, Kaori. What right do we have to risk their lives?"

"Such a paragon, aren't you? The mighty Arashi-no—"

"Oh, cut the Stormdancer bullshit!"

Kaori and Yukiko were nose to nose now. Kaori's hand was on her wakizashi, but Yukiko was yet to touch her katana. The blades were sisters, once wielded by Daichi, given now to his daughter and pupil; women he must have hoped would stand united after he'd fallen.

Buruu growled beside Yukiko, his rising anger mirroring her own. The girl's fury had also drawn Kaiah, the female arashitora swooping down from the clouds and landing on Daichi's ruined roof, looking over the rising tempers with narrowed eyes. Lanterns were being lit across the village, sleep-mussed people creeping out their doors to see what the fuss was about. Kaori seemed oblivious, spit flecked on her lips as she continued to roar.

"*We* are the ones fighting and dying, Yukiko! *We* are the ones paying the price while these rebels sit in their five-sided slave pits and count the days. Well, now they'll know what it is to bleed! Like we have bled! Like I have bled!"

"This isn't about you!"

"This is about *all of us*! Everyone in this village who called him father or friend." Kaori's eyes narrowed to papercuts. "He loved you too. You wear his sword on your hip, yet propose we lie with the dogs who stole him from us? Can you imagine what he's going through? Presuming they haven't already boiled him into fertilizer?"

"Godsdammit, this isn't about Daichi, either! You're killing our allies! We can work *with* the Guild rebellion, stronger together than we are alone."

"There is no 'we,' Stormdancer. There is us, and there is them. They deserve everything they get—Kin, Ayane, every one. You want me to weep for these rebels? I spit on them. I damn every one of them to the Yomi underworld! And you shame us all and everything we stand for suggesting we welcome any one of those bastards."

"You're so blinded by it," Yukiko breathed. "The hate in you . . . Everything you do, everything you say, it comes from the same place. The same moment. My gods, Kaori." Yukiko backed away, glancing at the woman's scar. "When Yoritomo cut your face, I'm not sure he realized he'd make you so godsdamned ugly."

It was an eternity, that moment. Yukiko saw Kaori's eyes widen, pupils to pinpricks, knuckles turning white on her wakizashi. And then the blade was in her hand, the sharp hymn of steel on the scabbard's lip, clear and bright. Akihito roared a warning, raising his warclub, Kaori's strike whistling toward Yukiko's head.

A deathblow.

Yukiko raised her katana, crying out as the swords touched. A burst of sparks and a brittle note of kissing steel, the blow deflected. Kaori stepped forward, kicking Yukiko hard in the chest, sending her tumbling.

Akihito cried warning, his words cutting the air like the steel in Kaori's hand. "Don't, she's pregnant!"

A roar. Like thunder a few feet overhead, the great booming echo of quaking skies. Buruu stood between Kaori and Yukiko, wings spread and spitting broken electricity. Kaiah landed astride the girl, shielding her with her own body.

Buruu's eyes were ablaze as he bellowed again, cruel beak open wide, just a hair's breadth from taking Kaori's arm off at the elbow, from scooping her insides out and spraying them across the village square before the children's terrified stares.

The Kagé closed in, weapons raised, broken lightning reflected in their eyes.

"*STOP!*" Yukiko screamed.

They felt that scream. All of them. Not just in the air around them, every bird in the canopy shrieking into flight, every hair on every body standing taut and tall and trembling. They felt it in their *bones*, somewhere old and reptilian at the base of their skulls, surfacing now only in hunger or thirst or lust. The beast inside every one of them.

And it was afraid.

"*Stop it*," she said.

Kaori's chest was heaving, frost tumbling from parted lips. Yukiko rolled out from under Kaiah, sheathed her katana, put one restraining hand on the thunder tiger's shoulder. Buruu growled so low and deep it felt as if the sky were falling. Thunder crashed overhead a final time, a pale wind rising. And with a single arc of brilliant lightning, it began to rain.

Clear as true glass, cold as ice and stinging with the promise of snow. As if Susano-ō had been holding it in his upturned palms for weeks on end, unleashed now in one colossal downpour. The heat amongst the gathering dissipated—water dashed onto a smoldering firepit. But deep inside the coals, fire still raged.

"Pregnant?" Kaori's voice was barely audible over the deluge.

". . . Twins," Yukiko said.

"Who is the father?"

"None of your godsdamned business."

"Your Kin?"

Yukiko licked her lips. Said nothing.

"Our would-be Shōgun Hiro, perhaps?"

Lightning clawed the skies, turning all to lurid, grisly white.

"To be honest," Kaori said, "I don't know which is worse. Either way, it explains much."

"We're done." Yukiko clawed damp hair from her eyes. "I'm gone."

"Gone?" Akihito stared at her, horrified. "Gone where?"

"Yama." Yukiko raised her voice, turning to the assembled crowd. "Anyone who wishes to come with me is welcome. I will stand by the rebels of the Lotus Guild. Speak to the Kitsune Daimyo and see if he'll accept my help. And when the Earthcrusher comes, I'll stand in its way. But I won't stand by and be a party to murder. And I won't stay in this village if that's what this rebellion has become."

"Go then," Kaori spat. "Go raise your bastards amongst your Guild dogs. They'll be in like company, no matter the name of the traitor you fucked to spawn them."

Buruu's roar shattered the shocked still. He took one step forward, floorboards crushed to splinters beneath his talons. Yukiko put out her hand, her face bloodless. The thunder tiger turned and looked at her, tail lashing just once, a spray of glittering droplets spilling between the rain. The girl shook her head, lips pressed into a razor-thin line. The arashitora turned back to Kaori with a snarl that made her flinch. But he moved no closer.

The faces of the assembled villagers spoke of astonishment. Of horror. Of an unraveling deep inside that left them breathless and gutted. A girl stepped forward, no more than a child, tears lost in the thundering rain.

"You can't go! Stormdancer!"

"I can't stay," Yukiko said. "Not like this. The Guild rebels see the wrong in this world we've built, and they've chosen to fight to make it right. How they fight is none of our business. We've no right to expose them, or put their lives at risk. We're no different from them. We're no better. As soon as we start thinking we are, we're just another Shōgunate, waiting to happen.

"But you can come. Any of you. All of you." She turned to the sky-ship captain, standing beneath his impossible straw hat. "Blackbird-san, will you carry them on the *Kurea*? Anyone who wishes to leave and come with me to Yama?"

"You saved my life. My crew and my ship." The captain nodded. "If you ask, it is yours."

As Akihito stepped forward, Buruu and Kaiah turned on him with a snarl. Wings flared, tails stretched behind them like whips. The big man stopped dead, his voice low.

"Yukiko, you can't do this . . ."

"It's done, Akihito. All that remains is for you to pick a side."

The girl climbed onto Buruu's back, looked amongst the villagers, the cloud-walkers, this tiny knot of rebellion now unraveling faster than any could have foreseen. A fortress made of clay, crumbling to the tune of falling rain.

"All of you," she said.

Thunder bellowed overhead.

"Choose."

2
CAPITULATION

Fair Kigen had lost her First Daughter.

The city was dressed in funeral black, boardwalk littered with the skeletons of gutted sky-ships. Spot fires still smoldered in Downside, filling the already choking air with smoke. Her people wore soot-stained clothes and bewildered expressions. Soldiers walked her cobbles, heads hung in shame. A mother wandered black riverbanks, her eyes as empty as the charred wicker stroller she pushed before her.

When the Stormdancer had landed in Market Square and urged Kigen's people to open their eyes and raise their fists, it had sounded an easy thing. A wonderful and powerful thing. And in a way, it was all that. But it was also an ugly thing. A brutal, callous, bloody thing.

Shima's people were learning what it meant to stand rather than kneel. Freedom is never given in tyranny's shadow—it is only taken. The Kagé rebels had done so, just as they promised. They'd burned Kigen city. They'd ruined Tora

Hiro's chance of renewing the dynasty that had ruled Shima for nine generations. And they'd murdered the Lady Aisha.

Her pyre was attended by almost every man, woman and child remaining in
the city. Their fair Lady. The last remnant of a proud lineage, the final link to
long-passed days of glory. As Shōgun, her brother Yoritomo had been respected,
obeyed, feared. But Aisha, with her wisdom and beauty and flawless grace—she
had simply been loved.

And now she was dead.

Her betrothed had watched her body burn, his armor painted death-white,
face smeared with ashes as if he too were to be consigned to the pyre. He hadn't
shamed himself with tears. But the Daimyo of the Tiger clan had spoken to the
assembled populace when the fire died, and in his eyes, they saw an emptiness
speaking of all they'd lost.

"That which has been taken can never be reclaimed," he'd said. "Kazumitsu's
last daughter is ended, and with her, all our hopes for tomorrow. But she will not
stand alone before the great Enma-ō. The Stormdancer, the Kagé dogs who
burned this city, those who made mourners of us all—they will join my betrothed
in death. I will lay her down on a bed of their ashes. And when I die, they will
greet me in the Hells."

Some had cheered. Some had wept. Most had simply stared. This was the hour
when words meant nothing. When talk of revolution and justice was washed
away, and all that remained was the reality of a gutted home, a bloodstained
thoroughfare, an empty stroller. This was fresh-faced troops marching onto
Guild sky-ships. This was mothers and wives kissing sons and husbands they
may never see again.

This was the pain before birth. The storm before spring.

This was what they asked for.

This was what they wanted.

This was war.

F*ifteen days.*
     Hiro stood with hands clasped behind him, green eyes staring at a gigan-
tic map of the Seven Isles on the floor beneath him. Long black hair tied in a
topknot, a pointed goatee on a handsome jaw, white ashes smeared all over his
face. The iron prosthetic where his right arm should have been spat chi smoke
into the soot-stained air, staining the rice-paper walls.

Six Iron Samurai stood with him, faces also smeared with ceremonial
ashes. Each stood seven feet tall in their death-white armor, masks crafted
like oni demons; tusks and horns and grinning fangs. Their eyes were those of
dead men.

"A fifteen-day march, Daimyo," said a voice like angry insect wings. "Then you and the Earthcrusher will be in the Iishi."

Hiro glanced at the figure looming beside him. Shateigashira Kensai was encased in his heavy brass atmos-suit. Instead of an expressionless mask like other Guildsmen, the Voice of the Lotus Guild in Kigen wore a sculpted brass face over his own. The features were of a beautiful boy in the prime of his youth, pouting lips open in a permanent howl and spewing segmented cable. Glowing blood-red eyes regarded Hiro, unblinking and soulless.

Three Guild Artificers stood with their Second Bloom, also encased in rivet-studded brass. Mechabacii clicked and skittered on their chests, counting beads moving back and forth in unfathomable patterns. Hiro wondered if any of them had helped design the replacement for the arm she'd torn from his shoulder.

He could feel his missing fingers, tried to ignore the urge to scratch.

The urge to scream.

The room in which the men stood was known as "the Face of Shima." It loomed in the heart of the Shōgun's palace, fifty feet square, two stories deep. The floor consisted of over a thousand interlocking tiles, forming an enormous map of the Seven Isles. A cluster of lights and scrims in the ceiling illuminated tiny armies in Kigen city, the Phoenix capital Danro, the staging ground near First House.

A nation poised on the brink of war.

Hiro's eyes were locked on the small inlaid peaks of the Iishi mountains, the tiny spotlight indicating the Kagé stronghold.

There she waits for me.

"North, northeast," he said. "First House to the Iishi. Magnify."

The servants in the control booth worked a series of levers and dials. The chatter of iron ratchets sounded below, and like a wave across a wooden ocean, each floor tile slipped down into the impossible mechanism beneath. New tiles slid up into place, flipping over one by one until the floor became whole again. The map now showed an enlarged version of the Imperium's northeast. A scrim was flipped, and the planned invasion route was traced in red light.

"We approach indirectly," Hiro noted. "Why not head straight to the mountains?"

"The Jukai deadlands should be avoided, Daimyo." Kensai indicated gray areas around First House otherwise referred to as "the Stain." "The Earthcrusher would not be troubled, but some fissures are too wide for a shredderman to cross. Besides, you need to muster your troops."

"The Phoenix fleet is already assembled," Hiro frowned. "Daimyo Shin and Shou have graciously given me command of their forces, and my Tiger troops muster as we speak."

"And the Dragon clan? The Foxes?"

"The Ryu flip back and forth like counting beads. And the Foxes are buried inside their holes. We do not need them. Between the Earthcrusher, a hundred shreddermen suits and the Phoenix sky-fleet, we have more than enough swords to destroy the Kagé."

"The Dragons and Foxes may yet bend their knee when they see the Earthcrusher."

"The destruction of the rebellion is all that matters, Kensai-san."

The Second Bloom's voice grew cold. "It is worth a detour to give Fox and Dragon a chance to join our endeavor."

"No."

"No?"

"I will not waste time in seeking their aid. Every day Yuki—" Hiro faltered, drew a calming breath. ". . . Every day Yoritomo's assassin lives is another day the Kazumitsu Elite live in disgrace. The Kagé burned my city. Killed my fiancée. They must die. Every one. Not next year. Not next month. Now!" The word was punctuated by an armored fist onto timber.

"I will repeat myself." Kensai folded his arms. "If the Kitsune and Ryu offer allegiance when they lay eyes on the Earthcrusher, you will accept it."

"You forget yourself, Guildsman. I am your Shōgun!"

"But you are *not* Shōgun, Hiro-san. Daimyo Haruka of the Dragon clan has not sworn to you. Daimyo Isamu of the Foxes did not even attend your wedding feast. You command the Tiger and Phoenix clans only through the strength of arms the Lotus Guild provides. So if Fox or Dragon capitulate at any point, you will welcome them with open arms. Though you may be intent on glorious suicide, some of us have a responsibility to the Imperium after this insurgency is quashed. The war against the gaijin *must* be renewed. We need more land. More slaves. More inochi. If we can save months of conflict against the Foxes and Dragons, we will."

"I will not simply—"

"You will do as you are *told*!"

As one, Hiro's samurai drew their chainkatanas and thumbed the ignitions. Lantern light flashed on spinning steel teeth, in the eyes of the death-white samurai in their demon masks. The air was filled with the screech of saw-toothed blades. Hissing pistons. Revving motors.

Kensai's hollow laughter.

"You draw chainblades against me? I, who provide the chi that fuels them? I, who designed the colossus you lead to the Iishi?" The Shateigashira chuckled behind that perfect, boyish mask. "The Kagé incinerated your fleet when they burned Kigen harbor, Daimyo. You cannot even move your troops without us, let alone fight when you get there."

"The iron rail still runs. Our forces can head north by train."

"And who do you suppose fuels them?" Kensai shook his head. "Put your swords aside, children, and remember what you are."

"We are warriors of the Tiger clan. We are samurai!"

"Above and beyond anything else you may be," Kensai sighed, "you are *ours*."

Hiro's jaw was clenched tight, his fists tighter. But at last, he glanced at his men, cut the air with his hand. With agonizing slowness, each samurai removed his gauntlet, blooded the drawn steel, then sheathed his blade. Kensai watched, expression hidden behind that impassive boy's face. His voice was the rasp of a thousand lotusflies.

"It was a stirring speech you made at Lady Aisha's pyre, Daimyo. But the time for pageantry is over. The Stormdancer poses a threat to this nation that cannot be overstated. In the space of weeks, she has turned the populace to rebellion and this nation's capital to ashes. But do not believe this Shōgunate's problems will simply disappear once she is dead. If *you* do not care for your country's future, at least have the sense to obey those who do."

His eyes burned bloody red, dying stars in a sky of brass.

"Are you hearing me, Hiro-san?"

Hiro was staring at his clockwork arm. The ball-joint fingers outstretched, iron-gray tendons now painted bone-white. The color of death. The death awaiting him at the end of this road. The death of honor. Of the Way. Of the girl who once thought him her love.

". . . I hear you."

"The sooner you rendezvous with the Earthcrusher, the sooner it marches," Kensai said. "And from then? Fifteen days."

Bone-white metal curled into a fist.

He nodded.

"Fifteen days."

3
SHEDDING SKIN

With every breath dragged over his teeth, pain flared like sunlight on broken glass. Daichi coughed, a handful of wet sputters leaving a black taste on his tongue. He was slumped in an iron chair inside a cell with no windows, manacles cutting into his wrists, stink of chi filling his broken nose. The thrum of countless engines vibrated through the floor.

How long had he been here? Days? Weeks? His stomach so empty it no longer growled, head still ringing from his last beating. But he hadn't broken. Hadn't begged. Not yet, anyway.

Only a matter of time, he knew. With enough raindrops, even mountains became sand. But the blacklung was working him too, in the long and quiet dark between one beating and the next. Even as the earthquakes shivered the walls around him, painting his skin with dust. Even when the Lotusmen weren't grinding him closer to his ending, the enemy inside his body was gathering its forces all the same. He wondered who would prove the victor in that race.

He had a favorite, to be sure.

The cell door opened, a shear of painful light cutting across yellow stone. Heavy iron boots rang on the floor, the heartbeat drumming of heel and toe mixed with the song of clockwork skins. How many had come to beat him this time? Four? Five?

Did it matter?

He felt smooth fingers pressing his pulse, pulling back his eyelids. He caught an impression of long, silvered arms, bloody eyes in a featureless face. A wasp-waist. Glossy skin. Noises, like an orchestra of insect parts.

"How is he?"

A male's voice, deep and growling. Daichi peered through the shifting haze, saw a face he recognized from years past. A boy-child's visage in burnished brass, iron cable squirming from open, frozen lips. The Voice of Kigen City—Second Bloom Kensai himself.

The lord of flies had come to the feast at last.

"He is weak, Shateigashira." A female's voice, thin and sibilant. "Malnourished, dehydrated and concussed. I imagine he is in considerable pain."

"We can do better than 'considerable,' surely?"

"We see only pointlessness in this, Shateigashira."

A soft voice, as of a man murmuring in his sleep. Daichi squinted at the one who spoke, caught the impression of a small man in dark cloth. A black breather shaped like a grin was affixed over his mouth, hissing plumes of sweet smoke, but to Daichi's surprise, the man's face was otherwise uncovered. His eyes were so bloodshot, the whites were simply red. The room seemed to grow darker when Daichi looked at him.

"I will judge what is and is not pointless here, Inquisitor," came Kensai's reply. "I am still Second Bloom of this chapterhouse."

"The boy has brought us this man as a gift. Is that not proof enough of loyalty?"

"Apparently not."

"He is destined for great things, Shateigashira. The son of Kioshi will rise to heights his father never dreamed of. The Chamber of Smoke speaks no lie."

"Then you have nothing to fear." Kensai turned to the door. "Bring him in."

Daichi watched another Lotusman enter the room, a slow, steady march with hands clasped before it. The suit marked it a member of the Artificer Sect—the engineers and technicians who designed the Guild's mechanical marvels. Ornate filigree decorated the brass, a pattern that put Daichi in mind of swirling smoke.

"Second Bloom," said the newcomer, bowing low.

Daichi's heart skipped, fingers curling into fists. Even behind the mask, he'd have recognized that voice anywhere. The boy he'd trusted. The boy who'd handed him over to these dogs to be beaten and burned.

"Kin-san." The little man in black returned the bow.

"Kin-san, is it?" Kensai growled. "Your father Kioshi gave you his name when he died. An honorable son would bear it with pride."

"The venerable First Bloom has promoted our young brother to Fifth Bloom after bringing this Kagé dog to justice, Shateigashira," said the little man. "It is surely within you to acknowledge he has earned his own name."

Daichi lunged upright, cracking lips drawn back from his teeth, chains snapping taut.

"You godless traitor," he spat at the boy. "Enma-ō damn y—"

A Lotusman's palm caught him full in the face, rocked him back with loosened teeth. Firm hands clamped down on his arms, mechanized strength pinning him still.

Not once did Kin glance in his direction.

"You sent for me, Second Bloom?" the boy asked. "What is your command?"

"The Inquisition have reviewed the information you gathered whilst on your . . . sojourn amongst the Kagé. It has been decided further questioning of this one"— a gesture in Daichi's direction—"is unnecessary. You have already given us the location of the rebel encampment. Numbers and disposition. Assets and strength."

"I seek only to atone for past mistakes," Kin said. "If my knowledge aids in bringing the Kagé dogs to justice, I consider the time I . . . wandered well spent. The lotus must bloom."

"The lotus must bloom." Pale smoke escaped from the little man's breather.

"Indeed." Kensai seemed unimpressed. "With that in mind, it has been decided to liquidate this prisoner immediately."

Daichi grit his teeth, fought down a rush of fear. He coughed, sudden and violent, swallowing thick. Stilling himself, he fixed his eyes on the floor.

Here? In this pit?

"If you are certain, Second Bloom . . ." Kin's voice drifted off into silence.

"And why would I not be?"

For the first time since entering the room, the boy looked at Daichi. The mechabacus on his chest clicked and skittered, counting beads shifting back and forth across their relays with timepiece precision, ticking down one second at a time toward Daichi's murder.

"I always pictured a public execution," Kin said. "To show the skinless the price of defying us."

"The opinions of the skinless are not your concern. The commands of First Bloom are."

"As you say, Second Bloom."

Silence descended, tinged by metallic breath, the burnished pulses of the skins these monsters coiled inside. Daichi strained against his manacles, earning nothing but more purple on his wrists and another slap from the Guildsman beside him.

"Then you will forgive me, Shateigashira," Kin spoke carefully. "But why did you call me here? I do not care whether this rebel lives or d—"

"Because you are to be his executioner. *Kin*-san."

Kensai reached into his belt, produced an ugly fistful of pipes and nozzles. Daichi had only seen a device like it once before, but he'd witnessed the damage it could wreak on ō-yoroi armor and the meat beneath.

An iron-thrower.

"You wish me to—"

"I do, Kin-san," Kensai said. "I wish you to kill this man."

". . . Here?"

"Now."

The boy seemed frozen, the breath in his bellows falling still. Daichi thought of his daughter, Kaori—all her fire and fury, those beautiful steel-gray eyes so like his own. The knife scar cutting across her features, the blow from a madman's hand that set his feet upon this path so many years ago. To think this was where it ended. That this was the sound of his funeral hymn. The clank and groan of retching machines . . .

Kin was staring at the iron-thrower in Kensai's hand.

"I . . ."

Daichi's lips peeled back in a snarl as Kin's voice faltered.

"Coward," he hissed. "How did you muster the courage to kill Isao and the others? Did you face them down or stab them in the back? Izanagi curse me a fool for thinking you'd have the strength to do what's right. You even lack the courage to face a man as you end him."

Kin looked at him, hands becoming fists.

"You know *nothing* of what is right," the boy spat. "Nor did Isao and his dogs."

"And so you crawl back to your master's feet? Because of the actions of a few? You'd give these monsters the location of our village? Where our children sleep? Our *children*, Kin?"

"Your children are rapists and murderers, Daichi. Pigs, all of them." Kin leaned in close, the old man's reflection snared in his single, glowing eye. "And pigs get put to slaughter."

Daichi spit at him then. A spray of black saliva, right into the smooth brass that passed for the boy's face. With a furious hiss, Kin snatched the iron-thrower from Kensai's hand, the device heaving a tiny, breathless gasp as he aimed between Daichi's eyes.

The old man looked down the barrel into bottomless black.

He nodded.

"Do it."

And Kin pulled the trigger.

S he should not be here.

Ayane stole up the access stairwell, silent and slow. A choir of machines sang in the chapterhouse belly, the mechabacus at her chest sang inside her mind, each false rhythm entwined with the other.

She stopped at the habitat level, pressed against the wall. Running her hands up her arms, she tried recalling the kiss of Iishi wind on bare flesh, the way it made the hair on her forearms stand tall and tingling. But she could barely feel anything now; encased once more in glossy earth-brown skin, hugging her tight and providing no warmth or comfort at all.

I should not be here.

These habitats were for the Shatei—the brothers. False-Lifers like her had their own quarters, far across the chapterhouse and two floors lower. Her business was with the nurseries, the surgical implants, the machines that emulated life within the chapterhouse. Male and female flesh did not mingle—even when it was time for a False-Lifer to bear a new Guildsman into the world, she met only with the Shatei's seed and an inseminator tube. Most Guild women lived their entire lives without knowing a man's touch.

But *she* had known. Had felt his breath upon her naked face, his lips pressed against hers, soft as strangled moonlight. She closed her eyes at the memory, pressed her thighs together, feeling goose bumps tingle across her flesh.

No, she thought. *My skin.*

She peeked through the stairwell exit, stole free when the way was clear. Silver arms curled against her back like a long-dead spider, she slipped along the corridor, searching the nameplates beside the habitat doors. At last, she found it—a thin brass slab, freshly engraved, the name he'd fought so long to keep and now had finally made his own.

Kin. Fifth Bloom. Artificer Sect.

She flexed the lever, watching the steel iris dilate and open into his suite. Fifth Blooms enjoyed accommodations only slightly less austere than the average Lotusman, but Kin's promotion at least afforded him a touch more space. A small workbench. A bigger bed. Ayane turned and pulled the lever, the iris contracting with a grinding sigh, slowly strangling the light beyond. And there in the dark, lit only by the red glow of her eyes and the purity monitor above the ventilation duct, she stood and simply breathed.

She must be mad for doing this. She risked everything by coming here—all she'd done, the blood, the lies, the hurt. But he filled her mind with daydreams, her belly with tumbling moths. The thought of their time together, the way he'd made her *feel . . .*

The purity monitors smudged slowly from red to green as the air filters hissed, finally signaling the all-clear with a bright metallic chime.

She worked the clasps at her back, above and below the empty silver orb swelling on her spine. Pulling the zip cord down, she bent double and peeled herself out of the slick membrane, stepped naked to Kin's bed and climbed inside. And there she lay in the dark, picturing him as he'd been in the Iishi, pale and perfect, lips against hers, electricity dancing on her skin. She ran her hands over her body, imagining they were his, waiting for the moment he'd open the door and find her there. Where she should not be.

What would he say?

Would he understand how badly she needed him?

She chewed her lip in the black.

I will make him.

She heard a clunk, a piston's hiss, the iris portal dilating with the tune of blade on blade. Sitting up in the bed, sheet clutched around her, she smiled at the silhouette outlined in the doorway. Tall and lean, cut from black whispering cloth.

Smoke drifting from the grin-shaped breather at its lips.

"Oh, no . . ." she breathed.

The figure stepped inside, followed by another, clad head to toe in black silk. Their breathers weaved vapor puppets in the air. She smelled chi-smoke. Unfiltered. Overpowering. Their eyes were red, but not aglow—simply bloodshot from the smoke they breathed every moment of their lives. She knew them. The brethren who enforced Guild doctrine, oversaw the Awakening ceremonies across Shima, safeguarding the Guild from corruption in all its guises.

The Inquisition.

They closed the door behind them, plunging the room into a darkness lit only by the purity monitor, shifted again from green to red. The first Inquisitor spoke as though he were not quite . . . *there.* As if some part of him drifted in a cold and distant dark, only a splinter showing above this surface.

"You have served well, sister," he said. "But now the time for service is over."

"No," she breathed. "Please . . ."

"You are lost, sister," said the other. "But we will show you the Way."

"No, not yet." Tears welled in her eyes, spilling warm down her cheeks. "I did what you asked me. I brought him back to you."

"You did," the first sighed, staring at outstretched fingers. "And you have our thanks."

"But you are poisoned," breathed the second. "We have watched it spread. Dragging you down, leading you here, where no sister who walks Purity's Way should find herself."

"Skin is strong," said the first. "Flesh is weak."

"Weak," came the whisper.

"I did what you *asked me*!" Ayane's voice rose, raw and growling, fistfuls of sheet clenched at her breast. "I turned him against them! Them against him!"

"We have been wondering at the how of it."

She looked between the pair, shame rising at the recollection, her litany of deceptions.

". . . I sabotaged his machines. The shuriken-throwers he built them. I rigged them to fail when the demons attacked the village. And when that wasn't enough, I . . . hurt myself. I made him think they . . ."

"A talent for deceit, sister."

"He killed for me. Do you know what that *feels* like—"

"Come." The first held out his hand. "You shame yourself."

"You knew this future would come to pass," the second said. "The moment you chose to step inside this room and seek the way of flesh."

"What did you think would happen?" Ayane pushed the tears down into her toes, felt them pushing back harder than she could hope to manage. "What did you think I'd become when you let me out of this cage? Feel someone touching me, really *touching* me for the first time in my life? Did you think I'd crawl back into this pit with a smile? What did you *think I would do*?"

"This." A gesture to the room around them. "Just this."

"You bastards," she moaned.

"Skin is strong," said the first.

"Flesh is weak," said the second.

"Come with us." The first stepped closer, hand outstretched. "There will be no pain. Not like for those who remain. This quiet parting is a blessing to you, sister. A gift."

"No . . ."

"She comes." The first shook his head slowly. "Her children also. In a handful of years, all will be ash. No place for a child of man. You or any other."

"Godsdamn you . . ."

"Come."

Fingers outstretched, gentle on her arm, the thought of another's flesh against hers suddenly utterly repulsive.

"Don't *touch me*!"

She snaked to her feet, quicksilver, the limbs at her back unfolding, air agleam with the shape of razors. Whistling chrome tore into the Inquisitor's face, chest, outstretched arm. He stood taller, eyes wider, like a man fresh woken from a dream.

"You dare . . ."

He lashed out with his foot, a thunderbolt in her chest, crushing her mech-abacus like it was paper. Blinded by sparks and pain, Ayane flew back against the wall, hit hard. She lashed out with her chrome arms again but he was gone, a hiss of smoke, an impression of black vapor moving along the floor. He coalesced before her, his fist demolishing her chin. She spun sideways, silver arms drooping as she crashed to her knees, chin slicked with red. She began weeping then, weeping as the chatter of the mechabacus died and she felt silence inside her head again. The same silence she'd known in the Iishi, blinking at the dappled day through a singing curtain of leaves.

She looked up into bloodshot eyes, wide and pitiless, tunic torn, pale skin that had probably never felt sunlight. And as his bloodied hands reached for her, she saw the ink on his right arm: a coiled black shape where the skinless bore the tattoo of their clan.

A serpent.

His hand was in her mouth, pushing past her teeth. She tasted ash on her tongue, in her lungs, filling her eyes. She tried to bite with her broken jaw, tried to speak. To whisper the name of her love, the dream dissolving into blossoms of brilliant white. But there was no breath in her lungs, not even for the tiniest of words. Only smoke. Blue-black smoke.

And so she held it inside. Close to her heart. And as the light became dark, and the blackness pressed down on her eyelids, her pulse spoke the word her lips could not.

"*Kin.*"

The light faded.

"*I'm so sorry.*"

And true silence fell at last.

C*lick.*

Kin blinked, his breath deafening, the iron-thrower in his hand refusing to roar. Daichi let out a ragged sigh, ending in a stifled cough. The weapon in Kin's hand felt heavy as mountains.

Empty . . .

"There," sighed the Inquisitor. "I trust you are now satisfied, Second Bloom?"

Kin stood taut as a bowstring as the Inquisitor took the iron-thrower from his fingers. He could feel Kensai's burning stare, his mouth tasting of lotus ash. He breathed deep to quiet his anger.

"You said First Bloom wanted this man dead."

"He does," Kensai said. "Just not yet."

"A test . . ." Kin realized.

"And one well conquered," said the Inquisitor. "Not only do you hand this rebel to us, but you would execute him with but a word. Admirable, would you not agree, Second Bloom?"

Kensai stared for a breathless age, boy-child face aglow with blood-red lamp-light. Kin watched him in silence this man who had been his father's closest ally. This man he'd once thought of as uncle. This man who, even after he'd betrayed the Kagé, handed over their leader, clearly trusted him as far as he could spit him.

"Admirable indeed," Kensai finally said.

"You have our thanks, Fifth Bloom." The Inquisitor paused, touched his mech-abacus, supple fingers dancing a reply. "Your presence is requested in the Chamber of Gears."

"I was headed to my habitat," Kin said. "The hour is late—"

"The brothers will not keep you long." The Inquisitor bowed. "The lotus must bloom."

". . . The lotus must bloom," Kin said, nodding and numb.

The air was filled with the rhythm of the machine, the clunk and clank of pistons and greasy iron, the rut and rumble of construct hearts inside concrete miles and black, metal shells.

Without another glance at Daichi, Kin stalked out the door.

4
SCARIFICATION

Kaori had honestly thought she loved him.

Nobody would have blamed her. She was only sixteen, after all. Her father had done his best to protect her from the hedonism of the Shōgun's court—it was understood amongst the nobleborn sons that Captain Daichi's daughter was off-limits. And though her beauty was almost peerless, all respected the blades of the Iron Samurai commander enough to admire her from minimum safe distance.

Her father's overprotectiveness left her frustrated, and as she grew older, hungry. She'd listen to the serving girls giggling about their trysts, see beautiful boys watching her from afar. And in her frustration, she began to hate them. Did they really believe her father would make good on his threat to decorate his mantel with the privates of the first to touch her?

They weren't warriors. Certainly not men. They were boys. Cowards, all.

Save one.

He allowed his stare to linger, when all others turned away. He would smile, his gaze roaming all over her. It made her shiver. And as she felt his eyes exploring her body, fierce and hungry as winter wolves, she found herself wishing they were his hands instead.

Yoritomo. Lord of Tigers. Shōgun of the Shima Imperium.

He was fourteen years old, barely a year within his reign, but already tall and broad, lean muscles and bronze skin. When he spoke to his courtiers and ministers, absolute stillness reigned. When he stared into their eyes, they would bow their heads and look away.

Fourteen years old, but more a man than any in this court of trembling children.

He'd smile when he saw her. And though she could sense the storm clouds roiling over her father's head, she would smile in return, flutter her breather fan before her face to cool the heat he brought to her skin. Daichi didn't approve of Yoritomo's blatant attentions, but Yoritomo was Shōgun, and Daichi his servant. Who was he to deny his lord?

She'd heard the rumors, of course. Talk of the Shōgun's cruelties. Even Yoritomo's sister Aisha talked to Kaori in private moments, warning that her brother's affections should not be encouraged. And though Aisha was a dear friend, still Kaori didn't believe. It was too easy to find her mind wandering along with her hands, alone in her bed at night, imagining herself seated at his right side. First Lady of the Imperium. Days spent in the halls of power, and nights spent in sweating, blissful collisions between silken sheets.

And so, when Yoritomo sent a missive that he wished to see her, she felt only the thrill. Not the fear born of open and clear eyes.

Her father had been sent to the Province of the Golden Road to punish a disobedient magistrate. Her matron was sent to bed early by a few droplets of blacksleep in her tea. And in his chambers, she met him, her honorable Lord, blood-red silk hugging her trembling body, a nervous smile hidden behind a shaking fan.

They'd sat and talked at first—or more truthfully, he had talked and she had listened. He spoke of his dreams, to see his Imperium stretch to every far-flung nation. And she'd pictured herself on a throne of gold—a Queen of the civilized world. And when he kissed her, she'd kissed him back, teasing at first, tasting at last, melting from the heat inside her.

This was bliss, she thought. This was love.

But he wouldn't stop.

His hands began roaming, clutching, squeezing, and though he was moving too swiftly, he was her Lord, and she wanted desperately to please him. He tore at the outer layers of her jûnihitoe, and she said nothing. He pawed at her breasts and she breathed not a word. But inside, her melting warmth turned to horrid chill. This was brutish. Ugly. And when he forced his hand between her legs, his fingers, Gods, his fingers . . .

She screamed. Cried no.

And he'd laughed.

The sound was a knife in her chest, as cold and hard as his hands. And she screamed again, louder, NO, slapping as hard as she could, fingers hooked, nails across his cheek.

He drew back, eyes wide, bringing those awful fingers up to touch the three ragged gouges in his face. She'd turned away, terrified, waiting for him to cry for his guards. Would she be arrested? Exiled from court? They'd know she'd come here unaccompanied. She would shame her father's name. Gods, what would he say?

But she heard no cry for the guards. Instead, he struck her. A closed fist sending her sprawling, a terrified cry on her lips. And then he was sitting on her chest and she couldn't breathe to scream again. She struggled, arms pinned, and as her lungs began burning she saw the blade in his hand, sharp enough to cut the air in two.

No breath to beg him.

No breath to scream.

"You deny your Shōgun?" he'd hissed. "You dare?"

He pressed the blade to her throat and the tears came then, black light burning before her eyes. And though it shamed her near to dying, though in years to come, she denied it to herself with everything inside her, she would have let him, then. She would have turned her head and closed her eyes and let him do what he wanted if only he'd have put the knife away. She was so afraid. Small and frightened and completely alone.

Sixteen years old.

"Have no fear." Amusement in his voice. "The mood has fled. I have no wish to take your maidenhood any longer."

Momentary relief evaporated as she felt the knife being pressed against her fore-head. Hard enough to cut her. To make her bleed.

Gods, oh gods, it hurt . . .

"But I think no other man should want for it either."

And she couldn't even scream.

K aori sat alone, staring at the empty pit where fire once burned. Listening to the rain's spatter-patter, footsteps, hushed voices, sky-ship engines idling amidst the shifting sea of leaves.

Exodus.

It was better, she told herself. War was coming, and she needed only warriors. Not bakers or carpenters or seamstresses. Not children or old men or babe-laden wives. Men and women prepared to do whatever it took to free this nation from the Guild, the Imperium, the blood lotus. Let the weak hide with the Storm-dancer in Yama city. The warriors would remain—Maro, Michi and the others. They remembered her father. They remembered the cause.

The lotus would burn.

"Kaori."

"Michi." She didn't look up from the firepit, black coals reflected on steel-gray. "When they've left, we must take stock of those who remain. There will be—"

"Kaori, we need to talk . . ."

She turned then, saw the girl in the doorway. Pale skin and bee-stung lips, chainblades crossed at her back. The girl Kaori had turned from a simple peasant child into one of the sharpest blades in the Kagé armory. The girl she'd trained to infiltrate the Shōgunate court. After years at Aisha's side, Michi had returned home. Older. Harder. So sharp the air fairly bled where she walked.

But there was a crude wooden scrollcase tucked under one arm, a satchel over her shoulder. And the look in her eyes nearly set Kaori's heart to breaking.

". . . You're leaving?"

The girl nodded. "I'm sorry."

"But why?"

"Aisha wouldn't have wanted this. It shames her memory."

"You think this sundering is my doing?" Kaori climbed to her feet. "Yukiko is the one leaving. I would have us stay and fight as we always have."

"It's more than this, now." Michi gestured around them. "Daichi always said this was never about us. The Kagé were about opening people's eyes, showing them they need to fight. We have a chance to win, with the Guild rebels on—"

"Rebels? Gods, call them what they are, Michi. Cowards."

"You don't know what it's like. To live in the quiet. To sit surrounded by brutality and injustice, knowing if you speak a word, as every part of you *screams* to do, nothing happens save that two die instead of one." A sigh. "But I know. I lived it every day for the past four years. And it takes a strength you wouldn't believe."

"When it comes to these Guild pigs? No. I wouldn't."

"Aisha showed me how to hide it. 'Let it burn slow,' she said. 'Keep it hidden until the day it will truly matter, when risking all will actually be worth the blood you wager. The day we can win.'" Michi shrugged. "This is the day we can win, Kaori. But not without Yukiko."

Kaori took one long, measured breath, exhaling poison. "You godsdamned traitor."

Michi stepped back as if Kaori had struck her.

"I brought you in here!" Kaori shouted. "I treated you as blood! I taught you *everything*, and this is how you repay me? You leave us now? *Now*, Michi?"

"There's something wrong in you, sister." Tears welled in Michi's eyes. "Something broken. I don't think you see the same world I do at the end of this. I see blue skies, and green fields and children dancing in clean rain. And I don't pretend it comes from someplace good and pure. It comes from hate, same as you. I want them to suffer, same as you. For my uncle. For my village. But I want something better afterward too. And all you want is to breathe the smoke. You don't even care if there *is* an afterward, as long as you can watch everything burn."

Tears spilled freely down Michi's face now, reaching out to touch Kaori's hand.

"And I want to fix you, and I don't know how . . ."

Kaori slapped Michi's hand aside, features contorted with fury.

"Don't touch me."

"Come with us."

"No. I will not stand beside the Guild. Not now. Not ever."

"Please, Kaori . . ."

"Begging? You shame yourself, sister."

The false smile dropped from her lips as Michi dried her tears, staring for what seemed an eon. But at last the girl turned, stalking from Daichi's ruined home. Kaori stood and stared, biting wind blowing the fringe back from her skin.

Everywhere she looked, she was reminded of her father. The chess set he'd brought with him from Kigen. The leather glove hanging on the wall, soaked with screams and scorched flesh stink, the memory of the day she'd asked him to burn off her tattoo still crystal clear in her mind. A handkerchief, soiled with black stains.

Gods, where was he? Already dead?

He'd been all she had left.

She sank to her knees, trying to breathe.

Gods, help me . . .

She heard footsteps on the decking outside, too heavy for Michi, too clumsy for one of her warriors—the tread of a man with a limp. She turned expecting to see Akihito, instead found herself looking into an eye of sapphire blue, another as white as sun-polished bone. Short dark hair and a pointed beard, a wisp of honey-and-cinnamon-scented smoke on his lips.

Yukiko's gaijin. The one called Piotr.

She stood, faced the round-eye, pushing the grief down into her feet.

Breathe.

She folded her arms, stared cold.

Just breathe.

"What do you want?"

"Yukiko," the gaijin said.

"She's not here."

"Da," he nodded. "Am knowing. But she wrong."

"Wrong?"

"Da."

"You surprise me, round-eye. I thought you a faithful dog. Is there no room on her lap for both you and the bastards in her belly?"

Sometimes the words just fell from her lips, cold and cruel.

Sometimes she didn't know where they came from.

Piotr shook his head. "No, on Guild, Yukiko is speaking true, and this is Kaori knowing, I am think. But Yukiko is wrong of saying Kaori ugly."

Kaori caught her breath. Whispered. "What did you say?"

He motioned to her face.

"Beautiful," he smiled.

Piotr turned to stare out at the village, the Iishi forest, the rolling storm clouds overhead. He seemed to be burning the picture in his mind, the sea of dead and evergreen leaves, the ancient trees, the jagged spires reaching toward the booming heavens overhead.

Finally, he turned to look at her again, honey-and-cinnamon smoke drifting from his smile. He clomped across the boards toward her, reaching down to take her hand. And staring into her eyes as she frowned in confusion, he brought her knuckles up to his lips.

"Good-bye, beautiful lady," he said. "Hoping I will see her near."

With a grimace, he turned and limped away, pistons at his broken knee hissing, heavy boot dragging across unfinished boards. She watched him go, not breathing a word. The wind danced amidst the trees, a gust pushing her fringe away from her face, cold and laden with rain. She reached toward it with outstretched fingers—the same fingers he'd just pressed to his lips.

It would have been a simple thing then, to tuck the hair behind her ears, to let the wind and the world see the scar he'd left her with. It would have been a simple thing, to exhale the vile inside, to accept and breathe and be. A simple thing. And the hardest thing in the world.

Her fingers clawed her fringe back down over her face.

And she sat alone in the dark, staring at the empty pit where the fire once burned.

5
WAKING

Hana squeezed her brother's hand, wrapped in the scent of new rain.

The siblings sat on the landing outside the guesthouse, feet dangling over the edge. Hana peered down to the dizzying fall between her toes. The wind howled like a wounded oni, the rain a constant drumbeat, drowning the sounds of the village around them. There was some kind of ruckus going on near the heart of town, but Hana couldn't bring herself to care. She swung her feet back and forth, letting tears tumble and misery roll over her in cold, lonely waves.

Poor Daken . . .

He'd been only a kitten when they found him, chewed by corpse-rats inside a Kigen city drain. He'd loved them, and they'd loved him back. He was Hana's best friend in the world.

And now he was gone.

She wiped at her good eye and hung her head, watching her tears spiral into the void. She tried not to think about how he'd ended, how she might have stopped it, how the yakuza who'd stomped him underfoot had died far too quickly at Akihito's hands. The bandage over the left side of her face was crusted with dry blood, the agony from where her eye had been ripped from her socket still gnawing and real. She tried not to think about that either.

Failure on both counts.

Yoshi had it worse. His skull was still wrapped in gauze from his beating, and his headaches weren't going away. Concussion, they said. It'll heal in time, they said. But when Hana looked into her brother's eyes, she didn't see the same Yoshi anymore. She saw the memory of a beautiful boy, cold and dead in a pool of co-agulating red.

A smile with no lips.

A face with no eyes.

Poor Jurou . . .

She wondered what they'd do. Where they belonged. The few days since they'd landed in the Kagé village had been all blurred visits to the healer, draughts of medicinal tea and pain. Hana hadn't had a chance to speak to Yukiko yet. She hadn't even really spoken to Yoshi about Jurou's death. Everything was happening so quickly. She just needed a minute to breathe . . .

A rush of wind blew her ragged bob around sodden cheeks, the thunder above sounding far closer than the clouds. She heard claws scrabbling on thatch, a tortured timber groan. Peering over her shoulder, she saw a pair of slitted amber eyes peering back. The female arashitora was perched on the guesthouse roof, half-spread wings dancing with faint electricity. The sight of her might have taken Hana's breath away, if she hadn't already spent it all on tears.

"Yoshi," she whispered.

Her brother turned and saw the beast, breath catching in his lungs. The hairs on Hana's arms stood rigid, ozone tickling her nose. And as she'd done with rats and cats since she was a child, she reached out to the heat, afraid it would be too hot for her mind to touch.

Hello.

– HELLO, MONKEY-CHILD. –

She blinked at the beast, wiped scabbed knuckles across her eye. Its voice was a thunderclap in her head. She squeezed her brother's fingers, whispered in amazement.

"Yoshi, she's talking to me . . ."

Yoshi turned away, staring out over the forest. "You been beast-speaking since you were a sprat. No news there."

"Her voice, gods, it's like a storm inside your mind. Try it."

Yoshi scowled, pointed to the gauze wrapped around his brow. "Headache."

Hana turned back to the arashitora, reaching gingerly toward its heat again. The sensation was like nothing she'd ever known, storm clouds in her mind, electricity dancing on her skin.

Your name is Kaiah, right?

– YES. –

I'm Hana.

– WHY YOU CRY? –

Hana blinked, taken aback. She sniffed, tucked her tangle of hair behind her ears.

No foreplay first, eh? No poetry or flowers. Just jumping right into it there.

– WHAT? –

. . . Doesn't matter.

The arashitora began preening, straightening the coverts of her left wing with a cruel black beak, the same color encircling those wonderful amber eyes. Hana watched her, fascinated, as if a picture from a children's tale had stepped off the paper into wonderful, full-color life. Her thoughts rang in Hana's skull; strobing, violent, deafening.

The beast blinked, tossed her head.

– WHY YOU CRY? –

Because my friend is dead.

– YUKIKO USES THIS WORD. NOT KNOW MEANING. –

Friend? You don't know what a friend is?

The thunder tiger tilted her head, tail switching side to side.

– FATHER OF YOUR CUBS? –

He was a cat.

– HOW CAN MONKEY-CHILD MATE WITH CAT? –

. . . What?

– WAS HE TALL CAT? –

Gods, no . . . look. He was my friend. We talked together, hunted together . . .

– AH. HUNT. YOU MEAN PACKMATE. –

. . . I suppose.

The thunder tiger puffed herself up, spread her wings.

- PACK I UNDERSTAND. THIS IS GOOD. –

Glad to help.

Hana heard raised voices over the driving rain, the thunder of wings. Yoshi quirked an eyebrow, looking toward the growing disturbance, the running foot-steps and shouts. A sky-ship engine sputtered to life somewhere in the distance, the propeller's drone chopping through the thunder. He put his hand to his brow and hissed.

"What the hells is going on over there? No respect for a body's aches, these yokels."

The siblings looked into the sky as another thunder tiger swooped overhead, coming in to land on the decking with a crunch. Hana knew from the tales the beast's name was Buruu. He was magnificent—broad chest and rippling muscle and fire flashing in his eyes, lightning flaring along his clockwork wings. But Hana was even more fascinated by the girl riding him. Yukiko. The girl she'd first seen in Kigen's Market Square. Blood streaming down her nose. The iron-thrower in the Shōgun's fist, leveled at her head. She could hear the words in her mind again, as clearly as if Yukiko had spoken them aloud.

"Let me show you what one little girl can do . . ."

Her hair flowed about her face in black waves, held in check by the goggles above her brow. She walked amidst the flurry of leaves that marked their arrival, pale as ashes. Hana could see why people spoke about her the way they did. There was something beyond the superficial beauty, a fierceness in the way she moved. An electricity humming in the air around her.

Yoshi inclined his head, a small crooked smile on his lips.

"Stormdancer."

The girl smiled back. "It's just Yukiko, Yoshi-san."

Kaiah locked eyes with Buruu, and Hana sensed disdain in the female's mind, a low growl in her chest. Hana looked between the pair, then to their savior. The girl who'd rescued them after the attack on Kigen. The girl Hana owed her life to. She saw Yukiko's face was flushed, her eyes wide. Somewhere in the Kenning, she felt anger. Anguish. Sorrow.

"Are you all right, Yukiko-san?"

The girl sighed, crouched beside the siblings. She dragged a stray lock of hair from her mouth, rain beading on her skin like jewels. Her voice was heavy as lead.

"I'm sorry to do this to you. I'm sorry you haven't had time to rest. But something's happened. The rebellion is splitting. I'm leaving here today. I want you two to come with us."

"Splitting?" Hana blinked. "Why?"

"There's an insurgency inside the Lotus Guild. I think we can use them as allies, but other Kagé refuse to stand beside them. It's all hatred and grudges and politics. Point is, Buruu, Kaiah and I are taking a ship and some of the less militant Kagé to Yama city. The Fox Daimyo slighted the Shōgunate by refusing to attend the royal wedding. He's no friend of the government or the Guild. And I'm hoping that'll make him friend to us."

"You're lighting out on your little rebel friends," Yoshi said. "Just like that."

"I'm going to keep fighting. But I can't be part of a rebellion that murders innocent people. I hope you can understand that. I hope you'll come with me."

Hana tried hard not to frown. "Where else would we go?"

"Anywhere you like. I don't want you to feel like you owe me anything. This is a war, and I'm in it up to my neck. Fighting to bring down the Guild and set this country free from blood lotus. The smog. The deadlands. The poison that is chi."

"I know," Hana smiled. "I've heard you talking on the radio."

"They call me a terrorist. They say I'm trying to destroy the whole country, not just the Guild. And for every person who listens to the pirate radio, there's a dozen who long to go back to the days of plenty." Yukiko shrugged. "Part of me can't blame them. There's no easy answer. We're in for hard times once the Guild is gone."

"We're in for harder times if it stays."

"Try telling that to a screaming mob."

"Three stormdancers are louder than one."

Yoshi scoffed, but for once, kept his opinions to himself. Yukiko looked between the pair, the question plain in her eyes.

"You're a smart girl, Yukiko." Hana's laugh brightened the deepening dusk. "But you're fucking crazy if you think we'd go back to sleeping in gutters after seeing all this."

"So you'll come with me? You'll fight?"

"We'll do more than fight." Hana took her brother's hand. "We'll godsdamned win."

Yukiko grinned and grabbed her in a bear hug, squeezing tight. Hana was taken aback at the sudden show of affection, but she felt the comforting strength in Yukiko's arms, Buruu and Kaiah's smoldering heat behind her, and for the first time in what seemed like her entire life, she felt absolutely righteous. Absolutely safe. And so she kissed Yukiko on the cheek and hugged her back, bathing in unfamiliar warmth.

The pair broke apart, the wind howling between them. And Kaiah stepped into the gulf and extended one wing, dipping her shoulder toward the ground.

– *FLY WITH ME.* –

T he wind was all screams and clawing fingers, tearing her hair and howling in her ears. As they soared through the swirling, soggy gray, the air grew brittle and Hana leaned close, arms wrapped tight around Kaiah's neck. Her clothes became soaked, hair clinging to her face as her stomach plummeted toward her knees, her missing eye burning like fire.

Ascending.

She could see Yukiko and Buruu off to her right, the sky-ship *Kurea* behind them. The vessel was a merchantman, four great propellers cutting through the chill air, its inflatable painted with an enormous dragon spitting fire across the canvas. Yoshi was somewhere aboard it—he'd flat-out refused to climb onto the thunder tiger's back. Hana's mind drifted to her childhood; the brief sky-ship journey she and her family had taken after her father had won his farm. She'd been awestruck, her stomach a storm of butterflies, the only time in her life she'd ever flown. Yoshi had spent the entire trip in their cabin, trying not to hurl.

The air grew sharp as razors, white plumes rolling from her lips. Hana clung to Kaiah's neck with aching hands, teeth chattering in her skull. And just when she thought they must turn back, that they'd never break through the cloud, the sky turned red and the gray fell away into a sea of rolling iron beneath them, stretching wide as forever. Iishi crags pierced the cloud cover, snow-clad and shimmering. Greedy winds snatched the blasphemy from her mouth, and all the world beneath the clouds was forgotten, submerged beneath the ocean of Shima sky.

For that one dazzling moment, everything she could see was perfect.

Gods above. It's beautiful.

– IT IS HOME. –

You can almost forget it all up here. All the hurt and the pain and the shit down there.

– WHY YOU WANT TO FORGET? –

. . . Sometimes it's easier than dealing with it, I suppose.

Kaiah growled.

– DO NOT UNDERSTAND. YUKIKO ASKS ME TO LEARN MONKEY-CHILD WAY AND I CANNOT SEE. SILLY THINGS. LITTLE THINGS MADE SO BIG. FOOLISH. –

Our way is real simple, Kaiah.

– OH YES? –

We're ugly. We're selfish and greedy and shortsighted, fucking each other over for a drop of fuel or a difference of opinion. That's pretty much the breadth of it.

Kaiah glanced across the red skies toward Buruu, and Hana sensed pure hostility, a low rumbling growl in her new friend's chest.

– HUMANS NOT THE ONLY ONES WHO CAN BETRAY, MONKEY-CHILD. –

You're talking about Buruu? What did he do?

– KINSLAYER. MURDERER. DISGUSTS ME. –

Kinslayer?

– DO NOT TRUST HIM, GIRL. NOT FOR A MOMENT. –

Why not?

– WILL BE REPAID IN BLOOD. –

Then why are you here? Why are you helping?

– REASONS NOT MINE TO TELL. –

The pair swooped back down through the cloud, fingers of jagged fringe kissing Hana's cheeks. She thought of Akihito charging in and saving her from death in the yakuza warehouse. Those big arms around her shoulder, brute strength wrapped in impossible gentleness, keeping all the hurt at bay. The air grew just a little warmer at the memory.

Not all people are evil, I suppose. Some are just stupid.

– SOME ARE GREATER. YOUR YUKIKO SEES TRUTH. WILL BE REMEMBERED. –

My people always forget, Kaiah. All the most important things.

– DO NOT MEAN MONKEY-CHILDREN. I MEAN BLUE SKY AND CLEAN RAIN. THUNDER'S SONG. THEY WILL SING HER NAME LONG AFTER ALL ELSE IS DUST. –

The beast glanced over her shoulder, eyes as deep as the fall at their feet.

– WHO WILL SING FOR YOU? –

Who says anyone should? I'm no one.

– NOT WISH TO LEAVE A MARK ON THIS PLACE? NOT WISH TO BE SUNG OF AS THEY SING OF KITSUNE NO AKIRA? TORA TAKEHIKO? –

Those are the names of stormdancers. I'm not a hero. I don't close hellgates or slay sea dragons. I rob drunkards and sleep in hovels and speak to rats. Sometimes I have fleas.

– NOT DREAM OF BEING SOMETHING GREATER? –

The wind thrummed with propeller song, whispering the plain and simple truth.

Everybody does . . .

She felt the heat inside the arashitora envelop her, fill her with a burning pride. Somehow she knew the beast was smiling at her. She found herself smiling back.

– THAT IS THE BEGINNING. –

Amusement enveloped the beast, bright and wicked like a child born to mischief. And before Hana could blink, Kaiah pressed wings to flanks and they dropped from the skies. Hana's stomach rose into her throat, screaming for all she was worth as they plunged straight toward the forest below.

Pull up!

– USED TO PLAY THIS GAME WITH MY CUBS. –

We're going to die!

– BREATHE. –

We're falling too fast!

– NOT FALLING. FLYING. –

The arashitora spread her wings, Hana's insides crashing downward as they leveled out and swooped into the air again. The pain of her missing eye forgotten, blood pounding, body shaking; tremors borne not of terror but exhilaration. The world flying by beneath them, hundreds of tiny life-sparks in the forest below, the beating of her heart, entwined with the beast's.

Alive.

So wonderfully, perfectly, impossibly alive.

She curled her fingers in the thunder tiger's feathers, laughing as though the world was ending, and the beast opened her beak and roared like thunder. Like a storm that would wash away everything she was and everything she'd been, all the dirt and filth and blood scabbing in the gutters, leaving her clean and whole and beautiful.

Take me back.

Kaiah glanced back at the sky-ship *Kurea*, amusement flickering in her mind.

– HAD YOUR FILL OF FLYING? –

No, not back to the ship. Back up to the clouds.

Hana held on tight, blinked the rain and tears from her eye.

Let's do it again.

6
INSURRECTION

It had been eight years since Yukiko last laid eyes on Yama city.

Eight years, one mother, one father, and one lifetime ago.

Two thunder tigers soared over the metropolis, the rumble of a gathering storm and the *Kurea* at their backs. The Kitsune capital was a smudge on polluted riverbanks; a crust of brick and dirty tile surrounded by struggling rice paddies and long, smoking tracts of deadland. Storm clouds filed in one by one to smother the sun, refinery smoke bruising the sky.

There it is, Buruu. Home of my clan. Seat of Kitsune power in Shima.

IMPRESSIVE.

You think so?

. . . NOT REALLY, NO.

Well you're in a lovely mood today.

I WAS TRYING TO BE POLITE.

Maybe stick to what you do best?

SARCASM IT IS, THEN.

They swooped lower, Hana and Kaiah beside them, watching the tiny bushimen on the walls below gathering to point and stare. Yukiko held her stomach, fighting mild nausea as the world rose up beneath them. The Fox capital was a fortress, built in the shadow of the haunted Iishi Mountains. Great walls encircled the city, topped with razor wire. The Amatsu river cut the capital in half, and a lone island sat in the middle of the flow, linked to either bank by broad bridges. Chapterhouse Yama was a pentagon of yellow stone in the island's center, and a dozen airships hung about the sky-docks on either bank. To the south loomed the knotted tangle of the chi refinery, the Warehouse District, shrouded with grime and smog. Atop a hill on the west side of the city glowered Kitsune-jō—the mighty Fortress of the Fox.

I was eight when we left here. I remember standing at the railing and watching the people grow smaller and smaller as we flew away. Mother and Father beside me.

THEY WOULD BE PROUD OF YOU, SISTER.

How do you know that?

YOU LEFT THIS PLACE A CHILD. YOU RETURN A STORMDANCER. HOW COULD THEY NOT BE?

She smiled, put her arms around his neck.

You always know the right thing to sa—

A thunderous boom split the skies, pulling Yukiko's thoughts back into the real. She looked down into the city, toward Chapterhouse Yama. The tower loomed on a flat spur of rock in the Amatsu river known as Last Isle. It was the symbol of Guild power in Kitsune lands. A bastion of razor wire and broken glass and dirty yellow stone.

And it was on fire.

The structure stood lopsided, smoke billowing from four of its five gates, covering the river with a soup of rolling black. Yukiko could see figures through the pall; insectoid shapes in burnished metal clashing on bridges and in dogleg alleyways on Yama's west side. Citizens were simply fleeing across the Amatsu in floods, husbands holding wives and mothers holding children. Subterranean explosions shook the city's spine, the *popopopopop!* of shuriken-throwers, the boiling hiss of flame-spitters. The smell of blood and fuel and burning meat.

She heard a shout behind, saw Akihito on the *Kurea's* foredeck, waving frantically and pointing to the ship's radio antenna. And as her belly dropped into her toes, Yukiko knew what had happened. Kaori had lived up to her word. She must have broadcast on the Kagé frequencies about the Guild rebellion. In a matter of minutes, she'd undone what had taken years, maybe decades to build. And all for the sake of hatred . . .

Another explosion tore through the chapterhouse, the building listing dangerously. Black smoke rose into the choking sky.

"Kaori," Yukiko whispered. "You *bitch* . . ."

Buruu sailed through the ash and smoke as Yukiko tried to make sense of the conflict. She slipped behind Buruu's eyes, saw dozens of Guildsmen clashing below, figures sprawled in the gutters, broken brass leaking red. So many . . .

I can't tell them apart! Fly lower, Buruu. We can see—

NO.

. . . What?

I WILL NOT DESCEND.

What the hells are you talking about? We have to help!

TOO DANGEROUS. FOR YOU AND THEM.

The rebels? You're not making—

NOT THE GUILDSMEN, YUKIKO. THE ONES INSIDE YOU.

Yukiko's hand went to her stomach, the sparks of warmth gathered there.

This isn't about them!

EVERYTHING YOU DO IS ABOUT THEM.

Oh my GODS, don't start going all male on me now.

I AM EQUIPPED FOR LITTLE ELSE.

I'm still the same person! I'm not some damn incubator you have to wrap in cotton-wool!

CHARGING INTO MELEE WITH A HUNDRED WARRING CHI-MONGERS—

There are people down there dying!

BETTER THEM THAN YOU.

Godsdammit, it's that kind of thinking that's led us here! That one life is worth more than another. Guildsmen worth more than citizens. Nobles more than commoners. Shimans more than gaijin.

YUKIKO—

No! Either all life is worth fighting for, or none of it is!

A thundering shock wave crashed against them, nearly knocking her from Buruu's back. Hana cried out, pointed at the chi refinery, the blossoming fireball rising into the skies. The complex shattered as if it were glass, claxon wails and screams lost under the explosion's rumbling yawn. Lazy flame stretched up and out, black smears across blood-red skies.

"What the hells is going on?" Hana yelled.

"Kaori outed the Guild rebels over the wireless! The rebels had no warning this was coming. We have to help them!"

"Help who? I can't tell who's a rebel and who isn't!"

RED.

Buruu's voice echoed in the place where the headaches lived.

Yukiko squinted down through the black and blood haze. She glimpsed two Lotusmen weaving amidst the tumbledown maze, one pursuing the other, rocket packs trailing blue-white flame. The one in front was marked with red paint; messy strokes across its spaulders, one deep line down its featureless face. The Lotusman in pursuit fired a popping burst of shuriken from a handheld thrower, metal stars glittering like fireflies.

"The ones trying to run!" she shouted. "They're marked with red!"

"You're right!" Hana yelled. "They must be the rebels! Go! Go!"

Hana leaned into Kaiah's spine and the pair dived into the smoke, spiraling as they fell. Kaiah clapped her wings together, an ultrasonic boom of Raijin Song rippling outward, scattering the Guildsmen in the streets below.

Buruu's eyes were locked on the carnage. Bursts of shuriken fire severing fuel lines, rupturing chi tanks. Gouts of flame, tangled knots and clumsy brawls, Lotusmen colliding midair, tumbling to ruin beneath collapsing houses. Citizens were running from the inferno where the refinery used to be, tiny figures hurling themselves into the Amatsu river, its filthy "waters" already ablaze.

Buruu, they're dying. We have to help them!

The arashitora said nothing, amber eyes locked on the carnage below. Yukiko's fingers ran over her stomach, the place she wouldn't let herself think about. She reached out with the Kenning and felt warmth there, resisting the urge to turn away.

Brother, I need you on my side. On our side. Now, more than ever.

Buruu sighed from the tips of his feathers. Muted daylight gleamed on the metal covering his wings, the polarized glass over her eyes, the Guildsmen fighting and dying below.

WHAT OTHER SIDE WOULD I BE ON?

And like a stone, they dropped from the sky.

T here was no room in Hana's head for understanding.

The girl was no stranger to violence and death—all their lives, she and Yoshi had fought for every inch, every scrap and desperate breath. But this was different. This was a battle they'd write about in history books. This was a day people would remember. Where were you when the rebels rose and set fire to Yama city? Where were you when the Guild War began?

Well, it just so happens I was there. Skies painted blood, flying through the smoke and flames on the back of a godsdamned thunder tiger.

She'd stalked Kigen's alleys for years inside Daken's mind, the tomcat's impulse of scent and sight and instinct augmenting her own. But Kaiah's mind was awash with a feral, predatory overload. Nothing like she'd felt with Daken, nothing so complex—it almost made her feel guilty, to form a bond so deeply and so quickly. She could feel the smoke in Kaiah's eyes, seething thermals beneath her wings, the weight of the tiny monkey-child on her back. But at the same time, Hana was still in her own head, wind-tangled hair stuck to her cheeks, exhilaration pounding against her ribs like a steamhammer.

The air was filled with metal shards, Kaiah banking and rolling between the shuriken spray. Guildsmen tumbled from the air as she passed, blue-white flame and mists of red, gurgling, metallic screams. Hana felt an impact at her shoulder, then realized Kaiah had been grazed, not her. She felt stabbing pain in Kaiah's leg, looking down to find a glittering metal star protruding from her own thigh. And there, in the midst of the smoke and the screams and the blood, she realized she couldn't tell where she ended and the thunder tiger began.

Tearing and biting, ripping and roaring, only those marked with red untouched. Swooping through the smoke, seeing soldiers; Iron Samurai tromping under the black Kitsune flag. Hana realized the Fox Daimyo must have sent out troops to restore order. She saw a general leading the soldiers, struggling to form words rather than a shapeless scream.

"General! The Guildsmen wearing red paint—they're rebels! They're on your side!"

She heard a roar behind, turned to see Yukiko and Buruu cutting through the air, blood spattered on snow-white feathers and snow-white skin. Yukiko was sitting tall, a naked katana in her hand, its blade gleaming in the inferno light.

"Rebels!" she cried, pointing to the *Kurea*. "We offer sanctuary! Head to our ship!"

Hana saw the loyalist Guildsmen thrown into panic at Yukiko's approach. Three Lotusmen beating on a rebel scattered like a flock of sparrows as her shadow fell over them. Dots of blue-white flame flared over the city, loyalists fleeing through the smoke and exhaust fumes toward their ruptured tower. Buruu roared, filling the skies with thunder.

"The Stormdancer!" one of them screamed. "Run while you can!"

And run they did. Fleeing to the docks in droves, the hulking shapes of ironclads gathered around the sky-spires. Artificers scuttling from their ruined tower, followed by wasp-waisted figures with silver razors on their backs. The Kitsune samurai charged over the Amatsu bridges, chainswords revving, calling for surrender as the Guild loyalists bundled into their ships.

Hana was bleeding, wound at her thigh, another on her forearm. But the red, red pulse thundered in her veins and the smoke and death filled her lungs and she knew, she *knew* with every ounce of herself that though this might not be right, at least it was *just*, and though the walls and ceiling might be painted red, this was the closest thing to a home she'd ever known.

Propellers surged at the sky-docks, the Guild fleet casting off and pushing their engines into the redline. The Kitsune fleet was moving from their own spires on the western bank, firing their net-throwers and snarling engines, ships on both sides listing and crippled.

The Guild ironclads laid down withering fire, forcing Buruu and Kaiah back from the largest and grandest of the sky-ships. A hundred and fifty feet long, name painted down its flanks in bold kanji: *Lotus Eater*. It was a floating fortress studded with shuriken turrets, lumbering upward and filling the skies around it with death.

"That must be the Second Bloom's sky-ship!" Yukiko shouted.

"Should we let him get away?"

Kaiah snarled, her bloodlust flowing into Hana and pounding in her chest.

– *SHOULD KILL NOW. STRIKE WHILE WEAK.* –

"I don't think we could get close!" Yukiko yelled. "It's too well armed. Besides, we have to regroup. Speak to the rebels. Dozens of them died today because of Kaori's bullshit—we have to mend that bridge. Having them as allies is going to be more useful than killing the Second Bloom of a ruined chapterhouse."

Hana nodded, sitting up on Kaiah's back and fighting against the impulse to tear anything moving from the sky. The Kitsune fleet shadowed the fleeing Guild ships, but they seemed more interested in protecting the city than preventing the Guild's departure. Two crippled Guild ships were being boarded, crews resisting with suicidal abandon. The skies echoed with chatter of shuriken fire.

"We should help the Kitsune," Hana said. "Those Guild crews aren't going—"

"Hana . . ." Yukiko pointed to the *Lotus Eater*. "Look."

Hana found herself falling behind Kaiah's eyes without thinking, her vision knife-sharp though the glare and smoke. She could see figures at a shuriken turret on top of the *Lotus Eater*'s inflatable—two Guildsmen struggling with a third. As she watched, the lone fighter kicked one assailant in the chest, sending him tumbling out into the open air. The falling Guildsman fired his rocket pack, bringing himself level with the deck. He shouted to the apparently oblivious crew, pointed at the struggle going on above their heads.

The arashitora circled closer, watching as a half-dozen Lotusmen leaped over the railings and rocketed up toward the melee. In the meantime, the struggling Guildsman had gained the upper hand, tearing a handful of cable from his opponent's backpack and kicking him out into the void. His atmos-suit was stained with soot and smoke, but certainly not painted red.

Hana shouted over the wind and engine roar. "If he's not a rebel, why are they fighting?"

Yukiko shrugged, shouted back. "Infiltrator?"

The Guildsman climbed into the shuriken-thrower turret and aimed the barrel at the inflatable. The 'thrower fired, punching through reinforced canvas. The air was filled with the screech of escaping hydrogen as the compartment began deflating. Standing at the tear's edge, the Guildsman tore the mechabacus from his chest in a blinding shower of red-hot sparks.

"Death to the Serpents!" he cried.

"Oh Gods . . ." Hana breathed.

A tiny flare of light; a bubble of flame, white hot. A split second of not-sound, nothing like silence. And then an explosion, a jagged shear of flame spreading faster than a brushfire on a summer's day. Hana held up her hand to blot out the light, the *Lotus Eater* shrieking with a voice of breaking timber and burning hydrogen and dying men. The great ship plummeted downward, trailing a skyful of smoke, ending with a screaming, nose-first dive into a fallow field two miles south of Yama's walls. The earth shook as the pair embraced like hateful lovers, the tremor lasting a good thirty seconds longer than it should have, dust and tiles skittering from the Yama rooftops and smashing on the cobbles below.

The rest of the Guild fleet tore away as fast as their engines would take them, south toward the Tōnan mountains and the fortress of First House.

He killed himself.

Hana's eye was locked on the *Lotus Eater*'s ruins, the smoking hole in the earth now serving as a mass grave. Kaiah's thoughts rumbled in her skull.

– WHAT? –

That Lotusman on the inflatable. He sacrificed himself to kill Yama's Second Bloom.

– BRAVE. –

I wouldn't call it brave. I'd call it sad.

She turned to Yukiko. "How could he do that?"

The Stormdancer's eyes were fixed on the smoking wreckage, her face pale as ash. She seemed older then—the weight of the world smothering the girl whose skin she wore, leaving her weary beyond all years and sleep. She raised her voice above the howling wind.

"This is war, Hana," she said. "It's bloody and ugly and people are going to die. Maybe you. Maybe me. Hells, maybe no one here gets out alive."

"Could you do that?"

"Do what?"

"Kill yourself like that? Walk gladly into the fire for a small victory?"

"I'm not sure there are small victories in a fight to the death. With stakes this high, every step closer to the finish is worth it."

"But could you die for it? Knowing you'll never see the end?"

Hana looked across the blackened skies to the girl on the back of her thunder tiger—this girl who'd slain a Shōgun, ended a dynasty, prompted a nation to rise. She saw Yukiko's hand pressed to her stomach.

"I don't know."

The hand dropped to her side.

"I'm guessing we'll find out before the song is sung."

7

IN THE SHADOW
OF COLOSSUS

Fifteen days.

Hiro stood on his bedchamber balcony, watching the city twitching below. The orchestra of engines and traffic and people was occasionally interrupted by a pitiful song—the sparrows who'd survived the Kagé attack, clipped feathers now singed from the fires that had almost gutted the Shōgun's palace. No matter how he tried, Hiro couldn't get the stink off his skin. He'd scrubbed so hard in the bathhouse last night the water was tinged red when he finished.

This city was a shell, people wandering the streets in a daze. Hiro had ordered the imperial coffers opened to alleviate the suffering, but the bakery lines still stretched around the block, prices spiraling higher as Chapterhouse Kigen pumped every drop of chi north to fuel the Earthcrusher. The black market was thriving, the yakuza gangs who ran it growing more daring by the day. And Hiro could spare no thought for any of it.

North. A fifteen-day march in the shadow of a colossus, into the depths of the Iishi mountains. An ending. To the weight of this false arm they'd drilled into his body, to this circlet of shame they'd placed on his head. Fifteen days would see the end of it all.

Gods, it seemed a lifetime.

Why did he still care? Why did the thought of choking the life out of her fill his dreams? He was dead already—the ashes of funeral offerings painted on his face every morning. Death's hue painted onto the armor he'd worn with such pride in fleeting yesterdays. It had meant so much to him once. But what had Yukiko meant?

An infatuation was all it had really been. An intoxication faded in the light of next dawning. And yet, it had brought the nation to war. Clan against clan. Blood against blood. This avalanche that had started so small—with a tear-stained kiss after Yoritomo littered the arena with severed feathers. They were teenagers. Maker's breath, they were *children*.

Who in the name of the gods did they think they were, to drag the nation to ruin?

The rap of soft knuckles on hard wood. The feather-light breath of his major-domo.

"Forgiveness, Daimyo. You have honored guests."

"I am about to depart for the staging grounds and war. You wish me to have tea with some bureaucrat before I leave?"

"No, great Lord. Forgiveness but—"

"Who is it?" Hiro turned on his cowering servant. "Some fat neo-chōnin wailing about the rising cost of slaves?"

"Lord Tora Orochi."

Hiro's belly flopped into his boots, blood drying up in his veins. The world was suddenly several shades too bright. Too loud. Too real.

After all this time . . .

His voice was a whisper under the broken sparrow song.

"Father . . ."

The throne room was as silent as Yoritomo's tomb. Muddy light filtered through tall windows, long slabs of illumination painted by a clumsy brush in the pall of ashes. A blood-red carpet marked the path to the Shōgun's throne, a charred breeze thumbing through the high tapestries. The throne itself was immense; a gaudy lump of golden tigers and silken cushions throwing a clawed shadow across the floor.

Hiro hadn't ever mustered the courage to actually sit in it.

Two figures waited at its feet. A woman, arrayed in a jûnihitoe as red as heart's blood, embroidered with golden flowers. Her face was painted white, jet hair swept into a layered coil pierced with glittering needles. She glanced up as Hiro entered the hall, and he met her eyes for the briefest of moments, dull pain in his chest.

Mother.

His eyes fell on the figure to her left, and all sense of joy or sadness fled, black nothingness in their wake. A voice from childhood, harsh with rebuke. A raised hand, and the memory of shameful tears.

Father.

He sat in the chair. That cursed chair that was his home, his concubine, his sentence. The breather over his face was a heavy, graceless thing of rubber and brass, affixed with fat buckles behind his head, long, graying hair still swept back in warrior's braids. But no warrior sat in that chair, no. A shell of one, perhaps, who dreamed of days before the gaijin rotor-thopters blasted his ship from the skies, left him twisted in the wreckage on some Morcheban plain.

His face was a knot of scars. His left arm desiccated, strapped in place. A bulky knot of pipes and bellows was affixed to his little iron throne, his thin chest moving with a measured cadence, like clockwork, like the arm at Hiro's side, like the voice in Hiro's head.

"Lord Orochi-san," he said. "Lady Shizuka-san. You honor me with your presence."

"Great Daimyo." His father's voice was a tortured wheeze, each pause punctured by a metallic rasp. "Blessing of Lord Izanagi . . . to your house."

His mother sank to her knees, pressed her forehead to the floorboards. "Great Daimyo."

Hiro stepped forward, hand outstretched. "Mother, do not—"

A sharp glance from his father, halfway between outrage and horror. The look dragged Hiro to a halt, caught him by the seat of his pants and hauled him to his feet, the pain of the skinned knee or bruised knuckles or aching back forgotten.

"A samurai does not show emotion. No pain. No fear. Never."

Hiro covered his fist and bowed.

"Lady Shizuka-san. You honor your Daimyo. Rise, please."

He could see it in her face: how she longed to throw her arms about him and shower his face with kisses as she'd done when he was a boy. But instead, she rose slowly, eyes to floor, mouth pressed firmly shut. As was fitting. As was *proper*.

"To what do I owe the honor of your presence in the Tiger's Palace?" Hiro said. "The journey from Blackstone province could not have been easy given your . . . condition."

"It is no trouble, great Daimyo." Orochi waved his good hand as if shooing away an insect. "News has reached us that you have consigned yourself to suicide . . . after the Shōgun's assassin is dispatched . . ."

Hiro looked at his mother then, but her eyes were still downcast. Could they have come here to talk him out of it? To step aside and leave all this behind?

"I . . . that is to say we . . ." Orochi drew a shivering breath, ". . . wished you to know . . ."

Could they?

"Your actions make us proud . . . Make *me* proud."

No.

Hiro found himself speaking in a voice that sounded nothing like his own.

No, of course not.

"You honor me, Lord Orochi."

"The shame of your failure . . . has been difficult . . . for your mother and I to endure. Many nights I sat with blade in hand . . . contemplating my own seppuku in protest that you . . . had not followed your Lord into death."

Orochi pressed the control lever beneath his withered hand, the chair trundling forward on fat rubber wheels. He stopped close enough for Hiro to see the gleam in his eyes.

"But I knew you would do . . . the honorable thing. That you and the Elite would spare your families the disgrace . . . of your failure."

Wooden swords in the yard outside their home. Wind blowing in the lotus stalks. No room for tears. No place for pain. To wield the long and the short swords, and then to die.

"I will not fail, Father. Our honor will be restored."

"I know it." A nod. "You are samurai . . . my son."

"Gracious husband," said his mother. "The letter?"

A cold glance over Orochi's shoulder silenced her like a slap.

"Letter?" Hiro looked between the pair. "What letter?"

"You sent it in the summer," Orochi finally wheezed. "But with news of Yoritomo's assassination . . . we presumed you would have committed suicide. Thus, we did not reply."

"You mentioned . . ." The woman looked at her son, desperate hope in her eyes. "You mentioned a girl you had met? Someone you wished to court?"

Orochi cleared his throat. "Understand, we enquire to determine if there were any . . . promises made . . . Promises your family must honor once you are dead."

She lay in his arms in the sweat-stained dark, cheek pressed against his chest.
He could smell her hair, her perfume, the taste of her still wet upon his lips.

"When the Shōgun has calmed down," he had said. "I will petition him for permission to court you. I have sent a letter to my father—"

"Court me?" Yukiko said. "What the hells for?"

"So I can be with you."

"Hiro, you're here with me right now," she laughed.

Her kisses had tasted like summer . . .

"No," Hiro said. "No promises were made. She is of no concern to you."

"Good," his father nodded. "This is good."

They stood there, silence washing against him like black salt water in Kigen Bay. Corroding. Eroding. Wave after wave breaking on him with each passing breath, taking a piece of him away as it rushed back out to sea.

Riding on his father's shoulders when he was too small to see above the lotus stalks, marveling at the world beyond their estates. Hefting his father's sword for the first time, watching light kiss the blade. The day he'd been accepted into the Kazumitsu Elite, the only time he'd seen tears in his father's eyes. All of it washing away, leaving only the stain. The burden. The failure he'd been taught to never, ever accept.

"I must leave for the staging grounds," he found himself saying. "My men await."

"Of course, Daimyo," his father nodded. "Do not let us detain you."

He swallowed. Bowed. "Good-bye, Father."

Orochi bowed in return. No light in his eyes. No tremor in his voice.

"Good-bye, my son. Lord Izanagi give you the strength . . . to die well."

He turned to the woman who had brought him into the world.

". . . Good-bye, Mother."

She broke then. Sank to her knees and wept, face hidden in her hands. Everything inside pressed him forward, the need to wrap her in his arms and tell her it would be all right, that it was not her fault. Everything inside him screamed he should move, speak, do something. Four whispered words from his father held him back.

"You shame me, woman . . ."

The weeping stopped, a door slammed shut, silence falling again. The moments ticking by in waves, every second spent standing there washing one more piece of him away. And when it was gone, when all he was had fled, what would be left?

What then would remain?

Without another word, he turned and stalked from the room.

8
LORD OF FOXES

The Guild rebels stood silent on the *Kurea*'s deck, Yama city still echoing with the explosions that had heralded their unveiling. A cluster of brass and blood. Scarlet splashes on their spaulders and faces, smudged with soot and smoke. No more than a dozen remaining.

Yukiko stood with Buruu, Akihito and Michi beside her. Hana and Kaiah were perched on the stern, the Blackbird's crew and Kagé refugees gathered in a knot as far from the Guildsmen as possible. Yoshi sat alone, up on the foredeck, looking out over the ravaged metropolis below. Smoke-scent whispered in the air, tongued the back of Yukiko's throat, clinging to Buruu's feathers amidst the promise of impending rain.

Thunder rumbled to the north.

I should speak with them.

YOU WILL NEED TO DO MORE THAN SPEAK, SISTER.

Come with me?

ALWAYS.

They stepped forward, slow, Yukiko's hands held up and out. The thunder tiger moved ahead, close enough that they still touched, tail curled upward as if he were stalking prey. She could feel him, hard as steel beneath feline grace, a roar bubbling just below his surface.

"I'm sorry," she said, eyes upon the gathered Guildsmen. "I didn't mean for it to be this way. I never wanted this to happen."

They were a motley bunch. Three Lotusmen, stained with blood and ash. An Artificer with his single rectangular eye and toolbox skin. Two False-Lifers clad in glistening membranes of earth-brown, spider limbs unfurling from their backs.

Behind them stood a clutch of smaller figures clad in simple atmos-suits of soft leather and gleaming brass. Half a dozen in all, some no bigger than toddlers. Yukiko heard one snuffling; faint weeping distorted within its helm.

My gods, they're children . . .

Their rebellion had been fermenting within the Guild for gods knew how long. Who knows what their plans had been? How close they'd come to fruition? And now, everything was ashes, their brothers and sisters slaughtered because of Kaori's mistrust. But could Yukiko really blame Kaori for all this? Maker's breath, the Guild had taken her father. The gods only knew what horrors Daichi had been through since.

Once again, it all came back to *him*. *His* doing. *His* betrayal.

Kin.

She drew a single, trembling breath.

Kin, godsdamn you.

"The Kagé broadcast news about your rebellion against my wishes," she said. "I never wanted any of you put in danger. I want us to be—"

"Do you know how many of us died today?"

It was one of the Lotusmen who spoke. Arms folded, skin splashed with blood.

"No," Yukiko said. "But I'm sorry anyone died at all."

"The great Stormdancer," the Lotusman sneered. "Slayer of Shōguns. Ender of dynasties. You expect us to believe the Kagé do anything without your say-so?"

"The Kagé existed long before I came along. And if dissent can fracture the Lotus Guild, you can be godsdamned sure a faction of anarchists, arsonists and fanatics can find a way to argue about the color of the sky."

"Ten."

The words came from one of the False-Lifers, her bulbous, glowing eyes fixed on Yukiko. A Guild child was cradled in her arms—an infant in brass and leather who couldn't be more than a year old. Her voice sounded like an iron boot stepping on beetle shells.

"We lost ten of us," she said.

"Enma-ō judge them fair."

"We do not believe in your gods, Stormdancer."

"Then I can only say I'm sorry."

"So are we," the False-Lifer hissed. "So are their children. Didn't the Kagé realize what the Guild would do when they *named me* over the wireless?"

"You're Misaki . . ." Yukiko breathed.

"They hung us out to slaughter. Not just us, our *children*! Animals! *Bastards!*"

"Misaki-san, I'm sorry—"

"STOP SAYING THAT!"

The child in her arms began wailing; a distorted, metallic cry that set Yukiko's teeth on edge. The False-Lifer pressed it against her cheek, eight silver arms encircling the babe as she rocked it back and forth, whispering words Yukiko couldn't hear. The Kagé refugees whispered among themselves, the wind whispering through the rigging.

My Gods, this is surreal.

THAT THEY MOURN THEIR DEAD?

No, I just . . . hidden behind those suits. Those masks. I never thought of them as parents who loved their children. I never realized . . .

"I have something for you, Misaki-san," she said.

"You have nothing I want or need, girl."

Yukiko reached into her obi, beside Daichi's katana, the short-bladed tantō her father gave her. The satchel was beaten leather, held out to the False-Lifer in Yukiko's upturned palm.

"What is that?"

"A letter," Yukiko said. "From your daughter's father."

". . . Takeo?"

Buruu bristling beside her, Yukiko handed the satchel over. Misaki cradled the snuffling infant in her arms, drawing out the letter with her false limbs. The paper was stained with blood and salt and rain. Yukiko could remember the words as if she'd read them yesterday: a missive from the Guildsman who'd saved Piotr's life, to the woman he loved until his dying moment. A plea that she fight on and bring the Guild to its knees. Death to the Serpents, whatever that meant. Freedom for Shima. A declaration of love, for this woman and the daughter in her arms.

She heard strangled weeping, saw Misaki's shoulders trembling. The woman sank to her knees on the *Kurea*'s deck, letter clutched to her breast. Another False-Lifer took the child from her arms as she curled into a ball and screamed; screamed in anguish and rage, so full of hurt it brought tears to Yukiko's eyes. The child began screaming also, echoing its mother's cries, setting off several of the other Lotuschildren. A chorus of wails filled the skyship's deck, Blackbird's cloudwalkers watching on uncertain, hands slack on their weapons.

Misaki began clawing at the bulbous eyes set in her mask. Gouging them loose, she tore at the artificial skin covering her head as if she were suffocating. Heavy lidded, bloodshot eyes and pale, tear-streaked skin. A gentle oval with delicate lips, lashless, browless, hairless. Pulsing veins. Gritted teeth.

The words "I'm sorry" sat pathetic on the tip of Yukiko's tongue, and she bit down hard, felt them die. Would it have made any difference if someone had told her "sorry" after her father died? Did "sorry" do anything to mend the hurt, the helplessness, the fear of walking life alone?

Sorry was just a word.

WORDS STILL HAVE POWER. EVEN HERE. EVEN NOW.

In some places, they have no power at all.

THAT IS NOT TRUE.

Winter draws near. The black rains will fall. The Earthcrusher will march. Blood like a river, you said, remember?

Yukiko shook her head.

The sun is setting on the time for words, Buruu.

A rush of wind, the creak of timber. A shadow fell over the assembled Guildsmen as Kaiah and Hana landed near the cluster of brass and wailing and tears. The Lotusmen tensed, the second False-Lifer flaring her razored arms in threat. But as the girl slipped from the thunder tiger's back, the look in her eye made the

Guildsmen step aside. Hana gently pushed through the group to stand before the woman weeping on the deck.

Kaiah nudged Misaki's shoulder with her head. The Guildswoman looked up, cheeks stained rose, staring at the thunder tiger in mute amazement. The arashi-tora nudged her again, looking from Misaki to her child in the other False-Lifer's arms.

"She says she knows what it is to lose a mate." Hana's voice was edged with sorrow. "I can feel it inside her. That loss . . . It hurts me just to look at it."

The girl knelt on the boards, took Misaki's hand.

"But Kaiah says at least you still have your daughter. You still have something of him to keep. And every time you look at her, you'll see him inside her and know he's still with you."

The woman pawed at the tears on her face, staring at the girl, turning to the False-Lifer who held her child and taking the infant back into her arms. She prodded a release at the child's neck, the brass throat unfurling like flower petals. Misaki pulled the helm from the babe's head, pressed her naked cheek to the little girl's skin. Eyes closed, she breathed long and deep. Thunder rumbled somewhere distant, a promise of the chaos to come.

Yukiko remembered her mother sitting by the fire, singing in a voice that made the mountains weep. Stepping closer to Buruu, she slipped her arm around his neck, glad for his warmth. She could feel them in the Kenning all around her, knife-sharp pain flaring at the back of her skull. The impossible tangles of thought; the cloudwalkers and refugees, the rebels in their shells of brass, the two knots of light resting in her belly. None of them dissimilar. Not sailors or insurgents or warriors or victims. Just people. All of them. Alive and breathing.

"Thank you," Misaki whispered.

"It's all right," Hana said. "It's going to be all right."

YOU SEE?

Buruu nodded, watching the sorrow fade, the light bloom in the woman's eyes as she kissed the tiny bow of her daughter's lips. The wind was cool water, mussing the feathers at his brow, the boards beneath him rumbling as he purred.

THERE IS ALWAYS TIME FOR WORDS.

Yukiko and Buruu stepped off the *Kurea*'s deck and dropped into blood-red skies.

They swooped over Yama city, Hana and Kaiah beside them. A thin haze of smoke drifted through the cramped buildings, Chapterhouse Yama now an empty, smoking shell.

Head for the Daimyo's fortress, Buruu. We need to have a chat with the Kitsune clanlord. Try to explain this shitstorm we started.

KITSUNE ARE YOUR CLAN. HAVE YOU MET THIS LORD?

No. Folk like me don't get to meet royalty, as a general rule.

She looked down at her frayed clothes, dragged her hands through her hair.

Gods, I look like I slept in a ditch.

SO?

I'm about to meet a Daimyo, brother. I could've at least had a bath first.

YOU ARE WHAT YOU ARE. WHEN YOU STAND BEFORE THIS FOX LORD, DO NOT FORGET WHERE YOU STOOD BEFORE. YOU HAVE STARED DOWN SHŌGUNS. HUNGRY DEAD. SEA DRAGONS. REMEMBER THAT. REMEMBER AND BE BRAVE.

When you're near? Always.

She curled her hands in the feathers at Buruu's neck, trying to smooth the disarray.

Speaking of shabby looks, we're going to have to give you a haircut soon.

. . . WHAT?

These feathers are getting messy.

LET ME UNDERSTAND THIS CORRECTLY. YOU WISH TO CUT MY MANE?

Thunder tigers grow manes?

OF COURSE! HOW ELSE WOULD YOU TELL MALES FROM FEMALES?

This is a trick question, right?

A MANE IS A SIGN A MALE ARASHITORA HAS REACHED MATURITY.

Her laughter rang out in his mind.

So it's going to be a few more decades growing, then?

HMPH. I'LL HAVE YOU KNOW MOST FEMALES FIND IT FETCHING.

Kaiah's distant roar wiped the smile from Yukiko's face, the mood between them somber once more.

Not all of them, it seems.

Buruu sighed.

NO, NOT ALL OF THEM.

Why does she hate you so much, brother?

YOU REALLY WISH TO KNOW?

You did something bad, right? Murdered someone. That's why she calls you Kinslayer.

I MURDERED MORE THAN ONE.

Why?

BECAUSE I THOUGHT IT WAS RIGHT.

She slipped her arms around his neck and squeezed.

Then I'm sure it was.

IT WASN'T. THEY WERE RIGHT TO TAKE MY NAME. AND KAIAH IS RIGHT TO HATE ME.

Yukiko could feel the hurt inside her friend, the shadow that had lain over him since the lightning farm. Being around Kaiah had awakened the ghosts of Buruu's past, and though she didn't want to push him into sharing his burdens, it made her feel helpless that she couldn't make it better. So she hugged him tighter, poured warmth into his mind.

You've the best heart of anyone I've ever met, Buruu. No matter what you did, no matter what anyone says, I'll love you forever. Do you hear me? Forever and always.

Silence was his only response, so Yukiko broke contact and slipped into Kaiah's mind. She felt a brief flare of pain, the familiar ache blazed across the base of her skull. Though she was getting better at holding the Kenning in check, sometimes it threatened to overwhelm her, along with the knowledge of why it had swelled beyond anything she'd known. Her hand slipped to her belly, to the pulses she could feel there, fear welling inside her.

Gods, what am I going to do?

– ABOUT WHAT? –

Yukiko blinked, realized her thoughts were leaking into Kaiah's mind. Hana was in there too; a knot of emotion and thought too intricate to comprehend. Yukiko remembered the Razor Isles and the gaijin boy who betrayed her, the way she'd pushed pictures into his head. And the thought occurred that a language barrier had lain between her and Ilyitch, but there was no such gulf between her and Hana. Using Kaiah as a bridge, there was no reason she couldn't . . .

Hana, can you hear me?

A pause, laced with uncertainty and the scent of ozone. A voice came to her across a vast space, dimmed by the roar of endless winds.

Yukiko?

Hello there.

I can hear you in my head! How the hells are you doing that?

I think you're hearing me through Kaiah. But honestly, I don't really know.

– THE ONES INSIDE YOU MAKE YOU STRONGER. I CAN FEEL THEM. –

The ones inside her?

Yukiko sighed, closed her eyes. If she said it, it'd be real. If she gave voice to it, there'd be no turning back.

. . . I'm pregnant, Hana.

Oh.

A pause, wind howling like wolves.

Should I offer congratulations or condolences?

I don't really know that either . . .

Ah.

Listen, we'll be at the fortress soon. The Kitsune Daimyo seems intent on making Hiro his enemy. We need to find out if that makes us his allies. This Guild War won't have helped, but getting him on-side would give us a real army. A sky-fleet and a fortress. This is important.

I should warn you, I'm not exactly a paragon of courtly matters. Not like I've met many Daimyo before.

Just follow my lead, you'll be fine.

All right, then.

She was about to break contact when Hana's voice rang across the gulf.

Yukiko?

Yes?

. . . Congratulations.

Atop a hill on the west side of the city glowered Kitsune-jō—the mighty Fortress of the Fox. Battlements of dirty gray stone studded with chi-powered ballista climbed heavenward in concentric rectangles. A crowd of people had gathered at the fortress gates; an ocean of upturned goggles, dirty kerchiefs and clockwork breathers. A dull roar grew in volume as Yukiko and Hana descended, the clamor of a hundred voices, one name, over and over again.

"Stormdancer!"

Yukiko held up a tentative hand and the roar intensified, thrumming in her chest. Bushimen struggled to press the mob back, calls for order falling on deaf ears.

Buruu roared and the crowd roared in answer; a thunderous, rumbling cheer.

This is madness, Buruu.

THEY LOVE YOU.

They don't even know me.

THEY SING YOUR SONGS. TELL YOUR TALE TO THEIR CHILDREN. THEY KNOW YOU AS THEY KNOW KITSUNE NO AKIRA, WHO SLEW GREAT BOUKYAKU. OR TORA TAKEHIKO, WHO CLOSED THE DEVIL GATE.

That's not me. It's only their idea of me.

DO YOU NOT SEE, SISTER? YOU ARE AN IDEA NOW.

The arashitora swooped over the crowd, close enough to tear hats from heads and kerchiefs from faces. They swung up over the outer wall toward the soldiers assembled on the castle's broad steps. Black flags embroidered with the white sigil of the Kitsune clan whipped like headless serpents in the wind. The Thunder God Raijin pounded his drums in the distance.

The arashitora landed, Buruu folding his mechanical wings at his side. Kaiah preened for a full minute afterward, as if flaunting her unmarred feathers in front of him. Yukiko remained where she was atop Buruu's shoulders, staring at the assembled Kitsune soldiers. She could feel Kaiah's agitation, turned to give a reassuring smile to Hana. The girl didn't remove her goggles, probably deciding a conversation about her eye would only complicate matters.

A huge figure in ceremonial armor descended the steps, Buruu growling softly as he approached. The suit was beautiful: embossed black iron, the face-guard crafted to resemble a snarling fox, a tassel of pale hair at its crown streaming in the wind.

The figure stopped within thirty paces of the arashitora riders, unbuckled its helm. Yukiko saw a broad face, battle scarred and hard. The man covered his fist and bowed.

"Stormdancer. I am General Kitsune Ginjiro, right hand of the Daimyo."

"Ginjiro-sama." Yukiko bowed in return. "This is my friend Hana. She is blessed with the Kenning like me, and has vowed to help rid these islands of the Guild and its poison."

"Do you bring violence to my honorable Lord's house?"

". . . No." Yukiko blinked. "Of course not."

"Um." Hana raised a tentative hand. "Me either."

"Do you bear malice to the Kitsune clan?"

Yukiko pulled up her sleeve, showed the beautiful fox tattoo on her right arm. "Your Daimyo is not my Daimyo, Ginjiro-sama. But I remember where I came from."

Ginjiro nodded. "Then enter, and be welcome at Five Flowers Palace, the beating heart of Kitsune-jō. My noble Lord, Kitsune Isamu, pledges you will be safe within these walls."

He covered his fist and bowed again, deeper this time.

DO YOU TRUST HIM?

Yukiko looked back toward the dark fortress walls, listening to the swell of people gathered outside. Mouths open and roaring. Fists in the air.

I think they'd be risking a riot if anything happened to me.

THAT WILL BE POOR SOLACE FOR SOME, SISTER.

We flew a long way just to insult the Daimyo's hospitality.

OH, YES. RAIJIN FORBID YOU INSULT ANYBODY. FAR MORE SENSIBLE TO RISK YOUR OWN BRUTAL MURDER INSTEAD.

Hana will be there. I'll stay in the Kenning. You'll know everything I do.

Buruu bristled, but said no more. She slipped off his back, felt the familiar pang as they parted. It was like stepping away from firelight and out into the dark, leaving everything warm and good behind. She walked toward the Kitsune general, Hana beside her. The girl looked distinctly out of her depth, plucking at the worn hem of her sleeve. Yukiko squeezed her hand.

Ginjiro's eyes were on the thunder tigers, as wide as a child's. Yukiko waited until he remembered himself, and coughing once, the general set his shoulders square.

"Follow me, please."

The wall of soldiers parted to allow them through. Yukiko smiled at Buruu and Kaiah, then stepped under the broad, rain-bleached gables of Five Flowers

Palace. Ginjiro led them through a massive entrance hall into a wide courtyard. Despite its formidable shell, the heart of Kitsune-jō was as beautiful as anything in the Shōgun's palace. It was odd to find such opulence inside fortress walls—like finding a beautiful courtesan inside an ancient suit of armor.

Ginjiro led Yukiko through towering iron-shod doors, down a hallway decorated with stunning tapestries depicting Shima's creation. Yukiko admired them as they passed—each stood twelve feet high and twenty feet wide, and must have taken a dozen artisans a year to make.

The first weaving showed Lord Izanagi and Lady Izanami, side by side as Izanagi stirred the oceans of creation with his spear. The following tapestry depicted the Goddess giving birth to the seven islands, face twisted in pain, sky filled with burning light. Yukiko averted her eyes and hurried past. Next came Lady Izanami's funeral, her life lost in childbirth. The following four tapestries showed the Maker God's failed quest to reclaim her from the underworld. The final tapestry showed Izanami on her bone mountain, surrounded by her demon children. The oni came in all shapes and sizes: tentacled monstrosities and snaggletoothed hulks and tall, muscle-bound demons with midnight blue skin. Lady Izanami herself was more terrifying than any of them, all corpse-pale skin and bottomless eyes. Mother of Darkness, they called her. She who would give voice to the song that slew the world.

Endsinger.

A small bowl of rice was set before this final tapestry to appease her hunger.

Yukiko remembered Daichi in the Kagé village, telling the story of Lady Izanami's fall, surrounded by smiling children. Sorrow gripped her so tight she couldn't breathe.

"Are you all right?" Hana asked.

"I'm fine." Yukiko squeezed the girl's hand. "It's nothing."

"Well, good. Because I'm about to mess my unmentionables . . ."

Their footsteps rang out on the nightingale floors as they approached the Daimyo's wing, boards chirping in a dozen discordant notes. Hana was pale as old bones as she ran her fingers through her messy bob, throwing another mournful glance at her shabby clothes.

Ginjiro stopped before another towering set of double doors, studded with fat iron bolts. He knocked three times, iron against iron. After a series of somber clunks, the doors split apart on rumbling hinges. The general stepped inside, calling in a deep voice.

"This humble servant begs pardon to present the noble Arashi-no-odoriko, Kitsune Yukiko and her comrade to his honored Lord."

A short man in black robes and a tasseled hat almost as tall as he was scuttled forth.

"Step forth and kneel before the Fivefold Throne, seat of Okimoto, first

Daimyo of the Kitsune zaibatsu, and his beloved descendent, Kitsune Isamu, immortal Lord of Foxes!"

Hands locked, Yukiko and Hana stepped into the room. Dark wooden floors lined a vast open space, lit by the extravagance of old-fashioned flower-oil lanterns. Thick pillars of the same wood lined the approach, shadows dancing in the stuttering light.

More than a dozen ladies and lords were gathered around the dais at the end of the room: dour-faced magistrates in jet-black, courtesans with kohl-rimmed eyes, scribes in skullcaps with ink-stained fingers. These were surrounded in turn by a small legion of Iron Samurai, watching behind their fox masks with fierce, narrowed eyes. And on the fifth step, ensconced on a mahogany throne of carven flowers, sat Isamu, supreme clanlord of the Kitsune.

He was dressed in courtly robes, chainswords paired at his waist beside the snub-nosed lump of an ornate iron-thrower. A golden breather crafted like a fox's face was strapped over his mouth. And though he was old and bent and shriveled, Yukiko could see the samurai coiled beneath his skin. Surrounded by courtiers, Isamu looked as out of place as a battle-worn blade amidst a sea of pretty fans. His brow was a scarred scowl. His moustache reached his waist.

"He looks about seven thousand years old," Hana whispered.

"Legend has it he's lived a hundred years. One of the greatest luminaries of my Clan."

"Gods, imagine what's going on under that robe. His luminaries would be hanging around his knees—"

Yukiko aimed a horrified glare at the girl.

The sentence died a quiet, if not dignified death.

"Stormdancer," said the Kitsune Daimyo. "We are honored by your presence."

"Daimyo Kitsune Isamu." Yukiko bowed low. "The honor is mine."

Hana was still squinting at the lord of the Kitsune clan, her expression slightly pained. Yukiko tugged her pants leg, and the girl gave a clumsy bow.

". . . Most Handsome Worshipfulness," Hana said.

The haunting music of koto and shamisen drifted in the room, and glancing around, Yukiko finally found the source. A machine stood against the southern wall; a collection of humanoid figures inside a crescent-shaped scaffold. Crafted in female form, the automatons were made of brass and tin; faces painted white, gowns of patterned gold and swirling black. Metal fingers flitted over the strings and skins of their instruments with inhuman precision.

The music was beautiful, yet somehow Yukiko found it empty. Perhaps it was the way the automatons moved, heads wobbling on their necks. Perhaps because they reminded her of Kin; the little metal arashitora he had made for her, the clockwork wings he'd built Buruu.

She turned away from the thought, throat squeezing tight.

"I won't usually see guests without invitation." The Daimyo's voice was hard behind his breather. "But for the mighty Stormdancer, I will make an exception. I trust the ruin and bloodshed you brought to my city did not inconvenience you on the way in?"

He leaned back in his throne, drummed his fingers on the dark wood.

He looks annoyed, Buruu.

THE KAGÉ JUST STARTED A WAR IN HIS CITY. YOU ARE A FIGURE-HEAD IN THE KAGÉ REBELLION. YOU WERE EXPECTING HIM TO NAME A STREET AFTER YOU?

. . . Maybe a little one?

"Great Daimyo," Yukiko began. "I deeply regret the chaos that befell your beautiful city today. Please know it was a chaos not of my making. I do not stand here as a representative of the Kagé council. I am a simple refugee, seeking safe harbor for my friends."

"A simple refugee." The Daimyo raised one gray eyebrow. "Riding a thunder tiger."

Yukiko risked a small smile. "A complicated refugee, then."

"My streets are awash with blood because of you and yours, Stormdancer."

"Great Lord, I am no longer a part of the Kagé rebellion. It was they who started the war within the Guild. I begged them not to, and when they wouldn't listen, I left their stronghold."

"So what are you now, then? A beggar? A freelance troublemaker?"

Yukiko squared her shoulders. "I am an enemy of the Lotus Guild. An enemy to their puppet, Tora Hiro. An enemy to the government that chokes our skies and murders innocents for the sake of blood to feed—"

"Gods, you've got a set on you, girl. Standing there and crowing about murder."

Yukiko blinked. "Daimyo?"

"You murdered our Shōgun. And while I loved Yoritomo-no-miya like I love my kidney stones, he was sovereign lord of these isles. The power vacuum he left behind is your doing. The civil war tearing these lands apart is your fault."

The words were a slap, draining the blood from Yukiko's face. She was taken aback for a second, pinned by the pale stare above the breather. The Daimyo seemed almost to be enjoying himself—she swore she could see a smile in his rheumy eyes.

"He murdered my father, Daimyo." She did her best to keep the righteous anger from her voice. "And my mother and her unborn child. So yes, I killed him. And I'd do it again."

"Rumor has it you slew him simply by looking at him." The old clanlord raised an eyebrow. "The Shōgun of this land, to whom all owed allegiance."

Hana rolled her eye, pressed her lips shut and stared at the floor.

"I swore no oath to him," Yukiko growled. "Never in my life did I make a promise to that baby-killing bastard."

A murmur rippled amongst the courtiers, as if a pebble had been dropped into quiet water. She felt dark stares on her, heard Buruu's voice rolling in her mind.

REMEMBER WHERE YOU HAVE STOOD. WHAT YOU ARE.

She stared at Isamu.

"The Kazumitsu Dynasty was a tyranny, and its alliance with the Lotus Guild has dragged this nation to ruin. You see it, too, Daimyo. Or else why give insult to Tora Hiro by not attending his wedding?"

"Tora Hiro?" The old man crowed with laughter. "That sniveling little upstart? I wouldn't drag my carcass out of this chair to piss on him if he were on fire, let alone all the way across the country to attend his sham of a wedding."

"So Hiro *is* your enemy."

"Hiro is an *insult*. I am descended from the first Daimyo of this zaibatsu— great Okimoto, the warlord who subjugated the clans of Serpent, Falcon, Spider and Wolf." He thumped his fists on his armrest. "This is one of the Four Thrones of Shima, mine by right of blood and birth. And I should bow before a *samurai's* son?"

THERE IT IS. HIS WEAKNESS.

Yukiko nodded.

Pride.

PRESS IT.

"We've heard through our agents the Guild are upset with your defiance," she said.

"I should be impressed?" The old man waved a hand, as if swatting a bothersome fly. "Everyone knows they withhold their boons after I slighted their would-be Shōgun."

"That's how they control you. Through the promise of fuel. In Kigen, they're offering payment to people who bring victims to the Burning Stones. People like Hana and I, who carry the Kenning. More innocents murdered, just for an accident of birth."

"So we have a common enemy. Your point?"

"My enemy's enemy is my friend."

"You have a fine way of treating your friends, girl. Setting their cities on fire."

"It's the Guild who burned your city, Daimyo. The same Guild who starve your armies of fuel until you do your duty. Obey the forms of Bushido. Kneel before your new Shōgun."

Isamu's eyes narrowed to papercuts.

"I fought the gaijin in Morcheba for twenty years. I sent all five of my sons to the war and *none* returned. I do not need Bushido or duty explained to me by some filthy chi-monger, and I do not kneel before anyone, girl. Least of all some crippled Tiger *puppet*!"

"Nor should you, honorable Lord." A grim smile lit Yukiko's face. "And I have no doubt you'll help us teach a lesson to those who think you will."

The Daimyo glanced at General Ginjiro.

"The pair on this girl . . ."

"Solid brass," the general nodded.

"Honorable Daimyo," Yukiko sighed. "It comes to this. We have common purpose and a common foe. I need a place for my friends to stay. A harbor for the Guild rebels. If you're actually serious about defying the Guild, now is your chance to prove it."

"Why should I help?" the clanlord asked. "What do you offer?"

Yukiko glanced around the room, the narrowed eyes above fluttering fans, the hiss of serpent's breath behind golden breathers. She looked again at the Daimyo—this withered old viper with razored teeth. Was he an honorable man, or just a grumpy old warmonger? Was he defying the Guild because he believed in their evil, or because he just wanted to pick a fight?

"Tora Hiro marches north with the Earthcrusher to make you kneel before him," she said. "I'll defend Yama from this Tiger army, the Guild war machine behind it."

Isamu leaned back in his chair. "You'll swear to me, then?"

"I swear to no throne," Yukiko said. "I pledge myself to Shima's people. The mothers and fathers and sons and daughters who choke under poisoned skies. Who sent their children off to die in a war made of lies. I pledge my life to them. Not you, Daimyo. *Them*."

Hana was staring at Yukiko, jaw hanging slack. Looking around at the assembled Kitsune court, the girl stepped up beside Yukiko and took her hand.

"Godsdamn right."

The Daimyo glanced at his general, a smile in his eyes. He looked down at the swords at his waist, the courtiers assembled around his throne, the two girls before him. The mechanical musicians played on in the corner, their song suddenly and terribly out of place.

"Solid brass," he muttered.

The clanlord stood, covered his fist and offered a bow.

"I accept your terms. If only because I can't wait to see the look on Tora Hiro's face when a pair of thunder tigers fly up his hindparts and start cutting his dogs to ribbons." Isamu nodded. "I offer you and your friends sanctuary in Kitsune-jō."

Yukiko sighed, relief flooding over her in warm waves.

"My thanks, great Lord."

Buruu's voice rang inside her head.

IS EVERYTHING WELL, SISTER?

Better than well, brother. Hana and I are coming out now.

Yukiko grabbed Hana's hand and walked from the throne room, a grim smile on her face.

And we're bringing an army with us.

9
WHAT WILL BE

Kensai had no time for a rebellion.

The Second Bloom strode the hallways of Chapterhouse Kigen, listening to the tumbling, jumbling clatter of the mechabacus in his head: reports of insurrection in Chapterhouse Yama, a suicide attack incinerating Second Bloom Aoi and the bulk of his command staff aboard his flagship. But worse, news filtered through command frequencies that the rebellion was not confined to Yama—that every chapterhouse in Shima was probably infested with insurgents.

And from the Yama frequencies themselves, where once there would have been noise and life and meaning, there was only a constant 50-cycle hum.

This should have been a moment of triumph. Hiro had mustered his troops, was sailing toward the Stain even now. In two days' time, the Tiger Lord would rendezvous with the Phoenix fleet and begin the march north. Fifteen days for the Earthcrusher to be unleashed on the Kagé—the nights, months, years of his life spent designing the colossus, agitating for its construction, all of it crystallizing in this single moment. And now, at the eleventh hour, to find traitors within the Guild's own ranks . . .

"How is this even possible?"

Kensai slammed a fist onto the stone tabletop of the Chamber of Council, glaring at the trio of Inquisitors at the other end of the room. His command staff was assembled, watching the show with blood-red eyes. The walls were lined with maps of the Shima Isles, chattering banks of instrumentation. The undertones of great engines growling and grinding in the building's bowels, overlaid with the rising uncertainty in the hallways outside.

"I have little time to waste on enigmatic silence," Kensai spat. "I suggest one of you wake long enough to offer explanation!"

"Explanation?"

The lead Inquisitor spoke, bloodshot stare aimed at the ceiling. Of the two others in the room, one peered at his fingers, moving them as if weaving invisible thread. The third watched the air directly above Kensai's shoulder, blinking once per second with timepiece precision. As each exhaled, blue-black smoke drifted from the grinning breathers over their faces.

"An explanation!" Kensai drew himself up to his full height. "The Inquisition is meant to recognize Impurity in all its guises. Is that not why you breathe lotus smoke every minute of your lives? To bring you clarity? How is it you failed to see rebellion festering in the Guild's heart?"

The lead Inquisitor looked sharply at the empty air to his immediate right. Taking one step left, the little man spoke with agonizing slowness.

"Who is to say we did not, Second Bloom?"

"Do you mean you foresaw—"

"We see much. Many possibilities."

"This is as it should be," said another. "This is . . . satisfactory."

"Satisfactory?" Kensai was incredulous. "A Second Bloom has been assassinated!"

"Are you certain?" The Inquisitor looking at his fingertips met Kensai's stare—the first of the group to have done so. "Did you see?"

"What *do* you see, Shateigashira?" the first asked.

"I see madmen," Kensai spat.

The statement was met with uneasy murmurs around the council table. Kensai ignored the rumblings of his lower Blooms, stalking toward the trio.

"I see charlatans who predict the What Will Be, but cannot see corruption growing before their own eyes. I see lotusfiends wreathing addiction in metaphysical nonsense, stumbling about in the dark and hoping one of their mumbled prognostications actually comes true."

The lead Inquisitor blinked again, eyes losing focus. "Then you see nothing."

"Soon you will," the second nodded. "Soon . . ."

Kensai seethed within his metal skin, bidding himself be still. Once the Earthcrusher destroyed the Kagé, once the gaijin war was renewed, he must speak with the Second Blooms of the remaining chapterhouses. Surely they must see the Inquisition's influence was becoming destructive? Surely they must realize the First Bloom's time was over?

The first Inquisitor spoke again, cutting Kensai's musings to ribbons.

"This insurgency cannot be permitted to spread. We assume you will remain here in Kigen and see to the dissent in your own house."

Not a question. A command.

"No," Kensai replied. "I will travel north with the Earthcrusher and destroy the Kagé."

"You are a Second Bloom, Kensai-san. Your first duty is to your chapterhouse."

"All my life has led to this day. It is *I* who should be standing on the Earthcrusher's bridge as it storms the Iishi. I designed its every—"

"You had assistance, did you not? Kioshi, former Third Bloom of this chapterhouse, was the genius behind its engines. And Kioshi's son sits here in this very chamber."

Kensai glared momentarily at his newest Fifth Bloom, the boy's single glowing eye downturned, not daring to meet his gaze.

Kin-san.

"You cannot mean to send him in my stead?"

"And why not? He is intimately familiar with the Earthcrusher's design. He knows the engine schematics better than any save perhaps yourself."

"Two weeks ago he was part of the Kagé rebellion!"

"And since then, has handed over the Kagé leader to us, and would have gladly executed him at our command. Of your entire chapter, there is none less likely to be a traitor than he."

"You do not know," the second Inquisitor breathed, "what he Will Be."

"But *we* know," said the third. "We have *seen*."

Looming over the black-clad trio, Kensai found himself contemplating heresy for the first time in his life. But to raise a hand to an Inquisitor . . .

"The Earthcrusher is my dream," he hissed. "*My* design. I will be dead before I see this child steal my glory after all he has done."

The first Inquisitor's voice was barely a whisper. "That is . . ."

". . . disappointing," finished the third.

"First Bloom will hear of this . . ."

". . . hubris."

"I will tell him myself," Kensai spat. "When I lay the Stormdancer's head at his feet."

The Inquisitors began drifting from the room, a brokenback trail of smoke in their wake. As they approached the doorway, the leader turned, eyes on Kensai's once more.

"First Bloom has sent word, by the by. We are to bring the Kagé leader Daichi with us to First House for execution."

"I thought he was to be executed publically in Kigen?"

A slow shrug. "First Bloom commands and we obey. At least some within these walls remember their place."

The iris doorway closed behind them with the sound of a headsman's blade.

The room seemed to grow lighter once the Inquisitors had departed, both the glow of the overheads and the breath in his chest. Uneasy murmurs and blood-red stares were exchanged. Kensai stilled the chatter immediately, planting himself at the table's head and glaring at the Third Bloom of the Purifier Sect.

"Kyodai Yoshinobu, you will seek out and eliminate any insurgents within Chapterhouse Kigen. You will make this your first priority, and report your findings *directly* to me. Not the Inquisition. Not any other. Do you understand?"

The Kyodai cleared his throat. "Second Bloom, all due respect, but my resources are stretched thin. With bounty now being offered on the Impure, accused are being turned over to us in greater numbers than ever before. Each of them must be tested. If guilty, they must be put to pyre. We simply do not have the manpower to continue processing, testing and purifying if we are also to oversee internal investigations into this rebellion."

"Conduct the testing at the Altar of Purity, then," Kensai said.

". . . In public?"

"Why not?" Kensai asked. "Hold one burning each weeksend, at noon. The skinless will bring their accused to the stones, the testing can be conducted then and there, anyone bearing false witness can burn on the pyres instead."

"Second Bloom, testing is usually conducted privately . . . There are rites to be conducted, forms to obey. I think it unwise—"

"I think it unwise to allow insurgents to roam this chapterhouse unchecked, don't you?"

"Of cour—"

"Assign your most trusted Shatei to the internal investigations. Leave no stone unturned."

". . . As you say, Second Bloom."

"The rest of you, attend your duties. Any aberrant behavior must be viewed with suspicion in light of events in Yama city. Any Guildsman found to be in allegiance with these rebels will be victim to the most heinous brutality we can fashion. Am I understood?"

The assembly spoke with one voice. "Hai."

"I depart for the Earthcrusher tomorrow. It is up to each of you to ensure this chapterhouse endures while I am gone. The lotus *must* bloom."

"The lotus must bloom."

The assembled Kyodai rose and stalked from the room in a cloud of smoke and suspicion.

All save one.

A small figure, seated at the opposite end of the table, his atmos-suit still gleaming with the shine of fresh-pressed skin.

"Fifth Bloom Kin," Kensai growled. "Do you not have duties to attend?"

The boy's eyes were aglow, cables from his mouthpiece rasping against each other as he shook his head. The smoke motif on his spaulders and gauntlets seemed to shift in the fume-choked air, blood-red light spilling from his eye socket.

"I don't trust them," Kin said.

Kensai reclined in his chair. "Trust whom?"

"The Inquisition."

"Trust is a rare thing these nights, Kioshi-san. Oh, but forgive me . . . you abandoned your father's name, did you not? Around the same time you abandoned this chapterhouse . . ."

The boy hung his head. "Will you never forgive me?"

"Were it my decision, you would have already been boiled into fertilizer."

"It was a mistake, Uncle . . ."

"Uncle?" Kensai scoffed. "What madness is this?"

"You and my father were as brothers. When he died, you treated me as your own son. Do you fault me for thinking of you as the uncle I never had?"

"We were as brothers, he and I." Kensai leaned forward. "So believe me when I say if he were alive today, your actions would have shamed him to suicide."

"I will never fail you again."

"I will give you precious little chance, believe me."

"You can trust me more than you can trust any member of this chapterhouse."

A hollow burst of mirthless laughter. "How so?"

"My father never told you, did he? What I saw during my Awakening ceremony? My glorious future laid out in the Chamber of Smoke?"

"We never spoke of such things. It would have been improper."

Kin spoke as if by rote, voice thick with reverb.

"Do not call me Kin. That is not my name. Call me First Bloom."

Kensai felt the words as a blow to his stomach. A cold fist sucking breath from his lungs, forcing him to steady himself on the table's edge.

Kin? As First Bloom?

The boy stood, a silicon-smooth hiss of pistons and chi exhaust. He approached Kensai, placed a gentle hand on his shoulder. That single eye burned with the heat of a thousand suns.

"One day I will sit on the Throne of Machines, Uncle. One day I will rule this Guild. You may have forgotten the faith you once held in me, but I still hold faith in you. I will do all I can to see this cancer in the Guild uprooted. And when you and the Earthcrusher burn the Iishi to cinders, I will be there in spirit beside you."

Kin turned to leave, heavy boots thudding in time with Kensai's pulse.

"Burn them for me, Uncle."

A nod.

"Burn them all."

"What Will Be . . ."

Kensai strode the hallways to his habitat, whispering the phrase over and over, thoughts all atumble in his mind. Could it be true? Could Kin be destined to lead the Guild once First Bloom Tojo was gone? The old man had ruled for longer than any could remember, but even he must eventually go the way of flesh. Was Kin really the one to take his place?

Kin?

All Guildsmen were shown visions of the future in the Chamber of Smoke, reliving it nightly while they slept. Some saw only snatches and riddles, some saw their futures clear as glass, some were driven mad by what they witnessed. For Kensai, his vision had been of the Earthcrusher—a towering goliath of iron and chainblades, sweeping entire armies before it.

The vision had always been there, a certainty he could set his back against, a desire that had driven him to excel. Designing the behemoth, convincing the other chapterhouses to invest the resources required to fashion this colossal deathblow for the Kagé and gaijin. And now to learn that Kin was destined to rule the entire Guild? While the Inquisition tried to rob him of his glory and see the boy stand in his stead on the Earthcrusher's bridge?

Kensai had long assumed he would be the one to supplant the First Bloom. He was Shateigashira of the most powerful chapterhouse in Kigen—it was only logical if Tojo fell, he would step into his boots. He'd dreamed of the changes he'd make, clipping the wings of those rampant spiritualists in the Inquisition, putting them back in the cages they'd long ago been allowed to fly. The thought of Kin ascending instead, of having to bow and scrape before that treacherous little boy-child . . .

But if those fools in the Inquisition couldn't even spot an insurrection brewing inside the Guild, who was to say whether their vision for Kin was true?

Who was to say any of it was right?

And if not them, who knew What Will Be?

Kensai spat a curse under his breath, stabbed at the controls for his habitat.

He had no time for a rebellion . . .

The chamber was vast, sparsely adorned. A bed dominating one wall, varnished oak and silken sheets of bloody red, his one real indulgence. A large desk loomed in a far corner, piled high with reports; deadlands percentile, crop forecasts, price fluctuations. An automated dictagraph sat beside reams of rice-paper, awaiting his voice to lurch into life.

He sat at the desk, clicked the dictagraph to record. The device was made of polished brass, gleaming and clean. He could see his reflection in its surface, the mask of the beautiful youth he'd never be again. He was an old man underneath his skin now, speeding toward middle age, thinning hair cropped upon his scalp, crow's feet and liver spots glaring every time he dared look with his real face in the mirror.

Less and less these days.

Skin is strong. Flesh is weak.

Leaning close, he spoke to the microphone.

"Kensai, Shateigashira Chapterhouse Kigen. Reporting seventh—"

The explosion cut his sentence to ribbons.

The dictagraph blasted apart, hurling Kensai clear across the room. He smashed into the far wall, felt his impact against the bricks, tasted blood in his mouth. Crashing to the floor, black flooded in, drowning the rising pain, the scent of his own charred flesh. Smoke filled his lungs, but he could barely manage a cough, fingers stabbing at his mechabacus—a stuttering, clumsy plea for help across the emergency frequencies.

Fading.

Falling.

All the while, a small voice in the back of his head was protesting. This wasn't the way it was supposed to happen, it assured him. This wasn't his What Will Be.

But who was to say any of it was right? Who really knew?

Kensai fought as the dark rushed in, pushing it back, flailing and clawing.

No, I don't die like this!

Kensai had no time for a rebellion.

And then Kensai had no time at all.

10
AN IRON SEA

The undisputed Lord of the Dragon clan stood in a hallway of his seaside fortress, listening to the rising storm outside his window.

Through the glass, Haruka could see the cliffs where he used to stand as a boy, watching the winter storms ravage his homeland's coastline. He'd spent hours at a time with his toes at the edge, electricity tingling his scalp as the lightning flashed and thunder rolled, the knowledge that a gust of greedy wind would be all it took to send him down into the Bay of Dragons below. He'd done it to master himself. To kill any trace of terror inside him, that he might grow up to be as fearless a Lord as any the Dragon clan had known.

At sixty-two years of age, Daimyo Haruka almost envied that boy on the cliff's edge. He couldn't remember what it was to feel afraid anymore.

He almost missed it.

The Dragon clanlord was short and wiry, a long goatee and gray locks swept away in a topknot. He was clad in a sapphire-blue kimono and a thick cuirass of solid iron. Black clouds hung over the Bay of Dragons, the seas whipped to rushing gray foam. The waters were the color of pitch, rolling out into a dull blood-red. On afternoons like this, Haruka could fancy the oceans were still filled with the spirits of his clan, thrashing in the breakers with long, silvered tails, teeth like katana gnashing amongst the waves.

But those days had passed now. The dragons had gone the way of the arashitora—chased back to the spirit world by chi fumes and the death rattles of the land they once called home. This was not a time for beasts of legend. This was a time for men.

Men and swords.

"Thuh-the most honorable and resplendent D-d-daimyo of the Ruh-Ryu Clan!" Young Daisuke heralded his Lord's arrival in the Hall of Warriors, voice echoing amongst high rafters. "Fuh-firstborn son of R-r-ryu Sakai, protector of the Suh-seven Seals of J-j-j-jimen-Jiro . . ."

Haruka stalked to his place at table, swept the long pleated skirts of his kimono aside, and sat cross-legged in one swift motion. His war council remained kneeling, waiting for the herald to finish stuttering through his announcement. Three spit-soaked minutes passed, the boy's face reddening with concentration. Haruka sighed inwardly, features impassive. His sister's son had been afflicted by the gods; it had been the honorable thing to offer place amongst his retinue. But still, his sister could have requested a more sensible role for the boy than godsdamned herald . . .

Daisuke eventually finished, face purple from exertion, pressing forehead to floor.

Relief drifted amongst the war council as the boy fell silent. A chill wind howled in off the bay, filled with the reek of chi sludge and dead fish. Yet Haruka enjoyed the sea's song despite the stink; the hiss and roll of black surf where his clan once roamed in long sail-ships, a terror to the merchants of the Hawk, the Mantis, and the Turtle. Before the twenty-four clans became four zaibatsu. Before his forefather knelt at a Shōgun's feet.

Haruka nodded to his assembled council, one hand on the chainsaw katana at his waist.

"My samurai," he said.

The assembled men pressed brows to table, murmured greetings as one. Haruka turned on his firstborn son, newly returned from scouting the eastern borders of their province.

"Reisu-san. Report."

"Daimyo." Reisu bowed his head. "The rumors are true. The Guild has fashioned an almighty war-machine for the Tiger clan. Three hundred feet high if it stands an inch, and an army of shreddermen beside it. The Phoenix Fleet is mustered at Midland Junction, with more Tiger troops arriving by rail every day. They prepare to march north. The upstart Hiro seeks to punish Daimyo Isamu for the temerity of not attending his wedding."

Haruka stroked his beard. "Think broader, my son. Why would the Tiger clan need shreddermen suits to attack Isamu's fortress? Is it made of wood?"

"No, Daimyo . . ."

The Dragon clanlord stood, began pacing the length of the table.

"The Guild intends to attack the Iishi forest. The Kagé stronghold. It is the rebellion's blood they seek, not the Kitsune. They will give the Fox clan a chance to join the fold, on my life. They will offer the same to us. This machine, this Earthcrusher . . . it is the flag the Guild's new nation is meant to rally behind."

"Will we pledge allegiance, Father?"

A small frown darkened Haruka's brow. "This Hiro . . . He holds the Phoenix Daimyo in his dungeons and their armies to ransom. I have met him, and there is nothing close to noble blood in his veins. When he was set to wed the Lady Aisha, at least he had thin claim to legitimacy. Now, he is little more than a puppet dancing to the Guild's tune."

Haruka turned to his samurai, fire in his eyes.

"I say this clan will not kneel before a mere boy-child. I say we would rather bleed the ground red than bow before a chi-monger's marionette. I say we will crush this pretender into dust, or perish in the attempt."

Reisu cleared his throat. "There are other rumors, Father. We heard them in our travels. Our clansmen to the south speak of horrors spreading from the Stain. Crawling from cracks in the earth. Talk of oni demons and creatures darker still—"

"We have no time for the babbling of superstitious peasants, my son. War is at our door. And will we rise to meet it?" Haruka turned to his men. "Will we stand with swords in hand? Does the blood of Dragons not flow in our veins? Are we not Ryu?"

"Hai!" A dozen shouts filled the room, Haruka's counselors beating their fists upon the table or the iron at their breasts. As the shout faded, a new sound stepped in to fill the space between crashing wave and howling wind. A sound born of metal on hollow metal, rimed with frost. A sound that had only been heard once in Kawa city since Haruka was born; the day his father, Daimyo Sakai, had passed on to his heavenly reward.

The song of iron bells from the Dragon Tooth Straights.

The samurai looked amongst one another in confusion. Herald Daisuke ran to the bay windows, staring out to the distant watchtowers perched on the Dragon's Teeth. Two long fangs of stone protruded from the mainland, forming a narrow pass into a natural harbor—the Bay of Ryu from which the old raiding fleets had once mustered. The towers were relics, manned only out of respect for the old ways. The chances of Kawa ever being invaded by sea nowadays . . .

Daisuke pressed one hand against the clouded beach glass, body stiffening.

The bells continued to peal.

Haruka frowned. "Daisuke-san, what do you see?"

"Guh," the boy said. "Guh . . ."

The war council frowned amongst themselves, muttering darkly. The position of Herald was no job for a halfwit. Any one of them had sons who could have filled the—

"Guh . . ." the boy said.

"Maker's breath . . ." Haruka stalked across the Hall of Warriors, clapped one hand on his stuttering nephew's shoulder, and looked out over the Bay of Ryu.

"Guh . . ." the boy said.

"Gods above," Haruka breathed.

Ships. Dozens of them. Metal-clad and sailless, towering above the waves and moving in phalanx formation. The flagship at their head as big as a fortress—wedge-shaped, great thrashing wheels on its flanks, churning in black water. Lightning arced across rivet-studded hulls, decks littered with the lopsided dragonfly shapes of rotor-thopters, each one painted with twelve stars down their bows.

Haruka had served twenty years in the Morcheban campaigns, could read gaijin writing if he put his mind to it. He squinted through the spray and mists, making out the name of the flagship in the vanguard.

Ostrovska.

Haruka was a warrior born. A Daimyo forged in fire and blood, veteran of brutal massacres and glorious victories. And as he looked out to the iron-gray shapes slipping like blades into the Bay of Ryu, he felt an odd sensation in his chest. Something that hadn't stirred in decades—not since he was a boy, standing on those cliffs and daring the storm to take him. It took him a moment to remember what it was . . .

Fear.

He turned to his council, eyes wide, lips flapping like laundry in the wind.

"Guh . . ." he said. "Guh . . ."

Herald Daisuke turned from the window, pale as cold ash. The boy drew his chainkatana in trembling hands, spoke with trembling voice.

"Gaijin," he said.

PART TWO
GRIEF

"Be you my brave love?"
Her voice sweet as plum perfume. "Will you stay with me?"
Izanagi sighed; took his Lady in his arms, held her in the dark.
"Lie with me now, love." Her breath, snow upon his cheek. "Make
    me warm again."
She pressed with black lips, and in her kiss he tasted,
Ashes on her tongue.

—*from the* Book of Ten Thousand Days

11
THE BATTLE OF KAWA

Kapitán Aleksandar Mostovoi smoothed a stray length of grimy blond hair from his face, breath hanging white in the bitter cold. He looked around the burning city, the troops pouring off the assault fleet in waves, draped in skins of mighty wolves and bears and snow leopards. The streets around him were awash with red. The falling rain as black as sin.

The slavers had put up a brief defense, paid for in slaughter, and had now retreated into their castle on the hill to prepare for siege. Their flags lay in the dirt amidst their corpses, blue slabs set with a Dragon sigil, now soaked in gore. The Blood-blessed were moving among the smoke—great, towering slabs of men, muscle heaped upon scar-tissue, clad in aprons of skin.

Aleksandar had once seen a Blood-blessed kill an Iron Samurai with his bare hands. The man had been split from belly to rib cage, half a dozen spears sticking from his back like a porcupine's quills. He'd used his own bloody innards to strangle the samurai leading the charge. Aleksandar recalled seeing four of the madmen roaming the battlefield after the stalemate at Fallow Pass, stooping to gather the blood of fallen slavers in human skulls, raising them in toast toward the surviving Shiman forces. Between them, the four berserks had slain fifty men.

The Morcheban Expeditionary Force that attacked Kawa included a host of two hundred.

Pulling his wolfpelt tight about his shoulders, Aleksandar trudged across the ankle-deep mire of the beachhead, cursing beneath his breath. Everything in this Goddess-forsaken country was filthy. The ground was either black mud, rotting fields or swathes of dead earth no soldier in his right mind would set foot on. The air weighed down their lungs, staining tongue, teeth and skin. No wonder the Shimans wanted to occupy his homeland—Aleksandar had only been here three hours and he already hated this bloody place.

As he pulled up his wolfpelt cloak, the Kapitán noticed it stank of slaver blood; sharp and vaguely rank. There was little to be done about it—the black rain only made it dirtier and clean water in this hellhole was rare as gold. He recalled the day he'd flayed the pelt, the taste of the strength he'd drunk, copperish in his mouth. Hands shaking on the knife hilt. Breeches stained with piss. A boy of thirteen, now a man.

Twenty years ago, next summer.

His father had been killed when Aleksandar was twelve. House Mostovoi had been the first to meet the marauders with their growling armor and swords that cut through men like fog. The Mostovoi coastal defenses were nonexistent; their walls were built to repel attacks from other houses, not strangers crossing the Faceless Sea. Their capital had been razed. His mother and sister taken by Kitsune slavers. He'd only escaped by running; running until his feet bled and his lungs screamed and he couldn't breathe or think or see. He still dreamed of it. Every night.

But in the dreams, the slavers always caught him.

He'd wanted revenge, of course. His family was a proud line, tracing their lineage back to the first Zryachniye, great Stanislava. But he'd need strength to fight this foe. A strength borne of a darkest heart. And so he'd walked into the Blackwood where the dire packs roamed, a boy with a spear and a knife and a will of cold iron.

And he'd returned a man.

That man now slogged his way across the slaughter to a newly-erected tent bedecked with standards of the Twelve Houses of Morcheba. He ran one hand over the House Mostovoi sigil on his breastplate; a rampant stag with three sickle-bladed horns. And breathing deep, he stepped into the gloom.

It took his eyes a moment to adjust. A long table was arrayed with a map of Kawa city, small disks indicating troop disposition, red for the Shiman dogs, black for the forces of her Imperial Majesty, Kira I of House Ostrovska. The Imperatritsa's flag hung between the tent poles; a black field arrayed with twelve red stars.

Marshal Sergei Ostrovska surveyed the map with a critical eye, barely looking up as the Kapitán entered. Beside him stood the Majór of the Imperatritsa's airforces, busy complaining about the damage being done to his rotor-thopters' engines by the black rain. A pack of six warhounds sat at the Marshal's feet, wheezing in the freezing, poisoned air.

Two Zryachniye priestesses stood on the other side of the table, swaying like saplings in the spring breeze. Blond as wheat before summer harvest, faces scarified with totemic blessings—lightning bolts torn down Sister Katya's cheeks, jagged claw patterns marring the features of Mother Natassja. Each right eye aglow.

"Marshal Sergei," Aleksandar said. "Columns are mustered. We await your orders."

The Marshal was a man of fifty, pitted and worn from two decades of constant warfare. His head was brick-shaped, his face just a touch too small. The sigil of House Ostrovska decorated his breastplate; a black gryfon clutching broadswords. Still glowering at the map, he grabbed a handful of salted meat from a bowl on the table and tossed it to the wardogs at his feet. The hounds remained motionless, licking at drooling chops.

"The slavers have retreated behind their walls, as expected," Sergei said, tapping a finger on the Dragon fortress. "The castle is well defended, easily held even by a small host." He raised one thick eyebrow at Mother Natassja. "You saw thirteen sky-ships, Holy Mother?"

"Aerial reconnaissance reported only six," the Majór said.

"Seven more lurk in the clouds over the keep," Mother Natassja murmured, running one finger down the claw patterns carved into her face. "I *see* them. They wait above, higher than your 'thopters can fly. Heavy ships. Well armed."

"The storm will grow fiercer close to noon." Sister Katya's glowing stare was fixed on the Kapitán. "I see lightning bright as sunlight. Airships burning in the tempest."

Aleksandar met the woman's stare, trying to show no emotion. Katya was easily the most fearsome of the two Zryachniye, her reputation well proceeding her. Where the Holy Mother wore soft leather adorned with totemic trinkets, Sister Katya wore flayed Guildsmen suits like armor, helms beaten flat on her shoulders like spaulders. He almost pitied the Lotusmen who'd crashed near the northern lightning farm and fallen under her blades.

"We wait until noon, then." The Marshal barked a command, and his warhounds pounced on their meat, drool flying. "We attack frontally once our 'thopters have cleared the walls. The Blood-blessed will run in the vanguard. You will lead the attack, Mostovoi."

"Your command." The Kapitán thumped his fist against his breastplate, turned on his heel. Mother Natassja's voice pulled him up short.

"Aleksandar Mostovoi. Slayer of Kirill, alpha of the Blackwood. Victor of Iron Ridge. Thrice-blooded in the service of his Imperatritsa. Son of Sascha, daughter of Darya, Matriarch of House Mostovoi."

He turned slowly. "Yes, Holy Mother?"

The woman's right eye was luminous, rosy light spilling into the ritual scars on her face. The glow turned her features vulpine, all hollowed cheeks and sharpened teeth, smile like a bruise on her skull.

"Your sons will remember this day. How they remember is up to you."

". . . Thank you, Holy Mother."

"Blessings of the Goddess to you."

"And you, Holy Mother."

The woman blinked, the glow in her eye fading like sunset's light. The room seemed colder for its absence, her gentle smile failing to hide the sadness in her voice.

"I will not need them," she said.

Aleksandar turned and marched from the room.

I t was a storm sent by the Goddess herself.

Just as Sister Katya had said, the winds began rising near noon bells, vast clouds blotting out Shima's accursed red sun and plunging the land into freezing gloom. Lightning lit the skies as if the Goddess wished a clear view of the slaughter to come. As the column commanders formed their lines, Aleksandar looked over the ruined city before him and smiled.

The Shima sky-ships were descending just as Sister Katya promised, tossed about as if in the grip of frost giants. One crashed into the keep walls thanks to vicious crosswinds, another was struck by lightning as it descended, burning to cinders. A bloodthirsty cheer had gone up from the lines as the cloud ship incinerated, hymns to the Goddess rolling down the ranks. Surely She'd sent the storm to punish these faithless pigs. Twenty years of slaughter. Twenty years of plunder and slavery. Payment long overdue.

The Blood-blessed were restless, pounding their mallets on the ground, the flayed skin draping their shoulders stained gray by the putrid rain. Aleksandar had tied a kerchief around his face, but his lips were cracked and burning, skin raw where the downpour leaked through his armor. Some of his soldiers had been so badly affected, he'd ordered them back to the medical stations and the ministrations of the Mercy Sisters. Every man in the legion was eager to get the attack under way—the less time they had to spend in this bastard storm, the better.

The engineer companies signaled they were ready to move. The last of the slaver cloud ships hit the ground. Aleksandar nodded to his signalman, gave the order for 'thopters to launch. The soft whine built to a throbbing pulse, the *lub-dubdubdubdub* of propellers vibrating in his chest. He turned, pale blue eyes watching the craft rise slowly, no more troubled by the brutal gale than a dog by a handful of fleas.

The 'thopters were shaped like crooked dragonflies, possessed of the slightly asymmetrical coarseness common among his country's engineering exploits. No two looked the same; cobbled together by mekaniks of different houses, each with his own theory on how to design a flying machine. But the fundamentals were similar—a round pod set with a tail, two glass portals resembling an insect's eyes, and three vast propellers left, right and aft.

They were as graceless as drunken whores. Slow as three-legged horses. Unable to achieve either the speed or altitude of the Shima cloud ships, and prone to catastrophic malfunction. Their crews called them "flying coffins," and the infantry called their crews "the winged dead." But they could fly in a storm, by the Goddess. And on a day like today, that was all the advantage the Morchebans needed.

The slaver fortress crouched on a steep hill, its back to a ragged granite cliff, towers set with heavy shuriken-throwers. Any siege engines sent against the walls would have to be crafted of metal, lest they be incinerated by the flame-spitters studding the battlements. And even if the towers themselves weren't flammable, the men inside surely would be.

Of course, the spitters would only work if there were slavers alive to man them.

The 'thopter fleet hovered fifty feet off the ground in rough formation, almost forty in all, wobbling in ferocious winds. A fierce gust sent one 'thopter crashing into two others, all three falling from the sky and ending as twisted, flaming shells on Kawa's cobbles. But the rest made their way slowly through the cramped and burning city, drawing closer to the slaver keep and the samurai scrambling like insects on its walls.

Hails of shuriken fire and catapult scatter-loads tore the skies as the 'thopters drew within range. Aleksandar could hear that hateful *popopopopopopop!*, his mind drifting back to the day his father had been cut down on the walls of Mriss. 'Thopters dropped from the sky, the men inside reduced to leaking bags of bloody meat. Explosions echoed across the city, bright flares and plumes of black smoke uncoiling from crashed aircraft. Aleksandar gritted his teeth, muttered a prayer. Ears straining. Eyes narrowed. Waiting for the storm to truly begin.

A grim smile twisted his lips as a hollow crackling sound burned in the space between his eardrums, and bright arcs of impossible blue-white spat from the lead 'thopter's snout, followed by half a dozen others. Raw lightning spewed from the belly-mounted cannon, shearing across the battlements in blinding patterns, leaving a green flare on the back of Aleksandar's eyelids and blackened, bloody ruins where samurai had once stood. Flame-spitters spewed into the 'thopter's faces, lightning boiling the black rain to steam. And turning to his signalman, Aleksandar gave the order for the second wave to begin.

The siege-crawlers started their engines, filling the air with the stink of burned skin and ozone. The vehicles were ugly fat hulks of riveted iron, wrapped in segmented tank tread. Eleven of them surged forward, smashing a path through warehouses and family homes as they drove toward the keep. The machines were a brand-new creation of the mekaniks at the Akmarr proving grounds—this attack on Kawa was their first real field test. They looked impressive enough; all black studded iron, and broad, spear-tip snouts. But 30 percent of their complement had been lost during the beach landing, mostly due to mechanical failure.

As if reading his thoughts, one of the 'crawlers coughed blinding sparks from its cooling vents, shuddered and ground to a stop. Hatches burst open, black smoke spilling into the air, charred troopers tumbling from the scalding innards. Mercy Sisters ran forward and dragged the poor bastards onto stretchers, hauling them to the medical trains at the rear of the line.

Aleksandar lifted his kerchief and tried to spit the taste of charred flesh from his tongue.

"Your sons will remember this day . . ."

He waited until the 'crawlers were fifty yards from the keep wall, and with one last prayer to the Goddess, he climbed onto a stack of packing crates, drew his lightning hammer and looked over the army before him. A legion of heavy steel and black banners set with twelve red stars, blue eyes glittering beneath their helms, lightning on their blades.

The Kapitán roared above the chaos of battle and engine and storm.

"Brothers! Before you lies your hated foe, trembling behind walls of stone! You will drink their strength! You will wear their skins! And tonight you will dine in the ruin of their halls, or with the Goddess in the Halls of the Victorious Dead!"

The men answered with a roar, all raised fists and gleaming iron.

"Today you are not men of Aushloss, Krakaan, Veschkow, or Mriss! You are not orphans of twenty years of bloody oppression. You are not fathers to slaved daughters, brothers to stolen sisters, sons of slaughtered mothers! You are not soldiers! You are a *reckoning*!"

Another roar, shapeless and deafening.

"Blood for the Imperatritsa! Blood for the Goddess!"

"Blood!" they roared. "Blood!"

"Chaaaaaarge!"

The men surged forward, a wall of iron and rage. Troop towers collided with the keep walls and his men barreled up the walkways, Blood-blessed swinging their great two-handed mallets at the samurai who charged to meet them. Aleksandar stalked through the streets, lightning cannon momentarily blinding him, eyes narrowed as he shouted orders to the column commanders over the rising sound of slaughter.

The Iron Samurai were fighting like demons; the unholy strength from their mechanical armor was a sight to behold. Aleksandar saw one slaver—a commander by the look—leap off the battlements and land on a rotor-thopter's snout. The man punched through the windshield and dragged the pilot out through the shattered glass, hurling him onto the ground below. The 'thopter wrenched hard left, plummeting after its master as the commander leapt back toward the fortress and scrabbled onto the battlements.

Aleksandar charged up a tower walkway, toward the castle walls. The Blood-blessed were on the battlements now, drunk with murder. A thicket of Iron Samurai waited with chainblades drawn, a wall of flesh seething into them, heedless of their growling swords. The ramparts were littered with corpses fried to cinders by lightning canon. A few shuriken-throwers were still operational, bathing Aleksandar's troops in steel.

The Kapitán waded into the melee, roaring like an ice devil. His lightning hammer was a hymn in his hand, each impact into some slaver's skull making his heart sing. He waded among the berserks, smashing chainswords from hands, heads from shoulders. Blood on his gauntlets. On his face. On his tongue.

A rotor-thopter wobbled in the sky above, an Iron Samurai leaping from the wall to plunge both chainswords through the windshield. The machine listed and dropped like a stone, the samurai calling out a prayer as the craft collided with a troop tower. Arcs of lightning spilled from sundered tanks, electrocuting the soldiers amassed inside. Raw current dancing on iron and flesh. Faces split in rictus grins. Smell of burning meat.

Aleksandar heard a loud voice, the song of chainblades. He saw a familiar figure—the slaver commander who'd torn the 'thopter out of the sky. He was shearing his way through dozens of soldiers, fighting like a demon possessed. A flag waved from atop the power unit of his armor, blue as real sky, a white dragon coiled upon it. Around and above, Aleksandar could hear songs of slaughter— chainblades roaring, mallets crunching, groans of the wounded and screams of the dying. Battle stench coiled in his nostrils. Burning fuel and burning meat, the reek of split bellies and shit, blood's metallic tang hanging so thick he could have waved his hand through the air and had it come away red.

He waded through the throng, smashed some slaver's head from his neck— just a boy, no more than eighteen summers old. His eyes were on the slaver commander, now badly outnumbered, his men falling all around him. But still the man fought on, seemingly fearless. A Blood-blessed charged with mallet raised high, and the samurai sidestepped, cleaving through the berserker's abdomen, entrails spilling out in long, rolling coils of red and purple. The Blood-blessed roared as the samurai commander spun on his heel, taking the berserker's leg off at the knee, skipping back as the man fell howling in a puddle of his own insides.

Three soldiers fell on him, a warhammer crashing down on his power unit. Fuel spilled down the back of his legs, thick and blood-red as he took out one soldier's throat, caved in another's face with his fist. But they were all around him now, a swarm with no craft—just a seething mass of iron and the skins of flayed beasts.

"Wait!" Aleksandar roared. "He's mine!"

The men stilled around him, pulled back half a dozen steps. Aleksandar hefted his shield, leveled his lightning hammer at the slaver's head. The man seemed to understand, his men parting around him. He reached up to his power unit, snapped his clan banner free. He thrust the flag deep into the bodies around him, the once brilliant blue now stained muddy gray. The Dragon sigil fluttered in the freezing wind, the rain seemed a final defiant hiss at the army come to avenge twenty years of slaughter. But not without a fight. Not on his knees.

The men around Aleksandar began chanting, a rhythmic shout like a pulse, a single word. "Blood, blood, blood." And to his shock, the Iron Samurai held his sword aloft and spoke in the Morcheban tongue.

"I salute you, brother," he called. "I am sorry."

Aleksandar looked across the bloody battlements at the samurai, storm crashing around him, the cacophony of slaughter thick in the air. He wondered who this man was. What drove him. Whether he lost any sleep at the thought of the butchery his people had committed. Was he a bloodthirsty warmonger? Or just a soldier following orders?

In the end, did it matter?

Aleksandar thought of his mother. His sister. His father. And then he replied in perfect Shiman, voice dripping hatred.

"I am not sorry," he said. "And you are not my brother."

And then he charged.

Aleksandar thundered across bloody stone, black rain in his eyes. The downpour made a noise on his shield like a thousand tiny drums, his lightning hammer raised high, poised to pound its own rhythm on this slaver bastard's skull.

Thunder cracked overhead as they met, hammer whistling harmlessly past the samurai's head as he sidestepped, a burst of sparks illuminating a spray of black water as the chainkatana sheared away a chunk of Aleksandar's shield. The Kapitán swung a backhanded blow, hammer ablaze with electricity, the samurai leaning back as the weapon crackled past his face. Within a heartbeat, the slaver was on the front foot again, clipping another corner of Aleksandar's shield away and tearing a jagged gouge across his breastplate.

Aleksandar lunged, two rapid strikes deflected, sparks bursting, blue-black smoke snaking from the clunking engine on the slaver's back. He dipped a toe into the gore at his feet, kicked up a clod of blood toward the samurai's face, landing a solid blow on his opponent's shoulder. The samurai went rigid as raw current crackled over his armor, smoke rising from his skin. Aleksandar was sure the electric shock would have finished him there and then, but a riposte sent him staggering back, sparks flying as chunks of iron disappeared from his shield. The slaver was a master swordsman, fully aware that his chi-powered armor gave him an edge. For Aleksandar to become entangled was to die. To drop his guard was to die. To parry the samurai's strikes was to risk his weapon being cleaved at the haft, and thus, to die.

Aleksandar fell back, sidestepping rather than deflecting and countering. Fuel spilled down the samurai's back from crumpled tanks, coating his legs with thick, bubbling red. It wouldn't be long before the tanks ran dry—the both of them knew it. The slaver sought to finish him before his armor's speed and strength failed, for then he would simply be a man. Not a terror towering over frightened children in the streets of Krakaan or Veschkow. Not a demon cutting through men like sunlight through motes of dust. Just one little man in a suit of lifeless iron.

Time was on Aleksandar's side. He could simply play defensively and wait for the armor to fail. But to topple a cripple in front of his entire command? He would not have his sons remember a day like that. He would have to defeat this man, stronger, faster, sharper, by using the one weapon the chi-mongers could not build for the oppressors.

His wits.

The chants of his men fell away, the army at his back fading alongside. He was back in the forest again, thirteen years old, all the bravado and energy of his hatred dissipating as the wolf stalked from the darkness, lips peeling back from fangs like knives. Great Kirill, alpha of the Dires. Terror of the Blackwood. Slayer of a hundred men.

Fooled and butchered at the last by a thirteen-year-old possum.

Aleksandar stepped forward with his lightning hammer high, allowing his shield to drop. Seeing the opening, the samurai struck, chainblade scything toward the Kapitán's throat. Ready for the blow, Aleksandar brought his shield back up, the blade tearing through the metal as if it were butter. But though the slaver was strong as five men, though the blow would have cut a body clean in half, it was not quite enough to shear through two feet of tempered steel. The sword was snarled in the ruined shield, three inches shy of cleaving it through. Aleksandar dragged it down, bringing the samurai's blade with it, and sent his hammer crashing into the slaver's face.

A burst of sparks. A spray of blood. The samurai staggering back as another blow crashed into his helm, wrenching his head across his neck, buckling the iron as if it were tin. Current danced across the samurai's armor, blood spraying between the rain as he dropped to one knee and Aleksandar brought his hammer down with both hands.

A bone-shattering crunch. Metal splitting metal. A wet sigh. The slaver collapsed, leaking blood onto sodden stone, belly-down before the Dragon flag. Aleksandar stood, shoulders slumped, trying to catch his breath from the poisoned air. The roars of his men were deafening, filling him to bursting. Finally, he stepped forward and tore the samurai's banner loose, threw it onto the stone at his feet. And turning to the legion around him, he pointed to the keep with his crimson-slick hammer and roared at the top of his lungs.

"Kill them all!"

Hammers high, his men set about the grim task of butchery. Aleksandar stood on the battlements in the rain, looming over his fallen foe. He rolled the body over with his boot, straining with the weight. As the corpse flopped onto its back, one arm fell outstretched, fingers uncurling from a tiny picture frame on a leather cord, gleaming in the black rain. Aleksandar plucked the prize from the fallen samurai's hand, looking down on a small portrait—a beautiful woman, a handsome boy, two pretty girls. Smiling faces, eyes shining with the joy of better days.

Not so different.

Not so strange.

He stared at the ruin of this man who called him "brother," heart slowing in his chest as chaos filled the air, hanging in the skies with the echo of Mother Natassja's words.

"Your sons will remember this day. How they remember is up to you."

Aleksandar picked up the Dragon flag, lying in the blood where he'd thrown it. He draped it over the fallen samurai's body, covered the shattered face. Thunder bellowed overhead, a deafening whip-crack rumbling down his spine. He could hear the carnage around him. Corpses toppling from the walls. Blood like rain. Men and boys screaming. His mouth tasted black, lips split and throat choking.

He said a prayer for the fallen samurai, tucked the portrait into his belt and began trudging back to command with the taste of bile in his mouth. The taste of blood. The taste that, for the first time in as long as he could remember, he would rather spit than swallow.

Victory.

12
THE HAND WE ARE DEALT

"Lady Fortune pisses on me again," Akihito growled.

The Blackbird laughed, leaned forward with a broad grin, dragging the pile of copper bits from the center of the table.

"Uzume is a capricious bitch, my friend. Only Foxes and fools throw prayers her way. Better off praying to Fūjin like me. At least the God of Wind and Ways can pick a direction."

Four figures sat cross-legged around a low table in the gardens of Kitsune-jō, listening to the sound of mustering troops, hammers beating anvils, distant thunder. Yukiko and Hana were in counsel with the Kitsune clanlord, organizing accommodations for the Kagé refugees. And though it was still bitterly cold, a feeble patch of sunlight had broken through the clouds, encouraging a few players to gather for a round of lunchtime *oicho-kabu*.

There was Akihito of course, still dressed in dappled Iishi green and brown. His trusty kusarigama was wrapped at his waist, the sickle-blade newly sharpened, a great iron-studded warclub that doubled as a crutch close to hand. His hair was bound in warrior's braids, beard not quite long enough to plait. One of the Kagé had given him some resin instead, and he'd fashioned his whiskers into a collection of impressive spikes.

Piotr sat beside him, the muted day reflected in the milk-white of his blind eye, the flower-blue of the other. Despite what anyone told him about the effect of Shima's sunlight, Piotr refused to wear a pair of goggles. He was dressed in a strange jacket of deep red, his wolf skin folded up beneath him as a cushion. When he laughed, the gouge below his right eye deepened, the hook-shaped furrow leading up to his missing ear like a new smile. He was no master's portrait, but the man had saved Yukiko's life. The round-eye could be missing his entire face along with his wedding tackle and Akihito would still have called him brother.

The Blackbird sat opposite, broad and barrel-chested, slouched beneath the brim of his enormous straw hat. In the ongoing war of the beards, the cloud-walker captain was the clear winner—whiskers thick enough to plant a rice crop in, plaited three times down his belly. The Blackbird had a deep, booming voice and a laugh Akihito could feel in his chest.

Lastly amongst the card players, there was Yoshi. The bruises on the boy's face had almost faded, but Akihito could still see the damage, within if not without. The boy's hair was tied in a plain topknot, blond roots showing. He didn't join in with the banter, but Akihito considered it a miracle he'd been able to drag the boy from his room at all. He couldn't remember the last time he'd seen Yoshi's infamous lopsided smile.

"All right, deal again, you Dragon dog." Akihito tossed the deck to the Blackbird. "And I'm watching you shuffle."

"I'm thinking you should quit while you're behind, Akihito-san." Michi looked up from her calligraphy desk. "You don't strike me as the lucky type."

The girl sat nearby, smoking some of Piotr's honeyweed, teeth clamped on the stem of a bone pipe. Bee-stung lips and pale skin bereft of paint, hair tied back in a simple braid. Without making an effort, she still turned the heads of many of the Kitsune soldiers, but the chainsaw blades at her back ensured most kept their stares to themselves.

She was bent over a small table, a rice-paper scroll weighted with smooth river stones, a paintbrush and pot of cuttlefish ink in her hands.

"What's that you're writing, girl?" the Blackbird asked.

"Mind your cards, Captain-san."

"The way this poor lump plays, I could win blindfolded."

Akihito hid his pout in his beard, sipped his saké.

"If you must know, I'm writing a book," the girl sighed.

Michi held up the scroll case in which she carried her work. It was crudely carved of unfinished pine, some hasty kanji etched into the surface.

"*The Lotus War . . .*" Akihito read.

"Mrnm. Not sure on the title." The Blackbird stroked his beard. "What's it about?"

"Fishing."

Piotr sputtered a mouthful of smoke. Akihito found himself chuckling, gave Yoshi a nudge. The boy just scowled.

"Very funny," the Blackbird bowed. "What's it really about?"

"It's a history of this war. Yoritomo. Yukiko. Masaru. Aisha. Daiyakawa." Michi waved her brush over the Kitsune fortress. "Us."

"Why?"

"So people will remember."

The Blackbird sipped his saké, made a face. "Sounds like a waste of good rice-paper to me. Nobody ever won a battle with a bottle of ink."

"You don't think people should know what happened here?"

"Oh, I think they should know, no doubt. I just don't think they'll care."

"How could they not?"

"Because it will be different next time. It always is."

"Different?" Akihito frowned at the cloudwalker captain.

"Different," the Blackbird nodded. "Whatever they fight over. It'll have a different name or a different shape—religion or territory or black or white. People will look back on us and say 'we could never be that blind.' People don't learn from history. Not people who count, anyway."

Michi's reply was sharp as steel. "Everybody counts."

"Not everybody is a Shōgun," Blackbird said. "Not everybody commands an army—"

"An avalanche starts with one pebble. A forest with one seed. And it takes one word to make the whole world stop and listen. All you need is the right one."

"You really believe that, girl?"

"I have to."

"Why?"

"Because there's something so wrong with this place it makes me want to scream. And I suppose you could be right, and all this counts for nothing. But suppose *I'm* right, and I *do* have the power to change things, but instead I sat back and figured someone else would speak up. That I shouldn't bother trying. What would that make me?"

The Blackbird scratched his beard, looking slightly abashed.

"Trying costs nothing if I'm wrong," Michi said. "But if I'm right, doing nothing costs *everything*."

Yoshi sighed, climbed to his feet. "Fuck this noise . . ."

"Where you going?" Akihito asked.

"Someplace a little heavier on the mellow and a little lighter on the drama." The boy slouched off with his hands tucked in his obi, eyes fixed on the rumbling sky as he walked away.

"Well, he seems lovely," Michi mused, turning back to her calligraphy.

"Don't mind him," Akihito shrugged. "He lost someone. Someone special."

"Just one? He should thank his stars, then."

Akihito turned back to the sky-ship captain, brow furrowed. "You make a funny sort of rebel, Blackbird-san. You don't talk like most of the folk around here."

"That's because most folk around here wouldn't know their tackle from their rigging."

"Well, why the hells are you helping us?"

"Blood-debt. The Shōgunate killed my baby brother."

"Forgiveness," Akihito covered his fist and nodded. "How did he die?"

"Yoritomo-no-miya blew his head off. After he failed to return with that damned thunder tiger your girl rides around on."

Akihito's jaw fell into his lap. ". . . Your brother was Ryu Yamagata?"

A slow nod. "Captain of the sky-ship *Thunder Child*."

"Then I ask forgiveness again," Akihito said. "I knew him. A good man. A brave man."

"Well, now he's a dead man. But he won't be sleeping in the hells alone." The Blackbird knocked back the last of his saké with a sigh. Scooping up his winnings, he stood and stretched. "Anyways, work to do. Kimono to chase. Thanks for the drink." A smile. "And the coin."

Akihito watched the captain saunter away, tipping his ridiculous hat to the serving maids as he passed by. The big man's brow was still creased and he fidgeted with his beard, running fingers and thumb down the resin-hard spikes.

"Akihito-san," Piotr said. "Talk me with you."

Akihito looked at the gaijin sideways. "So talk."

The gaijin cast a wary look over his shoulder to Michi, leaned in closer, his voice lowered to a conspiratorial whisper.

"Girl," he said. "Your pretty girl."

"Hana," Akihito frowned. "But she's not mine."

"She Touched. She Zryachniye."

"What does that mean?"

"I can still hear you, you know," Michi said, eyes still on her calligraphy.

Piotr scowled, leaned closer, pointing to his blind right eye. "Touched!"

"I haven't laid a finger on her, if that's what you mean. We're just friends."

Michi coughed, mumbled something inarticulate. Akihito ignored her.

"No, no, can't do for the touching." Piotr seemed alarmed. "She Zryachniye. Is white, da?"

"She's *half* white. Half Shiman. And I talked to her about her eye. If there's something special about it aside from the color, she hasn't noticed it in four years."

"Of course." Piotr looked at the big man like he was simple. "She sleeping."

"Sleeping?" Akihito rubbed his temples. "Listen, no offense, but you make as much sense as my grandmother when she's smoked her 'arthritis medicine.'"

Piotr sighed, exasperated. His eyes roamed the floorboards as if the dead leaves were scattered words, searching for the right ones to collect into a sentence.

"Gods?" he finally said. "You Shima have gods? Uzume? Fūjin? Izanami?"

"Izanami is a death goddess." Akihito made the warding sign against evil. "But we have gods. So what?"

The gaijin held his hand to the sky. "Gods."

He held his other hand down low. "Girl. You pretty girl."

"Izanagi's balls, she's *not* mine . . ."

Piotr reached down with his "god" hand and lightly touched his palm with one finger. Looking impossibly pleased with himself, he smiled and said "Zryachniye."

Akihito blinked, then downed the rest of his saké. "Zryachniye . . ."

"Da! Good is for him." Piotr clapped his hands, tapped his forehead. "Was thinking he for slow, but no, no, is good. Haha."

"Right." Akihito lowered his voice to a mumble. "Round-eye corpsefucker . . ."

The drum of pounding footsteps hushed Akihito's thoughts. The big man looked across the garden, saw Hana sprinting along the verandah toward them. Her jagged bob was tangled about her face, cheeks flushed, her eye wide and bright and all aglow. Akihito found himself swallowing a sudden lump in his throat.

The girl stopped beside the table, bent double, gasping for breath. Michi put aside her calligraphy, placed one hand on her chainkatana. Akihito leaned on his crutch, pulled himself upright and put one hand on Hana's shoulder.

"Are you all right?"

The girl shook her head, glanced at Piotr, trying to catch her breath.

"What is it? What's wrong?"

"Gaijin . . ." Hana gasped.

Akihito looked at Piotr. The gaijin was almost standing at attention in Hana's presence, his eyes downcast from the girl's face.

"What about him?" Akihito said.

"Not Piotr," Hana wheezed. "The gaijin have invaded Shima. A fleet. An army. They just hit the Dragon capital. Frontal assault on Kawa city."

"Izanagi's balls," Michi breathed. "Kawa city is a fortress. How many gaijin are there?"

Hana dragged sweat-soaked locks from her face, straightened with a wince. "Sounds like all of them . . ."

T his wasn't exactly the future Akihito had planned.

His father had been a hunter, his grandfather before him. In a clan of artistes, his were a family of destroyers. And though his head sang with poetry, though in his hands beauty was only a knife and chisel away, any desire to be an artisan had been beaten from him at an early age.

"*You can't make a winter coat out of godsdamned poems,*" his father had said. "*And there'll always be animals to hunt.*"

On reflection, the old man didn't have much talent for planning futures either.

When he'd been apprenticed to the Imperial Court at sixteen, Akihito had felt contentment rather than pride. He knew his future now. He'd hunt the hells-born black yōkai, find a wife (later), give his mother some grandchildren (*much* later) and that'd be that. A normal life. Not even worthy of a footnote in history. And here he was—twenty-eight years old, not a son in sight, and so far from a normal life he couldn't imagine what one looked like anymore.

Not what he'd planned for at all.

Eight figures knelt around the long, low-slung table, the scent of burning flowers woven amongst the lantern smoke. Old Daimyo Isamu at the head, thirty paces from his houseguests. General Ginjiro sat to his right, a dozen samurai around them. The warriors were dressed in armor old enough to have been plucked from a museum—Kitsune fuel stores were so low wearing chi-powered armor was out of the question for anyone but command staff now.

Michi, Hana and Yoshi knelt to the Daimyo's left, Akihito, Misaki and Yukiko opposite. Piotr stood by a window, blowing smoke rings. The table was laden with more food than Akihito had seen in years and yet nobody was eating, save Hana and, perhaps not so surprisingly, Yukiko, quietly demolishing a plateful as if it were her last meal.

The pale glow from Hana's eye refracted in the crystalware, and Akihito stared at her scar, the leather patch hiding her hurt. A life spent not knowing where her next meal was coming from had taught her to never waste a free feed, and she was busy scoffing a bowl of deep tuna. He found himself studying the lines of her cheek. The shape of her lips.

The girl caught Akihito staring, offered a shy smile around her mouthful. The big man turned away quickly, focused on the Iron Samurai's report to his Daimyo.

"The gaijin army numbers ten thousand, great Lord." General Ginjiro's expression was grim. "They caught the Dragons completely unaware. Before we lost communications from our scouts, Kawa city was ablaze. We have two separate reports stating your cousin Daimyo Haruka was killed in the defense of Ryu-jō, along with his son and most of his Elite."

"The fortress of Dragons is fallen." Isamu sighed. "After two centuries unchallenged."

"So say our reports, great Lord."

"And what of you, Misaki-san?" The Daimyo turned to the leader of the Guild rebels. "What do your brethren in Kawa tell you?"

Misaki was still clad in her membrane, spider limbs folded on her back. Her eyes were so heavily lidded Akihito had thought her half-asleep until she'd fixed him with a stare that might cut granite.

"First House is jamming our communications capability." The Guildswoman gestured to the silent mechabacus on her chest. "Our Artificers are trying to rig a shortwave transmission tower, but until then, we will hear no news from our Kawa brethren."

General Ginjiro turned to his lord. "We have received official missive from our self-styled Shōgun. Lord Hiro demands we ally with the Tiger Clan against these invaders."

"Send an appropriate response on the good stationery." Isamu stroked his moustache, brow creased in thought. "Something along the lines of 'the venerable Lord of Foxes declines your request with all due respect. May you choke on the thousand throbbing members of your Guild masters, you sniveling little shit. Yours sincerely, etcetera etcetera . . .'"

Hana protested through her mouthful of tuna. "Bdd vat's su'cide."

Akihito smiled at the girl's lack of courtly manners, tried to share it with her brother. But Yoshi was stabbing at his meal like he hated it, black clouds over his head.

"Suicidal it may be, but the Fox clan will not kneel to this puppet Shōgun," Ginjiro said.

Akihito was astonished as Yoshi spoke for the first time in hours, muttering and shaking his head.

"Samurai," he said. "So godsdamned predictable."

General Ginjiro blinked at the boy, surprise quickly turning to anger. "Tora Hiro is a usurper. He has no claim to the Golden Throne. Honor demands we—"

"Remind me again about the difference between honor and stupidity?"

"Yoshi . . ." Hana warned.

"They have a *fortress* here." Yoshi motioned about them. "An army of Foxes inside it. Another army of Tigers and Phoenix to the south. If everyone stopped for one minute and pulled their honorable heads out of their honorable asses—"

Ginjiro's voice rose. "It would be shameful to ally with a Guild lackey who has insulted our Lord and is poised to invade our homeland."

"Idiots," Yoshi muttered. "Little boys playing soldiers . . ."

Ginjiro slammed his hand on the table.

"I think everyone should take a breath," Yukiko said. "Think about this rationally."

"But that's not an option, is it?" Yoshi said. "Not when honor and Bushido and all that bullshit is concerned. They'd rather die alone than stand together—"

Ginjiro laughed. "So we push the gaijin into the sea together and then what? You think the Guild will forgive us for sheltering their rebels? Or insulting their puppet Shōgun?"

Daimyo Isamu's finger drummed on the iron-thrower at his waist. "Perhaps you suggest we withdraw our support and leave the Guild rebellion and you to rot, young man?"

"Of course not—"

"The Guild want your Kagé crushed, Yukiko dead, me kneeling at Hiro's feet. The cards are dealt. We play the hand we are given, or bow out of the game. There is no third option."

"So what's the plan, then? Hole up here and see who arrives to slaughter us first?" Yoshi turned to Yukiko. "We should have stayed in the godsdamned mountains . . ."

"This is what we asked for, Yoshi," Yukiko said. "Perhaps it's fitting. We warred on the gaijin for twenty years. Killed their people. Stole their children. Maybe we deserve retribution."

"Interesting that it comes now," Isamu mused. "I fought in Morcheba for years, and the round-eyes were never this organized. They were a mob. Fierce as rabid wolves, but never an army. Where did this fleet come from?"

"They mustered it to the north." Yukiko pushed her empty plate aside and sighed. "Away from their own shoreline so the Shōgunate forces wouldn't know their plans."

"But where did the orders come from? Who pulled it together?"

"Imperatritsa."

Everyone at the table turned to Piotr. The gaijin had been silent until this point, smoking ruefully at what looked to be the last of his honeyweed. Now he ambled over to the gathering, exhaled pale gray into the air between them.

"What the hells does that mean?" Michi asked.

"I've heard that word before," Yukiko said. "But I'm not sure what it is . . ."

Piotr gathered a bunch of empty cups from the tea service and arranged them before him.

"Twelve house," he said, gesturing to the cups. "Grigori, Baranova, Mostovoi, and is more, da? Twelve."

"Twelve gaijin clans?" Akihito suggested.

"Da," Piotr nodded. "Is clan, but not. Twelve *house*." He pushed several of the cups into each other, sending one rolling. "We fight. No peace. Many years. Then . . ."

He pointed to the Iron Samurai gathered around Isamu. "Shima is coming. Samurai. Making the war." He pushed at the cups again. "Then one is coming. Imperatritsa. She take twelve . . ." The gaijin scooped the cups together into one mass of wobbling porcelain. "Make one. Imperatritsa Ostrovska."

"A warlord," Isamu said. "A warlord who united the gaijin clans."

"I saw an image of her at the lightning farm," Yukiko nodded. "A woman on a throne with twelve stars in her lap. She wore the skin of a great black eagle."

"Not eagle." Piotr shook his head. "Gryfon. Much strength. Much prize."

Yukiko swallowed her reply before it had begun.

"She?" Ginjiro raised an eyebrow. "You are led by a woman?"

"She Zryachniye." Piotr pointed to Hana. "Like pretty girl."

Yoshi and Hana looked at each other, saying nothing. Silence descended, each stare settling on the girl and her impossible iris, glowing the color of rose-quartz. Akihito could see the blond roots in her hair—the gaijin blood she'd hidden for years creeping slowly to the surface.

"So, there's our history lesson for the day," Michi said. "But it still doesn't solve the problem of the fleet of gaijin berserkers now drinking the Dragon Daimyo's best saké. Nor Tora Hiro and his iron colossus."

Yukiko nodded. "If the gaijin march west, we'll sit between two armies. I don't know if we have the strength to repel one. But we have to try."

"This city was built to withstand an oni's siege," Ginjiro said. "It will withstand this."

"So that's the grand stratagem, General?" Michi said. "Just sit and wait?"

Misaki leaned forward, steepling her fingers at her chin. "Before the uprising, the rebellion had a plan to strike at First House. Destroy the chi stores there, along with the First Bloom. With no resupply, the Earthcrusher would not march long before running dry."

"Finally, someone speaks wisdom," Michi breathed.

"We'd been trying to infiltrate the complex for years, but only the Serpents and the Upper Blooms are allowed access."

"There's that word again," Yukiko said. "What does it mean? Who are these Serpents?"

"They call themselves the Inquisition." Misaki ran one hand over her bald scalp. "But they're a cult, really. More fanatical than the Purifiers. They live in a kind of perpetual dream from drinking lotus smoke all day, and they guard the First Bloom. Maybe they control him too. No one really knows. But they've been part of the Guild since it *was* a Guild."

"And why do you call them Serpents?"

"They visit chapterhouses to oversee the Awakening ceremonies. Whenever we got the chance, we'd set a drone on their trail. Years this took us, inch by careful inch. But they have serpents tattooed on their right arms."

"Their right arms?" Akihito frowned. "Where their clan ink should be?"

"As you say."

"A clan within the Guild?" Yukiko raised an eyebrow.

"That is impossible," said Daimyo Isamu. "The Serpent clan no longer exists, any more than the Cranes or Monkeys or Leopards. The twenty-four clans became four zaibatsu when Kazumitsu seized his throne. The rest are dead and gone. My own ancestor, great Okimoto, crushed the Serpents into dust. Even Kitsune children know the tale."

"Crushed?" Akihito blinked at the old clanlord. "When the first Daimyo took the Phoenix Throne, he offered peace to the clans in his territories. They were welcomed, not exterminated."

"Okimoto offered the same to the Wolves, Falcons and Spiders, Akihito-san. But the Serpents venerated Lady Izanami, Mother of Death. Their lands sat on the borders of the Iishi mountains, close to the ruins of Devil Gate. They built temples to her name in the wilds. Called upon her to sing the song that would end the world."

"The Iishi black temple." Yukiko looked at Michi. "Where the oni lived . . ."

"I studied history for years," Michi said. "The library in the Shōgun's palace was so big I got lost in it three times, and I never read anything about this."

"The Guild control the airwaves," Yukiko said. "Write the histories."

Misaki nodded. "And the Inquisition control the Guild."

"If they didn't want their clan spoken of, it wouldn't be . . ."

"This is foolishness," Isamu said. "The Serpent clan have been dead two hundred years."

Yukiko nodded. "About the same time the Lotus Guild has existed for."

"Conspiracies everywhere, eh?" Isamu smiled. "Perhaps you've spent too much time at the Court of Tigers, young lady."

Yukiko smiled in return. "Perhaps you haven't spent enough, old man."

The Daimyo chuckled as Yukiko turned to Misaki.

"What do these Inquisitors look like?"

"Black clothing. Bloodshot eyes. They walk and speak as if in a daze, wear breathers allowing them to imbibe lotus smoke every waking moment."

"In that case, perhaps we could ask about this Serpent clan," Ginjiro said.

Yukiko blinked. "What are you saying, General?"

"Our corvettes crippled three Guild ships during the rebel uprising. One was destroyed when it collided with a sky-spire, but the two others were successfully boarded. Our forces arrested and detained most of the crews."

He glanced around the table. Rose slowly to his feet.

"We have one of these Inquisitors in our dungeons."

13
ABOUT A GIRL

In Danro city, a rebel Guildsman walks into the Market Square, and, piece by piece, removes his metal skin. And there, sitting naked before the wondering crowd, he douses himself with chi from his tanks, and calmly sets himself on fire.

The same day, two False-Lifers contaminate the Chapterhouse Danro nutrient feed with blacksleep toxin. Thirteen shatei and two kyodai die before the cause is discovered. In the resulting arrest attempt, the False-Lifers kill three Purifiers before being killed themselves.

Upper Blooms of Chapterhouse Kigen call an emergency meeting to discuss the assassination attempt on Second Bloom Kensai. Ten minutes into the debate, a lone Lotusman enters the Hall of Council and detonates an improvised explosive device inside his chi tanks, killing almost every ranking kyodai in Kigen city.

The feeds from Kawa city speak of a gaijin horde rising from the sea. An army marching beneath a banner set with twelve red stars. The skies are filled with rotor-thopters, the boardwalk with blue-eyed devils clad in the skins of beasts, the streets with slaughter.

The First House feeds are now edged with steel, demanding the Tora fleet fly at maximum speed to rendezvous with the Earthcrusher. The Stormdancer's insurrection in Yama must be crushed. The Earthcrusher must then march east before the gaijin establish a firm foothold in Shima. The lotus must bloom.

The feeds from Yama still crackle with constant static.

The mechabacus hum is now tinged with fear.

A mask of brass hides his expression entirely.

W hen he was younger, Kin had thought it strange that cloudwalkers spoke about sky-ships like they were women. As a boy, he'd known ships only in schematic form, never really saw anything feminine in the designs. But he'd hear cloudwalker captains come to commission the Guild shipmasters, and noticed the men always referred to the vessels as "she" or "her."

He always wondered about that. Whether cloudwalkers spent so much time away from their families, they began to think of their ships as second brides. Perhaps when faced with the fury of a lightning storm, every sailor remembered a time when all they needed to banish the fear was the warmth of a mother's arms.

Kin didn't pretend to understand. He'd never known a wife or daughter or mother. He could only imagine what those things might feel like. Perhaps that was why the Guild named their ships as *things* instead. None of them knew. Not really.

Standing at the bow of the Daimyo's flagship, he watched the Guild navy dip and roll across iron-red skies. Even for someone who had apprenticed on a beauty like the *Thunder Child*, the sight was impressive; four lumbering ironclads and a dozen sleek corvettes, filling the air with metal thunder, the sky smeared blue-black behind.

Names were painted in broad, bold kanji down each vessel's prow—not tributes to mothers or daughters or wives, but names born of obsession with the weed at the Imperium's foundation. The *Scarlet Bloom* and the *Winter Harvest*. *Blessed Light* and the *Lotus Wind*. The thundering fortress Kin flew upon had been the only Tora sky-ship to escape the Kagé attack on Docktown relatively unscathed. Her name had been *Red Tigress* under Yoritomo's reign, but the pride of the Tiger fleet had been repaired and repainted just before they left Kigen, bold, fresh kanji now scrolling down her prow, proudly proclaiming her new name to the world.

The *Honorable Death*.

The ground below was a pockmarked wasteland, the rusting hulk of a chi pipeline snaking away through the deadlands fumes. Kin looked to the *Winter Harvest* blackening the skies four hundred yards off their stern. He didn't think of the man who'd trusted him, locked somewhere in that ship's hold. He didn't think of the night on the *Thunder Child* when she stood beside him, hand in hand as they laughed in the clean rain. He didn't think of her lips pressed against his in the Iishi, raindrops reflected like jewels in her eyes.

The world around him slowly unraveled; insurgency rising, gaijin plundering, total war drawing closer. And in all that chaos, Kin thought of nothing. Nothing at all.

Safer that way.

"I know you."

Kin turned from the fleet to the figure that had materialized beside him. The armor made a small din as he moved; spitting chi, hissing pistons, clockwork teeth. Painted death-white, the same as the ashes smeared on his face. The master of the Tiger zaibatsu. The one who would lead the Tora army to final victory. The corpse that hungered for its grave.

"Daimyo Hiro," Kin replied.

"I know you," Hiro repeated.

"I think not."

"You're the one," the Tora Daimyo nodded. "You gave the thunder tiger his metal wings, and that same thunder tiger took my arm." A small shake of his head, pistons hissing. "Of every ship traveling to the staging grounds, they would post you to this one, wouldn't they?"

Kin heard no anger in Hiro's voice. Simply the bitter resignation of a man already heaped chin-deep with indignity, suffering quietly beneath one more shovel load.

"Second Bloom Kensai is . . . indisposed," Kin said. "I stand in his stead. Apologies if this inconveniences you, honorable Daimyo."

"She called you Kin. That is your name, is it not?"

Do not call me Kin. That is not my name.

"Hai."

Call me First Bloom.

"Then as I say, I know you."

"As I say, honorable Daimyo, I think not."

"Tiger is not as blind as you think. My uncle's spy network still whispers to me on occasion. They speak of a Guildsman who joined the Kagé, only to betray them. Selling their leader during the Kigen uprising, handing him over in exchange for safe harbor." Hiro eyed Kin's new suit up and down. "And a promotion, it seems."

"Forgiveness, honorable Daimyo. But you know nothing."

"I know we're the same, you and I. I thought I loved her too, at first."

Kin turned sharply, atmos-suit hissing a plume of blue-black. The mech-abacus was a constant clatter in the back of his mind. Soothing. Silencing.

"Until I found out what she was," Hiro said. "Until she betrayed me. I'm wondering what she did to you, to see this story end with you beside me?"

"This is not about Yukiko."

Hiro laughed like a man who'd only read about it in books. "Everything we *do* is about her. Don't you see, Kin-san? We're both falling, you and I. And Yukiko? She's our gravity."

Silence, broken by churning propellers and hungry wind. Kin counted the spaces between each smooth breath, his bellows rising and falling. Second. By second. By second.

"The Kagé leader you handed over to the Guild was once Iron Samurai, did you know that?" A ghastly smile perched on Hiro's lips, as if they shared some private joke. "How did it feel when you turned Daichi over to your old masters?"

Kin glanced at the Daimyo's corpse-pale face. This was an answer he knew by rote.

"It felt like justice."

"I suppose if you were handed over to the Kagé, they'd call it justice too?"

"Do you think it matters what they say?"

"Not I, no." Hiro shook his head. "But I'm not the one who betrayed everyone he knew to join them. Dead samurai. Dead Shōgun. A clan in tatters and a nation in ruin. Did you ever stop to think none of this would be happening if not for you, Kin-san? If you'd simply left the thunder tiger to Yoritomo's mercies, and not deluded yourself with dreams of her affection? Do you ever think that? Does the thought of it wake you in the night?"

Kin remained mute, turning away to watch the distant storms.

"And all for nothing, eh?" Hiro mused. "For here you stand, where once you began. Did she at least take you for a roll before she cast you aside? That's her usual method of payment."

Counting the space between breaths.

Thinking nothing.

Nothing at all.

Hiro patted Kin's shoulder like an older brother, clockwork fingers rasping on new brass.

"Feel no shame she used you, Kin-san. She has a gift for making men look like fools."

"I think perhaps it is men who have a gift for it, great Daimyo," Kin finally said. "Women simply stand aside and leave us to it."

"Ah, such wisdom . . ."

"To some, perhaps."

Hiro stepped closer, his face inches from Kin's own. The engines' hum was a crackling static between them, tinged with the stink of chi, the promise of black rain.

"I wonder what you will be, when all this is said and done," Hiro murmured. "When she and I and everyone else in this drama is dead. When there's no one but farmers scratching in dying soil and puppets on zaibatsu thrones and the Guild standing triumphant as the earth shakes louder by the day. I wonder if you'll taste blood every time you breathe."

"I wonder something also . . ."

"Indeed?"

"I wonder why you hate her so much."

"Do you forget my Shōgun lies murdered by her hand?" Hiro spat. "This is about *honor*. Such a notion might seem quaint to one like you, but this is the life of a samurai."

"I know all that," Kin said. "How you all think dying gloriously will somehow make things better. But I'd think instead of spending so much of yourself hating her, you'd be giving her thanks. All of you. Right before you plunge the blades into your bellies."

"Thanks?" Hiro was incredulous. "What madness is this?"

"You're a warrior, and she's given you war. You seek your death, and she's given you something to die for. So why do you think you hate her so much?"

"It makes no difference—"

"If I didn't know better, I'd suspect you didn't actually *want* to die for the Imperium, Hiro-san. Maybe you'd rather go on living. Find someone to *actually* love. Raise a family? Scratch out a life in some quiet corner and find your happiness where you may. Maybe that would be better than dying for an empire that's already close to dead."

The pair stared at each other, inches and miles apart. A long moment passed in thunderous silence, every second drawing them closer to their final chapter.

"But where's the glory in that?"

Kin walked away, clomping across the rolling deck in a cloud of smoke, leaving the Lord of Tigers alone with his parting words. Mind alight with the mech-abacus hymn, the knowledge of what could have been, if only.

If only . . .

Thinking and saying nothing.

Nothing at all.

14
SMOKING AND SCREAMING

Yukiko stood in the dungeons beneath Five Flowers Palace, but in her head she was back in Kigen jail, Hiro by her side, walking to the cell where her father sat imprisoned. Her hand drifted to the tantō at her waist, her mind to the arashi-tora circling above.

Just a wordless touch; a squeeze of an old friend's hand to let him know you're there. Yukiko felt Buruu's warmth inside her head, static electricity crawling along his feathers. The ache to be up there with him was almost physical. She wondered how toxic the black rain would be this close to the Iishi, how badly it would burn them if they were caught in the downpour.

Be careful, brother. The rains here are not like the Everstorm or the mountains.

THE WATER IS WETTER?

They're poisonous. Black as night. They burn your skin if you stay in them too long. Even metal melts under them after a few years.

I PROMISE TO COME IN WHEN IT RAINS, MOTHER.

She smiled despite herself, lingering in the warmth of his mind. Ahead, she could see the silhouette of the Kitsune general in his ō-yoroi, a hand-cranked tungsten lantern held high. Misaki walked beside her, Michi behind, followed by four samurai in their ancient armor.

The rest of the group had stayed behind in the Daimyo's dining hall. Yukiko had asked Akihito if he wished to accompany her into the dungeon, and the big man had looked like she'd punched him in the stomach. She knew immediately he was thinking of Kasumi; the way she'd died in Kigen jail during her father's rescue. She'd given the big man a hug, told him to finish his dinner. He'd hugged her back, hard enough to make her ribs ache.

The dungeon corridors were cramped, pocked with rusted iron doors. Yukiko could sense the tumble of lives down here in the Kenning; hundreds of rats fighting amidst the rotten straw and sunless rooms. Dozens of Guildsmen locked in the dark, black bread and dirty water for solace. She knew they were her enemies—that if the situation were reversed, she'd be subjected to far worse before they dragged her out to the Burning Stones. But still, her stomach turned at the memory of her father's suffering in Yoritomo's dungeons. What Daichi might be suffering right now, if he still lived. A part of her wondered why these Guildsmen had to suffer the same.

I feel sorry for them, Buruu. How many really knew what they were doing? How many acted out of blind obedience, or because they were raised that way?

DO NOT BE ASHAMED OF YOUR PITY. IT SEPARATES YOU FROM THEM.

I'm not. But I still feel like shit.

WE ALL MUST LIVE WITH CHOICE AND CONSEQUENCE.

Speaking of which, is Kaiah up there with you?

SOMEWHERE.

Is she talking to you yet?

. . . NO.

One day you're going to have to tell me that story, Buruu.

ONE DAY.

Soon, I hope.

A HOPE I DO NOT SHARE.

"Here."

General Ginjiro's voice pulled her out of his head, back into the dungeon's bowels. The stink made her eyes water, and both she and Michi pulled kerchiefs up around their faces. Misaki seemed to be reveling in the new scents and sights now her face was uncovered, and she breathed deep despite the reek.

They'd stopped outside an iron door, nothing remarkable about it, save what lay beyond. Yukiko opened the Kenning just wide enough to feel inside. She sensed the impossible knot of human emotion beyond the door—a kaleidoscope of thoughts, too bright and numerous to look at for long. Her head began to ache like it was cracking.

"I think . . ." A frown. "I think there's something wrong with him."

"Stay back," Ginjiro warned.

The general pulled aside a viewing slot and peered through, eyes narrowed in the gloom. Unlocking the door, he led his samurai into the cell. Yukiko heard scuffling, a low moan. Ginjiro reappeared in the doorway, motioned the trio inside. His lantern hung on the wall, illuminating bare slick granite, a pile of dirty straw in one corner, and an empty, filth-encrusted bucket in another. Six by six.

The samurai had seized the Inquisitor, one on each elbow, another with his arm locked around the man's throat. The prisoner was barely an inch taller than Yukiko, sickly gray skin filmed in sweat, wrists manacled. His head lolled in the samurai's grip as if his neck were broken, bloodshot eyes rolled back in their sockets. An awful bruise purpled his cheek, left eye swollen near-shut. His jailers had stripped him of mechabacus and tunic, revealing a black serpent coiled down his bicep, beautiful and intricate—the work of a master inksmith. The bayonet fixtures in his skin reminded Yukiko of Kin, running his thumb around the input jack at his wrist, standing in the Iishi rain.

"I'd never hurt you. Never betray you. Never."

". . . I know that," she'd said.

"You mean everything to me. Everything I've done. All of it. You're the reason. The first and only reason . . ."

The Inquisitor was shaking, drool slicked on his chin. Yukiko recognized the look immediately—she'd seen it in her father on days he'd lost too much at cards and had no coin for smoke.

"He's going through withdrawal," she said. "He's a lotusfiend."

"I told you," Misaki said. "They breathe it every minute of their lives."

"But Kin . . ." Yukiko faltered. "I was told the Guild had to stay *away* from lotus. You eat purified food, live inside those suits. How is it these Inquisitors breathe it every minute?"

"Guild doctrine says it helps them to recognize 'impurity.' They look into the darkest places so the rest of the Guild don't have to. Lotus helps them 'see.'"

Michi's lip curled in disgust. "I wonder what he's seeing now."

The general reached into a satchel on his shoulder, pulled out a small combustion chamber on a leather harness, affixed with a grinning mouthpiece.

"He was wearing this when we found him. We found three others like him on the ships we captured, but they'd all committed suicide. This one was knocked unconscious during the attack, otherwise he'd probably have gone the way of his fellows."

Yukiko stepped closer to the Inquisitor, wrinkling her nose at his stink; smoke and sweat and something rotten. "Can you hear me?"

A shuddering moan was her only reply, and she sighed.

"We'll never get anything out of him like this."

Closing her eyes, she reached out into the tangle of his thoughts. She found them chilled and oily, edged in blue-black, just as impossible to untangle as any human mind she'd tried to touch. Wiping a trickle of blood from her nose she made a face, her head throbbing.

"We could give him some lotus?" Ginjiro aimed the question at Misaki.

"I do not know what will happen if we do that, General . . ."

The general tapped on the Inquisitor's forehead with his forefinger, held up the lotus breather in front of the man's mouth. "You want this?"

Mumbled nonsense. A spray of drool.

Ginjiro affixed the breather over the little man's face, fiddled with the nozzles on the combustion chamber until it started hissing. The change was astonishing. Within a moment the shakes had stopped. Within two the Inquisitor was supporting his own weight. Within three he'd opened his eyes, and was staring right at Yukiko.

Right *through* her.

"Can you hear me?" she asked.

A voice like a man woken from deepest sleep, still shaking the sand off his eyes.

"Kitsune Yukiko."

"How do you know my name?"

A rolling, bloodshot gaze roamed the room. "I have been here before."

"When?"

"Every night for as long as I can remember . . ."

Yukiko remembered Kin speaking of his Awakening ceremony. The visions of the future he'd seen. "The What Will Be."

The little man tilted his head, whispering. "Do I dream this now?"

Ginjiro slapped him hard, knocked the breather askew. "Feel real to you?"

His corpse-gray face twisted in a smile. "No . . ."

Yukiko put the breather back on straight, looked into those pools of blood-shot red. There was something familiar about this—a nagging déjà-vu sitting beside her splitting headache. The lotus scent made her think of her father, long nights sitting by the—

"Masaru-san sends his love," the little man said.

". . . What?"

"Kitsune Masaru. The Black Fox of Shima. He sends you his love."

Yukiko scowled, anger flaring in her breast. "My father's dead."

"I know. I see him often, in my travels."

"What the hells are you talking about?"

"Exactly," the little man breathed.

"He's a godsdamned madman," Michi growled. "This is a waste of time."

"I see your uncle too, Michi-chan." The Inquisitor's bloody gaze flickered to the girl. "Still bleeding from the cross-shaped cut in his belly. He wanders the dark, calling for his wife and children." A small shake of his head. "They never come."

Michi's eyes were wide, her voice a whisper. ". . . What did you say?"

The little man's eyes were affixed on the empty air just above Michi's shoulder. "Oh . . . look . . ."

Ginjiro's fist slammed into his belly, bending him double. The samurai hauled him back up into another fistful, a smoke-filled sputter underscoring the whine of Ginjiro's ō-yoroi.

"Enough lies," the general growled. "You speak when you're spoken to. You answer the questions we ask. One unwanted word and I rip this mask off and leave you down here in the dark to scream yourself to sleep, understand?"

The little man straightened with a wince, exhaled a ragged sigh. "Perfectly."

Ginjiro nodded to Misaki.

"What is your name?" she asked.

"Inquisitors have no names, sister."

"Amongst yourselves. What do they call you?"

"They do not call me. They call Her."

Another punch from Ginjiro. The little man rocked sideways, blood trickling from his ear. He started chuckling, as if remembering some long-forgotten joke.

"Her?" Misaki frowned. "Who is her?"

The Inquisitor caught hold of himself, laughter dying on his lips. "You will see."

The punch lifted him off his feet, a fine red spray mingling with the smoke, gurgling and wet as he inhaled. He sagged like a broken toy in the samurai's arms.

"Ginjiro-san," Yukiko warned, "you're going to kill him."

"It's all right," the little man wheezed. "I end here, I think . . ."

"The tattoo on your arm," Misaki said. "What does it mean? Are you Serpent clan?"

"The Serpent clan is dead. Food for Foxes."

"Do you control the First Bloom? Do you control the Guild? What do you want?"

"Nothing. We want nothing at all."

Misaki looked to Yukiko, shook her head. Michi still stared at the Inquisitor, eyes wide, horror etched in her expression. It felt cold in the cell, bitter and bleak. Not the shivering clean of the first snowfall. It was the cold of tombs. The chill of time and implacable, approaching death.

"Not long now," he whispered. "A season, perhaps two. There has been enough blood, don't you think? The little ones are already here, after all." His eyes drifted to Yukiko's belly. "Perhaps they can play with yours . . ."

Yukiko covered her stomach, backed away a step.

"Two seasons from now. Three at the most." His eyes crinkled as if he smiled. "Your little ones will be old enough to try and run by then."

"He's mad," she breathed. "Lord Izanagi save him."

In days to come, when Yukiko thought back on that moment, she'd swear the lantern light dimmed as if someone had thrown a veil over it. The little man's eyes widened, a sharp intake of breath through the breather. And then he screamed, awful and gut-wrenching, thrashing in the samurai's grip as his face purpled.

"Pray for me?" he shrieked. "Pray for *yourself*!"

A blurring of light, an absence of breath. Yukiko blinked, certain her eyes betrayed her. Where once the little man stood, there was now only smoke. Shifting and intangible, iron manacles dropping to the floor, samurai hands closing tight on fistfuls of vapor.

Michi cried out, Misaki's silver arms flaring wide. And in a blinking, the man stood before Yukiko, solid as the walls around them, lashing out almost too fast to see.

It was Michi who saved her, dragged her away and spun her around, wearing the kick across her shoulder blades. Yukiko felt as if she'd been hit by lightning, slamming her and Michi out through the cell door and into the wall opposite.

She heard a wet crunch, a ragged scream, blinking the tears from her eyes as the Inquisitor smashed a samurai into the floor as if he were made of rags. Another samurai threw his arms around the Inquisitor's throat, and again there was only smoke, roiling and midnight-shaped, slipping through his grip, past Misaki's gleaming razors and out into the hallway. And there he stood again, all too real, eyes shot through with bloody red, reaching toward Yukiko like something from a nightmare.

"Yōkai-kin," he breathed. "She awaits . . ."

Michi's foot connected with the Inquisitor's groin like a redlining goods train. It was the kind of kick that made one's testicles throw up their hands and move to a monastery in the Hogosha mountains. It was the kind of kick that made orphans of a man's grandchildren.

Her elbow spun him, knocked the breather from his face. He staggered, the girl's knuckles passing clean through the place his throat used to be, only vapor remaining. The Inquisitor coalesced behind her, hands reaching for her neck quick as lies. And Yukiko pulled herself up the wall, blood spilling from her nose as she reached inside his head.

And she *squeezed*.

The Inquisitor gasped, the last of his lungful drifting from his lips as he clutched his temples. General Ginjiro barreled through the cell door and collided with him, pistons and gears whining as his fingers closed about the man's wrists. The Inquisitor thrashed, tried to break the hold, twisting and kicking as his form shivered. The little man looked down at his breather swinging loose, wailing as Ginjiro wrapped him up in a bear hug.

"Don't let him breathe any more smoke!" Yukiko cried.

The Inquisitor slammed his head into Ginjiro's, face-first onto the jagged tusks of the oni mask. There was a sickening crunch, a spattering sound. The little man smashed his head into the iron mask again, its tusks painted with red and tiny fragments of bone. Yukiko put her hands to her mouth, Ginjiro crying out as the Inquisitor cracked his head a third time, a fourth, bone crunching, blood spraying. Other samurai seized the man's head to stop him inflicting further damage on himself, the hallway now filled with the smell of blood and awful, wet screaming.

The Inquisitor had put out his own eyes.

"Gods above," Michi breathed.

"I will see you there, Yōkai-kin!" The Inquisitor spat blood. *"I will wait for you!"*

"Izanagi's balls, get her out of here!" Ginjiro bellowed.

Michi and Misaki each grabbed an arm and hauled Yukiko away. She felt sick, head swimming, nose bleeding, ears ringing with the Inquisitor's screams. Ruined eyes, face torn and cracked, twisted with madness. She found herself reaching out with the Kenning, feeling for the two sparks of warmth in her belly. Reflexive, terrified, her thoughts echoing with his words.

"The little ones are already here, after all."

She tried to swallow, her mouth dry as ash.

"Perhaps they can play with yours . . ."

15
SEED

The looking glass saw right through her.

Yukiko stood naked before it, lost in her own reflection. Skin as pale as Iishi snow, long slender limbs, black hair spilling in soft rivers over her shoulders. Turning sideways, she searched the profile of her belly as if it contained the answer to every riddle, every question. She ran her hand down her stomach, feeling the curve of skin and muscle. It was beginning to swell.

She could see them now, as well as feel them.

A tiny island of herself, locked behind the wall she'd constructed in the Kenning. A fire inside her, waiting outside the barrier in her head. She lowered it now, pain flaring, like a flaming ice pick rammed into her skull. But in the midst of it, she could feel *everything*. Swallows in the midnight garden, vermin crawling the sewers, Michi's puppy dreaming. Buruu nestled on the rafters above her head, a growing guilt gnawing his insides. Kaiah soaring overhead, praying for thunder, her head filled with tears and portraits painted in blood. Little broken shapes. Black feathers and screams.

The people. So many people. Guards nodding at their posts and generals muttering over maps and blacksmiths sweating at forges and peasants filling sandbags and mothers comforting children. Daimyo Isamu, Yoshi, Akihito, Hana, all tangled and confused and impossible, but different enough for her to recognize their shapes. And finally, the little ones inside her. No thoughts to speak of, just the heat and pulse of womb's dark. Their whole world. In her.

In me.

So many. Too many. Her head throbbing, warmth and salt on her lips.

Stop.

She closed it off, slammed it shut, too much, too much. The face in the mirror was smeared to the chin in blood, overflow spattering on the floor. Running her hand down her stomach again, she could feel it. She was certain. A tiny curve. Too enormous to be real.

Was this what it should be like? Was this how it was for every yōkai-blooded woman whose children also carried the gift? She had no one to ask. Blundering in the dark, unsure and afraid, ever since this whole saga began. Stormdancer. Slayer of Shōguns. Ender of Dynasties.

Gods, if they could see me for what I really was.

But there was nothing for it. Nothing to do but win or die. She knew it, as certainly as she knew her own name. There was no doubt when she thought of the armies arrayed against them, no question she'd stand and fight—and if that was bravery, then she supposed she must be brave. It seemed an easy thing, when the only other option was to kneel and pray.

But to do more than fight and die—to actually fight and win? What little they had wasn't enough. Not to stop the gaijin *and* the Tora *and* the Fushicho *and* the Earthcrusher. Bravery wasn't enough to win this war. They needed swords. Swords and claws.

A knock at her door, soft as severed feathers.

"Just a moment," she called.

She washed the blood away, slipped into her clothes, still mourning black. An obi, wrapped twelve times about her waist. Her tantō slipped in and tied off; all she had left of her father, as comforting as fire in winter's chill. Daichi's katana, the blade he named after her rage, all she had left of the man who taught her anger was a gift.

This was all she was. All she had.

And they think me hero.

"Come," she said.

The door slipped open and Michi stepped inside, light as cats. She held a bundle wrapped in black cloth, bowing like the serving girl she'd once pretended to be. Yukiko could see her like it was yesterday: stepping into the bathhouse of the Shōgun's palace, arms laden with silk.

"I'm reminded of the day we met," Yukiko smiled.

Michi grinned. "Do you remember what I brought you?"

"A dress. Twelve layers and forty pounds of dress. Gods, I hated putting that thing on."

"You squirmed like a fish."

"I felt like an idiot."

"Not so in this, I think."

The girl padded to Yukiko's bed, put down her bundle and cast aside the wrapping. Yukiko caught her breath, fierce warmth in her chest, smile blooming on her lips.

"It's beautiful."

A breastplate of black iron, embossed with nine-tailed foxes. The metal was polished to a soft gloss, curved to accommodate a woman's body. The work of a master craftsman.

"I talked to the chief blacksmith when we arrived. Ironically, they don't usually make breastplates for ladies," Michi smiled. "But when I told him it was for the Stormdancer, he said he wouldn't sleep until it was finished."

Yukiko pointed to the breastplate's belly, all interlocking plates and straps and buckles, an unspoken question in her eyes.

"It's adjustable," Michi said softly.

"Oh."

"It makes it weaker."

"Does it."

"But you can wear it as you get bigger." Michi groped for the words. "I mean, if..."

Yukiko turned away, walking across the bedroom to the balcony overlooking the sleeping garden, the fountain's soft murmurs lost amidst the thunder. She leaned against the railing, watching lanterns moving across the verandahs below, servants flitting about like fireflies.

Michi stepped out beside her, just a shape in the dark. When she finally spoke, her voice was so soft Yukiko almost couldn't hear it.

"What Kaori said was wrong. About you." A wave to her belly. "About them."

"We were both angry. We both said things we didn't mean."

A long pause, heavy with the promise of black rain. "Do you mind if I ask..."

"Hiro."

"Oh."

The lanterns weaved below in the dark. If she squinted, she couldn't see the bearers at all. Just the light, disembodied, like she imagined real fireflies might look. If they existed anymore.

"I'm sorry," Michi said.

"I'm not sure why you're apologizing."

"It can't be easy. Knowing they're his."

"It isn't."

"You know there are..." Michi's voice drifted away, lost in the dark.

"...There are what?"

The girl licked her lips, her voice hesitant. "There are ways of dealing with it. If you don't want it. You know that, right?"

"It?"

". . . Them."

"And you know these ways?"

"I've used them."

Yukiko turned to look at her friend. "Really?"

"Sex is just another weapon in the halls of power. Aisha taught me that early. I used it to learn the secrets behind Yoritomo's throne. Used it to escape my prison." Sadness in her voice, swept away with a shrug. "But eventually the arrow hits the target. Even if the bowman is hopeless, let him fire enough shots, one will strike true. And gods, there are some awful bowmen out there, I assure you. How hard is it, gentlemen? You just aim for the little man in the boat."

A silence, filled with feeble smiles. Fading slowly.

"I'm not sure I could do that," Yukiko finally said.

"You drink it. It's easy. And you'll still be all right . . . later, I mean. If you want to start a real family."

"Real family?"

"With a husband. Someone who loves you."

"Will they be any less real, if I do it alone?"

"Why would you want to?" A slow frown darkened Michi's brow. "They're Hiro's get. He tried to murder you. Why would you want to bring his children into the world?"

"They'd be mine too."

"Yukiko, you're sixteen years old."

"Seventeen," she sighed. "It was my birthday last week."

"Oh." A weak smile. "Blessings of the Maker to you, then."

Yukiko smiled back, weaker still. "My thanks, sister."

"You *are* my sister, you know. You're blood to me. I'd die for you, Yukiko."

"Gods, don't do that . . ."

Michi laughed softly. "I'm in no hurry, surely. I need to finish my book, for starters. The godsdamned things don't write themselves."

"I love you, Michi." Yukiko squeezed the girl's fingers. "And it's not like the thought hasn't crossed my mind. Everyone has their own choices, and nobody can say if that's right or wrong. But I can feel them. Like two candles burning brighter by the day. I don't think I could make that stop. It's not about right or wrong. It's just about me. Does that make sense?"

"I suppose it might," Michi smiled. "If I were a stormdancer. But I'm just little me."

"There's nothing little about you, sister. You stand taller than mountains."

"You might think differently, when the Earthcrusher and the gaijin come.

When we look over Yama's walls and see iron and smoke all the way to the horizon, you might want for something more than one girl and her chainswords."

"If there were one girl in all the world I'd want beside me, it'd be you."

"Talking to that Inquisitor today, the way he spoke to you . . . Something else is coming. I feel it in my bones. We don't need an army of me. We need an army of *you*."

Yukiko shook her head. "I'm nothing without Buruu. And to win this war, we don't need an army of Yukikos. We need an army of thunder tigers."

"A pity there's only two arashitora left in Shima. Although Buruu and Kaiah *are* male and female. Where do little thunder tigers come from? Maybe we get some romantic music—"

"Oh my gods," Yukiko whispered.

". . . What?"

"My gods, I'm an idiot . . ."

Yukiko turned to Michi and embraced her, grinning to the eyeteeth.

"What?" Michi blinked.

"Where do baby thunder tigers come from?"

"How the hells should I know? Eggs?"

Yukiko dashed from the room without another word, the percussion of bare feet on mahogany loud enough to wake the rest of the guest wing. Michi was left alone in the gloom, confusion and concern vying for control of her expression.

Crawling into bed ten minutes later, there was still no clear winner.

T he groan of a storm wind and the scent of faint sweat woke her in the dark, heart lodged somewhere in her throat without quite knowing why. Hana sat up in the gloom, squinting at the figure on the edge of her bed. He was outlined by lantern glow filtered through rice-paper walls—shoulders broad as palace eaves, biceps carved from solid granite.

"Akihito?" she whispered.

"Hana."

"What time is it?"

His voice was sweet and dark as sugardew. "Time I stopped lying to myself."

"About what?"

"About why you look at me the way you do."

Sitting up straighter, she felt her pulse coming quicker, a stutter-step beat beneath bare skin. She was acutely aware of how thin her silk nightshift was, what the chill was doing to her body. Goose bumps all over. Her first thought was to fold her arms, cover her breasts, but the sight of him, the realization of what his presence might mean chased that thought away. Replaced it with butterflies.

"You've been looking at me, too," she whispered.

"... I shouldn't."

"Why not?"

"I'm too old for you."

"I'm eighteen next month."

"You're still a girl, for gods' sakes."

"You can change that . . ."

He looked at her then, and she could feel his stare as she sat up straighter, pushing out what little there was of her chest, wetting her lips slowly with the tip of her tongue. She leaned forward, the loose collar of her nightshift slipping down over her shoulder.

"Come here," she breathed.

"I shouldn't."

"Then why are you in my bedroom?"

"I don't know . . ."

She swallowed hard, mouth dry as ashes. And then she drew herself out from under her blankets, ever so slow. She prowled across a plain of tumbled silk, his features lit with the soft pink glow of her iris. Her face inches from his now, lips just a feather's breadth apart.

"I do," she whispered.

She drew her fingers down his face and he closed his eyes, sighed from the depths of his chest, stoking the fire building inside her. And then she kissed him, long and slow and deep, his mouth open to hers, her tongue seeking his as her hands descended, took his own, pressed them against her. She moaned, biting his lip, tasting blood. And as he drew back, pupils dilated, struggling to catch his breath, she could see he wanted this, every bit as much as she.

"Sis," he said.

"... What?"

His hand gripped her shoulder, shook her back and forth.

"Hana," he said. "Wake up."

Her eyelid opened a crack, letting in the garish lantern light. Yoshi loomed over her in the dark, shaking her. She woke fully, drawing her blankets up around herself and hissing.

"Izanagi's balls, what the hells are you doing in here?"

His face was creased with what passed for his smile nowadays. "Good dream?"

"What do you want, Yoshi? It must be fucking Cat's hour by now."

"I'm ghosting."

"You're what?" The phantom press of Akihito's hands faded as a chill slipped into her bones. "You're lighting out? For where?"

"Midlands." A shrug. "Then fair Kigen."

"You're going back to Kigen? Are you smoke drunk?"

"I can't do this anymore, Hana. It won't let me be."

She knew instantly what he was talking about—the shadow hanging about his shoulders like a shroud ever since they left Kigen. Every day between now and then had simply been a countdown. Fuse wire and spitting sparks.

She realized he'd shaved his head. Chopped off those long, gorgeous locks and trimmed the stubble back to his scalp. He was handsome as a fistful of devils, her brother. But it made him look older somehow. Harder.

She swallowed thickly, unsure where to begin.

"Yoshi, what happened to Jurou—"

"They threw a hammer party on him, Hana. Tore off his fingers. Took his . . ." Yoshi winced as he swallowed. "Well, you saw what they did . . ."

"I did." She took his hand and squeezed. "And I'm sorry, Yoshi."

"Motherfucker kills my boy? Lays claim on your eye? And then just walks free and clear?" Yoshi shook his head. "Hells no. Not while old Yoshi still got a pair. Not *ever.*"

"You think you can take the Scorpion Children on all by yourself?"

Yoshi smiled crooked, reached into his obi and produced a familiar lump. Snub-nosed. Lopsided. A handful of death, handle carved with laughing foxes.

An iron-thrower.

"Where the hells did you get that?"

"Lifted it from the Daimyo's room. Loaded, too. Awful nice of him."

Hana paused, looking for the words, knowing she was straying onto dangerous ground. Jurou had been her dearest friend, but Yoshi loved him with all he had. Anything he didn't keep for her, he'd given to him. And now, the place the boy had filled was flooded with the sight of him lying gutted in that alleyway, mouth lipless and silently screaming.

But . . .

"Yoshi, there are bigger things happening now."

Her brother fixed her in his sights, gaze shifting to glower.

"Don't you fucking dare, girl. Don't you spiel this rebellion shit on me. I'm not some dishpig gathered 'round an alms house radio, or some farmer fresh from the fields."

"I know what you're going to say, and—"

"Oh, doubtless? You know what I'm going to say?" Yoshi snatched his hand from hers. "Why don't you tell me then, little Stormdancer?"

". . . What?"

"Head still in the clouds? Ears full of thunder? Too high up to see the gutter you came from? Remember the people you came up with?"

"What the bleeding fuck are you talking about? I know *exactly* who I am and where I came from. I *loved* Jurou."

"Not like me. Not by half."

"Yoshi, there's a *war* coming. Tens of thousands of men. Machines that blot out the sun. Sky-fleets and Iron Samurai—"

"And what does one gutter-rat do against that? What exactly am I doing here, 'sides from taking up space at that senile old prick's table?"

"Yoshi, we need you."

"Room on that thunder tiger for two, you think?"

"Are you jealous? Because Kaiah chose me and not you?"

"It's not about that, and you know it. You've known me since you were knee high to a lotusfly. When have I *ever* fitted about the cards I got dealt? I do what needs doing. Always have. Always will. And what needs doing right now is that Shinshi and his band of painted pigs."

"But you look after me." Hana felt tears welling in her eye.

Yoshi shook his head. "Two tons of arashitora ought to sub just fine. You got an army behind these walls. Guildsmen and stormdancers and sky-ships and all. Up here, I'm just taking up air. But down there, there's some Scorpion Children that need doing, and state of play being what it is, I don't fancy their chances of getting shivved lest it's me flying the knife."

"Yoshi you can't leave me. Gods, not now . . ."

"Akihito will look to you. He's fine people. I like him, sis."

"You can't go!"

She threw her arms around his waist, digging her fingers in like the world was collapsing. Her entire life, he'd been at her side. The only one who knew what they'd been through, knew what it was to be clanless half-blooded gaijin filth. She'd noticed him drifting away over the last few weeks. But to leave entirely? Gods, she couldn't bear the thought . . .

"Got to stand tall now, Hana." Yoshi hugged her back. "Taller than most, on that arashitora's back. You're somebody special now. You don't need me."

"You don't have to do this alone. Just wait. When the war is over, we can—"

Yoshi pulled away, pressed his palms to her cheeks and looked her in the eye.

"Not later. Every day that motherfucker breathes, every mouthful, every moment, he stole. He doesn't deserve the dregs of it. And Jurou didn't deserve to go out like that. That boy was my beauty, Hana. That boy was my dawning and dusk. And they wrecked him with hammers and pliers and every time I spend a second in it, it grips me so tight I can't breathe. I can't *see* for the red in my eyes. And I just can't do it anymore."

She blinked at him in the dark, cupped the hand that cupped her cheek.

"You understand, don't you, sis? That this is about him, not us?"

A thick sniffle. "I understand."

"And you know I love you?"

She kissed his hand, tears coming in floods again. "I love you too, big brother."

"Hush now, girl, don't cry." He folded her in his arms again as she wept, great wracking sobs that shook her whole body. "Don't cry, sis. It'll be all right."

"It won't. You know it won't."

"You stand tall, you hear me?"

". . . I will."

Yoshi touched the golden pendant hanging around Hana's throat. The only thing they had left of their mother besides memories of sad blue eyes and the blond hair they both kept hidden. The stag embossed into the metal stared back at them, three sickle horns on his head. If the beast held any secrets, he kept them to himself.

"Stick with Akihito. Talk with that round-eye if you can make any godsdamned sense of him. He knows better than anyone what all this means. Ma. Your eye. All of it. You find out your truth, you hear? You tell me about it when I get back."

"All right," she sniffed. "I will."

"I've got to go."

"Don't," she whispered.

But he didn't listen.

16
BLOOD AND THUNDER

NO.

- NO. -

No?

Yukiko looked back and forth between Buruu and Kaiah, lightning ripping the clouds to ribbons overhead. Freezing cold in the Daimyo's garden, wind whipping amidst the cedars, thunder rolling between both arashitora and setting them apurr. But their eyes were flint hard, claws piercing the earth, feet apart as if bracing for onslaught.

What do you mean no, Buruu?

THE OPPOSITE OF YES?

Gods, I should've never taught you to sarcasm . . .

- FOOLISH PLAN. WILL NOT WORK. -

Yukiko turned on Kaiah.

And why the hells not? We need an army to fight the gaijin and the Guild. And there's an army of arashitora in the Everstorm.

- NO ARMY. A SCATTERED FEW. -

A few thunder tigers are worth a thousand sky-ships. Ten thousand men.

NO, YUKIKO.

You said that already, Buruu. You still haven't said why.

IS IT NOT ENOUGH THAT I SAY NO? DO YOU NOT TRUST ME?

- SHE LEARNS WISDOM AT LAST, KINSLAYER. -

AH, YOU SPEAK TO ME NOW?

- ONLY TO SPIT. -

Kaiah, you're not helping.

- IN THIS MADNESS YOU SPEAK? NO, I AM NOT. KINSLAYER CANNOT RETURN TO EVERSTORM. HE EXILED. MARKED FOR DEATH. -

And what about you? Why can't you go back?

- NOT CAN'T. WON'T. -

Why won't you, then?

- TORR. -

Who is that?

HE IS KHAN.

- FALSE KHAN. WILL NEVER BOW TO HIM. NEVER. -

What the hells does that mean? Izanagi's balls, Buruu, will you just speak to me?

- CANNOT SPEAK. EXILED BEFORE TORR CAME. REVILED. ACCURSED. -

All right, Gods, I don't care who tells me, as long as somebody does!

Kaiah growled low, tossed her head.

- KHAN RULES EVERSTORM. MIGHTIEST MALE. FIERCEST WARRIOR. TORR CLAIMED KHAN, THOUGH HE HAD NO RIGHT. -

No right? Why?

- NOT EVERSTORM BORN. TORR AND HIS PACK CAME FROM EAST. BLACK FEATHERS AND BLACK HEARTS. SEIZING EVERSTORM. KILLING MALES WHO STOOD DEFIANT. THEIR CUBS ALSO. BECAUSE OF HIM. -

Kaiah stepped toward Buruu with a snarl, hackles raised, wings unfurling.

- BECAUSE OF YOU. -

I AM SORRY.

- MY MATE AND HIS BROTHER STOOD ALONE, THE OTHERS TOO OLD, OR TOO AFRAID. AND WHERE WAS OUR KHAN WHEN USURPER CAME? -

THE LAW IS THE LAW. THE KHAN IS NO EXCEPTION.

- LAW WAS ALREADY BROKEN. KHAN MAKES LAW. -

SOME LAWS ARE WRIT IN STONE. IN THE BLOOD AND BONES OF OUR ANCESTORS. ARASHITORA DO NOT KILL OTHER ARASHITORA.

- PITY TORR DID NOT FEEL THE SAME. -

I DID NOT KNOW, KAIAH.

The female roared, snapping at the air a few inches from Buruu's face. Yukiko stepped between them, but Buruu simply backed away, wings pressed against his sides. No aggression in stance or thoughts—just a sorrow that filled Yukiko's heart to breaking.

She'd glimpsed it before in his mind; a shadow swimming just beneath his surface. But she'd never touched it, never sought to learn more out of respect for her friend. If he wanted her to know, he'd have told her. But it was close now. So close she could almost see its shape.

Thunder rocked the skies, faint spatters of black rain falling. Kaiah's tail was a whip, lashing side to side, hackles raised in jagged peaks down her spine.

- WHAT YOU THINK WOULD HAPPEN? -

I DID NOT THINK. THAT WAS MY FAILING.

- NOT THE FIRST. RAIJIN DAMN YOU, KINSLAYER. NOT THE FIRST BY FAR. -

YOU THINK I DO NOT KNOW THIS?

- THEN KNOW THIS ALSO. KNOW IF WORLD WERE FALLING, IF ALL THERE WAS AND EVER WOULD BE WEIGHED ON ME, I WOULD RATHER SEE IT END THAN FORGIVE YOU. YOU ARE COWARD. -

I AM MANY THINGS, BUT NOT THAT.

- THEN FIGHT ME. -

No, Kaiah. Stop this.

The female took another step forward, lightning cascading down her wings. Yukiko could feel the storm hung heavy in the air, ozone on her tongue, pulses racing.

- YOU KILLED THEM. AND IF YOU HAD COURAGE TO TAKE WHAT WAS YOURS, ALL THE DEATHS TO FOLLOW WOULD BE BUT A BAD DREAM. -

ARASHITORA DO NOT KILL OTHER ARASHITORA.

- A FOOL'S LAW! -

A KHAN'S LAW.

- THERE IS NO KHAN HERE, KINSLAYER. -

I WILL NOT FIGHT YOU.

- THEN DIE! -

Kaiah charged, ripping great clods of damp earth from the ground, eyes narrowed and gleaming like embers. Yukiko pulled back, terrified at the murderous rage inside the female's head. Buruu's roar shook the pillars of Kitsune-jō as the pair collided, crashing back into a twisted cedar and nearly tearing it from the ground. A resounding crunch, the tortured whine of Buruu's false wings, one brilliant snow-white feather torn free and spinning earthward amidst a hail of dead leaves, its end ugly and flat from the kiss of a Shōgun's blade.

Kaiah lashed out with her claws, a spray of bright red sailing into the darkness. Buruu roared again, furious, rearing up onto his hind legs, crashing breast to breast with the smaller female, locking her foreclaws in his own. She tumbled, the pair smashing an ancestor shrine to splinters as they rolled about in a roaring, screeching tangle.

Yukiko came to her senses, hands in fists by her sides.

"Stop it!"

Kaiah broke loose and lunged again, beak open and gleaming like a katana's edge.

"*STOP IT!*"

Her scream echoed in the Kenning, bouncing across walls of ancient granite, rocking both arashitora back onto their hindquarters. Lightning chased the thunder across the skies, illuminating the ruins of the Daimyo's garden. The two beasts glowered at each other, sodden and bleeding, flanks rising and falling with the fury of a blacksmith's bellows.

For the love of the Gods, we're on the same side!

APPARENTLY NOT.

- COWARD! -

Stop it, both of you!

"What the hells is going on?"

Hana stood on the verandah, night clothes and hair in disarray, surrounded by baffled guards and servants. She looked as if she'd been crying.

"It's nothing, Hana."

"Nothing?" The girl stepped down into the garden, put one protective arm around Kaiah's neck. "Doesn't look like nothing."

- HE *IS NOTHING. FOREVER AND ALWAYS. HEAR ME, KINSLAYER?* -

Buruu made no reply, eyes downcast. Kaiah snorted in disgust, flaring her wings.

- *IF YOU NOT HEAR, THEN YOU SEE.* -

Yukiko put hand to brow as Kaiah's mind flooded with images; faded memories bathed in bloody red. She saw two arashitora—one jet black, another white, clashing across storming skies. She saw the white arashitora smashed to pulp at the foot of a great black mountain, the seas around it boiling to steam. She saw a younger arashitora male, barely more than a cub, hit like a thunderbolt by a black shadow, sinking into the boiling ocean without a trace. And at the last, she saw that same shadow, dark and vast, looming like a nightmare over a nest of twisted branches and brambles. Beak open wide, talons descending.

Descending toward . . .

"Gods, no," Yukiko whispered.

Two arashitora cubs with soft down and fur, eyes wide as they looked up into the face of darkness. Too young to comprehend. Too small to flee. Able only to wriggle, to burrow beneath the blanket of old feathers, squalling and tearing each other in their fear.

Plaintive cries as the shadow seized them in claws as sharp as death.

Little wings torn from trembling bodies.

Trembling bodies hurled from the nest.

Down and down and down, skies painted red, falling into ruin.

"Oh my gods," Hana breathed, throwing her arms around Kaiah's neck and pressing her face into the thunder tiger's cheek. "Oh my gods . . ."

TORR . . .

- THIS IS WHAT YOU WROUGHT, KINSLAYER. YOU AND YOUR COW-ARDICE. YOUR PRECIOUS LAW. NO JUSTICE. NO PEACE. JUST THIS. -

Buruu hung his head. Thunder filling the skies. Rain falling heavier. Yukiko looked at him, folded down upon himself, misery written in every line, every curve. She reached out with herself, pouring her warmth into him. No judgment, no anger, just love—the same unquestioning love he'd always given her. None of it mattered. She was his and he was hers, from now until world's ending, and nothing would change that.

I love you, Buruu.

Yukiko stepped closer, black rain falling in earnest now. She knew she should get out from under it, that it would scald her. But Buruu sat beneath it, bent and thoroughly wretched.

Do you hear me? I love you.

I AM SORRY.

It's all right.

NO.

He climbed to his feet, spread his wings with a song of metal and canvas mesh, the iridescent frame creaking like old bones. He shook himself like a hound might, black water spilling from his flanks, eyes turning skyward.

NO, IT IS NOT.

With a single leap, he tore up into the air, pounding at the rain with his iron-clad wings. Up into the black, over the fortress walls as she called after him, his warmth fading as the distance between them grew. His sorrow lingered in her mind, a sour taste on her tongue, and she turned to glare at Kaiah. The beast stared back, prowling in from the rain to take shelter with Hana and the wide-eyed servants on the verandah. Yukiko snatched up Buruu's severed feather and ran under cover, skin stained with black, already beginning to tingle.

She stared at the pair for a moment, Hana with her arm about Kaiah's neck, three eyes staring in silent challenge. And without a word, Yukiko stalked back to her room, looking for clean water to wash away the black rain, sorrow's stain, the memory of those little shapes flung wingless and crying out into the void.

Her hand strayed to her stomach. The dread she found curled there. Rain pounding like mallets on the bleached tiles overhead, like a heartbeat, like the pulse beneath her skin.

And there she sat, hours in the dark, turning the feather over and over in her hands, waiting for Buruu to return.

Wondering if he ever would.

17
EARTHCRUSHER RISING

"Do you remember our chess game?" Kin stared at the old man across the embers, the fire burning in tired, steel-gray. "What you told me?"

Daichi stared back, unblinking, cold and reptilian. Wheels within wheels, weather-beaten and aged, weighed down by guilt and responsibility and the lives of those who needed him. Now more than ever. Now, when he was at his weakest.

A slow nod, black stains on his lips. "I do."

"Then we need to talk."

He nodded to the old man's daughter.

"Alone."

Blood in his mouth. Crawling on his tongue. Tasting death.

Daichi bent double, hugging himself as the coughing fit seized him, digging fingers into his gut, his throat, laughing somewhere in back of his mind. There was something altogether terrifying about living this way   knowing each inhalation could be the one that set it off. This pain. This helplessness. Living each moment afraid to breathe, the very motion that kept you living. Until you realize this wasn't living at all. This was just waiting to die.

No idea how long it lasted. No thought throughout, save that he wanted it to stop, please, make it stop. A just punishment he knew, this disease, twisting him on the cell floor and painting his palms black. He deserved it, for all he'd done. Daiyakawa village. Yukiko's pregnant mother, gods . . . how had he ever been a man who thought such deeds righteous?

This was his to cherish. Reward for faithful service to a regime built on murder and lies. He knew that. He *understood*. But in the grip of those seizures, he couldn't help but wish it over. To stand before the Judge of the Hells, and then, to kneel before the Endsinger on her throne of bones. To wander in the Yomi underworld as a hungry ghost, utterly damned for all time.

It could not be worse than this . . .

The coughing stopped, somewhere after an eternity and before forever. Silence fell, edged with humming sky-ship engines, vibrations creeping through the brig floor. And looking up through the cell bars, he saw them—three men with bloodshot eyes, swathed in black, the light dimming around them.

"You sound ill," the foremost said; a little man staring at his own outstretched fingers.

Daichi held back lunatic laughter for fear he might start coughing again. "Some would say."

"Do you believe in gods, Daichi-san? In heavens and hells?"

"In Storm and Sun and Moon?" whispered the second.

"In the great benevolent Maker and his divine order?" asked the third.

"Of course," he nodded.

"Will you walk, or shall we carry you?"

"Where?"

The Inquisitor's face was hidden beneath the smooth upturned lines of his breather, but Daichi could swear the little man was smiling.

"To see what your faith has brought you."

I n the end, they carried him.

One under each shoulder, the short one leading, up onto the deck. The skies were filled with ironclads, sleek, arrowhead corvettes cutting exhaust streaks across the sky. Daichi squinted, the dawn much too bright after days below. A storm was amassed to the north, the distant Iishi hidden by a curtain of black rain.

They propped him at the railing, holding his arms. The air overflowed with the burned-flower stink of chi, engine song, a choir of propeller blades. To the west he could see the Tōnan mountains, the cancer-black smear of the Stain spreading around their roots far below. Fumes hung over massive fissures in dead earth, little farms on the periphery being swallowed one foot at a time. And out there on the eastern edge, behind a perimeter of railway lines and barbed wire fences and a hundred shreddermen suits lined up all in a row, a giant stirred.

Black iron. Great foglamp eyes illuminating the blanket of smoke. Three hundred feet high, eight legs curled up under a bloated, rivet-studded belly; the limbs of some ancient spider god dredged up from the hells. Exhaust spires down its spine, great scythe arms edged with chainsaw blades big enough to level forests as if they were built from straw and dreams. The Guild's monster. Its masterpiece. Ready to be unleashed on an unsuspecting world.

Earthcrusher.

Daichi stifled a coughing fit, blinking fumes and tears from his eyes. Off at the distant Midland junction, he could see troop transports, banners flapping, blades glittering like breakers on an iron-gray sea. The Tiger lord's warhost, set to crush the Kagé into dust.

The shreddermen below started their engines; a hundred-strong choir of saw-blade arms and tree-trunk legs, crewed by Tiger pilots. An army of flesh and sharpened steel.

Gods, what could we have ever hoped to throw against it?

He looked to the Tiger flagship *Honorable Death*, floating off the starboard. A sharp intake of breath as he saw him, clad in new brass, eyes burning like hellsfire through the exhaust.

Staring right at him.

Kin-san.

He wished with everything inside him for five minutes alone with that boy in a windowless room. A few quiet words he would give his life to hiss.

But no. Trust had put paid to that ending long ago. Trust repaid with lightless cells and torture, ending here on these two ships, a few dozen feet and a thousand miles apart. They stared at each other, a bitter, vengeful wind moaning across the gulf between them. Staring until the skies split with a thunderous roar, a belching, crunching, clanking rumble felt from the tip of his spine to the base of his skull.

The engines of the Earthcrusher.

The Inquisitors lurked beside him, silent and still. Daichi realized it was freezing, thin air scraping his ravaged throat, but the trio seemed not to notice. They stood looking out over the Stain and the unfurling army, slow exhalations of blue-black breath lost amidst the exhaust.

The Earthcrusher spewed poison plumes a mile high, a jetwash of spattering tar, the garish oranges and yellows of the Phoenix Fleet nearly lost amidst the cloud. The very sky shook as it bellowed, deck vibrating beneath Daichi's feet, two vast foglamp eyes cutting through the pall.

The lead Inquisitor turned to the old man, a smile in bloodshot eyes.

"Where is your Maker now?"

K in climbed over the *Honorable Death*'s railing, and without a word, dropped into smoke-washed skies. Gravity clutching, velocity caressing his skin as he sailed belly down into the void, wind roaring in his ears.

The Stain stretched out below; a great tumor of ash and cracks torn through Shima's heart. The fumes blanketing the dead earth barely moved despite the prop-blasts from above. Kin closed his eyes as he descended, wondering if he would feel it when he struck the ground.

He worked at switches on his wrist, and the engines on his back roared to life, snatching him from gravity's embrace. He swooped under the fleet's belly, half a dozen Artificers flying with him—the team from Kigen sent to complete the Earthcrusher's crew.

The goliath loomed out of the exhaust veil as the Artificers descended. Kin didn't appreciate how colossal the machine was until they were within fifty yards. The giant towered over everything, the army of ten-foot-high shreddermen at its feet looking like children's toys. Kin banked around the crescent-shaped fore-arms, edged with chainsaw-blades large enough to decapitate buildings. This close, the engine's rumble was a suffocating pressure against his ribs.

The team landed on the machine's right spaulder, and a metal hatch in the Earthcrusher's neck creaked open, red eyes glowing at them from the dark. A Lotusman ushered them into a cramped corridor lined with thick iron piping, moist with steam. Looking down through the mesh gantry, Kin could see power cables and pressure gauges and combustion chambers, interlocking gears smeared with inch-thick layers of grease. There was a kind of poetry to it all, the motion of machines and men, the hiss of smoke and steam. He found himself smiling be-hind his mask.

"Welcome to the Earthcrusher, brothers," said the Lotusman.

Kin looked him up and down—barely more than an initiate judging from his voice, his skin still new and relatively clean.

"I am Shatei Bo, aide to Commander Rei. Our Kyodai requests you report to your assigned stations. We march within moments."

"Our thanks, brother," Kin said.

"You are Fifth Bloom Kin?" The aide's eyes glittered in the dark.

"I am."

"Commander Rei requests your presence on the bridge."

Kin nodded. "Lead on, brother Bo."

A cramped elevator carried them up through the goliath's neck, the engine song so amplified in the narrow space Kin had to adjust his aural dampeners. The lift doors hissed open into a wide, circular chamber within the Earthcrusher's skull. Two enormous glass portals stared out over the surrounding wastelands. The walls were lined with instrumentation; gauges and dials, punch-card inter-faces. The air left a greasy film over Kin's glass eye.

In the room's heart sat the pilot's station: a harness of iron and pistons and leather buckles, connected via segmented umbilicals to the instrumentation around it. Kin finally understood Kensai's frustration at being denied his place here—the thought of sitting at those controls sent a thrill of excitement skittering through his flesh.

But not to be. Commander Rei was ensconced on the throne, buckled in place. He was outfitted in a regular atmos-suit, eyes covered with telescoping goggles. Artificers were concluding the final stages of pre-walk check. Rei glanced over his shoulder, flicking a switch to close his comms channel.

"Kyodai Kin, I am pleased you saw fit to finally join us."

"Commander Rei." Kin covered his fist, bowed deeply. "Second Bloom Kensai sends regrets that he could not be here on this momentous day."

The commander turned to his aide as if Kin had not spoken. "Brother Bo, oil pressure is still fluctuating on leg seven."

The young Lotusman took his seat at the comms station and nodded. "Technician already dispatched. A seal ruptured during engine ignition. Repairs are under way."

". . . I should see to the Artificer crews," Kin said. "There is much I need to catch up on."

"No," Rei said. "You should bear witness. Your father assisted in designing this machine. It is only fitting you should stand on the bridge as it takes its first steps."

Kin stood beside the control rig, watching Rei from the corner of his eyes. The harness was suspended from the roof, able to swivel with the pilot's hips. The motion of his legs, arms and head would be transferred via relays to the Earthcrusher itself—the machine mimicking his movements. Control of the chainblades and air defense systems could be wielded via the control gloves, or ceded to secondary stations. The bridge was staffed with half a dozen, the Earthcrusher itself with over sixty, and there were a thousand ways things could go wrong. But presuming all systems were in working order, ultimate control was in the hands of one man.

That man nodded to himself, scanning his consoles. Seemingly pleased, he cleared his throat and opened his all-channels comms frequency.

"This is Commander Rei. Pre-walk check complete. Notify ground crew to stand clear."

Brother Bo began a countdown over the open frequency.

"Earthcrusher ambulation will commence in ten, nine . . ."

Rei turned to Kin, looked the Fifth Bloom up and down.

"You had best hold on to something . . ."

D aichi stood at the railing, feeling the volume rise, watching the ground crews and shreddermen suits back away from the Earthcrusher. Thunderous plumes of exhaust rose into the sky, an enormous burst of steam spewing from the machine's bowels. The old man spat black onto the deck, heart pounding in his chest.

The behemoth moved—trembling at first, a new foal trying to stand in a puddle of afterbirth. Its legs unfurled, one after the other, cacophony rising. And then, like some grotesque from a Docktown sideshow, some hideous collision between insect and machine, it thrust its legs up to the first knuckle into the ruined earth. And it stood.

The island shook, one impact after another as the beast began walking, four legs shifting forward and slamming into the ground in quick succession.

DOOMDOOMDOOMDOOM

The remaining four stepping forward now.

DOOMDOOMDOOMDOOM

A ragged cry went up from the fleet, Lotusmen raising their hands and calling its name; a testament to their power and ingenuity, now taking its first tentative steps toward the red dawn awaiting it to the north.

DOOMDOOMDOOMDOOM

DOOMDOOMDOOMDOOM

Daichi licked his lips, tasted black. The little man standing beside him turned, bloodshot eyes drifting aimlessly until at last they settled on Daichi's own.

"Do you see?" the little man breathed. "The end?"

Daichi's gaze was fixed on the Earthcrusher, breath caught in his lungs as the giant lumbered from the staging grounds, pursued by swarms of shreddermen, clattering and clanking like tiny soldiers after their emperor. All of them marching off to war.

"I see it," Daichi rasped.

"No. You do not."

The Inquisitor pointed at the colossus.

"Not there."

He pointed to the ground beneath their feet. The miles of deadland, wreathed in choking, soup-thick fog. Daichi swore he could see tiny figures moving in the vapor, watching the Earthcrusher depart. The little man spoke again, an unmistakable smile in his voice.

"There."

18

MOCKINGBIRD

The rain was warm as firelight, thick as treacle, black as midnight.

Yoshi trudged along the empty railway line, swathed in a hooded cloak of black rubber. Split-toed boots crunching in the gravel beside the rust-chewed tracks, gloved hands inside his sleeves. He'd not been able to find a handcart driver awake at Yama station, and trains weren't running since the refinery explosion. So, he was walking south, gale blowing black droplets into his goggles, soaking bitter into the kerchief around his face.

Had to start fucking raining, didn't it?

Minutes turned to hours beneath a thunder sky. A few Kitsune farmers were reaping the last of their lotus before the rain's toxicity ruined it, despite having nowhere to sell it anymore. The downpour finally dried to a trickle, and he slung the hood back from his brow, wrung out his kerchief. And glancing into the sky, he saw a winged silhouette sailing amongst the bloody-gray.

At first he thought it might be Hana and Kaiah, come to talk him down. But squinting hard, he realized its wings glinted metallic, and there was no rider on its back.

He watched the beast spiraling in broad circles, seemingly without point or purpose. There was something lonely about the figure up there in all that sky, something that spoke of a body who'd lost their way. Licking his lips and spitting, Yoshi reached into the Kenning, groping for the arashitora's mind.

Looking for me?

A long silence, broken by distant thunderclaps. He watched the beast for a slow minute, about to shrug and set boots to road when he felt the beast's voice thunder in his mind.

WHY WOULD I LOOK FOR YOU, MONKEY-CHILD?

. . . Who the hells you calling monkey-child, birdbrain?

AH, BIRDBRAIN. VERY GOOD. A BARB SO SHARP THE VERY AIR BE-TWEEN US BLEEDS, BOY.

Someone shit in your morning oats or something?

ARASHITORA DO NOT EAT OATS.

Can't hurl an ounce of blame if someone's been shitting in them.

YOU ARE NOT AMUSING.

Oh, doubtless.

OH, DOUBTLESS.

What, so you're a mockingbird now?

MOCKERY WELL DESERVED, BOY.

Fine. Go fuck yourself.

Yoshi ran one gloved palm over his stubbled scalp, pulled his hood back on, and resumed walking. He could feel the arashitora still circling above, languid, occasionally swooping toward the earth, pulling up at the last moment and hurling back skyward. Like a child, running for no reason other than he had legs and there was ground beneath his feet.

Yoshi found himself reaching out again, marveling at its texture—nothing like the simple beasts he'd spent his life inside. There was an element of Daken in there, a sense of the feline that bought hard-edged sorrow up in Yoshi's chest. But there was also a primal, razor-sharp edge, predatory and stained with frustration. He'd never felt anything like it in all his life.

I CAN FEEL YOU, MONKEY-CHILD. STUMBLING ABOUT IN MY MIND.

So?

SO GET OUT.

Say please.

PREPOSTEROUS. COULD GUT YOU LIKE A FISH. COULD DRAPE THE CLOUDS WITH YOUR INNARDS. WEAK. WRETCHED. USURPERS. TURN-ING SKIES TO RED AND—

Izanagi's balls, I've just figured it. You're out here sulking, aren't you?

. . . YOU KNOW NOTHING.

I know a tantrum when I see it. Gods know Jurou taught me all about them. Rich boys throw the worst kind, believe me.

AND WHO IS THIS JUROU? ANOTHER MEWLING MONKEY-THING?

Yoshi stopped short, reaching down and slinging a handful of mud into the sky.

Come down here and spit that shit! I'll teach you some respect for the dead, you whoreson. I'll fix it so you can apologize to his godsdamned face!

He drew the iron-thrower he'd stolen from the Kitsune Daimyo, dancing in a ridiculous, frustrated little circle. Finally he spat into the mud, thrusting the weapon back into his obi and marching down the tracks with thunderclouds crashing over his head.

. . . I AM SORRY.

Go to the hells.

I DID NOT KNOW HE WAS DEAD.

Then maybe you should think before you run your fucking mouth.

BEAK.

Whatever.

WHO WAS HE?

None of your godsdamned business.

FRIEND?

. . .

BROTHER?

He was my everything, that's what.

Yoshi heaved a sigh, lifted his goggles to run his hand over his eyes.

He was pretty much everything.

HOW DID HE DIE?

He didn't die. He was killed.

AH.

Ah.

AND SO YOU WALK ALONE, HOPING TO FIND SOME ANSWER FOR YOUR LOSS? YOU WILL FIND NONE IN THE CLOUDS, BOY. BELIEVE ME, I HAVE LOOKED.

I'm not looking for answers. I'm looking to kill the bastards who killed him.

REVENGE.

Godsdamned right.

YOU WILL FIND NO PEACE IN IT. THE STAINS NEVER WASH OFF. I KNOW.

Oh, you know?

YOU WOULD DO BETTER STAYING HERE. WITH YUKIKO. WITH YOUR SISTER. WAR IS COMING, BOY.

Do I look the kind who'll risk his stake for people he doesn't give a shit about? Hells, three months ago, those Yama folks would've happily chained me to a stone and lit me on fire.

MUCH CHANGES WITH THE SEASONS.

Not everything.

THE SHAPE OF HEROES, CERTAINLY.

So I look like a hero to you?

YOU LOOK LIKE AN ORDINARY BOY.

A blinding arc of lightning kissed the sky.

SO YES, YOU DO.

Save the speech for someone who cares, Mockingbird.

YOUR ANSWERS ARE NOT WHERE YOU THINK. DEATH CANNOT UNDO DEATH.

No shit.

WHY THEN? WILL YOU SPEAK LIKE THESE SAMURAI? OF HONOR? LOYALTY?

Think I left my honor in my other pants.

THEN WHY DO THIS?

Yoshi came to a sudden halt, boots scuffing in mud and bluestone. He looked at the silhouette above, sharp lines of mechanical wings, jet stripes and snow-white feathers against a seething gray sea. He ran a hand over his scalp again, pictured dark eyes alight with laughter.

The mouth he'd once kissed, bloody and lipless.

The hand he'd once held, gnawed and fingerless.

Because blood answers blood, Mockingbird.

He shook his head.

Because some motherfuckers just need killing.

Yoshi walked on. It started spitting again, thick droplets of viscous ooze pattering between rusted tracks, striking the metal in off-beat notes. Yoshi pulled his kerchief over his mouth. Walking along the bleached wood, he prayed the downpour would hold off a little longer. He didn't notice the arashitora until he'd almost bumped into him.

Yet there he was.

Sitting across the tracks, tail sweeping side to side. His feathers were stained gray by the rain, metal wings gleaming dully. His eyes were molten amber, bright as the hidden sun.

WHERE DO YOU LOOK FOR YOUR REVENGE?

Kigen city.

THAT IS TOO FAR FOR ME TO FLY. I MUST RETURN TO YAMA SOON.

If you say so.

BUT I CAN TAKE YOU TO WHERE THE METAL ROADS MEET.

. . . Midland Junction?
IF YOU SAY SO.
Why would you do that?
IT WILL RAIN AGAIN SOON.
So?
YOU WISH TO WALK IN IT?
No.
THEN GET ON MY BACK BEFORE I CHANGE MY MIND.

Yoshi tilted his head, looked the arashitora in the eye. He glanced at the clouds smeared overhead, the long stretch of rail track, the black rain spattering into one outstretched palm.

All right, then. My thanks.

He crawled up onto the thunder tiger's back, adrenaline turning his guts to tumbling, mumbling water. The arashitora stood, Yoshi swaying on his spine as the beast loped down the track, leaping once into the air, wings spread, crashing back down to earth with a jolt. Yoshi cursed, held on for dear life as the arashitora leaped up again, this time catching the air beneath his wings, tearing at the empty between clouds and earth and rising into the sky. The boy felt the blood flee his face, watching the ground fall away beneath him, swooping around in a long, loping arc that pushed his innards up against his rib cage. The beast's wings were a song of metal and gears and pistons, creaking with the uplift, soaring into the rain and cloud.

A severed feather drifted in their wake, tumbling out of the sky, over and over upon itself. The wind caught it, buoyed it, keeping it aloft for as long as it could.

Not forever.

But perhaps for long enough.

19
FALLING

A darkened room of greasy iron. The rumble of sleepless engines. Whispers of treason.

"Tonight," said the first.

"No. Too much risk," the second replied.

"We can make it look like an accident."

"No. Even if we *were* taking down officers, Commander Rei would be our priority target. Not this Fifth Bloom."

"If you kill Rei, they'll catch you. You're his aide, and the first they'll blame. We'll need all three of us to stop the engines when the time comes."

"Which is why we don't touch Rei *or* Kin until the time is right."

"You know our orders. All Upper Blooms are targets now."

"No. Too much rides on this. We lay low. And when we meet outside resistance, in the Iishi or outside Kitsune-jō, we take out the engines. Cripple this thing. That's the plan."

"This Kin was *promoted* by the Inquisition, Bo. He probably has their ink on his arm!"

"This isn't the plan!"

"I'm doing it. I can make it look like an accident."

"Shinji, no!"

"Death to the Serpents, Bo. Death to them all."

The rasp of brass on brass, an arm snatched from a clawing grip. A whispered plea overscoring rasping bellows, the clunk of a bulkhead door, heavy boots stomping into the dark. Bo standing in the gloom, glowing eyes downcast as he slammed his fist into the wall.

"Shit."

K *nife pressed to forehead. Yoritomo's face looming overhead in the lantern light.*

"But I think no other man should want for it either . . ."

Pain.

"No!"

Kaori lunged upright in bed, drawing her wakizashi from beneath the pillow, face slick with sweat despite the chill. She blinked, chest heaving, searching the gloom for her attacker. But he was dead now—long dead in the shadow of the Burning Stones. Killed for the Black Fox's murder. The Stormdancer's revenge.

Her own forever denied . . .

A faint knock at her door, a silhouette outlined in the rice-paper window. She rubbed her eyes, dragging her hair over her face. What time was it? Monkey's hour? Dog's?

"Kaori." Maro's voice.

"What is it?"

"A radio message. A transmission."

"You can't take it yourself?" she hissed. "Gods above . . ."

"He asked to speak to you personally. And alone."

A frown in the gloom. "Who is the transmission from?"

"I am uncertain. But he claims to be Isao . . ."

K in descended the service ladder, the space so narrow his skin rasped against the walls. Dropping down the last few feet onto a suspended walkway, he looked out over the engine room.

A wide space, ringed with iron gantries and ladders, a transmission block big as houses, the engine thrumming with the power of a thousand horses. The deck beneath his feet swayed with the Earthcrusher's gait, shock absorbers only partially compensating. Kin surveyed the room, stricken with déjà vu. Blinking in the chi-lantern light, staring at the glittering skins of the Artificers working below, struck to the heart with a single, burning thought.

I have been here before . . .

"Fifth Bloom Kin."

Do not call me Kin. That is not my name . . .

Kin turned, saw an Artificer on the gantry behind, red eye aglow. He looked to the small sigils marked beside the mechabacus, denoting the Guildsman's name.

"Brother Shinji."

The Shatei bowed. "You are here for inspection?"

"Forgiveness. I'm early, I know."

The Guildsman nodded. "I thought we might commence with the gear train? We will have a good view of the transmission from the upper walkways if you wish to see?"

"Very much so."

The Artificer bowed, motioned him forward. "After you, Fifth Bloom."

"My thanks, brother."

Kin turned and clomped along the walkway.

K aori closed the radio room door, locked it behind her, sweat-slicked from the climb. The listening posts were positioned up the mountainside south of the Kagé village—the better to escape magnetic interference. She'd covered the distance at a run, heart hammering, hair tangled about her face. Sitting at the radio table, she snatched up the microphone.

"Isao?"

The boy's voice was edged with static, dimmed with distance. "Kaori."

"What did you give my father on his last birthday?"

A pause, crackling with white noise. "Atsushi and I carved him a flute of kiri wood."

"What was the first tune he played?"

"Well, he tried to play 'The Ronin's Daughter.' But he was so awful, I wasn't quite sure. And then I got drunk and sat on it. Accidently, of course."

Kaori's heart ached at the memory, even as she smiled. "Gods above, it *is* you. How can this be? We thought you'd been killed when they took my father . . ."

"Are you alone, Kaori?"

"Hai."

"Are you sure? Look in the corners. Listen. Do you hear a clock ticking?"

"You mean the spider drone that Guild bitch Ayane let loose up here?"

". . . You found it?"

"And destroyed it. Would that I could have done the same to her."

"Izanagi be praised. Well done."

"How is it you still live? You were supposed to be guarding my father during the Kigen attack. If the Guild took him, they should have taken or killed you too."

"Kin *did* kill me. He stabbed me in the back. Atsushi and Takeshi too."

"What—"

"At least as far as Ayane was concerned . . ."

K in stood on the walkway above the gear train, looking down into an iron mouth full of chomping, rolling teeth. The Earthcrusher operated on a four-speed transmission, power transferred via a series of colossal cogs to the eight legs pounding the ground outside. The transmission was enclosed in an iron housing edged with safety railing, but from the top it was exposed to the open air, allowing technicians easy access to the gear train. An Artificer stood on a service ladder halfway up the housing, checking a lump of gauges.

Looking down on the poetry of gears and bearings, Kin was forced to admire Kensai's genius. The Second Bloom might very well be his enemy, but he spoke the language of the machine better than anyone. He was glad he'd never made the mistake of underestimating his uncle, or believing for a moment Kensai put stock in his story.

Thankfully the Inquisition hadn't shared the Second Bloom's suspicions. It was a blessing they put so much faith in their precious "What Will Be." In the future Kin even now fought tooth and nail to prevent.

"Call me First Bloom . . ."

Kin smiled grim behind his helm.

Not if I can help it.

He turned to Shinji, raising his voice over the clamor. "Tell me brother, how—"

An iron pipe crashed into his head, swung in a double-handed grip. The impact was almost deafening, head rocked sideways, helm buckling under sledgehammer force. Kin toppled forward over the walkway, pistons whining as he seized the railing with all his strength. White flowers bloomed in his eyes, blood in his mouth, pain overshadowed by terror of the gear chain churning below, waiting to chew him into mince.

He looked up at the Guildsman who'd struck him, raising his pipe for another swing.

"For the rebellion, bastard," Shinji spat.

"No," Kin rasped. "Wait . . ."

I sao, you'd best explain yourself swiftly . . ." Kaori hissed.

"Rat's blood." The boy's voice crackled in the speakers. "I had bladders of it strapped to my back. Kin used a fake knife with a retractable blade when he stabbed me. Easy enough to manage, even for a novice like him."

"You faked your murder at Kin's hands? You knew he'd betray us?"

"No, no Kaori. It was *Kin's* plan. He knew Ayane was a plant sent by the Guild to turn him against us. Or at the very least turn us against him. He *knew.*"

Stomach in knots. No spit in her mouth.

"How?"

"The shuriken-throwers. Ayane sabotaged them. Well, her spider-drone did anyway, while she was locked in the cells. But she did it too well. Kin figured it out by studying the wreckage. Nobody but a Guildsman would have understood the 'throwers well enough to have them all fail simultaneously, right in the middle of an oni assault."

"This doesn't explain what happened to my father in Kigen!"

Static hissed down the line as Isao drew a measured breath.

"Kin spoke to Daichi alone. He knew the drone would be listening—he figured it'd be following him everywhere. So they played chess, passed notes between moves. Out loud, Kin spoke of the plot to destroy Kigen refinery—the plan Ayane was told would end with his betrayal. But in the notes, he explained to Daichi what was really happening. Ayane. The drone. The sabotage. And finally, he outlined a plan to defeat the Earthcrusher, and end the Guild once and for all."

Kaori closed her eyes, dreading the answer.

"How?"

K in hunched his shoulders as the pipe smashed onto his helm again. Another blow, Shinji now battering at the fingers gripping the walkway, lost in frenzy.

"Stop! I'm on your side!"

Kin glanced over his shoulder, down at the transmission's rolling, cog-lined maw. Another blow landed on his head, stars bursting behind his eyes. One hand slipped and he gasped, teeth gritted, clinging on with everything he had.

When he was a boy, a fellow initiate told him in the moment before death, life was supposed to flash before your eyes. The triumphs, the mistakes, everything you'd ever been and done, rendered in white, strobing light, right before the lights went out forever.

And all he could think of was Yukiko.

That he'd never see her again.

Never make any of it right.

No.

Iron and brass sang as another blow landed, his grip failing.

No, not like this . . .

H e plans to destroy the Earthcrusher's engines, Kaori. His father designed the combustion chambers or somesuch. Kin knew their workings, but he had to be *inside* to take it down. And so, he'd have to make a convincing enough show for the Guild to take him back."

"He asked my father to—"

"No. Daichi volunteered."

"But why would—"

"He's dying of blacklung, Kaori. So why not make it count for something?"

Tears filled her eyes. Grief. Rage.

"Why are you only telling me this now?"

"Kagé radio doesn't exist in Kigen city anymore. We had to make our way north to the Endless Plains, the first listening station in Hatenashi province. We took a risk even contacting you now. For all we knew, the drone was still in the village."

"But why didn't my father tell me before the attack?" she hissed.

"Because he knew you'd never agree to it, Kaori."

"Isao, you *hated* Kin . . ."

"But we loved Daichi. His words made sense. Yukiko was gone. We had no other way to deal with the Earthcrusher."

"Yukiko has returned." Bitterness soured her voice. "She's thrown in with these Guild rebels, if you can believe it."

"We heard about the rebellion. Rumor is they've been killing Guild hierarchy. We figured if Kin managed to get back into the good books, he might become a target—the Guildsman who captured the great Daichi, leader of the Kagé insurgency."

Kaori bowed her head, grief-stricken. "Gods . . ."

"You have to tell them, Kaori. If Yukiko has the ears of these Guild rebels, you have to let them know not to touch Kin. He can take down the Earthcrusher. And the way Daichi talked, the explosion will take half the Tora army with it. *Kin is on our side.*"

Kaori closed her eyes, whispering.

"Father, how could you . . ."

F ingers slipping from the railing.

Pipe descending toward his head.

Denying it all, with everything he could muster.

Kin lunged with his free hand, stabbing the flight controls on his wrist as the blow crashed on his head. A burst of sparks fired, rockets igniting, another blow to his skull, another, another. Insensate, eyes filmed with blood, fingers slipping free. Twisting as he fell toward the transmission. Blue-white flaring at his back. Spinning and crashing against the safety railing. Teetering, rockets still burning, and with one last ragged gasp, pulling himself over, falling twenty feet to the engine room floor.

His rocket pack flared again and died, controls at his wrist spewing another bright burst of sparks. Blood in his mouth. Breath burning in his lungs.

The Artificer on the service ladder cursed, looked up at Shinji on the gantry above.

"Idiot, you missed!"

"Well, get down there and finish him!"

"Get down here and help me!"

Drawing an iron wrench from his tool belt, the Artificer dropped to the floor to end what his comrade started.

K aori, are you receiving me?"

Betrayal after betrayal . . .

"You must speak to Yukiko! Kin isn't to be touched!"

Yukiko. Michi. And now her father also? To trust that bastard Guildsman more than he trusted her? To throw away his life at the word of that traitor, and say nothing of it to his only daughter? Handing over his katana to Yukiko was bad enough. After all Kaori had given up. All she'd lost. Years at his side. And in a handful of weeks, Yukiko and that bastard Kin had more of his trust than she'd earned in a lifetime?

She stood slowly, lips pressed together, thin and bloodless.

"Kaori?"

Teeth clenched so hard, her jaw ached.

"Kaori, can you hear me?"

"No," she breathed. "No, I don't hear you."

She flicked the switch, Isao's pleas clipped into ringing silence.

S hinji pounding down a spiral stairwell, pointing at Kin, shouting to his fellow assassin.

"Stop him, he's on his mechabacus!"

Kin's fingers were flitting across his chest, a complex dance on the device's face, like a street minstrel on the strings of his shamisen. The message was being transmitted over the Earthcrusher's internal channel, a distress call heard by every Guildsman aboard the colossus.

"Assistance required. Engine room."

"Stop him, Maseo!"

The second Artificer crashed into Kin, trying to pull his hands from the device.

"Stop him!"

"Accident."

Maseo fell still, staring down into Kin's battered metal face. ". . . Accident?"

Shinji reached the engine room floor, stalking toward Kin, fists clenched. But as he drew close, an upper hatchway cracked open, another Artificer stepping onto the walkway, peering down at the three gathered below.

"By the First Bloom!" he called. "What happened?"

The two would-be assassins stared at each other, silent and grim. Kin dragged himself up on all fours and looked to the Artificer on the gantry above. His voice was matter-of-fact.

"I slipped," he said.

". . . You slipped?" The Artificer leaned over the railing, his voice incredulous.

Kin got slowly to his feet, gave a creaking shrug.

"My pack misfired. I nearly went right into the gear-train. Brother Shinji saved my life."

More Guildsmen began arriving in the engine room, all glowing eyes and chattering questions. They were met with the same explanation, repeated by a bloodied, battered Kin, now surrounded by concerned brethren. There was praise to the First Bloom, praise slapped onto Shinji's back, until finally it was resolved Kin should visit the medical station. The Fifth Bloom insisted it was too much fuss, that skin was strong though flesh was weak, but finally relented.

"Very well, brothers. It is better to be certain." Kin turned to his would-be killer. "Perhaps my savior would be generous enough to escort me?"

". . . Of course, Fifth Bloom." Shinji bowed. "I would be honored."

"The honor is mine, brother. I am in your debt."

The excitement faded, Guildsmen returning to their stations, several casting wary glances at the railing above the transmission. It was a miracle the Fifth Bloom had escaped unscathed. To think what might have happened if Brother Shinji had not been there . . .

Maseo stepped up and took Kin's arm, slung it around his shoulder. Shinji supported the other side, and the pair shuffled toward the spiral stairwell, Kin draped between them.

"Walk slowly, brothers," Kin said. "My legs are still shaking."

A humorless smile.

"And we have much to talk about, after all."

The listening post operator looked up as Kaori stepped onto the tower walkway. She dragged her fringe down over her face with one hand.

"Brother Isao has been compromised," she said. "Atsushi and Takeshi also. Send word throughout the network. Any intelligence from them must be viewed as suspect. Any transmission from them is to be ignored."

The signalman nodded. "Hai."

Without another word, she slipped down the ladder and off into the dark.

20
CAN'T AND WON'T

When it came to his "Ten Things I'd Rather Make Sweet, Sweet Love to the Dark Mother Than Do" list, Yoshi had decided "Flying On the Back of a Thunder Tiger" sat quite comfortably at number two.

"Falling Off the Back of a Thunder Tiger" was number one.

Oh, it was a pretty thing at first, to be sure. Storm growling at their backs as they sliced through the air, wind whipping through his clothes like knives. But once the initial thrill faded, Yoshi was left with a vague sense of wrongness about it all. The clutch of gravity. The vertigo as he peered into the drop below. If Lord Izanagi intended for him to be up here, he wouldn't feel like a virgin bride on her wedding night. And, to step aside from the metaphysical and into the practical for a moment, the saddle on Buruu's back had been made for a person with a different . . . configuration than his own.

Son of a ronin's whore, my balls are killing me.

YOU TELL ME THIS WHY?

Some sympathy would kill you?

I COULD KISS THEM BETTER FOR YOU?

You don't have lips, Mockingbird. You have a beak that can cut steel.

IT MAY END BADLY FOR YOU, YES.

Yoshi's hands were entwined in Buruu's feathers, freezing wind threatening to snatch the goggles from his face and hurl them into the mile-long drop beneath. He kept his eyes fixed on the southern horizon, squinting through the haze.

This smog is toxic. Makes me feel like tossing breakfast.

NOT ON MY BACK YOU WON'T, BOY.

Yoshi dared a quick glance at the land rushing away below them.

Looks so much worse from up here. I never knew it'd got so bad. You don't hear about it on the radio. You don't see the scope of it from the city. Fuckers have kept us so blind.

YOUR LAND IS DYING.

And here you are, fighting to save it. Not sure I see the point now. Even if the Guild was destroyed tomorrow, how the hells will you ever fix all this?

WHO SAID WE WOULD?

You must think there's a chance, or you wouldn't be here.

I DID NOT COME HERE TO SAVE YOUR HOME, BOY. I CAME BECAUSE I LOST MY OWN.

Family troubles?

ONE MIGHT SAY.

Know that feeling.

A curtain of rank black rain seethed across their path, so Buruu swept above the cloud cover, high into the freezing air. Yoshi curled into a ball of miserable shivers on his back, but peering over one wingtip, he realized he couldn't see the ground anymore—just a rolling floor of iron-gray that looked thick enough to catch him if he fell. And though he knew it preposterous, somehow the thought calmed him enough that his guts climbed down from his ribs.

Yoshi caressed the metal frame covering Buruu's feathers, watching the machinery at work as the beast's wings sliced the sky. The contraption was beaten, bent, held together by third-rate jury-rigging and a prayer. As he watched, a severed white feather fell away and drifted down into the abyss. Yoshi felt his stomach begin climbing again.

You sure these clockwork wings are flight-worthy?

THEY HAVE SEEN BETTER DAYS.

Where'd you get them?

A BOY MADE THEM FOR ME.

This Kin I heard about? The traitor?

YES.

Sounded like a little bastard to me.

NOT ENTIRELY TRUE. NOR ENTIRELY FAIR.

That knife in your back doesn't make you itch?

IT MAKES ME SAD. IF NOT FOR KIN, YUKIKO WOULD BE DEAD, AND I, A SLAVE. I WOULD NOT HAVE BELIEVED HIM CAPABLE OF BETRAYAL. PART OF ME STILL CANNOT.

We're all of us made of scars, Mockingbird.

IT IS WORSE FOR YUKIKO. SOON, THEY WILL BE ALL SHE IS.

You really care about her, eh?

ONE MIGHT SAY.

I don't want to offend you or anything, given our present altitude and the whole gravity thing, but she struck me as something of a bitch.

Buruu's growl traveled up Yoshi's spine as he added a hasty addendum.

Really nice cheekbones, though . . .

YOU DO NOT KNOW HER. WHAT SHE HAS BEEN THROUGH. THE WEIGHT OF THIS ENTIRE COUNTRY IS ON HER. SHE IS SEVENTEEN WINTERS OLD. HOW DO YOU THINK SUCH A MANTLE WOULD SIT ON YOUR SHOULDERS, BOY?

Badly. Why the hells you think I'm not in Yama right now?

Buruu remained silent, eyes narrowed against the howling wind.

Thing is, Mockingbird, I'm wondering the same thing about you.

WHAT?

Well, you love her so much, right? She's your dawning and dusk, I get it. So, if you don't mind me asking, why the hells are you flying my sorry ass around instead of being back there with her?

A long silence, battered by brief thunder.

. . . SHE ASKS WHAT I CANNOT GIVE.

Oh, really.

REALLY.

Might be I'm only eighteen summers aboard this ferry-ride, but couldn't say I've seen many fixes where folks genuinely can't *give what others ask. Most times it's all about won't.*

WON'T?

Won't pay the price. Won't do the dance. Won't kiss the girl.

Yoshi felt a grudging warmth in the thunder tiger's chest, something approaching a smile. Buruu dipped into the cloudbank, swooped up again with that same sense of abandon; a small child skipping across a field of sky.

YOU ARE A STRANGE ONE, BOY.

Yoshi laughed.

Hells, Mockingbird, coming from you, I'll take that as a compliment.

D ay frayed into night, and Yoshi did his best to sleep despite the cutting chill. They flew above the cloud cover, the white noise of distant rain like a lullaby. Anxiety chewed at him, and he could feel that same emotion building inside the thunder tiger's head. The farther away from Yama they drew, the worse it got. Close to dawn, Yoshi decided he'd used up enough of the arashitora's minutes.

Listen, you'd best be getting back. Yukiko will be fretting on you.

WE ARE NOT YET AT THE JUNCTION.

I can walk from here. Maybe catch a hand-car. Just drop me on the railway tracks.

AS YOU WISH.

Buruu swept down through the clouds. Thunder swelled, drumming on Yoshi's ears in a hymn of iron and engines. The cloud was thick as mud. Wet and freezing cold.

They were virtually on top of the sky-ship before they heard it.

As they swooped out of the gray, a three-man scout corvette flying Phoenix colors was cutting through the air alongside them, its arrow-tip inflatable adorned with a sunbird in flight. Yoshi and pilot caught sight of each simultaneously, both gawping in shock.

"Holy *shit!*" Yoshi cried.

The pilot roared in alarm, his marksman swiveling his shuriken-thrower just as Buruu came to his senses, banked hard and fell into a dive. Wrenching his controls, the pilot followed, motors screaming, spewing blue-black behind.

Yoshi and Buruu dropped like a stone, but looking over his shoulder, the boy was alarmed to find the tiny ship keeping pace. A chattering burst of shuriken fire filled the air, razored steel disks whizzing past his shoulders, skimming off Buruu's metal wings, and with a bang and a bright burst of sparks in his eyes, clipping the right side of his head.

"Ow, gods*dammit!*"

Yoshi reached up to the impossible pain, fingers coming away red and gleaming.

They chopped half my ear off!

OH. THAT IS TERRIBLE.

Fuck you, I needed that!

Buruu was spiraling down, trying to gain distance on their pursuers. Another burst of shuriken fire cut between the rain, Yoshi pressing low to Buruu's back.

THEY ARE SWIFTER THAN OTHERS I HAVE FOUGHT.

Up! Go up! No way they'll climb faster than you!

The thunder tiger pulled out of his dive and tore up toward the hidden sun. There was an awful moment as Yoshi glanced over his shoulder again—right down the 'thrower's barrel, down into that bottomless black, just waiting for it to open up and him along with it.

Fly, godsdamn you, fly!

HOLD ON TO ME.

The beast pulled up, wings tearing the iron-gray, Yoshi clinging with fingers and thighs and teeth. They looped up and over the sky-ship, the boy treating Buruu to the most imaginative burst of profanity he could conjure. The corvette's marksman lost sight of them, screaming for coordinates as Buruu completed his loop-the-loop, descending like a thunderbolt.

Their path took them through the dart. Not over or past, simply *through*—the dirigible shredding like paper, the ultralight frame disintegrating amidst the high-pitched scream of breaking metal and escaping hydrogen. The crew wailed as they tumbled free, trailing long sashes of bright Phoenix orange all the way down, like ribbons from the tails of dying kites.

Yoshi was sure the sound of them hitting the ground would come back to visit when the lights went out.

Izanagi's balls . . .

ARE YOU WELL?

Yoshi pressed hand to head, wincing as he touched what was left of his ear.

Hurts worse than my manparts, but I'll live . . .

He felt the thunder tiger tense, something close to fear rippling through the beast's mind. Buruu's eyes were fixed on the southern horizon, a low growl rumbling in his chest.

PERHAPS NOT MUCH LONGER.

What?

LOOK.

Yoshi squinted into the haze and rain.

I can't see anything.

USE MY EYES.

The boy complied, stepping into the warm dark behind the arashitora's eyelids, feeling his own lashes fluttering as the world snapped into shimmering brilliance. He was overcome with sensation; the vibrant predator rush, the thrill of the wind beneath his wings. Fear-tinged. And as he focused on the horizon, he felt it swell in his own gut—cold and slick and overshadowing the exhilaration of their brief victory.

A sky-fleet. So far away as to be mere specks, but Izanagi's balls, so many . . . A wall of black dust thrown up by the horde marching below. And there, towering above the ground, eyes aglow like vast ghost lanterns, a giant. A giant of black smoke and blacker iron.

EARTHCRUSHER.

Izanagi's balls . . .

The combined airpower of the Phoenix clan, a swarm of Guild ironclads—all of them looking like children's toys beside it.

. . . I MUST RETURN TO YAMA. TELL YUKIKO.

Think you better had.

YOU ARE STILL SET ON REVENGE? YOU WILL NOT STAND AGAINST THIS HOST?

What the hells is one gutter-rat going to do against that?

IF YOU DO NOT TRY? NOTHING AT ALL.

I owe a debt. And old Yoshi pays what he owes.

YOU COULD BE MORE, BOY.

Yoshi shook his head.

Not cut out to be a hero. I think this story has a few too many already.

They set down beside the railway tracks, a few hundred yards from a battered little station of corrugated iron. An old man in a broad hat was dozing against the cranks of his handcart, starting awake at the rumble of too-close thunder. He watched wide-eyed as the arashitora alighted on the bluestone, the boy hopping down lightly, the side of his face painted in blood.

You take care of yourself. Look out for my sister.

I WILL. IF YOU CANNOT LET IT REST, I WISH YOU LUCK IN YOUR HUNT, BOY.

Like I said there's can't and there's won't. Hope you can see the difference now. Or at least be honest about which is which.

The beast and the boy stared at each other, dirty rain filling the space between them.

PERHAPS WE WILL MEET AGAIN.

Never can tell.

FAREWELL, MONKEY-CHILD.

Fly safe, Mockingbird.

And with a creak of iridescent metal, the rush of a hungry wind, he was gone.

21
SLOWLY TO SCARLET

Her arms around his neck felt like coming home.

As if he knew what coming home felt like . . .

Gods, I was so worried, Buruu.

NOTHING TO FEAR. YOU ARE MY HEART, REMEMBER? I DIE WITH-OUT YOU.

Yukiko held him tight beneath the palace eaves as black rain sluiced down from above. He was soaked from his flight, eyes stinging from the tar. She pressed her cheek to his, heedless of the poison clinging to his quills.

Aren't I usually the melodramatic one?

NOT SO, LATELY, IT SEEMS.

I'll get some clean water. Wash this filth off you.

WE HAVE LITTLE TIME, YUKIKO. HIRO'S ARMY MARCHES. I HAVE SEEN THEM.

She licked her lips, nodded.

We have time enough to get you clean.

The girl padded away toward the kitchens, and Buruu stared at the storm raging above, lighting reflected in his eyes. Great Raijin, father of all arashitora, was busy on his drums, windows shaking with each rumbling peal. The chemical rain tumbled from darkening skies, slowly stripping all beneath it; poison pumped into lungs and earth and sky.

How completely it ruled this place. To think something so innocuous—one tiny flower—could transform the shape of the land so utterly. The engines and machines and treasures spitting tiny puffs of poison into once blue skies, turning slowly to scarlet. Killing the land one breath at a time, wrapped in a bow of blood-red petals.

Yukiko soon returned carrying buckets of almost-clean water from an underground Iishi spring. She began washing him down, black running through to gray and finally to pristine white again. He wasn't sure if the rain would eat at his feathers like everything else it touched, but his eyes felt full of sand, and Kin's device would surely be suffering.

I was worried about you, you know. When you flew away.

SO YOU SAID.

Where did you go?

YOSHI WAS HEADED SOUTH. I TOOK HIM PART OF THE WAY.

Hana told me he left. She never said why.

SOMETHING HE NEEDED TO DO.

It seems a selfish thing. To leave right when Hana needs him the most . . .

KAORI MIGHT SAY THE SAME ABOUT YOU.

. . . That's not fair, Buruu.

I THINK IT NEVER IS, STANDING ON THE OTHER SIDE.

Yukiko said nothing, scowling as she heaped more water over the contraption on his back. Black pooled around his feet, smelling vaguely of dead flowers.

I MUST GO ALSO.

Go where?

WHERE YOU ASKED. EVERSTORM.

Oh my gods! Truly? How far is it? How much food should I pack?

YOU ARE NOT COMING.

. . . The hells I'm not.

TOO DANGEROUS.

As opposed to staying here with the Earthcrusher and gaijin army?

YOU DO NOT UNDERSTAND. IT IS FIRE AND SCREAMING WIND. WHERE SUSANO-Ō PLAYS THE STORM ETERNAL TO KEEP THE GREAT DRAGONS IN THEIR SLUMBER. NO PLACE FOR YOUR KIND.

You're not leaving me. Not again. Don't you dare.

YOU ARE NEEDED HERE. THE PEOPLE WILL QUAIL WITHOUT YOU.

They have Hana and Kaiah.

SHE IS ONLY A GIRL.

What the hells do you think I am?

Buruu tilted his head, answered as if she had asked her own name.

YOU ARE A STORMDANCER.

And what's a Stormdancer without her thunder tiger? Where would Kitsune no Akira have been without Raikou? Who would have flown Tora Takehiko into Devil Gate if not Gufuu?

I WILL NOT LEAD THEM INTO DANGER.

His eyes flitted to her belly, to the iron breastplate covering the tiny bump of warmth.

Gods, don't start that again . . .

I DO NOT GO TO EVERSTORM FOR TALK, YUKIKO. I GO TO KILL OR DIE.

And you expect me to just sit here and pray?

WHO WILL BRING YOU BACK IF I FALL?

Why would I want to come back if you did?

FOOLISHNESS. YOU WILL BE A MOTHER SOON. MUCH TO LIVE FOR. MUCH TO FIGHT FOR. THIS WHOLE COUNTRY NEEDS YOU.

But I need you, Buruu. Don't you realize I can't do any of this without you?

She threw her arms around his neck, squeezing tight. He could feel the aching of her heart like a blade in his own chest, her fear turning his gut to water. This girl who meant more to him than life itself. This girl he loved with every moment, every breath, as much a part of him as the wind and the rain and blood in his veins.

I LOVE YOU, YUKIKO.

And I love you.

YOU MIGHT NOT SAY THAT. IF YOU KNEW.

He bowed his head, pushed his cheek against hers, the rumble of thunder overhead sending shivers down their spines.

IF YOU KNEW.

He felt her near that place; the place she'd never sought to enter despite the power and pain growing in her mind. A locked door, barred and rusted. The place he was at his worst. The place he'd lost his pride and his name and himself.

But she loved him. She'd always love him.

Wouldn't she?

Her thoughts were gentle as summer rain.

Show me.

And so he did.

To call it a storm would be to call the ocean a raindrop, a hurricane the spring breeze.

Lightning unending, the thunder a constant barrage. Rain like falling swords, a wind not so much a wall as a cliff, set against a vast blackness crashing like avalanches overhead. Jagged spires of dark stone, cracked at their summits and spitting fire into blackened skies. Ashes. Embers. Great floods of molten rock flowing from the earth's belly, cooling at the boiling ocean's touch until mountains stood tall and defiant in the seething oceans.

The throne of Susano-ō, god of storms. Here he made his music, the vibration seeping into volcanic water and lulling the great beasts beneath the waves. Vast as time they were. Old as gods themselves. Ancient and reptilian, a hunger ten thousand fathoms deep. Their children spiraled in the waves above their heads, scales of silver, katana teeth. But they themselves didn't stir. Not once had they woken since first Susano-ō offered to sing them to sleeping.

Their names were lost now to humans, swallowed in the shadows of myth and eon. But the arashitora remembered.

Niah and Ael. Father and mother of all dragons.

Atop the tallest volcano, now sullen and cooled, stood the aerie of the Khan; a series of tunnels in black stone, good and strong and warm. The wind kissed the fissure mouths, singing a haunting tune, all open endless vowels speaking of times long vanished, when Shima was but a dream in Lady Izanami's womb. Before her death. Before her fall. Before her vow of vengeance.

The whole pack would only gather when the Khan called a greatmoot, or when a female felt her first flushing and time came for the males to fight for her attentions. Then the pack would watch the blooding, the unmated bucks clashing across lightning-flecked skies, the mated males held in check by the musk of their own mates beside them.

But though they could go months without seeing each other, they were family. They were Pack. The last thunder tigers left in all the world, dwelling in their father's cradle and living free from the monkey-children and their burning flowers and poisoned skies.

The Others would come occasionally—young bucks mostly, black eyes and blacker feathers, flying from eastern lands to test themselves against the Everstorm's males. They would fight to the blood, a pseudo-war meant to test each other's strength. Occasionally, a thunder tiger female would go back with them, to the lands the monkey-children called Morcheba. Yet sometimes it was years between visits—years with none but the storm for company.

This was Buruu's world. All he'd ever known. Sitting atop the Khan's aerie now, looking out over the edge, stretching his little wings. Barely a year old, ready to fly for the first time.

His first real memory.

His mother beside him, warm and radiant. His brothers, Esh and Drahk, watching on. And circling above, their father. Mighty Skaa. The greatest arashitora alive. Khan of Everstorm.

Yukiko watched the memories in Buruu's mind, like a child watching a shadow pantomime. She felt his fear as he looked into the drop yawning at his feet—sharp fangs of black rock and frothing seas filled with hungry sea dragons. She felt him tremble.

You were son of the Khan?

ONE OF THREE.

That makes you a prince . . .

WE ARE NOT LIKE YOU. RULE IS NOT PASSED, IT IS TAKEN. ANY MAY CHALLENGE. WHO CLAIMS KHAN IS KHAN.

But the Khan is the strongest arashitora alive. And the strongest female will choose him. So his sons will be strong too, right?

STRONG IN SOME WAYS.

Buruu sighed.

WEAK IN OTHERS.

She watched from the cusp of memory as little Buruu pushed his fear down and dropped into the void. The wind snapped like starving wolves, threatening to dash him into the mountainside. The thunder was deafening, the Storm God's fury almost too much to endure. But he spread his wings wide as his father had told him to do, and he felt the air spirits beneath him, bidding him higher. He beat his wings, felt himself rise, elation and terror spilling out over his limits and filling the air. A roar of triumph. The first roar of their newest packmate.

The pack answered, young and old, thunder bellowing over all. A great day. A proud day. They were so few. Clinging to existence so tenuously, choked almost to extinction by Shima's poisoned skies. The toxins had ended most of the great yōkai—only those with the means and will to flee had survived the rise of the Lotus Guild. The phoenix had lay down and died of heartache as the skies filled with tar. The dragons had swum north as the oceans turned red.

The thunder tigers had departed at the behest of the last Khan of Shima. But still, they were not many. Even when the Khan's law ended ritual deathmatches for mating rights, proclaimed it unthinkable for an arashitora to kill another arashitora, they were slow to breed. Any day a cub first took to the wing was a momentous one; one step closer to crawling back from extinction's brink.

Buruu sailed skyward, pounding the wind with his little wings. He struggled toward the clouds, muscles straining almost to tearing. But at last he drew level, fell into place behind his father, calling out again to the packmates assembled below. Their answer filled him with pride.

The Khan was the last to answer, but also the loudest. And he looked back at

Buruu with unveiled pride and the special love a parent always holds for their youngest child.

I am proud of you, he called. *My Roahh*.

Yukiko frowned, ran her fingers through Buruu's fur.

"Roahh"?

THAT WAS MY NAME. ONCE. IT MEANS "TRIUMPH" IN OUR TONGUE.

Her voice was soft in his mind. Uncertain.

Would you rather I called you that? The name your father gave you?

Buruu hung his head.

THERE IS NO MEANING IN IT ANYMORE.

She released her hold, stepped away so she could look him in the eye. He saw no judgment, felt no dread in her chest. It didn't matter to her—the telling of this tale or what he'd done. All that mattered was that he was hers and she was his. Staring through the windows of her soul, he knew she'd forgive him anything. Everything.

Save perhaps if he left her alone again.

The Daimyo's palace trembled, thunder reminding him of the Earthcrusher's footsteps, even now trudging toward Kitsune-jō. His sigh was lost beneath the fury overhead.

THE REST WOULD BE BETTER TOLD AS WE FLY. WE MUST TRAVEL SWIFT IF WE ARE TO RETURN FROM EVERSTORM IN TIME. PRESUMING WE RETURN AT ALL.

Elation filled her, a fierce joy that brought tears to her eyes.

You'll take me with you?

TO THE HELLS AND BACK, IF YOU BID IT.

I should tell Michi and the others. And I should pack. Give me half an hour.

I WOULD GIVE YOU THE SUN AND THE MOON, YUKIKO. I WOULD GIVE YOU UNENDING JOY AND DAYS OF PEACE AND BLUE SKIES TO LAUGH AND SING BENEATH. BUT THESE ARE NOT MINE TO GIVE.

Just give me you. You're all I need.

YOU HAVE ME. ALWAYS.

Her hug was fierce as monsoon winds. They stood together, his wings folding about her with their broken, insect song, and the storm seemed to hush as if holding its breath. One last quiet moment. One deep inhale before the plunge. He closed his eyes. Felt her warmth, the warmth of the little ones inside her. His family now. His everything.

And then the storm fell again, her arms slipping away from his neck as she turned and dashed back into the palace, hair flowing behind her like black water. And he stood beneath the eaves, watching dark rain spilling in endless falls over the gutters, staining the withered leaves in the garden gray. Raijin's drums were no comfort. The stormsong, no lullaby. He looked at what lay ahead, what he must do and where he must go.

WHO CLAIMS KHAN IS KHAN.

He blinked up at the clouds, lightning in his eyes.

FATHER, FORGIVE ME.

22
SEVERED

Four figures stood in the shadows of the Daimyo's dojo.

Suits of teak and bamboo armor lined the walls, an honor guard of hollow warriors with wooden swords. The storm echoing overhead, wind slipping through the windowsills, shivering the circle of lantern light. And there they stood. In this nation of warlords and Shōgun. Of Daimyo and samurai and Lotusmen.

Four women who would change the face of the world.

"I can't believe this," Michi whispered. "You can't leave us now."

"I have to," Yukiko said. "There are dozens of arashitora in Everstorm. If Buruu and I can convince them to fight, we can win this war."

Misaki watched her with narrowed eyes, silver limbs rippling about her shoulders. "And if you cannot convince them? You will have taken our stormdancer and the people's hope."

"You have Hana for that." Yukiko nodded to the girl. "She can be the same figurehead I am."

"I'm not you, Yukiko," Hana said. "I'm not a hero."

"You can be anything you want. Fate deals us our hand, but we decide how to play it. We all of us choose the people we want to be."

"This is madness," Michi whispered. "What if the arashitora won't come with you?"

"She can make them," Hana said.

Michi raised an eyebrow.

"Kaiah told me about the Razor Isles." Hana was staring at Yukiko. "You held three sea dragons still with a wave of your hand. You killed men just by *looking* at them."

Michi looked at Yukiko in awe. "Gods above . . ."

"No," Yukiko said. "I don't want to make servants of these creatures. If I do, I'm no better than the tyrants marching against us."

"You may have no choice," Misaki said. "And at the end of the day, they are animals."

"They're more than that. And I won't be the one who enslaves them. *We* made this mess. *We* tore this country to shreds. If they won't help, we'll find another way."

"And what way would that be?"

Silence fell, edged with storm's teeth.

"The gaijin," Hana said.

The others turned to look at her. Her eye was glowing in its socket, warm light cast over her impish face, sharpened by a life spent fighting for scraps.

"Piotr said there's something about me. My eye. Maybe I should get to the bottom of it. The fact I'm half gaijin, this 'Zryachniye' thing . . . maybe it's something we can use . . ."

"The gaijin hate us," Yukiko said. "They're here to annihilate us. I can't understand what Piotr is talking about half the time. Who knows what he actually means?"

"I could try talking to him? Maybe something he'll say will make sense to me."

Yukiko pursed her lips, brow creased.

"Can't hurt," Michi said. "Maybe the gods brought Hana and Piotr together for a reason."

"Gods?" Yukiko scoffed. "What do they have to do with any of this . . ."

"Think about it. What are the chances of Akihito finding two gutter-waifs with the Kenning right about the time you find another thunder tiger? What are the odds we'd find ourselves standing here right now?"

"Kitsune looks after his own, Michi. It's just luck. Blind, stupid luck."

"In case you've forgotten your temple lessons, we have a god for that too," Michi smiled.

Yukiko licked her lips, finally nodded.

"All right, talk to Piotr. But don't do anything drastic until we return. It shouldn't take us more than a week to fly there and back. The Earthcrusher will be on our doorstep by then, but hopefully not ringing the bell." Yukiko turned to Misaki. "In the meantime, keep trying to get in touch with the other rebels. Maybe they already have people aboard the Earthcrusher."

Misaki nodded. "Almost certainly."

"And we need to think about First House. The Guild is throwing everything they have against us. That means their stronghold will be relatively undefended. We can take out their chi reserves when their backs are turned. Starve the Earthcrusher. Flee to the Iishi where they won't have the fuel to follow. Maybe even kill the First Bloom."

Michi nodded. "A wolf without a head is just a rug."

"Michi, stay close to Daimyo Isamu. He's a grumpy old bastard, but he seems a good man. You speak for me while I'm gone."

"Hai," Michi covered her fist and bowed.

"All right." Yukiko looked among them. "Everyone be careful until I get back."

Misaki bowed. Michi grabbed Yukiko in a fierce hug, Hana joining in, the trio standing motionless as the world around them shuddered in the storm's grip.

"You take care of yourself," Michi whispered.

"You too."

"Be careful," Hana said.

"Be brave."

They held on for a moment longer, there in the shivering light of their little circle, unwilling to let go. But each thunderclap reminded them of great iron legs pounding the earth, drawing closer every moment. And so they parted, slowly, arms falling to their sides, smiles from their lips, quiet tears from their eyes.

And without a sound, Yukiko turned and walked into the dark.

H e was waiting when she returned, slivers of curling cream piled around his feet. Sitting on a bench beneath the eaves, a wooden box in his hands. Buruu was watching him—those big, clumsy-looking fingers wringing elegant beauty from simple pine. His cornrows were fuzzed from the press of his pillow, flecks of sawdust caught in the resin tipped spikes of his beard.

Yukiko smiled.

"Akihito."

The big man looked up from his carving, put his knife away and brushed the shavings from his lap. He stood with a wince, one massive hand pressed to the wound that had never properly healed—the sword-blow he'd earned rescuing her father. Never complaining. Never questioning. As loyal as the day was long.

He looked her over, noting the overfull satchels across her shoulders.

"Leaving without saying good-bye, little fox?"

"I didn't want to wake you."

"Where are you going?"

"The Everstorm. Where the arashitora live. I'm going to ask them to help us."

"Didn't want to wake me, eh?"

A rueful smile. "Maybe I just didn't want a lecture about how dangerous it would be. How you're supposed to be looking after me now my father's gone."

"I think we're past that, little fox." The big man's smile was sad. "After Masaru died, I spent every moment trying to get back to you. To make sure you were all right. He would have wanted it that way. But now I find you, I see you don't need me at all." A shrug. "I feel a fool for thinking you ever did."

"Oh, Akihito . . ."

Yukiko hugged him, pressing her face into his chest. He squeezed her back;

one of his terrific, bone-grinding embraces that made her feel enclosed at the center of the world.

"You're such an idiot," she murmured. "I'll always need you."

"You're a woman now, little fox. A hero the whole nation looks up to."

"That doesn't mean I don't still need my friends. I love you, you big dunce."

"I love you too."

She stepped back, looked up into his eyes. "But my father is gone, Akihito. Kasumi too. The whole world is changing, but you're trying to hold on to the way it was."

He shrugged. "Other people is who I am. I've never been good at being alone."

"You remember when I was a little girl? You'd visit the bamboo valley when my father came home? You taught Satoru and I how to swim, remember?"

"I remember," he smiled.

"You'd stand in the middle of the river and get us to paddle out to you. And then you'd catch us in your arms."

"The water was like glass." He shook his head. "You could see clear to the bottom . . ."

"And in the summer after Satoru died, you took me down to the river and stood in the middle and told me to swim out to you. And so I climbed in and started swimming and you kept backing away. And at first I thought it was a game, but you kept backing off and I couldn't catch you. And I started to cry and I thought I was going to drown. Do you remember what you said?"

"I said, 'You're big enough to stand up by yourself now.'"

Yukiko smiled. "And I put down my feet and felt the bottom beneath me, and when I stood, the water only came up to my chin."

Tears shone in the big man's eyes, lips pressed tight as he tried to hold them back.

"You're big enough to stand up by yourself, Akihito," Yukiko said. "You've never needed my father. Or me. Or anyone. If you could see the you that I see . . ." She shook her head. "You're the strongest, bravest, kindest man I know."

He hugged her again, lifting her off the floor in that massive, crushing embrace. Not saying a word. Not even breathing. And then slowly, reluctantly, he put her down and let her go.

"You be careful," he said.

"Always," she smiled.

The big man turned to the thunder tiger, watching them both with wide, amber eyes. The beast he'd helped to hunt and bring down, what seemed like a lifetime ago.

"And you look after them, godsdammit."

Yukiko climbed up onto Buruu's back. "He promises."

"See you soon, little fox."

"Not if we see you first."

The creak of mighty wings, the roar of metal wind, and they were gone. Akihito looked down at all that remained—a single, snow-white feather lying on the damp boards, hacked in half by a madman's hands.

He stared at the poisoned rain, the tortured garden. This little fortress men had carved of iron and stone, heedless of the damage they were doing, the lives they were taking, the price they would pay. Not so different from a Shōgun and his katana. This was the bed they'd all made.

He stood in the dark and watched the rain fall.

23
A THOUSAND RED SUNS

THERE WERE THREE OF US. ESH, DRAHK AND I.

Shima was a muddy speck on the horizon behind, icy winds cutting through the woolens and oilskin Yukiko had wrapped herself inside. They flew above the storm, air so thin each breath was a knife in her throat, the frost leaving bite marks on her cheeks. She pressed herself to Buruu's warmth—the last fire in a world gone utterly black and cold.

You were the youngest?

YES. DRAHK THE OLDEST. FULL OF PRIDE AND FIRE. I LOOKED UP TO HIM AS IF HE MADE THE DAY BREAK AND THE MOON FALL. ESH THE MIDDLE SON. EVER UNSURE IN DRAHK'S SHADOW. EVER SEEKING TO PROVE HIMSELF.

Yukiko could feel a sadness in him, the same tinge of ashes and red she felt when she thought of her own brother. She could tell they were dead by the way Buruu spoke, and she hugged him fiercely, pouring into him with all the love she could muster. It was a long time before she could form the thought burning in her mind.

What happened to them?

Buruu sighed, eyes narrowed against the piercing wind.

WE GREW. HUNTING AND BRAWLING AS BROTHERS DO. ALL KHAN-SONS, EAGER TO PROVE OURSELVES. WE WERE NEVER HAPPIER THAN WHEN THE OTHERS CAME TO US FROM MORCHEBA; YOUNG BUCKS FLYING WESTWARD, FEATHER AND FUR AS BLACK AS NIGHT.

They came to fight you?

ONLY TO FIRST BLOOD. TESTING EACH OTHER. ARASHITORA DID NOT KILL OTHER ARASHITORA, AND IN OUR EYES, THEY WERE STILL

CHILDREN OF RAIJIN. THE MORCHEBANS HAD HUNTED THEM FOR THEIR SKINS UNTIL ONLY A FEW PACKS REMAINED. WE WERE ALL BROTHERS ON THAT BRINK OF EXTINCTION.

So what happened?

She saw an image in his mind's eye; a great, blood-red ocean, muddied by the perpetual storm overhead. A spire of gleaming obsidian rose out of the seething spray, flat-topped, like a nail piercing the ocean's face. She could see its name in Buruu's mind; the Bloodstone. Here the young bucks would meet, black and white, in summer when the tempest calmed and the hunger of the first sea dragons rose closest to surface. Their children would swarm in the oceans, thrashing through churning foam with long tails of glittering silver. The young arashitora males would gather and clash, their blood falling with the rain and driving the dragons to frenzy.

It was the fifth summer of Buruu's youth, his feathers and fur still off-gray, stripes not yet black. Esh was practically full-grown, and Drahk was old enough to be considered an adult—when next a dam came into heat, he would surely contest for the right to mate. They perched on the Bloodstone and watched the Others fly from the East, feathers as black as the spire beneath Buruu's feet. He sensed some familiar shapes and scents, others new, half a dozen in all. They landed on the stone's flat top, snuffling and preening before laying down to rest. The Everstorm bucks were in no hurry to commence hostilities—the contests sometimes lasted weeks.

Buruu watched the young females circling near the cloud line. They did an impressive job of appearing aloof, but all knew why they were here—scouting prospective mates among the Everstorm pack, feeding curiosity about the Morcheban blacks. He spotted one amongst the group, gray fur set with just the faintest impression of her stripes, dipping and rolling through the clouds. Buruu watched as if hypnotized, tail moving in confused, agitated arcs.

Who is she?

SHAI.

She's beautiful.

I THOUGHT SO, TOO.

The Others stirred, prancing for the females' benefit. This set the Everstorm bucks to growling, hackles raised, roaring challenge. Buruu took note of the new faces amongst the visitors—one particularly proud, a sleek head and a cruelly hooked beak, eyes burning emerald green. He roared his name was Sukaa, first-born of Torr, Khan of the Others. And though he was barely older than Buruu by the look, he would suffer no challenge from those not born of Everstorm's strongest. Prowling back and forth, he demanded to fight the sons of the Khan.

Drahk dismissed him with a glance. The buck was too young. No sport at all. Middle child and ever keen to fight, Esh accepted the challenge. And so the pair took to the air, two sleek, broad shadows on the wind, rolling amidst the thunder and circling like starving wolves around a haunch of bloody meat.

The arashitora below roared encouragement, and soon the pair joined, swooping comets of white and black shrieking across the skies. Sukaa was swift and fierce, but Esh was older, stronger by half. It soon became apparent the contest was one-sided. Buruu's brother toyed with the youngster, batting him about as a cat plays a mouse, embarrassing the arrogant Khan-son thoroughly before finally bloodying him with one great swipe down his flank. It was a fine blow, and would give Sukaa a nice, humbling scar to remember the encounter by.

The females roared their amusement in the distance as Esh returned to the Bloodstone amidst the approving crows of the Everstorm pack. The Others glowered darkly, displeased their Khan-son had been so thoroughly thrashed. Sukaa himself remained aloft, sulking, and soon two other males joined in battle, white and black lightning across the horizon. All eyes were on the contest. No one watched the thwarted Khan-son still circling above.

No one saw him dive.

Buruu noticed him in the final seconds, dropping like a thunderbolt toward his brother's head. He roared warning; Esh glanced up, flinched away—too late, too late. Sukaa crashed down atop him, flattening him on the stone, cracking bone. And raising his talons with a bloodcurdling shriek of rage, Sukaa struck at Esh's unprotected face.

Blood spraying. Shrieks of pain. Roars of outrage. Drahk and Buruu both charged the coward, smashing him from their brother's back. The Others joined in, and soon the top of the Bloodstone was a seething melee, flashing eyes and crimson sprays. Sukaa scrambled clear, torn and bleeding, taking to the wing. His pack followed, fleeing east, pursued for miles before the Everstorm bucks conceded the chase.

Back at the Bloodstone, Buruu and Drahk stood over their brother Esh, watching him struggle to his feet. His face was shredded, three bone-deep gouges running through his cheek. Where Esh's eye had been, Buruu could see only a torn and bleeding hole.

My gods . . .

SUKAA. THAT WRETCH. IF NOT FOR HIM . . .

Was he punished?

THERE WAS NO LAW ABOUT BLOODSTONE CONTESTS, BUT ALL WHO FOUGHT KNEW THERE WERE LIMITS. WE WOULD LEAVE OUR SCARS, YES, BUT NOT LIKE THAT. ESH WAS CRIPPLED. NO FEMALE WOULD WANT HIM, EVEN IF HE COULD WIN CONTEST FOR A MATE HALF-BLIND. WHAT FUTURE DID HE HAVE?

So what did your father do?

. . . HE DID NOTHING, YUKIKO.

Buruu dipped his wings, brought them closer to the clouds.
HE DID NOTHING AT ALL.

S he slept as best she could as night fell, binding her arms around his neck. It
was freezing above the clouds, her throat raw, teeth chattering like idle servants. The storm swelled as they flew ever closer to Buruu's birthplace, his past
coiled and waiting, patient as vipers. And so she curled up against his warmth,
listening to the rhythmic creak of his metal wings. The song of piston and gears
made her think of Kin, standing in Kigen arena with hurt plain in his eyes as she
accused him of betrayal.

"*I gave you my word. I gave Buruu his wings. I would never betray you, Yukiko.
Never.*"

Never . . .

She thought of their kiss in the graveyard, that brief wonderful beginning,
lips brushing soft as feathers against her own. And how it had all turned to rot in
the end.

Somewhere inside, she supposed she should feel sad about it—what could've
been. She should feel guilty for dragging Kin away from all he'd been, then running off to play hero and leaving him alone. But she thought of Daichi, probably
boiled into fertilizer inside some inochi vat. She thought of Isao and the others who
died during the Kigen raid, of Aisha in her machine bed, begging Michi to kill her.
She thought of the bloodshed to come, thudding its way toward Kitsune-jō. And
she grit her teeth and clenched her fists and whispered Kin's name like a curse.

*No matter how this ends, Kin. No matter who lives and who dies. I'll see you
pay for what you've done.*

She dragged freezing knuckles across burning eyes.

Tenfold.

YOU SHOULD BE SLEEPING.

She blinked, scratched Buruu at the join between neck and shoulder, her fingers numb inside her gloves. She could see tiny crystals of frost on his feathers.

How far are we from the Everstorm?

*CAN YOU NOT FEEL IT IN THE KENNING? CAN YOU NOT SIMPLY
REACH OUT AND TOUCH THEM, EVEN AT THIS DISTANCE?*

. . . I haven't tried.

YOU STILL FEAR THIS THING. THIS POWER IN YOU.

*Is that so wrong? I don't understand it. My father never told me it could be like
this. It's all I can do to shut it out sometimes. I can feel it building behind the wall
I've built. It hurts, even now, speaking to you like this. And I'm afraid of what will
happen if I let it go. Will I hurt you?*

She glanced down to her belly, hidden behind plates of reticulated iron.

Will I hurt them?

THE POWER COMES FROM THEM. FROM THE GODS. IT WILL NOT HARM THEM.

You sound like Michi. The gods don't have anything to do with this.

YOU RIDE ON THE BACK OF A CHILD OF RAIJIN.

That's nonsense. Your father was called Skaa. You're just flesh. Meat and bone, like all of us. You're no more the child of a deity than I am.

PRECISELY.

There are no gods in this story, Buruu. No hands reaching down from the heavens to help or hurt us. There's just us. Us and the enemy.

YOU MAY THINK DIFFERENTLY WHEN YOU FEEL THEM.

Who?

NIAH. AAEL. FATHER AND MOTHER TO ALL DRAGONS. SLUMBERING IN SUSANO-Ō'S SONG. THE GODS ARE NO CLOSER TO THE WORLD THAN IN EVERSTORM, SISTER. SAVE PERHAPS IN THE HELL YOUR KIND HAS MADE OF SHIMA.

Well, I can't feel them. We're too far away.

I CAN FEEL THE POWER WITHIN YOU, YOU KNOW. IT IS YOURS IF YOU CHOOSE TO CLAIM IT. STORMDANCER. THE GREATEST OF THEM ALL, SHOULD YOU WISH IT.

I don't.

YOU ARE AFRAID.

You would be too.

THERE IS NO SHAME IN FEAR, SAVE WHEN WE LET IT RULE US. I KNOW IT HURTS. I KNOW IT FRIGHTENS YOU. BUT THIS POWER WITHIN YOU MAY SHIFT THE TIDE THAT SWELLS AGAINST US.

You don't know that.

I KNOW IT IS PART OF YOU. AND I KNOW IF YOU DO NOT MASTER IT, IT WILL EVENTUALLY MASTER YOU.

Yukiko sighed, dug her fingers into his fur.

TRY.

I don't want to hurt—

JUST TRY.

. . . All right.

She breathed deep, feeling him inside her head, his heat entwined with the heat in her womb. And closing her eyes, she focused on the wall she'd built between herself and the force within. A dam of pure will, stemming the power in her mind. And focusing on the tiny crack she allowed the Kenning to leak past, she clenched her fists and stepped through.

A hurricane of fire. Blazing in her psyche with the heat of a thousand red suns. She could feel herself burning, scarlet warmth spilling down the lips of the flesh on the thunder tiger's back. Fear gripped her, an abyss opening up beneath her feet and willing her down. Buffeted by flaming winds, breath toiling in her chest, she opened her eyes and watched the fire dance. Immolating, enveloping, like the heat of all the animals and people she'd seen when last she opened herself wide. But it was different now—not just the heat of the beast she rode, the children inside her, the thousand lives sparkling in the waves below her feet. And, eyes open and gleaming, tears streaming down her face, she recognized the firestorm for what it was.

The Lifesong of the World.

The rhythmic existence of all around her—not just individual sparks, but life *itself*. The pulse of creation's totality. She could feel everything.

Everything.

Gods, it's beautiful . . .

She reached out to the Everstorm ahead, the flares of heat nesting and soaring around mountains of burning stone. The serpentine trails of sea dragons cutting the waves, long echoes of themselves trailing behind them in blazing ribbons, circling above the living infernos coiled around the islands' base. Vast and reptilian, ancient as moon and stars, slumbering in Susano-ō's lullaby. Scales as thick as city walls. Hearts as vast as fortresses, pumping blood like oceans through veins wide as avenues. Power and majesty like she'd never imagined.

I feel them.

The smile on her lips made her want to cry.

Buruu, I feel everything.

Reaching back the way they'd come, fingertips brushing Shima's edge. She could feel Kaiah, blurred in the impossible distance, sleeping fitfully beneath the eaves of Kitsune-jō. Little Tomo, curled up at Michi's feet and dreaming of dinner. She reached over the fortress, felt the pulses and life of everything within it: samurai on the walls, servants rising before the sun, the old Daimyo in his study, Guildsmen locked in his dungeons, even the blinded madman chained in the deepest, darkest cell, still aching with lotus withdrawal.

The Inquisitor.

His eyes were open. Bloody holes, black as deadlands fissures, splitting wider every season, every earthquake, leading down, down to gods knew where.

Gods knew where.

He can see me.

The Inquisitor was smiling at her. Rigid as iron, stretched against his bonds, lips peeling back from stained teeth. Empty sockets where his eyes used to be, swathed in bloody gauze, and yet she knew beyond any doubt that he *saw* her, just as she saw him. With those sightless holes the color of deadlands fissures, leading down.

Down.

The little ones are already here, after all . . .

And beyond him . . .

"No!"

She closed it off, fled behind the wall of herself and slammed it shut, lips and chin crusted with frozen blood. Curling up against Buruu's spine, shivering from nothing close to cold. The arashitora's concern was obvious, but she kept him locked outside, fingertips tingling, head still ringing with the Lifesong and the memory of those sightless eyes staring right at her.

Through her.

Buruu began fretting, growling and whining, until finally she opened up a crack and allowed herself to leak into his mind; an old, familiar warmth, the heat of a fireside in a favored inn, nestling down in the cushions and knowing you are welcome. You are safe.

WHAT DID YOU SEE?

I don't know.

She shook her head.

. . . Something awful.

WHAT?

Something's coming. Not so close that I could see. But close enough to taste.

I DO NOT UNDERSTAND.

Nor do I, Buruu. But we need to get to Everstorm and back to Shima. Quickly. All this, Hiro, Earthcrusher, everything we do . . .

She closed her eyes, tried to forget that bloody, sightless stare.

WE ARE A DAY AWAY. PERHAPS TWO.

We won't have much time to convince the arashitora to come with us . . .

THERE WILL BE NO CONVINCING. ONLY COMMANDING.

No, Buruu. I told Michi and I'll tell you the same. I'm not using the Kenning to force—

NOT YOUR COMMAND, SISTER.

Yukiko felt a faint growl building in his chest.

The thunder below was a rolling echo.

MINE.

24
WITHIN

Piotr stood in the muddy garden, heavy boots spattered black, eyes upturned to the clouds. He chewed his bone pipe, occasionally casting mournful looks into the empty honeyweed pouch inside his jacket. Face woven of scar tissue. Skin like a corpse.

The rains had ceased, but a freezing squall filled the skies, moaning amidst the rafters. Hana watched him for moments without count, burning curiosity finally bidding her speak.

"Piotr-san."

The gaijin met her gaze with those eyes of ice-blue and blind-white, instantly turning them to the floor. He stepped back, gave her a confused bow, one hand on his heart.

"Zryachniye," he murmured.

She stepped down into the garden, leaves and trees smeared with black rain. The glass-sharp stink of faint toxicity cut the air, a soft sear tickling her throat. Walking across the muddy ground to stand before him, she noted the way he refused to meet her gaze.

"I need to talk to you," she said.

"Is what for her talking?"

"My eye. I need to know what it means."

A shrug. "Is meaning for she Zryachniye."

"But what does *that* mean?"

"She sees." He pointed to the sky. To his chest. To the earth. "She sees."

"See what?"

"Cannot be saying. No one be knowing until she is for the waking."

She frowned. "But I'm not asleep . . ."

"She is." A smile deepened the scars on his cheeks. "She is sleeping, pretty girl. Eye still closed."

"All right, so wake me up then."

"Me?" The gaijin glanced up momentarily, something close to fear in that blue-blind gaze. "No, not for me to be the waking. She must stay for the white. Must be keeping for the self. Not me for her touching to be, no. Could not. Would never."

Hana slumped down on a stone bench, clutching the hair at her temples. "Izanagi's balls, I don't know what the *hells* you're saying . . ."

"Other Zryachniye." Piotr knelt beside her in the muck, hand outstretched as if seeking permission to touch her. When she didn't object, he held her fingertips, gentle as a child. "They wake you. They know. The others make she for seeing."

"Others like me?"

"Like her." Piotr dropped her hand as if it burned him. "They show. They know."

"But there *are* no others like me."

"The Imperatritsa, she Zryachniye. Many like pretty girl. And here." The gaijin pointed east. "Coming here. Army would not making for war without them. They see. See for the many big things. See for the victory."

"There are Zryachniye with the gaijin forces in Shima?"

"Must be." A nod. "Must. Sister Katya, at least. Maybe for more."

Hana licked her lips, reached beneath her collar to the leather thong hanging around her neck. The golden amulet her mother had given her years ago, set with the tiny stag and its crescent-shaped horns. Piotr's eyes widened as she pulled it out.

"Do you know what this means?"

"Where is she finding for this?"

"My mother gave it to me. My tenth birthday."

Piotr stared, pity gleaming in the sapphire depths of his eye.

"She Mostovoi." A nod, slow and heavy. "Your mother. She Mostovoi."

"What is that?"

"Mostovoi is first house to meet Shima. Twenty years past. City of Mriss. Great city, where your family live. But gone." A sigh. "All gone."

"They took her as a slave." The words tasted awful in her mouth, black and sharp and metallic. "Gave her to my father for saving the life of some samurai lord. He kept her. Hid her." Memories coming in a barrage: her mother dead on the floor, her father beside her. The truth of what she was and how she'd come to be came down like a hammerblow. "Raped her."

Her mother had never spoken of herself or her past. Never once in all those years. Maybe it hurt too much to remember. Maybe she was ashamed of what she'd become. Of the half-breed babies she'd been forced to bring into this hellhole.

Of us . . .

But that was self-pity speaking. Their mother had loved Yoshi. Loved her too. Why would she have given Hana this amulet, if not to instill some pride in what she was? If not to speak a truth words couldn't shape? Too painful to voice?

"We deserve it, Piotr." She scowled at the black mud under her feet. "Your people coming here. Killing and burning. Gods, part of me hopes they annihilate us."

"Not her, no." Piotr seemed genuinely appalled. He glanced at her hair, the blond roots clearly showing under the cuttlefish dye. "Kill for the Goddess-touched? No. Great shame. Black omens. Would never touch Zryachniye for the killing. *Never.*"

"Goddess-touched?" Hana looked up, heart beating quicker at the words.

"See." He held out his hand. "Pretty girl." Held another fist high in the sky.

"Goddess." He brought his hands together. "Zryachniye." The gaijin pulled up his sleeve, traced the blue lines of his veins beneath his impossibly pale skin. "In her."

"In me?"

A nod.

"In *you*."

S he wandered the palace halls, listening for his voice.

Past guardian statues of Fox in every doorway, coiled upon his nine flowing tails, stone eyes bright and laughing. In the days when Shima's kami walked the land with earthly feet, each had blessed their people with a touch—a gift from the spirit realm. Tiger had bestowed ferocity, Dragon gave courage, Phoenix an enduring vision and artistic spark. Fox had given his people the most capricious gift of all—the gift of uncanny good fortune. Imagining the army stomping over the deadlands toward Kitsune-jō, Hana wondered how long their luck would last.

She padded through granite halls, past the tapestries depicting Shima's myths: Lady Izanami's death; her husband's failed search through the Yomi underworld; his wife's vow to kill one thousand of Shima's residents every day. In the legend, Lord Izanagi had replied, "Then I will give life to fifteen hundred." Whenever she'd heard the tale, even as a little girl, Hana had always thought Izanagi's vow would be poor comfort to the thousand who'd already died that day.

So much death. Was this war the work of the gods, as Michi said? Were the hands of the Maker and the Endsinger behind this unfolding catastrophe? Was the gaijin Goddess somehow inside her, as Piotr insisted? Were they all just playthings of the immortals? Or was Yukiko right? Were the gods no more involved than the wind or rain?

Clanless as she and Yoshi were, Hana never had a kami to pray to. No Dragons or Foxes watching over her. No desperate prayers for a scrap of food or place to sleep answered.

If there *were* gods, they were hard to see from the gutter . . .

She glanced at her wrist, at the pale-blue scrawl just below the surface.

Maybe I was looking in the wrong place.

She wandered the verandahs in the bitter chill, searching the kitchens, snatching up a handful of honeysponge out of habit born of a lifetime's starvation. Through the barracks, cheeks stuffed and chewing quickly. Listening to the tune of steel and iron, soft murmurs of warriors looking down the barrel at a war they couldn't win. The percussion of servants' feet, the courtiers skulking in corners, appraising her with narrowed eyes—this gutter-trash who called herself Stormdancer. A pale shadow beside the girl of pure Kitsune blood who'd slain a Shōgun, ended a dynasty, urged the entire nation to rise.

Pretender, she could almost hear them say.

Counterfeit.

She thought of her brother. Gods knew where. Arms wrapped around herself, wondering if she should bother praying for his safety to gods who'd never answered. Everything moving so fast. She needed something to hold on to. Something strong as mountains.

And then she heard his voice. The baritone rumble sinking to her belly, setting the butterflies free. A smile on her lips, growing as she rounded the corner into the dojo and saw him standing there, surrounded by a forest of training dummies. Tall and scruffy-handsome, his beard fashioned into those ridiculous spikes, deep scars cutting through the Phoenix ink on one massive bicep. Akihito.

Akihito and Michi . . .

The girl stood before him, a beautiful flush on her cheeks and a pair of training swords in her hands, the dummy in front of her practically weeping with relief at this moment's respite. She was smiling, ribbons of raven hair plastered to the sweat on her face. Akihito was smiling too, those big hands wrapped around a box of beautifully sculpted pinewood; a scrollcase carved with a relief of cherry blossoms and the kanji for "truth."

Michi took the box, bowing from the knees and laughing like music. Akihito gave a clumsy bow in return, blushing, and the girl stood on tiptoes and kissed his cheek, one hand resting lightly on his forearm. And Hana's butterflies withered and died, and her stomach fell down into her toes and the smile on her lips faded until there was nothing. There was no one.

No one.

As she walked away, as fast as she could without breaking into a run, she looked down at her wrist. The pulse hidden just beneath the skin.

No one but me.

S he stood in front of the mirror hours later, bleach-burn scratching her eye. The air draped with bathhouse steam, the towel wrapped twice around her body, finger-thin from years of privation. She stared at herself, eyeline drifting up from her feet, over the subtle curve of her thighs and hips, her almost-flat chest. The leather thong around her neck, the tiny stag with the crescent-shaped horns meeting her stare with unspoken questions in his eyes.

A pointed chin in an impish face. Just like her brother's. Just like her mother's. A patch of leather over the hole the Gentleman had left behind—the yakuza boss with his dead stare and fistful of pliers. The memory made her tremble. The thought of Daken made her eye brim with tears. Images of Jurou made them fall. Iris softly glowing, the color of rose-quartz, telling the secret of her birthright. Of who she really was.

Stormdancer?

Or Zryachniye?

Finally, her gaze fell upon her hair, plastered flat, dripping wet. Childhood memories of her mother dyeing it burning in her mind. From the time she could talk, she'd been taught to pretend she was something else. Golden locks concealed beneath black ink, milk-white skin obfuscated behind fancies about Kitsune heritage.

Living a lie. Telling it so often she'd begun to believe it herself, so obsessed about hiding her truth she'd never discovered what it really was. Beyond the Kenning. Beyond the "Impurity" Guildsmen would have immolated at the Burning Stones. The truth of her blood, at last stripped of its black veil. She stared at it now; an unruly bob flattened by bathwater's weight, draped about her high cheeks and framing that eye of glowing rose-quartz.

Beautiful blond hair.

And in her mind, thunder flared. Wings pounding like a heartbeat. A storm-born ferocity, swelling inside her like a hurricane. An intent not just to be a stormdancer's shadow, not to be the girl others only looked to when Yukiko wasn't around. All her life, she'd fought. Every breath. Every scrap. The future of the entire nation hung in the balance. And if Piotr spoke truth, she had the power to do something about it. To find out who she truly was.

To *see*.

She ran her fingers through the natural blond, unveiled at last, staring at the girl staring back at her. A girl she didn't know. Had never bothered to. But she'd been there all along, waiting for this day. This truth. This moment.

Hana reached out through the storm for Kaiah's distant thoughts.

You want to fly with me?

- ALWAYS. WHERE? -

She touched the mirror, pressing her hand flat against the glass.

The girl she didn't know did the same.

Home.

T he walls of Kigen Station echoed with the hiss of pistons, violent sprays of water vapor, bubbling chi-exhaust. The platforms were lined with fresh-faced boys in unscarred armor, new-forged weaponry in hand, coughing in the rolling fumes. Lenses of polarized glass to hide frightened stares. Kerchiefs of dirty scarlet to conceal bloodless expressions. Platoons of brand-new bushimen, recruited from fair Kigen's slums with the promise of regular meals and a place to belong and a cause so glorious it was worth dying for.

Yoshi watched them as his train shuddered to a stop, shaking his head.

The rail-lines were still running, shipping soldiers northward. But as the engines sped back toward Kigen, the carriages were virtually empty, and some quick coin pressed into a conductor's palm had bought Yoshi a berth on a fast south-bound. So here he was, stepping onto the platform and ducking through the front-line fodder, pulling a broad, bowl-shaped hat over his head and thanking whatever gods listened it was them instead of him.

"Best of luck, gentlemen," he muttered, making his way through the forest of spears.

If any of the boys heard him, none replied.

He stepped into the smoke-stained boulevard, tempted to breathe deep but knowing he'd regret it. Staring out over the city where he'd grown, the alleys where he'd run, the streets he'd ever call home. The ramshackle cesspool of Downside, shrouded in exhaust and sin. The twisted refinery, spattering gray storm clouds black. The pentagonal spire of Chapterhouse Kigen. The Market Square and the Altar of Purity, where Guildsmen filled the skies with the screams of burning children. Yoshi saw posters on every wall, marked with the First Bloom's seal.

"*At weeksend, a one and two-thirds measure of chi and five iron kouka shall be granted to any loyal citizen who walks the path of righteousness and brings forth any Impure for judgment upon this city's Burning Stones.*"

People scurrying to and fro, blades hidden beneath their clothes. An auto-mated Guild crier lying broken in the street, clockwork guts spilled over broken cobbles. Beggar monks wandering amidst smoke and ashes, speaking of comfort and bringing none. Screams from an alleyway, the rhythmic hymn of violence. A hungry child, crying to a world that simply didn't care anymore.

The heart of Shima. Its mighty capital. This dirty, scab-kneed whore called Kigen.

How he loved her.

Yoshi reached into the Kenning, searching for the legion of flea-ridden ver-min crawling her nethers like lice. He sensed them all around, sleek and hungry, their shapes more comforting than an army of thunder tigers. Crawling the gutters, fighting in the filth, chewing on the bones of the dead. Harder than the iron the little soldier boys hid themselves inside. Harder than the walls these men built to cower behind. The city's eyes, her brood, her very blood, flowing along her alleys and seeing and knowing and feeling everything.

All her secrets.

All her sins.

He closed his eyes, breathed the stink. His voice echoed in their minds.

Old Yoshi is home, little friends.

His smile gleamed like broken glass.

And he's brought the Nine Hells with him.

25
HARBINGER

Enough waiting.

Enough thinking, debating, doubting. Enough wondering if this was the right way, if he should think of another. Enough images of an old man who'd trusted him with his *everything*, now probably heaving his last breaths in some lightless cell.

This road was paved with blood. Kin knew that before he first put his foot upon it. That he'd soon be wading knee-, waist-, neck-deep. Trying not to drown. But there was no room for doubt in this arena. His voice couldn't quaver, his hands couldn't shake. Too many had given up too much for him to get this far. To stumble now . . .

Kin shook his head, voice low. Four shadows gathered in a subsidiary exhaust shaft, whispering beneath cycling vents and engine's thunder.

"We're three days from Kitsune-jō." Sweat stung his eyes, and he longed to tear off his helmet and paw it away. "We need to speak with the other rebels. Tell them our plan."

"I'm trying," said brother Bo. "Every spare moment I get at the comm-station I'm trawling the Yama frequencies. But First House are jamming the rebel mech-abacii. Radio is the only way they'll hear us, and I can't speak openly up there."

"We need to talk to them, godsdammit. Didn't you plan for this?"

"We didn't know Chapterhouse Yama was going to be destroyed, Kin-san. When we were assigned to Earthcrusher, the rebels in Yama were still hidden."

"Don't fret, Kin-san," Shinji said. "I've converted one of the engine room comm-stations to receive outside transmissions. We just need to jack it into the bridge aerial relay and we can transmit and receive as we like."

"And I'm doing that tonight," Bo whispered. "You just worry about yourself. Unless I missed a meeting, nobody put you in charge of us."

"Peace, brother," Shinji warned.

"Maseo and I have rigged the engines," Kin said, keeping his voice even. "There's a grenade cluster hidden inside the primary venting shaft."

Bo nodded. "Good. When the battle for Kitsune-jō begins, you blow the primary cooling system and seal off the engine room. Then set the RPMs to redline. Shinji cuts access from bridge control so Commander Rei can't override, and the combustion chambers will overheat in a few minutes. That'll set the chi to boiling and blow Earthcrusher sky-high."

"How much time will we have to get out?" Shinji asked.

"Plenty for us upstairs. For Kin and Maseo, it'll be closer."

"Well, we tried to kill you once already, Kin-san." Shinji laughed. "Once more won't hurt, I suppose."

"Nobody else is dying." Kin looked back and forth between the three rebels. "Enough people have ended already because of this war. Nobody else dies in this story, agreed?"

"Hai," the rogue Guildsmen nodded, bloody eyes aglow.

"Bo, be careful setting up that comms intercept tonight. Commander Rei is Kensai's man, and Kensai was no fool. He wouldn't have let a fool pilot his master-piece either."

"Could be worse," Shinji said grimly. "We could be dealing with Kensai him-self. That old bastard is sharp as knives. Can you imagine trying to pull this off under his nose?"

Kin shook his head. "Kensai is still in a coma. The explosion almost killed him. Far as I know, they don't think he'll ever awaken."

"Kensai isn't our concern," Bo said. "Keep your eyes open and head down. When the Earthcrusher blows, it's going to take anything inside a kilometer with it. We can decimate the Tora infantry before the battle begins. We can win this war. But we must focus. We *cannot* fail."

Nods around the circle. Clasped hands, brass grinding brass. The shadows parted, heavy footfalls fading into the sea of engine noise as they drifted away, leaving Kin alone. Thinking of an old man who'd trusted him with his everything. Thinking of pale skin and long black hair like a ribbon of midnight, surrounded by Iishi perfume. Putting her arms around his neck, standing on tiptoes, eyelids fluttering closed.

"Kiss me," she'd breathed.

He closed his eyes. Hung his head. His whisper drifting in the air on crippled wings.

"Yukiko . . ."

B o stepped onto the Earthcrusher bridge with his heart in his windpipe. Swallowing hard, he peered around the chamber. Commander Rei was in his pilot's harness, accelerator stirrups at half-pressure, Earthcrusher plod-ding slow enough that the swarm of shreddermen at its feet could keep pace. The impact of each colossal step sent a tremor through the vessel, but Bo was accus-tomed to it. When the army bedded down for the evening and Earthcrusher came to a halt, it took him hours to find sleep. The silence seemed unnatural after a day of earth-shattering percussion.

DOOMDOOMDOOMDOOM.

DOOMDOOMDOOMDOOM.

The instrumentation lining the walls spat and chattered, gauges and levers and dials, speaking with the stuttering voices of countless punch-card interfaces. Greasy air, smeared thin over every surface, dampening color to a washed-out palette of grays and drabs.

Bo stood before the pilot harness, bowing low.

"Have you need of anything, Commander?"

Rei didn't turn his head. "I abide, brother Bo. See to your station."

"Hai." Bo sat at the communications hub, conscious of the signal splitter tucked into his belt. After a few moments, he allowed frustration to creep into his voice, turned to Rei.

"Commander, we are receiving inordinate background static on internal frequencies. The personnel decks are virtually inaudible."

Rei's head turned slightly. "The cause?"

"Apologies, Commander, I do not know. With permission, I will perform a diagnostic?"

"Swift as the wind, brother."

A shatei appeared at Bo's side, as if he'd coalesced from the greasy air.

"Can I offer assistance, brother?"

Bo nodded, kept his voice calm. "Can you head to the personnel deck and check if there is a problem at their end? It may not be the bridge hub."

"Hai." The Shatei marched into the elevator, doors ratcheting closed behind him.

Bo glanced around the bridge, looking for curious eyes. But every other Artificer seemed intent on their tasks. He unscrewed the communications hub faceplate, handfuls of insulated wire spilling out as if from an eviscerated belly. He searched spools of dirty reds, greens, blues, and reaching to his belt for the signal splitter, began splicing the device into the reception array. He was halfway through the installation when the Shatei on the personnel deck radioed in, reporting he could find no fault. Bo signaled thanks, licking sweat from his lips.

Glancing over his shoulder at Commander Rei. The other brethren. Listening to the elevator bringing back the Shatei from his fool's errand. Clipping wire, reconnecting, clamping circuits shut, hands definitely shaking now. If someone were to pass by, to glance over—

A metallic bang from the fuel gauges. A curse, rasping and metallic.

Rei's voice, demanding explanation. A hasty apology from the Artificers, one stooping to retrieve the tool he'd dropped. Bo gritting his teeth. Elevator doors opening. Heavy footsteps. Rasping breath. Engaging. Faint whispers of static. The brother's voice in his ear.

"Shatei Bo?"

Done.

"I found the problem, brother." Bo lifted the faceplate back into position with a nod, began driving the screws home. "Loose wiring, nothing complex."

"Always the little things."

Bo forced a laugh. "My thanks for your assistance."

"Always." A bow. "The lotus must bloom."

"The lotus must bloom."

A sigh of relief, a quick check to see if his surgery had upset any instrumentation. But no, all seemed in order. The splicer would allow Shinji's jury-rigged comm-system to piggyback off Earthcrusher's aerial—with a few hours spent trawling the prearranged stations, they should be able to contact the Yama rebels. The Kitsune could then prepare for the assault without needing to factor in Earthcrusher or the Tora infantry who'd die in the resulting explosion. The carnage would be almost unthinkable. But this was war. Those soldiers were their enem—

Bo's comm-station clicked into life, message incoming. A series of authentication codes identified the transmission source as Chapterhouse Kigen, and the transmission itself as Priority Red. After a burst of static, the message began, spoken swiftly by a distorted metallic voice. Bo's breath seized in his throat as he listened. He was barely able to acknowledge, send back the proper sign-off. He found himself sitting numb, struggling to breathe. Hands in fists, he swiveled in his chair and stood, stepping down the metal stairs to stand before the pilot's harness.

Rei's eyes were still locked on the horizon. "What is it, brother Bo?"

"Priority Red message from Chapterhouse Kigen, Commander."

That got Rei's attention. He pulled back on the stirrups, slowing Earthcrusher's advance, turning to stare at Bo with his shifting telescopics. "Report."

"Second Bloom Kensai has awoken from his coma. He is sorely wounded, but the False-Lifers say he will make a full recovery."

"First Bloom be praised. But why was this sent Priority Red? And encoded?"

"Second Bloom does not wish anyone outside this vessel to be aware of his intentions."

"Intentions?"

Bo nodded. "Second Bloom intends to oversee the destruction of the Kagé and all who abet them personally. He is traveling here to do so."

A murmur of delight rippled amongst the assembled bridge staff. Rei rose up in his pilot's harness, amazement in his voice. "Kensai is coming to the Earthcrusher?"

"Hai."

Bo nodded, dread dancing on his tongue.

"He is already on his way."

26
THIS MOMENT

Her ears had long ago gone numb and empty, the barrage of wind and rain and thunder turning all to hollow glass. There was no sunlight, not even a broken promise beyond the mile-deep cloud, as if Lady Amaterasu were afraid to show her face in the realm of her hated brother, Susano-ō. But Yukiko still wore her goggles, if only to spare her eyes the constant strobe of blinding blue-white. Spreading across the roiling gray like cracks in the sky itself, the ceiling of the world poised to crumble and crush everything below.

Like nothing she'd ever imagined. A war. A bedlam.

Everstorm.

Buruu thrilled to every lightning strike, purred with every thunderclap. His love of the chaos spilled into her, and she found herself grinning as if moon-touched, drenched to her very bones by the sideways rain. Wind like a hurricane. Thunder like a marathon pulse.

How close are we?

VERY.

What should I expect when we get there?

BLOOD.

Buruu's growl traveled up her thighs, settled in her belly.

BLOOD LIKE RAIN.

Torr?

YES.

Finish the story. What happened after Sukaa blinded your brother? You said your father did nothing? Wasn't he angry?

FURIOUS. BUT WE WERE ARASHITORA. NOT LIKE HUMANS. NO JUDICIARY. NO MAGISTRATES. THERE IS ONLY BEAK AND TALON. ONLY BLOOD FOR BLOOD.

Couldn't he demand Sukaa be blinded too?

HE DID. A MESSAGE WAS SENT TO MORCHEBA. KAIAH'S MATE DELIVERED IT—AN ARASHITORA CALLED KOUU. MY FATHER DEMANDED SUKAA RECEIVE A PUNISHMENT FITTING THE CRIME.

And what did Torr say?

HE SAID IF MY FATHER WISHED TO DICTATE JUSTICE, THEN HE SHOULD CHALLENGE FOR THE RULE OF WEST AND EAST. THEN HE GAVE KOUU A NICE SCAR TO REMEMBER HIM BY, AND SENT HIM ON HIS WAY.

So Torr was testing your father. Seeing how far he'd go?

INDEED.

Images swirled in the blood-warm depths of Buruu's mind, Yukiko watching through the eye of memory. She saw a gathering of the Everstorm pack, a great-moot attended by every buck and dam and cub. Buruu's father spoke of Torr's defiance, explained that to take offense would mean war between Everstorm and the Others. And then, for the first time in as long as any could remember, the Khan asked for counsel.

Amidst the howling silence, Esh raised his voice, bitter with hatred. It was not just, he said. Not right. Sukaa had taken his eye. Sukaa must pay. And if that meant blood in the skies, and death to the Others, so be it.

Drahk agreed with his brother. It would be the coward's way to let the insult go unpunished. Other bucks raised voice in agreement, blood rising, eyes flashing. Perhaps it had been too long. Perhaps this ritual combat and life of peace had made them soft. Afraid.

An elderly dam spoke then—a grand old beast, near blinded by the years, her stripes a dulled silver. Crea was her name, eldest of all in Everstorm, wise beyond counting. She stood amongst the other Elders, speaking of war's folly. The pointlessness of vengeance. How killing Sukaa, Torr, every arashitora in Morcheba, would not return Esh's eye.

The other Elders crowed assent.

Wisdom, they cried. *Wisdom.*

A tumult of roars drowned the Elders out, Drahk and Esh loudest of all. And amidst the cacophony, the Khan stepped forth, wings spread wide. Amber eyes aglow with storm's kiss, the brilliant cracks splitting the sky. He was muscle and beak and claw. The greatest ruler Everstorm had known. And he spoke a word that brought stillness, the bucks' fire dying as if freezing water had been dashed onto hot coals.

Extinction, he said.

They were so few. To fight a war meant to lessen themselves further, and drive a wedge between Black and White that would live for decades. They'd fled Shima for the sake of survival. To risk all now? Even over a wound as grievous as Esh had suffered?

There was one true law for the thunder tigers of Everstorm. One commandment, laid down by she who first led them from Shima's poisoned shores. Black. White. Young. Old. It did not matter. Arashitora did not kill arashitora.

Assent rippled amongst the greatmoot, the rage in the breasts of the males growing still. They were so few. Their grip so tenuous.

The Khan spoke true.

Buruu could see the pain of betrayal in Esh's eye. The unveiled fury in Drahk's gaze. But his brothers were young—too young to challenge their father and win.

And so they bowed their heads and submitted, like loyal subjects and loyal sons would.

The passing of years. The turning of seasons like dawn and dusk in Buruu's mind's eye. Yukiko saw him grow, flourish, becoming the thunder tiger she knew. Watching him soar amongst the clouds, chasing the female he'd called Shai through the lightning strikes. Watching Esh's resentment fester, hatred gleaming in his eye, poisoning Drahk along with him. It was only love for his father that kept the toxins from Buruu's own heart. But he knew the day would come when his eldest brother would challenge for the title of Khan.

But for now, Drahk was still too young. The Khan too strong. All knew it.

The Others hadn't been seen since the incident with Sukaa. But word came through a nomad who wandered the northern seas that Torr wished an end to hostilities. That the packs should once again meet in the summer, as they had in happier days. And though Buruu knew Torr was an opportunist, though Drahk counseled against accepting the Morcheban Khan's overtures, their father saw wisdom in it. To end the pointless standoff. To bring stillness after years of empty aggression.

Yukiko saw the Khan standing atop the aerie in the midst of the endless tempest. The nest was empty now, Buruu's mother having passed the previous winter, leaving Skaa alone in quiet grief. And Buruu stood at his father's back and watched the Khan watching his kingdom. The mighty thunder tiger seemed smaller somehow, bent with the burden of it all.

Esh will never forgive if you accept Torr's peace, Buruu growled.

No, his father agreed.

You choose Others over blood.

I choose future. For all our kind.

Future?

One day you rule, my Triumph. One day you understand. To think not of one, but all. One day there will be no black. No white. Only gray.

They will hate you. Drahk. Esh.

Then let them challenge.

Skaa turned to his son. His favored one.

Who claims Khan is Khan.

He sent Buruu the next day, the only son he trusted to deliver his words. Flying east to Morcheba, meeting with Sukaa. The Khan-son's arrogance seemed to have dimmed in intervening years, and Buruu saw something akin to regret in his eyes. He delivered his father's message—Everstorm would accept the Morcheban peace, if the rules of the Bloodstone were laid as law. No permanent injury. No death. Those who broke this law to be punished in kind.

Sukaa accepted, nodding deep before flying away. And Buruu flew back toward Everstorm, rankling at Sukaa's escape from justice, but beginning to see the breadth of it. The depth of it. That his father was wise to accept peace. To fight not to avenge past wounds, but to build the future. Something greater.

No black. No white. Only gray.

Shai intercepted him miles from Everstorm, breath heaving in her lungs, sorrow and dread in her eyes. And as she dashed toward him across darkening skies, he knew something terrible had happened. Something that would never be undone.

The Khan is dead.

The news like a blow. Gut to water. Heart to stone.

Unthinkable.

Impossible.

How?

Drahk and Esh.

. . . Two may not challenge one?

No challenge.

Grief in her eyes. Grief and rage.

Just murder.

A travesty. An outrage. Their own father? What madness had driven them to this brink? This betrayal? It was too much to comprehend. A blood-red tide rising in his sight, filling the endless mileage between dawn and dusk with fury, and turning all to scarlet.

Shai called his name as he flew away, begging him to stop. But there was no self in that moment. There was only red and the memory of the day he'd first taken to the wing beside his father burning bright in his mind. Everything gone before, everything to come after, all of it washed away by the blood-bright rush of rage. The Khan's aerie in the distance, growing closer with every breath, every beat of his wings, fury growing beside it.

Drahk circled the aerie, the mark of their father's talons etched down bloody flanks. He called to Buruu across the storm. Seeking parlay. Urging stillness. But there were no words. No moment in which to speak to this one he'd called brother. There was only a roar of challenge, striking like a thunderbolt, screaming fury. A moment of impact, ten thousand hammers strong, iron-gray and deafening. Brawling across storm-torn skies, strobing lightning, thunder pounding. The sea dragons goaded to frenzy in the oceans below, thrashing in the bloody rain. No thought. No pause. Simply doing, on and above and between, a whirling flurry of talons and beaks and furious roars. And when it ended there was heat and salt, rushing warm and slick down Buruu's throat and Drahk plummeting from the skies, trailing blood like ribbons through the rain.

His brother's body hit the water amidst the flash of silvered tails, sea dragons grinning with translucent katana teeth. Buruu turned to the Khan's throne below, the sibling lying curled in a puddle of tepid red, torn from throat to belly by their father's claws.

The Everstorm pack had gathered to watch the brothers clash, roaring outrage as Buruu dropped screaming from the skies. Shai's cry was a gentle murmur
under the pulse in his ears, the madness filling and flooding and pushing all else
aside. He landed atop his brother, Esh too weak from blood loss to even struggle,
the fear of death already gleaming in his one good eye. Broken wings flapping
feebly, a croak spilling from his bleeding throat.

Mercy.

He dared?

Mercy, brother.

Better to ask the sun not to rise and set. To ask mighty Raijin to still his endless drums. No father. No mother. No mate. No pack. No storm. No light. No dark.
Only death. Filling his veins, stealing reason and sight and sound. And Buruu
tore and bit until there was nothing left, until nothing remained of Esh but a
bloody smear of feathers and broken bones. Drenching himself. Drowning in it.
Mouthful after bloody mouthful.

Thunder in the aftermath. The percussion of his own pulse.

The cries of the pack.

Madness, they roared. Madness had taken the Khan-sons, and brought all to
ruin.

The Elders looked down, no pity in their gaze. Exile they called him. Outcast.
Thunder tigers did not slay one another. Such had been the law since the exodus
from Shima. Especially not their own blood. Their own kin. Wretched murderers
though they themselves might be.

Other voices were raised. Shai's in Buruu's defense. Kouu and Kaiah also. Buruu
was Khan now, they claimed. He *was* the law.

Arashitora do not kill arashitora, the Elders cried.

Who claims Khan is Khan, the response.

And the taste of blood hung thick on Buruu's tongue, the taste of the brothers
he'd laid to rest. And his father's words hung heavy in the air, stained with copper's tang.

*One day you rule, my Triumph. One day you understand. To think not of one,
but all.*

Buruu closed his eyes. His father's ghost standing beside him, turning his back
in shame.

I choose a future. For all our kind.

And this was the future his sons had wrought.

He could have claimed it. The seat of Khan. He'd challenged, and he'd won.
But the law was the law. Death had come to Everstorm, not in the guise of Father
Time or happenstance, but of brothers and sons. Of hatred and vengeance. No
true Khan would have it so. No Triumph.

They took his name. Cast him out. Drenched in his kin's blood. He and his brothers, murderers all, would never be spoken of in Everstorm again. And through the grief, beyond the beast he'd succumbed to, he knew it right. He knew it just. Shai begged him to stay. Kouu and Kaiah also. What would happen when the Morcheban blacks returned? With so many of Everstorm's warriors slain or gone? What if Torr claimed Everstorm for his own?

What of me? Shai asked. *What of us?*

No answer. No voice. Only shame. The memory of his father's words and the taste of his brothers on his tongue. He'd lost himself. Become nothing but a beast. Wretched. Broken. And he turned his back on Everstorm, everything inside it. The Elders' words ringing in his ears, the name they'd given to replace the one his father had bestowed.

No Roahh. No Triumph.

Only Kinslayer.

. . . ONLY KINSLAYER.

T here were no words. No words for miles.

Tears in Yukiko's eyes. Arms wrapped around his neck. All this time he'd kept it hidden. The shame. The guilt. She'd had no idea what she was asking when she'd begged him to come back here. No idea what he'd be returning to. Torr had come, just as Kaiah feared. And the Everstorm bucks who stood against him had been killed, along with their cubs, the Morcheban Khan laying claim to the Everstorm throne. Yukiko could see why Kaiah hated him. At last, she understood the female's seething animosity.

But . . .

It wasn't your fault.

OF COURSE IT WAS.

You weren't yourself. You weren't thinking.

THAT EXCUSES NOTHING. I MURDERED MY OWN BROTHERS.

You avenged your father.

AND FOUND IN VENGEANCE NOT ONE MOMENT'S PEACE. I BECAME AS THEY. JUST AS GUILTY. JUST AS STAINED. NOTHING BUT BEASTS, ALL.

In the distance, she could see islands; dark, gleaming stone, spewing fire and smoke into the endless chaos above. Cinders falling incandescent between the raindrops, clouds built of ashes and storms. Reaching out into the tempest, she could feel shapes—predatory and prideful. Arashitora, black and white, calling across the roiling clouds, roaring warning to their Khan.

The Kinslayer comes.

She felt helpless. There was nothing she could do to make him feel better. To make it all right. This shadow that hung about his shoulders, this loathing that had settled on his insides.

SO NOW YOU KNOW. THE TRUTH OF WHO I AM.

My brother.

BEAST.

My best friend.

MURDERER.

You're my everything.

She pushed her cheek into his neck, squeezed her eyes shut tight. Willing the pain gone, trying to fill him with warmth and light.

I love you.

. . . STILL?

Always.

A black shape stood tall and fierce on the spire of stone ahead, burning green eyes, vast wings spread in threat, edged with the light of molten stone.

IF I FALL . . .

You won't.

BUT IF I DO . . .

You can't.

The strength of him. Flooding her mind as Yoritomo took his feathers. As they defeated the Red Bone Warlord and his legion of oni. As they tore ironclads to flaming tatters, brought the nation to its feet, thousands of eyes alight with wonder as they soared overhead. She reminded him of it all, flooding him with images of every triumph, every moment they'd shared since all this began, since she first reached out from the *Thunder Child* and touched his mind.

It doesn't matter what you've done. Who you were. All that counts is what you're doing. Who you are. *Right now. This moment.*

AND WHO AM I?

You know as well as I do.

The black shape roared; a challenge echoing amidst smoking stone, rising steam, cinder rain. To challenge the new Khan of Everstorm was to challenge to the death. No quarter. No mercy. He could flee now, back into exile, back into shame. Turn from the scene of his failure, the ruin he'd made, the bloodstains he'd left behind on the stone.

I KNOW WHO YOU ARE, KINSLAYER.

The black shape rose from its throne, vast and cruel and cold. Yukiko squeezed him tight, pouring all she had inside him as Buruu opened his beak to roar above the endless storm.

YOU KNOW WHO I WAS. NOT WHO I AM.

AND WHO ARE YOU, THEN?

The song of the Thunder God filled the sky.

The thunder tiger roared in answer.

I AM BURUU.

PART THREE

DEATH

"You cannot leave, love!"
Her scream echoed in the black. "Stay you here with me!"
The Maker God wept, for Yomi had marred his bride, claimed her
    as its own.
Spurned, she spit her troth; one thousand deaths, every day. Her
    solitude's price.
"Then I will give life," great Lord Izanagi vowed,
"To fifteen hundred."

—*from the* Book of Ten Thousand Days

27

THE BOY WHO DOES NOT ASK

In the heart of the city sits a Boy.

A rooftop, damp and greasy, overlooking Market Square. The cobbles below glimmer with a black rain sheen, streetlights painting Kigen's filthy avenues with feeble stars. The clouds overhead move like oceans, and the dark is filled with eyes. And the Boy sits in the spaces between it all, palms upturned, head bowed.

Listening.

They come to him, one at a time. Like supplicants before a tumbledown throne. They know him, though they know not how or why. But the Boy calls, and they come, and they speak, whispering inside his skull with the tongues of sewer and broken cobble and alleys like scabbed and open mouths. Flea-ridden, yellowed teeth and flint black eyes. Yet he knows their names, old and young alike. And as they scuttle forward and speak, one by one by one, he reaches out and touches them, gently, like their fathers never did.

They tell him secrets. The seeings they have seen. The thieving and killing, the lawlessness rife, people fleeing the city in droves. The brass men in their yellow tower, calling for the Impure to be put to pyre at weeksend in exchange for a few drops of reeking fuel. The Boy looks down into the Market Square at this, dark eyes affixed on the four Burning Stones in the sunken mall, echoing with forgotten screams. And the Boy's face grows hard, and his fingers clench. But in the end he turns away.

More sewer-children come forward, offering morsels.

A Market Square baker murdered his wife and dumped her body in the Shiroi.

The guards who patrol Spire Row raped a streetwalker two nights past.

Three boys and a woman with arms like silver spiders are stockpiling weapons in a Downside flat.

Eyelids fluttering, filtering each snippet, searching for a particular loose thread.

A beggar keeps a bag of iron kouka beneath a stone near Railyard Bridge.

The Second Bloom of the Guild Chapterhouse is up and walking again.

The railyard master has been selling chi to black marketeers.

Finally, his voice cuts the clamor; a knife in the base of their skulls. He seeks news of painted men. The ones who rule Kigen from Wolf to Phoenix hour, now the boys in iron clothes have gone north to fight and die. And so they speak of a warehouse near the bay. There are traps there; poisoned meat that cut a bloody, heaving swathe through their number, and now the sewer-children stay away. But the tattooed men go there, with bags full of not-food, that *clank* and *clink* like the iron clothing of the boys who have gone north to perish.

And the Boy asks them, one by one by one, if they will help. Asks in a way that is Not Asking. Asks in a way that makes them fear. This Boy. This beggar prince. This lord returned.

And they bow.

And they scrape.

And they do as he Not Asks.

Jimen was in the parlor, counting out his money.

Stacks of it. Piles of it. Dull gray mountains of it. Rectangular braids of iron, stamped with the imperial seal. The little accountant pored over every one, stacking them into neat towers, counting off on his antique abacus. The spoils of war and markets black, growing ever higher as any semblance of order in Kigen disintegrated, and the yakuza gangs that had long suffered under the Shōgun's law stepped in from the dark to claim what was theirs.

The lieutenants would come and go, delivering more satchels, smelling of smoke and blood and alley sex. Jimen would barely look up from his ledgers. He supposed he could have pulled in more hands to help with the count, but the Shinshi's trust had all but evaporated in the wake of the robberies they'd suffered last month. That filthy rat-speaker and his friends . . .

The boy and his sister had escaped in the chaos of the rebel attack. And though they'd be fools to return, the Gentleman had demanded security be the Scorpion Children's watchword from here on. Thinking of the money and men they'd lost to that boy-child and his iron-thrower, Jimen couldn't help but agree.

The hour was late, and his eyes felt full of sand. Jimen stretched and yawned, listening to the rain, looking at the mural of Lord Izanagi on the wall. The Maker God was rendered in a familiar pose; stirring the ocean of creation with his spear, Lady Izanami beside him.

Life was never simple, Jimen thought. Such was man's fate. Even when he got what he wanted, it was seldom what he thought it would be. He could climb the tallest peak he sees, and still there would be another beyond, yet higher to climb. Only Lord Izanagi stood above all, higher than any mortal could ascend.

And even the Maker had an insane bitch of a wife to deal with . . .

Something moved in the shadows of the ceiling beams above, making Jimen start. The little accountant squinted at the shape and cursed, reaching for the tantō at his belt. A corpse-rat peered at him with eyes of black glass, gleaming and empty, lantern light flickering in their depths. The thing was over a foot and a half long, mangy ears, yellow teeth bunched in its mouth like an arena crowd. It snuffled the air, head tilted, blinking.

"Little bastard . . ." Jimen hissed. "How did you get past the baits?"

Shouts from the warehouse outside, dulled by distance and old timber. Jimen turned just as the door opened, a tattooed lump of muscle poking his head around the frame.

"Trouble," the gangster said. "Stay here, Jimen-sama."

The accountant flourished his knife, backed into a corner. The rat peered down at him with empty doll's eyes, black and dead. Jimen flinched as he heard a loud boom, a man's scream. Glancing at the knife in his hand, he set it aside, hefting a long tetsubo club sitting by the door. Four feet of studded iron, comforting and heavy in his hand. The rat on the ceiling tilted its head.

Blinked.

A second boom, then a third. Another scream, like a babe ripped from mother's womb—the tune of an ending no man really deserved. Jimen blinked sudden sweat from his eyes, backed farther into the corner and, despite the knowledge there were a dozen of his fiercest between him and whatever "trouble" approached, found himself wishing his office had more than one exit.

The wall pressed hard against his back.

Scuffling and screaming drawing closer, beating now on the door, hinges cracking. Silence followed, dark and cold and bottomless, broken only by the soft chittering of the rat above his head, the *drip-drip-drip* of something thick and viscous just beyond the door. Leaking in across the landing. Gleaming dark.

The handle turned slowly.

The door opened slower still.

Eyes. A legion of eyes. Jet-dark and shining in the gloom, a hundred tiny orbs reflecting the paper lanterns. A boy stood amongst them, tall and spattered red. Ghost-pale skin and shaven head, a blood-soaked bandage over a missing ear. An iron-thrower, ugly and smoking, clutched in one white-knuckle fist. Running a slow tongue along bloodless lips.

The boy spoke, voice dripping murder. "You know who I am?"

Jimen glanced at the corpse-rat sea around the boy's feet. "Hai."

"The Gentleman. Where is he?"

"I don't know."

Laughter. Grim and mirthless. Ending as suddenly as it began.

"What do I look like to you?"

"A dead man," Jimen spat, hefting the warclub.

The boy raised his finger, blood-slicked, eyes narrowing. And the horde rippled like black swell on a midnight bay, and forth they came, open mouths and bloody teeth, a swarm from some far-flung nightmare in the days when prayers were answered and the dark had eyes and monsters were oh, so very real.

The boy stood and watched. Listened as they began to chew. Smiling soft and deadly as Jimen screamed his mother's name, his own voice only a whisper.

"What do I look like now, motherfucker?"

T his was his moment of triumph.

The Gentleman dashed back another mouthful, wiped the sting from his lips. He stared at the irezumi on his flesh—the koi fish and cherry blossoms and geisha girls marking him as clanless trash. Not lucky enough to be born one of the four mighty zaibatsu, no. A child of gutters and a nameless family. He wondered who his people were. Where they'd come from, in days before the Empire crushed two dozen into four. Panda? Mantis? Cat? Monkey? Dog?

None of it mattered anymore. Tonight, he was Oyabun of the Scorpion Children. Master of the largest band of cutthroats, pimps, drug dealers and extortionists in all of Kigen. From lowborn trash, to a lord of the city. And all it had taken was a few hundred murders . . .

Eri stood in the doorway, the lantern behind throwing a long shadow on the floor. "Will you say good night to your son, Husband?"

"Soon, love."

She touched his face, swept the graying hair back from his brow and kissed his cheek. Tiptoeing up the hall to their son's room, to coo and sing the child into pleasant dreams.

How long did he sit there, drinking in the dark and dreaming of empire? A kingdom of shadows, wrought with his own bare hands. Eri's voice finally roused him, thin and trembling. There was something in her tone. Something close to . . .

The Gentleman pulled himself to his feet, padding up the stairs to the babe's room, door ajar, flickering with the dull flame of a single night light. He could hear little Kaito laughing—his firstborn son, the boy's voice high and bright, filling him with momentary joy.

Melting into fear.

It hit him like a hammerblow as he stepped into the room, seeing the boy in his crib, plump and rosy-cheeked, pawing at the sleek black shapes coiled around him. His crib infested with them, the smallest at least two feet long, dead doll's eyes and crooked yellow fangs.

The gasp caught in his teeth as he lunged forward. "Kaito!"

"Far enough, friend." A hiss. Behind.

He turned, caught sight of him then, standing in the far corner with hands in sleeves, Eri trussed at his feet like a corpse-rat in a butcher shop window. Blank expression. Pale and still. Only the eyes gave him away, swimming with the empty solace of murder. The eyes of a killer in a pretty boy's face—a face the Gentleman had last seen weeping and screaming as he tore his sister's eye from her socket.

The rat-speaker.

Rage flooded him, hot and blinding. He took two swift steps forward, tantō somehow already in his hands as the boy held up his finger and the corpse-rats shrieked, one sawing note that set Kaito to screaming, surrounded by hungry, open mouths.

"You think they'll fret or froth?" The boy glanced at the bedful of vermin. "If the fellow holding their leash slacks his grip?"

The boy nodded to the knife in the Gentleman's hand.

"Best be dropping that shiv. Supposing we can be gentlemanly about this. Gentleman."

"You threaten my family—"

"Oh, don't step there, little yakuza. Don't even dare."

A corpse-rat stood tall in the crib, licking Kaito's tears with a long, gray tongue. Eri's weeping was a distant waterfall. The tantō thumped into the floorboards, point down and quivering.

The boy's voice was soft as velvet. Black as night.

"There once was a clever boy named Yoshi. And being who he was, which was no one of much account in the grandest of schemes, and not half so clever as he thought, he took what wasn't his, and lost almost everything that was."

The boy stepped closer, footsteps lost under corpse-rat whispers.

"And at the last, with empty pockets and empty chest, he paid a visit to the man who'd taken all of it away. Because good or bad, favors are just like kisses. They taste sweeter when you give them back."

The boy unfolded hands from sleeves. The Gentleman was not the least surprised when he saw what he held in his fists.

A claw-tooth hammer and a rusted pair of pliers.

"Get on your fucking knees."

"Suppose then," the Shinshi said, "that I do not."

"Then I *suppose* you can listen to your son die."

The Gentleman blinked, gaze flickering from the rusted tools to the boy's eyes. No trembling in the gutter-rat's voice. No hint of fear or hesitation. An impressive display.

A peacock before wolves.

The Gentleman tilted his head, felt the vertebrae pop. His cheeks were saké warm, his tongue slightly too big for his mouth. Edges numb. Heavy as lead. But there was no pup on earth he couldn't whip, no matter how blurred the lines.

"Yoshi, isn't it?"

The boy made no reply. It would not matter if he had.

"It takes a peculiar kind of emptiness to murder children, Yoshi-san. I've seen the eyes of men who kill babes. It leaves a mark, that callousness. A stain, if you will. And forgive me, child, but for all your crowing, I do not see that mark in you."

Fists clenching.

"I called you coward once."

"Don't—"

"And to that measure I hold."

A quick step, feint and lunge, fist slipping past the boy's guard and into his solar plexus. A damp explosion of air, spittle-thick, the boy bending double, cheeks running red. The Gentleman lifted a knee into his throat, the boy dropping hammer and pliers, intertwining his fingers to stop the blow just short of turning his windpipe to sauce. The impact lifted him back, crashing against the wall. Coughing. Gasping.

A shrieking filled the room, tar-black and flea-ridden, little Kaito singing falsetto above their wails. The corpse-rats swarmed off the bed toward the yakuza boss, and the Gentleman dispatched a few in quick succession with his heel. Crunching skulls and spines, one, two, three, before a bucktoothed fellow with a mouthful of knives latched hold and started worrying his Achilles like old rope. He roared, tore the vermin away in a shower of bright red.

The boy hit him from behind, spine hyperextending, Eri screaming at the top of her lungs. The boy was on his back, a fistful of fringe in one hand, the other curled tight and slamming repeatedly into his head. The Gentleman howled as half a dozen rats seized hold, one tearing his face, another at the fingers scrabbling for the tantō he'd dropped. The boy sensed his intent, lunged for the blade himself, just a second too slow.

Knife in hand, whirling and stabbing, flailing at the scabby mongrel snapping at his eyes. He felt the knife bite the boy's forearm, shallow but long, spattering the walls scarlet. The boy rolled away, the Gentleman snapped up to a crouch as mangy shadows scrambled up his leg, onto his back, digging in between his shoulders, the screams of his wife and son filling his ears as the boy snatched up the rusty claw hammer and came to his feet, gods the noise, the pain, flailing at the razored shapes chewing his spine, slamming himself into the wall to dislodge them as the boy loomed, hammer raised, lips drawn back and grinning . . .

The rusted claw connecting with his jaw.

Bone splintering.

Teeth flying.

Spinning like a dancer, the world upending as he toppled backward, felt another blow, dim and distant on the back of his head. And the boy was cursing, spitting bile, raising the bloody iron for another blow and his legs went out from under him and he toppled earthward and between each blow, falling now like leaden rain, he heard the boy (gods, just a boy) spitting, hissing, voice thick with tears. The same refrain, over and over, like poetry laid over the splitting percussion etched into his skull.

Verse.

"You killed my boy."

Chorus.

"You killed my boy."

Finale.

"You."

Thump.

"Killed."

Thump.

"Me."

H*ush.*

Yoshi stood amidst the ruins, hammer dripping onto the boards at his feet. The rats were poised around the corpse, salivating. Always hungry. Always.

Hush now.

The woman was weeping, muffled behind her hair, eyes averted. The baby was screaming, red faced and snot-nosed. And Yoshi stood in the middle of it all and felt salty warmth cutting down his cheeks, smile like a tear across his face, trying to rid himself of the sight still hanging disembodied before his eyes—Jurou lying split and chewed in that alleyway. Crystal clear, tinged blood-red by the knowledge that all the killing in the world wouldn't bring him back, wouldn't make it stop, wouldn't fill the hole he left behind.

"Motherfucker," he breathed. "You motherfucker . . ."

The hammer fell from nerveless fingers, thumping onto the boards, slicked with ruby red. And Yoshi stepped over the corpse-rats, picked up the baby, the Gentleman's son, holding him at arm's length while the woman began screaming anew.

"Not my son, gods no! NO!"

He turned slowly, staring at her trussed on the floor. Holding the wriggling child, watching him wail. So tiny. So fragile.

"Murderer!" she screamed. *"Don't touch him!"*

And he saw it then, as if for the first time. The way *she* saw *him*. The thing he was. Had become. Death to more death. How the boy in his arms would one day grow to hate the one who killed his father. How eighteen years from now, it might be Yoshi smashed on the floor beside some screaming lover as this boy completed the circle. Began a new one. Violence upon violence upon violence. No kind of ending. Just a different beginning. And for what?

For *what*?

What would make it stop?

There was silence then. In his head. For the first time in as long as he could remember. And the corpse-rats looked up at the chubby squalling thing in his hands, gray tongues licking blood-matted whiskers, and he knelt amongst them with the babe in his arms.

Breathing hard.

Blinking sweat from his eyes.

All the world standing still.

Husssssh.

He lifted the bloody tantō from the floor. Cut the woman's bonds. Handed over her son. And as she crawled back into the corner, clutching the wailing babe tight to her breast, teeth barred and fierce as tigers, he felt something unwind inside him. Something release.

"Figure he might come stalking for me one day." He pointed to the boy. "Figure I'd probably deserve it. Just like your man deserved it." A shrug. "Assuming any of this is still here, I mean. Can't say as I'd pitch blame at either of you for that."

Yoshi walked toward the door, boots squeaking in the gore. The woman stared, saying nothing, pressing her son to her cheek.

"But I'm hoping you'll help him choose better," Yoshi said. "Better than I did, anyway."

He stopped at the threshold, not looking back. The rats left the cooling meat untouched, turned and flowed out the door like blackened surf.

"No hero, me."

And soon, there was nothing to mark their passing but bloody footprints on the floor.

28
SIGIL

Akihito beat one massive fist on his breastplate, shrugged expansively to test the fit. A stocky Kitsune blacksmith watched him, face covered by a breather of dirty brass. The forges inside Five Flowers Palace had been burning twenty-four hours a day since news of the gaijin landing at Kawa, and the master and his dozen apprentices were run off their feet.

"Fits good," Akihito nodded, thumping the iron again. "Nice work."

"From a Phoenix, I take that as high praise." The blacksmith bowed low. "But with your pardon, I have about a thousand more to make . . ."

The man trudged back into the steam and coalsmoke, barking orders at three apprentices working the smelter. Akihito flexed again, unused to the weight. He limped from the smithy, leaning on his studded warclub, surveying the muddy courtyard. Samurai shouting orders, bushimen running training drills, boys carrying weaponry. Hammers on anvils, the hiss of hot steel tempered in greasy river water, Michi's voice rising above it all.

"Akihito!"

The big man turned, saw the girl pushing through the mob. Hair tied in a long braid, chaindaishō strapped to her back, a hundred hungry warriors watching her pass.

"Akihito!" She caught his arm, breathless.

"What is it? What's wrong?"

"It's Hana."

"What about her?"

"She's gone."

"Gone?" Whispering fear uncurling in his gut. "Gone where?"

"She and Kaiah flew out early this morning. A guard said they headed east."

"East?" The whisper became a shout, cold as winter winds. "Toward the gaijin?"

Michi nodded. "And she took Piotr with her."

K aiah had been named for the clouds, but in truth, she flew like the wind. Hana was hunched against her spine, face swathed in scarves, three cloaks pulled tight about her. Growling chill chewed any exposed skin red raw in seconds, and the girl thanked Lord Izanagi for the goggles over her face—without them she was certain her eye would have frozen solid.

Piotr was huddled against Hana's back, doing his best not to touch her, clinging to the thunder tiger's hindquarters with his thighs. Every now and then, Kaiah would bank or dive sharply, and Piotr would be forced to grab Hana for balance, apologizing profusely in his broken Shiman. Hana would smile at Kaiah's laughter in her head.

You shouldn't tease him.

- WHY NOT? -

He's obviously terrified of touching me.

- WOULD BE WISER TO FEAR RETURNING TO THE PEOPLE HE BETRAYED, I THINK. -

"Won't the gaijin punish you for deserting the lightning farm?" Hana spoke over her shoulder, shouting above the wind. "Won't they be angry with you?"

"I promise." Piotr was shivering, teeth chattering. "Blood promise. Find his love. Bring her word. Takeo."

"The Guildsman who saved your life?"

"Da. In Morcheba, promising is most important thing. Blood promise mostly of all. Is the one that holds together many. Like black between brick, da? Is word. They know. My word. Must be for the holding. Must be for the true or else for the nothing. Blood in blood."

Gods above. I can only understand every second word he says . . .

- AND HE WILL BE TRANSLATING FOR YOU? -

Let's hope.

- LET'S PRAY. -

Hana pushed a smile into the thunder tiger's mind, felt warmth radiating in return. She rested her cheek against the sleek feathers at the arashitora's neck, watching the smooth movements of her wings from the corner of her eye. A perfect motion, precise and beautiful—a poetry of feather and bone and flesh.

I'm glad you're with me, Kaiah. I'm really glad you're here.

Howling stormsong filled the leaden pause.

. . . Although part of me thinks you should be with Yukiko and—

- SPEAK NOT HIS NAME. -

A flare of aggression in the arashitora's mind, turning warmth to bright heat.

I know you have your differences. But you know he's trying to do what's right, don't you? He and Yukiko are doing what they think is best.

- I LOST EVERYTHING BECAUSE OF HIM. MY MATE. MY CHILDREN. -

I know what it is to lose someone. I know what it's like to hate. But anyone can change. Grow. Look at me. Where I was three months ago. Where I am now.

- YOU ARE NOTHING LIKE THE KINSLAYER.—

More than you know. Everyone here wants the same thing. The Rebels. The Kagé. You. Me. Yukiko. Buruu. Gods, even the gaijin. We just want a moment's peace. A place to be happy. An ordinary life. So why the hells are we all fighting each other?

- THE THINGS YOU SPEAK. PEACE. HAPPY. HOW MANY YOU KNOW WHO ACTUALLY OWNS THEM? HOW MANY NOT TOUCHED BY HURT OR DEATH? -

Hana thought of her mother crumpled on the floor. Broken glass, blood-slicked, as clubbing became stabbing. Her brother lunging for her father's throat, murder in his eyes.

She could still hear the sound of her own screaming.

- FAMILY. LOVE. NOT ORDINARY THINGS. NOT IN THIS WORLD. SPE-CIAL. WORTH FIGHTING FOR. AND SO WE DO. -

And in doing so, we make sure nobody has them. Everybody loses except the man selling funeralwear.

- IT IS EITHER FIGHT, OR WATCH AS EVERYTHING IS TAKEN AWAY. YOU KNOW THIS. LIVING IN DREGS. WARRING FOR EVERY SCRAP. THEY TOOK YOUR MOTHER, YET YOU REMAIN. THEY TOOK YOUR EYE, YET YOU SEE. -

Hana turned her gaze to the horizon. The storm building between the edge of land and sky. The Tora army that even now must be stomping closer.

I wish it could be another way. That we didn't have to fight. Hurt. Kill.

- YOU KNOW YOU MUST. -

A sigh.

Yes. I do.

The clouds parted, and far below, she saw them. A long, twisting line march-ing east, near ten thousand strong, ironclad, drenched and grim beneath black drizzle. Her mother's people. The blood in her veins. She touched the amulet around her neck, trying to gather her strength, still the butterflies tumbling about her gut.

- I AM WITH YOU. -

I know that too.

- YOU ARE READY? -

A nod.

I'm ready.

- THEN WE BEGIN. -

Aleksandar stood shin-deep in black mud, commiserating with another of-ficer when the cry went up from the line. The Kapitán glanced up, shielding bloodshot eyes from the black rain, cursing the storm and this Goddessforsaken country for the hundredth time that day.

At least 10 percent of their number had fallen out from rain poisoning, an-other 20 percent were walking wounded, eyes and tongues swollen, skin peeling. He'd proposed they bivouac in the Dragon capital until winter deepened and the accursed rain turned to snow, but Marshal Ostrovska would hear none of it. The Kitsune lay east, and vengeance would not wait. The Zryachniye had concurred, eyes glowing bright, and all discussion abruptly ceased. They'd slogged on through this poison for days, shin-deep in filth, until the rains grew so heavy they were forced to halt, hunkered down beneath oilskin sheets until the storm spent itself.

What the hell are they yelling about?

More men crying out, pointing. Aleksandar followed their eyeline, breath catching in his lungs as he spied the silhouette above. Though its kind had not been seen in his homeland for decades, though it was snow-white, not black as the sigil of House Ostrovska was, he knew the shape instantly.

A gryfon.

Twenty-foot wingspan, pale as the deep snows of his homeland, fur torn with long stripes of velvet black. Eyes shining like fireside amber, roaring as it circled above, dipping its wing to reveal the riders on its back and the white flag held high in the toxic wind.

Riders.

Men emerging from tents, eyes narrowed against the rain, archers scrambling for their bows, lightning cannon crews arcing generators despite the fact the weapons would be useless against a foe with no ground. Hammers pounding shields, alarm rolling throughout the encampment. And the beast continued circling, just out of bowshot, the tiny riders waving that strip of white cloth back and forth. An overture any warrior would understand.

Parlay. Peace.

But this was war. Against a nation of slavers and butchers. Could they be trusted? Aleksandar could hear the rotor-thopter engines being started, the Majór obviously keen to cut this beast from the skies. What a prize. What strength it would bring to the one who wore it. Greater than a mere wolfpelt—even the pelt of the Blackwood's Alpha . . .

He heard muddy footsteps, splashing thick, turned toward the scrawny girl sprinting toward him. She stopped before Aleksandar, gave a salute, palms marked with painted eyes, the girl's own so bloodshot from the rain they were almost solid red.

"Kapitán," the girl gasped. "Word from the Zryachniye."

Aleksandar's eyes flickered to the command tent.

"Speak."

"Mother Natassja says she is to be allowed to land."

"She?"

The girl pointed to the gryfon circling overheard. "The Mother says you must bring the girl to her with all haste. That when you see, you will understand. It must be you. You alone."

Aleksandar sighed, ran one hand over the long stubble on his cracking cheeks. He watched the beast, sweeping in a broad spiral overhead, a murmuring dread in his gut. And finally, giving orders to each column commander that his men were not to engage the gryfon, no matter the promise of its skin, he set about finding a white flag to wave.

Kapitán," Piotr whispered. "Leader. Soldier leader."

Hana sat on Kaiah's back beneath her oilskin, eye hidden behind polarized glass, watching the man approaching over muddy ground. They'd landed far from the gaijin line, Kaiah ready to take flight again if trouble reared. The arashitora growled as the gaijin slogged closer.

"We can talk to him?" she asked over her shoulder.

"I will for the speaking."

Piotr grunted with effort, slinging his bad leg over Kaiah's back and slithering down into the mud. He limped a dozen yards closer and performed some kind of salute; fist to chest and then to the air.

The Kapitán returned the gesture.

Hana squinted behind her goggles, looking the man up and down. Early thirties, long blond hair, covered in filth and old blood. He carried a massive warhammer connected to some kind of generator on his back, oilskin wrapped over a night-black animal pelt—a wolf or bear that might have been as big as Kaiah when it was alive. There was something about his gait, the set of his shoulders. Something about him reminded her of Yoshi. The way he moved. Like a man born to be a dancer who'd never been shown the steps.

The Kapitán stopped twenty yards from Piotr, pulled down the swathes of cloth he'd wrapped his face inside, and Hana's heart almost stopped beating. Gods, his face. Square jawed, certainly, dirty and crusted with stubble. But still, it was a face that haunted her dreams, Mother lying on the kitchen floor, Father looming over her with the saké bottle in hand, screaming.

"Look what they took from me!" Face purpling, skin taut and blood-flushed. "Look at it! And all I have to show for it is you!"

"You pig." Mother's words were slurred around her broken jaw. "You drunken slaver pig. Do you know who I am? Do you have any idea what I was?"

Hana put her fingers to her lips. Trembling.

Mother . . .

The gaijin began talking in their alien language, thick and harsh as winter snow. A cold gust of wind caught the Kapitán's pelt, whipped it away from his chest, exposing the standard embossed on his iron breastplate. And Hana was sliding off Kaiah's back, the beast roaring warning as she sank ankle-deep in the mud, stumbling and scrambling, calling Piotr's name. The men turned toward her as she clawed at the leather thong about her neck, snapping it loose, tearing the scarves from her face. And as she stumbled closer, she held it up: the amulet her mother had given her on her tenth birthday, the little golden stag with his three crescent horns.

The same sigil adorning the gaijin's breastplate.

The Kapitán looked at her, sapphire eyes widening as she pulled the scarves from her head, jagged blond tresses flowing loose. His gaze flickered from the amulet to her face, his own turning pale as old starlight as he snatched the medallion from her hand, anger turning him hard and cold.

"Where did you get this?" He spoke in perfect Shiman, his accent dragging the words down into the earth. *"Where did you get this?"*

He grabbed Hana's shoulders. Kaiah's roar echoed across the ruined plain, wings spread, thundering through the mud toward them both. But the man's eyes were locked on Hana, heedless of the death approaching on crackling, silvered wings, the warning cries from the men behind him, the whine of motors, the ring of steel on steel.

"Where?" he shouted.

"My mother." Hana winced in his iron grip. "My mother gave it to me."

The Kapitán looked like someone had scooped out his insides.

". . . Your mother?"

"Anya." Hana pulled down her goggles, exposing her glowing eye. "Her name was Anya."

It lasted a moment more. The disbelief. The rage. He reached up to her face—that pointed, impish face with its too-round eye and the high cheekbones so like his own. And as Kaiah arrived in a hail of mud and wind, roaring as if the sky were falling, he pulled her close, kissed her brow, her cheeks, and holding her so tight she thought she might break, he began laughing, laughing even as the tears streamed down his face, as the storm rolled and roared, sinking to his knees in the mud, bringing her with him and rocking her back and forth like her mother had when she was a child, and all the hurt and dark in the world could be chased away by the sound of her voice.

"I found you," he whispered. "My blood."

She put her arms around him, closed her eye, lost in the sound of his voice.

"Goddess be praised, I found you . . ."

29
ANEW

Impact.

Yukiko felt it in her head, in her chest, compressing her spine and knocking her back onto the rocks. Roiling skies spat rain as hard and sharp as roofing nails, bottomless black in the moments between lightning strikes, sun-bright as the arcs bit the sky. An inverted landscape, shifting constantly as the Storm God and his children sang their hymn in the heavens.

She stood on an outcropping of stone, warm rock beneath her feet, stench of sulfur filling her lungs. Clawing cold. Shrieking wind. Hair slicked across her skin like black silk, eyes upturned to the tempest, heart in her throat, watching two titans clash.

Buruu stood out like a star against the dark, the iridescent metal of his wings glittering as lightning crackled across the clouds. She could feel the rage in him, the will, iron and blood singing here in the place of his birth. She could feel his pack watching fearful, hopeful, the pulse of blacks and whites intermingling with the enormous heat of the reptiles slumbering beneath the waves, so ancient and frightening her heart stilled whenever she . . .

No.

Don't look there.

Instead she focused on Buruu's opponent. Bigger. Stronger. Eyes burning like green flame. So black he seemed to swallow the light; just a shadow against the backdrop of deeper night. She could feel the pride in him, the grim amusement that this princeling had returned at last to challenge. This shadow of a thunder tiger with feeble metal wings, stooping so low as to allow a monkey-child to ride his back.

A slave who would be Khan.

The pair circled, each seeking altitude, lashing out when the other strayed too close. Buruu's wing assembly creaked and groaned, a canvas feather breaking loose and drifting down, down to the blood-flecked ocean, torn instantly to rags by the sea dragons swarming beneath. They were a multitude, already frenzied, awaiting the blood of royalty with serrated grins.

Torr clapped his wings together, giving birth to a peal of Raijin Song; a sonic boom splitting the skies and knocking Buruu aside as if he were a paper kite. The burst was so loud Yukiko covered her ears, Buruu dropping like a stone to escape Torr's swooping attack. The black spiraled into a dive and followed, snapping at Buruu's tail, the air trembling beneath their wings. The Khan's size made him heavier, less maneuverable, but Buruu's metal pinions were beginning to give under the strain, the months of constant abuse. Torr drew closer, talons outstretched. Fear blossomed in Yukiko's gut.

She reached out, touched the Khan's mind, a slight tweak telling him left was right and up was down. Buruu swept over and away as the mighty black reeled himself in, shaking his head and blinking hard. Glittering green eyes found their focus, then their prey, and Torr snarled and circled skyward again.

WHAT ARE YOU DOING?

Helping you, what the hells does it look like?

THIS IS MY FIGHT. LEAVE HIM BE.

There is no you and me. There's only us.

YOU MUST ALLOW ME TO DO THIS.

Godsdammit, I won't stand here and watch him kill you!

Buruu banked and dropped into a dive, hitting Torr like a falling star. The pair roared and spat, the challenger tearing a bone-deep gash across the Khan's chest, a riposte from Torr's hind legs sending him spiraling away in a shower of blood and feathers. They backed off again, wings thrashing the air, both seeking the precious advantage that lay in altitude. Wind screaming. Blinding lightning. Raijin pounding on his drums and shaking the black stone beneath her feet.

IF I CANNOT WIN THIS ALONE, I DO NOT DESERVE TO WIN AT ALL.

I won't let stupid pride get you killed!

I AM NOT RULED BY PRIDE. YOU MUST TRUST ME.

Buruu, I—

TRUST ME.

Buruu pressed wings to flanks, swooping across the skies and colliding with the Khan again. The pair fell into a snarling, bellowing flurry, foreclaws locked as they kicked, talons like sabers seeking the guts of their foe. Wounds earned on both sides, scarlet rain falling as they descended, down and down and down, ever closer to the blood-drenched waves. Buruu had his wings wrapped against belly and flanks, using the metal pinions as a shield, relying on Torr's wings to slow their descent. Sparks flew as the Khan tore at the metal, talons ringing bright on Kin's creation; a razorsong struck on dented, struggling clockwork. Buruu focused again on Torr's chest, purchasing more blood, more bone-deep gouges.

And still they fell.

Yukiko screamed warning as the pair finally broke their deadly embrace, each swooping up and away from the ocean's surface, broken feathers of black and white and bloodstained canvas in their wake. Sea dragons hissed their frustration as the pair spiraled out of reach, thrashing the water to blinding sprays.

Torr roared, rage and mockery spilling across the storm.

WEAKLING. HIDING BEHIND FALSE WINGS.

The black circled wide, rage building to a boil. Yukiko could feel the ache in his paws, cut bloody on pinions that refused to break. The Khan was confused about the clockwork on Buruu's back and wings—what it meant, how it worked. And though he was as ferociously intelligent as Buruu had been when they first met, Torr lacked a mind of men or metal. He didn't know what a machine was, how to overcome it. All he knew was that wings were an arashitora's greatest strength and greatest weakness, and the first to lose one would be the first to die.

NO KHAN, YOU.

A roar of frustration. Rage.

KINSLAYER.

Yukiko reached across the void, whispering into Buruu's mind.

Your wings. He doesn't know what they are.

I KNOW.

You have to stop using them as shields. They break, you fall.

TRUST ME.

Buruu, I can kill him with a thought. I could reach out right now and—

TRUST ME.

Thunder tore the skies, a battery of cannon rumbling up her spine. Fists clenched, mouth dry as she watched them circling. Torr roared again, spitting insults and hatred at the Kinslayer. Who was he to challenge? This monkey's pet? This son of a line gone mad? If not for Torr, this pack would have fallen to ruin. If not for Torr, Everstorm would be a graveyard littered with the bones of their race.

And through it all Buruu stayed silent as tombs. Why spend breath on insult? Waste strength on bravado? The human in him, the human in *her* in him, understood—a tempered intelligence layered over animal cunning, a soul-deep change wrought by the bond between them. She'd made him more. They'd made each other so much *more*.

Torr was older, stronger. But Buruu had the capacity for reason, subterfuge, and above all, patience. And for a moment, Yukiko found herself believing. That he could win. That he would triumph. But only for a moment.

A gust of wind caught the Khan's wings, buoying him higher. He wheeled and dove across the brink, colliding with Buruu like a thunderbolt. Lost in frenzy, targeting the metal wings that had thwarted blow after blow, now caught in his talons. The Khan clutched a fistful of the mechanism running down Buruu's spine, ripping and tearing, delicate gears tumbling like brass snow amongst the raindrops. Feeling them break, ripped to ribbons at last, at *last*, the Khan roared victory. Buruu twisted in his harness, kicking out with his hind legs as the pair once again fell from the clouds, blood and canvas feathers flying.

Spinning.

Plummeting.

Torr's claws digging into Buruu's shoulders. Ripping through the harness pinning the device to his back, tearing one false wing completely away, the broken pinion falling in a wretched spiral as Yukiko screamed and the Khan bellowed in triumph. Lightning illuminated the pair, light and shadow, spiraling toward the bloody waves. Clutching each other as death reached for them both. Inseparable as lovers all the way to their grave. With a desperate roar and the bright ring of splitting metal, Buruu tore free of the harness, twisting and seizing Torr's flank, claws finding purchase beneath the Khan's ribs. And with a kick that tore him free of the broken harness, leather snapping, bolts splitting and spinning bright into the void, Buruu's talons tore the Khan open from sternum to groin.

Torr roared, blood-flecked and defiant, tearing the contraption to pieces as his guts unfurled, trailing out behind him as the pair fell. Tumbling. Bleeding. Screaming. The Khan hit the water; a brilliant scarlet spray, foaming flurries, the dance of teeth like glittering swords. Yukiko's eyes were wide, scream frozen behind clenched teeth as Buruu plunged toward that same frenzy, wings spread to slow his descent. But he was too far from the broken islands to make it to safety, the water between filled with golden eyes and glittering, translucent fangs. Even if he managed to glide . . .

To glide . . .

Lightning crashed, illuminating the thunder tiger swooping away from the boiling froth. Wings outspread. Feather-tips rippling with faint electricity. Not the severed feathers left in the wake of Yoritomo's blade. Not the ugly, squared-off shapes that had grounded him in the Razor Isles, made him incapable of anything but a feeble, wobbling glide.

Feathers—pearlescent, whole and perfect and beautiful.

In her memory, she saw the severed feather she'd held in Five Flowers Palace as she waited in the dark for his return. Torn free during the clash with Kaiah in the Daimyo's garden.

No. Not torn free . . .

The pair of them flying over the Iishi, just days after her father had died.

How long until you molt? she'd asked.

I WILL HAVE NO NEW PLUMAGE FOR MONTHS. NOT UNTIL MY WINTER COAT GROWS IN.

Sitting together in the rain by the Kagé pit trap, alone in the wilderness, waiting for the hunters to become the hunted.

Father said you would molt your feathers. Like a bird. Is that true?

TWICE YEARLY. SUMMER AND WINTER.

Summer.

A smile on her lips.

And *winter.*

She'd missed it. Tangled in fears of Earthcrushers and gaijin hordes. Blinded by the storm clouds over the Seven Isles, her own traumas, failing to notice the feather trail he'd left scattered about the gardens. Speaking not a word. A tiger's cunning. An eagle's pride.

Buruu roared, echoing amongst the thunderclaps, the day-bright salvos of lightning. And Yukiko raised her hands into the air and screamed, laughing like a lunatic as he soared through the deluge, wings spread in all their glory—a beauty she'd almost forgotten. Lost eons ago on the *Thunder Child* beneath her father's blade. Lost again in the stinking pit of Kigen arena, sundered by a madman's pride. But no man or blade was here to touch him now. Just the Storm God and his children, bellowing triumph across tempest skies. Bloodied and torn, but beautiful. Beautiful and whole and perfect, as he'd been in the moment she first saw him, touching his mind for the first time, his voice as deafening as the peals of thunder crashing through the skies around her.

WHO ARE YOU? he'd asked.

Yukiko, she'd replied.

WHAT ARE YOU?

She flooded his mind with warmth, with love, relief and joy and the thrill of victory. Everything would be all right now. She knew it. As surely as she knew herself.

You're beautiful, Buruu. You're BEAUTIFUL!

He reared up in the storm, turned on the Everstorm pack, eyes ablaze. And the sky was filled with his voice, as loud as Raijin's drums, echoing in the spaces between the rain and the thrumming halls of their hearts.

I AM THE GET OF SKAA, KHAN-SON, EXILED AND NOW RETURNED. I AM A CHILD OF EVERSTORM, AND I CLAIM ITS RULE THIS DAY, IN THE EYES OF FATHER RAIJIN, AT THE SEAT OF HIS FATHER, SUSANO-Ō.

I AM HE WHO WAS ROAHH, THEN KINSLAYER, NOW REFORGED ANEW IN BLOOD AND THUNDER.

I AM KHAN.

Thunder rocked the skies; the triumphant bellow of the Storm God's son.

I.

AM.

BURUU.

30
PURIFICATION

Weeksend.

Rain spattered on corrugated roofs, a stutter-step beat filling the gutted warehouse district with the ring of hollow sticks on empty drums. Yoshi trudged through Downside, the stench of old smoke and char strung heavy in the air. He could hear the rhythms of Kigen Bay under the downpour's heartbeat, smell the stink of rot beneath the fire's leavings.

The satchel of Yakuza money slapped against his back as he walked, and he tossed fistfuls of coin at the blacklung beggars as he passed. The tsurugi sword was a comforting threat beneath his oilskin cloak, the bulk of the near empty iron-thrower nudging the small of his back. The Scorpion Children's money could have paid for some fancy digs in an Upside bedhouse, but he'd felt like sleeping rough. Like they used to back in the day, when every copper bit was a blessing, every meal a stroke of fortune. Before the entire world went mad.

Him, Hana, and Jurou.

Yoshi reached beneath his goggles, wiped at his eyes. The memory of the Shinshi's bride, the terror on her face as he'd picked up her babe . . .

"Don't you touch my son!"

He walked. Past refugees huddled in Kigen's burned-out shells, through crumpled, dirty streets and shadows of broken sky-spires. A motor-rickshaw roared faintly in the distance, his boots slapping the ash-choked floor. Figures brushed past him beneath filthy paper parasols, hungry eyes stared from dead-end alley mouths. But the blade showing just beneath his cloak and the dozen corpse-rats following him told even the most desperate folk that he wasn't a meal to be swallowed in one bite.

Head down. Shoulders slumped. Unthinking. Following his feet as the press of people grew thicker, sewer children spreading out about him, scampering through the riots' leavings. He didn't know where he was walking. What he was doing. Only the woman's face as he hoisted her son from the crib. Staring as if he were some kind of monster.

As if?

A phantom rising unbidden in his mind. Messy bangs hanging over dark, moist eyes. Lips soft as pillows, pressed sweetly against his own. And the ache, gods, the ache in his chest . . .

I got them for you, Princess.

Fist clenched beneath his cloak.

I got them.

So why didn't he feel better? Why didn't it go away? He could still smell the blood on his hands. Still hear the words of the thunder tiger in his mind.

YOU WILL FIND NO PEACE IN IT. THE STAINS NEVER WASH OFF. I KNOW.

Never wash off . . .

Jurou was still dead. The hole in him still empty. And his baby sister? The one person who mattered in all the world? He'd left her alone with the weight of a clan on her shoulders.

What was he still doing here?

He stopped amidst the crush, people pushing past into a broad, cobbled space. He realized he'd wandered to the Market Square, following the tide without thought. Gawpers and fanatics. Beggars and streetwalkers. One or two bushimen amidst the mob. And up ahead, in the sunken mall surrounded by four looming chunks of blackened stone, there they stood. Four Guildsmen in tabards of the Purifier Sect, the pristine white stained ugly gray. Black rain beaded on burnished brass, the horrid, blood-red eyes aglow, scorch marks smudged about the flame-spitters at their wrists.

Yoshi pulled his hat over his eyes, toxins dripping from the brim in a treacle waterfall. A Purifier stepped forward, hands held aloft. He spoke in a voice like dying lotusflies; a snatch of scripture from the *Book of Ten Thousand Days*:

"Soiled by Yomi's filth,
The taint of the Underworld,
Izanagi wept.
Seeking Purity,
The Way of the Cleansing Rite,
The Maker God bathed.
And from these waters,
Were begat Sun, Moon and Storm.
Walk Purity's Way."

A few hoarse cries went up from the mob, a few fists raised. The crowd swelled, threatening to knock Yoshi off his feet. Desperate faces and desperate stares—the wax-paper look of people running on no sleep, no food, families starving and children weeping. Refugees from the northern fronts, shell-shocked faces hidden behind dirty kerchiefs. Neo-chōnin merchants who'd lost their fortunes in the unrest. All of them drawn to this place like moths to flame—this one semblance of order remaining from better days.

Even if it was the worst those days had to offer.

A second Purifier unfurled a scroll, rice-paper stained by filth-spattered skies.

"By order of the First Bloom of the Lotus Guild, the Purifier Sect is charged with purging the taint of yōkai in Shima's bloodstream. The corruption of the spirit world, the poison of beasts in the minds of men, the stain of Impurity. As always, at this weeksend Purification, a one and two-thirds measure of chi and five iron kouka shall be granted any loyal citizen who walks the path of righteousness and brings forth any Impure for judgment upon the Altar of Purity."

The Guildsman rolled up his scroll, peered into the crowd with bloody eyes.

"Are there any who would lay accusation?"

"I do!"

A graveled bellow from the crowd. The sea parted before a burly man, a stalking tiger inked down his right arm, three linked rings of the merchant guild on his left. In one muscular arm, the man held another fellow, head lolling, barely keeping his feet.

"What is your name, citizen?" demanded the Guildsman.

"Tora Watari, a humble merchant. I run the Geisha House on Arena Boulevard."

"Come forward and be heard at this Altar!"

The merchant pushed past the gawkers, dragging the second fellow with him. Yoshi could see the man was elderly—long gray hair in bedraggled knots, skin cracked from a life beneath the red sun.

The merchant stopped before the sunken mall, cast a steady gaze about the Burning Stones. The Purifiers looked up at him, eyes aglow, merciless and insectoid.

"The cleansing of the Impure is our most sacred duty, commanded in the *Book of Ten Thousand Days* by the Maker God himself. But you should know, citizen, any bearing false witness against their fellows will take their place upon the Altar. To pervert this sacred right with slander is to pervert the will of the Maker God himself. You understand this?"

"I do," the merchant nodded.

"Then level your claim."

"This bastard," the merchant shook the old man, "moved into Arena Boulevard a few nights ago. A flute slinger who busked on corners. I thought little of it. But then I heard from my girls that he made the corpse-rats dance for the gutter-waifs' amusement. I saw this with my own eyes. The vermin moved to his music, standing on their hind legs as if they were people. And when one child asked how he did it, the old man said it was a gift from the gods."

"Blasphemer!" cried one of the mob.

"Burn him!" went the cry.

Yoshi shook his head. All the shit this world was in. All the chaos right outside those walls. Gaijin armies poised to wipe the lands clean. People set to fight and die against an army of iron and black smoke. And these fools waste time with this madness?

"Still yourselves, citizens!" The Purifier's shout drowned out the screeches. "Claim is leveled. Bring him forward, brothers, that we may know the truth of it."

Purifiers took the old man from the merchant's arms, dragging him beneath the Burning Stones. Brief lightning lit the skies, Yoshi squinting behind his goggles, catching a glint of metal in the crowd. A crooked face. Narrowed eyes. Gone now, too quick to see.

The Purifiers were gathered about the old man, forming a screen between themselves and the crowd. Even standing on tiptoes, Yoshi couldn't see for the mob and the rain and the wall of glinting brass. Eyelashes fluttering against his cheeks, the boy reached out in the Kenning, to the dozens of corpse-rats scattered about the Square, finding one little crooked mongrel crouched amidst the kindling at the Stones' feet. And as Yoshi's skin crawled with the bites of phantom fleas, he forced those tiny eyes of black glass up to watch the Purifiers work.

The Guildsmen held the old man in a pitiless grip. A blade gleamed, marked with kanji of the Guild. Blood flowed from a cut wrist, the old man struggling, scarlet dripping into a vial in a Purifier's hand. When the vial was full, the Guildsman carried it to a bench, stacked with half a dozen identical iron boxes, perhaps a foot square, again embossed with Guild sigils.

Yoshi watched through stolen eyes, fascinated despite himself. In days past, this ritual would have been performed within chapterhouse walls. He couldn't fathom why the Guild had taken to testing in public. Something to do with the Guild rebellion? Regardless, it was a glimpse inside the chapterhouse walls he'd never expected to see. This sect of zealots and their archaic rites, their devotion to gods that had never once made themselves known to Yoshi or his kin.

Madmen . . .

The crowd pressed in, all eager to catch a glimpse. The Purifier with his vial of blood was speaking some kind of incantation. Yoshi heard snatches from the *Book of Ten Thousand Days*, invocations of the Maker God. And finally, the Purifier slid back a panel in one of the iron boxes and, upending the black vial, dripped the blood inside.

A hush fell over the Square, broken only by the whispering rain. A shot of thunder rolled across the clouds. Onlookers blinked, mumbling disappointment, the merchant who'd leveled accusation looking distinctly uncomfortable. Yoshi scowled. What the hells were they expecting? Lord Izanagi to descend from the heavens to waggle his divine finger at this poor bastard? A choir of oni to rise from Yomi and howl the—

White noise.

An inversion of sound, as if his skull had been turned inside out.

Yoshi put his hands to his ears, found his shuriken wound bleeding anew. He felt as if someone had driven a fist into his stomach, tasted ash on the back of his tongue.

The iron box on the bench trembled, rattling on the table's surface, three hundred beats per minute. And with an utterance that was not so much a sound as an *absence* of it, the rivets popped and the sides buckled and the box twisted upon itself as if some invisible giant had clutched it in one mighty fist and squeezed.

Thin white smoke issued from cracks in the metal. Something black leaked from sundered seams. And though it was mad, Yoshi swore he could smell sweetness. A breath of Iishi wind, crisp with the scent of green and good, before the stench of exhaust fumes and ashes filled his nose and throat again, bringing stinging tears to his eyes.

"Impure!" cried one of the Guildsmen.

"Impure!"

The old man cried out, arms twisted behind his back as he was marched to one of the Burning Stones. Wrists dragged above his head, slapped hard into hungry manacles smeared in charcoal leavings of the hundreds before him—women and children and young and old. The fanatics in the crowd raised their voices, fists to the sky. The merchant smiled and bowed as the Purifiers handed him his chi in small metal drums. Bought and paid for in blood.

"Burn him!"

"Impure! Impure!"

"Are there any more who would level accusation this day?" A Purifier held up his hands, calling to the crowd. "Any more tainted by the Spirit World's stain, haunting this world of men? Bring them forth, that they may be tested and found as wanting as this wretch!"

An accusing finger was leveled at the old man, now shaking with terror.

"I only wanted to make the children smile! Gods have mercy!" He caught Yoshi's eyes amidst the mob, pinned him in that terrified stare. "Please! Mercy!"

Mercy . . .

Yoshi felt the tsurugi's hilt beneath his fingertips, hard and cool. His right hand around the iron-thrower at the small of his back, staring with stolen eyes at the tinder waiting beneath the old man's feet. It'd be mercy to put a shot to him. Flat-out end him before the sparks started to fly. But then what? There might not be many bushi about, but a mob would see to him straight, and the Purifiers would make him squeal. Probably chain him to that stone in the old man's place to sing in time while the flames danced over his skin.

The smart step was to ghost. Back to Kigen Station. Buy passage north with this yakuza iron. Get back to Hana and the war that would decide the future of the entire country . . .

And then what?

Lead an army? March in line? Send a corpse-rat horde against the Earth-crusher?

What then, boy?

A gutter-rat was what he was. This was his war. This city. This hole. This beautiful, ugly whore who'd suckled him when nowhere in the world felt like home. And if he was going to cash, it might as well be on home ground rather than some ash-choked battlefield. Might as well be for one of his own instead of a clan who would've gladly lit him up three months past.

Impure. Cursed. Tainted. Whatever. Something in this old man and Yoshi were the same. Something in the both of them, something the Guild wanted to eliminate. And whatever the reason, if the Guild wanted it gone, that meant it was worth fighting for.

Dying for?

Yoshi swallowed. He remembered the look in the woman's eyes—the Gentleman's wife screaming at the monster he'd almost become. He could still become. Even here. Even now.

MUCH CHANGES WITH THE SEASONS.

Buruu's voice ringing in his skull, tinged with the taste of thunder.

THE SHAPE OF HEROES, CERTAINLY.

A sigh from the depths of his chest.

Fuck it, then.

He engaged the iron-thrower pressure.

Fuck it all.

Shoving through the mob, paper parasols and straw hats, black clothes and yellow grins. Feeling the sewer-children around him; a hundred eyes in back of his head. And he pushed out onto the mall's edge, treading down the steps as the Purifier turned to glare with its glowing, blood-soaked eyes. Stare at this boy stepping lean and filthy toward him, bringing up his right hand, one little fistful of steel, and pulling gentle as a first kiss on the trigger.

The iron-thrower roared. A glass eye shattered, went dark. The Guildsmen spun in place and crumpled. The crowd roared. Panic. Outrage. Shock.

And then the world stopped making any kind of sense.

A burst of white light, spherical and blinding, right in the center of the Burning Stones. A soundless explosion, edges tinged with translucent, bloody red. A sudden stench of evaporating chi, the fuel lines in the Purifier's atmos-suits splitting wide, spewing plumes of blue-black vapor. The Guildsmen spasmed, dropped to their knees beneath brass deadweight, the chattering mechabacii on their chests falling silent as shapes loomed out of the crowd.

Half a dozen in all. Three boys around Yoshi's age—the first, sharp and quick with an angular face. The second, tall and swarthy, crooked features and a protruding lower jaw, as if someone had dropped him one too many times as a babe. A third, small and wiry—and none-too-hard on the eyes, if you'll indulge for a moment—dark hair drawn back in braids.

The other three were a motley crew: a tall man with lean muscles and skin like a hungry ghost. A young boy, also pale as death fresh warmed. And the third, a woman—gods, an *old woman*—casting aside her cloak as eight long, chromed arms unfurled from her back.

But Yoshi's eyes were on the three boys, raising their warclubs high. Each wore short-sleeved uwagi beneath their cloaks, heedless of the toxic rain, as if they *wanted* people to see the burn scars where their irezumi used to be.

No clan. No lord. No master.

Kagé.

The crowd rippled with panic, shock and dismay rising as the boys fell to with their warclubs, pounding up and down on the helpless Guildsmen until their helms split and the glowing eyes cracked black, and red, red, red seeped across the flagstones at their feet.

"We are the Kagé!" the first boy cried. "The clenched fist! The raised voice! The fire to burn away the Lotus Guild, and free Shima from the grip of their wretched weed!"

He pointed to the other three in his gang—the boy, the man, the woman and her razors.

"These folk were once Guild, now risen against the evil that breeds within that five-sided slave pit! If those born to the Guild and its lies have seen the truth of it, why can't you?"

The boy looked amongst the crowd, narrowed stare finding the merchant who had turned the old man over, still clutching his barrels of chi.

"Why can't you?"

Yoshi stumbled down the steps, ears ringing, eyes fixed on the iron boxes. As the crooked-faced boy unfastened the old man's manacles, Yoshi pried the lid from one of the untouched vessels, peering inside. He ran his hand through it, dark particles rising off the surface and dancing like dust. Black and greasy, reeking of old blood and burning hair.

Ashes . . .

He looked at the box sundered by the Purifier's testing ritual, split at the seams and spilling its guts over the benchtop. Scooping up a handful, he let it run from his fist, crumbling dry, turning to mud in his palm beneath the spattering black rain.

Dirt.

He blinked, giving an experimental sniff.

Just ordinary dirt.

What the bleeding hells . . .

"Bushimen." The old woman's warning to her comrades pulled Yoshi from his confusion. "More Guild. They're coming."

"Let's go," slurred the boy with the crooked face.

Yoshi reached out to the flint-black eyes stretched across the city, the thousand mongrel shapes in alleys and on corners, seeing all. The men in iron breastplates converging from north and east. The shapes in glittering brass, blue-black plumes trailing east to the chapterhouse that had spit them into the air. And he grabbed the boy who'd spoken to the crowd, pulling him up short as he turned to run.

"No," Yoshi said. "That's the way they're coming from."

The six rebels stared hard, eyes drifting from the iron-thrower still smoking in his hand to the Purifier whose brains he'd splattered across the cobbles.

"Do I know you?" said the boy.

"No, Kagé boy." Yoshi tipped his hat. "But I know you. And Yukiko. And Kaori. And pretty little Michi. You and yours, all."

The three boys blinked in amazement, shared a handful of confused glances.

"Time enough for the chit and the chat later, friends."

Yoshi nodded south, back toward Docktown.

"For now, follow me."

31
SEEING AND BELIEVING

The tent was as big as any house Hana had seen. A small palace suspended by poles as broad as tree trunks, the floor covered in dirty rugs and furs, fire burning bright in a pit of blackened stones. She blinked in the gloom, scarcely remembering to pull off her goggles as her eye adjusted to the darkness. A faint pink glow spilled into the dark as the storm swelled outside.

Hushed whispers. Hungry. Feminine.

Piotr stood behind her, the gaijin called Aleksandar beside her. It was still too much to think of him as her uncle. Too bizarre to look him in the face and see her own eyes, Yoshi's lopsided smile. She'd left Kaiah standing watch outside, glaring at the ten thousand warriors the way a cat watches a legion of hungry mice.

- *WALK CAREFULLY, HANA.* -

Don't worry. If I need you, I'll call in a heartbeat.

She made out figures in the dark; a man in iron armor with a face too small for his brick-shaped head. He was surrounded by gaijin hammermen, wreathed in pelts of wolves and bears and beasts whose shape she didn't know. At his feet sat six enormous hounds—the only living dogs she'd ever seen—growling softly.

She held up her hand, touched their thoughts, and they stilled at once, stubby tails between their legs. They whined to her about the dirty rain, the poisoned air, how they missed their birthlands. She pushed comfort into their minds, a smooth and soothing caramel warmth, laced with the scent of Iishi green.

She saw two figures near the fire, standing so close they touched. A woman, perhaps thirty, clad in the beaten brass skins of Guildsmen, lightning etched into cheeks and chin, glaring at Piotr as if she wanted to gut him. But it was the other who'd spoken: a woman near fifty, face patterned with claw scars, too symmetrical to have been the work of an actual beast. Ash-blond hair was entwined with bone and polished teeth, black feathers about her shoulders.

Aleksandar took Hana's hand, and with a reassuring squeeze, brought her into the firelight. Dozens of stares followed her, but her own was fixed on the women before her, their right irises glowing with the same watered-rose as her own.

"Hana Mostovoi," Aleksandar said, and Hana barely recognized the name as hers. "I present Holy Mother Natassja, and Sacred Sister Katya."

Hana stood tall despite the fear, her palms soaked to the wrists. The older woman spoke words she couldn't comprehend; a language tangled in faded snatches of childhood memory.

"The Holy Mother says you are welcome here," Aleksandar said. "Daughter of Anya, daughter of Sascha, daughter of Darya, Matriarch of House Mostovoi."

"Gods above . . ." she breathed.

Aleksandar translated and the women hissed between themselves, shaking their heads. The old one stepped forth, squeezing Hana's arms, poking her ribs as if she were meat in a market stall. And finally, as the girl flinched beneath her touch, the old woman pulled down the leather patch covering Hana's missing eye. She felt naked, heat rising in her cheeks.

- I AM HERE. FEAR NOTHING. NO ONE. -

The old woman spoke again, Aleksandar speaking afterward.

"The Holy Mother says you have the look of your grandmother. She sees her strength in you. Great things in your future. Great and terrible things."

"My grandmother?" Hana glanced at Aleksandar.

"A great woman. A true daughter of the Goddess. And your mother after her. Zryachniye, we call them. Those who See."

"See what?"

"Each is different." Aleksandar nodded to the fierce woman wearing the Lotusmen skin. "Sister Katya sees the riddle of the weather, sunlight and storm-pulse. The Holy Mother what may come, and what should not."

"Piotr said your ruler was Sighted too."

"Imperatritsa," Aleksandar nodded.

"What does she see?"

"The truth of men's souls."

"What will I see?"

Aleksandar repeated the question, and the Holy Mother smiled and replied in Morcheban. The language didn't seem as harsh in Hana's ears anymore. Surrounded by it, she found a deep music in the cadence and tone, tangled impressions of younger days, her mother singing to her and Yoshi when Father was passed-out drunk—

"The Holy Mother says that is for the Goddess to decide."

"You said my mother was a daughter of these Sighted. But her eye didn't glow."

"The Goddess flows in our family," Aleksandar said. "But she only manifests every few generations. Darya, your great-grandmother, she was Sighted. Priestess of our House. After many years of service, she left the Holy Order to take rule of House Mostovoi. To pass the gift of the Goddess to her unborn children. The bloodline had to be preserved."

"I don't understand . . ."

"You are daughter of a great tradition, Hana. Goddess-touched. We thought the Mostovoi bloodline broken. The gift is passed only to daughters. The hope of our House rested in your mother. My sister. When she was taken . . ." Aleksandar shook his head. "And now to find you amidst these murdering pigs, not only alive but *Touched* . . ." He caressed her right cheek, gentle as a first snow. "Goddess be praised, it is a miracle."

He turned to the assembled gaijin, shouted some kind of prayer. The cry was repeated among the men, murmured by the priestesses. Each woman stepped forward and embraced Hana, kissing her cheeks and lips, glowing eyes warming loving smiles. Like long-lost sisters.

Like *family*.

"Gods, I don't understand any of this," Hana breathed.

Aleksandar took her hands, gave her fingers a reassuring squeeze.

"Understand at least that you are safe, my blood. That you are home."

"I have a brother. Yoshi . . ."

"He will be welcome also. You are my blood, and I am yours. And when we have cleansed the slavers from this land, we will—"

"Cleansed?" Hana frowned. "What do you mean cleansed?"

". . . When the Shimans are dead."

"Dead? No, there are good people here—"

"Good people?" A frown. "Those people who stole our women and children? Who turned their island into a wasteland and now seek to steal ours? There is no goodness here, Hana."

"No, Alek—" She frowned. "Uncle. Listen. There *is* evil here. A group called the Lotus Guild. A clan who bear the Tiger flag. They're the ones who've driven us to war against you."

"Us?" Aleksandar blinked. "Hana, *you* are not one of *them*—"

"There are good people here. A clan who stands against the Guild. People who are risking *everything*, preparing to fight the chi-mongers even now. You have to help them."

Aleksandar glanced at his commander, the Holy Mother following the exchange with tilted head, Sister Katya beside her, swaying as if she heard hidden music.

"Help them?" Rage burned in his eyes. "Hana, we are here to *annihilate* them. To ensure they never steal another daughter. Another sister. Another son."

Hana looked among the group—the glowing eyes of the Sighted, the flint-black stares of the warriors. And taking Aleksandar's hand in her own, the Holy Mother's in the other, she brought them to the fire's edge and pulled them down beside her.

"You should get comfortable. This is going to be a long story . . ."

Y ou're out of your godsdamned mind!"

The Blackbird stood on the deck of his ship, the fair *Kurea*, arms folded across his belly, broad and round as a drum. He was nose-to-nose with a furious, red-faced Akihito, refusing to bat an eyelid. Breath hung in frozen clouds between them, the drone of the ship's engines underscoring their shouts. Michi leaned against the railing nearby, hands behind her back. Up here above the clouds, the skies were a brilliant, bloody red, but the temperature was still low enough to freeze the tears in her eyes. Wind draped her hair across her face, goggles spattered with frozen residue from the *Kurea*'s exhaust. Black ice gleamed on the boards under her feet.

Akihito and the Blackbird were both the size of small houses, rumbling like a couple of very angry motor-rickshaws. Akihito was pure muscle beneath his winter wools, but his leg would put him at a disadvantage if forced to brawl on the swaying deck. If the tiff turned violent, Michi honestly wasn't sure which man she'd lay odds against.

"Hana is down there amongst those gaijin!" Akihito shouted. "We have to help her!"

The Blackbird crooked one eyebrow and spat, saliva crystallizing on the deck. "First off, you effete Phoenix bastard, *nobody* tells me what I 'have to' do on my own ship. Second, we don't even know she's down amongst those round-eye bastards—"

"Because you won't fly close enough for a look—"

"And THIRD, if your little slip was stupid enough to fly off alone and land in the middle of ten thousand gaijin berserks, that's her own fault. I'm not flying this ship within spitting range of those 'thopters, and I'm sure as hells not taking her below the clouds in this storm!"

"Little slip?" Akihito's eyes grew dangerously wide. "You son of a ronin's whore—"

"Leave my mother out of this, little man. Liable to hurt my feelings."

"She could be in trouble. She could be *dead*."

"Best to grab yourself an umbrella then, Akihito-san. In case all the shits I don't give start falling from the sky."

"Gentlemen." Michi placed a restraining hand on their forearms. "I think everyone needs to breathe deep and think some happy thoughts. Spring days . . . The laughter of a carefree child . . . A woman with cleavage you could hide a boat inside . . ."

Akihito ignored her, still glowering at the captain. "Why fly us here if you were going to shit yourself five miles short of the mark?"

"You're welcome to get out and walk the rest of the way, if you think the leg can take it."

"It can take anything you dish out and more, you fat bastard."

"That so? Do you think it could take you kneeling down to suck my—"

"Izanagi's balls, will you two just kiss and get it over with?" Michi shouted.

Blackbird looked at her sideways, nodded to Akihito without missing a beat.

"His beard looks prickly. I have very delicate skin."

Akihito's face contorted as he tried to stifle his grin. The Blackbird skipped the pretense, bursting into a barrel-chested guffaw. The cloudwalkers around them relaxed and slouched back to their posts—it looked like there would be no sky-plank walking today.

Thunder bellowed in the cloud cover below, tension fading with the echoes.

"I'm sorry, my friend." The Blackbird patted Akihito's shoulder. "But flying any closer to that camp is suicide. *Kurea* is fast, but not armed for war. We fly low enough, those 'thopters will cut us to pieces. And given you were aboard *Thunder Child* when she died, I shouldn't need to explain what happens if Susano-ō decided to give our inflatable a little kiss."

Akihito sighed, running one hand over his braids. "We have to save her."

"She might not *need* saving, Akihito," Michi said. "Piotr is with her. You've seen the way he talks about her. I don't think he'd lead her willingly into danger."

"Can we at least drop below the clouds for a moment?" Akihito looked at the Blackbird, pleading. "See if we can spot Kaiah amongst the mob? She shouldn't be hard to spot."

Blackbird looked the big man up and down. "Well, well. Got it bad, don't you now?"

"Sick as a dog, this boy," Michi nodded.

"Stop talking foolishness," Akihito growled.

The Blackbird and Michi shared a knowing glance, the girl shaking her head. The Blackbird turned and bellowed at his helmsman (not entirely necessary given the man stood six feet away). Compressors were engaged, hydrogen crushed inside the inflatable with a vacant hiss. The *Kurea* descended, her crew striking up chi-powered lanterns as the clouds bubbled up over her edges and flooded the deck.

Michi took up vigil beside Akihito, shivering inside her cloaks. The cloud breathed down the back of her neck with clammy fingers. After what seemed an insufferable age, they broke through into the midst of a heavy squall. *Kurea* rocked like a pendulum, filthy black rain flooding over her decks. Michi cursed and pulled up her kerchief. In seventeen years, she'd never seen rain this toxic. Even swaddled inside a heavy oilskin, it still left her feeling dirty.

. . . No. Not dirty. That was the wrong word.

Unwholesome.

She peered over the side and saw the gaijin camp through the downpour; thousands of dirty gray tents, huge machines on tank treads carrying rows of rotor-thopters, like great metal insects with their broods clutching their backs. A black runnel had been carved in their wake, the mud churned by thousands of feet, metal treads, rubber tires as they marched inexorably toward Yama city. Lightning tore the skies a hundred yards to port, and Akihito flinched.

"You see anything?"

Michi roared over the howling wind. "Nothing!"

"They've sure as hells seen us!" Blackbird was peering through a mechanized spyglass. "Pilots are scrambling for those 'thopters!"

"Can you see Hana? Kaiah?"

"All I see is ten thousand round-eyes set to fuck our corpses! Helm, ascend one hundred and set her to full burn! We're off like a new bride's silkies!"

Michi turned on the captain and tilted her head. ". . . Silkies?"

"Well, what the hells do you call them?"

"Wait!" cried Akihito. "There they are!"

Michi peered over the side again and saw a flash of white through the falling black. Her heart surged as she recognized Kaiah, a small figure astride her that could only be Hana, ascending through the downpour. But the 'thopter pilots were still revving their engines, gaijin soldiers emerging from their tents, pointing skyward, clamor spreading across the camp. Was Hana fleeing them? Were they chasing her? Where was Piotr?

What the hells is going on?

She found one hand drifting to the chainkatana at her waist, jaw clenched.

The thunder tiger and her rider rose higher, Akihito pacing like an expectant father. As they drew level with the sky-ship, Michi recognized Hana under her heavy clothes. The girl had her kerchief and hood up, eye hidden behind her goggles—expression completely masked.

The crew cleared space on the deck as Kaiah drew closer, a few still murmuring in wonder at the sight of the magnificent beast in full flight. Blackbird groaned in sympathetic agony as the thunder tiger landed, talons tearing his ship's deck to splinters. Akihito bounded down to the main deck despite his injured leg, pushing through the mob as Hana slipped off the arashitora's back. Kaiah shook herself like a wet dog, spattering the assembled crew with reeking black. Hana pulled down her kerchief, tugged the cowl from her head. Akihito stopped in his tracks. Michi caught her breath.

Hana had bleached the dye from her hair, leaving it a gleaming blond.

An uneasy murmur rippled among the crew, hands drifting to weapons, a few backing away. The girl was pale as ghostlights, slender and fierce. What the hells had she been doing down there among the round-eye army? How was she still alive?

"Hana?" Akihito's voice was uncertain, sandpaper at the edges.

The girl pushed up her goggles, glanced around the crew, that strange glowing eye finally settling on Akihito. Her voice was as cold as storm winds.

"Why are you here?"

"You left without telling anyone—"

"We don't answer to you, Akihito."

The big man blinked, taken aback. "We were just worried about you."

That glowing gaze flickered to Michi. Back to Akihito. "I'm sure."

"What the hells are you doing out here by yourself?"

"Trying to save what's left of this hellhole." Hana shrugged. "Convincing the gaijin not to rub us off the map."

"Did Piotr put you up to this?"

"Put me up to it?" Hana frowned. "Isn't this what everyone expects me to be doing? Being a stormdancer? Playing hero and saving everyone's asses? I wish you people would make up your godsdamned minds about what you want me to be."

Michi cleared her throat. "Why would the gaijin listen to you, Hana?"

The girl pointed to her eye. "I carry the mark of the Goddess. My uncle, brother of the woman my father dragged back here to Shima—he's one of the commanders below. We've been speaking for the best part of a day. Him. The Marshal. The Sighted. And little old me."

Akihito glanced at the thunder tiger looming at Hana's back. "What did they say?"

"Lots of things." The girl's reply was cool, her gaze cooler. "But they're confused. To find someone who bears the mark of the Goddess born of a Shiman father . . . it's changed the way they see us. The way they think the Goddess sees us. I told them about Yukiko, the Kagé, the rebels in Yama. They're not sure what to make of any of this now."

"Are they going to press their attack?" Michi asked.

"Against the Guild? Most definitely. But as for the rest of us?" A shrug. "They honestly don't know. Not anymore."

"Gods above . . ." Akihito breathed.

"So." That cold, glowing gaze flitted back and forth between Michi and Akihito. "You two might just get to play happy families after all."

Akihito blinked in the lightning strobe. "What?"

"I understand, Akihito." Hana drew a breath, as if reaching deep for the words. "I can't say it doesn't hurt. But I understand. I need to be bigger than that. I need to be more."

"Wait, what?" Michi was incredulous. "You think he and I . . ?"

Akihito looked at Michi, terrified. "Me and her?"

Up on the pilot's deck, the Blackbird rolled his eyes at his first mate and sighed.

"I saw you," Hana said. "The courting gift you gave her . . ."

"Courting . . ?" Akihito frowned, remembering. "It was just a scrollcase for her book, Hana. She's writing a history of the war. I think it's important. That's all."

Michi held out her hands as if to take the world by the scruff and steady it. "There is *nothing* going on between us, Hana. Gods above, absolutely *nothing*."

Akihito glanced at her sideways. "You don't have to say it like *that* . . ."

"No. Really. I do."

Hana licked at her lips, dirty blond hair plastered to her face. "You mean . . ."

Kaiah watched with narrowed eyes as Akihito limped up to the girl, deck rolling beneath their feet, thunder filling the skies around them.

"I mean . . ." Akihito ran one hand over the back of his neck, looking like a newly landed fish. "I mean, I was really worried about you . . ."

The big man reached down, one clumsy paw encircling Hana's. The girl gazed up at him, uncertainty etched in her face. Her voice was a whisper, nearly lost in the thunder.

"But why?"

Akihito glanced around at the assembled cloudwalkers, to Michi, to Kaiah. Down at the deck, shuffling his feet, at the small hand in his own, fingers slowly entwining with his.

"Ah, hells with it . . ."

The big man stooped, and wrapping one arm around Hana's waist, lifted her gently off the ground. The wind filled the empty space between them, slowly shrinking. Hana's eye grew wide, a delighted smile curling the corners of her mouth as Akihito leaned in and pressed his lips to hers. She stared for just a moment longer, as if paralyzed by disbelief. And then her eyelids fluttered closed, and she pressed both hands to Akihito's cheeks, body against his, kissing him back with a hunger born of long starvation and breathing in his sighs.

Michi found herself smiling, shaking her head as she turned away with all but the most voyeuristic of the crew, leaving the pair alone in the crowd.

Up on the pilot's deck, the Blackbird gave a polite round of applause.

"About godsdamned time."

Yasuo sighed and inhaled another lungful of lotus, feet up on the controls of his locomotive. Kigen Station echoed with the faint clang of tools, the rumbling growl of power generators. He had ten minutes left on his break, then he'd have to move his train to Platform Two for the next troop shipment. Yasuo kept the thought to himself, but he couldn't help but notice how the soldiers were getting younger with every load sent north.

He pored over his newssheet with bloodshot eyes, the driver's cabin filled with a haze of pipe smoke. The headlines spoke of the great Tora army marching under Daimyo Hiro, set to crush the Fox Daimyo and his Kagé allies. The story insinuated Isamu's involvement in Lady Aisha's assassination, his desire to seize the Four Thrones of Shima.

"Bastards," Yasuo muttered. "The wise man never trusts the fox . . ."

He heard the soft scrape of footsteps behind, felt something hard and chill pressed against the back of his skull. A glance into the windshield revealed the reflection of a boy with a shaved head and a lopsided smile. Around the boy stood a handful of others—a tall, crooked-faced youth, another with a face of sharp angles, an old woman with silver glinting beneath her cloak.

"How do, friend?" said the boy.

Yasuo gawped, saying nothing.

"This is an iron-thrower pressed in back of your head, 'case you were speculating."

Yasuo slowly raised his hands.

"This engine we're riding fully fueled?"

"Hai," Yasuo nodded.

"Enough to get us to Yama city?"

". . . I have no authorization—"

The pressure increased at the back of Yasuo's head.

"Seems I've a whole fistful of authorization resting on your cowl, friend."

"Hai." A rapid nod. "We will get to Yama."

The pressure eased, the boy's reflection grinning like Kitsune let loose in a henhouse.

"Start it up, then. We've got a ways to go."

32
LEGACY

They stood in a circle atop Susano-ō's throne, gathered above thrashing waters beneath a thunder sky. Over two dozen in all, black and white, young and old, sleek feathers and gleaming talons. And each in turn, they scratched the stone at their feet and dipped their heads, acknowledging he who had slain Torr and claimed the seat for his own. Standing in the circle's center, dripping watery red onto the rock beneath, the pale monkey-child beside him.

Their Khan.

Yukiko swam in their thoughts, the overdose of predatory instinct. She focused on two above the others—two minds alight with more than subservience or uncertainty.

The first, a young buck around Buruu's age, black as murder. She recognized him from Buruu's memories—Sukaa, the Khan-son who had taken Esh's eye. She searched his mind and found thoughts of vendetta. Love for his fallen father and the desire for revenge. Nevertheless, the buck bowed to Buruu, growled he would serve. And with a glance at Yukiko that told her he'd enjoy nothing more than showing the sky her insides, he turned and took to the wing.

The second arashitora of note was a beautiful female, quick and cunning and sleek. Yukiko knew her from Buruu's memories also—the dam he'd chased across the clouds, the one who'd brought news of his father's death. And looking into the female's mind, she found a singular joy at Buruu's return. And amidst the feral thrumming of her heart, Yukiko found not just simple affection, but the bone-deep strength of a lifetime bond.

My gods . . .

Yukiko smoothed her hands over Buruu's feathers, bloodstained and sodden.

She's your mate.

Buruu looked to the female, tail lashing side to side, heart thundering with joy.

SHE IS.

You never told me.

I NEVER EXPECTED TO RETURN HERE.

Do you have any other secrets I should know?

The female stepped forward, bowed as the others had, lightning catching in the luminance of her feathers, a brief halo that seemed to set her ablaze. And then she stepped closer, ran her cheek across Buruu's, curling her head up under his chin and seeming to sigh.

Yukiko felt for the female's thoughts, wrapped them inside herself along with Buruu's, her own mind a bridge between them. As she stretched out to gently touch the female's mind, she felt Buruu's love for her fill her own. No hint of jealousy within her, no resentment at having to share his affections. The reunion of sisters who'd never met.

I am Yukiko.

I AM SHAI.

Her thoughts were warm, like a soft blanket near a roaring fireside. Alight with curiosity, instinctual aggression. Yukiko pushed her own warmth into the female's mind. Buruu curled his wings around them both.

You're Buruu's mate.

YOU ARE MONKEY-CHILD.

Buruu's voice echoed in their heads.

SHE IS MY SISTER. MY BLOOD AND LIFE. WITHOUT HER, I WOULD BE LOST.

SHE RIDES YOU?

SHE HAS EARNED THAT RIGHT. SHE IS YŌKAI KIN. FOX-CHILD. STORM-DANCER.

Shai's eyes gleamed as she looked Yukiko up and down.

*STORMDANCER . . . *

Buruu and I have been through much together. He saved my life, and I his.

BURUU?

THAT IS MY NAME NOW. ROAHH IS DEAD. KINSLAYER IS NO MORE.

WILL CALL YOU SUN AND MOON IF YOU WISH. YOU HAVE RE-TURNED TO ME.

I CANNOT STAY.

* . . . WHAT?*

I COME ONLY TO COLLECT OUR WARRIORS. THERE IS WAR IN SHIMA.

*WE NOT OF SHIMA . . . *

IT IS THE LAND WHERE OUR RACE WAS BORN. SINCE WE FLED, IT HAS TUMBLED TO RUIN. WE MUST DO WHAT WE CAN TO AVERT ITS FINAL FALL.

WHY?

BECAUSE IT IS RIGHT, SHAI. BECAUSE WE TURNED OUR BACKS.

Not all of us are evil, Shai. Some of us see the truth of things. The wrong we've committed. Some of us are fighting to change it.

The female's eyes flashed hand in hand with the lightning. Her glare could have cut steel.

ARASHITORA FIGHT YOUR BATTLES, MONKEY-CHILD? DIE FOR YOU?

HER NAME IS YUKIKO. AND ARASHITORA WILL FIGHT WHERE I COM-MAND. WHO CLAIMS KHAN IS KHAN.

Shai stared at Buruu, long and hard. She glanced at Yukiko, something between a purr and a growl rumbling in her chest.

PACK WILL THINK WRONG TO SERVE A MONKEY-CHILD'S WILL.

I don't want them to serve me at all.

The female snorted at her.

INDEED.

She turned back to Buruu.

*WILL YOU SEE RHAII? AM SURE HE WOULD SEE HIS KHAN WHILE
YOU STILL ARE KHAN.*

HE . . .

Buruu swallowed the dread in his gorge.

HE LIVES? BUT TORR . . .

*TORR ONLY PUNISH REBELS. YOU NOT HERE. I BENT KNEE AND
SERVED. RHAII SAFE.*

RAIJIN SAVE ME, I THOUGHT FOR CERTAIN . . .

WISH TO SEE HIM, THEN?

Buruu nodded.

BRING HIM HERE.

AS KHAN COMMANDS.

Shai turned and bounded across the stone, spreading pearlescent wings and
taking to the air. Yukiko's breath caught in her lungs, watching the beautiful figure cut the air, sweeping toward a spire of distant stone. Buruu watched her go,
eyes narrowed against the howling wind. She could feel the pain of his wounds,
gouged deep through feather, fur and flesh. But above that, she could feel an
emotion she'd never sensed in her brother before, so distant from his usual men-
tal landscape that she took a moment to recognize it for what it was.

Fear.

Are you all right?

I WILL ENDURE.

Who or what is Rhaii?

YOU COULD CALL HIM THE LAST SECRET BETWEEN YOU AND I.

Buruu heaved a sigh, shook himself beak to tail.

BUT IT WOULD BE SIMPLER TO CALL HIM MY SON.

"Kagé" was the Shiman word for "shadow."

A shadow isn't simply absence of illumination. They are born in the wake of the light, in the intercession between radiance and surface. They cannot exist in vacuum. They cannot be, in and of themselves.

All shadows are *made*.

Two dozen of them stood on a Phoenix sky-ship in the cold breast of night, bitter wind blowing off the western ocean, rocking the vessel like a squalling babe. The motors were a constant growl, metal beasts with empty bellies, seas of cloud rolling below their keel. Kaori stood on the mid-deck, snow-white breath billowing through the cowl covering her face. She was staring past the inflatable to the sky beyond. Even above the storm, the night was black as pitch, the pall of exhaust drowning all but the most stubborn stars.

Maro stepped up beside her. The Kagé lieutenant was swathed in black, just as she. A straight-edged sword and warclub on his back, smoke bombs and hand-flares at his waist.

"The captain says we should descend below the cloud cover soon," Maro said. "Get our bearings on First House."

Kaori nodded, eyes still fixed on the place where the stars should have been.

"The warriors are ready," Maro said. "Gear is triple-checked."

When Maro spoke, Kaori could hear rage underscoring every word. A fresh grief, born after his brother had perished bringing word of the Earthcrusher's construction in autumn. Maro and Ryusaki had been inseparable—both Iron Samurai serving under her father, joining him in protest, leaving Yoritomo's service and seeking the Kagé after . . .

After.

But rage was good. From rage came strength beyond strength. And they'd need every drop of it if they were to step knowingly into the serpent's maw.

"Take us down."

The bass-thick hiss of compressors kicked along the inflatable, the command to descend rolling over the crew. The ship was a fast-running merchantman called *Firestorm*, owned by a captain named Nori. The man had become a Kagé ally when his son was jailed by a corrupt magistrate who'd taken a shine to the boy's new bride. He stood on the pilot's bridge, both hands on the wheel as *Firestorm* slipped through the clouds.

"Brace yourselves, friends!" he cried. "High winds below!"

The merchantman pushed out into black skies, lightning shattering the dark off their starboard side. Cloudwalkers cursed in the rigging, several shouting prayers to Susano-ō and his vengeful son Raijin. The thought of the Thunder God brought unwelcome images of Yukiko and Buruu, and like a shadow after their passing, the ghost-pale form of Kin with his knife-bright eyes and plans within plans.

Anger seethed, bright and hot, fingers crushed into fists. She stalked across the deck, taking stairs two at a time up to the pilot's landing.

Nori was squinting into the black with a telescoping spyglass.

"A multitude of lights northeast," he nodded, handing over the device. "I fear, fair Lady, there lies your Earthcrusher and its army."

Kaori ignored the affectations in Nori's speech, the highborn accent. Even here, on the wrong side of the Tiger Daimyo and the Guild's law, the Phoenix captain couldn't help playing the artiste. Despite the hurricane winds, he'd even managed to strap his hat on at a rakish angle.

She peered through the spyglass, spotting a cluster of lights through the pummeling rain. She could make out a behemoth's silhouette, towering above the broken earth.

"Take us as close to First House as you're able and drop us near the chi pipeline."

"Lady, you do realize First House is a mountain bastion? Do you plan to sprout wings when you reach it?"

"We don't need wings, Captain, we have hands. Hands and the will to use them."

"And what of the Stain? Fissures in the earth running for miles, fumes stirring not a foot in the strongest wind. The oldest stretch of deadlands in the Imperium. Any who go there die, Lady. How in the name of the Gods will you walk it unscathed?"

Hers was a smile of midnight and ice.

"On the road the Guild built for us."

T he bridge staff were assembled, atmos-suits freshly polished, Kin standing at the end of the line beside Commander Rei. The group stood on the Earthcrusher's spaulder amidst howling wind. An ironclad loomed overhead, propellers blasting at the black rain, lightning crackling across the clouds above.

The ironclad's engines roared over the storm as it moored itself. Kin fancied he could hear rain spitting and popping on the red-hot engine housings. The captain must have thrashed the ironclad for most of the journey, driving the engines as hard as he dared. Kin could imagine a shadow looming over the captain's shoulder, eyes burning with the heat of the hidden sun, fixed on the horizon as they drew ever closer.

And here came the shadow now, stepping out over the ironclad's railing, winched down onto the Earthcrusher's spaulder. Come to pilot his creation to final victory.

Shateigashira Kensai. Second Bloom of Chapterhouse Kigen.

Kin wondered why the Second Bloom hadn't simply flown down to the gantry, but as he landed, Kensai sagged, steadying himself on an Artificer who'd come to his assistance. Kin realized the explosion must have done more damage than anyone had been led to believe.

"Shateigashira Kensai, we are honored to welcome you aboard Earthcrusher!"

Kin slapped hand over fist in unison with the other Guildsman, the multitude bowing in one fluid motion. Commander Rei was obviously overjoyed at the presence of his sensei, but a faint concern edged his voice as he spoke over the storm.

"Are you well, Second Bloom? Your injuries . . ?"

Kensai straightened slowly. Several other Lotusmen dropped down from the ironclad, landing on the gantry in a blaze of blue-white light. They hovered near the Second Bloom, intent on assisting him if needed, but careful not to actually touch him.

Kensai spoke, voice taut with pain.

"A simple scratch is not enough to keep me from this triumph, Rei-san."

"If you require assistance—"

"You have your own duties, Commander. But I believe my presence here renders at least one of your personnel redundant. Perhaps he would be kind enough to assist me during my stay?" Kensai turned his eyes to the end of the line. "If you can spare the time, Kin-san?"

"It would be my honor to serve you, Second Bloom."

"No doubt." Kensai hobbled to Kin's side, breath rasping, rain beating on their skins like a thousand metal drums. Like the pulse racing in Kin's chest.

Kensai placed a heavy hand on his shoulder, as if he required the support.

"Lead on, Kin-san."

Head high, Kin turned to the gaping hatchway and led Kensai inside.

H e hadn't coughed for fourteen minutes and eleven seconds. The count ticked over in Daichi's head, moment by moment, dry tongue catching on chapped lips. Every breath was edged with dull pain, black spreading across his lungs. A rag tied around his face was his only filter, but the air in the sky-ship's belly was probably cleaner than abovedeck, and for that at least, he was thankful to his captors.

Strange how a week of agony could make you thankful for the smallest mercy.

When he'd agreed to help Kin get aboard the Earthcrusher, he'd consigned himself to death. But he hadn't known the shape it would take. Seeing it coalesce before him, imagining the tortures the First Bloom might put him through for his amusement . . .

He willed himself still. Closed his eyes and thought of Kaori. The life she might have when all this was said and done.

The engine's hum dropped an octave, propellers slowing their pace. Daichi lifted his head, listening to the heavy tread above, the rasping of faint metallic voices. And there in the hold's gloom, he felt them—that now familiar absence of presence, that deepening darkness filled with the sorrow of flowers without sunlight.

"It is time," said the first Inquisitor.

"I am ready," Daichi whispered.

Laughter then, laced with something cold and not entirely human.

"No. You are not."

The laughter died quickly, as Daichi hoped he might.

"No one ever is."

34
SLUMBER'S END

. . . You have a son?

Buruu watched Yukiko, head tilted, studying her expression. Eyes wide as a full moon. Pale as the foam on the breakers below. Amazement scribed in every line and curve of the features he knew so well.

YOU SOUND SURPRISED.

Of course I'm surprised!

AND WHY?

Gods, I don't know. You just don't . . . You don't seem the father type.

AND WHAT DOES THAT SEEMING LOOK LIKE?

Hells, I don't know. Lotus pipes and gambling habits?

YUKIKO, I HAVE A MATE. WHY WOULD I NOT HAVE CUBS?

I suppose . . . You always struck me as so young. You don't seem much older than I am.

He glanced to the small swelling at her midriff beneath the banded iron.

IF I HAD EYEBROWS, THEY'D BE HEADED SKYWARD RIGHT NOW.

All right, all right. Good point, well made.

ONE PLUS ONE EVENTUALLY EQUALS THREE.

His name is Rhaii?

YES. IT MEANS "HOPE."

How old was he when you left Everstorm?

A HANDFUL OF MONTHS.

Buruu looked south, spying Shai winging her way back across the waves, a small, white shape beside her.

HE WILL NOT REMEMBER ME.

Yukiko put her arms around his neck, squeezed tight.

He may not remember. But he'll love you. You're his father.

"FATHER" IS JUST ANOTHER WORD FOR "STRANGER," TO THOSE WHO GROW UP WITHOUT ONE.

He felt sadness in her then, her hand straying to her belly's warmth, hanging her head as the rain dripped through the curtains of her hair. And he closed his eyes, cursed himself for a fool, so clumsy and fumbling and unused to human ways.

RAIJIN SAVE ME, I AM SORRY. THAT WAS NOT WHAT I MEANT . . .

It is what you meant. And it's true. I know what it is to grow up without a parent.

ALL THAT MATTERS IS THEY GROW IN A PLACE OF LOVE. ONE OR TWO SUNS MAKES NO DIFFERENCE. ONLY THAT THERE IS LIGHT.

She looked to the figures flying toward them. And in a moment, all the sorrow and heartache and worry melted from her face, lit with such a smile that it seemed Lady Amaterasu had come out from behind the clouds.

He's so beautiful . . .

He saw him then, a little bundle of fresh feathers and fur, still downy and gray in patches; infancy yet unshed. But though the winds were fierce as tigers, though he was probably too young to make the flight, on he came, tiny wings pounding with all the fury of Raijin's drums.

His contribution to the future of the arashitora race.

His little Rhaii.

His Hope.

My gods, Buruu, he looks just like you . . .

Shai came in to land, talons sparking on the sheer granite. She turned to watch her son, and Buruu curled his wing about her, heart filled with pride. The little figure struggled on, tossed about like a kite in the storm. But still he flew, brave as dragons, finally extending cub-sharp claws into a stumbling, tumbling landing that flipped him end over end and brought him to rest at his father's feet.

Oh, no . . . the poor treasure . . .

Yukiko knelt on the stone, reaching out toward him as he pulled himself to his feet, sneezed the rain from his nostrils and shook himself like a puppy.

Oh, you adorable little boy . . .

The cub caught sight of her, wide eyes growing wider still. He puffed up his hackles, spreading his wings in threat and let loose the most fearsome growl he could muster—a tiny mewl barely worthy of the title. Yukiko pulled her hands back as he snapped at them, bouncing backward toward his mother on clumsy legs, snarling with his tiny voice.

Gods above, he's got a temper . . .

HE HAS A FIGHTER'S SPIRIT. LIKE HIS FATHER.

Curiosity shone in the cub's eyes, peering up at Buruu from behind Shai's legs. His mother moved her head down, nudged him forward with an encouraging purr. Buruu knelt on the stone, the pain of his wounds forgotten, bringing his eyes level with the cub's. The last time he'd seen his son, he was barely more than a mouthful of fur and feathers.

The cub sniffed him, hackles still raised, prancing slowly toward him. Buruu shifted his wing and Rhaii bounced back, wings spread, growling. But slowly, ever so slowly, he crept forward again, head tilted as the rain continued to fall. He was perhaps two feet long, lustrous fur only faintly marked with the shadow of his stripes. But Buruu could see they would be bold and black, that he'd grow strong and fierce and carry the legacy of his forefathers into future years.

Buruu rested his chin on the ground. And little Rhaii walked up and pressed his forehead to Buruu's own, rested one paw against his cheek and purred.

He could hear Yukiko trying to muffle her sobs, joyful tears amidst the rain. He gathered her in one wing, drew her close, Shai nuzzling against his other flank. And he knew, with every ounce of himself, that this moment, this second, would live in his memory forever. That here, he was whole and he was perfect. That no matter what was to come, this would always be his.

MY FAMILY.

Always.

They gave him the time he was due. An hour to savor his homecoming, to play with his son, chasing each other amongst the clouds. But they were waiting when he returned to the aerie, black and white, young and old. Sukaa prowled in a wide circle around Yukiko, grief and anger etched in his gaze. Old Crea was there also, rheumy eyes filmed with white, perhaps a season from the endless sleep. And though the talesinger was the oldest and wisest arashitora alive, she obviously burned with curiosity at the whys of Buruu's return.

And so he came in to land, Shai gathering little Rhaii beneath her wing. Yukiko took her place beside him, grateful for his warmth. Two dozen stares were fixed on him, warriors both black and white, females, elders with faded stripes. And he planted his feet on the throne that had been his father's, and looked at the remainder of his race. Now his to command.

Old Crea was the first to speak, her growl hard with challenge despite her age. A monkey-child had never set foot in Everstorm, and she asked what the interloper was doing here.

Buruu looked to Yukiko, nodded slowly. He felt her in the Kenning, reaching out amidst the pack and catching them up, pulling them into the warmth of her mind. As she spoke, her thoughts echoed inside each thunder tiger's skull, burning with the combined strength of her mind and the ones within her. The heat of the song only she could hear. The combined fire of every living thing around her, immolating and inundating, rolling and seething.

The Lifesong of the World.

"My name is Kitsune Yukiko. I am yōkai-kin. Together, Buruu and I have changed the shape of Shima forever. Once we shared those islands, arashitora and human alike. And I would have it be so again. I would have you come back to us, help us reclaim the lands of your birth from the tyrants who would see them run to ashes and ruin."

Old Crea's thoughts were cool, creaking like a wooden door swollen with rain.

_ YOU ARE STORMDANCER. _

"I am. And Buruu . . . the one you knew as Roahh . . . he is my brother."

_ THEN I LIVE LONG ENOUGH TO SEE LEGEND. _

The black known as Sukaa snarled, voice echoing in the Kenning.

~ ARASHITORA FOLLOW STRENGTH, NOT LEGENDS. MONKEY-CHILDREN WEAK. WHY WE SAVE THEM? ~

Buruu growled, deep in his chest.

BECAUSE YOUR KHAN COMMANDS IT.

~ COMMAND WE SERVE THEM? WHAT KHAN SPEAKS SO? ~

THE KHAN WHO SLEW YOUR FATHER, SUKAA. THE KHAN WHO WILL SLAY YOU ALSO, SHOULD YOU CONTINUE TO DEFY.

Shai stepped forward, her bearing proud and regal, eyes locked with Sukaa.

I COME WITH YOU, MY KHAN.

Their minds rang with Sukaa's laughter.

~ A FEMALE? FEMALES DO NOT FIGHT. ~

Shai's growl was cut short by Buruu's voice in her mind.

HE IS RIGHT, MY HEART. ONE BUCK MAY REPOPULATE A SPECIES. BUT WITHOUT DAMS, OUR RACE IS LOST.

He looked among the other young females, eyes shining.

WE CAN RISK NONE OF YOU IN THIS WAR. YOU ARE OUR FUTURE. ONLY MALES. ONLY WARRIORS.

Shai blinked, anger burning in her eyes.

I YOUR MATE. I SHAKHAN OF EVERSTORM.

AND YOUR PLACE IS HERE. TO RULE UNTIL I RETURN.

Sukaa growled.

~ WILL HAVE NO RULE. NOT IF YOU ASK THIS. ~

I DO NOT ASK, SUKAA. I COMMAND.

The other Morcheban blacks growled, talons scraping on sodden stone.

Please, stop it, Yukiko said. *There's no need to spill more blood.*

~ SPEAK WITH WEAKLING'S VOICE, GIRL. WEAKLING'S HEART. ~

Weakling? You don't know anything about me . . . .

~ COULD GUT YOU WITH A THOUGHT. ~

Buruu roared, stepping toward Sukaa, hackles raised. Shai backed away, ushering little Rhaii with her wings, the other bucks clearing a space for the violence readying to break loose.

I AM KHAN. I COMMAND.

~ WHO CLAIMS KHAN IS KHAN, KINSLAYER. ~

THAT IS NOT MY NAME.

~ PREFER THE NAME MONKEY-CHILD GAVE? ~

Stop it, Yukiko growled.

YOU DEFY ME, SUKAA?

~ YOU ARE WOUNDED, MY KHAN. BLEEDING. WEAK. ~

UTTER CHALLENGE THEN, AND SEE THE DEBT YOU OWED MY BROTHER REPAID. I WILL SEND YOUR BONES TO JOIN YOUR FATHER'S. I WILL SPLIT YOU—

STOP IT! Yukiko roared.

The shout echoed in the Kenning, a thousandfold thunderclap that set every thunder tiger in the aerie staggering, blinking, growls rattling in their chests. The girl stepped up to Sukaa, the black towering over her as she stared into eyes of burning emerald green.

You call me weakling, Sukaa, son of Torr. You think me a frightened little girl. Another thought that of me, not so long ago. And I showed him his folly by ending his empire.

Sukaa snarled, wings flaring wide. Wisps of lightning crackled at his feathers, licking the air around them with hungry tongues. He stepped closer, beak inches from the girl's face, tail lashing like a whip.

Yukiko didn't flinch.

You think me weak? You think me a frightened little girl? Then I say to you what I said to him, right before I snuffed him out like a candle.

She spread her arms wide, closed her eyes.

Let me show you what one little girl can do.

Buruu felt her stepping out beyond the wall of herself into the firestorm beyond, into the seething chaos of the Lifesong. Its fury leaked through her into every one of them, the thunder tigers closing their eyes, shying away, growling and shivering. And yet she swam in it, immolated, stretching out beyond the aerie into the storm's fury, the rush and seethe of the waves below, to the titanic warmth coiled about the base of the Everstorm isles.

Older than time. Than life or death. The ancient ones who slumbered long and deep, their fury stilled beneath the thunder of Susano-ō's lullaby. And she reached toward them, burning with the heat of a thousand lives, a thousand hearts, a thousand voices. Brighter than the sun.

Niah. Ael. Father and Mother to all dragons.

Her lips moved, her voice a typhoon gale, louder that the song of the Storm God himself.

A single word, that set the entire world shaking.

Awaken.

35
EVE

In the house of the Lord of Foxes, eleven figures sit.

The first, a reed-thin girl, gutter-raised and ironwood hard. Hair of golden blond, a single eye aglow with pale-rose hue, the voice of a thunder tiger echoing in her heart. For the first time in as long as she can remember, she is starting to hope.

To her left, a tall man, broad and strong, Phoenix ink on one arm. He speaks with a gentle voice, and when he looks at the girl beside him, he cannot keep the smile from his lips.

To their right, a warrior from distant lands. Clad in a breastplate of battered iron, a stag with three crescent horns on its brow. Handsome but careworn. Golden-haired like the girl, but stained from weeks beneath black rain. He is a stranger here. Considered enemy by some. Friend by a few. Most do not know what to make of him at all.

Beside him, another man, quiet and watchful. His face is made of scars, left eye blind, the other blue and gleaming like ice. It drifts constantly to the blond girl, his palms pressed together as if he were praying. When the girl speaks, he falls still, like a child watching his first sunrise.

Next is a girl. Beautiful as falling flowers, sharp as razors, hard as folded steel. Long black hair, dark eyes smudged with kohl, swords crossed at her back. She does not think often of the one she stole them from—the man who called her his lady, his love. She does not think often of what might have been. She is not thinking of it now, here at the Fox Lord's table. But tonight, alone in her room on the eve of battle, she knows she will.

She promises herself she will not weep.

Beside her, a sky-ship captain. A chest like a chi barrel and a belly like a drum, an improbably broad straw hat slouched on his head. His eyes are sharp, his wits sharper, and inside him burns a thirst for vengeance. A thirst for Tiger blood.

Next to the captain kneels a general of the Kitsune clan, his armor enameled in black, a snarling fox helm resting in his lap. Beside him, three more generals of the Fox clan. They are mentioned here because they play a role—because armies are not led by one. But to linger on any of them would be to bring false hope, for by this tale's end, all three will be dead, and history will not speak of them overmuch.

Cruel as storms, is history. Cold as winter winds.

And last. At the table's head. The Lord of all Foxes. Master of this house, this han, this clan. He has armies at his command. Samurai and bushimen who would lay down their lives if he gave but a word. Men who look over Yama's walls at the approaching doom and waver not a foot, quaver not a moment. Like his sons did not quaver.

Even as they died.

All his life, he has known nothing but war. He has lost everything to it. Bride. Sons. Line. And here he stands on the brink of another. The last he will ever see. The last life he has to give.

Overhead, the thunder rolls, louder than an iron-thrower, echoing through his halls. He looks at his men, ready to fight and die in his name. He looks at his guests, these gaijin invaders now offering parlay, these Kagé rebels gathered beneath his banner, this stormdancer seated opposite, who may very well have given him the weapons he needs to win.

And all he wants to do is sleep.

Soon, he promises himself.

Soon.

T he gaijin army is over nine thousand strong, but only six thousand are actually battle-ready." Hana looked across the table at Isamu. "The black rain has hit them hard. With your permission, Daimyo, we can move their wounded into Yama, shelter them from the weather."

"That is unwise, Daimyo," Ginjiro said. "We invite those who annihilated the Dragon clan into our homes?"

"They will carry no weapons," Aleksandar replied. "I vow they bring no violence. The Zryachniye have spoken. It seems our war is with your Guild."

"Tell that to the samurai of the Dragon clan," Ginjiro said.

Akihito sighed. "General, the Earthcrusher is a day's march from these walls. Do you really want to spit in the face of six thousand gaijin warriors willing to stand beside you?"

"Who is to say they will not turn on us when the battle is done?"

"A vow holds great weight amongst Morcheban people," Hana said. "My uncle vows his troops will bring no violence to your door. They will not."

Ginjiro scowled, shook his head.

Hana stared at Isamu, brushing stray blond from her face.

"Daimyo, someone needs to start trusting someone here, or the Tora and their Guild masters will be toasting your death around this table tomorrow night."

Isamu fixed Hana in his stare; a viper watching a particularly chubby mouse.

"And the mystery of your"—he waved at her face—"peculiarity has been solved?"

Hana stared the old warlord down. She could feel Kaiah prowling behind her stare. The blood of a Goddess in her veins.

"I am one of the Zryachniye bloodline. We'd call them the Sighted in our tongue."

"Indeed?" A raised eyebrow. "And what do you Sighted see?"

"I don't see anything yet. The Sight must be awakened in me. The Zryachniye will perform the ritual tomorrow before the attack."

"Is that wise?" Michi asked. "Why wait until tomorrow?"

"The ritual must be performed at dawn. That's the hour of the Goddess."

"I don't like it, Hana . . ."

"Nor I," muttered Akihito.

"My great-grandmother could see people she knew, no matter where they were in the world," Hana said. "She could just close her eyes and see them as if she stood beside them. Imagine if I could see the future? Or the way toward the future we all want?"

"You might end up just seeing in the dark," Michi said. "Or what people have on under their kimonos."

The Blackbird wiggled his eyebrows. "Goddess be praised . . ."

Michi grinned, flashed the captain a particularly obscene hand gesture. The man roared with laughter, slapping the tabletop and setting the tea services shivering.

"I've made up my mind." Hana searched Akihito's face. "I need you to trust me."

The big man nodded. "I do."

The girl turned to the Kitsune warlord. "I need your trust too, Isamu-sama. Between us, the gaijin and the Guild rebels, we have a chance to take down the Guild once and forever."

"Have we heard from Misaki and her people?" Blackbird looked up and down the table. "I still don't think they have a chance in hells of pulling it off."

"They transmitted to us earlier today," Ginjiro nodded. "They will reach First House tomorrow. Their ship has been outfitted with Tora chapterhouse colors. They made radio contact with the rebels aboard the Earthcrusher yesterday, and have access to the priority transmission codes and passwords again. That should see them into First House. Once there, with any luck, they can detonate the chi reserves and blow the place to the heavens."

The Blackbird shook his head. "Did you send any of your people with them? Gods know they're going to need some old-fashioned Kitsune luck to pull that one off."

"Even without the attack on First House, we still have the Earthcrusher sewn up," Ginjiro said. "The rebels aboard will detonate the engines just as the battle begins. The blast will wipe out the Tora ground forces. Then we charge from Kitsune-jō, the gaijin attack from the east and we catch them on two fronts, covered by our own sky-ships and rotor-thopters."

"The Tora still have us badly outmatched in the air," Isamu said.

"We need Yukiko," Michi sighed.

"She's never let us down before," Akihito said.

"The odds have never been this bad before."

"And if she fails?" Blackbird asked. "What then?"

Isamu stroked his moustache and shrugged.

"Then let's hope Kitsune looks after his own."

Akihito stood at the window, watching the gaijin filter into Kitsune-jō's courtyard. Fox soldiers watched the round-eyes warily, but it was obvious they were no ambush in waiting. The gaijin were in terrible shape—many borne on stretchers, skin burned to blisters. The Daimyo's servants brought blankets and hot rice, the barrier of language between the two peoples overcome with small gestures of kindness and grateful smiles. The big man shook his head. A few days ago, these men had been set to destroy everyone on the island. Now all they were set to destroy was the contents of the Daimyo's larder. And all thanks to—

"There you are."

He turned at the sound of her voice, saw her leaning in the doorway. She'd smoothed her blond bob out as best she could, but it was still unruly, jagged bangs around her eye, the lopsided fringe doing its best to cover the leather patch. She was clad in a breastplate of dark, banded iron. Goggles and kerchief pulled down around her throat, that too-round eye watching him, unblinking.

Beautiful.

"Where's Kaiah?" he asked.

She rapped her knuckles on the breastplate in answer. "Getting fitted by the blacksmiths. Something to protect her from archery fire. They're making some for Buruu too."

"A good idea."

"You like it?" She ran a hand down the armor, over the faint curve of her hip.

Akihito swallowed. "I do."

"My uncle went back to report to the Marshal and the Holy Mother. He wanted me to go with him to prepare for the dawn ritual. Insisted, in fact."

"So why did you stay?"

". . . Don't you know?"

The rafters creaked, ominous and stuttering. The floor shifted beneath his feet, a vibration emanating from somewhere far below, windows rattling, a flower vase crashing to the floor. With a wince, he hobbled to the doorway, squeezed in beside her as the earthquake kicked into full swing. Ceiling fans rocked, tremors traveling from the soles of his feet to the base of his skull. He took Hana in his arms, braced against the doorframe as the palace shifted and rolled.

It was over in moments, dust drifting down from the beams, servants shouting in the distance. Not as bad as some he'd felt in recent months, but still, their frequency was unnerving. It seemed the very island was trying to buck them off its skin.

Hana was pressed against him, fingers entwined at the small of his back. She looked up at him through the mess of her fringe, gifting him a mischievous smile as the earth stopped moving.

"Was it good for you too?"

He laughed, and quick as silver, she stood on tiptoes and lunged at his mouth, throwing her arms around his neck. Hungry. Ferocious. He took hold of her thighs as she wrapped her legs around him, pressing him against the doorway. Her tongue darted out against his own, his breath coming heavy, losing himself in the sensation and returning the kiss with abandon.

He'd known women in his life—more than his fair share, truth be told. But though he'd lost himself in desire before, there had never been much in the way of true feeling behind it. Not the way this girl made him feel now. Fingernails entwined in his hair, pulling his head back as she bit his lip, almost too hard. He tasted blood, her lips grazing his cheek, nipping again, latching onto his throat as her hand slipped inside his uwagi, over his chest and down the muscles of his stomach, pulling the tunic away from his shoulder, biting again.

"Stop," he breathed, cupping her cheek, flushed with warmth. "Hana, stop."

She looked up at him, eye glazed with lust. "What? Gods, what?"

"Are you sure? I mean, have you ever . . ."

She was almost panting, lips bright pink from the rush of blood, the rasp of his stubble on her skin. But she found breath to laugh, slapping him playfully on his half-bared chest.

"You men. You're such godsdamned idiots."

"What?" he blinked. "Why?"

"Can't you tell I'm sure?" She tightened her fist in his hair, dragged him forward for another kiss, cinching her legs about his waist as she pulled away. Her lips brushed his with every word she breathed. "We could both be dead tomorrow. Tonight could be the first and last night I spend with anyone. I want it to be you. Do you need a herald to crow invitation?"

"I just don't want to hurt you . . ."

She fixed him in that glowing stare, veiled beneath charcoal lashes. "But do you want me?"

". . . Of course I do."

She kissed him again, mouth open, hungry, pressing against him with all her strength. Her lips were hot, almost burning, her heat making him sweat despite the chill. His hands ran up her ribs, over her back, and he cursed the metal she was encased in, blood pounding in his temples as she pulled away again, tossed the hair back from her face, breathing hard.

"Say it."

Her voice was almost a growl. Her movements predatory, the shadow of an arashitora flitting across her eye as her lips brushed his, pulling back again as he tried to kiss her.

"Say you want me . . ."

"I do."

"*Say* it."

". . . I want you."

"Then stop thinking." Her breath hot against his ear. "Stop talking. Tomorrow is getting closer by the minute, and there are better things you could be doing with your mouth . . ."

He lifted her up, slid the door closed with a bang, timbers trembling in their grooves. Staggering to the bed, her legs wrapped around him, her hands tearing his uwagi loose, fumbling with the straps and buckles on her breastplate as he cursed and she laughed, bright as summer sun.

Slow, he told himself.

Move slow.

Her lips and body crushed into his, breathing her sighs into his mouth. And as gentle as he wished to be, she was having none of it, pushing him down to happily drown, then dragging him up inside soaking heat, her teeth at his throat and her nails across his back.

"Hana," he whispered. "Oh, gods . . ."

He could see her smile in the dark, caught in the rose glow spilling from her lashes.

"Godd*ess*," she breathed.

36
BLACK SNOW

Midnight.

They'd marched through the dark, horizon echoing with the thunder in every footstep. As soon as Fox Hour had sounded, Kin had slipped from his bunk and descended to the engine room, into the rumble and clank of the gear trains, the bursts of dirty steam.

Evening was the only time he'd been able to steal away from Kensai's side since he'd arrived—the Second Bloom forced Kin to wait on him hand and foot whenever he was awake. His pointless tours of the Earthcrusher's innards, hours spent simply staring from the bridge. Kensai seemed to enjoy wasting Kin's minutes, every so often leaning on his shoulder as if his wounds pained him, just to remind the boy he was there.

Like he'd always been.

A man he should have called uncle. A man as close to blood as anyone left in this world. And Kin was set to destroy him, everything he'd worked for, everything he'd been raised to believe. Turning on the ones who trusted him. *Again.* Playing the loyal Fifth Bloom, nodding and bowing to the brethren passing him on the stairwells, knowing tomorrow they could all be dead. That all they knew would be gone.

Was everything inside him a lie? Where did deception end and his true self begin? And what would remain when all this was over and done?

Yukiko.

He whispered her name. The only truth in a world ringing more false with every breath.

He found Shinji in the Earthcrusher's bowels, at work on a ruptured piston. The boy asked loudly for assistance, and Kin stepped in to help, wreathed in filthy vapor.

"Is all in order?"

"Hai," Shinji nodded. "We've been in touch with the Yama rebels, and they're on their way to First House. The codes we gave them should see them past the perimeter."

"We may have a problem tomorrow when we hit Yama."

"Kensai?"

"He watches me like a spider. You might have to blow the cooling system alone."

Shinji nodded. "Maseo can do that. And I can cut control between here and the bridge. We can stage a fire on level nine, near the fuel filters."

"Good idea."

"It'll work out, Kin-san. Have faith."

"Faith? What the hells is that?"

"It's what keeps you going when everything turns to brown."

"Sounds like you're talking about ignorance. Or just blatant stupidity."

"Faith. Stupidity." A shrug. "Same thing."

They'd stripped him naked and scrubbed him clean, ridding him of sweat and filth, the dried blood from the Kigen raid and his torture still crusted on his skin. The bathhouse steam had loosened the phlegm in his chest and he'd fallen to coughing—awful, wracking fits that shuddered his core. The Inquisitors watched with bloodshot eyes, saying nothing at all.

They checked his hair, his mouth, every orifice that might conceal a blade. Dressed him in black cloth, combing his hair into a simple knot affixed with black ribbon. They were taking no chances, leaving him nothing with which to strike at the First Bloom in his house of lies.

Daichi closed his eyes. Washed the black from his mouth with a cup of almost clean water. The first Inquisitor's voice was a paper-thin sigh.

"You will not speak unless spoken to by the First Bloom."

"You will not look into the eyes of the First Bloom," said the second.

"You will show the respect that is due to the First Bloom," said the third.

Daichi's whisper was rough as gravel road. "Or what?"

The first Inquisitor titled his head. *Shifted*. One moment he was standing half a dozen steps away, the next he stood before Daichi, coalescing out of a cloud of blue-black smoke. His fist was a blur, the impact sending Daichi back several feet, down to his knees, lips wet with the taste of death and the tears he couldn't help but shed.

"Or pain," they said.

A darkness so complete Kaori couldn't see her hand in front of her face, nor the sweat fogging the glass over her eyes. The breather was strapped painfully tight around her head, but chi stench still drenched her tongue, seeping into every pore. Her head swam, echoes tumbling up and down the pipeline serving only to disorient her more. She could hear the other Kagé behind her—Maro and the rest. Two dozen in all, wading in the shallow, blood-red flow.

The pipeline was twenty feet in diameter, two inches thick, oxide clad. After the Phoenix captain had dropped them off beside the rusted serpent, they'd taken half a day to cut through the outer shell, finally slipping inside. After Yama refinery was destroyed, the Guild had drained as much chi from the northern pipeline as possible, but an ankle-deep river of dregs remained. The fumes were so thick Kaori could almost clutch handfuls from the air. But wading through the pipeline's innards was better than walking the deadlands outside. She swore she could hear voices out there. Claws scrabbling against the pipe.

Whispers.

The Kagé couldn't risk any illumination for fear of igniting the vapor. And so they walked in blackness, up to their shins. Sound was amplified, twisted until it was almost impossible to think. But on they pressed, knowing there was no wrong turn to make—only one destination the pipe could lead.

First House.

Kaori had no idea how long they trudged in that perfect darkness, footsteps like a funeral march. Forcing their way through heavy, one-way valves, into the vast chambers of silent pumping stations, the machinery standing motionless now the pipeline was empty.

The group would stop only when she could no longer breathe, when the fatigue threatened to bring her to her knees. No hunger in her, save to crawl from this pipe and into the Guild's blackened heart. No desire, save to rip First House burning from the mountainside. The explosives on her back were leftovers from the Kigen raid—the raid that had ended in failure, Kin's subterfuge and her father's surrender into Guild hands.

Gods, why didn't you trust me?

She came to a stop in the dark, cradled like a babe in mother's womb. Maro bumped into her, reached out to steady himself, his voice a tenfold whisper muffled by his breather.

"Kaori, are you well?"

She shook her head in the dark, eyes narrowed against the chi burn.

None of it matters anyway.

"Look to yourself, brother," she replied. "I am fine."

None of it matters at all.

And on she walked.

Dawn was a sulfur smear on the eastern horizon, echoing with the screams of freezing mountain winds. Storm clouds jostled overhead, laced with blinding cracks, each peal of the Thunder God's drums shivering the stone beneath him.

Akihito stood on the balcony, staring at western skies, praying for winged silhouettes to crest the walls of Five Flowers Palace and fill the air with Raijin Song. If he listened, he fancied he could hear it in the distance—faint, but growing stronger with each passing moment.

DOOMDOOMDOOMDOOM.
DOOMDOOMDOOMDOOM.

Night was slowly fleeing, the warmth of his bed with it. The chill bit bone-deep, stoking the pain of the old wound in his leg. He pulled up his goggles against the black drizzle, wondering what the day would bring. Trying not to think of the night before, to banish the freezing chill with memories of the warmth between Hana's thighs. Lover's thoughts were liable to get a man killed on the battlefield. And he was only a man. No samurai. No stormdancer. Just a hunter turned . . . what? Warrior? Babysitter? Fool?

The sound of wings in the dark. Mighty pinions beating the freezing air, raising gooseflesh on his arms. He looked up into the graying sky and saw a majestic arashitora, sleek and snow-white and beautiful. And on her back, a girl, more beautiful still.

Kaiah was clad in dark iron—a thick breastplate running throat to ribs. Reinforced leather guarded her hindquarters and neck. Over her skull sat an iron helm, black glass covering her eyes, pierced at the crown with a long tassel of hair. The blacksmith had even taken time to emboss prayers to the Thunder God into the armor.

Hana was wearing her banded breastplate, messy blond bob held in check by the goggles over her eye. She wore a tsurugi sword on her back, though Akihito had no idea if she knew how to wield it. But as the pair landed in the courtyard, the wounded gaijin bivouacked beneath the eaves stared in wonder, jaws to the floor. She drew the blade and Kaiah reared up, lightning crackling across her feathers. The thunder tiger split the air with a deafening roar.

Hana looked up at the balcony, head tilted, lips twisted.

"Coming?"

Limping slowly down the stairs, across the courtyard beneath wondering eyes. Hana took his hand and pulled him up onto Kaiah's back with a grunt. As he slipped behind her, she pushed back against him, gave him a wicked grin.

"You slept late."

"I'd like to think I earned it," he smiled, slipping his arms around her waist.

"Don't be getting a big head on me now."

"I'm surprised you're up so early."

"I couldn't sleep for your snoring."

"I do *not* snore."

Hana turned away with a smile, mumbling just loud enough for him to hear.

"Thought it was another earthquake . . ."

A surge of muscle beneath him, a moment of insistent gravity, pushing him down as Kaiah leaped skyward. He could feel the power in her, the brutal majesty, his stomach left far behind as they rose higher, over the walls and through the lightening sky. He clutched Hana's waist, gripping Kaiah's ribs with his thighs, trying to keep some semblance of control over the grin on his face. He'd flown on sky-ships before, but it had been *nothing* like this.

Yama city was spread out below them, the distant horizon growing steadily brighter. As they climbed, he felt something cold and wet on his cheek, a black spot fluttering in his vision.

Akihito frowned behind his goggles. And all around them, they began falling, tumbling and spinning like forgotten jewels from the glowering sky overhead. Frozen and tiny and perfect.

Snowflakes.

He caught one in his open palm, looking down with narrowed eyes. It was fragile, beautiful, possessed of a symmetry and complexity that would make the greatest artisan weep. And if it were white, it might have struck him as a gift from the heavens themselves.

But it was black. Just like the rain. Just like the ruin they'd made of this country. And just at the edge of hearing, he caught it again, beating and rising like a trembling pulse.

DOOMDOOMDOOMDOOM.

DOOMDOOMDOOMDOOM.

He looked south and his stomach curled up against his ribs. Just an impression in the muddy light of the almost-dawn. But he could see great clouds of sky-ships, swarming around a shape so vast and horrifying he had to force himself to stare.

"There they are," he breathed.

Hana reached back, gave his hand a reassuring squeeze.

"Breathe easy," she said. "We're about to have a goddess on our side."

37
ACCORDING TO PLAN

Michi knelt beside a low table in her room, calligraphy brush in hand, her dog Tomo snoozing amidst crumpled blankets in her otherwise empty bed.

Her brush strokes were swift, tiny ink droplets spattering on the page. She'd been up most of the night writing, fingers stained and back aching. But she'd reached the dawn of today's battle in her history of the Lotus War, taking a moment to describe the aroma of the breakfast fires and exhaust, the clash of boots and swords as bushimen marched out onto Yama's walls.

The Iron Samurai had once more donned their armor, the last drops of the Kitsune chi stores fueling their final stand. Michi had refilled her chainblades the previous evening, trying not to think about the man she'd stolen them from. What might have been.

Ichizo.

A knock at her door. Tomo opened one eye, but failed to stir further.

"Don't get up or anything," Michi muttered.

She straightened with a wince, padding to the door and sliding it open. The Blackbird stood beyond, clad in a thick breastplate, a studded tetsubo in his hands. Iron covered his forearms and shins and knuckles—he'd even riveted some metal plating to his ridiculous hat.

"Well, aren't you a sight, Captain-san," Michi smiled.

The Ryu captain flashed her a rogue's grin. "I was thinking the same thing."

"We're ready to depart?"

"Well . . ." Blackbird glanced behind her. "We could always stay in. Warmer in bed."

"Not one for the subtle art of seduction, are you?"

"I'll have you know I've been working on that one most of the night."

She gave him a little pat on the shoulder. "Needs more time in the oven."

Blackbird chuckled as she scooped up her chainblades and strapped them to her back.

"Working on the book?" Blackbird eyed the paper and quills on the table.

"I know, I know. Bottles of ink don't win battles . . ."

"Just seems a shame to have spent what could be your last night alive on it."

She leaned down and kissed Tomo's nose, pointed to her scroll still drying on the table. "I'll be back to write the ending tonight, little one. Guard it for me while I'm gone."

Tomo licked her face with his bright pink tongue, closed his eyes. Michi squeezed the wicks of her candles, snuffing them out, one by one by one. Smoke uncoiled from melted wax, weaving fingers of pale-gray in the frozen air, the scent of warm honey making her sigh.

And without a backward glance, she turned and walked away.

Hiro stood on the bow of the *Honorable Death*, watching black tumble from the clouds. Eyes fixed on the city lights, river like black glass in the almost-dawn. The fleet filling the skies about him, the clattering tread of the shredder-men below, the barrage of the Earthcrusher's footsteps—all of it stirring the butterflies in his belly, the adrenaline gnawing his veins.

"Daimyo Hiro, forgiveness."

Hiro turned to find one of his samurai behind him, head bowed.

"We have received a transmission, marked for your eyes only."

The samurai handed over a square of rice-paper, embossed with an authentication seal. Hiro looked at him briefly, face daubed with fresh ashes, armor painted the color of death. They stood all around him—the glorious Kazumitsu Elite. Men who had failed their Shōgun, now consigned to death. This was the day their shame would be expunged. To destroy Yoritomo's assassin, crush the insurrection, and then to step before the great judge Enma-ō and *know* they had fought bravely, for as righteous a cause as any left in this nation.

"You look tired, Koji-san," Hiro said to the samurai. "Did you sleep?"

"I confess I did not, Daimyo."

"Nor I," Hiro smiled. "Time enough for sleep when we are dead."

"I long for it," Koji's whisper rolled in freezing wind. "Every breath since Yoritomo's murder has been drawn in disgrace. But today my family may hold their heads high again."

"Did they not hold them high before?"

"My wife . . . She said it didn't matter. That she'd rather live with me disgraced than lose me for honor's sake. But she is a woman. She does not understand the Way of Bushido."

"And your sons? What did they say when you told them you were headed to your death?"

". . . I did not tell them. They are too young to understand."

"One day they will, Koji-san. They will look back on this day, and they will know their father was a hero. They will grow to be honorable and brave, just like him."

Koji covered his fist and bowed. "My thanks, Daimyo."

The Iron Samurai clomped away, his ō-yoroi spitting chi into the greasy air. Hiro remembered his father's words in the throne room, an insistent echo inside his head.

"*Lord Izanagi give you the strength to die well.*"

He looked at the note in his hand, recognized his father's seal. No doubt a final message from the ruined war hero, some last words to ensure his son didn't falter. He snapped the authentication seal, unfolded the message within. The wind moaned around him, tiny black snowflakes falling on his lashes, the deck beneath his feet. His gaze was fixed on the calligraphy, painstakingly rendered— handwriting he recognized instantly.

> *My beloved son,*
>
> *It is duty that drags you north, far from those who love you. It is duty that would see you end, before you have truly lived, so that our honor may be restored. And it is my duty as a wife to honor my husband and wish you the courage to die well.*
>
> *But I cannot.*
>
> *There is no sense to this. No honor in any of it. We have built a world*

where we murder children to feed our soil. War upon those different for the sake of greed. We hold the ease the machine brings above the wellbeing of the land around us. We should be ashamed.

A man needs no courage to die. He need only close his eyes. It takes courage to fight on, when all hope seems gone. To struggle through, when the hurt and shame seem too much.

It is your father's dream to see our shame expunged. But if I must mourn you, I would have it be for something more than avenging the Shōgun who oversaw our fall from grace. For the dream of a father who has never created anything worthwhile, except that which he would now destroy. For it is only when we are asleep that we dream, Hiro. It is only when we close our eyes that such dreams make sense. That we believe them real.

Open your eyes, my son.

Wake up.

Hiro clenched his fist, metal knuckles gleaming, his prosthetic arm spitting out a small plume of chi. He looked again to the horizon, the lights of Yama, slowly rousing from slumber. The faces beside him, painted with the ashes of their own funeral offerings.

Too late.

He looked down at his arm again. The arm they'd gifted him after she tore his flesh away. Left him with nothing. No one.

Far too late, Mother.

He lifted a small microphone to his lips, speakers across the fleet crackling to life.

"Soldiers of the Tora clan! Today we bring an end to Yoritomo's assassin, her accomplices, those who have betrayed their oaths to Lord and land! Do you stand ready?"

A roar from above, below, all around. Blades torn from scabbards. Hilts pounded on the decks. Shreddermen revving their engines and lifting chainsaw arms to the sky.

"Know no fear! Show no mercy! And tonight, should you stand before the Judge of all the Hells, stand proud and tall! For you have died in glorious battle for the honor of the Tora zaibatsu, and in the name of our Shōgun Yoritomo-no-miya!"

"Yoritomo!" A thousand voices took up the cry. "Yoritomo!"

"Death to the Kitsune! Death to the Stormdancer!"

"Death!" they roared. "Death!"

"Banzaiiiii!"

K in stood on the Earthcrusher's bridge, listening to Hiro's voice crackle over Yama's barren fields. The sun had almost crested the horizon, bleak light piercing the storm. Black snow crusted the Earthcrusher's viewports, hundreds of tiny lights moving below as shreddermen took up position. The sky-fleet spread out in wedge formation, the Daimyo's flagship front and center: Hiro seemed intent on leading his troops into the thick of battle.

The bridge was strangely calm, Shatei watching their instrumentation like spiders watching prey. Bo sat at his communications hub, speakers propped on his helm. Kin stood beside the pilot's harness, Kensai looming behind, that horrid, childish face staring out to the city beyond. Commander Rei was conducting a final systems check.

"Commander." Bo turned from his comms console. "Scouts report the gaijin army is stationed two miles east. They are fully mustered, and preparing to launch 'thopters."

"Clever dogs," Rei mused. "Waiting for us to hit the Kitsune, then swoop on the wounded victors."

"The gaijin have nothing capable of harming Earthcrusher," Kensai rasped. "This vessel was built to end the gaijin war, Commander. A ragtag invasion presents no obstacle. Proceed."

"Hai," Rei nodded. "Shatei Bo, I want one vessel with eyes on the gaijin at all times."

"Hai," Bo bowed.

Kensai limped up next to Rei, his breathing labored. He flicked a switch and spoke into the PA system, his voice bellowing across Yama's towering walls.

"People of Yama, warriors of the Fox clan, I am Shateigashira Kensai of Chapterhouse Kigen, loyal servant of Tojo, First Bloom of the Lotus Guild. Hear me now.

"You are not our enemies. But you have been deceived by this so-called Stormdancer and her thirst for revenge. We seek only justice for the assassination of our Shōgun, Yoritomo-no-miya and his beloved sister Lady Aisha. We have no quarrel with you.

"Daimyo Isamu, I beseech you—cast out the rebels from your city. Turn the Stormdancer over to our authority, and join us in expelling the gaijin from our home. Today can be the dawning of a new age for the Imperium. United, there is nothing we cannot accomplish.

"Open your gates to signify your acquiescence. You have five minutes to comply. If in such time, we have not received word of your assent to Guild authority, with heavy hearts, and heavier hands, we will wipe your clan from the face of Shima."

Kensai turned off the address system, clasped his hands behind his back. Kin could feel sweat creeping down his face despite the chill, the behemoth's engines thrumming in his ears.

"Do you think they will concede?" Rei asked.

Kensai shrugged. "We will know in five minutes."

Rei tensed in his harness. "Perhaps sooner."

Kin engaged his telescopics, squinting in the dim light and falling snow. He could make out Yama's walls—towering gray stone, studded with shuriken-cannon and razor wire. All along the battlements, he could see soldiers' silhouettes. Floating above the city, he saw the sky-fleet—sleek ships painted Kitsune black, nine-tailed foxes adorning their inflatables. Their decks lined with cloudwalkers, bushimen and samurai, all cut like shadow puppets against the lightening sky. Every one of them—every man on the walls, the decks, every single one—struck the same pose, swelling Kin's heart in his chest.

Fists in the air.

Thousands of hands, raised as one. A gesture of defiance in the face of crushing odds, of courage and solidarity before abject tyranny. It was all he could do not to raise his fist in reply.

"So be it." Kensai turned to Bo at his comms station. "Send word to all commanders. Full attack on my signal."

Bo was stabbing at his console, tapping at his microphone. "I seem to have lost communications, Second Bloom . . ."

Kensai cursed, engaged the public address system again. "All forces, full attack!"

With a shriek of iron and pistons, the shreddermen charged—a scuttling, thumping horde of towering bipedal engines, saw-toothed arms raised. Bushimen stalked behind, crossbows and naginata spears in hand. The sky-fleet spat plumes of exhaust, gunning forward with hollow roars. And with the casual arrogance of a butcher on the way to the slaughterhouse, Commander Rei kicked his stirrups, urging the Earthcrusher into action.

The controls spat a dull clunking cough. The engines revved, great clouds of black smoke spewing from its chimneys. But for all the sound and fury, Earthcrusher didn't move an inch.

For the first time in as long as he could remember, Kin was thankful for the brass skin covering his face—he didn't have to hide his grin.

"What in First Bloom's name is happening?" Rei hissed.

M isaki stood aboard the sky-ship *Truth Seeker*, looking out over the Tōnan mountains. The Guild rebels aboard the vessel were gathered topside, all clad in gleaming new skins courtesy of a salvage raid into Chapterhouse Yama. Fresh paint gleamed down the ship's flanks, a cluster of scarlet flags at her aft signifying allegiance to Chapterhouse Kigen.

The spider limbs at Misaki's back twitched as she waited for the inevitable challenge from the First House patrols. She thought of Suki, her baby daughter, back in whatever safety the Kitsune fortress could provide. She found herself wishing she had gods to pray to.

A message chattered across the secure frequencies.

First House control tower seven to unidentified sky-ship. This is restricted airspace. Transmit ident code and security clearance package now.

Misaki's fingers danced upon her mechabacus, deft and graceful; the fingers of a musician who had never learned to actually play.

Truth Seeker—*5676-1814-4852-7951. Package transmitting.*

Acknowledged, Truth Seeker. *Processing* . . .

Misaki sucked the inside of her lip, cast wary glances at her fellows.

"Be ready to turn and redline it," she whispered.

Package confirmed. Truth Seeker, *you are logged as having departed for Earthcrusher yesterday morning. Why have you returned to First House?*

Starboard engine malfunction. We reported yesterday evening. Did you not receive?

I show no record of said report, Truth Seeker.

We were ordered to return to First House. Should I notify my Kyodai?

A pause, laden with the drone of engines, the smog-thick reek of chi.

Negative, Truth Seeker. *Dock at sky-spire four. You will be met by First House security forces, acknowledge.*

Acknowledged, First House.

The lotus must bloom.

The lotus must bloom.

Misaki cut the connection, grinning like a madwoman. The subterfuge had held—First House was allowing them to land. So far, Kitsune seemed to be looking after his own.

The *Truth Seeker* flew on through the mountains, her captain ordering the starboard engine shut down. The propeller sputtered and died, spitting a brief smear of exhaust into the building snowstorm. Black slurry was accruing on the deck, Misaki shivering despite the poreless skin coating her body. Her eyes were on the clouds, noting the shadows of lurking ironclads, the three-man corvettes flitting amongst snow-clad mountaintops.

Finally, she spied it in the distance, atop an immense granite spur, wreathed in smoke. A pentagonal fortress of filthy yellow stone, rooted by mighty buttresses to sheer black cliffs. The pipelines converged here, winding up the mountainside and vomiting into First House's belly. A service road spiraled up from the valley, dotted with guard towers, ending at a goods elevator one hundred feet below the summit. Misaki thanked the heavens for their stolen sky-ship—there was no way in hells anyone was making it into First House without wings.

As the *Truth Seeker* cleared the outer wall, Misaki and five other rebels gathered at the railing. At a signal from the helmsman, cloudwalkers in the *Seeker's* gut spilled smoke bombs into the exhaust filters, and an enormous plume of choking tar spewed from the starboard engine. The *Seeker* spun on its axis, smearing black across the skies.

Misaki waited until they'd drifted over the First House fuel dumps. With her brethren behind her, she leaped over the railing and dropped onto the tanks. The *Seeker* drifted over the First House complex, spewing smoke cover, an iron claxon singing duet with a shrill siren. With slightly overdramatic effort, the crew forced her down onto landing pad four. Ground crews were waiting, fire gear ready, shrouded in black fumes from the "faulty" engine.

Hunkering down by an access hatch, Misaki tuned in to the First House security feeds with her mechabacus, listening for an alert. She noted chatter about a priority prisoner being escorted to the Chamber of Void. But hearing nothing about intruders on the chi silos, she nodded to her brethren, and they set to work breaking open the hatch.

Misaki nodded to herself, trying to calm the storm in her stomach.

So far, so good.

The ascent was torturous, fumbling in the dark, fingers scrabbling against the pipeline's greasy innards. Kaori was soaked with chi-stink, blood-red reek seeping into every pore. The incline had been gentle at first, but as they climbed higher, the slope deepened, their footing growing ever more treacherous.

Kaori had finally relented to Maro's demands, lighting a hand-cranked tungsten lamp, throwing long shadows on concave walls. They'd passed through two more pumping stations, forcing through the heavy one-way hatches into cylindrical chambers, twenty feet in diameter. Pistons loomed overhead, frozen in place with no fuel to pump.

Eventually, they heard the rhythmic pulse of machinery ahead, echoing in the oily dark. Shining the light into the gloom, she saw their pipeline curving downward into another below, the join sealed with a heavy, one-way valve. Beyond it, they could hear another pumping station, an intermittent current, like a river of butter sloshing against the pipeline's guts.

"This must be where the Yama pipe meets the other flows," Maro muttered. "This is where the fun begins."

The man had his head tilted, listening to the pistons' pattern. The pump station below would be a duplicate of the dry stations they'd already passed through— three massive piston chambers, driven by hydraulics. The pistons would draw themselves up, sucking chi into the chambers. Then, one at a time, the pistons would descend, like massive plungers in a syringe, forcing the chi along the pipe. Subsequent pumping action kept the chi flowing once it had moved through, like train commuters being pushed along by people flooding in behind.

"Ten seconds for the chambers to fill," Maro concluded. "Each piston takes six seconds to hit bottom. Once the third piston hits, all three ascend. Then it starts again."

"Twenty-eight seconds to swim sixty feet," Kaori whispered. "That will be tight."

"The pumping action will help force you through the valves. I'm more worried about breathing. There won't be much air once we drop into that current. And it's going to be black as night. Once we're inside, there's no turning back."

Kaori was staring ahead, feeble light reflected in the glass covering her eyes.

"There has never been any turning back," she murmured. "For any of us. Everything we are, everything we've done has brought us to this moment. This minute. This second."

She looked at the Kagé gathered in the dark, each in turn.

"And I am not afraid."

T he wind was a thousand knives, flaying skin from bone. The frost left bite marks on Hana's skin, black snow frozen on her goggles. She leaned into Akihito for warmth as they spiraled down to the gaijin camp. Remembering falling asleep with his breath kissing the back of her neck. Brute strength wrapped in gentle tenderness.

She could feel Kaiah's apprehension, spilling into her and setting her hands to shaking. The arashitora rankled at the thought of returning Hana to this army of fools—these monkey-children who skinned beasts and wore them in some preposterous attempt to usurp their strength.

- WHAT DOES THIS RITUAL ENTAIL? -

I've no idea.

- DANGEROUS? -

I don't know that either.

- THEN WHY DO THIS? WE SHOULD BE WITH THE OTHERS, PREPARING FOR BATTLE. LITTLE FOXES ARE OUTNUMBERED TWO TO ONE. -

I trust Uncle Aleksandar.

- A MAN YOU MET TWO DAYS AGO. -

Family is everything to him. He promised to protect me.

- PROMISES ARE ONLY WORDS. -

Piotr promised to get the Guildsman's letter back to his beloved, and he betrayed his own people to do it. That's how much a promise means to a Morcheban.

- AND THE FOOLS TAKE HIM BACK. EVEN AFTER HIS BETRAYAL. -

Because he found me. That's how much I mean to them.

- DO NOT LIKE THIS. IF YUKIKO WERE HERE . . . -

Yukiko told me to be brave. That's what I'm doing. The Goddess could give me the power to see the way to victory. To see the future. Who knows what I'll be after this ritual is done?

— NOBODY KNOWS. THAT IS WHAT TROUBLES ME. —

This is a part of me, Kaiah. Every bit as much as the Kenning. We can still fight. The sooner this is over, the sooner we can join the battle for Yama.

The thunder tiger was silent, brooding. Head swimming with vague notes of sadness, of loss, of tiny bundles thrown wingless and bleeding into the void.

Nothing is going to happen to me, Kaiah. You're there to protect me. Akihito too. The first sign of danger, we get the hells out of there. It's going to be all right. You'll see.

— NOT THE ONLY ONE, I HOPE. —

Hundreds of gaijin watched them glide down to the frozen earth, many lowering their heads, parting like a wave as she slipped down off Kaiah's back. Akihito grunted as he pulled his bad leg over and slithered down beside her. Hana noted dark stares aimed at the big man, aggression hanging in the air.

Aleksandar pushed his way through the mob, spitting Morcheban words she could only guess were curses. Piotr limped alongside, bowing when he saw her. Her uncle was wearing his wolfpelt, the battered breastplate embossed with House Mostovoi's sigil, the same stag gleaming around her neck. She was wearing her mother's gift openly now, after years of hiding it. Hiding who she was. Gold gleaming in the rising sun.

"My blood, come, come," Aleksandar said. "We have little time."

She noted her uncle refused to touch her, to take her hand and drag her along as someone in a hurry might be expected to. With a reassuring smile to Akihito, and a flood of warmth into Kaiah's mind, she walked toward the command tent. Aleksandar strode behind, followed by Akihito and the thunder tiger, Piotr limping in the rear.

Soldiers in grubby uniforms and the pelts of mighty beasts lined her approach. At the end of the path stood the two Zryachniye. Sister Katya, for all her apparent ferocity, embraced Hana like they'd known each other all their lives. The Holy Mother Natassja also held her close, surprising strength in her bony arms. Wrinkled lips were pressed to Hana's cheeks, the glow of the old woman's right iris spilling into the furrows on her face.

Natassja spoke, Aleksandar translating her words.

"Welcome, Hana Mostovoi, in this, the hour of the Goddess. Are you prepared to meet her?"

"I don't know," Hana said. "I think so."

"The Holy Mother bids you go with her," Aleksandar said. "She has felt an illportent since late last night. But there is nothing to fear. You are amongst your sisters now. It is time to meet your mother."

Katya held the tent flap wider, motioned into the dark. Hana turned, uncertain. Akihito had lifted his goggles, was looking right at her, a reassuring smile on his face. She reached out to Kaiah, feeling strength and ferocity prowling behind her stare.

- IF YOU NEED ME, CALL. -

I will.

A crackling voice echoed across the valley, edged with metal and static amidst the distant roar of sky-ship engines.

"*People of Yama, warriors of the Fox clan, I am Shateigashira Kensai of Chapterhouse Kigen, loyal servant of Tojo, First Bloom of the Lotus Guild. Hear me now . . .*"

This was who she was. And the longer she spent hovering on the edge, the longer it would take to help her friends. Michi and Blackbird, the Kagé and the Guild rebels. Even Daimyo Isamu. They were counting on her. She could do this. She was *born* to do this.

The words she and Yukiko shared at their parting rang clear and bright in her mind.

"*I'm not you, Yukiko,*" she'd said. "*I'm not a hero.*"

"*You can be anything you want. Fate deals us our hand, but we decide how to play it. We all of us choose the people we want to be.*"

And with a final smile to Akihito, she stepped into the dark to make her choice.

38
DISINTEGRATING

"Report!" Commander Rei bellowed. "All stations, immediately!"

A tumult of voices erupted, brethren reporting losses of all bridge-based functions. Kin smiled like the Kitsune who stole the Emperor's dinner. Any second now, they'd hear the alarms heralding Shinji's fire, drawing crews away from the engine room. Maseo would then be free to blow the cooling system. All according to—

Kensai glanced up from his mechabacus, fingers dancing as he spoke with a sandpaper voice. "Calm yourself, Commander. All is as it should be."

An icy certainty in Kensai's voice. A fistful of dread in Kin's stomach. The Shateigashira turned to two Lotusmen stationed near the elevator.

"Take him."

The Lotusmen marched across the bridge and seized Bo's arms, hauled him back from the communications hub as he squawked in protest. Pistons hissed, the air filled with short bursts of exhaust as the pair dragged Bo before the Shateigashira, forced him to his knees and tore off his helm. The elevator doors opened with a shuddering groan and two more Lotusmen marched onto the bridge, dragging brother Maseo. The rebel's helm had also been removed, and he'd been beaten bloody, cheek and lips split, one eye swollen shut.

"Shateigashira?" Rei's voice was incredulous. "What is this?"

"An operation, Commander," Kensai replied. "To remove the cancer taken root aboard this vessel. The third conspirator will be in hand momentarily."

Kin was trembling, a thousand thoughts skittering through his head, a million beats per minute. The third conspirator would be Shinji—Kensai must have discovered the rebel infiltrators aboard the Earthcrusher somehow. Perhaps they captured another rebel in Kigen, forced them to talk. Maybe Bo and the others had been observed before Kin arrived. However the trio had been uncovered, Shinji would be in hand within moments. Everything ruined.

But they didn't know about him. Kensai had only mentioned *three*. He wasn't officially part of the rebellion—however Kensai had unraveled the plot, Kin had avoided detection. If he kept his mouth shut, he might have a chance to escape, detonate the charges himself—

Kensai drew the iron-thrower at his belt; the same weapon Kin had aimed at Daichi's head. The Second Bloom's voice echoed throughout the Earthcrusher's innards.

"Attention rebels aboard this vessel," Kensai said. "Your coconspirators are in custody. Your plans are known to us, and already thwarted. Surrender yourselves, or I will execute your brethren here and now. You have ten seconds to comply."

Kin grit his teeth. Sweat in his eyes. Breath coming harder. Faster.

Kensai engaged pressure, pointed the iron-thrower at Bo's head.

"Eight seconds . . ."

He's going to kill them anyway. Turning yourself over will only mean you die too.

"Six . . ."

If you stay hidden, there's still hope.

"Five seconds . . ."

Bo and Maseo didn't look into Kin's eyes. Didn't plead. Didn't falter. Prepared to die for their beliefs. For the rebellion.

"Four . . ."

Too many people have perished to get you aboard this vessel. If you give up now, Daichi's sacrifice was in vain. Every rebel who died in the Yama rebellion. The Danro attacks. The Kigen suicide bombings—

"Three . . ."

And what's a few more murders now, eh?

"Two . . ."

A few more bodies for the pile?

"One . . ."

Gods, what have you become . . .

"Stop. Uncle, please."

A dozen burning glares turning on him. Kensai's eyes drilling into his skull.

"Kin-san? You have something to say?"

"This is my idea. It was me. All me."

Bo hissed, glanced toward Kin at last. "You fool, shut—"

A slap sent the boy to the floor. Kin stared hard at the Shateigashira's horrid, childlike face. "It was my doing, Uncle. All of it."

The Second Bloom tilted his head.

"I know, Kin-san." Kensai's smile curled in every word. "But I truly wondered if you would have the courage to admit it yourself."

A small bow.

"My respects."

And with a squeeze of the trigger, Kensai blew Bo's and Maseo's brains all over the floor.

They marched through halls of yellow stone, black carpet underfoot. His coughing echoed on the masonry, the Inquisitor on either arm pausing when it grew too violent. But as soon as he regained his breath, they were moving again, through steel doors expanding like the iris of a human eye, the crisp sound of blade kissing blade accompanying their dilations.

The air was freezing, walls glistening with moisture. Long paper amulets ran floor to ceiling, protective mantra scribed in soulless kanji. Daichi could hear motors thrumming through the floor, smell chi-stench curled in the air, clinging to the inside of every breath.

They finally stopped outside another iris door, looming and black. The Inquisitors seemed distracted, watching the corners or staring into space, the leader actually sidestepping as if to avoid collision with something that wasn't there. After long minutes, the iris dilated, opening out into a vast hollow of black stone. The room was too large to see the edges, a domed ceiling stretching overhead, the floor lit by strips of glowing halogen.

As his eyes grew accustomed to the gloom, Daichi made out a granite pillar in the room's heart. Ten feet high, riddled with fat lengths of cable, like boreworms in rotten fruit. The pillar's base was ringed with thousands of mechabacii, chittering and skittering—the hum of some obscene hive. And atop the pillar, a figure crouched like a parasite king upon his throne.

Red glowing eyes, a thin, pointed helm with hollow cheeks like a death's head. Cables ran from throne and ceiling, plugged into his chest, legs, arms. His back was a cluster of metal shafts, like sea-urchin spines, glowing with scalding heat. Despite the brass shell, the cruel barbs and sharp lines, the figure seemed frail, old and thin and bent under the weight of his skin.

Daichi could sympathize.

The figure was watching the ceiling as they entered, staring at the impenetrable black above their heads. As Daichi was brought before the throne, it looked down on him, breath straining through the breather bellows encircling the chair. When it spoke, its voice echoed around the room, amplified by speakers in the walls.

"*Kagé Daichi. I am Tojo, exalted and venerable First Bloom of the Lotus Guild.*"

"A pleasure," Daichi rasped.

"*No doubt.*" A smile lurked inside the wheeze, dry as summer grass. "*I fear it will be short-lived.*"

The command tent's ceiling had been peeled away, ushering in the rising sun's feeble light. Black snowflakes drifted through the gap, hissing as they ended in the roaring firepit. The room was pitch-dark behind her goggles—Hana could barely see a thing. But Katya and Natassja held her hands, one apiece, and Hana was afraid of doing or saying anything wrong. So she remained mute and near-blind behind polarized glass, stumbling as she was led to the fire's edge.

She could make out trophies lining the walls—ō-yoroi from dead Iron Samurai, chainkatana, bloodied flags set with the standard of the Dragon clan. The Marshal's six huge warhounds sat in one corner, softly wheezing, but their master was nowhere to be seen. She reached out to caress their minds before slipping back into Kaiah's thoughts, the bottomless strength she found there. A courage born of endless, raging storms.

I will not be afraid.

Natassja circled the flames, her eye a burning point of brightness even through dark glass. Katya pulled Hana down to kneel opposite, entwined her fingers in the Holy Mother's. Each woman's right eye was aglow, fierce and bright, hands joined around the flames.

I will NOT be afraid.

Natassja began speaking, her voice low, musical—a supplication before a power both feared and respected. Natassja closed her eyes, Katya followed suit, and Hana felt the air grow heavier, the tang of iron and blood in back of her throat as the Sisters joined voices, a tune that at any other moment might have seemed terrifying, ending in a rhythmic chanting, breathed at the last like the words of lovers into the ears of their desire.

Natassja opened her eyes, that rose-clad glow spilling into the scars lining her face. Her expression was indulgent, full of love—the smile of a parent watching a clumsy child in an innocent blunder. The old woman spoke softly, pointed to her face, but Hana couldn't understand the words. She licked her lips, again tasting bloody oxides.

"I don't understand," she said, panic rising.

Had she done something wrong? Had she offended?

Katya bared her saw-tooth smile, leaned across the firelight, pulling Hana's kerchief down around her throat. The girl felt the momentary fear evaporate, finally realizing they just wanted to see her face.

"Oh," Hana smiled. "Forgiveness, please."

Katya smiled in return. And reaching up, she pulled the goggles down from her eyes.

Firelight gleamed bright, dazzling after the gloom.

And then everything came undone.

K aori dropped down through the hatchway, sinking into the blood-red flood, warm and sticky-thick. She kicked to surface; a few feeble inches of air at the top of the pipeline, spitting her breath and sucking in another reeking lungful. Maro and the others dropped in beside her, the tungsten lamp sputtering out and plunging all into darkness.

Almost immediately they were moving, sucked farther up the pipeline by a tumbling current. Kaori's head smashed against a low-hanging seam, stars bursting in her eyes. Dazed and near-senseless, sputtering, the gash in her scalp burning at the fuel's touch. The current choked off as pump chambers filled and valves closed, silence falling like a feather. She was able to collect herself, pressing her hands against the curved ceiling, trying to suck down more of that awful choking air as twenty-eight seconds ticked by, lifetime by lifetime.

As if into the lungs of some titanic beast, the current kicked in again, dragging them farther along the pipeline, tears in her eyes. So it went on; torn up the pipe like a rag doll, floundering for a handful of heartbeats, then hauled along again. The motion was violent, sickening, the current dragging her down, down toward the bloody dark where her screams would go unheard. The pumps grew louder, nausea rising, threatening to spill from her lips and fill her breather, leave her choking on the contents of her own innards. She swallowed hard, another pulse gripping her, flinging her, a child at the mercy of some unholy tempest.

She heard Maro's voice over the thunder, the deafening beat of her own pulse.

"We must be close! Breathe deep and swim for your life!"

But how could she breathe deep when every breath threatened to choke her? When the air itself was poison, wringing the bile from her throat, retching dry, gods, gods help me—

And then it took her. That colossal undertow. Dragging her down through the great valve, sucking her into the black beyond. Head over heels, up and down meaningless, utterly dark. The groan of the great pistons to her left . . . or was it behind? Was she even here at all? Curled up in her bed in the Shōgun's palace, all her life before her, a father who loved her, a princeling who wanted her, a golden throne beckoning and all the treasures and pleasures of the Seven Isles laid glittering at her feet . . .

Swim, godsdamn you.

A shuddering moan, all along her spine, dread rising with the puke in her throat. A thrumming pulse. A crushing weight. Which way? Gods, which way?

Swim!

Kicking blindly in the dark, struggling toward the light. Except there *was* no light. No air in her lungs. And even if she did make it through, even if she did light a fire in the Guild's heart and burn it all to cinders, would it change a single thing? Would it bring back all the things she'd lost? Burn away the hate inside her? The rage at what she'd been and become?

Swim!

Would it bring her peace?

SWIM!

Would any of it make any difference at all?

Akihito leaned on his warclub crutch, staring across the valley at the Tora army lumbering into motion. The Earthcrusher had vomited an enormous plume of exhaust into the air, but hadn't actually moved an inch. After everything—all the talk and prayers and risk—it looked like the rebel plan was working. The big man found his face decorated with a broad smile.

The Guild sky-fleet charged headlong toward the Kitsune ships amassed over Yama. The shreddermen pounded across the open ground, carrying mighty metal boardwalks to bridge the Amatsu. Legions of bushimen moved like a glittering, scarlet flood behind. But the army had no siege towers, no battering rams, and without the Earthcrusher to clear the way, they were in for hard times when they reached the walls. Any second now, the behemoth would blow, vaporizing anything nearby.

But still, some of the Tora fleet would survive. The ships were better armed than the Kitsune ironclads—they needed something to equal the scales. And not for the first time that day, Akihito found himself searching the clouds, ears straining for the thunder of beating wings.

Yukiko, where the hells are you?

Hana's uncle Aleksandar stood a few paces away, Piotr beside him. The big man glanced toward the tent, Kaiah sitting outside and preening. The thunder tiger seemed alert but calm, and he knew she'd react at the first murmur of Hana's distress. But still, he couldn't help the anxiety stealing his spit, unspooling like ice-cold worms in his belly.

"How long does this ritual take?" he asked.

The gaijin commander raised an eyebrow, looking him up and down. "Why do you ask?"

"They could probably use a stormdancer soon." Akihito pointed to the skyfleet. "Besides, I'm worried about her. That's allowed, isn't it?"

"I admire my blood's courage," the gaijin said. "And that of her friends. And I know she will fight for her people this day, her friends beside her. But you should know, much will change after the ritual."

"What do you mean?"

"Hana will not be the same. No matter what happens this day, you should prepare yourself for a parting. When this war is done, my niece will return with us to Morcheba, to serve her House and the Goddess as is her duty."

"What?" Akihito frowned. "Have you spoken to her about this?"

"What is there to speak of?"

"Maybe she doesn't *want* to go to Morcheba . . ."

"What she wants is not entirely relevant. All Zryachniye—"

"Izanagi's balls, it's not relevant. That girl has been through the hells. All her life, she's never had a choice. And now she's had all these doors opened, all these riddles answered, you're going to take any choice she has away? She *trusts* you, Aleksandar. And for that girl, trust—"

A harsh cry, guttural and fierce; a tumbling nonsense Akihito had no chance of translating. He saw one of the Sacred Sisters stalking toward them, Guild faces beaten flat against her shoulders, sharpened teeth bared. Kaiah was on her feet, growl building in her throat. Akihito hefted his warclub, limped forward, eyes on the thunder tiger.

"Hana?" he called.

"Akihito-san." Piotr was looking at him, horrified. "What you do?"

"What?" He glanced at the gaijin, at the woman stalking toward him, scarred face twisted in fury. "What did *I* do? What the hells are you saying?"

"What you *do*?" Piotr asked again, voice rising.

Kaiah turned toward him, hackles rippling as she roared. The woman with the lightning scars shouted again, the Kapitán hissed and seized Akihito's arm. The big man cursed, shoved Aleksandar away. Kaiah was bounding toward him, gaijin soldiers were drawing weapons, outrage etched on every face. Piotr grabbed his arm, eyes wide and bright with panic.

"Akihito-san, run you."

He heard Hana cry out. The Sacred Sister shouting again, pointing. He shook Piotr off, stalking toward the holy woman, warclub raised high.

"What did you do to her?"

"No!" Piotr yelled. "No, run *you*!"

"What the hells did you do?" he growled. "If you've touched a hair on her head—"

The woman stepping toward him.

A blade, long and cruel and sickle-shaped.

Piotr shouting warning.

Kaiah's roar.

Hana's scream.

A blur of leather and brass, the priestess stepping close, whirling, braids flailing as she came. The sun finally cresting the horizon, a bright spray of blinding red, a soft hissing as the blade passed clean through his throat.

Ear to ear.

Black snow tumbling from the sky. Tumbling just like him. Hands at his neck, the flood of his blood almost scalding in the clawing chill. Collapsing to his knees. Dull roaring in his mind. Bubbling foam between his fingers, pink and bright. Falling face-first into frozen mud, disbelieving. Stupefied.

Taste of salt and copper on his tongue. Sticky on his lips. Those same lips he'd pressed to hers, sighing and laughing and whispering in the dark.

Together.

In the dark . . .

39

AN ORCHESTRA OF BONE AND BLOOD

Iron-thrower smoke curled in the air. Bo and Maseo lay twitching in a puddle of their own ruins. Kin roared, raised his fist. And Kensai lifted the iron-thrower, and blew a hole clean through the boy's leg.

The pain was breathtaking, bright and sickening, an unwanted scream spilling from his lips as he fell, crashing onto steel mesh smeared with his friends' blood. Staring into their sightless eyes, the whites ruptured, filling slowly with red. He clutched his leg, rolling on the floor, crimson painting the brass on his thigh.

"Understand me, Kin-san." Kensai loomed above him. "I will spare your life. To drag you before the First Bloom as proof of the Inquisition's fallibility—their feeble prognostications and their Chamber of Smoke. For if *you* are the one they hold up as Tojo's successor, *everything* they have ever said is suspect. But simply because I need you alive, does not mean I need you whole. And nothing would please me more than seeing just how much of you we could lose before we lose you entirely."

Kin clutched his leg, eyes locked on Kensai's.

"How did you know?"

"You were betrayed," Kensai sneered. "By the one nearest and dearest to you."

Kin blinked, mind racing. Kensai leaned down with a labored hiss and fumbled at the releases on Kin's helmet, pulled it away, staring at the boy's naked face.

"It was *you*, Kin-san. No matter what the Inquisition murmured in their smoke-drunk haze, I have known you for a traitor ever since you returned from the Iishi. I know your true self. I know the words you have whispered in the long quiet of the night."

Kensai made a fist, pistons hissing, an explosion of pale sparks filling the air as he tore the mechabacus from Kin's chest. The boy gasped in agony as the input jacks were ripped from his skin, the Second Bloom rummaging in the machine's guts until he produced a coiled length of wire, a small transmitter, the black button stud of a tiny microphone.

"I have heard them."

Kin groaned, hands pressed to the holes torn in his chest.

"Tell me," Kensai said. "Did you plant the bomb in my quarters yourself?"

Kin hissed, blood in his mouth, "Hai."

"I should have known. And yet I live. A failure to the last."

"I didn't want to kill you, Uncle. I don't want anyone to die who doesn't have to."

"Ah, such mercy, Kin-san. But what of Ayane? Have you spared a thought for what became of her? Your friend Daichi? Tell me, when you pulled the trigger at his head, you had no idea the iron-thrower was empty, did you?"

". . . No."

"And you would have killed him all the same. Killed almost anyone. Sacrificed almost anything. Just for the chance to be here, am I right?"

"The lotus must burn. The needs of many outweigh the needs of one."

"Except if *she* is the one. Your precious Yukiko. And perhaps yourself. Everything else is expendable, am I right? Those soldiers outside you planned to incinerate. The brothers aboard this vessel who trusted you. I'm sure you could happily throw the whole world away if you and she were standing together in the final chapter. And you call me monster."

Kin lashed out at Kensai's shin with his good leg. Metal kissed, the dull *whunng* of brass drums. The Second Bloom staggered, clutching the railing to stop his fall. Lotusmen descended, punching, kicking. Kensai seized Kin's collar and slapped him, gauntlet ringing on breaking skin. A Lotusman stepped forward, concern underscoring his rasp.

"Shateigashira, your wounds . . . If you exert yourself . . ."

Kensai still glared at Kin, his perfect, childlike face devoid of rancor. But his voice was black, poisonous, like the snow falling all around them.

"The things we do for love," he wheezed. "The things it does to us . . ."

Kensai released his hold, allowed Kin to slump to the deck. Standing with a smooth hiss of gears, he turned to his lackeys, breath rattling in his lungs.

"He is unworthy of his skin."

The Lotusmen swarmed, snapping the release clasps and tearing the atmos-suit from Kin's body. They were intentionally cruel, twisting into the bayonet fixtures at his wrists and spine, tearing them out, bruises and blood behind. Kin refused to groan—unwilling to give the bastard looming over him the satisfaction.

An Artificer turned from his console, bowing in apology.

"Forgiveness, Second Bloom, weapons systems are back online."

Another Shatei spoke up. "Communications back online."

Rei gave his stirrups an experimental nudge, and the Earthcrusher took four thundering steps forward, all aboard the bridge clutching at support to keep their footing.

DOOMDOOMDOOMDOOM.

"We have drive control again, Shateigashira," Rei reported, somewhat needlessly.

Kensai stepped forward, glaring through the viewports at Yama city.

"Leave no brick unbroken. No blade unshattered. Let this day be spoken of with shock and awe for one thousand years. Let Yama's ruins serve as a tomb for the corpses of this rebellion, and her tumbled walls a marker for the graves of those who defy us."

Kensai pointed one bloody finger at the city walls.

"Annihilate them."

M ichi stood on the *Kurea*'s deck, frozen breath billowing from bruised-blue lips. The sky-ship floated above Yama, watching the shreddermen suits lay their iron walkways across the Amatsu, storming across the tar-thick flow with floods of Tora bushi' following. She glanced at the Daimyo's flagship, the *Lucky Fox*, seeing old Isamu surrounded by his samurai guard and command staff. The Guild fleet was bearing down on them, but the Kitsune warships were holding back for fear of being caught in the Earthcrusher's fiery demise.

Except the Earthcrusher wasn't doing anything that resembled exploding.

"Shouldn't we be seeing fireworks by now?" Blackbird roared from the pilot's deck.

Michi grit her teeth, watching the Guild fleet draw ever closer. A dozen ironclads, fat and heavy and armed to the nines. The air swarmed with three-man corvettes, crisscrossing the skies like swallows on the mate. The Phoenix fleet was amassed to the west, sleek and beautiful ships armed for slaughter, circling to starboard. If the Kitsune fleet sat still for much longer, if the Earthcrusher didn't pop its cork soon, they'd be crushed like a thumb in a vise.

Her heart skipped as the behemoth groaned; a shuddering, rumbling exhalation, a mile-high spray of black from the chimney spires dotting its spine.

"Here it comes!" she yelled, covering her ears.

Poor choice of words, as it turned out.

The behemoth lifted four of its massive limbs, smashing them earthward in quick succession. The ground split asunder, clods of freezing black as big as boulders spraying in all directions. The remaining legs rose up, stretching and groaning. And with dread clutching her innards, Michi realized the Earthcrusher wasn't exploding.

It was charging.

Warning sirens howled amongst the Kitsune fleet, the Yama walls rang with the panicked peals of a hundred iron bells. Michi turned to the Blackbird, roaring over the din.

"Look alive, Captain-san! You might not have the chance much longer!"

"What the bloody hells is happening?" Blackbird roared.

"We have a war after all!"

Michi looked left, saw the *Lucky Fox* engage its propellers and lunge forward, followed by the other Kitsune ironclads. The Fox corvettes swarmed west to engage the Phoenix, Isamu standing on the pilot deck and waving his sword above his head, pointing toward the enemy.

Michi drew her chainblades, thumbed the ignitions. The motors roared to life, sending warm vibrations through her forearms. She searched the line of incoming Guild ships, eyes narrowed in the falling snow. But at last, she saw it, fresh painted and adorned with flags of the Tora Daimyo, deck glittering with a hundred blades. Down her bow, Michi could see her name in fresh kanji—a threat or promise that right now seemed about the best she could hope for.

The Honorable Death.

"There!" she screamed. "Full ahead, Blackbird. Right at that flagship!"

She could see him on the pilot deck, standing tall and proud amidst his samurai.

Hiro.

She remembered him sitting in the bleachers of Kigen arena as Yukiko pretended to train Buruu, the mock frowns she'd throw in his direction when she caught him staring too long at the Kitsune girl. She remembered teasing him, gathered with the other handmaidens and whispering as he passed, giggling as he smiled. So young, all of them.

And then she remembered Aisha. Chained to that awful half-life by those Guild machines, breath rattling in her lungs. What they'd done to her.

What he'd *let* them do.

"*The line of Kazumitsu needed its precious son. The Guild needed to cement their Shōgun's legitimacy. So do you know what they used?*" Aisha grit her teeth, spit the words. "*A metal tube. A handful of lubricant. As if I were cattle, Michi. As if I were livestock.*"

Blackbird was bellowing over the engines, the opening salvos of 'thrower fire, battle cries splitting the air. "You want us to ram the Daimyo's flagship? Have you gone mad?"

Michi licked her lips, eyes locked on Hiro.

"Not mad, Blackbird-san," she growled. "Just thirsty."

B urning.
        Lungs. Eyes. Skin. Throat.
All.
Burning.

She tumbled out into the void, up and down and left and right, abstracts with no real meaning. Instinct bidding her reach for a handhold, something, anything to slow her fall. Because Kaori knew she was falling, some tiny reptilian part of her brain screaming above the blur of chi fumes and vertigo and nausea and fear.

She hit the surface in a spray of bloody red, plunging down into treacle-thick darkness, kicking and thrashing with everything left inside her. Breaking into the vapor soup that passed for air, spewing and heaving, clinging to slick walls with trembling arms, struggling to regain what she could of her breath. Blinking in the near dark. Trying to understand where she was.

And gods, she'd made it . . .

An enormous tank, cylindrical, at least a hundred yards across. The interior was lit by a circle of tiny red globes, burning sun-bright after the pipeline's constant darkness. She saw rivet-studded walls, an outflow spewing intermittent blood-red jets into the sea of fuel all around her. The ceiling hung thirty feet above—only gods knew how deep the chi below her ran. A service ladder scaled the wall, up to the circle of lights she finally recognized as an access hatch.

A figure in black plummeted from the outflow mouth, tumbling down into the chi with a splash. Kaori swam over, dragging him to the ladder. She recognized Maro, his long braids soaked through with fuel.

"Izanagi's balls," he gasped, coughing thick inside his breather. "Next time, we take the bloody front door . . ."

Another body tumbled through the outflow and down into the darkness. This time it was a girl, Megumi, her breather flooded to the eyeholes with bloody-red, floating facedown in the fuel. More bodies followed, some breathing, most not, crushed flat or torn to pieces. The empty ones slowly spinning in the outflow's vortex, sinking down into the dark—people who had dreamed and laughed and died for something worth fighting for.

Did she still really believe that?

At the last, they counted each other by the light of that morbid red, discovering only five of them left. Kaori. Maro. Botan. Fat Yuu. Little Eiko.

Five of two dozen.

They climbed the ladder onto a suspended walkway leading to the access hatch. Waterproofed satchels were peeled open, explosives lifted out onto iron mesh. Maro looked them over with a critical eye, Kaori's head cocked as she listened to the dull sounds outside the tank. Motors and propellers, the latter growing louder by the moment.

The reservoir walls began trembling, what sounded like a sky-ship passing overhead. Maro glanced up sharply as several thuds sounded on the ceiling above. Kaori motioned for silence, drew her wakizashi. The other Kagé followed suit, blades drawn softly, smeared with lamp black to hide their sheen.

She could hear voices, hushed and metallic. A claxon in the distance. The red globes circling the access hatch winked off, one by one, and the six-studded lock contracted, the circular handle turning slowly, almost soundless in the oily air.

"Go!" Kaori hissed. "Go!"

Fat Yuu and Eiko had resealed their explosives, descending the ladder and slipping back into the chi below. Maro affixed climbing claws to his boots and palms, swung below the gantry and hung inverted, like some black, dripping spider, Botan behind him. Kaori followed suit; rolling over the gantry, she swung beneath, hung beside Maro with sword in hand.

The access hatch opened slowly, hinges buttered black with grease. A blinding spear of light flooded the tank. She made out a silhouette, burning eyes peering down into the dark. And as soundless as anyone wrapped head-to-foot in brass could move, three figures swung through the access hatch and climbed down to the gantry.

Guildsmen.

Two Artificers and a False-Lifer, gleaming chrome arms unfolding from her back. The sight of the arachnoid limbs put Kaori in mind of Ayane, of the spider drone in the village, deceit and betrayal curdling on her tongue. She glanced at the Shadows hidden below, Maro and Botan beside her, well aware that if it came to blows, any luxury they'd had in stealth would be gone.

The False-Lifer spoke, bubbling and sibilant.

"Be swift, brother."

One of the Artificers pulled a large package from a satchel: a fat blob of sticky, black resin, sealed in wax paper. He clomped to the wall, pressing the substance against a seam. The resin held in place, malleable as warm dough. The False-Lifer's hiss echoed in the dark.

"Set the timers for fifteen minutes, just in case radio control fails."

"In case we're captured, you mean?" asked one Artificer.

Kaori could see Maro's frown through his breather's viewports. Just as baffled as she.

"We cannot be captured, brother. We know too much. Defiance or death."

"Defiance or death," the second Artificer nodded, made a fist.

What in the name of the gods?

The second Artificer was unwrapping small sticks of what looked like copper, topped with radio receivers. Though she was no expert, Kaori knew enough to recognize a detonator when she saw one. The black, taffy substance was chi residue mixed with sulfur and sawdust—the same explosive that filled their own chi bombs.

They're planning to blow the tanks?

Could it be true? These were the rebels Yukiko spoke of? And now they were in First House with exactly the same plan as the Kagé?

Could it be?

The first Artificer knelt on the walkway directly above her head, rigging a timer. Perhaps it was light refracting off her breather. Perhaps the faint labor of their breath. But the Artificer looked down through the mesh, sucked in an astonished gasp as he spied them hanging below, and within the beat of a sparrow's wing, all thought vanished from her mind.

Kaori kicked off the wall, pivoting on her palms and swinging up over the railing. Her heel connected with the False-Lifer's jaw as Maro took one Artificer's legs out from under him. The Guildsman wobbled and tumbled off the walkway, brass-gauntlets shrieking on the railing as he arrested his fall, clinging like a tick over the drop.

The second Artificer drew an iron-thrower, aimed it at Kaori's head just as she seized the False-Lifer's throat, wakizashi ready to strike. Eight razored needles uncurled in the dark, gleaming in the garish light spilling through the access hatch. Poised at Kaori's throat, chest, eyes, just like the blade she pressed at the False-Lifer's jugular. Maro raised his katana, ready to strike at the Artificer aiming at Kaori's head.

Six of them, frozen in place, each hovering a breath away from murder.

The False-Lifer's voice was a whisper.

"You would be the Kagé, I presume?"

The Earthcrusher hit the walls of Yama like an avalanche, shearing through battlements as if they were dry grass, the men atop them mere dandelion seeds. Chunks of masonry were tossed about like a child throwing unwanted toys, Kitsune soldiers falling like black snow onto crushed granite below.

Each blow from its chainsaw arms was accompanied by a tortured metal shriek, a bubbling blast from its chimney stacks. Kitsune corvettes swarmed around it like mosquitoes, the pilots trying to draw the behemoth away from the city. But the Earthcrusher ignored them, kicked its way through the outer walls of Yama and stomped slowly toward Kitsune-jō.

The shreddermen poured in through the breached walls, each suit a giant in its own right. Ten feet high, legs as thick as old sugi trees, long, chainsaw arms hooked like scythes. Pilot lights shearing through smoke, glittering on the swords of the Tora bushimen who stormed in their wake. Howling fury, Tiger banners whipping in the wind. And having no chance of stopping the Earth-crusher, the men and women manning Yama's walls screamed their challenges in return and dropped into the storm of blades.

Iron Samurai leaped from the walls and crashed onto the shreddermen roll cages, stabbing and hacking at the pilots within. Shuriken-throwers singing *pop-popopopopop*, spraying death into the Tiger warriors, hoping to stem the red tide. But on they came, like blood from a wound in Yama's skin, flooding her streets with mayhem and screams.

In the skies above, the fleets were joined, shuriken fire filling the air. The first Kitsune ironclad to charge the Guild fleet had been cut down on all sides by withering hail. As it tumbled earthward, it had fired its grapple lines into a Guild ship, dragging it to its doom, the pair exploding in a rush of wailing hydrogen. The Kitsune Daimyo's flagship *Lucky Fox* had followed into the breach, firing its own grapple lines into the Guild ship *Blessed Light*. Their crews were already locked in deadly battle across the decks.

Michi roared aloud as the *Kurea* plummeted toward the *Honorable Death*. The sky between them was filled with dueling corvettes, the glittering rain of shuriken spray, flurries of black snow. A glance west revealed the Phoenix fleet cutting around the Kitsune, encircling despite the desperate charges of the Fox corvettes. Surrounded on all sides, the Kitsune captains had no choice but to charge into the enemy's open arms.

At least one other sky-ship—*Kitsune's Courage*—seemed to have the same idea as the *Kurea*. Her engines roared as she charged, firing a storm of grapples before plowing into the *Death*'s flank. Her crew withered under a battery of shuriken fire, cloudwalkers and bushimen left minced across the deck. *Kurea* collided with the *Death* a few moments after, and Michi was already leaping across the gap, chainswords shrieking.

The clash of steel all around, the growl of ō-yoroi, chaindaishō, screams of dying men, shrieks of sundered metal. Iron Samurai from the *Courage* were also boarding, roaring challenge in their Daimyo's name. She moved swift and sure, cutting along the railing toward the pilot's deck until three Iron Samurai inter-cepted her advance. She lashed out, plunging her chainwakizashi through the eyehole of a samurai's oni mask. The man was dead before he had a chance to cry out, the bone-white demon's face drenched red.

She deflected three lightning-quick strikes, dancing backward until her backside was pressed against the railing, sparing a quick glance for the drop below. Another samurai stepped up to replace the one she'd slain, and Michi realized she'd bitten off more than she could chew. Not simple bushimen like the kind she'd slain in Yoritomo's palace here. These were men born to soldiering, bigger and stronger, and thanks to their ō-yoroi, just as fast as she was. She could see Hiro on the pilot's deck, but there was no way she was cutting her way through twenty Elite to get to him. Best to seek another path to the prize.

She relieved one samurai of his chainkatana as he lunged, another of any chance he had of having children as he slipped on the blood-slick deck. Seizing her chance, she flipped back onto the *Death*'s railing, sheathed her swords and began climbing the rigging, two Elite close behind.

Monkey-swift, she pulled herself up onto the *Death*'s inflatable. The skies were a storm of corvettes, dark snow and darker smoke. Fire gleamed on her goggles as another Kitsune ironclad went up in flames, dropping like an anvil, her captain steering her into the Tora soldiers below as his final act of defiance. A dull explosion tore the air to ribbons, the rumble of collapsing buildings and the Earthcrusher's tectonic tread, the chatter of a hundred propellers, screams of the dying, cries and curses and prayers.

The Elite behind her climbed up onto the inflatable, cresting the balloon's gentle curve. She turned and charged toward them, a soundless howl on her lips. Using the inflated canvas like a springboard, she leapt toward one Samurai's chest, planting both feet on his breastplate. The man grunted, lost his balance and spilled backward into the void, silent as he fell. Kicking off the samurai's chest, Michi bounced back onto the taut canvas, flipping up to her feet as the second Elite swung at her head, once, twice, shearing clean through her braid and filling the air with wisps of long black hair.

Michi fell back under the onslaught, parry and riposte, feint and lunge, her swords a blur. She could see the samurai's eyes through slits in his demon helm—dark and narrowed, his skin crusted with ashes. The man was a master, pressing her back over the spongy surface, giving no opportunity to launch a counter-attack. Heart thundering in her chest. Sweat clawing at her eyes. Feeling suddenly small and alone, up here in the storm.

Just we two . . .

The wind howled like hungry wolves, teeth of ice and lolling tongues. She sheathed her katana, reached into her obi as she ducked one scything blow, side-stepped another, growling blades shearing through the cloth at her elbow. And drawing out a tiny clay bottle from her sash, she snapped off the cork and hurled it, an arcing stream of jet black, right into the samurai's face.

The ink splashed across the oni mask, into the samurai's eyes. The man staggered back, blinking furiously, but it was already too late. The girl moved, like a scalpel, a razor, a double-handed blow with her chainwakizashi shearing through his wrist. Spinning on the spot as he fell, collecting him just beneath the chin, where the long cheek guards of his helm kissed the iron collar at his neck. A spray of blinding red, great gushing gouts of it falling like rain as the samurai clutched the new smile she'd carved, dead before he fell.

She stood panting, mouth dry as dust, looking at the empty ink bottle in her hand and hurling it into the void with a roar.

"And you said a bottle of ink never won a battle, Blackbird-san!"

The sky ablaze, ironclads roaring as they plummeted from the clouds, metal groaning, shuriken fire and propellers chewing the haze, blue-black smears daubed across it all. And beneath the cacophony, below the shrieking orchestra of metal and bone and blood, she heard distant shrieks, thunder like the pulse in her veins, heart pounding in her chest.

Distant shrieks.

Thunder like a pulse.

Growing closer.

"About *godsdamned* time. This dramatic entrance bullshit is getting out of hand . . ."

A roar splitting the air, the song of lightning and thunder, the rhythm of mighty wings. The cry echoed through the valley, the city, bouncing amidst burning streets, off broken walls, repeating amidst the clash of steel, the war cries and death rattles, curses and prayers. And glancing up into the lightening western skies, Michi realized there *was* no echo—no trick of feeble sound in the hollow, bloody places. Instead of one thunder tiger descending from the black above, there was almost a dozen, filling the sky with their cries. Yukiko and Buruu at their head, screaming together as they fell, the air about them flooded with shrieking arashitora.

What did the old tales call a group of thunder tigers?

"Pack" seemed too simple. Too soulless and tiny to describe the sight. Wingspans as broad as sky-ships, cruel talons and hooked beaks, feathers of pristine white and darkest jet. Fierce and brilliant and beautiful, descending like hammers and flawless blades of folded steel—a sight no one had witnessed in over a century.

A flight?

A host?

A cloud?

No.

She shook her head, held her blades aloft as she roared.

Not a cloud.

And all around, all across the brightening skies, the thunder tigers roared in answer.

A godsdamned storm.

40
FLOWERS FALLEN

"Oh," Hana smiled. "Forgiveness, please."

Katya smiled in return, ran glass-smooth fingertips over Hana's cheek. And reaching up, she pulled the goggles down from her eyes.

Firelight gleamed bright, dazzling after the gloom.

And then everything came undone.

Katya's eyes widened, lips peeling from sharpened teeth. Hana thought the woman was going to bite her until she saw tears welling in her eyes, pulling back as if horrified to touch her. The Holy Mother stared across the flames, despair and outrage mixed on her face.

"What is it?" Hana asked, looking among the Zryachniye. "What's wrong?"

The Mother spoke words Hana couldn't comprehend, anguish in her eyes. Katya was climbing to her feet, face darkening in fury, Morcheban falling from her lips in leaden mouthfuls.

"What's wrong?" Hana wailed. "For the love of the gods what is it?"

Mother Natassja drew a curved, gleaming knife from within her furs. Hana tensed as the woman stood, reaching out to Kaiah's mind, just a heartbeat shy of screaming for help. But it was clear from the Mother's expression she meant no violence, only sadness in her eyes as she limped around the fire, holding up the flat of the blade so the girl could see her own reflection.

- ARE YOU WELL? -

Oh gods . . .

- WHAT IS WRONG? HANA? -

Trembling fingers stretching up to her face, her reflection doing the same. The leather strip, the pale skin, the wisps of burned blond. But beneath her eyebrow, where she should have seen an iris glittering like new rose quartz, there was only muddy brown.

Her eye had ceased to glow.

Katya stormed from the tent, a flurry of black snow tumbling inside as she tore the flap away. Hana took the blade from Natassja, pawed at her cheek, rubbed her eye, silently pleading for some explanation, some word to make sense of a world that suddenly made none at all. The old woman knelt beside her, and taking Hana's hand, she whispered in the Shiman tongue. Three words that sent the ground falling away from Hana's knees.

"No man," she said. "Zryachniye. No man."

"Gods, no . . ." Hana breathed.

"Spoiled."

She slipped into the glass-smooth warmth behind Kaiah's eyes, crying warning. The thunder tiger was on her feet, hackles rising, ready to charge into the tent and tear all asunder.

No not me, Kaiah! Akihito!

Hana forced the arashitora to turn, looking toward Katya as she stalked toward the big man. She saw the woman reach behind her, draw one of those awful sickle-shaped blades. Akihito strode toward her, warclub raised, demanding explanation. Kaiah roared warning, began bounding forward, lightning crawling across her feathers. Too far away.

Far too late.

And as Katya whirled in place, slicing Akihito from ear to ear, Hana started screaming.

Aleksandar was climbing to his feet as Katya cut the big man's throat, her face twisted in fury, those razored teeth gleaming. And then the Zryachniye was screaming, screaming at the top of her lungs for the Marshal, for warriors, to arms, to arms.

"Sergei!" she shrieked. "We are betrayed!"

The gryfon roared, turning on the command tent and charging into the dark where Hana and Natassja were sequestered. Aleksandar drew his lightning hammer, engaged the current, roaring at the top of his lungs as static electricity crackled up his arm.

"Protect the Holy Mother!"

He sprinted toward the tent, heard the warhounds baying within. A dozen warriors reached the tent before him, charging into the dark, now thick with screaming. Not just Hana, but the guttural, choking cries of men meeting their deaths—a bubbling choir of battlefields and slaughter Aleksandar had heard a hundred times before. A corpse flew back through the canvas wall, knocking him down, the body torn near in half. Thunder rolled, the tent collapsed, roof bending inward as the crunch of snapping timbers rose above pitched screams. Soldiers cried out in alarm, hundreds more charging the tent now, hammers and swords drawn.

Another thunderclap, the roar of a typhoon and shriek of tearing sails. A white silhouette burst through the tent roof, thick canvas shredding as if it were silk. The gryfon tore into the sky with Hana astride it, the pair painted in blood. She had a Zryachniye blade clutched in one hand, daubed red, the beast roaring in outrage as arrows rained around them.

Katya was stalking toward him, bloodied knife in hand as he pulled himself free of the sundered corpse.

"Katya, what in the Goddess' name is happening?"

The woman pushed past him into the tent, not saying a word. As Aleksandar stepped into the ruins, she started keening, stumbling to the firepit's edge, falling to her knees beside the corpse laying amidst a mound of others. Warriors of House Ostrovska, Goraya, Dmitriyev, Zubkov, soldiers of the Imperatritsa, all. But their loss was nothing, *nothing* compared to that of the woman lying dead by the smoldering coals—Mother Natassja, savaged to death by the warhounds lying dead all around her. Two dogs remained, blinking and comatose in a corner, muzzles smeared in gore.

"What did she do?" Katya moaned, rocking back and forth. "Goddess, what did she do?"

"What did *you* do?" Aleksandar demanded. "You killed Akihito! What—"

The Sister whirled on him, eyes catching the lightning above. "You dare speak his name to me? One who defiled a daughter of the Goddess?"

Aleksandar swallowed. "He . . ."

"We are betrayed, Aleksandar. Your niece is despoiled. Plucked by the hands of man."

"The girl is still my blood. She is still—"

"She has slain the Holy Mother!"

"You slew her lover! By the Dark, what did you think would—"

"Aleksandar Mostovoi!"

The bellow cut through the red haze clouding Aleksandar's eyes. He turned and saw Marshal Sergei standing in the tent flap, horror and rage scrawled across his face. "What in the name of the Living Goddess happened here?"

"We are betrayed, Marshal," Katya said. "The Mostovoi girl and her beast have slain Mother Natassja."

"*After* Sister Katya slew her lover," Aleksandar growled.

"Lover?" Ostrovska frowned. "No Goddess-touched may—"

"The girl has lost her flower," Katya hissed. "Left unattended by her fool uncle in a den of bastards and liars. She can no longer bear the Goddess' blessings. All is come to ruin. The tie binding us to the Shimans is undone."

Aleksandar turned to his commander, begging for calm, "Marshal, she is still born of both our lands, she is still—"

"Order your troops to attack, Marshal," Katya spat. "Rally your men and destroy every one of those filthy slaver pigs."

"And what of the iron behemoth?" Aleksandar demanded. "How shall we topple it? With prayers? I beg pardon, Sister, but you are not a strategist, and not a soldier."

"I am *Zryachniye*!" Katya stepped up to Aleksandar, shouting into his face. "I am the Imperatritsa's word made flesh now Mother Natassja is dead, and I say *attack*!"

Aleksandar shook his head, stared at the Marshal. Sergei licked his lips, spat hard. In the background, they could hear the chaos of battle, engines, shuriken fire and screams. The slavers were tearing each other to pieces. A barrage of thunderclaps sounded overheard, a multitude of roars filling the skies. Aleksandar squinted westward through the torn roof, spying a dozen black and white shapes descending from the clouds, sowing slaughter and flame. Shiman ships were dropping from the skies, fire reaching up to kiss the lightning.

The gryfons had arrived. Their stormdancer, Yukiko.

What price will we pay for the murder of her friend?

Sergei sighed, gave Katya a small bow.

Aleksandar's heart sank down to his toes.

"As the Imperatritsa wills," the Marshal said.

And turning to Aleksandar, he gave the order to attack.

I can feel them, you realize."

The First Bloom lifted one clawed hand, tapping his brow. "*Up here.*"

Daichi scanned the dark, taking in the figures of a dozen other Inquisitors around the chamber, silent and black as shadows. He kept his breathing steady, stance relaxed. Though he was unarmed, there was a time when his punches could smash cedar boards, his kicks crush brick. Just because he had no weapons didn't mean he was weaponless . . .

"Feel who?" he said.

"*Every member of the Guild,*" Tojo hissed. "*The Lotusmen on their ironclads. Kensai in his little behemoth. The Inquisitors in this room, uncertainty battling with their faith. They wonder about me, you know. If I am truly . . . here. Where all this is heading. Do you not?*"

Tojo stared around the room, at the shadows breathing their plumes of smoke. Hollow laughter spilled from his tentacled maw. The mechabacii clustered around his throne chittered.

"*I could even feel your friend, Daichi-san. Little Kin. Before Kensai tore the mechabacus from his chest. I quite enjoyed it, lurking on the cusp of those thoughts. Such an oddity, that one. The Inquisition expects great things of him, when I am gone.*"

Daichi could hear motion around him; men shifting their weight, as if discomfited.

"*It would shame any of them to admit it, but they are glad it will be soon. I frighten them, you see. I see that which they do not. Cannot. Will not.*"

Daichi was calculating the distance to the First Bloom, the unfathomable machines he could use to vault up the throne, reaching out and seizing that helm in his hands, twisting . . .

Gather your strength. Keep him talking.

"You can feel them in your head?" Daichi stifled a small cough. "Every Guildsman plugged into one of those accursed machines? How do you stand the noise?"

"*With difficulty. But I have been doing this for . . . quite some time.*"

"How long?"

"*Centuries? Something akin . . . I used to tally the years when I was younger. It kept me sane. A countdown to rebirth. Until I realized the truth we all should know.*"

"Truth?"

"*What Will Be, Will Be.*"

"Fatalism." Daichi smothered a cough. "I know how that feels."

"*Every man who has seen the face of his death does. You and I are very much alike.*"

"You have seen your death also?"

A slow, creaking nod. "*When I was a young man. When first we used the lotus sacrament to see the Truth. My lungs full of smoke and my eyes full of tears.*"

"And you have lived with that knowledge for two hundred years?"

"*Lived?*" Mirthless laughter. "*I would not call it that. I have not lived since before the rise of the Shōgunate. Since the twenty-four clans were consumed by four zaibatsu. Since my family, my wife, my people were annihilated by the Kitsune. Serpents, crushed underheel.*"

"I do not understand . . ."

"*You will,*" Tojo nodded. "*We talk now for a time. We will feel like old friends before we speak our last to each other. Before you do what it is you do.*"

". . . And what is that?"

"*Ah, the eternal question. 'Why am I here?'*"

"And?" Daichi frowned. "Why *am* I here?"

Tojo tilted his head, the smile plain in his voice.

"*To bring my death, of course.*"

You would be the Kagé, I presume?"

Kaori stood stone-still, wakizashi poised at the leader's throat. The False-Lifer's silver razors were a hairbreadth from her jugular, carotid, eyes. Gleaming in the garish light, the echoes of dripping chi filling the spaces between each breath.

"You are the rebellion," she said.

"But a few," the woman replied. "We are legion."

"As are we."

"I count but three."

"Count again."

"You are the Kagé who remained in the Iishi." The False-Lifer glanced at Botan and Maro. "The ones who refused to follow Yukiko to Yama. She told us about you."

"I'm certain she did."

"You came up through the pipeline system? I am impressed at your valor."

"Coming from one such as you, that means absolutely nothing."

"My name is Misaki."

"I care as little for your name as your praise."

"You would be Kaori? Yukiko told us of the betrayal. The one called Kin. Not all of us are like him."

"You all look the same to me."

"We *all* share similarities, it seems. Or are you here to admire the view?"

"We are here to burn the Guild's heart out. To destroy this pit and all within."

"Then we have common purpose. So why do we have blades poised at one another's throats?"

Long silence, filled with distant claxons, rhythmic drips from chi-sodden clothes. Breath burning in her lungs, sweat in her eyes, blurring the world and all within. Misaki simply stared, blades hovering at Kaori's throat, the breath of her brethren rasping through the bellows on their backs. The breath of living men. Living, thinking, feeling . . .

"Kaori . . ." Maro cleared his throat, his voice soft in the dark. "Perhaps there is wisdom in alliance. The explosives they planted speaks to the truth of their words."

"Why are you here?" Kaori whispered to the Guildswoman. "Why are you here really?"

"To destroy this house."

"That is a purpose. Not a reason."

Misaki stared back with those bloody eyes, her mask expressionless. When she finally spoke, her voice burned with a passion Kaori could scarce believe.

"I have a daughter. Suki. Her father is gone. Dead. But his last words to me were a plea to build a world in which our daughter might live free. To dance in the light with the sun upon her skin. He died for that dream. And I will die to see it done, if needs be. There is nothing I would not do to keep her safe. To see her breathe

the free air. I would die a thousand deaths to see my daughter live one lifetime in happiness."

Kaori blinked in the dark, a sting rising in the corners of her eyes. Misaki's voice, her father's thoughts. The *truth* of what he'd done. What he'd sacrificed for her. Why he'd *chosen*. Not Kin. Not any of them. His choice and his alone.

Misaki touched Kaori's wakizashi, gently pushing it aside. "The lotus must burn, Kagé."

"Burn," echoed her companions.

Kaori sighed, held out her hand, her voice a whisper.

"Burn."

Thopters lurched into the air, swaying like drunkards in a howling wind. Drums pounded, siege-crawlers roared, lightning crackling down their treads and arcing into black snow. And with howls of rage and bloodlust rolling up and down the line, flags of a dozen houses hoisted in the poisoned air, the gaijin army charged down the hillside toward the city of Yama.

A solitary figure remained.

Piotr stood in the black snow, staring at Akihito's body, the blood still steaming in the chill. It was strange how such a big man could suddenly seem so tiny, all the power in him, all the strength reduced to an empty bag of slack meat and tumbled bones.

The gaijin winced, kneeling beside the big man's corpse, the metal at his knee creaking. Reaching out, he folded Akihito's arms across his chest, closed his sightless eyes. Head bowed, he kissed his fingertips, pressed them to the big man's brow, whispering a prayer.

"Good-bye my friend," he sighed. "Am so sorry."

41
THE SHAPE OF LOSS

Yukiko could feel them all. Every one. Waiting in the burning fire beyond the wall in her mind. The arashitora, black and white, swarming in the air around her. Her Khan beneath her, fierce and proud and sharp as swords. Cloudwalkers and Iron Samurai clashing aboard sky-ships. Corvette pilots dogfighting through blinding fumes. Kitsune soldiers fighting and dying to defend their home. Tora soldiers fighting and dying to avenge their Shōgun. Gaijin warriors charging down the hill to avenge their fallen Mother. All of them, tumbling and burning and seething, one flame burning brighter than the rest. A flame that touched the Kenning just like she did, sending ripples across flaming water.

Hana. Grief-stricken. Furious. Screaming as she and Kaiah weaved among the gaijin rotor-thopters, tearing them from the sky.

Blood dripping from her nose, pain flaring hot at the base of her skull, Yukiko reached out through the storm, crossing a sea of death and pain. Gentle as she could, she reached inside the girl's head, saw the source of her heartache: Akihito lying motionless on the frozen ground.

Oh gods, no . . .

Grief seized Yukiko's heart, almost stilled it. It was a physical pain. A punch in the chest with jagged, frozen knuckles. One more piece of herself lost in this fucking war. One more person she loved taken away. Aisha. Kasumi. Her father. Now Akihito too. Gods above. His huge crushing hugs lifting her off the ground. His bad poetry. His clumsy, big brother hands, encircling her own. Gone now. Blood-slicked. Cold and still.

She reached out into the storm of talons and feathers all around her, filling them with her rage. Flooding their inputs with bitter, broken-glass grief, the desire for revenge burning white and blinding. They roared in reply, deafening and furious.

The Phoenix sky-fleet was now attacking the Kitsune fleet from behind, shredding their crews with bursts of shuriken fire. The arashitora fell on them like hammers from the sky, talons shearing through inflatables, the shriek of venting hydrogen layered over the roar of the thunder tigers as they fell on this tiny swarm of wood and flimsy metal, ripping it to tatters.

Enemy corvettes swarmed to engage, and an arashitora named Eii was caught in a three-way burst of fire from the incoming ships, shredded in the hail, dropping from the sky. The rest of the pack shook the clouds with their outrage, turned from the larger ships to pursue the smaller craft, the pilots trying to maneuver the thunder tigers onto the heavier ship guns. Razored steel filled the air, cutting the snowflakes to black mist.

Yukiko and Buruu flew east, over the plains outside Yama. Looking down, she saw a horde of gaijin storming toward the Tora assault bridges over the Amatsu, siege-crawlers roaring in the vanguard. Looking back, she could see the Earthcrusher slowly crunching toward Kitsune-jō, the Fox sky-ships tangled with the Guild fleet, boarding parties engaged in brutal hand-to-hand. But Hana's pain was like a fresh wound in her skull, the girl's grief amplifying Yukiko's own—impossible to ignore. She could see Kaiah and Hana moving like a chain-blade amongst the gaijin rotor-thopters, smashing them from the air with bursts of Raijin Song. Their formation in utter disarray, Kaiah and Hana pursuing the ships and opening them like love letters, remnants fluttering to the earth in clouds of burning perfume. And still the pilots fought on, spitting lightning, seemingly filled with suicidal rage.

And then they spotted Yukiko and Buruu swooping from the clouds—a second hellsborn girl on the back of a *second* thunder tiger, the sight turning all valor to water. One by one the remaining 'thopters fled, tearing back east across the smoking skies.

"*Hana!*" The cry spilled from her lips into the Kenning, echoing in the red warmth between them. "*Hana, listen to me!*"

The girl turned in her saddle, lightning gleaming on the edges of her armor. Her face was contorted, goggles dragged down around her throat, tears frozen on her cheeks.

"They killed him!" she screamed. "They killed Akihito!"

Yukiko could almost taste the girl's grief in the air. She could see fragments in Hana's mind; the pair lying together in the dark, her head on his chest, wrapped in gentle strength. Tears welled in her eyes—for her friend, for Hana who'd lost him almost as soon as she found him. But there was no time for grief now, not unless they wished to mourn the entire country along with him.

"*Hana, I know what they did. But thousands more are going to die if we don't stop this.*"

"I don't give a shit about any of them! At least Akihito won't be in the Hells alone!"

"*What about your brother? What about Yoshi?*"

"He's not here . . ."

"*Hana, if we fail today, the entire country is lost, do you understand that? No one is safe. The Guild will live on and everything that was good or pure in these islands will be gone. Everything. Do you think Akihito would have wanted that?*"

"You didn't know him like I did . . ."

"*I knew him since I was seven. He held my hand at my brother's funeral. And though I didn't love him like you did, don't you dare tell me I didn't know him. He'd want you to fight now, Hana. Not to avenge him, but to save these islands and the good left in them.*"

They stared at each other across the snow-filled sky, the smell of black smoke and fire and blood, the cacophony of sky-ship engines and the Earthcrusher's march, the stampede of gaijin drawing closer to the Tora river crossings. Hana was still crying, shoulders heaving as she struggled for breath. Kaiah cut the air in sweeping circles, tail stretched like a whip.

- *SHE SPEAKS TRUE, HANA. THOUGH PRECIOUS FEW, THERE ARE THINGS HERE WORTH SAVING. HE WOULD HAVE YOU FIGHT. -*

The girl hung her head, scraping frozen tears from her lashes. Yukiko could feel her fighting with herself, the grief and rage and spite locked tooth and claw with Kaiah's words, Yukiko's, Hana's own sense of right. Wavering on the brink; the same abyss that had almost swallowed Yukiko when her father died. But in the end, Hana caught her grief and swallowed it, rusted and sharp. And Yukiko could see the reason Akihito had loved her.

"I'm with you," the girl nodded.

"*All right.*" Yukiko pointed to the assault bridge over the Amatsu, the gaijin army charging toward it. "*We stop the gaijin getting into Yama. Then we deal with the Tora fleet. Then we take out the Earthcrusher.*"

"Hai," Hana sniffed.

Yukiko slipped into Buruu's thoughts, all warmth and folded steel.

Are you ready, brother?

ALWAYS.

All right. Let's cut this thing off at the root.

His name was Vladimir Grigori. Seaman, second ribbon. Fifteen years old. His application to enter the service had been a string of half-truths held together by lies, although in fact, the recruiters didn't question too vigorously once they discovered he was from Krakaan. The slaughter perpetrated by the slavers, the abduction of every woman, child and half-hale man from the city . . . well, the tale had already become legend before Vladimir and the ragtag bunch of survivors had limped east to Tarnow. For a boy to want revenge after everything he knew had been destroyed? Anyone could understand that, fifteen or no.

Vladimir was a fisherman's son, and he supposed if he were to serve in the Imperatritsa's forces, a ship would be the sensible place to do it. He just hadn't realized it would be so accursedly boring.

The muster had been magnificent to be sure. The assault on Kawa city glorious. But now the landing was done, there was precious little for seamen to do. They were moored in the smoking ruins of the slaver harbor, awaiting the return of Marshal Sergei's forces. Vladimir's days were spent on games of chance, listening to battlefield reports, or, as he found himself now, standing on a watchtower, smoke in one hand, spyglass in the other.

The skies were black and the sea iron-gray, the wind as cold as ice devil's breath. Someone had told him the slavers called this place the "Bay of Dragons." Staring down into the water, Vladimir exhaled a plume of smoke and shook his head at their folly.

Something silver moved in the depths, long and whiplike. A flash and it was gone.

Vladimir blinked, frowned at the swell, smashing against the hull in crests ten feet high. Another flash of silver passed beneath the bow, quick as Old Man Frost, twenty feet long if it was an inch. Vladimir dragged the smoke off his freezing lips and drew breath to shout, glancing up at the horizon. The words died in his throat, panic hitting him like a pail of ice water. Reaching down, he began grinding the warning siren, yelling at the top of his lungs.

"Stations! All hands to stations! Tidal wave!"

Cries of alarm running the ship's length, the siren's wail echoing in his head. Vladimir felt the engines start, the drumbeat of hundreds of boots as the crew scrambled. The *Grigori* began shifting, propellers churning waves to froth as the bow swung slowly about, the entire fleet following suit, helmsmen leaning hard on their wheels and gunning the engines to set the ships facing the threat cresting the horizon. Vladimir could see it with his naked eye: a vast, churning wall of water, black and cold as night. He peered through his spyglass, breath catching in his lungs. He wiped away the frost on the lens and peered through it again, a wondering curse on his lips.

"Living Goddess, save us."

A wave bigger than any he'd ever seen, made not only of water, but of teeth. A thousand serpentine shapes swirling in its depths, cresting and crashing through its face—shapes the battery farm crews spoke of with fear and awe.

Sea dragons.

But deeper within the wave, he saw two vast shadows, longer than the entire fleet end to end. Creatures so huge and terrifying they beggared belief; teeth as tall as houses, eyes like great glowing suns. Something primal awoke at the sight, something born in long winter nights of his childhood; a fear so bottomless his heart almost failed in his chest. And as they crested the wave, one serpent of gleaming silver, the other so black that light seemed to *die* inside it, Vladimir found himself screaming at the top of his lungs.

"Abandon ship! Goddess help us, abandon ship!"

Dragons.

Dragons such as the world had not seen for a thousand years.

And they were coming.

S he could feel them, reaching out across the island between her and the eastern seas. To the things she'd awakened, the slumbering giants curled in Everstorm's warmth, held still by Susano-ō's lullaby. But she'd been loud enough. Strong enough. The fires in her belly giving her the power to hear it all, every pulse, every heartbeat; the Lifesong of the World. And she'd reached into their minds and shouted, echoing in the black, until eyes as big as sky-ships had cracked open, until hearts as big as castles began to pulse faster, until that which had slept for as long as any had lived roused in the depths and demanded to know her name.

She had told them.

And they told her they had been waiting.

She saw them now in her mind's eye, rising from the deeps.
In their wakes, whirlpools.
Their heralds, tsunami.
The Bay of Dragons, men called it?
Time it lived up to its name.

Yukiko and Buruu swooped down through the snowstorm, Hana and Kaiah beside them, hovering above the troop bridge crossing the Amatsu. The arashitora seized hold of the railings, trying to drag it sideways off the riverbanks. The structure was impossibly heavy, Buruu and Kaiah straining for all they were worth.

- *YOU ARE WEAK, KINSLAYER. NOT EVEN TRYING.* -
THAT IS NOT MY NAME.
- *IT IS YOUR TRUTH.* -
I AM KHAN OF EVERSTORM NOW.
- *AND THIS IS NOT EVERSTORM. SO LIFT, CURSE YOU.* -

Even their combined might wasn't enough to shift the structure, so Yukiko called to the rest of the Everstorm pack. The arashitora responded, black and white, peeling away from the airborne melee and speeding toward them. But the gaijin troops were almost on them, archers setting up on the hills above, hammermen and blood-drinkers howling as they charged. Every one of them knew if the structure was dragged away, they'd have to call in their own engineers to forge a crossing. The battle for Yama would be over before they arrived. And so they threw themselves down the hill, intent on cutting the stormdancers to pieces.

"Get back!" Hana shouted to Yukiko. "Buruu has no armor!"

Yukiko and Buruu leapt into the skies, away from the storm of falling arrows, Hana and Kaiah charging the gaijin troopers. Kaiah clapped her wings together, gaijin clutching their ears and falling like saplings under a shredderman's blades. Arrows rained amidst black snowflakes, blasted to splinters by the thunderclap. Kaiah unleashed another burst, timing it with the archers' second volley, shivering the arrows to pieces as another wave of gaijin dropped like lotusflies. But the handful of blood-drinkers stumbled on, blinking and blinded, blood pouring from their ears even as they raised their mallets to attack.

Buruu roared warning, plowed into the wave, a flurry of talons and beak, Yukiko swinging her katana from atop his shoulders. When Daichi had given her the blade, he'd named it "Anger." The embodiment of Yukiko's rage at her father's death, the land dying all about her. But as she wielded it, she felt only sorrow that it had come to this—that all this blood was being spilled for no reason, that everyone on this field was fighting for the same thing.

She reached out into their minds, past the pain, into the song of the world. If she could *see* them, she could *touch* them, reach through the storm of death and hurt filling her head. And she flooded the minds of every man she could see with images of ancient dragons thundering into the Bay of Ryu, gaijin sailors fleeing in tiny boats, tsunamis made of teeth smashing the bayside buildings to splinters. Taking hold of the leviathans' primal fear and flooding the soldiers with that same terror; that fear born in the minds of little boys, huddled beneath their blankets as the winter winds blew outside their windows and the monsters beneath their beds dragged long fingernails on the undersides of their cots.

Run.

A single word in every mind, chilling the marrow of every bone, halting the charge of every man, breaking, turning and screaming from the girl atop her thunder tiger, hair whipping around her eyes as the winds howled and the snows fell and thunder tore the skies.

RUN.

The Everstorm pack arrived in a hail of black snowflakes, half a dozen landing on the troop bridge. Kaiah and Buruu turned from the routed gaijin, grasping the railings with their foreclaws. Each thunder tiger beat their wings, keening with the strain. And between them, ever so slowly, they tore the bridge from the banks, frozen earth ripped away, the iron walkway screeching at its joins, twisting beneath its own weight, the arashitora roaring as they dragged it up, back, finally releasing it and allowing it to fall, welds snapping, metal groaning as it hit the tar-black Amatsu in a blinding spray and sunk down into the depths.

The gaijin army was in utter disarray, halfhearted arrow fire falling about them like feeble rain. Yukiko looked down on them, stepping into the Lifesong, filling their thoughts. The sorrow of Akihito's death, the loss of her friend, gentle and kind and brave, gone now forever. Like the gaijin mothers and sons and daughters taken into the slave-ships' bellies, never to be seen again. The same pain, the same grief, no matter the color of their skin or the names of the gods and goddesses they believed in. The simple pain of a thing loved—a thing taken, never to return, no matter the blood spilled in revenge. All of them the same.

All of us the same.

And those who were not fleeing with the shapes of dragons in their minds hung their heads, tears filling their eyes without knowing why. Bows falling from numb fingers, breathing the names of mothers or daughters, fathers or sons, struck to the heart and bleeding anew.

The arashitora took to the skies, a swarm of black and white, eyes of burning amber and brilliant green. Flying west, Yukiko could see the Earthcrusher cutting through Yama like a slow avalanche, concrete dust and screams in its wake. She could see the Guild fleet above Yama city, entwined with the Kitsune, all smoke and fire and gleaming steel. A swarm of shreddermen had cornered a crowd of Fox bushimen near the broken wall, cutting through them like a hot blade through black snow. Behind the soldiers, a crowd of helpless civilians cowered in the ruins, just a minute or two from slaughter.

YUKIKO . . .

I see them.

FOX NOT LOOKING AFTER HIS OWN, IT SEEMS.

She grit her teeth, clutching her katana so hard her fingers hurt. And at last, she felt the anger Daichi had named the blade for. Flooding up her throat and bubbling over her tongue, one hand pressed to the iron at her belly, knuckles white on the sword's hilt.

All right, then. Let's look after them instead.

H e'd felt his fingers twitching as the pair flew past, Yukiko and her thunder tiger, roaring east toward the gaijin horde. Not the fingers of the prosthetic—the flesh they'd taken away. A phantom reminder of the battle in Kigen arena, repaying her betrayal with his own, casting aside love for the sake of honor. Loyalty. Servitude.

Only hatred left behind.

"There she is!" Hiro tore his chainkatana from its scabbard. "Can we pursue?"

"My Lord, we can't move!" the helmsman spat. "The Kitsune have us entangled!"

Hiro looked down on the *Honorable Death*'s deck, the brutal melee between Fox and Tiger samurai. Chainsword kissed chainsword in bright bursts of growling sparks, gore slicked over polished wood as men fought and screamed and died in puddles of themselves. But the *Death* was wedged firmly between two other sky-ships—a Kitsune ironclad and some Ryu merchantman. Boarding tethers were tangled in her rigging, grapples embedded in her hull.

Hiro turned to his personal guard—six Elite standing nearby. "Get down there and cut us loose. Yoritomo's assassin flies free while we flail amongst Isamu's rabble. We should be wetting our blades in her, not these Kitsune dogs!"

"Hai!"

The samurai drew their swords, charging into the storm of blades. Hiro turned back to the Eastern skies, watching the tiny shape flying farther and farther away.

She hadn't even *looked* at him.

"Soon you will," he whispered. "And I will be the last—"

Soft footsteps across the deck, the ignition of chainblade motors behind him, a cry of pain. Hiro turned with a gasp, bringing up his chainkatana and parrying the blow aimed at his head, feeling a chainwakizashi slice deep into his left arm. Blood sprayed, hot and thick, and he spun away from the railing as the wakizashi scythed toward him again, shearing clean through the wood. Skipping back, he raised his katana into guard position, left arm hanging useless and bleeding by his side, staring at the girl who had almost decapitated him.

Small and light and sharp as knives. Black hair chainsawed into a jagged bob. Plump, beestung lips twisted in a snarl as she tore the chainwakizashi from the railing, revved the motor. The last he'd seen of her, she was wrapped in a beautiful scarlet robe, flitting through the Shōgun's palace. Now she wore black, a breastplate of dark iron. But still he recognized her instantly. Recognized the swords in her hands—once wielded by his cousin, dear Ichizo, found dead in her room after the insurgents burned his city to cinders.

"Michi," he hissed.

"My Lord Daimyo."

He glanced up at the inflatable she'd dropped from, down at the helmsman she'd cut near in half. He couldn't feel his left hand; blood dripping from numb fingers to spatter at his feet.

"An impressive entrance."

"Your exit will put it to shame."

The girl charged across the deck, sliding down onto her knees and aiming her shrieking blades at his legs. Hiro leaped into the air, flipping over her head and landing in a crouch behind, aiming a blow at her exposed back. Michi blocked blind, spun up to her feet and launched a flurry at Hiro's face, neck, chest. His prosthetic was a blur, moving faster than any flesh, twisting at the joints in ways a real arm never could as he parried each strike. Bright sparks burst in time with each kiss, each impact marked with sub-harmonic notes of tumbling frequency, as if they played a tune on each other's swords.

The girl finished her barrage, stepped back and parried the two rapid ripostes, ducking beneath a vicious swipe that would have taken her head off. Her form was perfect, her blades a blur. But the iron arm was as much a part of him now as his flesh had ever been; a constant weight on his shoulder, a chill across his chest in the dead of night. And her every lunge, strike, stab—all of them were met by his blade on hers, chainsaw teeth snarling like starving wolves, sparks on their tongues.

He struck again, aiming a whistling blow at her throat, roaring as he swung. She caught his attack against both blades, blazing fragments of metal spitting and sparking in the air, the soles of her boots squeaking on the wood as she skidded back three feet across the deck.

Michi was panting, her expression incredulous as she adopted a backfoot stance, blades growling in guard position. He could read her thoughts, as plainly as if she'd spoken them aloud.

Little Michi, the Kagé sword-saint. Any other man she'd faced would have been dead by now. Her blitz attack had failed. Every second he lived was another second he could simply call for help from the dozens of Elite fighting on the deck below.

But no. Where was the honor in that?

Hiro laughed instead, flexed his clockwork arm back and forth.

"Say what you will about the Guild, Michi-chan." He revved his chainkatana. "They seem to have this flesh problem solved."

"Can your masters craft you another head?"

FeintLunge.

ParrySparks.

"They are not my masters," he found himself growling.

Now it was Michi's turn to laugh. "Did Buruu take your eyes when he took your arm?"

Rage came then. Sudden and burning. He could feel the ashes on his skin cracking as he snarled, brought his sword down toward her head. Michi deflected the blow into the deck, his blade churning through the boards as she brought her wakizashi up toward his throat and kicked at the trapped blade. Hiro released his grip, bent backward as the blow clipped his chin, trimming his goatee. Tumbling away, he came up on his feet, drew his wakizashi and thumbed the ignition. Michi plucked his katana from the deck and tossed it over the railing.

Sloppy.

"Truth hurts, little Daimyo?" she smiled.

"Shut your mouth, bitch."

StrikeParryLungeParrySparks.

"Gods, look at you." Michi tossed the hair from her eyes, glancing at the carnage around them. "All this death—all because Yukiko chose to stand tall instead of kneeling in Yoritomo's shadow. And you kneel there still."

"Do not speak her name to me."

"She loved you, you realize."

Hiro drew back as if she were a jade adder, coiled and ready to strike.

"I could see it in her eyes when she spoke your name. Like a flower unfurling in the first light of spring . . ."

"Shut up!"

"You were her first, you know. And she yours, am I right?"

"SHUT YOUR FUCKING MOUTH!"

A tiny part of his brain screamed he was being played, manipulated into a clumsy, howling attack. But that voice drowned under the indignation, the fury, the blood flowing from the scabs this little Kagé bitch had so casually torn away. And so he charged, watching those bee-stung lips curl into a smile, the girl moving like water over river-smooth stones. Deflecting his strike, she brought her wakizashi down on his sword arm, crunching through the crossguard, cleaving fuel lines, the blades falling still. Spinning down into a crouch, kicking his ankles as he stumbled past, momentum sending him crashing to the deck, colliding face-first with the railing and rolling over onto his back, gasping as blood spewed from his broken nose.

Riding on his shoulders through the lotus fields. Reaching up to touch his swords, so heavy he could barely lift them, little eyes alight.

"Will I grow up to be like you, Father?"

Her foot came down atop his chainsword, her own growling in her hands. Wind in her hair, a tangled knot of raven black in her eyes, staring down at him with nothing close to pity.

"You don't even know what you took from me, do you?" Michi hissed.

"Lord Izanagi give you the strength to die well . . ."

"Still you talk?" Hiro spat. "Finish it, for the love of the gods . . ."

Michi brought the katana's buzzing teeth close to Hiro's throat.

"A parting gift before you leave us," the girl said. "To repay the kindness you showed my Mistress. You remember Lady Aisha, don't you, Daimyo? Chained to a bed of machines for the sake of your glorious dynasty. Raped nightly by Guildsmen and their honorable inseminator tubes? And all the while, your dynasty was already assured. Growing in the belly of the girl you once professed to love." She drummed her fingernails on her katana hilt. "Two of them."

"What did you say?" Hiro's eyes grew wide.

"Would that I could sing it, bastard."

"Yukiko is . . ?"

"You'll never see their faces. Never hold them in your arms or hear them call you 'father.'" A smile, as cold and empty as tombs. "And now . . . *now* you know the shape of loss."

The girl raised her sword, steel teeth slicing the air as she drew it back to strike.

Licking his lips, tasting the ash of the funeral offerings. Eyes open wide.

A good end. A warrior's end.

A father's?

Gods . . .

"Wait," he said.

"No," she replied.

Everything in that final breath was hyper-real—every nerve singing, every sense alive. The wind on his skin. A black snowflake melting on his cheek. Men screaming. Swords clashing. Running footsteps. 'Throwers spitting. But amidst all that input, that storm of touch, sound, smell, all he could see was that falling blade.

Falling.

Tumbling.

Clattering on the deck.

Her hand at her throat, the spray of blood that bloomed there as the shuriken passed clean through. The report of the 'thrower, hanging in the air like smoke. Her eyes wide as she spun about, bringing her wakizashi to bear as the second marine opened fire, sparks dancing on her breastplate, crimson spraying from her forearm, shoulder, face. Features twisting, charging into the hail, but so frail now, so small, this little engine of death and deception who'd played him like a shamisen, unable here, at the last, to speak even a word.

She killed them both—brave men with the sense enough to look toward the pilot's deck, rushing to their Daimyo's defense when all others were concerned with their own lives. She cut them to pieces, not realizing she'd spent the last of herself doing so. And turning back to him, she fell to her knees, wakizashi clattering into the blood beneath her, one palm to her throat.

So much blood.

On her face, twisted with hatred as she tried to crawl, eyes locked with his. Collapsing on her belly, fingernails clawing the wood, legs kicking on the deck. Running only on hate now, the blood fleeing her body in steaming floods. And he, helpless, but to stare.

And at the end, her face bled all hollow and white, she tried to talk. Ruby red, bee-stung lips, mouthing the word she couldn't speak. Her last will and testament. Something profound, perhaps. The name of a loved one? Some word of wisdom to carve on her stone? To make sense of all she was, and why this, of all places, was the place she ended?

Hiro crawled through the blood, pressed his ear against her lips. The faintest whisper, a single syllable, fragile as glass.

A prayer.

An epitaph.

Wreathed in smoke.

"Burn . . ."

42
WHAT WILL BE

Charges set. Timers ready. Kaori's smile, grim in the dark.

The chi reservoir was rigged with four bombs, each one enough to ignite the fuel vapor and set off a catastrophic reaction. None of the rebels seemed to know how deep the reservoir stretched, but there was certainly enough chi to blow First House off the mountainside.

When each device was triple-checked, Misaki turned to Kaori.

"How is it you planned to escape from here, Kagé?"

A shrug. "Steal an ironclad. Fly it as best we could."

"Our crew is waiting at our ship for us to return. One of our brothers is planting explosives beneath another landing platform, to serve as distraction. We will be under heavy fire if we launch without clearance. But we can bring you with us if you wish."

A glance at Maro and the others. A slow nod.

"We will ride with you."

"And what about your father?" Misaki said.

Kaori blinked. Knife in her gut.

Twisting.

". . . My father?"

"He is in First House. They spoke of him in the security reports." Misaki shrugged. "I presumed that was why you were here."

"He . . ." Kaori's voice cracked, ". . . he still lives?"

"Can it be any surprise the First Bloom wished to speak with the Kagé leader?"

Kaori's eyes narrowed behind her breather. "He's with the First Bloom?"

"In the Chamber of Void," Misaki nodded.

"How do we get there?"

"You do not. To attack the First Bloom in his sanctuary is to commit suicide."

Kaori took one step closer, stared into those bloody eyes. "I asked how we get there . . ."

A metallic sigh. "This mission is too important to risk on the life of one man."

"A great man," Maro growled. "A man who has given all to save this land."

"If he had given *all*, there would be nothing left of him to rescue."

"You told me you do this for your daughter," Kaori said. "That there is no greater love than that of parent for child. Well, I have no children. No family save him, and these brothers and sisters beside me. And I will not leave one of them behind today. I'll die first."

Misaki was motionless, glancing amongst the Kagé, one by one.

"The Chamber of Void is an observatory. A domed roof. Climb through the hatchway and you will see it immediately. But your chances of making it there unseen . . ."

"We are shadows," Maro said. "Leave that to us."

"Fifteen minutes. After that, there will be nothing left of this place but rubble."

Kaori nodded. "We understand."

"The Inquisitors who guard First Bloom Tojo," Misaki warned. "They have strength born of madness. They move like the very smoke they breathe. You will have to fight every inch of the way. You will need the intercession of the gods themselves to have any hope of victory."

Kaori smiled. "Just another day, then."

She nodded to her brethren.

"We move."

D aichi blinked, scarcely believing what he heard. He stared at the First Bloom atop his Throne of Machines, breath rasping in blackened lungs.

"You want me to kill you?"

"*Want has little place here. This is where I die, and it is you who brings me my death.*"

"The What Will Be . . ."

"*Ah, you have heard of it. From young Kin-san, I presume? Did he tell you what he saw within the Chamber of Smoke?*" Tojo gestured to his throne, eyes aglow. "*Did he tell you he will be First Bloom when I am gone?*"

Tojo flipped a lever on his armrest, and a rumbling creak reverberated through the floor. A hollow song of mighty gear chains sounded in the walls, and the great domed ceiling began rolling back, inviting in a brutally sharp daylight Daichi winced to see. Cold wind howled through the widening gap, bringing stabbing pain to his lungs even as it banished the chi stink dripping from the walls.

Blinking in the burning light, Daichi made out vague shapes of the Inquisitors gathered around him—two dozen, black-clad, midnight smoke drifting from their breathers.

"*It is time,*" Tojo ordered. "*Leave us, brothers.*"

"First Bloom—"

"*I will give her your greetings, little Serpents. Your new First Bloom rises this day. Go, and prepare for his coming, the ashes of Foxes upon the soles of his feet.*"

The Inquisitors bowed, low and solemn, palms pressed together, speaking as one.

"For the Mother."

"*For the Mother,*" Tojo nodded.

The Inquisitors filed from the room, through the aperture of an iris portal, the metal grinding closed behind them. Only four remained now, standing at the room's periphery. Daichi found himself alone, just a few footsteps away from the heart of Guild power in Shima.

Staring down at his upturned palm.

None of the Inquisitors were close enough to stop him. Once his eyes grew accustomed to the light, he could snap this old man's neck like tinder. There was no way in the hells Kin would serve as First Bloom in this place—he knew the boy's love for Yukiko would never allow him to rule the Guild. If they were relying on him to step into the void Tojo left behind . . .

"If Kin will be the Guild's next leader, why is he not here in First House? Protected?"

"*Because he* Will Be *the Guild's next leader.*"

"But should you not be keeping him safe? Why risk his life in the Yama assault?"

"*We risk nothing. What Will Be, Will Be.*"

"That is madness. Nothing in this life is a certainty."

"*Foolishness. All is preordained. Tell me you do not feel it, since first the blackness took root in your lungs. And tell me that certainty has not brought you a clarity. A peace. A strength. You know it, Daichi-san. You were* meant *to be here, speaking with me, right now.*"

"I *chose* to be here. For good or—"

"*We are slaves to fate. To a design beyond our comprehension.*"

"That makes no sense. There are no strings. No puppeteers."

"*You do not believe in gods, then?*"

"Of course, but—"

"*I have seen the future, Daichi-san. I have seen this moment, every night in my dreams. In the Chamber of Smoke, we pry our inner eye wide, looking into the tapestry of fate. Those of us with strength see the most pivotal moment of our lives. How could that be, if those lives were not predetermined? If all the events leading to that moment were not set in stone?*"

"But if everything is predestined, what is the purpose of living at all?"

"*There is no point. None whatsoever. That is the truth she whispers to us in the dark.*"

"She?"

Tojo gestured to the walls with one creaking sweep of his arm. Daichi looked around, eyes still narrowed after weeks spent in gloom. But on the room's edge, carved deep into the granite, he could see murals. Lord Izanagi stirring the oceans of creation with his spear. Lady Izanagi, perishing in the birth of Shima. The Maker God's quest to retrieve his beloved, ending in failure. And at last, the Lady sitting on a throne of human bones, waiting in the dark.

Alone.

"*Endsinger, Daichi-san,*" Tojo said. "End. *Singer.*"

"Lady Izanami."

"*Hai.*"

"But why? What does she—"

"*One thousand people. Every day.*"

"And you fools in the Guild seek to aid her? To bring about the end of all things?"

"*Not all within the Guild know. Most are as blind as you. Never questioning.*"

"But how? She is forever trapped in Yomi . . ."

"*She sought to reclaim this world once. Tricked a child into opening the gate*

Lord Izanagi had sealed. And through that gate, she sent her children to war on the world of men."

"The War of the Hellgate."

"*Indeed.*"

"But the stormdancer Tora Takehiko charged into Yomi and sealed the gate forever."

"*And so, with the Iishi gate reduced to rubble, she sought a new way into the world. A new key to unlock it. A new altar, watered with the blood of thousands.*"

"Blood lotus . . ."

"*Hai.*"

"The deadlands . . ."

"*Hai.*"

"My gods . . ."

"*No, no,*" Tojo chuckled. "*Your Goddess.*"

"So all this . . . lotus, the gaijin war, inochi . . . all to start another hell war?"

"*There will be no war.*" Tojo shook his head. "*More than oni will crawl from the cracks we tear in this island's face. The little ones have already begun arriving, but when we are done, the fissures will be large enough to unleash the greatest denizens of Yomi. Horrors beyond imagining. The Dark Mother herself will walk these isles. And in her wake? Ashes, all.*"

"Madness . . ." Daichi breathed.

"*We could not have done it without you. Oh, you wonderful little skinless. So enamored of the trinkets we gave. Engines and sky-ships and chainswords to fight your wars and stock our larders with gaijin slaves, their blood watering the earth from which She will spring.*"

Tojo shook his head, sighing.

"*You cannot imagine the magnitude of the task when first we began. So few of us left, we Serpents. And if you had told us then we could convince the entire country to become complicit in its own death, to not merely sit back and let us work, but actually aid us . . . well, we would have called you insane.*"

Tojo's laughter was the flutter of a thousand metal wings.

"*But you are blind. So blind.*"

"You lied to them," Daichi growled. "No one could have known . . ."

"*Should they need to? You people are not eyeless. You could see the damage you were doing to your world. Red skies. Black rivers. Mass extinctions. And nobody lifted a finger. Because it was easier, wasn't it? The world we gave you? We never forced anyone's hand, Daichi-san. We simply gave you the blade and let you cut your own throat.*"

Daichi spat black onto the floor. "Not all of us are blind to what you do."

"*And for that, you have my thanks.*"

"So why?" Daichi rasped. "Why tell me all of this?"

"Because there is nothing you can do to stop it. What Will Be, Will Be."

Daichi couldn't see Tojo's face, but he swore the old man was smiling. A toothless grin behind a chitin mask, sallow skin and ricket bones held together by its cage of brass. He could feel the rage inside; that burning, blinding hate he'd drawn so much strength from. The gift he'd urged Yukiko to embrace. Here he was—in the heart of Guild power. Their leader near-helpless before him. The man responsible for all of it—poisoned sky, blackened earth, mass graves.

Tojo deserved to die. Here and now. Head twisted until his neck snapped through, his last sensation the severance of his spinal cord and the slow choke that followed.

He deserved it. And if everything he said was true, there was no escaping it.

"Death is too good for you," Daichi hissed.

"Death does not think. Merely takes. Good has nothing to do with it."

Daichi coughed. Once. Twice. Holding his belly as a fit started, gods no, not now . . .

"If it did, you would not be dying. For are you not a . . . good man?"

"No . . ." Daichi wiped his lips, breathing hard and spitting dark. "I am a murderer. Ten years of rebellion won't atone . . . for a lifetime of service to a regime built on butchery and lies."

"Feel no shame. You are what was intended. All you have done is what you were meant to. Accepting this brings freedom. Freedom to do whatever it is in your nature to do."

"And you would have me kill you," Daichi wheezed. "For such is my nature. I've devoted my life to stamping out your kind . . . Here you are, within my reach, and I have no reason *not* to do it. For though you think Kin will rise in your remains, I tell you now I know that boy better than any smoke dream . . . He will *never* rule this place."

"What Will Be, Will—"

"Spare me." Daichi glared up at the chattering throne. "You say all this is foretold—this room, your tomb, and I, your killer. But your dreams have no power over me, old man. Mine is the world I build . . . My triumphs, my mistakes, my loves, my losses. I *choose* what I am. Every day. I rise, and I stand. And the world you describe is one where I only kneel."

Daichi straightened, shoulders set, fists clenched.

"And so while I have every reason to kill you . . . I stay my hand. This, I *decide*. Your What Will Be will only *be* if I choose it. And I choose to defy it." He spit on the ground. "So much for your predetermination. So much for what you *know* to be true."

Tojo stared down at Daichi for a long, silent moment, distant thunder the only sound. And then he began clapping, metal striking metal, the sound of hammer hitting anvil underscored with a hollow sibilance Daichi finally recognized as laughter.

"*You skinless,*" he said. "*How you love your delusions.*"

"Speak your lies all you wish." Daichi spat again. "I will die as I have lived this past decade. Free. I will not give you the death you desire."

"*I never said you would give me death, Daichi-san. I said only you would bring it to me.*"

Tojo tilted his head to the sky.

"*I think . . .*"

A shadow, falling like an arrow from the clouds. A gleaming blade in an outstretched hand, golden cranes in flight across black lacquer. Folded steel piercing burnished brass, in through the join between shoulder and throat, out through the chest, crimson-drenched.

The First Bloom gasped as Kaori tore her wakizashi free.

"*At last . . .*"

"Daughter, no!"

And raising the blade, face twisted in hate, Kaori struck off the First Bloom's head.

43
BRIGHT AS THE SUN

Kin lay in a puddle of blood, ruby-slick hands pressed to his thigh. A Shatei had rendered some rudimentary first aid—hurried sutures and a wad of bandages; just enough to stop him bleeding out. He was propped against a railing, staring out the viewports at the carnage below.

The Earthcrusher seemed unstoppable, plowing through houses, temples and tenements on its torturous plod toward Kitsune-jō. Commander Rei was merciless, pausing every few steps to clear great swathes of concrete and timber and soldiers with sweeps of the massive arms, fire spewing from flame-spitters on the Earthcrusher's belly, setting the rubble around them ablaze.

"Commander, lookouts report four arashitora incoming from the southeast."

"Air batteries are armed?"

Kin heard a deep metallic whine, slowly building in intensity.

"Hai."

"Then let them come."

Dread gripped Kin's insides, eyes wide as the Earthcrusher turned its head to watch the incoming thunder tigers. He could see four shapes: two black, two white, headed right into the Earthcrusher's fire zone. He looked for a flash of metal wings, a rider amidst the mob, and was ashamed to feel a flood of relief as he realized Yukiko wasn't among them.

"Those creatures are almost extinct," he said. "There's probably only a handful alive anywhere in this world."

"Now the handful will be easier to hold," Kensai rasped. "Fire."

The beasts soared closer, peeling off into four different directions. Rei waited until all were in range, then engaged the firing studs. With a deafening crackling, as if a thousand kindling wheels had been set off simultaneously, the air around the Earthcrusher was filled with iron-thrower shot—a hail of tiny metal balls shredding feathers, meat and bones, the magnificent creatures reduced to shapeless pulp, smashing to the ground in bleeding ruin.

"Godsdamn you!" Kin cried, trying to get to his feet. "When will you be happy, Uncle? When there's nothing left but ashes?"

A Lotusman slammed one brass-soaked fist into Kin's gut, dropping the boy to his knees. Kin rolled onto his side, gasping for breath.

"March on," Kensai said.

D aimyo Isamu stood on the *Lucky Fox,* watching the battle unfold about him. Kitsune Iron Samurai were clearing the decks of the Guild ship *Lotus Wind,* moving amongst the remaining cloudwalkers and cutting them to pieces. It was nearly impossible to tell how the battle was faring through the ash, exhaust, and smoke, but the Kitsune seemed to be holding their own in the air.

The ground was another matter entirely.

The old clanlord watched through a telescoping spyglass as the Earthcrusher stomped closer to Kitsune-jō, obliterating everything in its path. His heart had soared for a brief moment when he saw the four arashitora swooping to attack, but as the Earthcrusher blasted the magnificent beasts from the skies, the Daimyo's heart had sunk to his toes.

More thunder tigers streaked past the stern, barely half a dozen, black and white, Isamu crying aloud when he saw riders on two of the arashitoras' backs.

"Stormdancer!"

The crew took up the call, the shapes wheeling about and circling the *Fox,* flashing eyes and bloody claws. The thunder tigers alighted on the deck, tearing the planking to splinters. The one called Buruu roared, and the other arashitora found perches on the bow, the inflatable, the railings—creatures of impossible grace and beauty, even amidst this godless slaughter.

Yukiko slipped off Buruu's back, Hana beside her. The girls were both blood-spattered, pale as hungry ghosts. Yukiko tore her goggles down around her throat, bloodshot eyes beneath, tear tracks cutting along ash and smoke-stained skin.

"It is good to see you, girl," Isamu nodded. "We feared you were among those arashitora who fell to the Earthcrusher."

"I lost track of them." Yukiko's voice trembled, barely audible over the engines' roar. "We cut off the gaijin assault, then destroyed a group of shreddermen near the breach in the walls. I didn't know they were going to attack it . . . They should have waited . . ."

Hana was breathing hard, lips pulling back from her teeth. "Guild bastards . . ."

"The fault is not yours," Isamu shook his head. "The machine is unstoppable."

"If I could see where the pilot sits, I could turn his brain to soup," Yukiko said. "But we can't get near enough. The 'throwers will cut us to shreds."

"The rebels must have failed," Hana said. "Without them, we have nothing to throw against it."

Isamu gripped the railing, looked at his city. He felt tired in his bones. Tired in his heart. Five sons buried. Wife gone. His line broken. A war built on lies and a nation on blood.

All for nothing?

"No, Stormdancer." He turned to Hana. "We have something to throw."

The old clanlord stepped to the edge of the pilot's deck, called in a booming voice. "Soldiers of the Fox clan! Kitsune-jō stands in peril! We head for the Earthcrusher!"

Grapple lines were cut, the *Lotus Wind* set adrift on the choking skies, crewed now by ghosts and dead men. The *Fox*'s helmsman brought her about, redlined the throttle, smearing their wake with spattered blue-black fingerprints. The arashitora clinging to her flanks peeled away, dismantling any Tora corvettes foolish enough to cross their path.

"Daimyo." Yukiko's eyes widened. "You can't intend to—"

"There are no weapons in this fleet that can dent that thing's hide, girl."

"You mean to ram it." Her voice incredulous. "Use the fleet itself as a weapon."

"That is what I mean, Stormdancer."

"This is madness . . ." Hana said.

"To wield the long and the short swords and then to die, girl."

"Gods, not again!" Yukiko cried. "Honor and glory? What the hells is wrong with you people? Why are you all so eager to kill yourselves?"

"If you have another suggestion, Stormdancer, I am willing to hear it."

Yukiko grit her teeth, looked to her thunder tiger. Isamu watched her scowl deepen, but she stayed silent as graves.

"I thought not," he said.

"There must be another way . . ."

"Not all sacrifice is in vain. Not all who give their lives do it for glory, or honor. Some do it for love. Of clan, or future, or family. Something greater than ourselves."

". . . My father said something like that to me. A lifetime ago."

"A wise man." Isamu looked at his empty hands and sighed. "Wiser than most fathers."

The city of Yama blurred beneath them, the flaming trail of destruction in the Earthcrusher's wake visible through the veil of smoke and fumes. Shreddermen suits stomped through the rubble, thick knots of fighting raging in the sky-harbor, the market district, the refinery ruins. The behemoth's footsteps had cracked the ground like broken glass.

The *Lucky Fox* was soon joined in its charge by four Kitsune corvettes, all converging on the Earthcrusher's position. The helmsman adjusted altitude, bringing the *Fox* level with the Earthcrusher's head, pouring every drop of chi into the shrieking engines.

The cloudwalkers, bushimen and Iron Samurai gathered on the pilot's deck, every eye locked on the goliath. Isamu turned to them, a smile on his ash-streaked face.

"You men have fought bravely this day, but the battle is not yet done. Take the escape pod and continue the struggle against the Tora below."

A bushiman not even old enough to shave stepped forward, covered his fist. "We stand with you, Daimyo! We stay to the end!"

"Your duty is to your families. This battle is far from won. Go now. See to our city."

Isamu was met with defiant stares, mute disobedience, shuffling feet. His lips peeled back from his teeth, five decades of command turning his words to steel.

"This is a direct order!" he barked. "Go! Now!"

The Kitsune soldiers reluctantly covered their fists, bowed slow and deep, sorrow in their eyes. As the men began filing into the escape pod, the clanlord turned to Yukiko, placed a gentle hand on her belly. The girl tensed at his touch, but didn't move away.

"Do good by them," he said. "Never let them go."

Yukiko swallowed hard, said nothing. Hana threw a hasty embrace around the old man's shoulders, kissed him on his cheek.

"Maker bless you, most Handsome Worshipfulness."

The pair trudged down the stairs toward Kaiah and Buruu. The male thunder tiger watched him with glittering eyes, tail lashing like a slow whip. Isamu held up a hand, signaling farewell. And with a rush of wind, the pulse of the storm, the beasts took to the skies.

Isamu turned back to the Earthcrusher, took position at the wheel, tossed his helmet to the deck. White hair streamed out behind him in the burning wind, flailing at his eyes; the pepper gray his lady had so loved to tease him about. He thought of Morcheba, the horrors he'd witnessed and helped inflict. He thought of his sons, his lady. But mostly he thought of the time he'd lost to war. The things he'd missed out on, fighting other men missing out on the same. Love. Family. And for what? Glory or greed? A soldier or a tool? A warrior or a weapon?

Too late to wonder now.

The Earthcrusher loomed out of the blinding smoke, its turrets whining, spitting a storm of iron-thrower shot. He could see two corvettes diving through the hail of fire, shredding and bursting aflame, colliding with the Earthcrusher's belly and glancing off its shoulder. A great scything chainblade arm tore another corvette from the skies, painting the clouds inferno-red. The *Lucky Fox* bore down, Isamu wrenching the wheel to avoid one lumbering swing of the goliath's arm, just as a corvette collided with the Earthcrusher's back.

The ship burst into flames, a blinding flash of blue-white, curling into sunburned orange and up into coal-black smoke. Isamu roared, the *Fox*'s engines screaming with him, the Earthcrusher's arm tearing the keel away in a shower of splinters just as the other arm came down atop the inflatable, cleaving it in two.

The war cry catching in his throat.

The sensation of flying, weightless.

A fireball above, bright as the sun.

Impact.

The explosion was deafening, deck shifting beneath Kin's feet as the Kitsune ironclad collided with the Earthcrusher's head. Vents exploded, sparks and flame, Guildsmen flung like toys to the floor. Rasping cries, tortured metal shrieks, hissing pipes, crackling flames.

"Damage report!" Rei bellowed from his pilot's harness. "Report, all stations!"

A brother limped to his console, every mechabacus chittering and clacking, the stuttering percussion of a hundred tiny drums. Kin looked about him, saw Kensai being helped to his feet by two Lotusmen, blood leaking from his skin's buckled collar.

One side of the Earthcrusher's head had caved in, the left viewport shattered, consoles toppled and spewing sparks. A ventilation duct had been torn from the wall, a bucktoothed grille hanging from broken screws. Kin grit his teeth against the pain of his wounded thigh, gathered himself for a spring.

"By the First Bloom!" Kensai swore. "Commander, what are you doing?"

"Forgiveness, Shateigashira, there were too many!"

"It was an ironclad, man! A hundred feet long! How did you miss it?"

"Due respect, Shateigashira, but I *did* hit it. Its momentum carried its—"

"Get out of that chair!"

Kin crawled closer to the ruptured vent, wreathed in smoke and steam as the Commander raised his voice in protest.

"Shateigashira—"

"Out!" Kensai bellowed, slapping aside the hands of his concerned lackeys. "The Earthcrusher is *my* creation! This plan of *my* design! No one will jeopardize it! Not you, not the Inquisition, not the First Bloom, no one!"

We'll see, bastard . . .

And with a gasp of pain, Kin rose to his feet and dove into the ruptured vent.

H is landing turned out to be a little softer than he'd expected. Bouncing down the greasy air vent, his cursing rose over the engines' roar. He fell near forty feet, head over heels, finally crashing to rest at the bottom of the duct. Even though he'd been stripped of his skin, the impact wasn't quite bone-jarring, but he still cracked his head on the metal, breath leaving his lungs with a sprayed curse. An agonized minute passed as he tried to inhale, finally realized the floor was groaning underneath him.

"Off," it pleaded. "Get off me."

Kin blinked, barely recognizing the voice without the suit-distortion.

"Shinji-san?"

"Kin-san? What the hells? Did you fall down the vent shaft?"

"Fall would imply . . . it was accidental . . ."

"I think you broke my godsdamned ribs . . ."

"I think I broke my godsdamned everything," Kin groaned.

Rolling off the other boy, Kin was astonished to see Shinji had removed his skin, the boy clad only in the skintight membrane every Guildsman wore beneath his outer shell. His skin was pale, hair cropped short, chin sharp and pointed.

"Why are you naked?"

"Look who's talking, skinny boy." Shinji was feeling at his rib cage, wincing. "Nice ankles."

"Shinji, what the hells are you doing in here?"

The boy shrugged. "Maseo managed to warn me as they grabbed him. I figured the vent system was a good place to hide, but my skin was too big to crawl around quietly. So I stripped. Kept my tool belt and mechabacus, but that's it." Shinji glanced overhead. "What the hells happened up there?"

"Kitsune suicide attack. Their fleet rammed the Earthcrusher."

Iron creaked, the vent echoing with the engines' guttural song. Kin felt the ground shift beneath them as the *DOOMDOOMDOOMDOOM* of the behemoth's tread began again.

"Not hard enough," Shinji said.

"Apparently not."

"So what the hells do we do now?"

"We can't proceed with the plan," Kin sighed. "They had me bugged. A transmitter in my mechabacus. They know we intended to overheat the Earthcrusher. They'd have removed the explosives from the coolant clusters by now."

Shinji scratched his head, looking a little rueful.

"And what about the heat diffuser arrays?"

Kin glanced at the boy. "You didn't mention any—"

"I confess, I was feeling a little guilty about it too. But I feel better now."

"Shinji, what the—"

"We didn't tell you about our redundancies," Shinji shrugged. "Bo didn't trust you enough. But we planted secondary charges. Not in the coolant cluster. In the heat diffusers. If Kensai only knows what *you* knew, the explosives might still be there."

"Surely they would have checked everywhere?"

"They're well hidden. Besides, the crew probably have bigger problems, what with Kitsune ironclads dropping from the sky. But even if the charges are still in place, we can't blow the cooling system. Earthcrusher is inside Yama walls. We'd level the entire city."

Kin nodded, wiping at his split brow. The pair sat in the dark, bleeding and bruised, listening to the behemoth's footsteps, the roar of its motors, the song of its gears.

Kin blinked in the dark, sudden light gleaming in his eyes. "Unless . . ."

"Unless what?"

"Our chance to take out the Tora army is gone," Kin said, a slow smile blooming at his lips. "But we can still stop Earthcrusher."

"How?"

"Drop those charges . . ." Kin winced, rolling to his hands and knees. ". . . into the transmission. Blow a drive rod, we'll be immobilized."

"The charges are *in* the cooling system, Kin. Right on the diffuser arrays. That place will be an inferno now."

"Let me worry about that. You just worry about keeping up."

Shinji sighed, pulled himself onto all fours with a wince.

"It was always going to be a risk, getting out of bed today."

And through the belly of the beast, they crawled.

44
INCENDIARY

The First Bloom's head hit the floor, severed arteries bathing her in blood, sizzling on the heat sinks rising from the Guild leader's back. Kaori slashed the cables linking the body to throne and ceiling, gave it a savage kick and sent it tumbling to the ground.

The other Kagé had rappelled from the chamber's roof, down behind an Inquisitor on the periphery, the four of them cutting him to pieces before he could cry out. The other Inquisitors made not a sound as they rushed across the vast, bloodstained space. Kaori leaped from atop the Throne of Machines, throwing her arms around Daichi's neck.

"Father . . ." she breathed.

"Daughter." Daichi wheezed. "What have you done?"

Kaori dragged her goggles from her eyes. "It's wonderful to see you too."

"You killed him . . ." Daichi looked around the room, at the murals of Lady Izanami etched on the walls. "All of this, just as they planned . . ."

A cry of pain rang out in the chamber, and Kaori saw Yuu go down in a spray of blood. Three Inquisitors were locked in combat with the Kagé, shifting from one spot to another amidst coiling trails of smoke. With a shout, she charged across the black stone, Daichi beside her, breath rattling in his chest. She saw Eiko get kicked so hard she cracked the wall behind her, bloody vomit spraying from her lips.

Kaori lunged, took the attacker's arm off at the elbow, the man turning, utterly soundless, bloodshot eyes aglow. One moment he stood at arm's length, the next he *shifted*, and before she could blink he was inside her guard, touching her solar plexus, smashing the wind from her body. Daichi landed a flying kick on the Inquisitor's chin, knocking his breather loose, his jaw snapped clean and hanging below his broken teeth like a door left ajar. The man stumbled to one knee, exhaled blue-black through bloody gums. Daichi brought a heel down on his head, a sickly crunch resounding in the chamber as the Inquisitor hit the floor.

Daichi coughed, deflected three punches from a second Inquisitor before the man's fist turned to smoke. Knuckles coalesced against Daichi's chest, knocking him back ten feet as if he'd been hit by a motor-rickshaw. Kaori was back on her feet, swinging her wakizashi, collecting four of the Inquisitor's outstretched fingers and then burying the blade in his ribs.

The Inquisitor rippled like a heat haze on a summer's day, her blade moving inside his chest as easily as it would a cloud of smoke. A strike to her throat, a headbutt to her cheek, white stars exploding in her eyes. She drew her sword back, struck blind, felt meat parting like water as a kick took her feet out from under her and she hit the floor, cracking her skull on the stone.

Blinking hard, she had the vague impression of flashing steel, Maro's voice fierce and hate-filled, a soft wet thud. Strong hands pulled her to her feet, and she pawed the blood from her eyes. Her cheek was broken, scarlet across her vision. Botan was dead, disemboweled with his own sword. Yuu lay motionless, neck twisted at a ghastly angle. Eiko knelt against the wall, clutching her belly and vomiting. Daichi was on all fours, coughing hard, chin smeared black.

Four of them, unarmed, did all this. And we had surprise. What would happen if . . .

Kaori heard the crisp sound of steel blades scraping together.

The iris portal into the room began to dilate.

Maro looked at the door, back at Kaori and Daichi, up at the silk rope still hanging from the lip of the dome above.

"Go," he said.

"Maro . . ."

His stare silenced her protest. The shadow of his brother lingering behind his gaze, calling for vengeance. Blood. Death.

"Go," he said.

And then he was running, katana drawn, a war cry on his lips as he charged the Inquisitors stepping through the doorway. No time to wonder, to feel, to think. Just motion. Just action. Thinking by doing. Kaori hauled Daichi up and put his black-slicked hands on the rope.

"Climb!"

Pulling Eiko to her feet, she manhandled the girl to the rope and screamed to get up, climb, go, just go. At the doorway, she saw Maro flying backward in a spray of blood as a smoking wheel kick nearly took his head off his shoulders. Kaori ripped her satchel off her back, reaching inside to arm her remaining explosives. With a shapeless cry she hurled them toward the Inquisitors, leaping up the rope as a blossom of seething fire unfurled at her back.

The blast wave smashed her against the wall and she almost slipped, palms torn as she hauled herself skyward. She could see Eiko climbing slowly, her father coughing and spitting black. Claxons screamed. Running footsteps. Roaring engines.

She felt tension on the rope below, looked down into a smoldering face; an Inquisitor climbing toward her like a twisted, smoking monkey. Drawing her wakizashi, she slashed the rope below her, and the man fell twenty feet, splashing onto the stone as a cloud of smoke, reforming and glaring up with empty, blood-shot eyes. She heard a distorted voice above, looking up with a sinking heart as

Lotusmen landed on the dome's lip. Silhouetted against the sky, peering down with glowing, bloody eyes, patient as spiders for her to crawl into their arms.

Daichi had stopped, spinning in place, Eiko beneath him. More Inquisitors gathered below. Kaori grit her teeth, knuckles white, staring down at her death.

"I am sorry, Daughter," Daichi coughed. "I did not want you here."

"You should have trusted me, Father. *Neither* of us had to be here."

"Not here, in this place," Daichi rasped. "In this life. I would not . . . have chosen this for you. I would have seen you happy . . . far away from all this."

She pictured the timers on the explosives in the chi reservoirs, ticking down. Second.

By second.

By second.

"Fear not, Father." A small smile. "Soon we'll both be far away."

F ucking hells . . ."
     Yukiko cursed as the Earthcrusher shook off the Kitsune suicide attacks, began lumbering toward Kitsune-jō again. Its hull was blackened and smoking, its head buckled, but still, it marched. Hana and Kaiah circled close by, along with the three remaining bucks from the Everstorm pack, Sukaa still among them. The black was dripping blood, green eyes alight with the thrill of the kill, glancing at Yukiko with something close to hunger.

"Izanagi's balls, what does it take to stop this thing?" Hana shouted.

Yukiko turned her mind from Torr's son, back to the problem at hand.

"There's nothing for it! I have to get inside! If I can see the pilot, I can kill him!"

YOU SAW WHAT HAPPENED TO MY BRETHREN.

"And how the hells do we get you inside it?" Hana's shout echoed Buruu's thoughts. "Those iron-throwers will shred us before we get close!"

. . . YUKIKO, BEHIND US.

She felt warning flicker across Sukaa's mind, Kaiah roaring and swooping about as shapes coalesced out of the pall of smoke and black snow. Four Guild ironclads, battle-scarred and limping. Hulls torn by grappling irons, inflatables scored by flame, boards washed with blood. But she could see them on the decks, demon helms painted bone-white.

The last remnant of the Kazumitsu Elite, chainswords drawn, screaming challenge as they saw her—slayer of Shōguns, ender of dynasties. And standing on the bow of the largest ship, face caked with ashes and spattered blood, he stood tall and fierce as tigers.

Hiro . . .

INDEED.

As Buruu wheeled about, her hand strayed to her belly, the lives swelling inside her. So tiny. So strong. Filling her with power enough to wake ancient dragons, to feel the minds of every soldier in this battle, to swim in the thoughts of every thunder tiger floating above the butchery. A part of her, every bit as much as the heart in her chest.

But part of him too?

She stared across smoke-stained skies, remembering how she'd felt the first time she'd seen him. Heart in her sandals. Those sea-green eyes, nothing like the color of the sea at all. Because the oceans were red as blood, just like the poisoned skies. And the Guild who'd ruined it all was the same Guild propping Hiro on his splintered throne, who armed the Tora soldiers committing butchery in the city below, who built that towering goliath just minutes away from turning the Kitsune palace to rubble.

They his masters, and he their slave.

But still . . .

WE MUST MAKE SURE THIS TIME.

Meaning what?

MEANING WE DO NOT SIMPLY TAKE HIS ARM.

Buruu growled low and long, eyes locked on the Tiger Daimyo.

WE TAKE HIS HEAD.

Thunder tigers roared, tearing across the skies toward the Guild ironclads. Shuriken fire glittered amongst falling snow, catching the lightning on their edges, turning all to broken, spinning glass. Hana and Kaiah peeled left, swooping under an ironclad's bow, Sukaa heading right with another Morcheban black. Yukiko and Buruu soared over the shuriken storm, accompanied by a swift Everstorm buck named Tuake, the pair splitting off in different directions, headed toward the *Honorable Death*'s inflatable. The topside 'throwers opened up, catching Tuake along one wing and sending him spiraling away, roaring in rage. Yukiko narrowed her eyes, one hand wrapped in Buruu's mane, the other pressed against her stomach, fingertips skirting the hand-flares stuffed into her obi.

They hit the inflatable, tearing through reinforced canvas, the air behind them filled with shrieking hydrogen, the *popopopopopop* of 'thrower fire, roars and Raijin Song. Yukiko drew out a flare, striking it against her breastplate. Flame bloomed in her hand, bright and hot. The warmth on her face made her shiver, sparks trailing through the falling black behind them.

Just a flick of her wrist.

Just to let go. Let it fall. Watch it burn.

Him burn.

Like this?

YUKIKO . . .

She wavered, staring into the light in her fist.

. . . He's their father, Buruu. The father of these babies inside me.

HE IS A DESTROYER. ALL THIS DEATH. THIS PAIN. FROM HIS HANDS.
I know.
YET YOU FORGIVE HIM? AISHA. DAICHI. AKIHITO. KASUMI. EVEN
YOUR OWN FATHER. ALL OF THEM DEAD BECAUSE OF THIS WAR. AND
HE LEADS THEIR HOST.
I never said I could forgive him.
YET YOU STAY YOUR HAND.
No, Buruu. Hiro still dies today.

Yukiko tossed the hand-flare away from the torn inflatable, the light spitting
and spinning down to the ruined earth below.

I just want to tell him why.

K in dropped down behind the cooling system and collapsed into a ball of
pain, clutching the hole in his thigh. He was sweat-soaked, the ambient
temperature almost enough to scald his bare flesh. But despite the heat, he felt
a terrible chill, greasy and nauseous, his hands shaking like autumn leaves. Hard
to breathe. Hard to think.

You're going into shock.

Shinji dropped down next to him with a soft grunt, arms wrapped around his
broken ribs, the clicking chatter of his mechabacus muted with the palm of one
hand.

You're going to die in here . . .

Kin hauled himself up on all fours, head down, dripping sweat, struggling to
breathe. Fingers curled into fists. Vomiting on an empty stomach.

"Are you all right?"

". . . Hai."

He could hear Guildsmen's boots, patrolling on overhead gantries and walkways. Kensai must have some inkling as to what he was thinking—there were
only a few reasons why he'd have fled into the vents. He had to get those explosives to the transmission. Quickly.

"Where are the charges?" he breathed.

"Up there." Shinji pointed. "Tight squeeze."

Risking a glance from his vantage point, Kin saw the explosives welded to the
diffuser array, twelve feet above the ground. The cooling system filled the entire
floor above the engine room; a twisted sprawl of pipes bubbling with coolant.
The air hung thick with steam, the roar of engines and thunder of the Earthcrusher's tread underscoring a sea of hissing iron.

Shinji leaned against an inflow pipe and stifled a yelp, his skin sizzling where
it touched the metal like cuttlefish on a skillet.

"How the hells did you get it up there?" Kin asked.

"We planted them before anyone fired the engines. We never expected to move them."

Kin heard approaching footsteps, rasping metallic voices. There was no time, not even a spare minute to look for an alternative. Every second brought the patrols closer, brought the Earthcrusher nearer to Kitsune-jō. Every moment wasted was a moment another arashitora or Kitsune soldier or, gods help him, even Yukiko herself, did something suicidal to stop its march.

This was why he left the Iishi, why he left *her* behind. This is why Daichi sacrificed himself. So Kin could be here, at this moment, the power to bring the Earthcrusher to its knees just a few feet away.

"Give me your membrane," he said to Shinji.

"What are—"

"Just give it to me."

Shinji complied, grasping the thin, gleaming fabric and ripping the arms off, the torso, the legs at the thighs. Kin could see the bayonet fixtures in Shinji's skin, the cables leading from the boy's mechabacus into his flesh. And wrapping the webbing around his hands, knees, feet, he crawled from behind the pipes. Down on his belly, thigh ablaze, hands shaking, beneath the potbellied bulk of the diffuser array and into the space between it and the wall.

The air rippling, too thick to breathe. The chill in his gut evaporating in the narrow, scorching space. Back pressed to the wall, wincing at the furnace heat, slithering up to his feet. And then, whispering a prayer to whoever was listening, he pressed his hands to the metal and began to climb.

The heat took a moment to penetrate Shinji's membrane, and he'd made it at least three feet off the ground before the fabric began melting. Pain arrived then, a rapid escalation from mild discomfort to searing agony, stink of burning meat in his nostrils, membrane blackening, smoke rising, every instinct screaming to let go, get away, fall. But he thrust his feet and knees and hands against the diffuser, back to the wall, pushing higher as the agony mounted. Blistering. Charring. Shaking away the encroaching numbness from the iron-thrower wound, the shock his body had tried to wrap him inside, dunking him headfirst into incendiary pain.

Smoke rising from his skin wherever it touched metal. Scream strangled behind his teeth. But he could see it through the haze, the cluster of explosives, just inches out of reach now, smoke in his eyes, tears spilling down his cheeks stretching toward it blistered fingers brushing the edge almost slipping gods it's too far it hurts IT HURTS.

And if you let go now it will have all been for nothing
every lie every death every second of your
life
leading here to this
moment this place pushing higher back scraping

skin staying behind reaching
out farther just a
little farther and he could smell himself
charring little
Kin
in the fire
gods
nothing left nothing
more don't you
dare
let go now DON'T
YOU
DARE
LET
GO.

He fell, skin tearing, face smashing on the diffuser, a layer of cheek left behind to sizzle. Collapsing on steel mesh, hissing as it burned his chest, rolling away from the bundle he'd dragged with him as he fell. A cluster of cylindrical shapes, a tiny radio receiver mounted atop handcrafted detonators, making soft crinkling noises as it slowly cooled.

A blistered gift.

A smoking promise.

An explosion unborn.

Kaori held her breath, waiting to die.

Rope twisting in her fingers, spinning slowly above the Chamber of Void. Any second now, the chi reservoirs would blow, ripping First House apart. An end to Guild power. An end to everything.

"Climb up slowly, citizens." The Lotusmen gathered about the chamber's lip peered down with burning eyes. "No sudden movements."

Eiko was holding her breath lest she sob, trembling grip setting the rope aquiver. Kaori looked up at the girl, pity in her heart. Barely seventeen. So much strength in youth. The wisdom to see and the courage to act. Still doomed to die in this pit with the rest of them.

"Courage, girl," Kaori said. "It will be over soon."

Tickticktick . . .

"I don't want it to be over . . ."

"Want seldom matters in life, child. We do what we must."

"What we must . . ." Daichi murmured.

Kaori looked at her father on the rope above, his eyes affixed on the First

Bloom's headless corpse. She saw a pale fear in them; a shadow of doubt never present before. And she realized it was not Eiko making the rope tremble.

It was him.

"Citizens!" The Lotusman raised the flat barrel of his shuriken-thrower. "If you are not climbing within five seconds, you will be falling."

Weapon aimed at Daichi's chest.

Finger tightening on the trigger.

Tickticktick . . .

She didn't want him to die like this. Afraid. Alone. Not after everything he'd been through. And if these moments were to be their last, she knew they shouldn't be stained by past mistakes or words unsaid. The anger inside her, burning so brightly after he'd left her alone—it wasn't enough to consume the bond between them. Ties deeper than blood. Here and now and always.

Tickticktick . . .

"Father."

Daichi's eyes were still locked on the First Bloom's body.

"Father, look at me."

His gaze drifted up to meet hers.

Tickticktick . . .

"Father, everything is going to be all right. I promise."

"Kaori . . ." A shuddering cough stole the words from his mouth.

"I know, Father," she smiled. "I love you too."

"You were warned," rasped the Lotusman.

The hollow *popopopopopopopopop* of shuriken-thrower fire, razored steel glittering in the air. Forcing herself to watch, not to flinch, not to turn away. Droplets of blood, perfect globes, falling like rain. Lotusmen corpses tumbling after them, brass skins torn wide and ragged, bodies tumbling end over end as the *Truth Seeker* roared overhead, propellers chopping snow-laden air, the engines' thunder lost amidst her own heartbeat. Misaki was leaning over the railing, tossing a rope ladder and screaming words too distant to hear, deck-mounted shuriken-throwers spitting death at the remaining Lotusmen, down to the Inquisitors turning to smoke amidst the hail of sparks and steel.

Misaki screaming again. Pointing.

What is she saying?

"Go!" Eiko screamed. "Gods above, jump!"

The girl leaped from the rope, snatched at the ladder, feet flailing for purchase. Shuriken fire shredded the *Seeker*'s hull, the roar of more sky-ships rising over the pulse throbbing in her temples. Eiko was screaming, holding out her hand as the *Seeker* began to rise. Daichi hurled himself at the ladder, wrapping one fist on the bottom rung. Kaori at last woke from the dream, leaping into the void, hand outstretched, catching his, rough as stone. The *Seeker* rose up into the light. Sirens wailing, the roar of ironclads, the percussion of 'thrower fire, metallic shouts. Engines pushed to full burn, sweeping away from the First House complex, wind tearing at Kaori's face, her skin, the ladder swaying in its grip.

She looked down at the monastery, the ruined valley, the rusted pipeline snaking up the mountainside. Rising higher, sweat greasing her palm and her father's. Hard to breathe, hard to think, impossible to climb, looking up to the Kitsune cloudwalkers and Guildsmen as they began hauling the ladder up, foot by agonizing foot. Knuckles white. Fingers numb. Slipping.

"Hold on to me!" Daichi roared.

"I can't!"

"Don't let me go!"

Shuriken fire filling the air, another burst from the pursuing ironclads. She felt a projectile whistle past her cheek, the ladder bucking as another struck it, dropping them a jarring foot and leaving them dangling by a single fraying cord. Eiko screaming. Freezing wind bringing tears to her eyes, crystallizing in her lashes.

Fingers entwined in his.

"Father!"

Slipping.

"Kaori! Hold on to me!"

Slipping.

"Hold on!"

Squeeze.

S udden chaos. Panicked voices echoing in the Earthcrusher ducts, empty murmurings of the Shatei standing stupefied and staring at nothing at all. Whispers coalescing into a fact almost too impossible to comprehend.

Shinji grasped Kin's arm, eliciting a hiss of pain as his fingertips touched cauterized flesh. But the boy's eyes were saucer-wide, hand pressed to the skitter-chatter of his mechabacus. And when he spoke, his voice was breathless, as if he'd been slugged in the gut.

"First Bloom is dead . . ."

An echo beneath the duct they hid inside, listless steps dragging across steel mesh. "First Bloom is dead . . ."

Kin stared at Shinji, incredulous. "Gods above . . ."

"Two hundred years . . ." Shinji breathed. "Two centuries he's sat inside First House. Who the hells could possibly take his place? They're *done*, Kin!"

Kin said nothing, rolling onto his back, almost weeping in pain. Hands, forearms, shins and feet—all blistering, layers of skin left behind like snake scale. Sweat burned in the wounds, tremors shaking him head to toe. The agony was enough to dislocate consciousness from flesh, shock flooding every receptor. But he couldn't stop here. Not this close to the end.

The Earthcrusher came to another halt, its deafening footsteps silenced as word of Tojo's demise spread across the frequencies. The body fell still without its head, anguish echoing through its gut. But Kin hurt so badly he could barely move.

"Do you have any opiates?" he hissed. "An aidkit?"

"No," Shinji said. "I'm sorry."

"Gods, it's killing me . . ." Eyes squeezed shut. Teeth clenched.

Just breathe . . .

"A little farther. We're almost above the engines. I'll plant the charges. But we have to hurry while everyone is still reeling from Tojo's death."

"Just leave me here."

"I can't do this alone, Kin. You have to move."

Kin tried to roll onto his belly, face contorted, teeth gleaming white against broiled flesh.

"I can't . . ."

Shinji stared, lips pursed, drumming his fingers on the vent's innards.

"Why are you here, Kin-san?"

"In this vent?"

"I mean, why did you rebel against the Guild?"

Kin closed his eyes. Took a deep, calming breath that shivered all the way into his lungs. "Because what they do is wrong. Killing the land, choking the sky—"

"No." Shinji shook his head. "People don't just wake up one day and throw away everything they've been raised to believe. Why are you *really* here?"

Kin opened his eyes. Licked at cracking lips.

"A girl . . ."

"Ah."

"Yukiko."

"The Stormdancer?"

He shook his head. ". . . She's just Yukiko to me."

"Then picture her at the end of this duct, Kin-san. Waiting for you. All you need to do is crawl to her."

"But she's *not* there . . ."

"Kin." Shinji's voice was like iron. "Crawl."

And so he did. Rolling onto his belly and dragging himself as best he could. The texture of the metal like sandpaper on his flesh, soldered joins like hooks in his skin. Sweat burning his eyes, blisters popping, drool slicking his chin, head down, papercut eyes, crawling just one more foot. One more inch. Just to the next solder line. The next corner. The next level.

Eyes closed now, every movement that of a machine. One that didn't feel pain. Skin sloughing away. Raw meat rasping on greasy iron. Feeling nothing.

Nothing at all.

Her picture in his mind, faded and curled at the edges like an old lithograph—an image burned into his thoughts a lifetime ago. Standing in the rain by her father's grave, eyelids fluttering shut as she leaned in close. Lips like bruised roses brushing his own, feather-light. A curtain of night falling in sweet waves about her shoulders. All for her. All of it.

Crawl, godsdamn you.

Light on his skin. Engines increasing in volume. He opened his eyes, saw a ventilation grille to his right, staring down through the slats to the engine room floor. The growling pistons, the transmission churning like an open mouth full of clockwork teeth. Artificers standing in one corner, heads bowed. Uncertain voices barely audible above the engine's din.

Kin rolled away from the vent, let Shinji get to work, unbolting the grille from the inside. A crackling announcement spilled over the intercom.

"*Brothers.*" Kensai's voice—sorrow underscored with something else. Energy? Elation? "*Grievous news has reached us that Tojo, resplendent First Bloom of the Lotus Guild, is dead at the hands of Kagé assassins. Though it wounds the very soul, do not lose yourselves in sorrow. Turn your pain to rage, and light a fire in your hearts. A fire to guide us through this darkness, and incinerate any who defy our will.*"

Shinji pulled the grille aside with a faint metallic squeal.

"*There can be no Lotus Guild without a leader.*" Kin could hear the thrill in Kensai's voice plainly now—words the old man had waited a lifetime to utter. "*And thus, I claim the title of First Bloom until Tojo's successor can be named.*"

Shinji stowed the grille to one side, nodded to Kin.

"All right. I'll crawl down, plant the charges in the transmission. Hopefully, the explosion will pop a bearing housing. Maybe even a drive rod."

"And what do I do?" Kin whispered.

With a grin, Shinji reached into his belt and pulled out an iron-thrower. "You cover me."

"Where the hells did you get that?"

"Munitions locker. Broke it open after I cut drive control. Seemed like a good idea at the time."

"Fine thinking." Kin held up his blistered hands. "But I can't shoot it, Shinji."

"You have a good vantage point from up here. It'll be like shooting koi in a cup."

Kin grit his teeth and grasped the weapon as best he could, wincing as the grip scraped his blistered palms. Shinji produced a flat block of burnished iron, studded with a tiny aerial, a switch of gleaming chrome. The boy pressed a flat button, a red diode lighting up on the explosives, another atop the block in his hand.

Detonator.

"Wish me luck."

"Good luck, Shinji-san."

"What, is that it?" Shinji blinked. "No kiss?"

With a grin, the boy slipped out of the ventilation shaft, explosives clutched tight. He dropped down to the floor with his armful, stealing through the steam and shadows toward the transmission. Kin set sights on four Shatei gathered around the PA speaker, took trembling aim.

"*I will rule this Guild as Tojo has done.*" Kensai was building to his finale. "*To see his death avenged, and all who incite insurrection purified with flame. The lotus must bloom!*"

Shinji was at the transmission, climbing the outer housing with his arms full of explosives. He slipped, seized the rungs, almost dropping the bundle.

"The lotus must bloom!" The cry echoed in the Earthcrusher's innards.

Gods, they're all so used to following.

Kin shook his head.

None of them stop to think where following might lead . . .

"Battle stations!" Kensai cried.

The vent seethed under Kin's belly, and the engines roared as the Earthcrusher began marching again, the thunderous cadence of its tread bouncing around the inside of his skull, vibrations threatening to dislodge Shinji from his perch.

DOOMDOOMDOOMDOOM.

DOOMDOOMDOOMDOOM.

The Shatei hurried back to their posts, mechabacii chattering, blood-red eyes gleaming in the gloom. The stink of burning chi was almost overpowering—that chemical, grease-fire stench of oil and burning flowers. Kin squinted through the haze, saw Shinji crest the transmission housing, staring down into the exposed, churning mess of cogs and iron teeth.

The boy couldn't simply drop the bomb into the transmission—the gears would crush it to powder without setting off the charge. Shinji leaned into the gap, legs hooked in the ladder's rungs as he searched for the place it could do the most damage.

Kin cursed beneath his breath as he saw an Artificer clomping around the transmission housing. If the Artificer glanced up, he'd see Shinji's legs hooked in the ladder rungs, pale as some Kitsune maiden's nethers.

Hurry up, godsdammit . . .

Sweat in Kin's eyes, the reverberation of the Earthcrusher's steps bringing new pain. He aimed at the back of the Artificer's head, the iron-thrower trembling in wounded hands.

No way to signal Shinji without drawing attention to himself.

No way to warn the boy about the Guildsman drawing closer every step.

Shinji propped the explosives between the spacer plate and gasket of the lowest gear setting and pulled himself back up. Wiping sweat from his brow, he saw the Artificer passing below, freezing as still as a statue in the Shōgun's gardens. If he made no sound, if he didn't move, perhaps the Artificer wouldn't notice . . .

"First Bloom's name!"

The cry came from the gantry above Shinji's head. Another Artificer stood there, bloody eye aglow, locked on the near-naked boy. The first Artificer looked up, caught sight of Shinji.

"Saboteurs!" it cried. "They're here! Sound the alarm!"

Kin caught his breath, finger on the trigger.

Squeeze.

S tanding in the fire, one foot in both worlds, eyes open wide.

Yukiko could see them—every one. She could feel them, their rage and their hate, clad in snow white, ashes on their faces. Servants of the great Yoritomo-no-miya. The last of his Elite. Killers, every one, and her death, their life's only purpose.

She and Buruu landed on the pilot's deck of the *Honorable Death*, splinters and cracking boards, sundered rope and rigging. Hiro stood before them, one arm of cold iron, the other hanging bloodied by his side. The Elite heard them land, turned to face them. Shouts of alarm. Swords drawn. Charging. All the world moving in slow motion.

The *Honorable Death* was losing altitude, hemorrhaging hydrogen from her inflatable. Yukiko surveyed the decks, boards awash with blood and bodies. Kitsune samurai and cloudwalkers and Elite. All of them brave in their own way. Each fighting for a belief, a truth, a reason. And some part of her wanted to respect that. To understand none of them were so different. That Daichi had once been like these men, and they too might only be a step away from seeing the world the way he did.

And then her eyes fell on the girl. Crumpled in a puddle against the railing. Dark hair hacked short, pale skin bled paler still, bee-stung lips parted as if to breathe. Except she wasn't breathing. Or moving. She wasn't anything at all.

"Michi . . ."

Too much.

Too much loss. Too much death. Too much taken from her. And if this were one of the grand old stories, and she the great hero in it, a noble stormdancer like Kitsune no Akira or Tora Takehiko, she might have found something inside to cling to. This would be the chapter where she'd find it in herself to show mercy, to cling to Bushido or honor or the knowledge that none of them were so different. None of them were truly "wrong."

But this was not one of the grand old stories. And if she were a hero, Michi

wouldn't be dead. Akihito wouldn't be dead. Or Aisha and Kasumi and her father. She would've saved them all. She *could* have saved them all. If she were a
hero. But only if.

"*No*," she breathed.

She reached into the Kenning, into the flames where the dragons writhed,
tsunami and fire and flood. And she touched the minds of each man charging
her down, their ashen faces twisted in hatred. Reaching out and wrapping them
up in herself. Hands outstretched, fingers beckoning. On they came. Swords raised.
Spitting curses. Murder uncoiling.

She closed her eyes.

She closed her fists.

And every one of them clutched his temples.

Bled from his eyes.

Collapsed upon the deck.

Every.

One.

Samurai and marines and cloudwalkers. Young and old. Living and breathing and thinking no more. Emptying the deck of every man who'd see her slain.
Now slain in turn.

All save one.

Those eyes that had once held her spellbound, gleaming now like flat, polished glass. Face caked white, daubed the color of death; the same color they'd
wrapped her father inside before they lit his funeral pyre. The same color they'd
wrap Akihito and Michi in, presuming any of them survived this day.

DOOMDOOMDOOMDOOM.

"You killed her," she said.

"Not I." Hiro blanched at the ruins she'd made of his Elite. "My men."

She could see Michi's death in his mind, etched in something that tasted like
regret. And as she stepped toward him, she saw Hiro's eyes drift to her belly, the soft
curve swelling under banded iron. Buruu's growl shook the deck beneath them.

HE KNOWS.

"Michi told you. About them."

"Hai."

"So now you know."

"Now I know."

She reached across the space between them with her thoughts, slipping into
his synapses, just a tweak to let him know she was there. He stifled a gasp, eyes
widening as she pinched.

But not yet.

Buruu growled, low, tectonic, a wall of fire at her back.

FINISH HIM.

Soon.

WHILE YOU SAVOR THIS MOMENT, THE EARTHCRUSHER MARCHES.

We can't stop the Earthcrusher, Buruu. We'd need a miracle.

KITSUNE LOOKS AFTER HIS OWN.

Akihito is dead. Michi is dead. Aisha, Daichi, Kasumi, my father. If this is Kitsune looking after me, I think I'd prefer if he left me the hells alone.

"Are you happy, Hiro?" She gestured at the battle raging across Yama. "It's all for you. Every drop. Does it make you proud?"

"Proud?" Hiro laughed, short and bitter. "Gods, you never understood me, did you?"

"No. But I was just a girl. A girl who thought she was in love."

"No more than I."

"You betrayed me, Hiro."

"And you betrayed me. When you betrayed my Lord Yoritomo."

"Yoritomo was a pig," she spat. "A rapist. A baby-killing bastard."

"You knew what my oath meant to me." Hiro shook his head. "I told you I was samurai before all else. I never pretended to be anything different."

"You pretended to be a good man. An honorable man."

"I *am* an honorable man!" A bellow, face twisted into a snarl. "Do you know what I've sacrificed for honor's sake? Do you think those men you just murdered would—"

"Don't you *dare* preach to me about murder—"

"I am sworn to the Kazumitsu Dynasty! To defend my clan! My lord! Without those oaths I am nothing! I told you that from the very beginning!"

"This isn't about clans or oaths. This is about *you and me!*"

"Gods, how you flatter yourself . . ."

"You should be *dead*, Hiro! You failed Yoritomo, and you should have *killed yourself* to restore your honor. But when the Guild offered you a chance to come after me, you grabbed it by the throat and held on for dear life!"

Yukiko stepped forward, Hiro stepped back, muscles ridged, blood trickling from his nose. The *Honorable Death* shuddered as her belly clipped Yama's outer walls, the sky-ship sinking lower as her sundered inflatable continued to collapse.

"You never wanted to rule an empire. You didn't want the Tiger throne or to reforge a dynasty or to marry Aisha. You wanted revenge. To hurt me the way I hurt you. You call yourself honorable, but underneath your codes and oaths, you're just a spoiled little boy. Stamping his feet and dragging the nation to ruin because he didn't get his way."

She waved her hand at the destruction going on all around them.

"You know what the Guild are. You know what will become of this land if they remain. But you didn't give one solitary speck of *shit* for your family or your clan or your country when they offered you your noose. You didn't sacrifice a gods-damned thing *except* your honor when you got into bed with those bastards."

"And you?" Hiro spat. "What have you sacrifi—"

His question was snapped in half by a hoarse cry of pain. He sank to his knees, iron fist at his temple, thick, salty floods spilling from his nose.

"My father isn't enough for you? My friends?"

"You . . . you did not give . . . them. They were . . . taken."

"They were taken," Yukiko leaned in close, teeth bared. "By people like you. But not anymore. You won't ruin this place, or our children. You won't do to them what you did to me. I want you to know that as you die. Everything you've done has all been for nothing. It's all going to burn. And I'm the fire you helped create."

"And years from now . . . when you speak to those children . . . will you tell them you killed their own father?"

Her smile was the color of murder.

"Who says I'm ever going to speak to them about you, Hiro?"

She tightened her grip on his mind, hand clenching to fist.

"They'll never even know your name . . ."

Squeeze.

45
ALL THAT WOULD HAVE BEEN

"Father!"

"Kaori!"

The *Truth Seeker's* engines drowned their shouts, hissing trails of shuriken fire filling the space between each breath. Their ladder unraveled thread by thread. They swayed in the grip of the wind, momentum, gravity, skies filled with pursuing Guild vessels, spitting death. Daichi's muscles were tearing as he clung to the ladder with his right arm, his daughter's hand with his left. Black on his lips. Bubbling from his lungs.

Gods, not now, please . . .

Kaori's scream. Paper-thin across a bleeding sky.

"Let me go!"

"N-no!"

"If you don't we'll both die!"

Fingers numb. Grip melting.

"I will not let you go!"

Guild corvettes swarmed about them, the *Seeker's* 'throwers riddling the closest with spinning steel, the craft splitting open and dying on the deadlands below. But three more skipped and spun through the glimmering hail, blood-red eyes staring down iron sights at the pair who'd slain their father. Their foremost. Their First Bloom.

Popopopopopopopopop.

Shuriken fire tore his shoulder, his stomach, deep into his chest; bursts of bright pain. Kaori screamed as he lost his grip, fading beneath the rushing wind as they fell. And still he held her hand, pulling her close as they tumbled earthward, the space between them wet with blood, the pain nothing at all. End over end as he held her tight, just as he'd done when she was a girl. She wrapped her arms around him and closed her eyes, tumbling, spinning, over and over. Nothing mattering save they were together, here, at the last.

"I love you, Daughter."

The wind snatched the words like a thief. Carried them away with sticky fingers. But she squeezed him tighter. She knew.

Its roar filled him now, muting all else. Nothing but wind. Sight fading as the blood fled, painting her face and the black snowflakes behind. The roar filled his ears, swelling until it engulfed him, the color of new snow on Iishi peaks. Glittering with metallic opalescence, cut through with swathes of deepest black.

Amber eyes.

Iron-gray claws.

Snatching them from the air, gentle as mountain streams, strong as the stone beneath, swooping low and slowly up, past the ruined corvettes, falling from the skies like rain. The air filled with beautiful, savage cries, Daichi's fading eyes filling with tears of wonder, a half-dozen arashitora cutting through the air and the Guild ships like katana. Sleek and sharp, smaller than Buruu, somehow more graceful, a peerless verse penned by the Thunder God's hands.

Females . . .

No strength to lift his head, warmth fleeing his body. Kaori was screaming to hold on, don't let go, Father, please. But hadn't they fallen already? Were they falling still?

He wanted to sleep. Close his eyes and rest. So tired. Years of war, of blazing lotus fields, of striving with every breath to make this a world in which she might bloom rather than rot. And all for nothing. All had come to pass, exactly as Tojo promised.

So tired.

Wood beneath him, the smell of exhaust smoke and rumble of engines. A woman with silver razors at her back, pressing the wounds in his chest and belly. Coughing black, distant pain, hands and feet already numb.

"Father."

Kaori's plea, desperate and tear-stained.

"Father, hold on."

"Tojo's ending . . . was just as he said." He looked down at her hand, wrapping his like a bloody bow. "Everything we did . . . brought all this to pass. We *helped* them . . ."

"Father, don't talk. Hush now . . ."

"No, you must listen."

"Please—"

"No!" Fear bubbled on his lips. Despair. Weightlessness. "There is no escaping fate. No defeating an enemy . . . who knows the shape of things to come. Shima will die . . . The Endsinger comes. What will be, will be . . ."

"The Endsinger?"

"I am sorry, Daughter. I sought—" A cough, tearing his chest; bloodied, broken glass. "I sought to give you . . . a future. But I . . . I only ensured *their* future came to pass . . ."

Kaori turned to the others, tears in her eyes. "Help me with him. Get him up."

The woman with the silver arms spoke. "We should not—"

"Get him up!"

"All for nothing . . ." he breathed.

He felt hands on the edge of his numbness, pulling him to his feet. He had no strength to stand, but they held him, Kaori by his side, keeping the cold at bay. Blood on his tongue amidst ashen paste, staring over the railing at First House; a yellow stain amidst a deadlands sea.

"You *have* given us a future, Father. The Guild can't see all things. This I promise you."

Her face was wet with tears. But in her voice, he heard a fire to match the one he'd lost.

"If they could foresee all, they'd have foreseen this . . ."

She pointed to First House, the sky between filled with Guild ships and shrieking thunder tigers. The edges of his vision darkening, closing like slow curtains; the onset of night after a long, cold day. But as he watched, a tiny spark bloomed—just a match-flare at first, burning in his growing gloom. The spark became a blossom, a sun-harsh flare, lighting the sky like summer days, a series of concussive blasts arriving seconds behind. The bricks, mortar, glass and stone of First House disintegrated in the light, blown away like dust in a winter wind. A blast of heat hit his face, banishing the awful chill, melting the fear. The certainty. The seed of fatalism threatening to steal all he was, here at the last.

"Do you see, Father?" she cried over the growing thunder.

". . . I see . . ."

"*We* decide! Not gods! Not fate! *We* choose!"

The explosion was impossible, splitting the Tōnan mountains asunder, the clouds now made of boulders and dust. Their ship shuddered through a trembling sky, cries of alarm spilling across the deck. He sank to his knees, daughter holding him tight. Concussion after concussion, mushroom-shaped, the pair lost in all but each other's arms as the *Seeker* was tossed like a paper kite in a burning wind.

Years passed? Moments? He couldn't tell which. Only that there was no pain now. Kaori laid him down on the deck as the air finally fell still, skies bruised with dirt, debris like rain.

"We choose . . ." he rasped.

Kaori looked down on him, face streaked with blood, tears, steel-gray eyes shining bright in a mask of ash and grit. So like her mother. A smile that stole his breath, if only she allowed it to bloom. With all the strength he had left, he reached up, cupped her cheek, running his thumb down the scar on her face. The wound on her soul never fully healed.

"Choose, then," he breathed. "To be free . . . of him."

"Father . . ."

"Choose . . . to be happy."

She closed her eyes, weeping, her whole body wracked with the sobs.

"Promise me, Kaori."

Her arms around his neck, cheek pressed against his, his daughter in his arms.

"Promise me."

"I do."

A gentle sigh.

A smile on his lips.

The skies about him raining the ruins of all that would have been.

"I promise."

The Artificer screamed as the iron-thrower shot punched through his shoulder, dropping him to his knees. Kin gasped, blistered palms tearing wide. Cries of alarm spread through the Earthcrusher's belly as Shinji dropped from the transmission housing to the deck, the floor beneath him seething as the Earthcrusher continued its march.

DOOMDOOMDOOMDOOM.

DOOMDOOMDOOMDOOM.

The wounded Artificer seized the boy's ankle. Kin fired again, the shot going wide, sparking bright on greasy metal. More shouting, brass shapes rushing through steam and smoke. Shinji dragged the detonator from his belt, but a savage kick sent the device spinning off into the darkness. Kin fired again, the shot ricocheting off the Artificer's helm, sending him reeling into cover. Rocket packs flared, Guildsmen closing in on Kin's vent. He fired off a handful of shots, hoping they'd just keep their heads down. Shinji cried out as the wounded Artificer wrapped him in a headlock, the boy's strength no match for a fully-suited Guildsman.

Another shot. Another. Sweat in Kin's eyes. Chi on his tongue. Shaking so badly he could barely breathe. An Artificer landed on a gantry just across from his vent and Kin fired, hitting the Guildsman's thigh and dropping him like a stone.

"Kin!" cried Shinji. "The detonator!"

Another shot, cracked off at a brass shape ducking behind the drive train. The iron-thrower clicked empty. With a ragged gasp of pain, he pulled himself from the vent, crashed onto the mesh below, crying out. Flares of blue-white flame. Boots pounding metal grilles.

DOOMDOOMDOOMDOOM.

"Check the transmission!" A rasping metallic cry.

"They planted something!"

DOOMDOOMDOOMDOOM.

Kin caught a glint of metal beneath a knot of cooling pipes, the scarlet globe atop the detonator winking at him. He pulled himself to his knees, burned skin tearing wide, lunging across the floor just as two Artificers rounded the corner, a third landing in a halo of blue-white on the gantry above. Dragging himself under the narrow space between pipes and floor, hand outstretched, fingertips brushing the burnished metal case and failing to find purchase.

"There are explosives in the transmission!"

DOOMDOOMDOOMDOOM.

"Get them out!"

DOOMDOOMDOOMDOOM.

The shuddering jolt of impact, great scythe-arms smashing ancient walls to splinters, the bastion of Kitsune-jō within striking range at last. Kin felt a vise grip seize his ankle, dragging him back as he roared in pain. He lunged at the detonator once more, just touching the edge.

Stretching.

DOOMDOOMDOOMDOOM.

Gasping as the Guildsman dragged him back.

DOOMDOOMDOOMDOOM.

Too far.

The pain too much.

Her lips were soft, a feather-light brush against his own, gentle as falling petals.

DOOMDOOMDOOMDOOM.

"Yukiko . . ."

DOOMDOOMDOOMDOOM.

He lunged, ligaments tearing, seizing the detonator as the Artificer tore him out from under the pipe. An explosion filled the engine bay, deafening in the confined space, Kin crying out as the air caught fire. The concussion knocked everyone to the floor, pieces of atmos-suit and bloody meat falling like red snow over the din of buckling, tortured metal. A ragged, ear-splitting shriek, the broken-tooth growl of snapping drive rods and popping rivets.

The floor swayed, like the deck of the *Thunder Child* on the night he and Yukiko stood together in the clean rain. It dropped away on one side, the behemoth listing, Kin tumbling away and coming to rest against the cooling pipes, chest heaving, squinting through the choking fumes at the transmission housing, the black smoke spilling from its innards.

The great engines trembled, stalled, and went silent. Metal shuddered and breathed one final sigh. And at last, the Earthcrusher fell still.

But only for a moment.

Yukiko was closing a final grip around Hiro's mind when the flare scorched the southern horizon. She turned to stare, watching the sky brighten, almost as if a second sun were cresting the island's lip. The deck shook beneath them, the wounded hulk of the *Honorable Death* smashing houses away with her belly as she slowly fell. Smoke drifted across the deck as aftershocks from the Tōnan explosion finally reached them, the very air shuddering.

Hana and Kaiah swooped in from the west, a flaming ironclad tumbling from the skies behind them, the girl's voice burning bright in the Kenning.

The rebels did it! First House is gone!

The groan of tortured metal caught her ears next, Yukiko looking up to see the Earthcrusher toppling to its knees, great clouds of smoke spilling from its belly. The scythe-arms still twitched amidst the splintered walls of Kitsune-jō, but the behemoth seemed incapable of walking any farther. Elation filled her heart, the sky about her now ablur with the bloodied remnants of the Everstorm pack, calling to each other across the smoke and ash. Blood-smeared. Amber and green eyes alight with victory. Even Sukaa seemed aglow with it.

"Do you see, Hiro?" She smiled down at the Daimyo, on his knees, face painted in blood. "First House is gone. Earthcrusher paralyzed. Yama still stands. Everything. All you've done. All for nothing."

The *Honorable Death* hit the ground, gouging a furrow through the Market Square. The ship trembled, crashing nose-first into a temple to Amaterasu. Yukiko clutched the railings as the skip came to a shuddering stop. Clouds of dust, the sound of distant fighting, crackling flames.

She lifted her hand, brow creased in concentration as the Daimyo of the Tora zaibatsu clutched his temples and curled up in a ball on the deck.

"Good-bye, Hiro . . ."

A tremor.

Just a whisper at first, the faded echo of a quake long past. The ground aflutter beneath them, small stones dancing on broken cobbles, roof tiles falling to their end. But growing louder now, stronger, the earth shaking, bucking, a rumbling, crumbling groan seeping up from underground. Sukaa's voice rang in her mind.

~ BEWARE. ~

Buruu roared, eyes flashing.

YUKIKO, GET ON MY BACK!

Yukiko leapt onto his shoulders, the mighty thunder tiger taking flight as the ground roared, like a spoiled child in a tantrum, flat on its back and screaming its displeasure.

Yama's walls split and crumbled, the entire city shaking, houses collapsing, dust pall rising, flagstones splitting wide and tumbling down into new fissures, grinning like toothless smiles. Terror spilling across the city, taller buildings now crumbling to ruin, the five-sided tower of Chapterhouse Yama listing, sky-spires toppling into twisted wreckage, the ruins of the Amatsu bridge dropping away into black, shivering water.

What in the name of the gods . . .

EARTHQUAKE.

Like none I've ever seen . . .

They flew above the city, looking south toward the Kitsune deadlands, the great swathes of choking, ashen earth. Yukiko felt dread in her chest, cool and sickening, watching the pall of ash-gray fumes roiling as the cracks in the tortured earth split wider and wider, crumbling into a darkness her eyes wanted to slip away from, faint screaming in the back of her mind.

. . . WHAT IS THAT?

You hear it too?

THROUGH YOU. WHAT IS IT?

Gods . . .

She remembered the Everstorm, the darkness she'd glimpsed as she looked toward Shima through the Lifesong. She reached into the Kenning, into the fire of every living thing around her, the storm of self and spirit and breath, feeling the pulse of the world.

The screaming grew louder in her ears, Buruu roaring in fear, the other arashi-tora echoing his unease. Distress in her womb, her hand pressed against the swell of warmth and life growing there. She focused on the sound—that horrid, glistening wail, like bloody nails drawn shrieking down the chalkboard of her skull—and amidst the terror, the primal, paralyzing fear of it all, she heard an inverted rhythm, drummed onto the skin of madness by the claws of stillborn children. And she realized it wasn't the sound of screaming at all. Not a wail or a howl or a cry. It was . . .

IT IS A SONG.

A mother's voice, black with hate and longing, drifting from the edges of time. The blind Inquisitor's words echoing now in her head, his grin that of a corpse-mask.

"The little ones are already here, after all . . ."

And looking into the deadlands fissures, guts clawing the insides of her throat in their bid to escape, she saw them. Silhouettes against a deeper darkness, crawling up from the cracks, coated in ashes, eyes glowing bloody red. Humanoids with midnight blue skin, long, sinuous arms, underbites overfull with grinning teeth. But beyond them, dragging themselves up out of the widening pits leading down to gods knew where

i

know

where

came shapes carved of nightmares, all mouths and eyes and skinless meat, things of wings and fangs and ash-smeared flesh, backward fingers and razor smiles and names all children know in the deep black of night and grow in the light and choose to forget.

Oni . . .

They rose in a swarm, only a handful, but still, but *still* . . . Voices raised with Hers, with *Hers*, and looking to the south, to the Stain, to the heart of the corruption humanity had planted in its own skin, Yukiko knew the true shape of fear.

She knew at last where all this had been leading.

What was coming.

Who was coming.

She *knew*.

"Lady Izanami," she breathed. "Great Maker, save us . . ."

The sky about them was ash-choked, seething, the remnants of the Tōnan mountains and First House falling among the black snow. A wave of fumes rose from the Stain below, fissures crumbling, the deadlands dropping down into bottomless black—just a great, seething hole where the entire plain once lay. Kaori looked down into that darkness, felt it looking back; a black too vast and bottomless to comprehend. A bone-snapping wind rose from the fissure, the stench of funeral pyres and burning hair, her mind alight with a tuneless, screaming hymn, a roar of pure psychic terror, and she clawed her ears bloody in her attempts to block it out.

"Fly!" she screamed to the comatose helmsman. "Godsdamn you, get us out of here!"

The female thunder tigers roared in terror, tearing away north as *things* rose up from the darkness, seething at its edges, shapeless winged nightmares, slithering, skinless horrors, fingers with too many joints, faces with too many mouths, heads with no faces at all. And beyond it, swelling pregnant in the gloom, Kaori could feel it, feel *Her*, a fear and hatred so perfect she could sense her sanity splitting, clawing its own eyelids as it screamed.

Her father's body lay on the deck in front of her. Eyes closed. At peace. How easy would it be to lie down beside him? To sink into the arms of the things rising from the maw beneath them, to welcome them home, to smile and hum along with the song that would slay the world?

You promised.

The thought dragged her in from the dark. Dug fingers into her skin.

You promised him.

She crawled across the deck, grabbed the helm and dragged herself to her feet. Misaki lay on the boards beside her, gleaming spider arms dancing a twitching, terrified jig, her head beating against the deck with a stuttering, off-beat time. Eiko was curled up in a corner, screaming, just *screaming*, knees against her chest as she rocked back and forth. And Kaori spun the wheel hard north, pushing on the throttle as if by will alone she could make them fly faster.

A chill wind rose at her back, frozen fingers entwined with her hair, a whisper in her ear, old as creation itself.

"I am home, oh my children . . ."

Eyes locked on the skies ahead, teeth gritted, refusing even to blink.

"And I have missed you so . . ."

A howl in his mind, a wail from a time before the womb, before the dark, when all was void. Kin rolled onto his belly, hands to his ears as he screamed, the ground splitting beneath him and crumbling away, dragging him down into bottomless, empty black. But no, he wasn't falling, he wasn't, all in his mind, his mind, gods *what is that noise?*

The air was filled with the stuttering clatter of mechabacii, every Guildsman twitching on their backs as the machines on their chests spat the same broken-beat rhythm, the backs of their heads beating against the floor in time. Kin crawled to the closest Shatei, dragged out his aidkit with shaking hands. Filling a hypo of opiates, he stabbed the needle into his arm, sighing as the pain disintegrated. Bliss rose up on shadowed wings, whispering for him to sleep, close his eyes and let all of it just wash away.

Hush, child.

Eyelids fluttering on his cheeks like the wings of butterflies he'd only seen in paintings.

Hush now.

The kind that didn't exist anymore thanks to the lotus poison spewing ever skyward . . .

And he raised his head, clutching his thigh. He stood on feet he couldn't feel and stumbled through the smoking dark, finding Shinji twitching and drooling, smashing his head against the floor in that stuttering rhythm. Kin unplugged the mechabacus from the boy's chest, the machine falling silent, the seizures slowing until Shinji opened his eyes wide, pupils like saucers, teeth chattering as if he were freezing to death.

"Shinji?" Kin touched the boy's arm. "Can you hear me?"

"Gods above . . ." Shinji blinked, wiped the tears from his eyes. "Kin . . ."

"Are you all right?"

"I could hear Her," the boy breathed. "My gods, She was *singing* to me."

"Can you walk? We have to get out of here before they wake up."

Shinji looked down at the mechabacus strapped to his chest. The cables burrowing like worms into his flesh.

"I don't think they will." The boy shook his head. "Not while She's singing . . ."

"Get up." Kin stood, dragged Shinji up with him, faintly aware that his palms had no skin, that his forearms and knees were bleeding, shedding and frayed.

Shinji raised an eyebrow. "First Bloom, are *you* all right?"

Kin pointed to the empty hypo on the floor, a mirthless smile on bloodless lips. Shinji grabbed another aidkit from a comatose Guildsman, fishing out pressure bandages and wrapping Kin's wounds. The boys limped across the listing floor, through near-blinding smoke, the *ticktick* of cooling metal accompanied by the beat of a dozen heads bashing into the floor. Climbing the stairwell, along the upper gantries, Kin felt lighter than air, tongue slightly too big for his mouth.

Passing more Shatei in the tight corridors, all flat on their backs, twitching in time to the soundless tune. They reached the service elevator at the Earthcrusher's spine, stabbing the control and watching it descend. Kin licked the taste of smoke and bad dreams from his lips, breathing deep. Dislocated in the opiate haze, reminded of the Iishi again, the burns he'd suffered there, he and Yukiko sheltering in their little cave by the rock pool.

"I won't tell them. N-never tell anyone. I won't let them hurt you. I promise, Yukiko."

Kensai towering over him in the hospice, eyes ablaze in that perfect, beautiful face.

"Tell me everything you know . . ."

He opened his eyes as the elevator reached their floor, stepping inside and pressing the button for the bridge. Shinji frowned.

"Our best exit is down in the nethers. Why are we headed to the bridge?"

Kin smiled, closed his eyes as they ascended.

"Someone I need to see . . ."

———

H ana screamed a war cry as the arashitora swooped from the skies, down onto the twisted nightmare shapes rising from the deadlands fissures. Yukiko and Buruu were at their head, blade raised high, flurries of black snow falling amidst ashes and smoke. Hana had stolen a chainkatana from a dead Iron Samurai, now holding it aloft and gunning the motor. The vibrations up her arm felt good and strong, gifted her with something close to courage as they flew toward the abominations rearing up from the deadlands wounds.

They cut through a thing made of gibbering mouths and leathery wings mounted on spurs of bone, Kaiah tearing and clawing, Hana chopping away with her chainblade. The thing's blood was black, steaming, filling the air with the stench of rotten corpses and burning hair. It fell screaming, back into the pit below, the pair turning and swooping on a tall, long-limbed demon, midnight blue skin crusted in ash, a belt of skulls about its waist. It was standing at the fissure's edge, blinking like a newborn, one hand up to the light as they fell on it from behind, hacking at its throat, blackened blood spraying through the air, burning where it touched their skins.

What the hells are these things?

- DARK ONES. DEMONS FROM THE DEEPEST HELLS. -

Yukiko's voice echoed in the Kenning amidst the blood-soaked roars of the Everstorm pack, falling on the demon brood and tearing them to bloody rags.

"They're oni. Children of the Dark Mother. We fought them before in the Iishi mountains. But nothing quite like these."

What the hells are they doing here?

Kaiah tore the throat from a faceless monstrosity, disemboweled it with a vicious kick and sent it tumbling back into the wound that had birthed it.

- DYING. -

Hana sliced at a thing with too many faces shrieking backward words she could somehow almost understand. A nameless terror shook her insides, pressing her to reach out to Kaiah's heat, her strength, the thunder tiger's iron will entwined with her own. And still, her hands trembled on her blade.

- COURAGE NOW. I AM HERE. WE ARE TOGETHER. -

Gods, how can you be fearless when the whole world is splitting apart?

Kaiah tore the demon's head from its shoulders in a spray of thick black, the mouths still gibbering as the carcass tumbled into the pit.

- ONLY FOOLS KNOW WHAT IT IS TO BE FEARLESS. SEEK ONLY TO BE AFRAID AND STAND TALL ANYWAY. THAT IS WHAT IT IS TO BE BRAVE. -

They moved amidst the horrors, Hana gritting her teeth, pushing down the cold, deep in her belly. She could see Kitsune soldiers on the Yama battlements, watching the thunder tigers and stormdancers cut the demons down, send them back to the dark that had birthed them. The men's eyes were alight, cheering as each horror fell. She remembered Kaiah's promise in the Iishi—the thunder ti-ger's vow to the wounded, frightened Burakumin girl she'd once been.

You asked who would sing for me.

- NOW YOU KNOW. WE WRITE THE WORDS EVEN NOW. -

Yukiko and Buruu were circling, picking off the demons still crawling from the pit. One of the Morcheban arashitora had been eviscerated by some nameless horror, falling into the darkness. Only four packmates left now, but they were unharmed. The demons had seemed dazed; confused somehow, like newborns blinking through their first dawn.

Hana wiped black gore from her face, spitting, still tasting it on Kaiah's tongue. The soldiers on the battlements raised their blades, roaring in triumph. She looked to the girl leading their pack—pale skin spattered with bloody tar, hair streaming in the wind—and she saw what the soldiers saw. What they must see in her also. Not a girl who was small and afraid and bleeding from a wound in her heart too deep to even acknowledge. Not a thing of flesh and blood and hurt and tears.

A legend.

A stormdancer.

Hana flicked a sluice of black blood from her chainkatana, glanced into the darkness beneath them. An open, yawning mouth, spitting the children of Yomi into the world of men. A crack in Shima, leading all the way down to the Hells. Her eye ached to look at it.

"What the hells is going on, Yukiko?"

The girl's reply echoed in the Kenning, laced with the same dread Hana felt in her belly.

"I don't know."

Yukiko turned her eyes to Kitsune-jō.

"But I know someone who does."

46
INTERSECTION

They sat in the forward carriage, swaying with the motion of the tracks, inhaling chi fumes as the train sped north toward Yama city. It was Isao's turn to mind the engine driver, and Yoshi was staring out the window, watching the deadlands fly by to the west. The Stain lay sprawled out on their left-hand side, endless miles of cracked earth, wreathed in choking fumes.

"A terrible sight."

Yoshi turned to stare at the False-Lifer, watching him intently. She'd told him her name was Kei, that she'd joined the rebels some years past, recruiting the big man Jun, and the young one, Goro, who never seemed to stray far from her side. Her face was thin, lips thinner, fierce and calculating and sharp like the chrome razors on her back.

Yoshi shrugged, turned back to the window.

"You can find pretty in anything if you look hard enough."

"And what beauty is there to be found in the Guild's desolation?"

Yoshi looked down at his wrist, the pale blue veins etched just below the surface. He made a fist, watching the tendons flex, the muscles at play beneath his skin.

"Maybe the one we make."

"Always riddles with you . . ." Kei shook her head.

"Why do the Guild burn folks with the Kenning?" Yoshi looked up from his wrist, eyes narrowed. "Why torch us?"

"The Purifiers teach that you are tainted by the Spirit World. That in order to achieve Purity, we must cleanse all taint of yōkai blood from our land."

"But *why*? What is this Purity they talk about all the time? What happens when you 'achieve' it? The heavens open up and blowjobs rain from the sky? What?"

"Yoshi-san, the Purifier's doctrine means little to me," Kei said. "Always I questioned it, even as a girl. But understand: if you are taught the gaijin are your enemies by everyone you trust, you will believe it. If you are taught children must be put to the pyre for a matter of faith, you will believe that too. Especially if no one else in the crowd raises their voice in dissent."

"That doesn't answer the question . . ."

"If I knew the answers, I—"

Bright light bloomed to the southwest past the deadlands, a blinding sheen cutting through the beach glass windows and Yoshi's goggles. The boy hissed as the western sky grew summer-bright, pulsing, burning even on the backs of his closed eyelids. Kei cursed, Isao shouting a warning from the driver's cabin. The flare slowly died, flared again and dimmed, Yoshi standing and staring out the window, hand pressed to the glass as he saw an enormous mushroom-shaped cloud rising on the western horizon above the Tōnan mountains.

"Izanagi's balls . . ." he breathed.

The train began to tremble, a crumbling, bass-deep shifting of the tracks beneath them, the entire island shivering in its boots. The train rocked side to side, bucking on the rails as the driver slammed on the brakes, a hail of sparks falling outside the window amidst the agonized shriek of metal, a hundred tons of momentum grabbed by the crotch curls and dragged up short.

Yoshi was pushed forward by the sudden deceleration, losing his grip and bouncing off the bulkhead. Jun, Kei and Goro all went flying, slamming into the foremost wall, Takeshi crying out from the aft carriage, followed by a loud thump. The train bucked and rolled, brakes screaming, tremors intensifying, flinging everyone about like a mob of rag dolls. Yoshi cracked his head on something hard, slammed into something soft, heard a grunted exhalation of pain. And then they were tilting, tilting, the crashing screech of snapping axles, wheels leaving the tracks and hitting gravel, and the world turned upside down and over and over, Yoshi grabbing a pillar as the train flipped onto its side, its roof, metal shrieking, iron and steel shredding like paper, glass splintering, people screaming, sparks and smoke and popping rivets, rolling over and over again as Yoshi roared and flopped about, blood in his mouth, the deafening kaleidoscope of sound, of momentum and inertia and gravity and mass, coming to rest at last in a twisted, smoking, moaning heap.

The engine died amidst the hiss of escaping pressure and creak of spinning wheels.

"Raijin's fucking drums . . ." Yoshi groaned.

The boy lifted his head, one eye gummed shut with blood, the wound at his ear bleeding fresh. The ground was still shaking, a colossal roar building in his ears. Yoshi looked around, saw Kei lying dead, her skull smashed open, the boy Goro hanging half out the shattered window, crushed beneath the train. But beyond the boy's corpse, Yoshi could see a dust cloud rising miles into the sky, like a tsunami across a waterless sea. Moving fast as the wind.

Right toward them.

He dragged himself up, eyes locked on the incoming cloud, blood dripping from his cracked brow and spattering on the broken glass at his feet. The door to the driver's cabin was torn aside and Isao staggered in, bleeding from a broken nose, a horrid gash in his forearm.

"Gods, is everyone—"

"We need to go," Yoshi breathed.

"Where's Takeshi? Atsushi?"

Yoshi pointed at the incoming dust cloud. "Isao, *we need to go!*"

The boy paled, and the pair fell to their knees, crawling out through the shattered windows on the eastern side of the train. Yoshi stood, head swimming, rappelling up a service ladder and looking back west. The ground bucked and rumbled, roar building until it was almost deafening, and as Yoshi squinted through the rising cloud of deadlands ash, he realized the Stain was *collapsing*, a massive chasm spreading its arms out toward them, miles upon miles of earth falling away into nothingness amidst the howl of a colossal, tectonic unmaking.

"Run . . ." he told Isao.

"What do you see?"

"RUN!"

Yoshi dropped from the ladder, bolted away, Isao struggling to keep pace. Over the broken stone and gravel at the side of the tracks, into the fallow lotus fields on the other side, tripping and tumbling on the snow-sludged earth. The ground bucked and rolled away from them, throwing them down and tossing them up, the roar near deafening now, impossible to think or speak, but only to run, to run as fast as you could, the aches of your body a distant second to the raw panic in your chest, pumping your veins full of adrenaline and bidding you to run, *run* until there was nothing left inside you.

A roar overhead, scattered shrieks. Yoshi dared a glance up and nearly choked as half a dozen familiar silhouettes darkened the sky above. Blade-sleek and slender, all feathers and fur and cruel hooked beaks. He had no idea under heavens what the beasts were doing there, but there they flew, as solid as the shuddering earth beneath his feet, and Yoshi locked his eyes on the leader and screamed, screamed into the Kenning with everything he had left.

Help! Help us, please!

A voice touched his mind, loud as thunder and as beautiful as sunset lightning.

*YUKIKO?**

Isao stumbled and Yoshi dragged him to his feet, risked a glance behind him and saw the chasm spreading closer, closer, swallowing the locomotive, twisted carriages tilting and tumbling down into the bottomless maw.

I'm a friend of Yukiko's! My sister Hana rides the arashitora called Kaiah!

The lead thunder tiger wheeled around, swooped low, followed by her pack-mates. Yoshi grabbed Isao's hand, ran toward them, stumbling and almost falling, screaming with his voice and his mind and waving his free hand high.

Here! Over here!

The earth bucked, threw him forward, crashing face-first into the dirt. Yoshi gasped, spat out black soil, scrambling up onto his hands and knees, throwing a desperate glance over his shoulder as the chasm yawned behind him, the earth shivering and groaning and dropping away beneath him. Isao fell down into the dark, his screams fading to nothing. And as Yoshi began to fall beside him, as weightlessness seized him and the bitter, bone-shattering chill seeping up from that impossible hole stabbed his heart to stilling, he felt an impact at his back, the thunderous beat of mighty wings. He was torn skyward, the arashitora grasping him in its claws. The ground dropped away as they soared higher, chasm yawning wide and groaning its hunger, denied at the last by Raijin's daughters. Filling the skies all around him with their cries; a moment of sheer beauty amidst total calamity.

Yoshi grasped handfuls of feathers, crawled up between the arashitora's shoulder blades, refusing to look down. Breath ragged. His whole body trembling.

Balls of the fucking Maker God . . .

INDEED.

Yoshi put his arms around the thunder tiger's neck, fighting to regain control of his pulse, his trembling, freezing limbs. He looked down into the pit that had swallowed Isao whole, unable to suppress a shudder. The beast's warmth banished the chill of that awful abyss, and gratitude swelled up to replace the terror, flooding over his edges and out into the beast's mind.

My thanks, great one. Truly.

GREAT ONE?

Faint amusement bubbled in the female's thoughts.

YOU I WILL LIKE.

Yoshi looked around at the pack, all sleek ferocity, feathers of snow white and jet black. Behind them, just in front of the enormous ash cloud rising out of the collapsing Stain, Yoshi could see a Guild sky-ship, engines roaring with the strain of full burn, tiny figures on its deck.

DO NOT FEAR. THEY FRIENDS. WE CAME HERE SEARCHING FOR OUR MALES. FOUND THEM CHASED BY MEN IN METAL SUITS.

Her growl was a vibration up his thighs into his belly.

BUT THEY CHASE NO MORE.

Yoshi ran one hand down the thunder tiger's neck.

Can I ask your name?

SHAI. SHAKHAN OF THE EVERSTORM PACK.

Where are you headed?

DO NOT KNOW. SEARCHING FOR YUKIKO AND OUR KHAN.

They'll be in Yama. The Kitsune city to the north.

MUST BRING NEWS OF RISING DARK. HORRORS WITHIN.

Well, Yama was where we were headed.

INDEED.

If I ask nice, you figure I might trouble you for a ride?

HOW NICE CAN MONKEY-CHILD ASK?

Well, if you were a pretty boy with prettier lips, I might think of something fancy. But I think I'll have to do with "pretty please," oh mighty Shai, Shakhan of the Everstorm pack.

MIGHTY SHAI.

Amusement rippled in the Kenning, warm as a new spring breeze.

* YOU I WILL DEFINITELY LIKE.*

The elevator doors split apart with a hiss, iron grinding in buckled furrows. Kin limped out onto the Earthcrusher bridge, the air filled with the smell of burned insulation, chi exhaust and blood. All around him, Guildsmen lay on the floor, heads beating against the decking with that off-beat rhythm, arms and legs twitching.

Kin and Shinji made their way down to the deck, Kin's eyes fixed on the figure sitting in the pilot's chair. That perfect, childish face, eyes aglow, blood leaking from his collar—the man Kin had called Uncle. Second Bloom Kensai.

No, Kin reminded himself. *First Bloom now . . .*

Shinji grabbed a piece of broken iron railing, tore it free, standing beside Kensai's prone form as Kin thumbed the latches at his collar, watching the throat unfold like a flower, unfastening the lengths of cable at the child's mouth and pulling the helmet free.

It wasn't a monster waiting for him behind the mask, not a horror twisted and deformed. Just an old man, eyes creased at the edges, slack jowls, balding pate dotted with liver spots. Kensai's eyes were wide, pupils fixed, and he continued to bash his head into the harness, his mechabacus echoing the stuttering beat spitting from every Guildsman's chest.

"Do you want to do it?" Shinji proffered the iron bar. "Or should I?"

"Why would we kill him?"

"He's the First Bloom of the Lotus Guild. He killed Maseo and Bo. Why the hells would we keep him alive?"

Kin looked out to the smoking ruins of Yama city. He thought of the arashitora cut to pieces by the Earthcrusher's defenses, the brave samurai who'd crashed their ships into the Earthcrusher to try and halt its advance, the countless soldiers who must have lost their lives. And at the last, he thought of Daichi. This victory the old man had bought with his life.

"For all he's done, Kensai deserves justice in the cold light of day. Not a clumsy murder in the dark."

Kin replaced Kensai's helm to spare the old man's skull further punishment. Then he began unfastening the pilot's harness, the pain of his burns a distant, cutting ache.

"Help me with him, brother."

Shinji stood, uncertain, the air filled with the stuttering beat of Guildsmen skulls on metal grilles. But at last, he took hold, straining with the weight, and the pair hauled the First Bloom out of the pilot's rig. Half carrying, half dragging him to the elevator, the boys staggered out into the loading bay, finally reaching broad double doors marked with diagonal stripes of yellow paint. The hydraulics were disabled, and the pair propped Kensai against the wall as they spun the locking wheel, finally cracking the doors open and blinking out into blinding light.

Kin winced, held his breath, the poisoned air tasting impossibly sweet after the Earthcrusher's choking confines. He looked out over Yama, the smashed walls of Kitsune-jō all around them, the bushimen and samurai moving out of cover slowly, weapons raised. Smoke and ash, fire and blood, the ground trembling as an aftershock from the colossal quake hit the city.

Ruined walls toppled to dust, Kin and Shinji crouching low with Kensai between them as the city shivered and fitted, just like the man they clutched between them.

"Gods above," Kin breathed, eyes roaming the carnage. "Just look at it all . . ."

Shinji extended the loading ramp down to the broken ground. Palace guardsmen were surrounding the Earthcrusher, crossbows raised, cadres of bushimen preparing to advance.

"Hold!" Kin called.

"You give no commands here, Guildsman!" A tall Kitsune man stood amidst the rubble, broad as a doorway, a general's sigil on his tabard. "You stand within the walls of Kitsune-jō, the Fortress of the Fox and our Lord, Daimyo Isamu!"

"We are rebels!" Kin shouted. "We have Shateigashira Kensai here as our prisoner!"

"An obvious ploy." The man spat on the ground. "You think us fools?"

"A ploy? Who the hells do you think sabotaged this thing?" Shinji slapped one palm against the Earthcrusher's hull. "Didn't you notice someone stopped it stone dead forty feet from your Daimyo's bedroom door? Or did you think it ran out of fucking chi?"

"Quite a mouth you've got on you, boy."

"That's just what your daughter said!"

The general laughed. "Quite a pair too. What's your name?"

Kin cut off Shinji's reply. "My name is Kin, General. My exuberant friend is Shinji."

"I have heard your name. This very day, in fact . . ."

The man lowered his head in a slow bow.

"I am Ginjiro, general of the Kitsune Army."

Kin did his best to return the bow with Kensai's weight on his arm, the pain of his burns rearing up beneath the fading opiate haze. "My honor, General."

"Is that really the Second Bloom of Kigen city in your arms?"

"Technically, he's First Bloom of the entire Guild, now Tojo is dead."

General Ginjiro signaled for his men to stand down, a cold smile on his lips.

"Then I bid you welcome to Kitsune-jō."

Yukiko and Buruu swooped toward the Kitsune fortress, Kaiah and their other packmates beside them. Limping through the skies behind came a few wounded Kitsune ships and the battle-scarred hulk of the *Kurea*, a bloodied and bruised Blackbird at the helm. The city had been decimated, pockets of fighting still ongoing between Kitsune bushimen and Tora shreddermen. With no way out of the city, the Tora had barricaded themselves on Last Isle, uncertainty rising in the wake of the earthquake, the destruction of First House, the rise of those demons from the pit.

The gaijin army had been halfway through bridging the Amatsu when the quake hit, their structure collapsing into tar-black waters. Now they stood amassed on the eastern banks, their commanders pacing along the black shores as their engineers began work again. Only one among them walked with his head bowed, swathed in guilt.

But Yukiko only had thoughts for the blind Inquisitor, locked in the fortress dungeons. A man who'd hold all the answers, who could tell them how to defeat the darkness spreading from the ruins of the Stain.

The Earthcrusher loomed out of the smoke ahead, the behemoth listing, its engines silenced. It had smashed its way through the outer walls of Kitsune-jō, but fallen short of the mark. Fox clan soldiers had surrounded it, blades glittering in the light of the fading day. Snow still fell in fitful flurries.

Yukiko felt Buruu tense beneath her, falling instinctively into the space behind his eyes. And then she saw him, picking his way through the ruins at the Earthcrusher's feet, supporting what looked like the Second Bloom of Kigen city in his arms. Soldiers closing in all about him.

Rage flared in her heart. Rage at his betrayal. At everything it had cost her. *"KIIIIIIN!"*

Buruu roared along with her, diving from the skies with the Everstorm pack behind them, her katana drawn. The boy beside Kin quailed, released his grip on the Second Bloom, turning and running as the Shateigashira collapsed. Kin's eyes were wide, but she seized hold of his limbs, holding him frozen to the spot as they swooped in to land, broken rubble and shale beneath their talons, whipping dust and ash into the air.

She was off Buruu's back in a blinking, the katana in her hand gleaming in the fading light. Drawing the weapon back, picturing Isao, Takeshi, Atsushi, Akihito, Michi, Daichi, Aisha, the soldiers who'd died defending this city, the ideal of freedom this boy spat on with every breath he could muster. Sorrow in his mind, bursting the banks of his subconscious, rimming his eyes as she drew within striking distance, knuckles white on the blade Daichi had named for her Anger, given to her by the very man this boy had sent to his end.

And without a word, without giving one more breath of herself to this wretched little bastard, she stabbed toward his heart.

The bright note of steel on steel, a burst of sparks as her blow was deflected, clipping Kin's shoulder and giving birth to a spray of blood. Yukiko turned, eyes wide, Buruu roaring, faint incomprehension swelling in her thoughts.

General Ginjiro stood before her, warclub in his hand.

"Hold, Stormdancer."

"Stand aside, General," Yukiko growled, "before I lay you down."

"I am pleased you still live, girl."

Four thunder tigers gathered at Yukiko's back, filling the air with menacing growls.

"Step. Aside."

The general seemed unfazed.

"This is Kitsune-jō. The Fortress of the Fox. Daimyo Isamu is lord here. Not Stormdancer Yukiko."

"Daimyo Isamu is dead! All of them dead! Because of this traitor!" Her eyes flashed, staring at the still-paralyzed Kin. "I could smash him open with but a thought—"

"And grieve that second's folly for the rest of your days, girl."

"It wouldn't be folly, it'd be *justice*! He betrayed us! Betrayed Daichi!"

"Kaori's father."

. . . THIS MAN HAS NEVER MET KAORI.

Yukiko blinked, hesitation breaking through the rage.

"How do you know Kaori? Daichi?"

"Misaki sent missive wirelessly from the deck of the *Truth Seeker* barely ten minutes past. She returns from the ruins of First House, the remnants of a Kagé sabotage squad with her. Their leader, a woman named Kaori, bid us spread the word amongst the rebels and other loyalists here. The boy named Kin is not to be touched."

"Kaori hates Kin. She wants him dead more than I . . ."

The general stroked his beard. "Seems this boy and your Daichi formulated a plan between them. A stratagem unknown even to Daichi's daughter. A ruse to get the boy aboard the Earthcrusher and stop it from within."

Ginjiro glanced up at the lopsided goliath, then back at the bare forty feet of ground between the machine and the inner walls of Kitsune-jō.

"Fortunately for us, it seems . . ."

. . . COULD IT BE?

"That's impossible . . ."

"Says the lowborn girl leading a pack of thunder tigers."

Yukiko's katana fell from nerveless fingers. She looked at Kin, anger slipping away as she searched his thoughts. All of it there for her to see, if only she'd taken the time to look. Kin and Daichi hunched over their chess game. His infiltration of Chapterhouse Kigen, then the Earthcrusher itself. The agony of his burns, the 'thrower wound in his thigh, all he'd risked and suffered laid out in the glittering pathways of his mind. But above all, reflected in the tears in both their eyes was the moment she'd accused him of betrayal in Kigen arena. When she'd thought Kin sold her to Yoritomo and been proven wrong, now proven so again, his words then echoing now in her thoughts, like a rusted knife in her chest.

"I gave you my word. I gave Buruu his wings. I would never betray you, Yukiko. Never."

"Oh gods, Kin . . ."

She released her hold on his body, and he sagged, the heat of his burns flaring blood-red in his mind. Despite it all, he still stood, eyes filled not with the pain of his body, but the pain of a single thought—that again, and despite everything he'd done, she'd thought the worst of him.

She stepped toward him, hands fluttering helplessly at her sides.

"Oh gods, Kin, I'm so sorry . . ."

The wind howled in the frozen gulf between them. A single foot and a thousand miles wide.

He looked down at the swelling at her midriff, wiped the tears from his eyes.

"So am I . . ."

47
A GRAND WAY TO DIE

THERE IS NO TIME NOW, FOR GRIEF.

They sat perched on the highest point in Yama city—the lopsided head of the Earthcrusher—looking out over the ruins of the Kitsune capital. Events of the last hour played over and over in her mind; a broken sound-box breathing a white-noise hum.

She'd marched straight into the dungeons, Hana at her side, intent on questioning the Inquisitor and finding some truth in all this. But the warrens had collapsed in the earthquake following the destruction of First House; the Inquisitor's cell and dozens of others had been buried under tons of fresh rubble. Yukiko had stood before the wall of crumbled masonry, felt beyond the ruins with the Kenning, searching for those pitch-black eyes, that empty smile, any sign of life. She found nothing. A desolation, devoid even of corpse-rats. Despair in her heart, she realized any answers the Inquisitor held had died with him.

General Ginjiro had ordered the helpless Guildsmen removed from the Earthcrusher and placed under lock and key. Kin had begged his brethren be taken to the hospice, and with no dungeons to lock them inside, the general had acquiesced. Kin had overseen the operation despite his injuries, unplugging each Guildsman from their mechabacus by hand, ending their convulsions, helping them to their feet, bleary-eyed and trembling. It was only after the last Guilds-man had been removed that he'd allowed himself to be taken for treatment.

All the while, he'd not said a word to her.

She'd returned to the crash-site of the *Honorable Death*, unsurprised to find Hiro gone. Tears smudging her face, she'd collected Michi's body, winging her back to Kitsune-jō. She was laid in the gardens beneath white sheets and black snow—just one among hundreds, their ranks swelling by the second.

Yukiko knew they'd have to deal with the gaijin soon to collect Akihito—or at least what was left of him. But for the moment, it was all she could do to stop it spilling out of her in a flood without ceasing. Here in the quiet, loss amplified by the thunder tigers mourning their fallen brethren, the girl circling astride Kaiah above, mourning her love.

Grief.

SORROW WASTES TIME WE DO NOT HAVE.

I can't help it, Buruu. If anyone was going to make it through this, I thought it would be Michi. She was fiercer than a thousand sea dragons. And gods, poor Akihito . . .

ALL THIS WAS PRELUDE. THE REAL BATTLE HAS NOT EVEN BEGUN.

She stepped into the Kenning and felt her way south, a headache kick-starting itself somewhere in the back of her skull. She could sense the impossible dark-ness swelling around the Stain's ruins, writhing, seething, the faintest of echoes in her mind, a broken, skull-bending rhythm trying to draw her in. She pulled herself back into her brother's warmth. Shivering.

You can't even imagine what's growing down there . . .

I HAVE A NOTION.

How do we even begin to fight it? A hellgate, Buruu. A wound in the world lead-ing right down into Yomi. The demons we fought here were nothing. The things crawling from that hole . . .

WE SHOULD RUN, THEN? LEAVE THIS PLACE TO DIE?

We can't do that.

SUKAA AND THE OTHERS WOULD SEE IT AS JUSTICE.

And what about you?

Buruu sniffed the air, gazed at his few remaining packmates circling above. His eye was on Sukaa, the black sweeping across the city like a crow in the old tales; a herald of death walking in the wake of war.

I AM MORE THAN THAT NOW. AND I DO NOT THINK IT RIGHT TO LEAVE THESE PEOPLE TO THEIR FATE, NO MATTER THE HAND THEY HAD IN ITS MAKING. HERE AT THE END, ESPECIALLY IF THIS IS THE END, WE MUST DO WHAT IS RIGHT. NOT WHAT IS JUST. AND THERE IS A DIFFERENCE.

This isn't your fight, Buruu. You have a bride at home. A son. There's nothing stopping you going back to them now. Living the life you longed for.

YOU THINK MY EXILE IS THE REASON I STAYED?

You've done enough, brother.

YOU ARE MY LIFE AND MY HEART. I GO WHERE YOU GO.

Your kind has lost enough already because of us. They fight because you command them, not because they see any worth in us. Five of them died today. And knowing what awaits us to the south, I'm afraid you'll be sending the rest to their deaths.

I DO NOT THINK THE GODS WILLED US HERE TO SUFFER SUCH A FATE.

The gods? What the hells do they have to do with this?

SURELY YOU CANNOT DOUBT THEM NOW? WITH THE ENDSINGER RISING?

Well, where the fuck are they? Why aren't they helping us?

WHO SAYS THEY ARE NOT?

You sound like Michi . . .

SHE SPOKE TRUTH. THINK ON IT. YOU AND I. ALL THESE EVENTS TRANSPIRING FROM A SINGLE MOMENT—THE HUNT FOR THE LAST ARASHITORA ALIVE. WITHOUT IT, KIN WOULD NEVER HAVE MET YOU. THE REBELS WOULD NEVER HAVE ALLIED WITH THE KITSUNE. THE EARTHCRUSHER WOULD NEVER HAVE FALTERED. FIRST HOUSE NEVER FALLEN.

It's all chance, Buruu. We met because of a madman's dream.

AND WHO GAVE HIM THAT DREAM?

Yukiko scowled, pressed her lips tight.

And what have we achieved? What did we gain?

WHATEVER SCHEME THE INQUISITION HAS BEEN WORKING TOWARD, IT HAS NOT UNFOLDED AS THEY FORESAW. THE INQUISITOR BENEATH KITSUNE-JŌ SPOKE OF YEARS PASSING BEFORE THEIR PLAN SAW FRUITION. THE ENDSINGER'S REBIRTH, THIS CALAMITY—IT IS PREMATURE. THE ONI CRAWLING FROM THAT PIT WERE LIKE NEWBORN BABES, BLINDED BY THE LIGHT. THEY ARE NOT YET READY TO BE HERE. THERE IS ADVANTAGE IN THAT. STRENGTH.

But how? How do we fight a goddess?

WITH AN ARMY.

Yukiko looked across the river, to the gaijin forces amassed on the Amatsu shores. To the Tora soldiers holed up on Last Isle, surrounded and outnumbered but still unbroken.

No time for grief.

Buruu nodded.

TIME ENOUGH FOR TEARS WHEN THE WAR IS WON.

A storm of arrows raged across the sky as they flew above the gaijin camp, plummeting back down to kiss the frozen earth. The remaining rotor-thopters hung in the skies below, but refrained from engaging—the pilots obviously had no desire to battle thunder tigers unless forced to. Yukiko reached into her satchel and dragged out a long white flag, circling over the camp until the arrows stopped, until every soldier below had seen her symbol of parlay.

And then, they descended.

The soldiers cleared a wide circle, Kaiah and Buruu tearing the frozen ground as they came in to land. Every gaijin carried a weapon—a broadsword or mallet or longspear, and Yukiko found herself surrounded by a wall of cold, glittering steel. Every soldier's eye was on Hana, distrust and rage in every gaze. The gaijin commanders stayed well behind their men, standing atop one of the squat siege-crawlers so they could see above the throng.

Yukiko could see Hana's uncle: a tall, blond man with scruffy whiskers. Next to him stood the priestess from the lightning farm, the beaten brass skins of Guildsmen covering her body. The camp was lit with barrels of burning fire, long shadows dancing in growling wind.

"Aleksandar Mostovoi," Yukiko said.

"Da." Blue eyes gleamed as lightning arced across darkening skies.

"I cannot speak your language. Will you translate to your priestess?"

"Da." He glanced at Hana. "My blood, are you well?"

Hana did her best to keep her voice from trembling. "What the hells do you think?"

"He seemed a good man, Hana. I am sorry—"

"Where is Marshal Sergei, Uncle?"

"He died at the river today." The man stared at Yukiko. "You killed him."

"I'm sorry," the girl sighed. "I only wanted—"

Sister Katya spat a series of incomprehensible words, and the Kapitán breathed deep.

"The Sacred Sister bids you speak your piece and be on your way."

Yukiko stared at the blond woman, bitter winds blowing dark tendrils across her eyes. She clawed the locks from her mouth, remembering the last time they'd seen each other. Yukiko had been a prisoner, helpless and terrified. But now she stood tall, reaching across the island's bleeding face, into the impossible, ancient strength still roaming its waters.

"Your fleet is destroyed. Every Morcheban seaman has fled the Bay of Dragons or now slumbers beneath it. Every ship in your armada lies rusting on the bottom of the bay."

A brief exchange passed between Mostovoi and the Sister.

"You tell us nothing we do not know, beast-speaker."

"Know then, that the dragons who destroyed your ships did so at my command."

As Mostovoi repeated her words, an angry murmur rolled amongst the gaijin troops. More than one took a menacing step forward, stopped in their tracks by Buruu's bellowing roar.

"You tell us this, why?" the Kapitán asked.

"Because we must trust each other now, Aleksandar Mostovoi. Because if we do not, all of us will die in this place. And trust cannot grow in a field of lies."

"You killed our people. Brave soldiers, all."

"You killed my—" Hana's voice cracked, tears in her eye. ". . . You invaded our country. Burned Kawa city. Women and children—"

"The Shimans took *our* women and children!" Mostovoi growled. "My mother. My sister. Love of the Goddess, Hana, you are a daughter of *rape*. The rape of my family, my country, all at the hands of these slaver pigs!"

THIS WAY LIES RUIN. BLOOD FOR BLOOD.

Gods, I know but—

THE FIRST STEP MUST BE YOURS. RAISING ANCIENT DRAGONS FROM ENDLESS SLUMBER. SLAYING DEMONS FROM THE DEEPEST HELLS. RIDING A THUNDER TIGER. THESE ARE EASY THINGS FOR ONE LIKE YOU.

Easy? Gods above . . .

AKIHITO IS GONE. MICHI IS GONE. DO YOU NOT THINK THEY WOULD WISH, AS YOUR FATHER DID, THEIR SACRIFICE MEAN SOMETHING?

Yukiko wrapped her arms about herself, shivering in the bitter chill.

Something greater.

She looked at Mostovoi, at the soldiers around her. Hundreds of miles from home. All driven by that same thirst for revenge, caught in that same downward spiral. And she'd seen exactly where it led . . .

"I know we've wronged you, Kapitán." She softened her voice, palms upturned. "If it were within my power to undo, I would. But you should know it will never happen again. The Lotus Guild was destroyed this day. By my people, my friends—men and women who could no longer live in a country built with the blood of your kin. I'm sorry for your loss, I truly am. But we face a greater threat now than you can possibly imagine. And we need your help to defeat it."

Mostovoi paused for a cold, empty forever before repeating the words. Yukiko watched Katya's eyes narrow, bitter laughter spill over sharpened teeth. Her words were a viper's hiss.

"Hana has killed the Holy Mother. The hand of the Imperatritsa herself. There can be no peace between us, girl."

"Then we'll die," Hana spat. "All of us. All of you."

"Threats, my blood? This is your overture of peace?"

"Hana speaks no threat." Yukiko shook her head. "An evil rises to the south. A wound in the world, bleeding demons. They're weak now. Stunned by their birth. But soon they'll come. From the tip of Seidai to the isle of Shabishii. From the eastern seas to the edge of Yotaku. The children of the Endsinger will march, and everything before them will perish. Everything."

"And this concerns us how?"

"You have no fleet, Uncle," Hana said. "You're trapped here like the rest of us."

Yukiko stepped forward, pleading eyes aimed at Sister Katya.

"We have wronged you, gods know it. But if you cannot find it in yourself to forgive us, every living thing on this island will die." She looked down to her stomach, felt the warmth within her, growing by the day. "I . . ."

The words caught in her throat. The impossibility of it all. The enormity.

"I will be a mother soon," she said. "These babies will come into a world I help shape. And the thought absolutely terrifies me, Katya. But what terrifies me more is the thought they may never have a chance at all. And a part of me wonders if I shouldn't just fly away, leave all of this behind. To tell myself that I tried as best I could, and hope that lie will let me sleep at night. But I think of the other mothers and fathers on these islands, who all played their part in your people's suffering to be sure. But still, they love their children. And those children deserve a future, just as much as mine. And if I can fight to give them one, if losing my life and the life of my own means a hundred thousand more can be saved . . ."

She pawed the tears in her eyes, leaned into Buruu's warmth.

"I'm sorry." She looked around the assembled gaijin. "All of you. I'm sorry for what was done to you. And though I have no right, I beg you to help us as you help yourselves. Though precious few of us deserve it . . . I can think of at least two who do."

She looked back at Katya, the word catching in her throat.

"Please."

Lightning arced across darkening skies, the wind a tuneless dirge. The priestess stared, long and hard. At the soldiers gathered around her. At the girl and her thunder tiger and the tears shining in her eyes. At the Kapitán leaning in close and whispering in her ear.

"Please . . ."

Yukiko put her arm around Buruu's neck, pressed her stomach to his warmth. Sister Katya spoke, her voice low and measured, her eyes locked on Yukiko. The girl turned to Mostovoi, watching him exhale, deflate, broad shoulders slumping.

Disappointment?

Relief?

"Sister Katya says it would disgrace the memory of our Zryachniye, of all those who have fallen against your people, to ally with you against an evil of your own making. She forbids any and all troops loyal to the Imperatritsa to fight at your side."

Yukiko sighed, the words a cold knife in her gut. Hana's jaw clenched, fighting back bitter rebuke. Katya spit on the ground, pointed to the sky.

Heart sinking into her belly, Yukiko pulled herself up on Buruu's shoulders.

"I am sorry," Mostovoi said. "Morcheban folk are not known for their forgiving ways. We have suffered twenty years of atrocity beneath your Shōgun's flag."

Hana's voice was taut, her lips almost unmoving. "Where's his body?"

Mostovoi spoke a few words to his men, and the sea of swords and hammers slowly parted. The Kapitán pointed to a shape near the command tent, wrapped in blood-soaked cloth.

"Wait." Piotr pushed through the crowd, limping as he came, cursing and shoving. He stopped before Yukiko, stared at her with half-blind eyes.

"I come with her." He cast his glare around the mob. "If no other."

Yukiko smiled despite her sorrow. Piotr helped lift Akihito's corpse onto Kaiah's shoulders, then struggled up onto Buruu behind Yukiko. Mostovoi moved closer before a low growl from Kaiah pulled him up short. He looked at Hana, grief plain in his eyes.

"I am truly sorry about your man, my blood . . ."

"You said Morcheban folk are not known for their forgiveness, Uncle," Hana murmured. "Perhaps there's more of my mother in me than either of us knew."

A bounding dash across frozen ground.

A rush of wind, freezing beneath.

Flight.

F ive figures sat in the Kitsune Chamber of Counsel—an old wardog, a cloud-walker captain, a rebel Guildswoman, and two girls who had changed the face of the world. The seat at the table's head was conspicuously empty.

The seats around them, more so.

"We spend two days repairing the fleet," Yukiko said. "Then we march south with everything we have and meet the oni in the field."

"Sounds like a grand way to die," Blackbird sighed, knocking back a cupful of saké.

"We have a fortress here, Stormdancer," General Ginjiro replied. "Why ride out from behind our walls with the gaijin waiting across the river?"

"I don't think this hellgate was meant to open yet. The Stain's collapse was set off by the First House explosion, not by whatever ritual the Serpents were intending. If we strike now, we have a chance. If we wait, the oni simply build their strength and move when they're ready. Besides, your walls are breached. Once the gaijin bridge the Amatsu, they need only to walk up to your front door and knock."

"Fools," Ginjiro murmured.

"They're not fools," Yukiko said. "They're just angry. They've lost as much as we."

"With the legions of the Hells just days from annihilating us all, they still press old grudges? Time and place?"

Hana spoke, her voice dark and low with grief. "If it was your mother crushed into fertilizer, your might sing a different tune, General."

"My Lord and Master lying dead is not sacrifice enough for you, girl?"

"Don't call me 'girl,' motherfuc—"

"My gods, we're on the *same side!*" Yukiko slammed her hands on the table. "If we don't put aside the past and look to the now there will *be no tomorrow.*" Her glare switched between Hana and Ginjiro. "Do you not understand that?"

"Hana has a mean streak," said a low, graveled voice. "Gets it from her da."

Hana looked up, eye wide, saw him standing at the doors with a crooked grin. Misaki stood beside him with her chrome arms unfurled, daughter in her arms.

"*Yoshi!*"

Hana flew across the room, feet barely touching the ground, into his open arms. Spinning on the spot as if they danced, tears streaming down her face as he laughed and squeezed her tight. Time stood still as Hana clung to him for dear life, until anger replaced relief and she pulled away, punched him once in the chest, wiping her face on her sleeve.

"Where the hells have you been?"

"Pretty much the size of it." He was staring at her eye, running a gentle thumb across her cheek. "I like the new look. Very fetching."

"Later, all right?"

Yukiko had joined them in the doorway, covering her fist and bowing low to Misaki.

"Stormdancer." The woman bowed in return. "I am glad you live. I would greet you properly, but my arms are blessedly full."

"Hello, little one." Yukiko tickled the chin of the little girl in Misaki's arms. "Your mother is very brave. Did you know that?"

The girl smiled shyly, turned her face into her mother's breast.

"First House is gone." Yukiko turned her eyes to Misaki. "First Bloom dead. All Shima owes you a debt, Misaki-san."

"Not us alone," Misaki said.

A figure stepped from the shadows. Steel-gray eyes and high cheekbones and full lips, her fringe cut short to at last expose the scar on her face.

"Kaori," Yukiko breathed.

"He is dead, Yukiko." Tears shone in Kaori's lashes. "My father is dead."

Yukiko closed her eyes, sagged inside. "Gods . . ."

"Kin lives?" A hopeful gleam in steel-gray.

"He does. Barely."

"I learned the truth of it." The woman stared at her hands, clenching and unclenching her fists. "Of his plan with my father. But I said nothing. My deceit could have cost his life. Your life. Anyone's." She shook her head. "Forgive me. I did not see . . ."

Yukiko took Kaori's hands in hers.

"Past is past, sister."

". . . Sister?"

Yukiko smiled. "Always."

The pair embraced, fiercely, eyes closed against their tears. The storm rolling overhead hushed itself, black snow falling still, as if to give them one tiny moment's peace before the final plunge. The five walked back to the council table, Yukiko speaking to Ginjiro.

"General, this is Kaori, leader of the Kagé. You have already met Misaki-san, leader of the Guild rebels, and Yoshi-san, Hana's brother."

"Not much of a leader of anything, I'm afraid." The boy smiled crookedly.

Yoshi knelt beside his sister, one arm around her shoulder. He stared across the table at Blackbird, at the saké bottle before him.

"How do, Captain-san?"

"Alive," Blackbird grunted. "So, better than most."

"Doubtless."

"You?"

"Parched."

Blackbird smiled, filled a cup, watching as Yoshi gulped it down. Wincing against the burn, the boy wiped his lips and shook his head.

"Beats the shit out of that brown rice seppuku me and Jurou used to drink." He smiled at his sister. "You remember that?"

She smiled back. "I remember."

The boy blinked, frowned about the room. "By the by, where's Akihito?"

Hana's smile dropped to the floor, shattered into a million pieces. Yukiko placed her palms on her knees, head down, hair a black curtain over her face.

Yoshi looked back and forth between them. "Oh hells, no . . ."

"We have a lot to talk about, Yoshi," Hana said. "But later, all right?"

Yoshi squeezed her tight, kissed her brow. Hana leaned in close, closed her eye, so grateful to be back with him she could barely breathe.

"We all have paid dearly," Kaori said. "But we must put aside grief. The Endsinger and the Yomi horde will not be so kind as to give us time to indulge it."

"You saw them?" Yukiko asked.

"I only glanced over my shoulder as we fled, for fear the madness would take me. Fingers of burning chill scraping through my head. A tune etched in my spine. Darkness." Kaori shook her head. "Hunger and cold unending."

"A hellgate," Blackbird breathed, reality finally settling in. "Great Maker's breath . . ."

Misaki hugged her daughter, smoothed hair from the child's brow. "I cannot believe we triumphed over the Guild and the Tora, only to be struck down by a mad goddess."

"Can't fault her, really," Yoshi shrugged.

"What?"

"Think about it. She dies giving birth to creation, and her husband leaves her in the Hells to rot."

"Lord Izanagi tried to rescue her," Kaori said.

"And he failed," Yoshi shrugged.

"So you think it right for her to destroy the world in retaliation?"

"Well, she's the one who had to squeeze it out. Can you imagine what it's like popping *seven islands* out of your delightfuls? Hells, give the woman some sympathy."

"Madness," Ginjiro breathed. "Blasphemy."

"All I'm saying is betrayal like that leaves a scar." Yoshi shrugged. "If it happened to anyone here, they'd probably go mad too. I'm not saying I'm all for dying or anything. Just saying I feel sorry for her, is all . . ."

Hana was watching her brother, firelight gleaming in her eye. "Did you find what you were looking for in Kigen? Did it help?"

"Didn't help. But I *did* find something. An answer maybe."

"To what question?"

The boy chewed his lip, saying nothing. He passed his cup to the Blackbird for a refill.

"So," Kaori said. "What do we know of hellgates?"

"Legends," Blackbird said. "Children's tales."

"Tora Takehiko," Yukiko nodded. "One of my father's favorites."

Piotr finally stirred from amidst his cloud of honeyweed. "He stormdancer?"

Yukiko nodded. "He ended the last hellwar. Lady Izanami tricked a young boy into moving the boulder sealing Yomi shut, unleashing her hordes upon the world. Tora Takehiko flew inside the hellgate and closed it again."

"He died in the process," Kaori said.

"But saved the Seven Isles by doing so."

"Sacrifice," Hana nodded.

"My father once told me, 'One day you will see that we must sometimes sacrifice for the sake of something greater,'" Yukiko said. "I can't think of much greater than the lives of every man, woman and child in Shima."

"You mean to do this?" Kaori frowned. "Fly into the hellgate?"

"I don't see a better option, do you?"

Misaki shook her head. "But once inside, how will you close it?"

"I don't know," Yukiko sighed. "The legends don't ever say how he did it."

"Yukiko, you are pregnant. And you are not the only stormdancer at this table."

All eyes turned to Hana. The girl met their stares, one after the other, then turned to Yukiko. She nodded, jaw set, lips thin. Unafraid.

"Kaiah and I can do it."

"No," Yukiko said.

"Yukiko—"

"No, Hana. I dragged you into this. And you and I are *not* going to sit here arguing about who gets to kill themselves."

"Who says I plan on dying? Just because Tora Takehiko fell, doesn't mean one of us—"

"We place the rickshaw before the runner," General Ginjiro said. "The point is moot unless we have an army with which to fight the Yomi hordes. Sealing the gate alone will be pointless. From what you say, the legion already spat through the hellgate would be enough to wreak untold havoc. They must be dealt with also."

"Two days," Yukiko nodded. "As I said, we repair the fleet, march south with everything we have. Buruu and I deal with the gate once we get there. Agreed?"

Uncomfortable silence fell, dissent bubbling just underneath. It was obvious none at the table were keen on the idea of Yukiko or Hana sacrificing themselves in some suicidal charge, but no other option presented itself.

Blackbird finally knocked back his saké and sighed.

"A long day. I think we'll all see clearer on the morrow."

The council-goers left in silence, each burdened with dark thoughts. Yoshi remained at the table, staring into his empty cup. Hana hovered by the door, pale and fragile.

"Are you coming, brother?"

". . . Hai."

Running his palm over the stubble on his scalp, he heaved a sigh, scooped up the saké bottle and went in search of sleep he knew would never come.

Lightning from his father's hand, etching blue-white poetry across the clouds above. The warmth of his bucks at his side, gathered like crows for a feast on the eaves of the Daimyo's palace, black and white, eyes gleaming with every arc thrown across the heavens. Watching the females descending slowly, coming in to land on the roof opposite the Kitsune garden. Angry growls. Rumbling discontent. Awful sorrow in the eyes of those who had lost mates or kin.

Mocking amusement in Sukaa's glare.

Buruu stared at Shai, watching as she settled on the rooftop, preening with a beak like a saber. Tail switching, breathing slow, as if this were any other day.

He roared that he had commanded them to stay in Everstorm. That it was not a female's place to fight. That they endangered their race's future by coming here.

Shai glanced at Kaiah, and made no reply.

That is different, Buruu roared. *Kaiah is different.*

Niah and Aael awoken. Black and white share one Khan. Endsinger rises. All is different.

Buruu glanced at the assembled pack, growling softly.

Fly with me.

Shai's eyes glittered.

As Khan commands . . .

The pair took to the sky, circling into the storm, static electricity building and bursting along their quills. Shai flew close enough that the outstretched tips of their feathers touched.

You disobeyed me, Buruu growled.

I am Shakhan of Everstorm. My place to challenge, when no other will.

I will not see you fall here.

Nor I you. Pack needs you. Rhaii needs you.

The future of our race lies with mothers, not fathers.

No future if Dark Mother ends world. Without us, the silver-tongue monkey-child would have died. He spoke in my mind. May have a way to save this place.

What way?

Did not speak it. But certain in his heart.

. . . Where is our son?

The Elders watch. Watch them all.

That is wise.

I know.

Thunder rocked the skies, thrumming in his bones.

. . . I am glad you are here, my heart.

She dipped her wing, glided closer.

Know this also.

Is there anything you do not?

Shai looked to the south, to the cold and rising dark.

How this will end . . .

48
BEFORE THE DAWN

She wept.

She wept until her voice was splinters and her throat was chalk. Until Yoshi's uwagi was soaked through, her face pressed to his chest, his arms around her shoulders.

They sat on her bed. The same bed where she and Akihito had lain the night before, now cold and empty, ten miles wide, the thought clawing the inside of her chest, leaving her hollow.

Yoshi said not a word. Didn't breathe platitudes or sympathies or promises everything would be all right. He simply held her, his warmth keeping the pre-dawn chill away. And after an hour of emptying herself, she found it all too much to hold on to, and he laid her down with a pillow beneath her, pulling up her blankets, still touched by Akihito's scent.

He knelt beside her, whispering in the gloom.

"Dark now. Blacker than black, I know it. And words are tiny things in the face of all that dark and all that cold. But hear these words, little sister. Hear and know. Tomorrow is coming, just as fast as the turning of the sky. And as sure as it's black now, the sun will rise. Always. No matter how faint the glow." He leaned in and kissed her brow. "I love you, Hana."

"I love you too, Yoshi," she whispered. "Don't ever leave me again."

"I'll try my best."

"You promise?"

"Doubtless."

He kissed her brow again, gentle as feathers.

"Go to sleep."

And into the dark, she fell.

Smooth, polished pine beneath her feet, singing in time with her tread. Drowning in the crushing dark before the dawn, sleep a thousand miles away, wandering aimless through the halls. Buruu's thoughts echoing in her own.

I KNOW WHAT YOU ARE THINKING.

Do you.

YOU CANNOT THINK I WOULD HELP YOU.

No. But I can make you. Whether you want to or not.

YOU CAN. BUT YOU WON'T.

What choice do I have, Buruu? Can I ask Yoshi or Hana to give up their lives?

YOU DO NOT HAVE TO ASK. BOTH WOULD BE WILLING.

Yoshi doesn't seem the heroic sort.

THOSE HEROES ARE THE GREATEST KIND.

Hana has lost too much. We can't take her brother away too.

SHE WOULD GLADLY GIVE HERSELF.

She's heartsick over Akihito. She doesn't know what she's saying.

AND YOU DO?

I started this war. I should finish it.

AND WHAT OF YOUR CHILDREN? THE ONES INSIDE YOU?

What of the thousands of children who will die if the Endsinger rises?

YOU WILL FIND NOT ONE THUNDER TIGER TO BEAR YOU TO THE HELLGATE.

Sukaa would carry me gladly.

HIS KHAN WILL FORBID IT.

We must close the gate. One of us must die, or this whole country dies instead.

IT WILL NOT BE YOU.

Buruu, I—

IT WILL NOT BE YOU.

Yukiko winced, hand to brow, the force of Buruu's thoughts overcoming her wall. Thunder rolled inside her mind, the fury and heat of a lightning barrage, strobing bright as he shut himself off; a sullen, seething fury pushing her out into the cold.

She closed it off, everything, stepping out of the Kenning and into herself. And there she stood in the empty hallway, struggling just to breathe.

Gods, how did it come to this?

A servant shuffled past carrying an apology and an armful of bloodstained linen. Looking up, she realized she'd wandered to the makeshift infirmary. It stretched the entire western wing of the palace, filled with the wounded and dying. Gaijin. Guildsmen. Kitsune. And reaching out into the Kenning, feeling room to room through the hundreds of pain-stricken lives, she found him, stirring in fitful sleep, his mind haunted by a familiar, terrifying dream.

Lashes fluttering against her cheeks, she walked toward the sound of his thoughts.

H*e held his arms wide, fingertips spread, the lights of their eyes glinting on the edges of his skin. The gunmetal gray filigree embossed upon his fingertips, the cuffs of his gauntlets, the edges of his spaulders. A new skin for his flesh; the skin*

of rank, of privilege and authority. Everything they had promised, everything he
had feared had come to pass. It was True.

This was Truth.

They called his name, the assembled Shatei, holding their hands aloft. And
even as he drew breath to speak, the words rang in his head like a funeral song, and
he felt whatever was left of his soul slipping up and away into the dark.

"Do not call me Kin. That is not my name."

In the dream, he felt his lips curl into a smile.

"Call me First Bloom."

Kin awoke with a start, eyes wide, groaning as the pain took hold. He considered calling out to the guards on his door, demanding more opiates to numb it. But the drugs made him sleep, and sleep meant the dream, louder and more insistent than ever before.

"That's what you see every night . . ."

He opened his eyes again, saw Yukiko beside him, hair framing her face and draped across her shoulders like a wave of black velvet. His pulse quickened, tongue cleaving to the roof of his mouth. And then he looked lower, to the small swelling beneath her kimono, cold rising to still the lurch of his heart, twisting and tearing it wide open.

"That was the future you'd never speak of," she said. "Your What Will Be."

He frowned. "You can see my dreams?"

"If I try hard enough. I can see the thoughts of everyone in this palace."

"A wondrous gift."

"To some."

"A shame you didn't use it before you tried to kill me."

"I'm sorry, Kin. I thought—"

"Don't," he sighed. "Don't make excuses. At every turn, you've thought the worst of me."

"Gods, can you blame me? You fooled *everyone*, Kin. People who've known you your entire life. How can you hold it against me that I believed you too?"

"Because I promised I would never betray you."

"I know." She knelt beside him. "And I'm sorry. I swear I'll never doubt you again."

"Even when my dreams show you I will one day lead the Guild?"

She reached out, brushing his bandaged fingertips. "I *swear it*, Kin."

"No one can stop What Will Be, Yukiko."

"You will," she insisted. "You won't *let* it be. I believe in you."

"Gods, I wish I understood you." He blinked at the ceiling. "I wish I could see inside your head the way you see in mine."

"Be careful what you wish for."

He glanced at her stomach, then to her eyes. She met his stare, unashamed and unafraid.

". . . Ask me. I know you want to. I can feel it."

"It's none of my business."

"I thought I loved him."

"You don't owe me explanations, Yukiko."

"You said you loved me once."

He said nothing. Felt nothing. Nothing at all.

"You don't feel that way anymore?" Yukiko asked.

". . . Do you care?"

"Of *course* I care . . ."

Kin sighed, ran a hand over his stubbled scalp. "General Ginjiro came to me earlier. He told me you want us to march south and detonate the Earthcrusher. Incinerate the demons already born from the hellgate."

"What does—"

"I already agreed to help. You don't need to maneuver me onto your side. You don't need to pretend."

She shrank back as if he'd raised a hand to strike her. ". . . You think I'd do that?"

"Honestly?" He met her horrified stare. "I don't know what you'd do. I don't know what you're thinking. I don't know you, Yukiko. And it's obvious you don't know me, either. So I don't know why every time I close my eyes I see you there. But still, I do."

"So you *do* love me. Still."

He looked down at his bandaged hands, licking at cracked lips. "I think I love the *idea* of you. The thing you represent. The life I could never have. The person I could never be."

". . . And that's all?"

"I don't know." His gaze roamed her face. "I don't know."

"I know when I thought you'd gone back to the Guild, it felt like someone had cut my heart out." Her voice was small in the dark, as if a weight crushed the breath from her chest. "I know you risked everything for us. I know you're the most courageous person I've met. I know there is a strength in you that puts me to shame. I know you make ten of me."

She touched a patch of bare skin on his arm, the brush of her fingertips bringing up goose bumps on his flesh.

"I know I'm sorry we left things . . . the way we did."

He looked up into her eyes, wide and hopeful.

"I know I missed you," she whispered.

He looked at her fingertips, the static electricity crackling between her flesh and his. The pain of his burns a distant memory. The pain in his chest too real to believe.

"I don't know how all this is going to end, Kin. I know I'm not the person you wanted me to be. I know I made mistakes. But they're *my* mistakes. I chose them. I own them. But I know I don't want to add to them by leaving us like this. Because if I did, I know I'd never forgive myself. I've lost enough today. Enough in the telling of this story. I can't lose you too."

It seemed an age passed, there in the guttering light, as the wind sang in the rafters and the black snow danced in the clouds above. The weight of yesterday and the threat of tomorrow and tomorrow and tomorrow, and the clutch of his chest and the tightness in his throat and the thought that all of it might be over soon— that they both could be skirting the edge of their last dawn, discolored by the anger and disappointment and pain of it all. But he looked up, and there she was, in full and blinding color. This girl who'd been just a dream—the promise of a life he could never live. But beneath that impossible, shattered facade, there she was still, pale as Iishi snow and stronger than folded steel, standing tall no matter how small she felt inside. Beautiful and frail and flawed and perfect. And just a heartbeat away.

His hand found hers; a feather-light touch of his fingers on her skin.

"I missed you too," he said.

Her eyes flooded with tears and she bowed her head, waves of raven black spilling forward to cover her face. Her hand was trembling, and he squeezed it tight, heedless of the pain.

"Don't cry," he pleaded. "Don't cry, Yukiko."

"Will you do something for me?" she whispered.

"Anything."

"Will you hold me?"

". . . I'd like that."

She crawled onto the bed, careful of his injuries, resting her head against his shoulder. The burns on his arms, the torn cable plugs in his chest, the iron-thrower wound in his thigh, all of it faded away as he lifted his hand, smoothed her hair from her face, closing his eyes.

"Would you do something for me?" he asked.

"Anything."

"Wake me up. If I start to dream."

"What if you dream of this? Of us?"

"I won't. I never do."

"Maybe one day?"

"One day."

She sighed from the depths of her, her tension melting in his arms. He lay there, listening to her breathing slow, her body against him, his arms around her. Leaning down, he kissed her brow; a long, silent moment, skin to skin, eyes closed, breathing her in.

She sighed, the shadow of a smile on her lips, pressing tighter against him.

"I love you, Yukiko," he whispered in the dark.

And in the dark, she whispered back.

"I love you too."

H*ow do, Mockingbird?*

Buruu sat perched on the rooftop of the Kitsune fortress, staring over the ruined city. He'd heard the boy climbing up, swift and sure, now crouching on the eave beside him. A thin carrion bird, looking over the leavings of a day's war. The wind was a howling, open mouth, teeth of frost, and the boy pulled his cloak tighter, eyes narrowed against the chill.

COLD OUT HERE, MONKEY-CHILD. YOU WILL CATCH YOUR DEATH.

Only if I chase it.

Buruu rested his head on his forelegs, sighed deep. The remainder of his pack were scattered across the rooftops, Shai curled up against a chimney close by. The snores and fitful growls of the few remaining bucks shivered the cedarwood tiles beneath them.

HOW IS YOUR SISTER?

Bleeding. Real bad. Yours?

He could feel her in the distance, asleep in Kin's arms. The thought filled him with a smile, momentarily banishing the dread he felt when he considered what lay before them.

SHE SLEEPS.

She still pondering her legendary charge? Down into the hellgate and whatever lies beyond? Fixing to be another story for the ages?

SHE WILL HAVE TROUBLE WITH THAT. UNLESS SHE GROWS WINGS.

Not keen on the idea of her ending?

TO FLY HER AND HER UNBORN CHILDREN INTO YOMI? AFTER ALL I HAVE BEEN THROUGH TO KEEP HER SAFE? YOU WOULD BE AS MAD AS THE ENDSINGER TO THINK IT SO, MONKEY-CHILD.

Yoshi nodded, spit through his teeth out into the darkness. They sat in silence for a few moments more, flakes of black snow curling in the air between them.

You were right, you know. What you said about revenge.

YOU KILLED THEM, THEN. YOUR FOES IN KIGEN.

Doubtless.

AND WHAT IS DIFFERENT?

Not a thing.

I TOLD YOU. ALL THINGS FADE WITH THE SEASONS. PAIN IS NO DIF-FERENT. ALL THINGS DIMINISH WITH TIME.

Time isn't something we have a barrel of anymore, Mockingbird.

WHY ARE YOU HERE, MONKEY-CHILD?

Need a ride.
WHERE?
Out to the deadlands.
WHY?
Test a theory.
WHAT THEORY?
Never tell a story when you can put on a show.
The boy stood with a lopsided smile, brushed his palms on his hakama legs.
Come on. Let's fly.

Yoshi slipped off Buruu's back, snow crunching as his boots hit earth. The stench of blood and iron hung thick in the air. The fires of the gaijin encampment were a flickering glow in the eastern foothills, distant drums underscoring the thunder's tune. Drawing close to the deadlands pit, Yoshi swore he could hear singing: a broken clockwork rhythm eating itself and spilling metal crumbs from a blacktooth grin. The stink of burned hair stabbed his nostrils, the oily haze hanging over the tortured earth barely rippling despite the howling gale.

PUT ON YOUR SHOW, THEN. AND LET US BE AWAY.

Yoshi pulled up his kerchief, wincing at the nagging ache of his severed ear.

Patience, Mockingbird. Not exactly sure how to play this tune.

WHY ARE WE HERE? WHAT IS YOUR MIND?

Purifiers in Kigen. They were burning folks at the Stones, even up until a few days ago. I don't know what forced them out of the chapterhouse, but they were conducting their purity testing in the open. Not exactly in plain sight, mind, but I had eyes to see it.

AND WHAT DID THEY TEST?

Yoshi pulled his cloak around him, shoulders hunched against the wind.

Some old fellow. Bled him and dripped the gravy into an iron box.

WHAT WAS INSIDE IT?

Yoshi nodded to the deadlands.

Looked like ashes. Except when this old fellow got bled on them, the ashes popped their cork. All violent, like. Split the box apart. And what I saw spilling out wasn't ashes anymore.

I AM WEARY OF BEING THE AUDIENCE IN YOUR SHOW. SPIT IT OUT, BOY.

It was dirt. Just regular dirt.

Yoshi spit into the deadlands, watching the fumes roll and eddy like a full moon tide.

Got me to thinking. The Guild is run by the Inquisition. They set the policy on yōkai-kin, order the Purifiers to burn folk with the Kenning. But they're also the ones trying to split the island down to the Hells. So what if those purposes dance hand in hand? What if this vendetta against "impurity" was just a grift to stitch the only folks who could stop them for real?

Buruu watched the boy, eyes narrowed, saying nothing.

You heard of Tora Takehiko?

A STORMDANCER.

That's right. Flew inside the hellgate during the last war, sealed it closed.

AND?

Doesn't it make sense every stormdancer had the Kenning? How else could they tame thunder tigers? Ride them to war?

SO?

So watch.

Yoshi reached to his hip, to a tantō he'd lifted from one of the bushimen. He drew the blade, gleaming with the distant city flames, then glanced at Buruu.

Best to step back. Not sure how impressive this is going to be.

The thunder tiger growled, stood his ground. With a small smirk, Yoshi pressed the knife to his forefinger, a few drops of blood pearling on the blade's edge. And running his hand over the stubble on his scalp, he lifted the tantō and flicked the scarlet into the wind.

The blood glittered as it fell, a dark, somber red in the bitter night. It sailed five or six feet, fell through the fumes hanging above the scar and hit the ashen earth.

Nothing.

Yoshi scowled, praying under his breath.

YOUR SHOWMANSHIP NEEDS—

White noise.

That same inversion of sound, as if someone had reached inside his skull and turned it inside out. Yoshi put his hand up to what was left of his ear, gasped, the thunder tiger staggering as if someone had king-hit him. Yoshi felt a fist in his stomach, spitting breath, the stink of char and ash on the back of his tongue. Blinking hard. Shaking.

The earth trembled; a tiny earthquake for his feet only. And with that same utterance that was not so much a sound as an *absence* of it, the deadlands exploded.

Not enough to split the island apart to be sure, but enough to knock him off his feet, send him sailing back into Buruu, colliding with the arashitora's broad chest and tumbling earthward in a knotted heap. White smoke snaked up from the deadlands, filling his lungs with that same momentary sweetness—as if the spring breeze were reborn in winter's depths. Black fumes peeled away, a rumbling seeping from ashen earth. Yoshi staggered to his feet, a soft growl uncurling in Buruu's throat.

The pair stood awestruck, mouths agape as they stared at the deadlands. A circle of good, dark earth lay where once there had been only smoking, scarred soil. An impact crater, ten feet in diameter, forged by a single drop of Yoshi's blood.

IT IS TRUE.

The boy nodded.

The Way of Purity. The Burning Stones. All of it created to wipe out the blood of yōkai—the one weapon we can use to alley-fuck the Serpent's soiree.

MAKER BE PRAISED.

Not ready to praise him just yet. But I might stop swearing about his balls for a while.

Buruu blinked, the frost wind ruffling feathers at his brow. He tilted his head, looked the boy up and down, understanding dawning in his mind.

THEN TORA TAKEHIKO . . .

Now you're starting to see, Mockingbird.

Buruu looked back at the distant lights of Yama city. The thousands of lives within those walls, his Yukiko and her unborn babes among them.

NOW I SEE.

Yoshi stared back at the deadlands scar, licked the ashes from his lips and spit.

Doubtless.

P atient as cats and quiet as mice, he waited in the dark for his mistress to return.

Curled up in the blankets, still rich with her scent. His belly was growling, his bowl was empty. But he knew if he waited long enough, and quiet enough, she would come. She liked it when he was quiet. When she knelt by the wooden thing that was not a tree, and put black marks on the flat thing that smelled like rice but was not food. He didn't understand it. But he understood she liked quiet. So he stayed quiet and waited. Hoping she'd come soon.

He heard footsteps outside her door. Too heavy to be hers. But still, it was *some-one*, and he'd waited in the dark and the quiet for so long. So he pounced from beneath the blankets and ran to the doorway, dancing in delighted little circles as it was dragged wide. And he stared up at the man who was not his mistress, and growled with his little puppy voice.

The man was big. A beard like a bush. He'd been here this morning, had taken his mistress away. And Tomo growled, unsure of himself, but knowing all gooddogs growled at strangers. But then the man knelt and scruffed his ears, and made sounds that were not speakings in a soft voice, and Tomo flopped onto his belly and allowed the big man to scratch him, his little legs kicking as the man found the spot he liked best, right under his left shoulder.

The big man stood finally, and Tomo rolled over, walked with him toward the wooden thing that was not a tree, tail wagging, because the big man was carrying a flat white thing that smelled like fish, and fish was his favorite. The big man put the white round thing down on the floor and yes, it *did* have fish, and Tomo scoffed it down as quick as he could, licking the top and sniffing beneath in case more was hidden underneath (there was never any hidden underneath).

The big man knelt and made fire on the burning things, which made the light by which his mistress used to see. And Tomo watched the big man unroll the flat thing that smelled like rice (but wasn't) on top of the thing that was not a tree (though Tomo had used it like a tree once and his mistress had been very cross), and he picked up the thing that made the marks and dipped it in the black water that was not water (it did not taste good *at all*) and he heaved a sigh louder than the wind.

Tomo watched, one ear cocked, head tilted.

The man began making marks. Many marks, on the thing that was not food.

Tomo looked to the door, hoping his mistress would come soon.

He climbed onto the bed where it was warm, and he watched the man making the marks and stopping occasionally to wipe at his eyes as if they hurt him. And he thought the big man was nice, and that the big man could watch for his mistress to come back (it must be soon) and so it wouldn't matter if Tomo closed his eyes for just a little while.

The puppy licked his lips (lovely fish) and snuggled down in the blankets.

He could hear the big man scratching with the thing that made the marks. It reminded him of the sound in his mistress's chest, her heart beating at night as he curled up beside her.

And hoping she'd come soon, the puppy closed his eyes and slept.

49
OR NOTHING AT ALL

The entire city seemed to wake before the sun.

Smithy fires burning bright, the chime of hammer upon iron and the burn of coal smoke. The Everstorm pack was outfitted with the same barding Kaiah wore, breastplates and helms with eyeholes of black glass. They soared above Yama, filling the dispirited populace with wonder. Yukiko rode at the lead, bringing supplies to the dispossessed, assuring all would be well. And if the people were shaken to their bones by the shifting of the world beneath their feet, they took some heart in her words, the Kitsune ink bared on her arm despite the freezing cold, this daughter of foxes who now carried the future of their nation in her hands.

The gaijin wounded were moved from the Kitsune fortress, ferried back to their people on the opposite shore of the Amatsu. Hana oversaw their deportation from astride Kaiah's back, ensuring neither side attempted violence. The wounded were met with fierce hugs from their countrymen, wondering stares at the girl and her thunder tiger. Hana's face was stone, her eye cold behind polarized glass, belying the heart bleeding within her chest.

Kaori spoke with the remaining Kagé, and Misaki of the rebellion. She oversaw funeral preparations for the slain Kagé—Michi, Akihito, and her father Daichi, along with the other brethren who had lost their lives. But in quiet moments, she sat in the garden, Piotr beside her, and the pair spoke of tiny unimportant things in the face of the chaos around them.

Things that sometimes made her smile.

The Blackbird sat in Michi's chambers, emerging only to make polite requests for food or drink. A puppy lurked at his heels, tail wagging constantly. The Blackbird's fingers were stained with ink. So were the puppy's ears.

The Earthcrusher crew were given their skins back, minus their mechabacii, and asked to muster in Chapterhouse Yama's ruins. Each was free to walk away if they wished. Only Kensai remained under guard, the self-proclaimed First Bloom locked in a guest room in Kitsune-jō.

And Yoshi.

Yoshi crouched on the rooftops, a bottle of expensive saké unopened beside him. Despite the motion all around, his stare was fixed on the dark gathered across the southern horizon.

His thoughts were of a beautiful boy, and simpler days.

His hands were fists.

P ain lancing his chest with every breath. Soft carpet beneath him, a bed with silk sheets—his one real indulgence. A cage with art on the wall, guards at his "guest room" door. The bayonet fixtures in his flesh like mouths, hungry for input. The silence in his head as black and terrifying as any he'd ever known.

Alone. For the first time in a long time.

Utterly alone.

"Uncle."

The voice pulled Kensai's eyes open, chased away the muddy dreams in his skull. No visions of greatness from his Awakening anymore. Confusing, twisted nonsense; a tumult underscored by a tuneless hymn, a horror too vast to look at with his mind's eye . . .

"Uncle."

Kensai wheezed, sat up in his bed. "I heard you, Kioshi-san."

". . . That is not my name."

Kensai peered at the boy in the doorway, thin and pale and blurred, eyes sunken in gray hollows. Wrapped in bandages, shoulders slumped, pupils dilated. If he did not know better . . .

"Forgive me, Kin-san. Old habits perish reluctantly. As do you, it seems."

"You keep calling me by my father's name."

"It is *your* name. Given when your father died. An honorable son—"

"Would wear it with pride. I know."

"But you are not an honorable son, are you? You are a cur who betrayed his family for the love of an impure whore. If Kioshi could see you now . . ."

"I did not come here to fight with you, Uncle."

"Why then? To caper? To crow?"

"To tell you the truth."

"You know not the meaning of the word."

"I know I warned you not to trust the Inquisition."

"You did come to gloat, then."

"The deadlands, Uncle. The deadlands we helped create. Planting lotus in every corner of this land. Poisoning the soil, splitting it wide. Watered with innocent blood. All part of the Inquisition's plan. First Bloom also. We were deceived, all of us."

"It is you who—"

"The Guild was founded by the survivors of the Serpent clan. All of us— you, me, the Inquisition—we are of Serpent blood. But only the inner circle knew the full truth. Did you not wonder why you were never brought fully into Tojo's trust?"

Kin shook his head, ran one bandaged hand over his eyes.

"They were disciples of Lady Izanami, Uncle. As our ancestors were. Determined to bring about the rise of the Endsinger and the death of this world."

"Are you crazed, boy?" Kensai spat. "Serpents and Dark Mothers?"

Kin turned, nodded to someone beyond the door. "Come in."

Two men with close-cropped hair and bayonet fixtures at their wrists entered the room, dragging a body between them. A third followed, carrying a stained hessian bag. The men lay the corpse on the carpet, placed the stained bag by the boy's feet. Each favored Kensai with a poisoned stare as they left.

The corpse was reasonably fresh, parts of it crushed to pulp. Kensai could see its skin was the gray of a smoke addict.

"You bring a lotusfiend's corpse in here to frighten me?" Kensai sniffed. "If this is a threat, it falls far short of the mark, boy."

Kin leaned down with a wince, tore the corpse's uwagi away. Kensai saw its chest was dotted with the bayonet fixtures for mechabacus input. Trailing down its battered right arm was a beautiful tattoo, coiled and deadly—a serpent inked into the gray chalk of its flesh.

"This is the corpse of an Inquisitor captured in the fall of Chapterhouse Yama. The Kitsune burned the corpses of two more after the schism. All marked with this same irezumi. Serpent clan. Servants of Lady Izanami. All of them, Uncle."

"One corpse does not a legion make."

Kin reached down to the hessian bag, upturned it with a flourish. A severed head rolled across the carpet, upside down and grinning. Skin of midnight blue, a serrated freakshow grin, rusted iron rings through its broad, flat nose and pointed ears. Kensai had seen the same visage on the faceguards of every Iron Samurai in the Shima legions. A demon of the deep hells.

"Oni . . ." he whispered.

"With the drama aboard the Earthcrusher, you would have missed it, but this monster crawled from the Kitsune deadlands, along with a dozen of its fellows. Each put down by the Impure whore you so despise. The cracks tore wide when First House exploded, the Stain tearing wider still. Only the gods know what crawls now from the pit."

Kensai stared at the demon's head, saying nothing.

"We have been raised on a lie, Uncle. Every moment of your life has been a *lie*. Purity. The Guild. Skin is strong, flesh is weak. All a ploy to bring the Endsinger back to Shima."

Kensai frowned, shaking his head. "My vision . . ."

"The What Will Be?" Kin sighed. "I don't know. I think there is a kind of truth to be found in the Chamber of Smoke. I think those who saw too far, who saw what would come at the end of all this—they were the ones who went mad during the Awakening. The ones the Inquisition would boil in the vats before they could speak of what they'd seen."

"This is not possible . . ."

"You heard Her, Uncle. I know you did. Shinji told me all about it. Echoing inside anyone who wore a mechabacus when the Yomi gate opened. She sang to you, didn't she? And now in the place where the dreams of your Awakening used to be, you can only hear Her."

Horror in his heart. In his eyes. Reflected in Kin's own.

"You were born to the lie, Uncle." The boy's eyes were pleading. "You can't blame yourself for believing. But now you have a chance to right the Guild's wrongs. Help me."

". . . Help you?" Kensai whispered.

"Repair the Earthcrusher. March south to fight the Yomi horde. Close the gate threatening to engulf the Seven Isles and everything on them."

Kensai stared down at his open hand, the bayonet fixture at his wrist, back up to the severed head and its sightless eyes. In the back of his skull, he could feel that tuneless rhythm, crawling in the place his dreams used to live. Cold lips brushing his skin.

He'd known.

Somehow he'd always known.

"Get out," he whispered.

"Uncle, help me. Help *yourself*—"

"*Get out!*" Kensai lunged from his bed, across those silken sheets, heedless of the pain. He collapsed to the floor, fingers twisted into claws, face contorted. Kin looked at him with pity and Kensai screamed, howling, a thing of wretched meat and feeble bones, longing to be encased inside a skin of cold metal. Impervious. Invisible. Hidden behind a perfection of molded brass, a beauty unmarred no matter how hideous the flesh beneath.

"Don't look at me like that!" he screamed.

"I'm sorry, Uncle," Kin murmured. "I'm so sorry."

Kensai curled into a ball to the tune of Kin's fading footsteps, clawing the bloody carpet. He couldn't breathe, couldn't see, the floor crumbling beneath his feet and letting him fall, down and down and down into a blackness bathed in the blood of thousands. Torn wide in the womb of the world, birthing monstrosities; a mouth that swallowed the feeble truths upon which his reality had been built, leaving him with a question to which he could find no answer.

"Who am I?"

D O YOU REMEMBER THE FIRST WORDS WE SPOKE?
     They were perched atop the walls of Kitsune-jō, surrounded by the Everstorm pack. Mercifully, the snow had stopped, toxic drifts lying four inches deep on the ground, covering the corpses littering Yama's streets. Hana was somewhere in the Kitsune library, searching for any record of Tora Takehiko and his exploits. Shai sat nearby, watching Yukiko, tail lashing side to side as if she were irritated. The girl ran her hands down Buruu's armor, working her fingers between the plates at the join of his shoulder and neck—his favorite spot.

Of course I remember, brother.

AND WHAT DID I SAY?

You asked who I was.

YOU TOLD ME YOU WERE YUKIKO.

It was all I could think of to say. I don't think I knew the answer to that question then. Didn't know who I was, or who I'd become.

BUT YOU KNOW NOW?

I know I'd be nothing without you, brother. I would be ashes and bones.

WHO WILL YOU BE THEN, WHEN I AM GONE?

Yukiko looked to Shai, watching with narrowed, amber eyes. She thought of the Everstorm, of the little bundle of feathers and claws waiting for Buruu—the son he'd flown with for that brief, blessed hour before returning to fight a war not of his making. She'd known this moment would come—that he would leave her one day, go back to the life he'd made, the family he'd built. She knew even if they somehow bested the Endsinger, they'd have to say good-bye.

I know it's not fair to ask you to stay. I know you have your pack to lead. Your family to raise. And I want you to be happy. But when you go back to Everstorm . . . you know it's going to break my heart, don't you?

The thunder tiger surveyed the ruined landscape, sigh rumbling in his chest.

YOURS NO MORE THAN MINE.

But you have to go.

THERE IS NO OTHER WAY.

I know it's true. But don't ask me not to weep when you leave. You mean every-thing to me, brother. You are my blood and my heart and I love you with all I have inside me.

AND I YOU.

She put her arms around his neck, rested her cheek against the steel he was encased in. This thing she'd turned him into. This weapon. And she knew in her heart she'd asked enough.

SO. WHO WILL YOU BE WHEN I AM GONE?

She sighed. Shook her head.

I don't know. A teacher? A leader? A mother? There will still be so much—

NO. NOT WHAT.

The arashitora shook his head.

WHO *WILL YOU BE?*

"Yukiko!"

A voice from below pulled her stare into the courtyard. She saw Ginjiro and a dozen Iron Samurai, thickets of bushimen gathering about them.

"General?"

"Word from Last Isle! The Tigers are gathering. They look to be preparing for an assault. Will you come with us?"

HIRO.

She pulled her goggles down over her eyes, called into the Kenning. Fierce cries split the air, the bucks and dams answering her call. Yukiko drew her katana, folded steel ringing bright against its scabbard. Eyes fixed on the blade, she nod-ded to Ginjiro.

"Lead on. We will follow."

Kitsune troops were stationed at the two bridges leading from Last Isle. Yukiko and the Everstorm pack flew above, wheeling and diving; a picture of majesty Kitsune historians would speak of for centuries. The day the storm-dancers came to Yama.

Tora troops gathered on the other side of the river; row upon row of bushi-men, banner-bearers, a few Iron Samurai in bone-white armor. The tiger standards were brilliant red—the red of blood. The blood spilled repelling the Tora assault.

The blood Kitsune must spill again in futile combat against their own cousins, while the true threat swelled to the south.

The thought boiled in Yukiko's veins, jaw clenched as she listened to the field commanders briefing General Ginjiro. The Tora numbered near one thousand, but the bridges would bottleneck their charge. The Kitsune shuriken-throwers would cut them down like lotus fronds as they streamed across—it seemed the Tigers wished for one last, suicidal battle to bring some measure of glory to their doomed endeavor.

"The Tora have few sky-ships, General," Yukiko said. "Their air support will not last a moment against a pack of thunder tigers. Save your men. We'll deal with the Tora."

The Tiger troops parted like water, a retinue of Kazumitsu Elite stomping to the edge of the bridge. Buruu growled, a long rumbling note of hatred that set his armor squealing. Yukiko saw Hiro at the forefront, skin painted with ashes. His sword knot was still tied, his men carrying the white flag of parlay.

"Who is he?" Ginjiro asked.

"Tora Hiro, Daimyo of the Tiger zaibatsu," Yukiko spat. "Not a man in this city is more deserving of a wretched end. If you'll excuse us for a minute, we'll go give it to him."

"Puppet he may be, but he is still a Daimyo. I will obey the forms of Bushido. I will hear his words."

Ginjiro nodded to his retinue, walked to the opposite end of the bridge, surrounded on all sides by Iron Samurai. Yukiko rode beside him on Buruu's back, the air around them crackling with static electricity. She stared at Hiro across the bare expanse of snowcapped stone, the wind between them mournful and hungry.

"Kitsune Ginjiro," Hiro said, covering his fist.

"Tora Hiro." The general bowed. "It pleases me to put face to reputation."

"Rumor has it you intend to march south to confront the Yomi legions spilling from the ruins of First House."

"You hear much from your cage, Hiro-san. My compliments. But you speak true. When you and your men are stains upon the stone at my feet, we will turn south and face the true enemy, still marveling at your folly."

Hiro glanced at Yukiko, his face a mask, one hand on the hilt of his chain-katana. "Forgiveness, General, but we do not wish to fight against you. We wish to march beside you."

Buruu's claws cracked the flagstones to rubble, the packmates soaring overhead bringing the thunder with their wings.

"You're a godsdamned liar, Hiro," Yukiko spat. "You murdered Michi, along with a thousand other Kitsune warriors. And if not for the deeds of a brave few, most of whom are dead now, you'd be toasting this city's conquest with the skulls of the dead."

"Yukiko." Hiro looked at her, those perilous green eyes hard and cool. "For once, this is not about you and me."

Thunder rolled overhead, fanged winds chewing at the gulf between them. Yukiko grit her teeth, hands in fists. Tempted to just reach in and *squeeze* . . .

"What you said on the *Death* . . ." He looked around at the ruins he'd made. "You were right, Yukiko. I came to this city to die. I gave no thought for afterwards. All I wanted was to feel clean again. But I was blind. All of us, blind. To the world we built and the monsters we served. And She rises, or so we hear. The Mother of Demons, spoken of in the *Book of Ten Thousand Days*. And if the code we followed and the lives we lived led us here, to this place, where the Hells themselves have opened, then what good was any of it? The code? Our lives?"

"Who told you about the Endsinger?" Yukiko said. "That She rises?"

"I did."

Yukiko turned, saw Kaori step from the Fox soldiers, black swathed, pale skin.

"Forgive me, sister, but you said yourself we must put aside the past. We are stronger with the Tora than without them. And we will need all our strength in the days ahead."

Hiro nodded. "In the *Book of Ten Thousand Days*, the people pray to the Heavens to save them. But I think it within us to save ourselves."

"So now you command your men to fight beside us?" Yukiko growled. "Where once you'd have gladly slaughtered us?"

"I command nothing," Hiro said. "Each man behind me was presented with the choice. Each has chosen to fight. As I have chosen. For the future of this nation."

"You cared nothing for the future yesterday."

His eyes betrayed him; a quick glance to her belly then back to her face.

"Yesterday, I had no stake in it."

Hiro walked across the bridge until he stood face-to-face with Yukiko and Buruu. And there, he drew his chainkatana, and with obvious difficulty, lifted his left hand from its sling and sliced his palm. He offered it to Yukiko, blood spattering onto the stone in tiny, steaming droplets.

She blinked. Searched his face. Finally spoke.

"Nothing has changed. Nothing is different between us. You must know that."

"I know it. But I know they will grow in the world I help create. Even if they never know my name, I'll know I gave all I had to ensure the sun rises for them tomorrow. That is a cause worth fighting for."

She stood for an age. Empty winds howling between them. Miles and lifetimes. And finally, she drew the blade her father gave her and opened her palm, and took his outstretched hand in hers.

"Something worth fighting for," she said.

Hiro glanced down to the blood between them. Up into her eyes.

"To the end."

W hat Will Be, Will Be.
       Kin stood in the antechamber, listening to distant engines and the hiss of smelters, that single thought floating through the haze in his head. The chapterhouse around him felt semiconscious, echoing with distant sounds of life, too sparse to mimic the bustling, thrumming atmosphere of the house he'd grown up in. The rebels had restarted the machine-works yesterday evening, a skeleton crew cobbling together components under Shinji's instruction, hastily drawn plans of the Earthcrusher's innards spread upon the walls and floors.

Shinji entered the room now, his new atmos-suit gleaming in the dim light. Watching Kin pace back and forth, clenching and unclenching his fists.

"Nervous?"

Kin shrugged, said nothing. His burns were a strangled ache beneath an opiate glow, and the atmos-suit felt heavier than any he'd worn in his life. His head was full of black velvet, smothering his thoughts along with his pain, the taste of dead flowers on his tongue.

"Are you well?" Shinji asked. "Does the new skin not fit? We can have—"

"It fits well enough."

His voice echoed as if it came from far away. He looked at the gunmetal gray flourishes at his gauntlets and spaulders, chilled fingers of déjà vu caressing his spine.

"Although I wish you'd found something less ostentatious."

"It's a Kyodai's suit. Most of those gathered out there are just regular Shatei. You were a Fifth Bloom, the son of an honored line. With First Bloom dead, they will look to the Big Brothers for leadership."

"Will they see me as brother? Or the traitor who laid Earthcrusher low?"

"It was you who unplugged them from their mechabacii, Kin. You who freed them from that nightmare song. If that doesn't warrant a moment's consideration, nothing will."

Kin gnawed his lip, longing to rub his eyes. A question rolled behind his teeth; improper, dangerous even. Though he'd been through fire and blood with Shinji, he was still uncertain if he should give it voice . . .

"What did you see, Shinji? On the night of your Awakening?"

The boy tilted his head, breathing slow. A minute passed, the hollow spaces between one breath and another laden with the memory haunting his every—

"A tangle," the boy shrugged. "A baby made of iron twisting on its back. White noise. Green fields. Nothing I could make much sense of. The Inquisitor who guided me seemed content, but I was disappointed. I'd heard the most blessed Guildsmen saw their What Will Be clear as day when they Awoke. Reliving the greatest moment of their lives, over and over. Before I had my eyes opened to the Guild's hypocrisy, the whole thing sounded rather glorious."

"It isn't."

"Why do you ask, Kin-san? What did you see?"

"This moment. This place. What lies at the end of this corridor. I'm sure of it."

". . . This is your What Will Be?"

Kin nodded.

"I don't want this," he sighed. "I've never wanted it. And now I'm here, standing on the brink, I have no idea what I'll say."

"Maybe you should try the truth. Hells know it would make a welcome change."

"And why will they listen?"

"Do they listen in your dreams?"

Kin said nothing, staring at the traceries of black and warmth behind closed eyelids.

Shinji patted his arm. "Come. They await. If this is your What Will Be, there is no escaping it. Best look it in the eye as it comes for you, then kick it in the balls."

Kin drew a ragged breath, nodded, sick to his stomach. The boys clomped from the antechamber, down a corridor of pus-yellow stone, machine-song thrumming in Kin's bones. Cold sweat lit fires across his burns, his skin weighing heavy as he stepped onto the gantry.

Sparks and fire, groaning iron and glittering brass. They gathered below, an ocean of skins; every Guildsman who'd served on the Earthcrusher or the Tora Fleet, every rebel who'd survived the Yama insurrection. More than a hundred— Artificers and False-Lifers and Lotusmen. All staring with their faceless faces, eyes burning like funeral candles in the dark.

Misaki stood on the gantry, spider limbs swaying like feathers in the breeze. She nodded to Kin, descended with Shinji, down onto the machine room floor, leaving him alone beneath those glittering, blood-red stares. The air crackled with expectation, fear, anger, bringing the taste of battery acid to the tip of his tongue, the contents of his stomach to the back of his throat. He tried to keep the tremors from his voice as he spoke.

"Brothers and sisters of the Lotus Guild. Brother Shinji bids me speak the truth here tonight. But instead I think I should speak of lies. The lie to which we were born, taught before we could crawl. The lie we swallowed and regurgitated and perpetuated every day. Blinded to others' suffering behind eyes of red glass. Shielded from their agonies by suits of clockwork brass. The lie that skin is strong, and flesh is weak."

Kin plucked at the metal he was encased in, fingertips ringing on the brass.

"I challenge you to look outside these walls and find weakness in the skinless of this city. In the men who stood tall as the shreddermen charged their lines, who fell burning from the sky as the Tora fleet ripped them to shreds, or sacrificed their lives to slow the Earthcrusher's march. Who mourn their loved ones, even as they prepare to march south and face the darkness growing there by the moment. You show me weakness in that flesh. You show me strength in the ones who brought this nation to the edge of ruin."

Uneasy murmurs floated in the darkness below, echoing on walls of stone.

"We have been lied to. By our leaders. By the Inquisition. By those who'd see the Endsinger rise, and all this world come to nothing. But more than that, we lied to ourselves. Placing the Guild above the people. The notion of Purity above the lives of innocent children. The lotus harvest above the blood of the gaijin. All of us are stained. I don't know if that stain will ever wash away. I don't know if they can ever forgive us for what we've done.

"But I know this: I know we have a chance to make a difference now. To take the Earthcrusher south with the Kitsune and the stormdancers, and send those demons back to the Hells. We owe it to the skinless. But more, we owe it to ourselves. We owe ourselves the truth: that we are no better than any outside these walls. That the suffering in Shima and Morcheba is a suffering of our creation. That we were wrong, and that we have to help make it right.

"You are my blood. We were raised to see each other as brothers and sisters. But we are also kin to the men and women outside these walls. And I ask you now, as your brother, to help me. To believe something good can come of all this, and fight to make it so."

A hollow silence filled the machine room, the groan of engines and metal mouths the only sound. Finally, a lone voice rang out in the gloom, echoing from one corner to the next.

"And you will lead us?" Commander Rei cried. "You who betrayed us?"

"The First Bloom is dead!" cried another. "All we know is dead!"

A murmur spread amongst the throng; ripples on molten brass.

Shinji turned to the crowd, his voice rising above the whispers.

"Who would you have lead you?" he cried. "Who saved you? Who had eyes to see the truth, and the will to stand for what was right? Who laid the Earthcrusher low? Who saved you from madness? There is only one, and you know his name!" Shinji pointed aloft. "Kin-san!"

The words spread like fire on wet tinder—spitting and smoking at first, finally unfolding into bright flame. He heard them calling his name as they always did. As they always had. This cup before him, this choice he'd vowed never to choose. He didn't want it—had never wanted it. He wanted them to stand on their own feet, speak with their own voices. They'd lived so long without faces or identities of their own, they couldn't see the freedom just a breath away.

"Kin-san!" they called. "Kin-san!"

He looked down over the railing, destiny unfolding, life unraveling one thread at a time.

All of it. Again.

And again.

And *again*.

Hundreds of eyes, red as sunset, staring up at him with as much adoration as glass could muster. A sea of brass faces, stretching into dark corners, smooth and featureless. Walls of stone, dripping wet, the songs of engine and piston and gears blurring into a monotone hum, a broken-clock rhythm that seeded at the base of his skull and sent out roots to claw the backs of his eyes.

As if remembering the steps of some forgotten dance, he held his arms wide, fingertips spread, the lights of their eyes glinting on the edges of his skin. He stared at the gunmetal gray filigree embossed upon his fingertips, the cuffs of his gauntlets, the edges of his spaulders. The skin of rank, of privilege and authority. Everything they had promised, everything he had feared had come to pass. It was True.

This was Truth.

They called his name, the assembled Shatei, holding their hands aloft. And even as he drew breath to speak, the words rang in his head like a funeral song, and he felt whatever was left of his soul slipping up and away into the dark.

The multitude below fell silent. He looked down at the scarlet pinpricks in the dark, swaying and flickering like fireflies on a winter breeze. His voice was a fierce cry, hollow and metallic behind the brass covering his lips.

"Do not call me Kin. That is not my name."

He felt his lips curl into a smile.

"Call me First Bloom."

A cheer echoed in the dark, spilling from brass lips and iron lungs, an awful, shapeless roar that turned his insides upside down. He cut it off with a wave of his hand, voice ringing over the silence falling like a hammer. The smile grew wider, heart racing as he scrambled toward the light, the way out he could see, the final truth he'd always meant to speak in this waking dream.

He tore at the clasps about his neck, pulling off his helm and hurling it away. He could taste old chi and blood in the air, iron heavy on his tongue. He could hear the gasps below, the astonishment at seeing naked flesh beneath a brother's skin.

"I am First Bloom, and this is my first and final command." He looked among the multitude, his truth singing in his veins. "The Lotus Guild is ended. Disbanded. Forever. No more sealing ourselves off in suits of brass. No more filling the skies with poison, the rivers with tar, the earth with ashes. We will be *part* of this world. Not above it. Not outside it.

"No more Shatei. No more Blooms. No more Artificers or Lotusmen or Purifiers. Simply brothers and sisters. Orphans, all. United in fleeting grief at the death of our past, and hope at the birth of our future."

The crowd hung motionless, petrified, the air crackling with electricity. Kin limped down the spiral stairwell, onto the machine room floor. He walked over to Shinji, Misaki beside him. He looked at them both, pleading, sweat burning the corners of his eyes.

"My name *is* Kin. Call me that, or brother, or nothing at all."

Shinji looked to Misaki, clawed suddenly at the seals at his throat, compressed air escaping with a high-pitched sigh. He pulled the helm from his head, throwing it to the ground with a sharp bang. And grasping Kin's hand, he nodded, pulling him into a fierce embrace.

"My name is Shinji," he said. "Call me that, or brother, or nothing at all."

Misaki was clawing at her face, tearing the membrane from her head, the light of her eyes dying in a pale burst of sparks. She turned to the crowd around her, offered her hand to a Lotusman beside her, searching that featureless mask with desperate, breathless hope.

"My name is Misaki. Call me that, or sister, or nothing at all."

The Lotusman stood rooted to the spot, looking among his fellows, back and forth across that sea of faceless faces. Every bellows fell still, every heart catching in every chest, time itself slowing to a crawl and treading upon tiptoe for fear of it all. The air was smoke and cinder, iron and chi and blood, humming with possibility. And slowly, deliberately, the Lotusman popped the seals at his throat, lifting his helm away with both hands.

The flesh beneath was middle-aged, creased with time, thinning gray hair sheared to a shadow on his skull. His eyes were crouched in gray hollows and rimmed with tears.

"I have carried my father's name for thirty years," he said. "I have served this Guild longer still. It is all I have ever known. That skin is strong and flesh is weak."

He looked down at his open palm, ensconced in leather and brass. And as the entire room watched in silence, the old man took Misaki's hand, a trembling smile on his face.

"But I was born Shoujou. Call me that, or brother, or nothing at all."

H e'd thought him asleep at first.

Lying in his bed, head drooping slightly to one side. Kin had returned from the chapterhouse, so buoyed by elation that even the rising pain of his burns and the hole in his thigh barely slowed his step. His head still rang with names, unmasked faces, the hope and fear burning behind their eyes. He'd left Shinji to oversee work on the Earthcrusher, returning to the guest wing of Kitsune-jō. Ready to plead. To argue. To scream if need be.

"Uncle," he said. "Wake up."

He walked into the room, sitting beside him on the bed. It was then he noticed the faint stain seeping slowly through the sheets, peeling them back to find Kensai's open wrists, a bloody knife, mattress soaked in scarlet.

"Uncle!"

Kin clutched the slashed wrists, roared for the guards, blood on his hands. Soldiers arrived, cursing, pushing Kin aside and trying to staunch the nonexistent flow. Kin backed into the corner, staring at the red across his palms, blinking mutely as the guards pounded on Kensai's chest, trying to resuscitate the fallen Second Bloom.

"You're too late," he said.

Shaking his head. Tears in his eyes.

"Too late."

50
THE VICIOUS HORIZON

Sky-ships cresting a swell of black snow, exhaust trails misting the skies above a city all but reduced to a catacomb. Sigils of the Lotus Guild, of Fox and Tiger, joined now by the remnants of the Phoenix fleet—the three remaining zaibatsu of the Shima Imperium united in a final desperate throw of the bones. One Dragon ship among them all, her captain striding her decks with ink-stained hands, a promise to a dead girl fresh on his lips.

Lines of troops, the light of a choking dawn refracting on enameled iron and folded steel. Clanking shreddermen towering above the infantry, battle-scarred and smoking, legs pounding with a wardrum rhythm as the Shiman army marched from Yama's gates.

The skies around the fleet were filled with talons and feathers and rolling thunder, the arashitora pack weaving amongst ironclads and corvettes. Black and white, male and female, sleek and beautiful. Three stormdancers riding at their head: Yukiko upon Buruu, katana in hand, clad in freezing iron and black cloth; Hana astride Kaiah, unruly blond locks tousled about her eye, a chainkatana at her waist and a prayer in her heart; Yoshi last of all, clinging to Shai like a waterlogged rat to a piece of driftwood. Refusing to look down.

And behind them all, lumbering with all the grace of a headless drunkard, the Earthcrusher marched. Shaking the ground with every step, splitting flagstones to the core, shells of fire-gutted houses collapsing to rubble around it. The behemoth was dented and scorched, its engines skipping and clunking. But still it came, held together by will and belief, its innards crawling with men and women who now called each by true names. A young man sat in its pilot's harness, inside a metal skin that felt nothing like his own, mind smudged with pain and pain-lessness, staring out through the cracked portals of the Earthcrusher's eyes.

South.

To the swelling black.

To the vicious horizon.

DOOMDOOMDOOMDOOM

DOOMDOOMDOOMDOOM

Across the river, an army awaited. Twelve standards raised in the bitter-black wind, swathed in frost. Twelve houses assembled on the Kitsune plains, grim and proud. Goddess-sworn, children of a war decades long, a mandate of bloody ven-geance clad in skins of wolf and bear. Ghost-pale skin and cobalt-blue eyes, stained and scarred by black rains.

Facing south.

The Stormdancer called a halt at the newly-repaired Amatsu bridge, her army poised before the gaijin's backs. She did not dare hope.

Yet still she prayed.

Yoshi felt Yukiko's voice echoing in his head, felt her strength reverberating in the Kenning, the heat behind her eyes and swelling at her belly. The girl reached out into the minds of the others: Hana and Kaiah and Sukaa and Shai and Buruu, forming a bridge between them all—a hub through which each could speak and feel and know. Yoshi winced as he felt the thoughts of the other thun-der tigers, Yukiko's own blazing psyche, a headache digging in at the base of his skull. He wiped one hand across his nose, blood smeared on his knuckles.

"*Be ready for anything. We've suffered dearly for trusting gaijin in the past.*"

Buruu growled across the latticework of their thoughts.

IF THEIR PLAN IS TREACHERY, THEY WILL COME TO RUE IT.

I can see Uncle Aleksandar, Hana nodded. *But not Sister Katya.*

Kaiah growled, her eyes narrowed.

- WOULD THEY BETRAY? AFTER WE RETURNED THEIR WOUNDED? -

"*I don't know,*" Yukiko replied. "*But expect no less.*"

Yoshi sniffed hard, hawked phlegm and blood past Shai's wing.

Seems sensible keeping Yukiko and Buruu up here, out of harm's way. Hana and I can go make with the talking. I've a notion to meet this uncle of mine.

"No Yoshi, we go tog—"

I AGREE.

Shai growled over the fading echo of Buruu's interruption.

AS DO I.

Yoshi smiled across the snow-filled skies at Yukiko, tipped the brim of an imaginary hat.

No sense risking all of us, Stormgirl. On the chance it does throw down, best if our ace in the Endsinger's hole stays out of bowshot. We'll return presently.

Yukiko bit down on her reply as Hana and Yoshi swooped away, circling down in a gentle spiral toward the assembled horde. The Morchebans had cleared a wide space around their commander, standing tall in his black wolfskin, staring south. He glanced back only as Kaiah and Shai came in to land. Yoshi jumped off the thunder tiger, desperate to get his feet back on solid ground. Hana slid down beside him, standing close, their hands touching.

The Kapitán looked at the pair wistfully. "You must be my nephew. Yoshi."

The boy ran a hand across the pale fuzz on his chin, looked the big gaijin up and down. "You must be the fellow I've never laid eyes on before."

"You have the look of your mother." He smiled. "Some of her fire too."

"What are you doing here, Uncle?" Hana asked. "Do you plan to stand against us? Or attack Yama once we've marched south?"

"Morcheban and Shiman strategy may differ in many ways, but in one respect we are very similar: we seldom begin our attacks facing the wrong way."

"You're facing south," Yoshi nodded.

"Then south must be the right way."

Hana looked around the assembled troops: the stern-faced men and boys, the Mercy Sisters with their hooked hammers and bonesaws, the frothing Bloodblessed. Banners of each House flapped in the wind, but she saw no flag of the Imperatritsa—no twelve stars to represent the unity of the Ostrovska Peace.

"Where is your Empress's flag, Uncle? Where is Sister Katya?"

"Up on the hill. She will not be joining us. We will have to guess the coming and going of the storm on our own, and pray the Goddess finds us without the Sister to point the way."

Hana was mute, staring at the Kapitán with a wide, hopeful eye.

"We know little of your gods. If there is a doom on the horizon, we cannot see it. So last night I proposed to my Houseguard we head south, along with any who cared to come, in order to conduct reconnaissance. The return of our wounded did much to win the hearts of the other House Kapitáns, and thus, they joined our march. Simply to see what we can see, of course."

Aleksandar's crooked smile cracked his frost-encrusted beard.

"We cannot ally with Shiman forces—such would violate our Imperatritsa's command. But . . . if Shiman forces happen to be marching in the same direction, I am certain the road is wide enough to carry us all."

Tears filled Hana's eye. "Thank you, Uncle."

"When all this is said and done, I will take you both back to Morcheba. Show you the Godstooth Ranges and the Endless Ice. The Maw and the Moonstag Keep. The family you have never known." He looked at Hana. "The House you were born to rule."

"But my eye," she said. "The Goddess . . ."

"You may not be Zryachniye, but the Goddess still flows in your veins. She will flow in your daughters also."

Yoshi watched the older man carefully, eyes hidden behind his goggles. He pulled a scarf up over his lips, his breastplate so cold it burned his skin.

"I'll confess the thought of my little sister sitting at the head of the table plants a warm and fuzzy square in the chest. But we're putting the rickshaw before the runner, maybe."

"True." The Kapitán turned to the horizon. "First, we march south. To blood and victory."

Hana put her arm around Kaiah's neck, squeezed tight. "Blood and victory."

The arashitora purred, tail switching from side to side. Yoshi looked to Shai, to the skies above, to the sea of pale faces all around. He sighed.

"First part goes without saying."

Days upon days upon days.

Trekking south into rising chill, raking wind, black snow crusted in her hair. Ashes in her mouth, a greasy film on her skin, thick with the stink of burned hair and corrosion and exhaust from the Earthcrusher's chimney spires. Corpseflies swarmed about the ships, the men, clustering around their eyes or at the corners of their mouths. Storm clouds rolled overhead, like the tsunami that had heralded the approach of ancient serpents into the Bay of Dragons.

Yukiko could feel them if she tried—stepping out into the fire behind her wall. But the Lifesong was quieter now, muted by the black to the south, a chill creeping into her bones if she stared too long. The ancient dragons circled through the northern sea, surrounded by swarming children. But they and all their brood couldn't help her now, she knew it. And so she kissed each one and sent them on their way, back to the Everstorm, her thanks ringing in their minds.

This battle wouldn't be won by leviathans from the dawn of time. It'd be won by men and women and a handful of thunder tigers, a limping giant and the dream of a future unborn.

Presuming it would be won at all.

On they marched. The air thundering with the Earthcrusher's tread, the storm above, the arashitora's wings. Flies growing thicker along with the stink of charnel pits and dead flowers and open drains. Yukiko and Buruu spent much of their time on the *Kurea*, standing at the bow with the wind in their faces. Not much in the way of words were shared for the first few days. The shadow of what lay ahead, what *needed* to be done lay between them like a fissure through the Stain. But she pressed against him regardless, simply standing in each other's warmth, the solace of each other's company. Let the Endsinger's legions come.

Let a thousand oni stand between them and victory. None of it mattered in this moment before the plunge.

I love you, brother.

AND I YOU.

She sighed, licked at cracking lips. To the south, she could see the haze darkening to muddy gray. If she squinted, she could see shapes swimming in the distant black. If she slipped too far into the Kenning, she could hear that awful song.

Yukiko ran her hand down Buruu's cheek, across the barding at his throat.

You cut a fine figure in this armor. A portrait for the ages.

I DO NOT CARE ABOUT THAT. I AM NOT LIKE KAIAH.

She drew her hand away, falling to her side.

. . . We haven't spoken . . . about what we plan to do . . .

I THOUGHT YOU HAD DECIDED. YOU WILL FLY INTO THE HELLGATE, AS TORA TAKEHIKO DID BEFORE YOU. DESPITE THE FACT THAT IN THE LEGENDS, HE PERISHED. AND THOUGH YOU HAVE NO IDEA HOW, YOU WILL SEAL IT CLOSED.

I have to try, Buruu.

WILL YOU SPROUT WINGS? PERHAPS MANEUVER ONE OF THESE CLUMSY SKY-SHIPS THROUGH AIRBORN SWARMS OF YOMISPAWN?

Obviously I need an arashitora to fly me there. But it doesn't have to be you.

DOES IT NOT?

Buruu, Tora Takehiko died when he closed the Devil Gate. Whoever goes in there . . . I'm not sure they'll come back alive . . .

AND YOU WOULD HAVE ME SEND A PACKMATE IN MY STEAD? YOU CANNOT ASK YOSHI OR HANA TO STAND IN YOUR PLACE, BUT YOU WOULD ASK ME TO—

No. I just . . .

She sighed, looked toward Sukaa flying off the starboard side. The thunder tiger had refused the armor the Kitsune smiths made for him, making him faster, more maneuverable; a black blade, cutting the air to ribbons. Shai flew in wide circles around the fleet, sleek and effortless, speeding past the *Kurea* every few minutes, Yoshi clinging to her shoulders like a terrified child. Yukiko swore she could feel a vague jealousy in the dam's mind, a distrust, perhaps even anger. But despite it, the girl couldn't help but be awed at the sight of her.

She's beautiful, Buruu.

The Khan turned to watch his mate, swooping up and over the *Honorable Death*'s inflatable. Yukiko could feel the smile in his mind.

SHE IS.

You have a family. Shima is my home. But you have your own home now.

I DO NOT DO THIS FOR SHIMA. I DO NOT DO IT TO BE REMEMBERED IN SONGS, FOR A FUTURE OR AN IDEAL OR EVEN BECAUSE IT IS RIGHT.

He turned to look at her, and she could see her reflection in the bottomless black of his pupils, ringed by circles of molten gold.

I DO IT FOR YOU.

She put her arms around him, wrapped in the warmth radiating from his body and mind. The home, the brother, the life she'd lost. All of it, she'd found inside him. This soul tied to her own, so far entwined she could no longer tell where she ended and he began. Part of her always.

Forever and always.

I don't know what we'll find in the hellgate. I don't know how we're supposed to close it. But no matter what happens, whatever comes, we'll face it together.

TOGETHER.

Do you promise?

I PROMISE. TOGETHER.

He stared southward, black reflected on black, the darkness staring back.

UNTIL THE END.

They marched through sunlit hours, Lady Amaterasu's light dying as they drew farther south. The ashfall grew heavier, tumbling drifts coating everyone and everything in gray. The flies were legion, clustered on each soldier's back, so thick on the kerchiefs over their mouths it seemed every man had grown a beard overnight.

When darkness fell along with the temperature, the flies would mercifully flee, and they'd bivouac down, huddling around roaring fires and listening to the dark. They could hear things moving beyond the fleet floodlights; a shapeless gibbering and a broken clock rhythm, snatches of a dark tongue no man could understand. Some swore they could hear voices of people they knew to be dead, bidding them leave the firelight and come out into the dark. The gaijin marked their foreheads with the sigil of their goddess—a circle drawn in blood on every brow to keep the evil at bay. The Shimans burned offerings in Lord Izanagi's name, begged him to stay his wife's hand in the battle to come. Prayers and pleas and grim vows.

Just words in the midst of that freezing black.

The sun would rise each morning, each dawn fainter than the last, and they'd discover more of their number missing—seemingly vanished in the night. Nerves were stretched to breaking beneath the corpsefly hum. Morale unraveling one thread at a time.

The warband leaders met on the *Kurea*—Ginjiro for the Kitsune, Hiro for the Tora, Misaki for the rebels, Kaori for the Kagé, Aleksandar of the Morchebans, the Khan of the arashitora, and the stormdancers themselves. It was decided to march through the night, so they'd arrive at the Stain mid-morning and fight with whatever advantage lay in daylight.

Every face was smeared with ashes, every hand trembling from the marrow-deep cold. Yukiko looked over each one in turn, even the Daimyo of the Tiger clan, watching her with his sea-green eyes. She wished them luck, bid them remember what it is they fought for.

As the meeting concluded and the members drifted away, Hiro caught Yukiko's gaze, opened his mouth as if he wished to speak. He stood motionless, staring at the girl staring back at him, the space between them filled with flies.

"I wish . . ."

His voice faltered and he stared at his clockwork arm, the iron hand clenching and unclenching. He met her eyes again, tongue frozen to the roof of his mouth.

He shrugged helplessly.

The ice in Yukiko's stare cracked. Just a hairline. Just a sliver.

"They'll know," she said. "It's all I can give you. But they'll know, Hiro."

She left him standing there in the snow, staring at his hand.

Fingers closing one by one.

T he warriors were gathered in the floodlight glow, Morcheban and Shiman alike, an army the likes of which the island had never seen. Yukiko flew down from the *Kurea* on Buruu's back, surrounded by arashitora of black and white, all of them smudged with gray. Spiraling to the frozen earth, the chill seeping into her very core. Slipping from Buruu's back, she surveyed the crowd around her, the thousands of expectant stares.

She was a tiny thing amidst the warriors—slender limbs clad in black cloth and scars, loose hair drifting amidst the falling ash, like fingers of smoke painting the lines of her face. Each man could see the swell at her stomach; the new life growing amidst this ocean of flies. Some took heart, knowing if a mother would carry her children into the battle to come, there must be *some* hope of victory. Others felt their hearts sinking in their chests, knowing if the girl risked her unborn babes in this gambit, their plight must be more desperate than any supposed.

She thought back to the day they'd left Kigen at Yoritomo's command, barely six months ago now—gods, it seemed a thousand years. Akihito and Kasumi and her father beside her, friends and family, loved ones all. All of them dead now. She pictured Michi braiding her hair in front of the looking glass, speaking in fierce whispers of the will it took to swim against the flow. Aisha's deadly beauty and deadlier mind. Daichi . . . gods, poor Daichi, his wisdom and his rage and his righteousness in perfect balance, her sensei in her darkest hours.

So much death.

EVERYTHING DIES, YUKIKO.

But so soon? So young? Some of these people aren't old enough to have lived at all. And at the end of this story, all of them could be dead.

ALL STORIES END. ALL SONGS CEASE. ALL OF US HAVE OUR ONE FRAGILE MOMENT IN THE SUN, THEN SLEEP FOREVERMORE. BUT MOST SPEND THAT MOMENT OF WARMTH IN MUTE DESPAIR, NEVER KNOWING WHAT IT IS TO LIVE A LIFE EXTRAORDINARY. NEVER KNOWING A SINGLE BREATH WHERE THEIR BLOOD WAS FIRE AND THEIR HEARTS WERE SINGING, A MOMENT THEY COULD GAZE BACK ON AND SAY IN TRUTH "THEN, IF NEVER AGAIN, I WAS ALIVE."

He smiled into her mind, and her blood became fire in her veins.

SPEAK YOUR HEART. THEY WILL SEE THE TRUTH OF IT.

She drew a breath, staring into the black behind her eyes. She could feel Buruu's warmth, even here in the cold belly of winter, the darkest depths of night. The stone she set her back against. The mountain never crumbling. And she raised her voice, and began to speak.

"I'm not a hero," she said.

She looked at the faces around her, expectant, ashen pale. She heard Aleksandar's voice amidst the wind, translating her words for the sake of his countrymen. Out in the dark beyond the ship lights, gibbering voices whispered in tongues too black for men to know. She raised her voice over them, over the storm above, the rolling thunder and crackling lightning.

"I know you want me to be. You think me to be. But I'm not. A hero would speak great words to you now. True words. Fierce words. Words that would ring in the ages, long after everything of us is dust. A hero would have words to turn your sword arms to steel and your hearts to iron, crown your shoulders with wings. And you'd march toward the enemy with the song of those words in your souls."

She shook her head.

"But I'm not a hero.

"I'm just like you. Just as lost. I'm small and afraid and I wonder if anything I do here will make the slightest difference. If it's worth trying at all. I wonder if any victory could be worth the price we've already paid. I've lost so many people I loved, so much of who and what I was. I look to the sky and I can't see the sun. I look in the mirror and I can't see myself."

Her gaze roamed the crowd, the eyes locked on her own.

"But I look around me. And I see all of you. Just like me. Just as small and just as lost. But when we stand side by side, we are twice the size. Twice as brave. Twice as loud. Look around you now, and see there are not just two of us, but *thousands*. Thousands of voices. Thousands of fists and minds and dreams, all of us together, in this moment. Because we believe.

"We can light a fire to burn through this dark. We can scream loud enough to be heard over this storm. We can say 'no.' We can say 'enough.' And hand in hand, stronger than we could ever be alone, we can change the shape of this world. All of us. Together."

She walked into the crowd, the soldiers parting before her, every heart stilled, every breath held. Yukiko took the hand of a Kitsune bushiman—a young boy barely older than she, his ash-smeared face alight with awe. With her other hand, she clutched the gauntlet of a gaijin hammerman—a mountain of muscle and scars and plaited blond hair. She squeezed each hand tight, looked each man in the eye, her voice as fierce as a thunder tiger's roar.

"All of us." She looked between them. "Together."

"Together."

It spread like a ripple across mirror-still water, like a flame across the bone-dry leavings of a breathless summer. One hand grasped another, and another, and another, each man and woman latching hold of the one beside them. Up on the sky-ship decks, on the Earthcrusher, every hand finding another and squeezing tight, strength found in the press of another's grip on their own. Silencing the whispers in the dark, black voices fading beneath the vow, the prayer, the hymn, repeated amidst fierce smiles and glowing faces. Over and over again.

"Together."

"*Together.*"

Up on the *Kurea*, the Blackbird closed his eyes, burning the picture below in his memory—a portrait to be repainted in black ink on rice-paper scrolls, testament to a night that must surely live in people's hearts and minds for a thousand years.

"Maker's breath." A wistful sigh. "And she says she's not a hero . . ."

51
ENDSINGER

Dawn approached like a thief, nothing but a skulking glow to herald its arrival. The army marched through knee-high snow and ash, beset by swarms of accursed corpseflies. The ground trembled beneath the shreddermen legion, the Earthcrusher plodding behind, the true terror of what awaited them coalescing from the gloom before Yukiko's horrified eyes.

Where once the Stain had lay, there was now only a bottomless hole, cracked at its edges like sores at a beggar's mouth. Rolling mist clung to the rim for a few hundred feet, shrouding it in a pall reeking of dead flowers and burning hair. She found her eyes slipping away when she looked at the pit, headache flaring, chill gripping her bones. The air was a sea of frozen swords, so cold her tears froze on her lashes, her hair crackling whenever she turned her head.

An awful fear took root inside her, the warmth in her belly diminishing to a dull ebb. She pressed her hand there, feeling for them in the Kenning. The heat of the Lifesong beyond her wall was faded, a dull, sullen tempest rather than the inferno she'd grown accustomed to. She reached out, felt the dim pulses of the people around her; fireside sparks dying between winter's teeth. The thunder tigers still burned strong enough to hold, and she caressed each mind with her own, willing them to be strong. But the soldiers were too muted and dim to cling to.

Whatever strength the lives inside her had brought was gone—negated by the awful chill emanating from that wound in the world.

And then of course, there were the things born from it.

A legion of horrors arrayed at the hellgate's edge: malformed children clinging to a dead mother's kimono. But gods above, what children. Nightmare forms, hundreds upon hundreds, dragged screaming from the depths of subconsciousness into strangled light. Blinking and stupefied, fixing glazed stares on the humans marching out of the wastes, gurgling hatred. The smallest were the oni she knew—blue-skinned, humanoid monstrosities. Some no bigger than human children, the skulls they wore still crusted with fresh meat and skin and hair, open-mouthed and silently screaming. The larger ones stood twelve feet high, tree-trunk warclubs in their hands. Features pierced with iron rings, twisted, as if their Dark Mother had taken a fistful of each face and squeezed. But they were nothing compared to the horrors looming beside them.

Abominations in the blackest sense of the word. Parodies of life, of forms once gracing the living world. Great hawks made of bone and corpsemeat, rotten feathers and worm-ridden flesh stitched together by blackened tendons. They rose in a great swarm, circling the hellgate like flies over a fresh cadaver, clad in the reek of open graves.

Towering goliaths of dripping flesh, piles of corpses, mashed and pulped together into shambling monstrosities. Yukiko saw the skinless shapes of beasts long gone from the Isles—what might be pandas or monkeys or big cats, crushed together like putty around frames of tree-trunk bones, mouths like fanged furnaces, burning blue with awful cold.

Other horrors amidst the mob—pale, naked men with skins several sizes too big, sloughing and dripping as they shuffled, keening and eyeless. Bone-thin things with too many joints and too many fingers, eyeless faces with flat noses, snuffling at the air, long red tongues darting across needle-lined maws. Others still without static form—just writhing mountains of worm-ridden meat, trails of congealing blood left in their wake as they dragged their carcasses along frozen ground. When they roared, clouds of corpseflies spewed from their mouth amidst the wails of screaming children.

A brood born in utter darkness, suckled at a breast turned black with hatred.

The children of the Endsinger.

A song hung like mist in the air, growing louder with every passing moment. Echoing from the hell in which She'd been abandoned—the hymn heralding the end of the world.

Lady Izanami's song.

Commanders yelled up and down the line, gaijin wardrums pounding in time with the Earthcrusher's tread. The army formed up—a legion of folded steel and embossed iron and grim, bloodless faces. First came the shreddermen, their scythesaw arms cutting at the air. They were backed by infantry—Shiman and Morcheban. Standards waving proud in the corpseflesh wind, sigils of Fox and Tiger and Phoenix side by side with the stags and gryfons and frostlions of the gaijin Houses. The sky-fleet gathered above—lumbering ironclads, bristling with shuriken-throwers and flame-spitters. Gaijin rotor-thopters and Phoenix corvettes weaving between them. Amidst the *DOOMDOOMDOOMDOOM* of its colossal tread, the Earthcrusher stomped into position on the right flank, vomiting black tar into the skies.

Yukiko stood on the war-machine's bridge, staring through cracked viewing portals to the horrors beyond. Her hand found her tantō—the blade her father had given her for her ninth birthday. She could almost feel him beside her, smell the smoke from his pipe. If he were here, he'd smile, call her "Ichigo," press his lips to her brow and tell her to be brave.

But he wasn't here. He'd died for her, fighting for what he loved. For something greater. Just as Tora Takehiko had done before her, flying beyond the hell-gate and somehow sealing it closed. What awaited her beyond that black? Would she ever return to the ones left behind?

She turned to Kin, strapped into the pilot's harness, his brass skin gleaming in the light of the control boards. The suit looked strange without a mechabacus on its chest—stranger still without the helmet, the boy inside watching her with his knife-bright eyes. He'd refused painkillers for fear they'd dull his wits. A sheen of sweet gleamed on his brow. His face was pale, etched with fear.

But not for himself.

"I don't want you to do this," he said.

"I have to." Her smile trembled at the edges. "Time to be the hero."

"Did you ever notice our heroes never live to be happy? Kitsune no Akira, Tora Takehiko, all the stormdancers of legend. None of them died in their beds. None of them got to enjoy the victories they fought for, or live in the world they defended."

"Would we love them as much if they came home when the war was done?"

"I would," he sighed. "I'd love them more. With every breath I took. With every beat of my heart. I'd love with everything I had to give if she came back to me."

"She?"

He whispered then, a single, tiny syllable as wide as the sky.

"You."

Yukiko stepped up to the pilot's harness, to the boy encased in brass. The boy who'd suffered like no other for the sake of his heart. A boy who'd do anything, risk everything for the one he loved. For her.

She stood on tiptoes, cupped his cheeks with her hands. And drifting close, so close she could feel the heat radiating from his skin, she pressed her lips to his.

Her eyelids fluttered closed and the world fell away. The noise and light, the grief and fear. Only them, the pair of them, her mouth on his, soft as the dreams of clouds, lighting a flame inside her, melting away the frost, leaving only an aching, blissful warm. The taste of him, the feel of him, his breath in her lungs, sighing from the depths of herself and breathing into his mouth. A declaration. A farewell. A kiss that would burn in her mind, that would make her ache every moment she had left beneath this poisoned sky.

A kiss worth dying for.

She drew away slowly, reluctantly, Kin lunging forward and keeping his lips pressed against hers for just a few more desperate seconds. But at last they parted, looking into each other's eyes. So much unsaid between them. No time left to say any of it.

"Come back to me," he whispered. "Please."

She said nothing, tears welling in her eyes. He took her hand in his, the brass gauntlet engulfing her fingers, gentle as falling snowflakes. And then she pulled away, feeling her heart tearing in her chest, a pain so real she could taste blood in her mouth.

"Good-bye, Kin."

"Don't say that . . ."

"Too late," she smiled, tears spilling down her cheeks. "Too late."

Head bowed, eyes flooding, she turned and walked away.

The Everstorm pack greeted them with roars of approval as they rose into the air, their Khan and the girl upon his back. They could see adoration in the eyes of the monkey-children on the sky-ships, fixed upon this slip of a thing clinging to their Khan's back—this tiny girl who moved entire nations with the sound of her voice. If anyone could return from the black and freezing depths, it would be her.

She spoke aloud, but her voice rang in the Kenning, in each arashitora's mind, burning with the heat of a pale white flame.

"Each of you know what you must do."

Kaiah growled, long and low.

- WE KNOW THE PATH. WE WILL MARK IT FOR YOU IN DEMON BLOOD, YUKIKO. -

"When the gate is closed, the iron giant will incinerate all around it. Go no farther than you have to, risk nothing more than you need to. Your lives are precious, and I would see each of you back in Everstorm, to tell the tale of this day to your children."

Shai circled alongside Buruu.

WE WILL TELL THEM. THEY WILL REMEMBER.

The voices of the pack echoed in the Kenning, their thoughts as one.

THEY WILL REMEMBER.

Sukaa growled low and deep, emerald eyes on the rising dark.

~ LET US WASTE NO MORE TIME. LET THERE BE AN ENDING. ~

Yukiko looked to Hana and Yoshi, calling to them above the howling wind.

"You two, stay as close to Buruu and I as you can. If we fall before we get to the hellgate, one of you will have to enter Yomi instead. I have no idea what awaits you there or how to fight it. But one of us must finish this story!"

"We will!" Hana cried. "Whatever happens, one of us will see it done!"

Kaiah was flying close-by, gaze fixed on Buruu. She reached out with her thoughts into the bridge, her words echoing in Yukiko's mind, laced with something close to regret.

- CAN YOU HEAR THE THUNDER, KINSLAYER? OUR FATHER RAIJIN IS PROUD. THE STONES AND THE SKY WILL SING OF YOUR COURAGE FOR A THOUSAND YEARS. -

THAT MATTERS NOT TO ME, KAIAH. IT NEVER HAS.

- I SEE THE TRUTH OF IT. THE LACK OF SELF. THE WILL TO DO WHAT OTHERS WILL NOT. TO PLACE YOUR PACK ABOVE YOURSELF. THE MARK OF A TRUE RULER. -

She nodded, pushed warmth into his mind.

- MY KHAN. -

Buruu purred, nodding once. Yukiko smiled, reached out and touched the mind of every thunder tiger, one by one. Finally she settled on Shai, looked at the pale boy clinging to the Shakhan's shoulders. She called out, the wind snatching her words from her lips.

"You're awfully quiet, Yoshi."

The boy blinked, the corner of his mouth curling into a smile.

"Makes a pleasant change, I'll wager."

"There's no need to be afraid."

"Can't say I'm not, Stormgirl. I'd be a liar if I did. But it's not fear that's got me stilled."

"Then what is it?"

He shrugged, looked toward the gathering black.

"Seems a time for doing, not talking . . ."

Yukiko turned to the Yomi hordes below, the swarms of hellspawn clustered around the blackened pit. The corpse-hawks were a seething cloud, the skin-things and corpsefly maws filling the air with blood-thick roars. She fixed her gaze on the darkness, narrowing her eyes and trembling as the headache bloomed and the tuneless, mournful song echoed in her mind.

That was it. The utter dark. Where they must go.

She nodded.

"Not talking. Doing."

She drew her katana and held it aloft, the blade's edge gleaming as lightning arced overhead. Thunder shook the sky, Susano-ō and Raijin gathered to cheer on their struggle against the Endsinger's horde. The Thunder God's drums rolled across the clouds, echoed by the gaijin wardrums below, roaring sky-ship engines, thousands of hammers pounding on shields, revving of chainsaw katanas. The army below rippled, rearing back and tensing for the spring.

Yukiko drew a deep breath, the song of the storm filling the sky.

"Not alone!" she roared. "Together!"

She leveled her sword at the enemy.

"BANZAI!"

The Earthcrusher roared and lumbered forward, retching lungfuls of billowing black. The army cried out with one voice, charging headlong through the mist and snow toward the Yomi horde, shreddermen in the vanguard, scythe-saw arms chattering and raised for the kill. The sky-fleet engines thundered, propellers shredding the soup-thick air, steam and exhaust spewing from their flanks. The *Honorable Death* came first, flanked by the fair *Kurea*. Captain Blackbird stood at his ship's helm and roared into the storm. Kaori beside him, manning a shuriken-thrower, eyes fixed on the incoming swarm.

The corpse-hawks shrieked, beaks of bloody bone open wide, milk-pale eyes bulging in rotting sockets. The fleet opened fire, cutting a swath through the cloud, black blood spraying as razored steel tore the air. The beasts came on, not slowed by mortal wounds, only tumbling from the sky when their wings were too shredded to keep them aloft. The Everstorm pack swooped through them, cutting like chainblades, ripping heads from necks and wings from backs. The sky was filled with screams, with the *popopopopopop* of the shuriken-throwers, the hiss and woosh of flame-spitters lighting the dark. Above it all, Raijin pounded his drums, lightning spreading across the clouds like cracks in the face of the sky.

The Earthcrusher hit the Yomi horde like an avalanche, cutting a swath through a dozen demons with one sweep of its arm. Blood like a river, an ocean, gurgling screams and shearing bones. But where one demon fell, another two took its place, charging headfirst into flame-spitter fire, withering bursts of shrapnel from the iron-throwers. One gigantic, headless monstrosity collided with the 'Crusher's belly, latching hold with tentacled arms as long as buildings. The behemoth staggered, a hundred smaller gibbering demons hitting its legs and climbing; a rising tide of open, shrieking mouths.

Inside the cockpit, Kin cursed, fighting to keep control of the war-machine beneath the weight of the demonic tide.

"Portside hydraulic pressure dropping!" roared Misaki from her console. "They've sundered one of the lines!"

Damage reports came one after the other.

"Shrapnel-throwers seven and ten disabled!"

"Legs seven and five unresponsive!"

"Loading bay! Get to the loading bay!"

"Godsdammit!" Kin swung one of the Earthcrusher's arms, feeling the impact rock the goliath, painting the viewing portals with great sluices of black blood.

Shinji's voiced crackled over the PA. "Kin, demons are at the loading bay doors! If they breach, there won't be anything left of the Earthcrusher to blow!"

Kin blinked the sweat from his eyes, swung at the seething mob again and again. His voice was a whisper. A prayer. Not to the gods roaring in the skies above, but to the girl who now held all their fates in their hands.

"Hurry, Yukiko . . ."

Yukiko pressed low to Buruu's back, watching him tear a corpse-hawk's head clean off its shoulders as they flew past, wheeling and spinning through storms of rotting flesh. The sky was black with them, screaming, shrieking nightmares on leather wings, claws like knives. The thunder tigers were faster, fiercer, but there were so many of the creatures that individual might meant nothing. The pack split apart, sweeping and diving through the air, dismembering one foe only to be pursued by a dozen more. A Morcheban dam fell from the sky, half a dozen hawks tearing at her belly and ripping at her eyes. Tuake had his wing sheared off at the shoulder, roaring in agony as he tumbled to his ruin on the ashen earth below.

The pack regrouped near the fleet, keeping close to the withering hail of death spewing from the shuriken-throwers. Yukiko could see Ginjiro at his flagship's prow, roaring commands to his crew. A Phoenix corvette called *Flameburst* lived up to its name, exploding into a billowing cloud of fire as it was torn from the clouds. The *Honorable Death* loomed close by, Hiro storming across the deck with his Elite Samurai, hacking at the corpse-hawks who'd managed to break through the 'thrower fire and attack his crew. The Guild ship *Resplendent Glory* was spiraling out of control, her decks overrun by seething black, the piercing screams of men being devoured alive rising above the roar of engine and storm.

Hana screamed over the slaughter. "Yukiko! The Earthcrusher is being overrun!"

"I can see it. But there's too many of these godsdamned things!"

Spiraling through the scent of ozone and death, thunder crashing in time with her pulse. She could feel wind in her feathers, blood on her claws, the acrid tang of the kill in her mouth. Sweeping through the sky as easily as fish through a rushing stream, Buruu's heart pumping in her chest, her eyes in the back of his head. Rolling and swooping and roaring, feathers crackling with wisps of lightning, blasting dozens of horrors from the skies with each burst of Raijin Song. Hana chopping and slicing with her chainkatana, Yoshi blowing withered heads off rotting shoulders with his iron-thrower. Slow and bloody work, but on they flew, the girl and her thunder tiger and the pack around them, closer to the deepening dark.

And then the darkness moved.

A ripple in the impossible black, the shriek of a thousand tortured gulls across a bleeding sky, a knife of burning ice in her mind. Yukiko hissed, Buruu and the pack broke away as a *thing* rose up from the hellgate, too horrifying for her eyes to focus on.

A vast winged shape, hundreds of feet across, twisted and monstrous. Its stink hit Yukiko like a punch to the face, vomit rolling in back of her throat. It was a horror wrought of corpses—the bodies of dead birds, maggot-riddled, two eyes burning with freezing blue flame, the beating of its wings like a hurricane laden with the suffocating aroma of death. And she knew it for what it was: the tortured spirit of every sparrow that had fallen choking from blood-red skies. Every crane or eagle that had spiraled from the clouds with a lungful of poisons and a bellyful of blood, reborn in the Hells, bringing death now to those who had destroyed them and all their kind.

It screamed again—the agonized wail of ten thousand denizens of the air, dying in pain beneath a burning red sun.

"Great Maker," Yukiko breathed. "Protect us now."

A leksandar smashed the skull of a wailing, faceless horror with his lightning hammer, bursting the creature's head apart in a spray of bone and brain. The Kapitán kicked the flailing corpse back into the oncoming wall of flesh, introducing another abomination's face to his shield. His arms were slicked in black blood, the ground beneath him a mire of melting snow and gore, the stench bringing tears to his eyes. All around him, men were fighting and screaming and dying, swords and hammers falling, the crunch of bone and the spray of blood interspersed with the buzzing choir of chainsaw katanas. Shreddermen were reaping demons by the armful, but for every dozen that fell, a brave man was borne to the ground and torn asunder, a shredderman was toppled and the pilot inside ripped limb from bloody limb. There seemed to be no end to the hell-spawn, all glowing eyes and reeking flesh and *snik-snak* claws. His lungs burned and his sight blurred, and every step felt a tortured mile.

Worse, there was the song. Rising in intensity, so loud he could almost hear the words. It was bloody fingernails drawn across a chalkboard of skin. A sliver of metal behind his eyeball, a constant, conscious, breathing wrongness in the marrow of his bones. Some men fell still at the sound, stupefied, staring into the gaping wound in the island's face and lifting not a finger as the demons fell upon them, smiling like simpletons as they were dismembered.

Aleksandar recognized it—the dulcet tones he'd not heard since he was a boy. The voice of his mother, calling across long and empty years. He felt the need to be held, cradled to a warm breast as he'd been as a babe, when all the world revolved around her, *her*, the one who bore him, who carried him inside her, who would always be a part of him no matter how tall and strong he grew. He felt the wrong-ness of it all, the mother betrayed, left alone in darkness to rot and plot and dream of revenge. A revenge now come unto the world she had died birthing.

But he knew it was a lie. Some evil magik born of the Shiman's hell. Whatever this Dark Mother was, she was not *his* Goddess. And so he clutched the pendant about his throat and prayed for vision, for clarity and will, and smashed another demon's head from its shoulders.

"Do not listen!" he roared. "Do not listen to the song!"

The ground shook, the abyss rippling as if a stone had been dropped into black water. He looked beyond the demon lines and saw the vast carrion bird rising from the pit, the reek of old death and worms like a hammerblow to his face. A vast and terrifying shadow fell over the battlefield, throwing all into chaos and darkness.

"Everliving Goddess," he whispered. "Protect us now."

The mighty carrion bird screamed, swooping across the smoke and rolling black, a cyclone reeking of open graves beneath its wings. The repeating chat-ter of shuriken fire rang in Yukiko's ears, the revving of sky-ship engines pushed to full burn. Blackbird, Kaori and the crew of the *Kurea* were engaged in bloody battle with a deck full of the smaller corpse-hawks; the *Lotus Wind* had been overrun, but the rest of the fleet had set course for the beast, scrawling exhaust across the sky as they charged. At the forefront, Yukiko could see the *Honorable Death*, Hiro standing at the prow with chainswords drawn, roaring at the top of his lungs.

Hiro . . .

THEY BUY US TIME. WE CANNOT WASTE IT.

Hana screamed into the choking wind. "Yukiko, go! Go!"

Sukaa swooped past, first into the breach, the buck's words burning in her mind.

~ FLY, MONKEY-CHILD. FLY! ~

The thunder tigers banked left and cut through a small swarm of corpse-hawks, buffeted by blasts from worm-riddled wings. Thunder rolled about them, ruined bodies falling from the sky as they wove between the snapping beaks and slashing claws. Yoshi's iron-thrower roared, blasting the face off a snarling monstrosity swooping toward Yukiko's back. Hana circled high, burning bright in Yukiko's mind, overcome with the battle around her, the fury of the arashitora she rode. The girl was laughing, if one could believe it—*laughing* as she and Kaiah split half a dozen corpse-hawks into ribbons, black blood falling like rain. A brutal symbiosis, a oneness Yukiko couldn't help but find beautiful, reaching out to Buruu and feeling the same, the pack tearing away over the bottomless black, the clouds above lit by blinding blue-white.

She heard an explosion behind her, a rush of boiling air around her, as if she walked on the face of the sun after days of freezing cold. A roar of rage and agony, a glance over her shoulder to see the giant shadow aflame, wings smoldering as it screamed. The air about her awash with black and teeth and talons, bursts of iron-thrower fire, roaring chainswords, writing a poem in blood across a canvas of smoking cloud. Buruu inside her, around her, above and between her, so close she felt she wore his skin, saw the world through his eyes, focused now on the rippling darkness before them, growing wider, colder, deeper, the song scratching at her eyeballs, rising above the wall between her and the Lifesong, seeping through the cracks she allowed herself to have. She could hear the tuneless song, twisting the vertebrae up her spine one by one by one until it lodged like a splinter in the back of her skull. And in the midst of that awful, soulless dirge, she heard a voice calling from the dark.

"*Ichigo . . .*"

She knew it. That voice. Still graveled from a lotus pipe kiss, the countless days spent in sunless bars. The pet name he'd called her since she was a little girl, running with her brother through the bamboo valley, sitting on his shoulders and feeling as tall as the clouds.

"*Ichigo, I'm here . . .*"

Tears in her eyes. The word lodging in her throat like a splinter of black glass.

"Father . . ."

52
THE ART OF RUIN

It loomed out of the black before him, bringing the darkness with it.

A horror from the muddy mists of childhood, dragged kicking and screaming from beneath his bed into sullen light. Real as he'd always known it to be. Bearing down on his ship, blotting out the lightning's glow with the maggot-clad breadth of its impossible wings.

Hiro glanced past the ironclads to his port, the arrow-sleek flight of Phoenix corvettes beyond, at last finding the thunder tiger pack. Yukiko had taken her chance, cutting her way through smaller flights of demons, around this looming horror fresh from the world's ruptured womb. He stared for a moment at all that could have been, gradually growing smaller. And smaller. And then he tore his gaze away. No time for regrets, for good-byes, for dreams of paths untrodden. This is what it came to. All that was left.

Here.

Now.

The few remaining members of his Elite stood around him, eyes locked on the foe. Their presence was a comfort, here at the last—his brothers, ready to die for something real. Not a dream of Shōguns or dynasties. Not the dream of a father drowning in regret, embroidered with faded tigers. For a future unborn. For something to be proud of, if not remembered for. Here at the ending of the world, standing before the edge and saying "No."

Saying "Never."

And so he roared it. Raised his chainkatana and screamed it, staring into the swelling eyes of the monstrosity before him, its beak splitting open to reveal a pit as black as the rift below. The *Honorable Death* and all her crew would scarcely be a mouthful, the sword in his hand no more than a humming splinter on its tongue. But still he roared, lips peeled back from his teeth, face twisted in a maddened, howling smile. The beast seemed not to notice, blotting out all sight and sound, a perfect dark intent on swallowing them utterly.

And there, as the black swelled and the chill shivered his bones, he pictured his mother's letter. Her tears at their parting. Her final, desperate plea.

"Open your eyes, my son."

He turned to the pilot, gave his signal. An Artificer belowdecks cranked an oil-slick handle. The winged abomination opened its maw.

"Wake up."

The *Honorable Death*'s engines coughed once, spat flame, the chi within her belly igniting as the thing's beak closed on her inflatable. A dull roar filled the sky, the *Death*'s hull splitting apart in a superheated ball of flame, a savage kiss to the lips of escaping hydrogen, right into the mouth of the monstrosity closing all about them.

A brief burst of blinding, beautiful daylight.

A second of dawning's dazzling beauty.

Awake at last.

K in shielded his eyes against the burst of flame, watching the shadow above the hellgate burned away in the flare of the *Honorable Death*'s demise. But he had no time to stare, the Earthcrusher rocking back as a tentacled fist slammed into its head, the iron around him reverberating with tortured groans. Hydraulics were blown, the 'Crusher's left arm torn almost completely from its socket, its other chainblade jammed elbow-deep in the chest cavity of some towering, skinless monstrosity.

The Earthcrusher's innards echoed with the bass-thick report of explosions. Distant screams. Kin stabbed at the intercom, roared into the microphone.

"Engine Bay, this is the bridge! Shinji, report!"

The boy's voice crackled down the line. "Loading Bay and the nethers are overrun. They're at the second bulkhead. We don't have long!"

A shower of sparks burst from Misaki's instrumentation panel. "Left shoulder is moments from breach. If they get in on the spaulder level, the brothers below will be cut off!"

Kin cursed, pressed the intercom again. "All right, we can't wait any longer. Shut down the cooling system and get the hells out of there, Shinji!"

"If Earthcrusher blows now, it'll take out the army around us! Everyone will die!"

"I can control the temperature manually from the bridge. I'll shut down nonessentials, keep the 'Crusher running hot, but not enough to ignite the chi until the army is clear."

"But that means—"

"Maker's breath, Shinji, just do as I say!"

A hollow boom. A burst of static.

". . . Acknowledged. Izanagi watch over—"

Kin snapped the channel shut, opened all-deck communications. His voice crackled over the PA, bouncing through the behemoth's greasy innards as it shuddered beneath another violent impact. Roars and blood-soaked screams.

"All hands, all hands! Coolant system is offline! Evacuate Earthcrusher, now! Repeat, all hands, evacuate!"

Kin flipped a trigger on the console, and a stream of green flares exploded from the goliath's belly, raining bright into the sky and drifting down over the howling sea of bone and teeth and flesh below. He tore the 'Crusher's arm free, swept away a few dozen monstrosities with a wave of the shrieking sawblades.

Misaki watched him from her console, expression soft with concern.

"We will stay with you, Kin-san."

The brothers around him murmured assent.

"No, you won't." A boom, a pained wince. "Get down to the spaulder exit now. I'll clear you a path with what's left of the anti-air."

"But we—"

"Misaki, you have a daughter. You owe it to her to make it back alive."

The woman walked to the pilot's rig, clutched his hand. The silver arms unfolded about her like a flower coming into bloom, glinting with the light of exploding sky-ships. "Kin-san, we will fight beside you until the end. Alone is no place to die."

He gifted her a grim smile.

"No one who is loved dies alone."

He nodded to the elevator.

"Go. Live well. Tell Yukiko . . ."

His words faded as the Earthcrusher was rocked by another blow. The viewing portals splintered, a gleaming chunk of glass falling away, letting in a cold wind laden with the stench of death, bitter chill, the hollow, soulless un-rhythm of that awful song.

"What?" Misaki clutched his arm. "Tell her what?"

He smiled, shook his head.

"She knows."

The elevator doors hissed open, the endsong rising in pitch.

"Go. Before it's too late."

She watched him, torn with indecision, clouds over her eyes. But at last, she chose—chose as she must, for her daughter, for the promise she'd made to her beloved. Misaki ran to the elevator and stepped inside with the other brethren, lifting her hand in farewell.

"I will remember you, Kin."

And spinning back to the horde, the rising tide of flesh and bone, the boy lifted the Earthcrusher's arm, kicked the stirrups and turned once more to the fray.

The air swam with burning green, a cascading waterfall spilling from the Earthcrusher's belly. Aleksandar caught sight of the flare-barrage, roaring over the song of carnage and chaos.

"The signal! Retreat! Back, in the name of the Goddess!"

The line shifted, the rearmost men turning and running, the front lines fighting a slow and bloody withdrawal. Arrows fell like black rain amongst the shambling deadthings, the screaming abominations. Men fell as they pulled away, more bushimen, samurai, hammermen. The few remaining Blood-blessed refused the call to retreat, charging farther into the melee, heedless of their wounds. Aleksandar saw one berserk beating a demon with his own severed arm, another torn asunder from the waist down, still crawling toward the enemy with a gurgling cry on his lips, glistening ropes of entrails dragged behind him.

He heard a dangerous groan from the Earthcrusher, a burst of flaming exhaust tearing the sky. The goliath was locked in battle with three towering abominations, the staccato beat of iron-thrower fire flaring at its collar, clearing its shoulders of the hellspawn encrusting it. As the burst faded, a swarm of Guildsmen spilled from a hatch, leaping into the air and fleeing back across the waste amidst bursts of blue-white flame. But the Earthcrusher still moved, still battled its monstrous opponents, another blast of fiery exhaust scorching the clouds.

Someone had stayed behind to pilot the giant through its final moments.

Someone who'd not see the morrow.

Lifting his lightning hammer in salute, Aleksandar called again for his men to fall back, and turned his thoughts to full retreat.

G o back," the voice echoed in the blackness. "*Go back home, Ichigo . . .*"

Yukiko grit her teeth, shook her head.

"You are not my father . . ."

Black and cold all around, a whispering wind underscored by that empty, tuneless song. She reached for Buruu in the dark, could feel nothing but the cold, an empty forever, tinged blue-black by the perfume of her father's pipe.

"*You are my daughter,*" the voice said. "*I love you, Ichigo . . .*"

"My father is dead," she hissed.

"*Where do we go when we die, Daughter? Down to the Hells to dance forever with the Hungry Dead. Your mother is here. She longs to hold you in her arms.*"

"My father gave his life for me. The Great Judge would never damn him to Yomi's dark. Nor my mother or brother, before you wrap yourself in that lie."

"*The Great Judge? So you believe in gods now? In their power?*"

"I believe what I see with my own eyes. And I cannot see you, demon."

"*But I have seen you, Daughter. As summer turned to autumn, and autumn to winter's deep, I have felt you bloom. Those within you. So beautiful. So dazzlingly bright. All around you love you. Your passing shapes the face of the world.*"

"Is that why you hide in the dark? Show yourself!"

"*. . . But you have lost so much. The ones you love and who loved you. Do you* *not long for peace? Do you not tire of the weight of the world upon your shoulders? You are too young to be so exhausted, daughter mine.*"

"And you would have me lay down? Run?" Her lips peeled back in a snarl. "You are not my father. He'd never bid me turn away when I could make a difference. Enough lies!"

Akihito's voice echoed in the black, dipped in regret. "*Where were you, Yukiko? What difference did you make when they killed me?*"

"*Or me?*" Michi breathed, somewhere near her ear. "*You can save the world, but not the ones you love?*"

"*You failed me,*" Kasumi whispered.

"*All of us gone,*" her father intoned. "*All sleeping now in the dark. But it is better here. Quieter. No pain. No loss. Stay with us.*"

"No," Yukiko hissed, pawing at the tears of rage welling in her eyes.

"*Stay with us . . .*"

"You have no right," she breathed, her throat squeezing tight. "You have no right to claim their voices, or speak their names. You didn't know them. You didn't love them. All this loss, all this agony is because of *you*. You began it all. This rot, this war. *You're* the reason they're dead. I know who you are. I know your name."

A voice in the dark, rolling and hollow.

"*Speak it.*"

". . . Endsinger."

"*That is what they call me.*" Whispers upon whispers. "*But that is not my name.*"

"Izanami, then." Yukiko searched the darkness, turning on the spot, wisps of hair caught at the corners of her mouth. "Lady Izanami. The Maker's bride. The Earth Goddess who died birthing the Seven Isles. Mother to demons. Hater of all life."

"*Hater?*" The voice softened, coalesced into something gleaming and feminine. "*Oh, daughter, I do not hate you . . .*"

Something pale moving in the black, distilling out of the roiling abyss.

"*I love you,*" she breathed.

And there she stood before Yukiko's wondering eyes. A paper lantern in one hand, a soulless, freezing light spilling from its folds. The air vibrating around her, thick with corpseflies and that awful, tuneless song. She was slender, white-clad, pale as milk and soft as silk. Black tresses flowed about her like water, cascading over the smooth curve of her shoulders, down over the swell of her hips, all the way to the floor. It writhed across her skin like a living thing, like serpents, insubstantial as shadows. Blood lotus flowers bloomed in her wake, filling the dark with cloying sweetness. Her face was impossibly beautiful; a perfect, timeless grace, heart-shaped and death-pale, pouting lips filmed in moist, glossy black.

But her eyes.

Gods, her *eyes* . . .

Punctures in her skull. Bottomless yawning pits, sucking all life and light from the air around her. Her lashes were worms, tiny and sightless, writhing toward Yukiko's warmth. Her outstretched hand was painted elbow-deep in blood. Dripping on the floor.

"*I love you,*" she repeated.

"And so you seek to destroy us? To unmake everything you helped create?"

"*Helped?*" The sightless eyes blinked. "*There was no helping, daughter. I did create this place. My beloved planted the seed, but it was I who sheltered it in my womb. Who knew the pure and perfect agony of its birthing. Who suckled it at my breast, even as I lay dying. You killed me, and still I love you.*"

"Then why?" Yukiko stepped closer despite herself, hands to fists. "Why do this?"

"*What have I done?*" Izanami tilted her head. "*You speak as if it was I who filled the skies with poison. I who choked the life from sea and earth.*" She gestured to the flowers blooming at her feet. "*I gave you something beautiful, and you turned it to atrocity. Into the tool of your own unmaking. But the choice was yours, daughter, doubt it not. You and all your kind.*"

She shook her head sadly, sorrow in her voice.

"*I forced no one's hand. Twisted no one's will. Such is not within my power to do. This, your ruin, is a product of your own artistry.*"

"You knew what blood lotus would do. You *knew* where it would lead us."

"*To me.*" A bottomless smile. "*Into my arms.*"

"But why?" Yukiko screamed. "It's not our fault you died! We didn't want this. We didn't ask for any of this!"

"*Because I love you . . .*" She shook her head, black tresses moving like the tides. "*Because I miss you. Because I made you. You are mine, all of you. You belong with me.*"

A whisper of wind, Yukiko's hair drifting about her face as if in a breeze. And then the goddess stood behind her, gentle arms snaking around her waist, caressing her belly with bloody hands, black lips pressed cold against her ear.

"*You do not know a mother's love. It is only a concept for you. The pale shadow of an idea. But once you lay eyes on those within you, once you bring them into life, you will know what it is to love absolutely. To wish to be with them, always. The cruel press of time or fate dragging them away. It will break your heart. It will end you, as it ended me. As now, I end you.*"

"Not today," Yukiko hissed. "I won't let you . . ."

Black lips pressed against her cheek, so cold they burned. Her voice was the wind howling through cemetery gates, blowing across fields of newly made corpses.

"*Mother knows best, child.*"

Yukiko pulled away, turned to face her, horror and rage in her eyes. Her hands were pressed to her belly, smeared with the blood Izanami had left behind.

"You know nothing . . ."

"*You never wanted them, did you? That poisoned cup in your womb. Is that why you seek this grand sacrifice? Because it is easier to die gloriously than face a future so terrifying?*"

"I haven't died yet. And I'm sure as hells not planning on doing it today . . ."

Izanami blinked, a slow, deadly smile forming on blackened lips. "*Oh, my dear. Oh my dear, precious girl. You do not know, do you?*"

". . . Know what?"

"*The gate. How to close it. What it will cost you . . .*"

"Tell me."

Hollow, soulless laughter. The cry of lonely wolves, the wind moaning through granite crags crusted with winter's bite.

"*She does not even know the part she plays. I should have known. This, their hero. Beloved of all. And neither they nor you can see the truth of who you really are.*" The goddess shook her head. "*A coward. A weak and tiny child, now begging the answer from she whom it would thwart. I love you dearly, but do you think me fool, my daughter?*"

"I *am* frightened," Yukiko said. "But that doesn't make me a coward. And I may be young, but that doesn't make me weak." Her hand slipped to her waist, to the tantō tied there. Her father's gift. "But no, I don't think you're a fool."

"*Oh?*" The goddess tilted her head.

"I think you're afraid. Of me. Of us. Together."

A smile.

"You're afraid."

She drew the blade, a gleaming flash of folded steel in the light of Izanami's ghostly lantern. She heard a faint tearing sound, chill laughter, a rushing, roaring gale. And then she was cold, the freezing air cutting her like knives, the brightness of gloomy daylight almost blinding after the black. The heat of the burning shadow bird at her back, Buruu's warmth beneath her, the skies filled with blood and thunder and the roars of the arashitora pack all around.

Back in the world again.

YUKIKO!

Buruu's voice echoing in her mind, edged with bright fear.

YUKIKO!

I'm here brother. I'm here.

I COULD NOT FEEL YOU. AS IF YOU HAD CEASED TO BE.

I saw her. Izanami. She spoke to me in my mind.

AND SHE SAID WHAT?

Yukiko closed her eyes amidst the chaos, the screaming, swirling death all around, replaying the conversation in her head. The goddess assumed she was here to sacrifice herself, that she already considered death a certainty. As if there was *no way* to close the hellgate and survive. But if so, how? How had it been done before? Tora Takehiko had closed the last hellgate, but he'd never returned to tell the tale.

But there must be a way.

There *must* be . . .

"Hana!" She looked to the girl circling above. *"Hana!"*

The girl split an abomination's skull apart, her face and arms drenched in dark gore, Kaiah's frenzy filling Yukiko's mind.

"What?"

"The tales of the last hell war! What did they say about Tora Takehiko's charge? Exactly! Word for word!"

"They said nothing, I told you!" Hana ducked a fistful of talons, struck at the shapes around her. "Only that he and his arashitora charged into the hellgate and sealed it closed!"

Pulse pounding in her ears.

That tuneless song, scratching at the back of her mind.

So hard to breathe, let alone think. Blood and murder all around. The heartbeats of a dozen arashitora, the roar of Yoshi's iron-thrower, the growling screech of Hana's chainblades. Beak and talon and claw, Buruu diving and spinning, the screams of dying soldiers, sky-ship engines growling beneath Raijin's drums.

. . . Only that he and his arashitora charged into the hellgate and sealed it closed . . .

Lightning bright across the sky, burning in her mind's eye. The answer was there, she knew it. Hand in hand with the death Izanami promised. All she needed was one second's clarity.

. . . he and his arashitora charged into the hellgate . . .

The wail of tortured metal from the Earthcrusher. Roared commands to retreat from the gaijin soldiers. It was falling apart. She had no time. Think, godsdammit, think. What did she say? What did she mean?

. . . charged into the hellgate . . .

"Gods," she breathed.

. . . charged into . . .

"That's it . . ."

. . . into . . .

Elation and dread, her right hand at her belly, her left slipping beneath the plates of Buruu's armor and finding the feathers beneath. A wash of fear, breath too fast to catch, heart pounding in her chest like a steamhammer. All of it. Everything. Every word, every deed, every moment leading to this, poised on the brink, staring into blackness below. The blood raining from the sky. The blood in her veins, the blood of yōkai, the blood the Inquisition had tried to exterminate from

Shima entirely. And why? Unless it held some power, some strength in the spilling that would close the breech, end the song that would otherwise end the world?

Buruu . . .

She pressed her hand against him. Her foundation. Her mountain. The stone she'd set her back against. The one certainty in this world of quakes and fires and storms. All this time.

"*Oh, my dear. Oh my dear, precious girl. You do not know, do you?*"

"I know," she breathed.

Buruu.

YES?

Brother, I know what we have to do. Tora Takehiko didn't fly into the hellgate. He flew INTO it. Collided with it. There was no battle in the dark of Yomi. No wrestling with the Endsinger to seal it closed. There was nothing beyond the charge itself. It was his blood, his sacrifice *that sealed the rift.*

She looked down into the dark below, the rolling, ink-black chill.

I know what I have to do . . .

Sorrow in his chest, bleeding and raw, reaching out and filling her own.

You don't have to carry me all the way, brother. No one does. Just take me to the heart of it and let me fall.

THE SKY IS FULL OF DEATH. IT WILL CATCH YOU BEFORE YOU LAND.

It doesn't have to be you.

I PROMISED, REMEMBER?

Until the end . . .

THIS THEN IS THE END?

She looked around her, the raging storm, the dark beneath, the island stretching away in every direction to press its lips to the sky.

I think so . . .

SO BE IT.

He nodded, spread his wings wide, slowing their pace. It seemed for a moment all the world hushed, gravity pulling her down, momentum pushing her forward. The pair of them, hanging still, like a single, perfect raindrop in the second before it began to fall.

I LOVE YOU, SISTER. NEVER FORGET. BUT AS YOU SAY, THERE IS NO NEED FOR BOTH OF US TO DIE THIS DAY.

A blindside from above.

An impact from behind.

Buruu dipped his wing, twisted his body. The blow knocked her loose, senseless, tumbling from his shoulders and out into the void. A gale roaring all around her, gravity seizing hold as she plummeted toward the dark. Toward the maws of a hundred deadthings, roaring up from below on rotten wings.

FORGIVE ME, YUKIKO.

She closed her eyes, trying and failing to swallow her fear, her heart shattering into a million pieces.

FORGIVE ME.

And toward the gate she fell.

Alone.

K in could hear bodies slamming against the shoulder-level entry, the tortured screech of buckling iron, the engine's rising tempo as he pushed them into the redline. Turning the Earthcrusher's head, he could see his brethren speeding away, flightless False-Lifers or wounded soldiers cradled in their arms. Soldiers were fleeing across the black snow, blood and gore and bodies in their wake. Hundreds had been cut down as they fled, but the monstrosities seemed incapable of straying more than a few hundred feet from the pit's edge, howling in frustration as the army pulled back. And when they'd emptied their lungs in rage at being denied their prey, they turned toward the Earthcrusher, lips splitting beneath the press of jagged fangs beneath.

The goliath positively crawled with them now, staggering under the weight of hundreds, crusted like limpets all over its body, smashing seams, tearing hatchways. The loading bay doors were torn wide, the Earthcrusher's belly now overflowing with hellspawn, more flooding through the breach by the second. Towering abominations were locked with the behemoth—twisted giants of skinless flesh, all tentacles and eyes and seething hatred. Kin was swinging the only functional arm with all his strength, sweat slicking his brow.

Freezing wind moaned through the shattered viewing portals. Izanami's song hung in the air, almost clear enough to make out the words, a pale whispering layered upon itself, an echo of a mother he'd never known. The temperature gauges were trembling in the red, warning lights flashing, a claxon wail deep within the Earthcrusher's belly driving the demons to frenzy.

He heard the spaulder hatchway give, the clattering and screaming of the oni pouring through, tearing the elevator doors apart. It'd only be seconds until they clambered up the shaft on talons of bone and black glass, smashing their way onto the bridge to find him in his feeble metal shell. Death so close he could taste it, feel its breath upon his neck.

Kin peered through the bloodstained viewports, looking for a distant speck in glowering skies. Some final sight of her, some last moment to share. But he could see only darkness, brief strobes of blinding lightning, smoke and blood and death. His words to Misaki hung in the air, their warmth fading now in the face of finality, their truth slipping up and away into the gloom.

"No one who is loved dies alone."

A prayer on his lips. A fragile hope in the face of hopelessness.

He slammed the throttles forward, flooding the intakes with burning, boiling chi.

The alarms rose in pitch, one final desperate plea to the madman at the controls, pushing the Guild's mightiest creation beyond the edge of tolerance.

A spark flared somewhere in the Earthcrusher's belly.

Vapor rushed toward it with open, hungry arms.

Ignition.

Plummeting.

Weightless.

The song of the wind and the stench of death all around, tears of ice crusted in her lashes. A black snowflake, falling, falling, down into the nothing she wished she'd always known. She could feel it below her, shying away from the blood in her veins. The ending she'd bring. But the carrionbirds would tear her to pieces before she reached the dark. She closed her eyes, welcoming the finale that would drown the fear of being finally and truly alone.

The rush of wings, an intake of breath, the tang of ozone. Something hit her out there in the black beyond her eyelids, feathers and fur and warmth, dragging her back up into hateful sky.

Yukiko opened her eyes, fingers digging into jet-black fur, lightning crackling along the edges of his wings. A mournful cry split the air, and she reached into the Kenning, recognizing the shape of the one who'd saved her.

Sukaa . . .

~ *YES.* ~

Why?

~ *BECAUSE HE ASKED.* ~

. . . He asked?

~ *BECAUSE I WILL BE KHAN WHEN HE IS GONE.* ~

She looked above, saw Buruu speeding across the clouds, twisting and rolling between the flailing swarms of corpse-hawks. And as he flipped over, dipping his wing to the earth, she saw a figure on his back, a smoking iron-thrower in his hand, fist wrapped in Buruu's mane. The pair moving together like poetry, cutting the sky to ribbons and the Yomi birds to pieces.

The one who'd knocked her from Buruu's back.

Leaping from Shai's shoulders . . .

Pushing her . . .

Yoshi . . .

Sukaa ascended, a slow spiral bringing them up from the rift below. Hana and

Kaiah fought on above, the girl screaming into the wind as her brother flew away, Shai blocking their pursuit with flared wings and flashing eyes. The rest of the pack were pressed tight to Buruu's heels, cutting down all that stood before him, clearing a path toward the deepest blackness, the heart of the wound, the place she'd been prepared to plunge. But Sukaa was flying *away* from the hellgate, bearing her back to safety beyond the abyssal edge.

What are you doing? Take us back!

~ SUCH IS NOT YOUR FATE. ~

Hana raised her chainblade, screaming into Shai's mind.

Get out of my fucking way! Yukiko, make her move!

Yukiko blinked, slow horror rising inside her breast, crashing down into dark and cold and crushing despair.

No. No, he can't . . .

~ THE BOY CHOSE. KHAN AGREED. BETTER TWO THAN FOUR. ~

Shai shook her head, sorrow welling in Yukiko's mind.

BETTER THEM THAN YOU.

"No," she breathed. "No, he *can't . . .*"

She seized fistfuls of Sukaa's feathers, digging fingers into the flesh beneath, screaming into the minds around her.

You can't let him! You can't let him do this!

~ KHAN'S WORD IS LAW. ~

Rage in Shai's breast, run through with bitter sorrow.

HE DOES THIS FOR YOU, GIRL. THE ONES WITHIN YOU.

"NO!"

Yukiko stepped into the Kenning, reaching out for Buruu's mind, struggling against the bitter, roiling chill spilling from the rift below. The thought too awful to comprehend. To permit.

It couldn't be. Couldn't end like this.

Not after everything they'd been through.

"*Buruu!*" she screamed. "*Buruu!*"

Blood pounding in her temples, spilling from her nose, reaching down into the depths of herself, stretching to her limits across the void below, the hatred rolling across its surface. Clutching at him, refusing with every ounce of herself that it must be this way. Her voice was a ragged scream, her throat torn and bleeding.

"BURUU!"

And in the distance, fading with every breath, she heard his faint reply.

YUKIKO.

She clawed the hair from her mouth, eyes filled with tears.

You can't do this, brother. You can't!

I MUST.

No. No, it doesn't have to be this way . . .

WE KNEW, THE BOY AND I. THE PATH WE MUST WALK. A YŌKAI-KIN MUST DIE THIS DAY. BUT WE LOVE OUR SISTERS TOO MUCH TO ALLOW EITHER OF YOU TO FALL. SO WE FALL FOR YOU.

Not you, Buruu, please, not you . . .

WHO THEN SHOULD CARRY HIM? MY PACKMATES? MY BRIDE?

You said we'd be together!

WE WERE. AT OUR GREATEST. AT OUR BRIGHTEST. WE WERE GLORIOUS, YOU AND I.

A smile in her mind.

WE WERE LEGEND.

But you promised! You promised we'd be together until the end!

BUT DO YOU NOT SEE, SISTER?

His voice growing ever fainter.

THIS IS THE END.

Buruu, please. Come back. Please gods, COME BACK!

I WAS LOST WHEN I MET YOU. EVERYTHING I WAS. AND IN ALL THAT DARK, ALL THAT DESPAIR, YOU FOUND ME. YOU WHO NAMED ME. ONLY YOU. MY SISTER. MY EVERYTHING.

But you can't leave! You're leaving me alone!

YOU ARE NEVER ALONE. I WILL BE WITH YOU IN BLUE SKIES AND CLEAR WATER. YOU WILL SEE ME IN THE EYES OF THOSE CHILDREN WITHIN YOU, HEAR MY VOICE WHEN THEY CALL YOUR NAME.

He filled her with a loving, crushing warmth.

THIS IS NOT THE END FOR YOU.

Sobs wracking her body. Aching in her lungs. Too impossible to grasp. Too cruel and unfair. Of all things, this was the price they had to pay?

This is what their folly had cost them?

Him?

I CHOOSE THE EASY PATH, SISTER. IT IS A SIMPLE THING I DO NOW, TO CLOSE MY EYES AND SLEEP. IT IS YOU WHO MUST ENDURE. WHO MUST REMAIN AMIDST THE WRECKAGE, AND TEACH THOSE WHO COME AFTER OF WHAT WENT BEFORE.

Buruu . . .

GOOD-BYE, SISTER.

Don't. Please gods, don't say that . . .

WHAT THEN SHOULD I SAY?

Tell me you'll see me soon. Tell me we'll be together again.

BUT WE WON'T.

We have to be! I can't go on without you!

YOU DO NOT MEAN THAT. YOU ARE STRONG AS MOUNTAINS. ALWAYS HAVE BEEN. ALWAYS WILL BE.

But you're the best of me. The one who makes me strong. Who will I be without you?

YOU WILL BE WHO YOU HAVE ALWAYS BEEN.

His voice almost lost beneath the flood of her tears.

YOU WILL BE YUKIKO.

Just a whisper now.

I LOVE YOU.

Just a breath.

GOOD-BYE.

They hurtled across the sky, water-swift, formless and perfect. The gloom was filled with horrors and the snows with poison and all about them was death and sorrow and suffering the color of raven's claws. But they walked between it all, hand in hand, voices echoing in the dark of each other's minds, here in this ringing solitude.

Here we are, Mockingbird. Tiptoes at the edge.

ARE YOU READY?

Yoshi thought of a beautiful boy, a smile he'd see again soon.

Doubtless.

They fell, down through the flood of shrieking black, spiraling toward the ripples on the face of the dark. Closer. They could hear it as they approached, louder with each passing second, the song, the words within, clear enough to finally discern. A song of love and hate, of loss and longing, of the fear and sorrow entwined with abandonment. Forgotten. Alone.

Closer.

Yoshi focused on the deepening dark, drawing near, eyes wide, every sight, every sound sharper than he'd ever known. Behind him, he heard the Earthcrusher crack wide and daub the sky with fire, a blast-wave of heat and impossible light filled with the screams of the Endsinger's children. A burning sponge to wipe the chalkboard clean. And to his utter amazement, he found his lips curling in a crooked smile.

Strange thing, this life.

Thunder rolled in the black, a woman's scream beneath, almost too faint to hear.

IT IS INDEED.

If you'd told me last summer what winter would bring, I'd have called you liar, Mockingbird . . .

MUCH CHANGES WITH THE SEASONS.

. . . Not everything.
THE SHAPE OF HEROES, CERTAINLY.
So I look like a hero to you?
The thunder tiger smiled into his mind, speeding toward the black.
A blinding arc of lightning seared the sky.
YOU LOOK LIKE AN ORDINARY BOY.
All became bright.
SO YES, YOU DO.
And daylight bloomed.

53
EPITAPH

All was ashes.

Ashes on her skin and in her eyes. Caked upon her face and painted on her lips and smeared thick across her tongue. Tears cutting through the snow-white mask on her cheeks.

A ringing silence filled her ears. Echoing with the thundering boom of the Earthcrusher's demise, the fading remnants of the Endsinger's song. But all around her was still. All within her was empty. Nothing at all.

She stood on the snowcapped ground, numb and freezing. Hana knelt amidst the frost, wailing, screaming, fingers into fists and tearing at her hair. But Yukiko couldn't hear a thing. Couldn't grasp it, didn't want to, any or all of it. Swimming insubstantial in the air around her, flakes of ash and black snow filling the space where understanding once lingered.

There had been light as he left her. Sound that wasn't sound. An inhalation as wide as the sky, bringing all down to nothingness.

Nothingness.

The hole seemed gone. The wound in the world closed, replaced with rup-tured earth—just ordinary dirt where once the rift had lay, a gentle rain of ashes tumbling from the sky to press it with frozen lips. Its edges were crusted with metal shrapnel, demon corpses, fallen soldiers, incinerated to charcoal and black sticks amidst melted snow.

The hole seemed gone. But she could still feel it. Inside her.

In the space he'd once filled.

Men drifted through the ashen fog, coalescing from the mist to stare. Morche-ban and Shiman, rejoicing, embracing, weapons thrust to the sky, to the storm raging overhead. The Thunder God pounded his drums, echoing the victorious howls. Amaterasu gleamed behind the clouds, the darkness abating, drifting back to the gloom of any normal winter's day.

She could hear none of it.

Not a thing.

The remnants of the Everstorm pack stood about them, feathers fluttering in kindling winds, black and white caked with gray. So pitifully few. Dragged once again to the edge of extinction. Grief in their minds for their fallen packmates, their fallen Khan, this hollow victory bringing cold comfort in the face of their loss. Shai hung her head low, couldn't meet Yukiko's eyes. Sorrow like a flood, drowning all inside her. A loss too vast to comprehend.

Sukaa stood tall, emerald eyes burning in the ashen wind, the strongest and fiercest of the bucks who remained. The one whom the Khan had entrusted to wing his sister to safety.

~ *NEVER AGAIN.* ~

His thoughts echoed in the Kenning, in the bridge still lingering between them in the weeping girl's mind.

~ *WILL NEVER HAPPEN AGAIN, THIS. IF BOND WITH MONKEY-CHILDREN CAN BRING OUR RACE TO RUIN, WE WILL BOND NO MORE. WE GO. NEVER RETURN. LEAVE YOU TO YOUR ASHES.* ~

He turned to Kaiah, standing vigil over Hana's weeping form.

~ *COME. THERE IS PLACE FOR YOU IN MY PACK. BLACK AND WHITE TOGETHER. WE ARE GRAY.* ~

Kaiah growled, hackles flaring, glancing down at the girl at her feet.

- *I STAY WITH HER. ALWAYS.* -

The Khan stared hard, finally nodded.

~ *SO BE IT, SISTER.* ~

He turned to his pack, his gaze imperious.

~ *WE GO HOME.* ~

Sukaa took to the wing, tiny whirlwinds of ash and snow rising beneath the thrashing of his wings. The other arashitora followed, leaping into the air one by one after their Khan, black and white, until only Kaiah and Shai remained.

The females looked at each other across the ruins, the shared loss of mates between them, pity welling in Kaiah's eyes. Shai's gaze shifted to the girl standing still and numb in the cold, arms wrapped about herself, hair whipping in the ash-choked wind.

GOOD-BYE, YUKIKO. WE WILL NOT MEET AGAIN.

The beating of mighty wings. The rush of frozen gales. The warmth of Shai's thoughts, fading slowly. Yukiko closed her eyes.

She could feel them again, the lives around her, the swelling of the Lifesong beyond the wall of herself. Aleksandar the Kapitán, making his way through his men, kneeling in the snow beside his niece and cradling her in his arms. The tattered remnants of the sky-fleet above, *Kurea* last of all, Captain Blackbird's ship barely aloft, her struggling engines spewing blue-black smoke. Kaori stood at the bow, Piotr beside her, fingers entwined.

Fingers entwined.

Even in the midst of all this death . . .

Yukiko put her hands on her belly, felt for the warmth there, her power surging anew now the dark had swallowed itself. Their strength in her, flooding, burning, an affirmation of everything they'd fought and suffered and died for.

. . . there is life.

All around her, thousands of sparks flaring in the space beyond the wall of herself, the song of life drowning the fading echoes of the Endsinger's hymn. Yukiko looked out over the ashes to the new plain the hellgate once filled, the ruins of the sundered Tōnan mountains to the west, the heart of Guild power in Shima now reduced to broken rock and good, fresh earth.

The snows would fall. The chill would reign for untold nights ahead. But soon enough, the weather would shift, the sun would rise. Spring would come, and with it, the children inside her, the seeds now sleeping in the ground. This place would be a forest again. Trees would grow here. Birds would sing. Life would bloom. She could feel it in her head, in her heart, reaching out across the ruin, feeling the sparks all around her. The pain of her headache a welcome sensation after the numbness, the warmth of the blood dripping on her lips a relief after the wind's freezing bite.

And then.

And then . . .

She began walking. Slowly, blinking, unbelieving. Aleksandar called to her, the soldiers cried "Stormdancer!" as her walk became a jog, then a flat run, one hand at her stomach. She heard nothing. Nothing except the pulse of it. Sprinting now, staggering and stumbling over broken ground, snow and ash all around, blinding, choking. But still she ran, fresh tears in her eyes, not daring to hope, not daring to believe what she could feel with her own mind, reaching out across the Kenning to the faint and fluttering spark somewhere beyond. Running faster than she could have dreamed, feet barely touching the earth, skidding to a stop beside a pile of dirt and ash and twisted metal, still steaming from the heat of the Earthcrusher's demise.

She could see it in his mind's eye as she reached him, down on her knees, tearing a sheet of buckled iron aside, clearing away the black slurry and dirt covering him.

The oni legion gathered all around him, the iron giant's hide crawling with every child of the Endsinger yet moving, belly filled, throat gurgling with them, breaking through the elevator doors. His hands, slamming the throttles forward, bending and jamming them in place. Slipping from the pilot's harness and diving toward the shattered viewports, down through the broken pane and out into the freezing air. His rockets flaring blue-white, shuddering with exertion as he flew away at full burn. The Earthcrusher's tortured scream flaring red-hot, then incandescent, the spark catching behind him amidst the deafening detonation of the behemoth's chi reserves. The blast wave hitting him midair, thrusting him farther away, buoyed on a pillow of fire and shock as the Earthcrusher tore itself apart and incinerated the seething horde around it.

Crashing to earth. Too hurt to move. Almost too hurt to breathe.

Almost.

"Kin," she sobbed.

He blinked up at her, face caked with ash and soot. He tried to speak, but no words would come, cracked lips painted white. And there, in that sea of gray, his head cradled in her arms, he fixed his gaze on hers, watching with those knife-bright eyes. She could feel it within him, even if he couldn't speak it.

Even in the midst of all this death, there is life.

He lifted his hand, clad in beaten brass, and gentle as falling snow, he wiped away her tears. And he smiled.

There is love.

54
EULOGY

Sumiko prayed.

Head bowed before the shrine of Susano-ō. Begging he would not cover Lady Sun's face today, that rolling gray would not cast a shadow across the muddy purple of the sky. Today there must be light. Today there must be warmth. Lady Amaterasu must burn bright in the heavens, smiling on the festivities to come.

She heard floorboards creaking, the shrine door sliding open. Faint birdsong in the garden, her children playing amidst the struggling trees. It had been a good winter—the rains had fallen heavy, washing yet more poison from the skies above, falling from the heavens no longer in floods of reeking black, but of fading, injured gray. The air was light today, a hint of freshness and new green amidst the lingering chi stains. She'd noted some people had even stopped wearing kerchiefs and breathers in spring, but Sumiko still insisted her girls not play outside unprotected. The memory of her mother's passing, the black she'd coughed at her ending would never truly fade. All wounds heal with the passing of long years, but it would be some time yet before the air was clear enough to risk her loves outside.

She'd lost too much already.

Everyone had.

Footsteps across the floorboards, bringing a smile to her lips. Her husband knelt behind her, put his arms around her, kissed her neck. She leaned back into him, felt the muscle and cable at play beneath his skin, ran her thumb over the empty input jack at his wrist.

"Shinji," she sighed.

"Are you ready, love? It would not do to be late."

"I'm ready," she smiled.

"Then come."

A hundred flags and a thousand ribbons and ten thousand smiling faces. People were gathered in the fields outside Kigen city; an endless sea, rolling and shifting like the gray waters of the bay. Clan banners whipping in the wind—the sigils of the Tiger, Fox and Phoenix alongside the twisting design of the Serpent clan—a viper eating its own tail, forming an endless, unbroken circle. Though small in number, the remnants of the Lotus Guild had built their homes in the ruins of Dragon lands, setting up new factories with the help of Morcheba's Ordo-Mechanika. After a decade of toil and failure, at last the works were producing marvels for the populace; creations born of ingenuity and alliance with the gaijin technicians, powered not by the deadly bloom that had brought their nation close to ruin, but by the same fuel the Morchebans had almost conquered the country with.

A gift from the sky.

The people had traveled from every corner of the islands—jammed into carriages aboard the new lightning-rail, or booking passage on the new airships being produced in the Serpent machine works. There was no man or woman or child alive who wished to miss this day, this glorious moment in their nation's history—the moment Lady Yukiko would stand before the people and heal the last patch of deadlands in all of the Shima Isles.

Every heart beat faster, every breath came quicker at the thought. Though she'd worked tirelessly in the decade since the Lotus War ended, traveling from province to province, town to town, she never lingered long, and very rarely spoke publically. She traveled with a small entourage it was said—just her children, a historian and a handful of volunteers. Beginning in the north and working her way south, months melting into years, ashes before her, and only good, dark soil in her wake. It had been over ten years since Sumiko saw her—that day she'd never forget, when the Stormdancer arrived on her arashitora in Kigen's Market Square and bid the nation to raise their fists. As their train pulled into Kigen Station, Sumiko wondered how the years had treated her, the marks the war had left behind.

She disembarked, forced her way through the throng, Shinji beside her, daughters between. Though her husband was a chief of production in the Serpent machine works, he insisted they travel by lightning-rail, just like everyone else. No special treatment. No man above another. But as a hero in the Lotus War, as one of the rebels who'd sabotaged the Earthcrusher and saved Kitsune-jō, Shinji was to be afforded a special place in the celebrations today.

The thought made Sumiko's heart swell with pride.

They were met by Tora bushimen, the fresh soldiers bowing low. There was something close to awe in their eyes as the young men escorted Sumiko and her family to the gala grounds outside Kigen. A massive stage had been erected, semicircular in shape, shrouded at its rear by a large curtain of billowing black silk. It encircled a tiny crop of ruined land—rumor spoke it had once been a lotus farm, won years before by some Burakumin soldier in a Kitsune smoke house, and then left to rot. The crowd was gathered around it—a sea of people stretching for miles, all bright eyes and smiling faces. Vendors moved through the throng, selling saké and barley wine, sushi and rice cakes, pork and crackling and sticks of sauced beef—produce from the midlands breadbasket where once the Stain had lay, now known as Yoshi Province.

Sumiko looked around the stage at the other players, unbelieving at the company she found herself keeping. She'd read the history of the Lotus War of course, but to be standing in the presence of the man who had completed it set her heart to fluttering. The Blackbird was every bit as impressive as Shinji had told her, tall and broad, his graying beard spilling over his girth, his laughter felt somewhere deep in her chest. He was busy flirting with several young ladies of the Tora court, their blushing cheeks hidden behind fluttering fans. An old hound sat beside him, wagging his tail. Sumiko smiled, and despite her desire to speak to the great historian, resolved not to interrupt.

Misaki caught her eye, bowed to her, to Shinji, and Sumiko returned the smile, walking over for a swift embrace and a kiss to each cheek. The silver arms at Misaki's back rippled, the woman's smile like bruised strawberries, her cheeks aglow. Her daughter, Suki, stood close by, tall and elegant, long hair bound into braids and held fixed by brass rings.

"I feel utterly out of place up here," Sumiko whispered.

"No more than I," Misaki smiled. "But be at peace, sister. Today is a good day."

Sumiko squeezed her friend's hand, turning back to the others she shared the stage with. She saw the Daimyo of the Tora court opposite her, fierce as the Tigers her clan was named for. Dressed in a blood-red kimono and an iron breastplate,

long hair drawn back in a braid, steel-gray eyes matching the wakizashi and katana she wore at her waist, golden cranes in flight down the black lacquer. She
wore no makeup, made no attempt to hide the long, jagged scar cutting through
her beautiful features.

At her side stood a fierce-looking gaijin man dressed in the robes of a courtly
emissary, his face a patchwork of scars. But when he smiled, which was often,
Sumiko could see the kindness in him. And when he whispered into the Daimyo's
ear, she would smile too.

A small girl ran out from behind the black silken curtain, chased by a younger
boy, and Daimyo Kaori knelt, held her arms wide. The pair ran to her arms, all
the cold and ferocity melting from her face, kissing each brow and holding them
tight.

"Michi, you behave better around your brother," she half-scolded. "Daichi is
not so old as you. You must set an example."

The little girl bowed. "I will, Mother."

Kissing the boy again, the Daimyo stood, searching the eastern horizon. Pulling down her goggles, she raised one hand against the glare—still harsh after a
decade of industry without chi. The wounds of land and sky were healing slowly,
but none knew for sure if the scars would ever truly fade from sight. The sun still
burned kiln-hot. The rivers faded from black to gray, but not to crystal clear. And
though the ocean and sky longed to return to their brilliant blue, it seemed they
might never rid themselves of blood's hue.

A figure walked through the crowd toward Shinji, a smile on his face, reflected in knife-bright eyes. Speaker for the Serpent clan. First amongst equals.

"My friend," Kin said, holding his arms wide.

"My brother," Shinji replied, hugging him fiercely.

The pair embraced, eyes closed for a long, silent moment. Kin was dressed in
a simple black kimono, a leather obi at his waist arrayed with all manner of tools.
Dark cropped hair and black, twinkling eyes, the skin on his hands marred by a
slight sheen—the mark of awful burns earned in years long past. But there was
no trace of that old pain in his eyes as he turned to Sumiko, bowed low, looking
at each of her daughters in turn.

"It is good to see you again, Sumiko." He knelt by her daughters, shyly peering
out at him behind curtains of long, dark hair. "My, you two ladies have grown!"

"It is good to see you also, Kin-sama." Sumiko bowed from the knees.

Kin smiled, holding up one scarred hand. "Just Kin."

"Where is your Lady, brother?" Shinji gestured to the massive crowd gathered
around the stage. "The whole country waits for her appearance."

"You know her. Dramatic entrances are her favorite. The later, the better."

"I remember," Shinji smiled.

Sumiko looked again over the restless crowd, murmurs rippling through the throng. She could feel an electricity in the air, butterflies tumbling in her stomach. A gentle spring breeze kissed her skin, the soft perfume of young flowers and new life running fingers through her hair.

And then she heard it. A lone voice, crying aloud, a single word that dragged her back a decade to Kigen's Market Square, to the day she'd raised her fist in the air and witnessed the birth of a legend.

"Arashitora!"

The cry spread; a fire on bone-dry tinder, blooming like wisteria and laden with promise. All eyes turned eastward, every finger pointing, every mouth open in wonder, every heart lifted from the shackles of its mortal shell and set to singing.

"Arashitora!" they cried.

The majestic figure flew toward them out of the rising sun, circling above, its wings making the sound of thunder. It was sleek as knives, cutting the air like folded steel, dipping and swooping to the crowd's delight, awe and joy written on every face. And as the beast came in to land, talons shredding the fresh earth near the ruins of the little farmstead, Sumiko caught sight of the rider astride it.

A beautiful woman, slender and graceful, moving like a dancer as she slipped down from the arashitora's back. Her skin was pale as Iishi snow, hair rippling in the wind like molten gold, a ribbon of sunlight framing her impish features. She was clad in iron; an embossed breastplate set with the sigil of a stag with three crescent horns, a golden amulet around her neck bearing the same. A band of black leather covered one eye, the other settling on the Speaker of the Serpent clan as he leapt down off the stage and caught the woman in his embrace.

"Hana," Kin said.

The woman closed her eye, hugged Kin tight. When she spoke, her consonants were hard, a hint of the Morcheban accent creeping into her inflections and tone.

"It is good to see you again, my friend."

"How fares your family?" Kin asked as they parted.

"Well enough," Hana smiled. "My eldest insisted she ride here with me, though she stands only five summers deep. Screamed for hours when I told her she couldn't come. She has the fire of the Goddess, that one."

Sumiko gazed at the arashitora looming behind the woman, peering down at Kin with bright, amber eyes. The beast was impossibly beautiful; deep bands of black marking her hindquarters, feathers possessed of a wondrous opalescence. But the feathers around her eyes were graying, the black in her stripes running to charcoal. Sumiko was filled with melancholy to look at her—the last thunder tiger, as frail and mortal as anyone. Time would claim brave Kaiah, as it would claim them all. What would be left, when the last stormdancer was gone?

"Where is your lady, Kin-san?" Hana said. "Where is my sister?"

"Here I am," said a voice.

The black curtain parted, sunlight gleaming on rippling silk. And there she stood, quiet and fragile and beautiful. A simple kimono of embroidered black flowed off her shoulders, hugged her waist, the handle of a black lacquered tantō at her hip. She was thin, pale as wisteria blooms. Her hair flowed about her face like black water, rolling down her back in waves. Her face was careworn, her eyes tired, but still, they blazed with light at the sight of her friend, the smile on her face as fierce as the Lady Amaterasu's light.

At her side, two children stood, a boy and a girl perhaps ten years old, both tall and beautiful, black hair and pale skin. She held a third child in her arms, little more than a toddler—a boy with bright inquisitive eyes as sharp as knives. All three were looking at the arashitora, spellbound, the thunder tiger dipping her head as if to bow.

The crowd was awash with jubilation, cheering wildly at the sight of the woman and her children, the legend made flesh. She looked over the mob and smiled, raising one fist in the air. The gesture was returned, ten thousand fists and a single name, shouted over and over again.

"Yukiko!"

"Yukiko!"

When the frenzy abated, after what seemed an impossible age, the twins looked up at their mother, an unspoken question in their eyes.

"Go on, then," Yukiko nodded.

The twins whooped and dashed away, jumping off the stage and running to the arashitora's side. They stopped a handful of paces away, staring at the mighty Kaiah with wide eyes, holding out their hands together, palms outward. The thunder tiger stalked toward the pair and lowered her head, flared her wings, pushing her cheeks against one palm and then another to euphoric roars from the crowds.

Yukiko made her way down off the stage, a frailty in her tread. Kin stepped up beside her, took the babe from her arms, and Hana fairly flew into her embrace. Both women were weeping, holding each other as a drowning man clutches floating tinder.

"I knew you'd come," Yukiko breathed.

"Even if all the oni in the Hells stood in the way."

"I missed you, sister."

The pair parted, Hana turned to the twins standing beside Kaiah, wondering at the luster of her fur, the softness of her feathers.

"Hello, Masaru," the woman said. "Naomi. You don't remember me, do you?"

The children stared mute, as children are wont to do, and Hana laughed, loud and fierce, a glint of lightning in her eye. She turned to Kin, to the little boy in his arms, reaching out to caress the child's cheek.

"And who are you, little man?"

"His name is Arashi," Yukiko said.

"Arashi," Hana smiled. " 'Storm.' Very fitting."

Yukiko motioned to the small tract of deadlands around them. In the distance, thunder rolled, the edges of the sky darkening with the press of an oncoming storm.

"Shall we do this? Before the rain?"

"I still remember this place," Hana sighed. "Our house was right over there. Broken windows and broken dreams . . ."

"Then let's be rid of it. And all shadows of the past alongside."

Hana nodded, took Yukiko's hand and walked to the edge of the deadlands, Kin beside them. A thin wash of black vapor roiled on the surface, feeble and near translucent in the light of the sun. But still it lingered—the last mark of blood lotus left in Shima. Tora bushimen stood vigil around the perimeter, but there was no crush to touch the stormdancers. A strange hush descended over the crowd, a gravity that took hold and pulled them back down to earth, all jubilance and joy stilling, silence echoing in the mournful breeze, laden with the promise of distant storms.

Yukiko brushed a stray lock of hair from her face. Her lips were bloodless, and she seemed so small amidst that sea of people—somehow utterly lost. But she reached out for Kin's hand, smiling as he placed a gentle kiss on her brow. She looked to the children at his side, the people gathered up on the stage behind her. All of them wounded, but walking still. And she drew a deep breath, and she spoke, and her voice was strong as the roar of a thunder tiger.

"People of Shima," she said. "Hear me now."

Yukiko raised her hand, and Sumiko saw the flesh of her palms was covered in scars; hundreds of knife wounds scored across her skin.

"Ten years. Ten years I've walked, the length and breadth of this place we call home. I have seen rivers black and choked with corpses. I've watched poisoned winds blow across deserts where forests once stood, looked into empty skies where once there were as many birds as stars across the face of night. We came so close to the abyss, you and I. I stood on its edge and looked into its eyes. I heard it speak. I learned its name.

"In the tavern tales, I hear stories of the Endsinger. Of a goddess who sought to swallow the world, and the stormdancers who stood in her way. I hear the honors given to those who paid the steepest price, who gave more than anyone may ask of a brother or friend."

She shook her head, tears welling in her eyes.

"Their sacrifice should live in legend. But that is not the truth of this tale."

Kin squeezed her hand. She squeezed it back, tight as she dared.

"The truth is, the abyss lives in us. In our greed. In the way we look at things different to us, and see things lesser. In the way we see the smaller, or the weaker, and think them prey.

"It begins with the beasts of the land, the birds of the sky. And in a blinking, we find ourselves seeing our lessers in people with different-colored skins. Different gods. Different creeds. We see them as lessers, and we hurt, and we kill, and we think nothing of it. Because they are different, we think ourselves just. Because we are stronger, we think ourselves righteous.

"That is the abyss in all of us. And we stand close to the edge still. Closer than any can dream. We need but stray for a moment and we will find ourselves back again, staring down into that black. And who will save us? When everything that was different to us is already gone?"

The woman shook her head, her eyes downturned.

"We choose this. This place. This life. What it will be, and how we live it. We are not slaves to gods, or fate, or destinies woven in veils of smoke. We choose the people we want to be, and we choose the shape of the world in which we live. Nothing worthwhile comes without sacrifice. There is nothing so easy as swimming with the current, nothing so difficult as being the first to stand up. To say no. To point at a thing wrong and name it so. There are none so brave as those who choose to stand, when all others are content to kneel. None so worthy of the title 'hero' as those who fight when there are none to see it. Who choose a life bereft of accolade or fanfare, a life of struggle for the idea that we are all the same. Every one of us. And every one of us has the right to be happy. To know peace. To know love."

She searched the faces of the crowd, young and old, man and woman and child.

"You can choose this. Right here. Right now. You can choose to be the one who fights to make things better. You can choose to see how close we came to the edge, and how easily we can fall there still. Or you can close your eyes. Go back to sleep. Hope someone else will fight for you. Or you can hope for nothing greater at all.

"It is within all of you."

As Kin let go of her hand, Yukiko drew her tantō, held her palm aloft and ran the blade down over the old scars. Blood welled, streaming down the whorls of the folded steel. Hana drew a long dagger from her belt, held her palm aloft and did the same, cutting deep. The women pressed their hands together, the blood of Foxes and Burakumin and distant lives across the seas, mingling upon their skin.

Yukiko turned to the crowd, her voice calling high and clear.

"Choose," she said.

Open palms.

Scarlet droplets, flung into the breeze.

An inversion of sound.
White light.
Silence?
"Choose."

EPILOGUE

She sat alone on the stage in the dark.

A curtain of storm clouds drawn overhead, shutting out the glow of the smothered moon. The distant lights of Kigen city, the flares from kindling wheel and dragon cannon, fireworks blazing up toward the clouds. Never high enough to reach. Always falling short and tumbling back down in gravity's hateful grip.

The wound at her palm ached. Just like the wound in her chest. Kin had bandaged it gently, pressed his lips to hers, then left her with her thoughts. As he always did.

She looked at her other palm, made of scars; a thousand marks from a thousand knife cuts to spill a thousand drops and heal a thousand wounds in the earth. But never the one inside her. Never the ache he left behind. She was blessed and she knew it. The love of a wonderful man, beautiful children, a life spent in the making of a brighter tomorrow for the ones she'd brought into this place. She loved them with all she had to give. But it was on nights like this . . .

Nights like this . . .

When the storms would roll down from the Iishi, laden with rain's promise, a deluge so powerful it seemed the God of Storms had been saving it all for her. When Raijin would fill the heavens with his drums and hurl arcs of brilliant blue-white from all corners of the sky. When all was tempest, all was chaos, she'd look above to that rolling sea of black and miss him so badly her chest would ache. Her soul would bleed. Her breath would catch in her lungs and her throat would seize tight and it would be all she could do not to scream, *scream* at the heavens that it wasn't fair, that it wasn't right, that it should never have been him.

Never have been him.

She hung her head, sodden hair falling over her face as the rain began to fall, pawing at her breast and the hurt behind it, sobbing from the depths of herself.

"I miss you, brother . . ."

Thunder across the skies, settling in her bones.

"Gods, I miss you so much . . ."

Face crumpling like paper beneath the barrage, curled over on herself, forehead pressed to grain, hair strewn in black drifts all around. She could see him, just as she'd seen him on the night they met, a night like this, a sight etched in lightning and snow-white feathers before her wondering eyes. The things they'd done. The places they'd seen. The bond they'd shared. The hole he'd left behind that all the love in the world couldn't fill.

No victory without sacrifice.

No parade without a funeral.

No heroes dying in their beds.

She rose slowly, the sobs wracking her body, climbing to her feet and staring at the storm above. She watched lightning split the sky, great banks of black clashing like ironclads across the heavens, the thunderous boom of explosions echoing in her memory, shreddermen and Earthcrushers and vast shadows of death, and the voice of a goddess reverberating in her mind.

"*Oh my dear, precious girl. You do not know, do you?*"

She wiped her eyes.

"*What it will cost you . . .*"

And her heart fell still in her chest.

For there, up in the black, etched in brief brilliances by the lightning's hands, she saw it. A momentary flash, the flare left behind on your eyelid after you stare too long at the sun. The impression of vast, white wings, feathers as long as her arm, broad as her thigh. Black stripes, rippling muscle, a proud, sleek head tipped with a razor-sharp beak. Eyes like midnight, black and bottomless.

"Izanagi's breath," she whispered, squinting into the black.

Lightning flashed again, illuminating the beast before her wondering eyes.

The impossible.

The unthinkable.

She reached into herself, into the place she'd refused to go since that day, that ending, a decade old and caked in dust. The quiet fire of it, impossibly dimmed since the sparks inside her had been born, walking with lives and minds and dreams of their own. But still she found it, waiting, like an old hearth of char-black stone, cold with the press of years. But still stone. Still strong. Unbreakable. Waiting for the tinder to catch again, to flare bright, to bring warmth where all had been darkness a moment before.

She reached up into the clouds and felt him. A flash of aggression. Curiosity. Wild and vibrant and seething hot, so alive and bright she couldn't help but laugh for the joy of it, fingers pressed to her lips as it spilled out of her, a bubbling flood from the depths of someplace dark and deep.

So beautiful . . .

He circled lower, down through the deluge, skimming between the rain. His wings crackling with lightning, set afire with each arc across the skies. Down and down and down, Yukiko leaping off the stage and running out into the mud, splashing through the muck to where he finally set himself down, spattered in black, shaking himself like a soggy hound. She stopped a handful of feet away, stretching out one hand, thinking herself crazed, moon-broken, the grief and loss finally getting the best of her and tipping her down into the black.

And then he roared. Thunderous. Deafening. Pressing on her chest, thrumming in her belly. A roar of warning, of a beast when territory is pressed, hackles raised, tearing at the ground with his talons, tail stretched like a whip. Radiating pride, aggression, a beautiful, imperious will.

She stopped short, fell still.

Perfectly.

Utterly.

Still.

KNOW YOU.

His voice rolled like a thunderclap in her mind, in the place once filled with warm and wonderful thoughts—a love that had borne her higher than the clouds. She ached with the song of it, the fire of it, wrapping her arms around her chest and knowing it wasn't a dream, not a vision, recognizing him at last. At last.

You're his son, aren't you?

She pushed warmth into his mind, the sensation of her cheek pressed against his. The memory of a little bundle of feathers and fur sneezing and snarling at her as she reached out to hug him on Susano-ō's throne, cub-sharp claws scratching on the stone.

You're his Hope.

She filled him with a smile.

Little Rhaii.

A snarl, shifting the earth beneath him, rumbling and tectonic.

NOT LITTLE. NO MORE.

He spread his wings, lighting flaring bright.

SUKAA IS GONE. SO IS HIS LAW.

She stepped closer, through the falling rain, smoothing the hair from her face. He was as beautiful as any sight she'd seen in her life. As tall and broad as his father had been, amber eyes ablaze with a rage, a questioning, filling her with the sense she'd come home; stepping into the heat of a well-stoked hearth after a decade of wandering in the dark. The storm raged about them, a song as old as the world itself, the rains washing everything away. Flooding earth and filling sky and waking new seeds in fresh ground. All that had gone before. All that would come after.

RHAII IS KHAN OF EVERSTORM NOW.

She heard cries above, roars akin to the thunder. And looking up, she saw them, sleek and razor sharp, cutting through the skies and filling her heart to bursting, her tears lost in the falling rain. She turned on the spot, crying out in sheer, bottomless, maddening joy, arms outstretched as they soared overhead, more than thirty of them, black and white and gray, buck and dam and cub, filling the clouds with their song.

REMEMBER YOU.

She lowered her arms, stared at the thunder tiger, rain and tears in her lashes. She took one step closer, a smile on her lips, filling him with her joy.

KNOW WHO YOU ARE.

And who am I, mighty Khan?

She felt warmth in him then, the beginnings of a smile deep inside.

He spread his wings.

Bowed his head.

Purred.

YOU ARE YUKIKO.

GLOSSARY

GENERAL TERMS

Arashitora—literally "stormtiger." A mythical creature with the head, forelegs and wings of an eagle, and the hindquarters of a tiger. Thought to be long extinct, these beasts were traditionally used as flying mounts by the caste of legendary Shima heroes known as "Stormdancers." These beasts are also referred to as "thunder tigers."

Arashi-no-odoriko—literally "Stormdancer." Legendary heroes of Shima's past, who rode arashitora into battle. The most well-known are Kitsune no Akira (who slew the great sea dragon Boukyaku) and Tora Takehiko (who sacrificed his life to close Devil Gate and stop the Yomi hordes escaping into Shima).

Blood lotus—a toxic flowering plant cultivated by the people of Shima. Blood lotus poisons the soil in which it grows, rendering it incapable of sustaining life. The blood lotus plant is utilized in the production of teas, medicines, narcotics and fabrics. The seeds of the bloom are processed by the Lotus Guild to produce "chi," the fuel that drives the machines of the Shima Shōgunate.

Burakumin—a low-born citizen who does not belong to any of the four zaibatsu clans.

Bushido—literally "the Way of the Warrior." A code of conduct adhered to by the samurai caste. The tenets of Bushido are: rectitude, courage, benevolence, respect, honesty, honor and loyalty. The life of a Bushido follower is spent in constant preparation for death; to die with honor intact in the service of their Lord is their ultimate goal.

Bushiman—a common-born soldier who has sworn to follow the Way of Bushido.

Chan—a diminutive suffix applied to a person's name. It expresses that the speaker finds the person endearing. Usually reserved for children and young women.

Chi—literally "blood." The combustible fuel that drives the machines of the Shima Shōgunate. The fuel is derived from the seeds of the blood lotus plant.

Daimyo—a powerful territorial Lord that rules one of the Shima zaibatsu. The title is usually passed on through heredity.

Fushicho—literally "Phoenix." One of the four zaibatsu clans of Shima. The Phoenix clan live on the island of Yotaku (Blessings) and venerate Amaterasu, Goddess of the Sun. Traditionally, the greatest artists and artisans in Shima come from the Phoenix clan. Also: the kami guardian of the same zaibatsu, an elemental force closely tied to the concepts of enlightenment, inspiration and creativity.

Gaijin—literally "foreigner." A person not of Shimanese descent. The Shima Shōgunate has been embroiled in a war of conquest in the gaijin country of Morcheba for over twenty years.

Inochi—literally "life." A fertilizer that, when applied to crops of blood lotus, delays the onset of soil degradation caused by the plant's toxicity.

Irezumi—a tattoo, created by inserting ink beneath the skin with steel or bamboo needles. Members of all Shima clans wear the totem of their clan on their right shoulder. City dwellers will often mark their left shoulder with a symbol to denote their profession. The complexity of the design communicates the wealth of the bearer—larger, more elaborate designs can take months or even years to complete and cost many hundreds of kouka.

Kami—spirits, natural forces or universal essences. This word can refer to personified deities, such as Izanagi or Raijin, or broader elemental forces, such as fire or water. Each clan in Shima also has a guardian kami, from which the clan draws its name.

Kazumitsu Dynasty—the hereditary line of Shōgun that rule the Shima Imperium. Named for the first of the line to claim the title—Kazumitsu I—who led a successful revolt against the corrupt Tenma Emperors.

Kitsune—literally "Fox." One of the four zaibatsu clans of Shima, known for stealth and good fortune. The Kitsune clan live close to the haunted Iishi Mountains, and venerate Tsukiyomi, the God of the Moon. Also: the kami guardian of the same zaibatsu, said to bring good fortune to those who bear his mark. The saying "Kitsune looks after his own" is often used to account for inexplicable good luck.

Kouka—the currency of Shima. Coins are flat and rectangular, made of two strips of plaited metal: more valuable iron, and less valuable copper. Coins are often cut into smaller pieces to conduct minor transactions. These small pieces are known as "bits." Ten copper kouka buys one iron kouka.

Lotus Guild—a cabal of zealots who oversee the production of chi and the distribution of inochi fertilizer in Shima. Referred to collectively as "Guildsmen," the Lotus Guild is comprised of three parts: rank-and-file "Lotusmen," the engineers of the "Artificer" sect and the religious arm known as "Purifiers." "False-Lifers" are a sub-sect of the Artificer caste.

Oni—a demon of the Yomi underworld, reputedly born to the Goddess Izanami after she was corrupted by the Land of the Dead. Old legends report that their legion is one thousand and one strong. They are a living embodiment of evil, delighting in slaughter and the misfortune of man.

Ryu—literally "Dragon." One of the four zaibatsu clans of Shima, renowned as great explorers and traders. In the early days before Empire, the Ryu were a seafaring clan of raiders who pillaged among the northern clans. They venerate Susano-ō, God of Storms. Also: the kami guardian of the same zaibatsu, a powerful spirit beast and elemental force associated with random destruction, bravery and mastery of the seas.

Sama—a suffix applied to a person's name. This is a more far more respectful version of "san." Used to refer to one of much higher rank than the speaker.

Samurai—a member of the military nobility who adheres to the Bushido Code. Each samurai must be sworn to the service of a Lord—either a clan Daimyo, or the Shōgun himself. To die honorably in service to one's Lord is the greatest aspiration of any samurai's life. The most accomplished and wealthy amongst these warriors wear chi-powered suits of heavy armor called "ō-yoroi," earning them the name "Iron Samurai."

San—a suffix applied to a person's name. This is a common honorific, used to indicate respect to a peer, similar to "Mr." or "Mrs." Usually used when referring to males.

Sensei—a teacher.

Seppuku—a form of ritualized suicide in which the practitioner disembowels himself and is then beheaded by a kaishakunin (a "second," usually a close and trusted comrade). Death by seppuku is thought to alleviate loss of face, and can spare the family of the practitioner shame by association. An alternative version of seppuku, called "jumonji giri," is also practiced to atone for particularly shameful acts. The practitioner is not beheaded—instead he performs a second vertical cut in his belly and is left to bear his suffering quietly until dying from blood loss.

Shōgun—literally "Commander of a force." The title of the hereditary military dictator of the Shima Imperium. The current line of rulers is descended from Tora Kazumitsu, an army commander who led a bloody uprising against Shima's former hereditary rulers, the Tenma Emperors.

Seii Taishōgun—literally "great general who subdues eastern barbarians."

Tora—literally "Tiger." The greatest of the four zaibatsu of Shima, and the clan from which the Kazumitsu Dynasty originates. The Tora are a warrior clan, who venerate Hachiman, the God of War. Also: the kami guardian of the same zaibatsu, closely associated with the concept of ferocity, hunger and physical desire.

Yōkai—a blanket term for preternatural creatures thought to originate in the spirit realms. These include arashitora, sea dragons and the dreaded oni.

Zaibatsu—literally "plutocrats." The four conglomerate clans of the Shima Imperium. After the rebellion against the Tenma Emperors, Shōgun Kazumitsu rewarded his lieutenants with stewardship over vast territories. The clans to which the new Daimyo belonged (Tiger, Phoenix, Dragon and Fox) slowly consumed the clans of the surrounding territories through economic and military warfare, and became known as "zaibatsu."

CLOTHING

Hakama—a divided skirt that resembles a wide-legged pair of trousers, tied tight into a narrow waist. Hakama have seven deep pleats—five in front, two at the back—to represent the seven virtues of Bushido. An undivided variant of hakama exists (i.e. a single leg, more like a skirt) intended for wear over a kimono.

Jin-haori—a kimono-style tabard worn by samurai.

Jûnihitoe—an extraordinarily complex and elegant style of kimono, worn by courtly ladies.

Kimono—an ankle-length, T-shaped robe with long, wide sleeves, worn by both men and women. A younger woman's kimono will have longer sleeves, signifying that she is unmarried. The styles range from casual to extremely formal. Elaborate kimono designs can consist of more than twelve separate pieces and incorporate up to sixty square feet of cloth.

Mempō—a face mask, one component of the armor worn by samurai. Mempō are often crafted to resemble fantastical creatures, or made in twisted designs intended to strike fear into the enemy.

Obi—a sash, usually worn with kimono. Men's obi are usually narrow; no more than four inches wide. A formal woman's obi can measure a foot in width and up to twelve feet in length. Obi are worn in various elaborate styles and tied in decorative bows and knots.

Uwagi—a kimono-like jacket that extends no lower than mid-thigh. Uwagi can have long, wide sleeves, or be cut in sleeveless fashion to display the wearer's irezumi.

WEAPONS

Daishō—a paired set of swords, consisting of a katana and wakizashi. The weapons will usually be constructed by the same artisan, and have matching designs on the blades, hilts and scabbards. The daishō is a status symbol, marking the wearer as a member of the samurai caste.

Katana—a sword with a single-edged, curved, slender blade over two feet in length, and a long hilt bound in crisscrossed cord, allowing for a double-handed grip. Katana are usually worn with shorter blades known as wakizashi.

Nagamaki—a pole weapon with a large and heavy blade. The handle measures close to three feet, with the blade measuring the same. It closely resembles a naginata, but the weapon's handle is bound in similar fashion to a katana hilt—cords wrapped in crisscrossed manner.

Naginata—a pole weapon, similar to a spear, with a curved, single-edged blade at the end. The haft typically measures between five and seven feet. The blade can be up to three feet long, and is similar to a katana.

Ō-yoroi—suits of heavy samurai armor powered by chi-fueled engines. The armor augments the wearer's strength, and is impenetrable to most conventional weaponry.

Tantō—a short, single- or double-edged dagger, between six and twelve inches in length. Women often carry a tantō for self-defense, as the knife can easily be concealed inside an obi.

Tetsubo—a long warclub, made of wood or solid iron, with iron spikes or studs at one end, used to crush armor, horses or other weapons in battle. The use of a tetsubo requires great balance and strength—a miss with the club can leave the wielder open to counterattack.

Wakizashi—a sword with a single-edged, curved, slender blade between one and two feet in length, with a short, single-handed hilt bound in crisscrossed cord. It is usually worn with a longer blade, known as a katana.

RELIGION

Amaterasu—Goddess of the Sun. Daughter of Izanagi, she was born along with Tsukiyomi, God of the Moon, and Susano-ō, God of Storms, when her father returned from Yomi and washed to purify himself of Yomi's taint. She is a benevolent deity, a bringer of life, although in recent decades has become seen as a harsh and unforgiving goddess. She is not fond of either of her brothers, refusing to speak to Tsukiyomi, and constantly tormented by Susano-ō. She is patron of the Phoenix zaibatsu, and is also often venerated by women.

Enma-ō—one of the nine Yama Kings, and chief judge of all the hells. Enma-ō is the final arbiter of where a soul will reside after death, and how soon it will be allowed to rejoin the wheel of life.

Hachiman—the God of War. Originally a scholarly deity, thought of more as a tutor in the ways of war, Hachiman has become repersonified in recent decades to reflect the more violent warlike ways of the Shima government. He is now seen as the embodiment of war, often depicted with a weapon in one hand and a white dove in the other, signifying desire for peace, but readiness to act. He is patron of the Tiger zaibatsu.

The Hells—a collective term for the nine planes of existence where a soul can be sent after death. Many of the hells are places where souls are sent temporarily to suffer for transgressions in life, before moving back to the cycle of rebirth. Before Lord Izanagi commanded the Yama Kings to take stewardship over the souls of the damned in order to help usher them toward enlightenment, Shima had but a single hell—the dark, rotting pit of Yomi.

The Hungry Dead—the restless residents of the Underworld. Spirits of wicked people consigned to hunger and thirst in Yomi's dark for all eternity.

Izanagi (Lord)—also called Izanagi-no-Mikoto, literally "He who Invites," the Maker God of Shima. He is a benevolent deity who, with his wife Izanami, is responsible for creating the Shima Isles, their pantheon of gods and all the life therein. After the death of his wife in childbirth, Izanagi traveled to Yomi to retrieve her soul, but failed to return her to the land of the living.

Izanami (Lady)—also called the Dark Mother, and the Endsinger, wife to Izanagi, the Maker God. Izanami died giving birth to the Shima Isles, and was consigned to dwell in the Yomi underworld. Izanagi sought to reclaim his wife, but she was corrupted by Yomi's dark power, becoming a malevolent force and hater of the living. She is mother to the thousand and one oni, a legion of demons who exist to plague the people of Shima.

Raijin—God of Thunder and Lightning, son of Susano-ō. Raijin is seen as a cruel god, fond of chaos and random destruction. He creates thunder by pounding his drums across the sky. He is the creator of arashitora, the thunder tigers.

Susano-ō—the God of Storms. Son of Izanagi, he was born along with Amaterasu, Goddess of the Sun, and Tsukiyomi, God of the Moon, when his father returned from Yomi and washed to purify himself of Yomi's taint. Susano-ō is generally seen as a benevolent god, but he constantly torments his sister, Amaterasu, Lady of the Sun, causing her to hide her face. He is father to the Thunder God, Raijin, the deity who created arashitora—the thunder tigers. He is patron of the Ryu zaibatsu.

Tsukiyomi—the God of the Moon. Son of Izanagi, he was born along with Amaterasu, Goddess of the Sun, and Susano-ō, God of Storms, when his father returned from Yomi and washed to purify himself of Yomi's taint. Tsukiyomi angered his sister, Amaterasu, when he slaughtered Uke Mochi, the Goddess of Food. Amaterasu has refused to speak to him since, which is why the Sun and Moon never share the same sky. He is a quiet god, fond of stillness and learning. He is the patron of the Kitsune zaibatsu.

Yomi—the deepest level of the hells, where the evil dead are sent to rot and suffer for all eternity. Home of demons, and the Dark Mother, Lady Izanami.

ACKNOWLEDGMENTS

Jay Kristoff would like to offer Big Scary Hugs to the following outstanding human beings:

Amanda, for just about everything.

Pete Wolverton and Julie Crisp, for giving me permission to kill my babies.

Brunch Bitch, Sharkgrrl, and The KitKat for still being on speaking terms with me after the trauma of crit-reading this screaming murderfest.

Matt Bialer and LT Ribar for breaking the right thumbs and always shooting straight.

As always, a special shout-out to the fantabulous Anne Brewer, Mary Willems, Justin Velella, Melissa Hastings, Paul Hochman, Cassie Galante, Courtney Sanks and the PR/Marketing posse at St. Martin's Press, Bella Pagan, Louise Buckley and all @ Tor UK, Charlotte "Don't call me Reetard" Ree, Hayley Crandell and crew @ PanMacMillan Aus, and all the ground crews in all the countries my book has visited before I did.

Scott Westerfeld, Pat Rothfuss, K. W. Jeter, Stephen Hunt, Marissa Meyer and Kevin "Droogie" Hearne for the pimpage.

Lance Hewett, Narita Misaki, Sudayama Aki and Paul Cechner for being my sounding boards and guides in all things Japanese.

Kira "Imperatritsa" Ostrovska for her help with the Rus.

My web-mastah Brad Carpenter, for not punching me in the throat every time I make a change. And to the inimitable Mr. Hart, for the crash space.

Marc, B-Money, Rafe, Weez, Surly Jim, Eli, Beiber, The Dread Pirate Glouftis, Tomas, Steve, Mini, Sam, Patrick, Lucky Phil, Dave, Handsome Tom, Xav, Snack-Daddy and all other splendid members of my nerd posse, past and present, for preventing my slow spiral into Howard Hughes-esque isolation and madness.

Dr. Sam Bowden, for advice on all things doctor-y. Yes that's a word, shut up.

Eamon Kenny, for his help on the airwaves.

Araki Miho, once again, for her beautiful calligraphy.

Jimmy the Orrsome for our clan logos and company at all things metal, and Sir Christopher Tovo for bringing out my handsome side.

Jason Chan, again, you killed it, dude. So many beers do I owe thee.

The book bloggers—always too many to mention, never too many to remember. Your passion and energy and dedication never ceases to amaze me. You know who you are. I know who you are. Never stop being awesome.

My family for always being there. Sorry I'm not most of the time.

Anyone who made me poetry or music or artwork or helped spread the word, anyone who got a Lotus War tattoo (!!!) or came out to see me at a con or show, or wrote/tweeted/FB'ed me about the series, anyone who has accompanied me on this amazing journey, even if it was simply by visiting these pages. This series changed my life in more ways than I can describe, and for your company on this long and often lonely road, I am forever grateful.

And finally, Yukiko and Buruu, for opening the door to this, the most amazing chapter of my life. I'll miss you guys.

The rest of you—see you in the next world. It's a killer.

Jay Kristoff
April 2014